SUPERNATURAL
BULLIES & BEASTS
BOOK 7

Z A

AQUA TERRA IGNIS AER

ZODIAC ACADEMY
HEARTLESS SKY

CAROLINE
PECKHAM

SUSANNE
VALENTI

Place
Terra House
Hall
Mars Laboratory
King's Hollow
The Howling Meadow
The Wailing Wood
The Orb
Earth Observatory
Venus Library
rcury
mbers
Aer House
Fire Arena
Ai
Co

This book is dedicated to the piece of our souls we gave to it.
Here lies Clive the soul crumb. He was chipped off during the
painstaking days and nights we put in to get this book done.
From the 3 am starts to the midnight ends.
The tears, the laughs, the pain, the heartache, the joy.
The hot cross buns, the buttered toasts, the countless teas and our
parents who ducked in and out of our office asking if we were good,
and the readers who cheered us on and waited patiently for Clive to be
sacrificed into this story.
We gave it our all. We hope it was enough.
This is the beginning of the end.
See you on the other side.
!

WELCOME TO ZODIAC ACADEMY

Note to all students: Vampire bites, loss of limbs or getting lost in The Wailing Wood will not count as a valid excuse for being late to class.

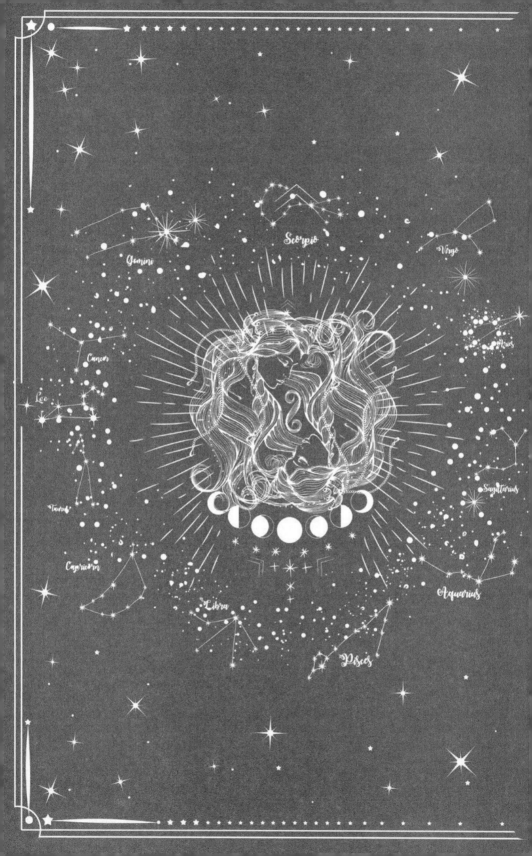

DARCY

CHAPTER ONE

Adrenaline, fear and relief tumbled through me in a potent mixture as I tried to calm the frantic racing of my heart and cling onto the fact that we were okay. Here, now, against all odds almost all the people I cared most about in this world were surrounding me and we were once again out of reach of Lionel Acrux and the Shadow Princess. Though I had to wonder how many more times we would be forced to run from them before we managed to tear them down from their stolen throne and return Solaria to the peace which could only be brought about by their end.

Dante circled down through the fluffy white clouds and I marvelled at the incredible feeling of riding a Dragon while my thoughts spiralled over everything that had happened. His midnight blue scales buzzed with a faint but constant tingle of electricity and the sheer size of him was unbelievable. The only other time I'd ridden on a Dragon's back had been when I'd escaped the graveyard after retrieving the Imperial Star but the rush of the escape and sudden end to that flight had meant I'd barely gotten a moment to appreciate it. Now that we were soaring across an endless sky with the stars bright overhead and the moon silently watching our passage, I couldn't help but feel the pure magic of this moment.

I was a girl who had grown up in the foster system in the mortal world. Fighting tyrants and riding Dragons had been the kinds of dreams I never would have even dared to try and wish into reality. Yet here we were. Caught in the thick of a world we'd been born to rule among all forms of magical creatures and cruel twists of fate, and I couldn't help but feel like we'd truly found where we belonged.

Tory squeezed my hand as I clung to her, and I gave her a smile threaded with tears of relief as I let myself bathe in the fact that she was finally free of her bond to that monster. Free of the shadows, free of the curse which had been keeping her and Darius apart. Shit, so much had changed that I didn't even know where to begin with it all, but I was just so glad to have her in my arms. And to know she'd never be forced to return to Lionel's side ever again.

So many of us could have been lost today, but somehow here we were, sailing away from our enemies on the back of a beast of legend, with breath in our lungs and hope in our hearts. At least for now.

The air was icily cold, but my Phoenix had awoken to burn away the chill, and I leant Orion warmth as he held onto me, feeding it from my skin into his. I wanted to just linger there, in that moment with his arms surrounding me and my hand in my sister's, the night opening up all around us and nothing but peace in this unforgiving sky.

"You took Lionel's hand, Tor," I said, in awe of my badass sister.

She glanced back at me over her shoulder, her dark hair whipping around her and I found tears brimming in her eyes, some of relief, some of fear, but the wind stole them away from her as it drove against us.

"He took a lot from me in return," she replied darkly, a flicker of some untold horror in her eyes which she blinked away hard as she glanced at the others who still surrounded us.

I wanted to ask her more about what had happened since the last time I'd seen her. I knew Lionel must have done something terrible once he'd figured out that she'd broken free of his hold on her, but I also knew my sister and even with the aid of a silencing bubble, she wouldn't want to discuss any of that here with so many people surrounding us.

Though I couldn't help but notice the way she was holding Max's hand where he sat on her other side and the furrows in his brow gave me clues to the emotions he was helping her contain which set my gut churning with an ache that wouldn't quit. We'd all suffered at the hands of that tyrant. But I guessed the best thing we could do now was focus on the freedom we'd just managed to claim from him.

"Your Star Crossed rings are gone," I told her in disbelief and she nodded like she knew, like she could feel it. "Maybe he did something so you could be together?"

"Maybe, but…he married Mildred," she murmured, her gaze dropping to her lap as she gritted her jaw against the pain of that truth and I squeezed her fingers even harder, shaking my head despite the fact I knew it was the truth.

Xavier had filled us in on that when he'd landed on Dante's back and shifted into his Fae form to rest for a while. Tory had looked out towards the horizon and said nothing while the Heirs, Orion and I grilled him for every detail. The only comfort any of us had managed to find in his story was the fact that Gabriel had contacted the Heirs to tell them they needed to strike at Lionel to rescue Orion and I from the Nymphs, and he had assured them that he was getting Darius to safety.

But none of us knew any more than that aside from the fact the bonds had broken.

We still hadn't heard a single word from either of them and only my faith in our brother and his gifts gave me any kind of reassurance about them being okay wherever they were.

"What has Darius done?" Tory breathed, the concern in her tone making my chest ache and I hugged her tighter.

"I don't know, but we'll find out," I promised, and she nodded, leaning against me as we just held each other in the wake of so much destruction.

I didn't let my mind wander to the curse that had been cast on me, the feel of it somehow absent now as I half expected some terrible fate to befall me at any moment. But nothing came. We simply kept riding away to freedom with the wind at our backs and the sense of our small victory surrounding us.

"I can't feel anything of him anymore," Orion said in fear and Tory looked at him over my shoulder.

"I'd feel it if he was dead," she said firmly and Orion's grip on me relaxed slightly, the tension in his body speaking of how much he feared for his friend's life.

"Are you sure?" he rasped and she nodded, her eyes blazing with the fire of her Order and I believed her. She was his mate, Star Crossed or otherwise. If anyone knew the truth of Darius's fate, it was her.

"All of our enemies were at the battle," I agreed, stroking my fingers over Orion's arm where it was latched around me, my fingers finding the bare skin where the Leo brand had once marked it. "He must be alright."

"Yeah," he said heavily. "Must be." Though there was a weight behind those words that said he wasn't going to relax until he could see Darius for himself, but I had faith in my sister. If she was sure he was okay, then he was. Perhaps he was waiting for us wherever we were headed.

I couldn't bear the thought of him dying. Tory needed him, his friends needed him. And Orion had already lost Clara today, how much more would the stars really take from him? From us?

Xavier whinnied as he flew beside us, his wings cutting through the clouds and his mane trailing purple glitter out behind him. Dante answered him with a soft roar and my gut lurched as he descended through the mass of clouds, dropping down at speed while Xavier chased after us, his hooves cantering through the air.

As we made it beneath the canopy of white, my gaze fell on a snowy expanse stretching out in every direction over rolling hills. An endless forest bordered the horizon, the pines capped with a frosting of snow and the darkness thick between the boughs.

Magic rolled over us as we dropped lower, the hairs rising on my arms and I shivered as an old farmhouse was unveiled below with a large barn standing to one side of it.

There was a crowd of Fae filing inside the house, half of them naked from recently shifting and others in blood splattered, battle marked clothes.

Hamish stood in the doorway, beckoning people past him. His large form, bushy black moustache, mutton chops and bald head were unmissable among the masses. "That's it! Bring your Nelly Nancys inside. Hot showers and buttery bagels for everyone!"

"How can so many people fit in one small house?" I questioned in dismay as more and more of the battle survivors headed inside.

"There must be some enchantment at play," Orion said in my ear.

"Hello, fellow warriors – good day – look upon the sky to see the true queens descending among you!" Geraldine called out and my cheeks warmed as the whole crowd looked up to watch us land and a bunch of them started cheering.

She suddenly stood up on Dante's back, yanking her silver breast plate off and hurling it in Max's direction, forcing him to catch it, followed by the chainmail, the rest of her armour and her flail until she was butt naked and he was cursing her, demanding she cover herself up again.

But Geraldine ignored him, leaping from Dante's back as he closed in on the ground and shifting into her enormous Cerberus form, the three heads of her gigantic dog Order lifting to the sky as her paws skidded in the snow and she began to howl.

I had no idea how she was managing it, but between the howls of her three heads, she somehow managed to sing a tune which sounded a whole lot like a royal fanfare and my blush intensified as the rebels all cheered even louder as they spotted us.

I braced just before Dante hit the ground, a tremor rocking through the earth and dislodging some snow from the roof of the barn beside us as he tucked his wings in tight against his powerful body and crouched low to let us all climb off of him.

We made our way down from Dante's back, most of us using air magic to lower ourselves to the ground while Caleb just leapt down with the agility of his Order.

Xavier landed lightly beside us in his lilac Pegasus form, the shift rippling along him as he fell still and a second later he stood in front of us naked in his Fae form.

"The Acrux spare!" a man cried in alarm nearby, pointing at him. "Quick – someone capture him before he reveals our location to the false King! Somebody – quickly!"

Orion flicked a finger that sent a snowball slamming into the guy's mouth to shut him up, making him stumble over his own feet and land on his ass and Tory barked a laugh without even bothering to try and hide it. Honestly, the two of them were bad influences on each other, but I couldn't help but like their little friendship all the same.

"He's an ally," Orion barked, glaring at anyone giving Xavier a fearful look.

The people closest to us exchanged glances then looked anywhere but at Orion, the words 'Power Shamed' passing between them in horrified mutters. A growl built in my throat and fire magic twisted through me as my rage grew hotter at their dismissal of him.

"Looks like you're invisible, bro." Seth's hand clapped down on Orion's shoulder, as he stood with his dick out right beside him – his leaf pants apparently having blown away on the wind - and Orion shoved him away so fast, he stumbled into Caleb.

"Xavier is our ally," Tory confirmed to the crowd and they quickly paid her attention, bowing their heads and nodding their agreement.

"That's right," Geraldine piped up, moving to step in front of us and thrusting out her chest as she placed her hands on her hips. She'd shifted back into her Fae form now that she was done howling our arrival to the sky and the hoody someone had draped around her shoulders fell off into the snow, leaving her completely naked in front of them, her ass cheeks clenched tightly. "He is our pure hearted Pegasus friend, a Fae who is as kind as a kimmenfrog on a kipper, and who has fought valiantly beside us this very day."

"For the love of the moon, Gerry," Max growled, hurrying forward to grab the hoody and trying to drape it over her again, but she kept elbowing him away as she continued her speech.

"And yes, he may be an Acrux, raised by the vagrant vagabond who has stolen the throne from the true queens, and yes, we may look at him and accuse him of being a cowardly creature with a spine as slippery as a sallion slug. But hear me this day, and hear me ever more, for Xavier Acrux has proved he will fight in the name of my lady Tory and my lady Darcy. He has shown that every glittering speck of his essence is devoted to the true cause, the rightful cause-"

"Can we hurry it along? I'm freezing my cock off here," Seth called and I glanced over at him as he fashioned himself some more pants out of leaves.

Caleb reached out to touch his arm, the heat of his fire Element blazing under his fingers, making Seth shiver as it flooded into him and he grinned at his crush with so much adoration in his eyes that I had to wonder how Caleb hadn't noticed it yet.

Xavier's cheeks had pinked from all the attention that was on him, standing awkwardly to one side as he held his junk beneath his hands.

"Come forth – come forth! Make way for the true queens!" Hamish cried, barrelling his way through the crowd and Geraldine abandoned her speech, running forward to embrace her huge father.

His moustache was flecked with snowflakes and he was dressed in a shaggy fur coat that gave him the appearance of a giant beaver. He had a pile of sweatpants and sweaters in his arms, throwing them out to whoever needed them so our friends could get dressed. The Heirs all moved forward to pile up their Phoenix weapons in the arms of one of the rebels, like they expected to be waited on by these people. The man's knees nearly buckled under the weight of them all, but he didn't drop them, even when Caleb grabbed Orion's sword and tossed that on top of the pile too and a little squeak of exertion left the guy.

Assholes.

Dante shifted into his Fae form, pulling on some sweatpants but leaving his muscular chest bare as he nodded to us and strode off into the crowd like he was searching for someone and I wondered if his family were here.

"Oh daddypops, you fought like a clandestine clatterpuss out there," Geraldine gushed.

"My dear Gerrykins, you fought like a true warrior of the Naggaluff," Hamish exclaimed.

"Xavier?" a woman's voice reached us as she pushed through the crowd and I looked up at the stranger as she darted towards him. "It's me," she said, flicking a hand across her face so that her true features were revealed for the briefest of moments and he gasped as he recognised his mother Catalina, running to meet her, the two of them embracing hard and making my heart squeeze. "Where's your brother?" she begged, a note of terror in her voice.

"I don't know," he said uncertainly as she placed kiss after kiss on his forehead and hair, making him turn even brighter red as people watched them, clearly wondering who the hell she was. Though I guessed in that moment she didn't care about hiding her connection to him or her own identity despite the concealment that hid her true face.

Tory moved forward to hug her too and they exchanged some words quietly as Catalina took in the lack of rings in her eyes, surprise and hope crossing her features. For a moment, I envied the way Catalina looked at my sister, caressing her cheek and checking she was alright. It was almost motherly, something I had never experienced in all my life. But then I remembered everything both of them had been through and buried the feeling deep. Tory deserved that more than I ever would.

I glanced at Orion, finding him watching them with something of the same yearning in his eyes and I recognised the ache in him that lived in me. He was as good as an orphan with his mother aligned with Lionel Acrux, and I wished his father hadn't been taken from him so young. Catalina's eyes fell on him and brightened as she rushed toward him, hugging him tight while he fell still in her arms.

"I'm so glad you're alright," she whispered and Orion's eyebrows arched in surprise as she checked him over for injuries like he was one of her own sons. I stepped back to give them some room, knotting my fingers together as I watched them.

"I owe you the deepest apology I can offer," he said to her, pressing Catalina back and squeezing her hand.

Catalina shook her head in refusal. "You didn't know he was controlling me."

"I should have," Orion growled, his brow pinching with regret. "You weren't the same woman you were when I knew you as a child. I just thought…I don't know what I thought. But I should have realised you needed help." He dropped his head in shame and Catalina cupped his cheek, drawing his eyes back up to meet hers.

"Don't you ever blame yourself, Lance," she insisted. "Lionel is the one who did this."

Orion nodded, though the guilt didn't leave his expression as she released him and returned to Tory and Xavier, tears of happiness swimming in her eyes.

Orion moved toward me with intent and a gasp rippled through the crowd as he reached out and his fingers brushed mine. He paused, his gaze moving to the onlooking rebels who had a mixture of horror and disgust written into their features as they glared at him and he immediately retracted his hand.

I was about to snap at them for daring to look at him like that, but Tory called my name.

"Darcy?" She beckoned me over with anxiety in her eyes and I moved hesitantly toward her, finding Catalina smiling warmly at me beside her.

"Everything okay?" I asked.

"Xavier still has the shadows, but I think I can remove them now. And I think together it might be even easier."

She held out her hand to me and I took it, my Phoenix rising to meet hers like they were two halves of the same soul, and maybe they were. That was the way it had always felt between us, like we were made of the very same thing, detached but never quite whole without the other. Calm washed over me and Xavier glanced nervously between us as Tory reached out to place a hand against his chest. My heart beat with trepidation, knowing we needed to remove the shadows from him to protect him from Lavinia so that she couldn't use them to control him or even worse – to find us here in this place.

"Just don't freak out," I warned, and he nodded stiffly.

"Got it," he said, though a little whinny of worry left him. But I knew we could do this now. After burning the shadows out of Orion, I could feel how to do it, it was like connecting to the best and brightest emotions within me and guiding them forward. It was love and hope and all the things we'd never let Lionel take from us.

I felt Tory's Phoenix fire twisting around mine and it burned beneath her palm as Catalina stepped closer anxiously, clearly concerned for her son. But Xavier's eyes told her to trust in us, and a minute later the fire rippled over his flesh and burned within his eyes as it sought out every shadow in his veins and banished them from his body.

He sighed as the Fifth Element left him, the relief on his face clear as we freed him from Lavinia's control and he sagged forward a little as Tory dropped her hand.

"Thank you," he breathed, hugging us both tight, and suddenly Catalina wrapped her arms around us too and I looked up to find tears rolling down her face.

"You're a gift sent from the stars," she whispered and a blush filled my cheeks as I shook my head in denial of those words.

When they released us, I tucked a lock of blue hair behind my ear, heat burning up the back of my neck.

Max tugged on my arm and I turned to him. "Come on little Vegas, they're not gonna let us in unless you two lead the way."

I realised the crowd were watching Tory and I closely, and wondered if Max was right about that.

Hamish beckoned us forward again and I moved to walk beside Tory as we followed him through the rebels. Orion walked at my back, so close to me that I could feel him everywhere, and I took comfort in knowing he was there, especially after all we'd been through, but every time I tried to turn back and draw him closer, he fell further away, the distance between us making my heart hurt. And I had the awful feeling it was intentional.

People bowed their heads to Tory and I, muttering thanks to the stars and my breaths grew uneven as the eyes of the rebels followed us. It looked like a lot of these people were royalists, die hard supporters of the Vega line, and it was strange to be the subject of so much attention at once. Even the A.S.S. club hadn't made me feel this scrutinised.

My heart pounded harder as we made it to the farmhouse and Hamish bowed so low his nose nearly touched the ground, his right arm held out in a gesture for us to head through the door.

"Welcome to The Burrows, Your Royal Highnesses," Hamish said proudly.

Another cheer went up and Tory glanced at me, our hands finding each other's instinctively as our souls drew us together. This moment felt endlessly important somehow. Like we were stepping into a future that had been laid out and waiting for us to accept it. Like we were finally treading the path we would need to follow if we ever intended to truly claim the throne for ourselves. And now that Lionel had sat his scaly ass on it, I wanted it more than ever.

Tory leaned in close to whisper to me, "If we ever become queens, my first law will be that no one is allowed to stare at us. And that'll probably deal with your little stalker problem too."

"Huh?" I laughed and she jerked her chin to point over my shoulder.

I glanced back, finding Orion hot on my heels again and looking right at me.

"What are you gonna do, throw me in prison?" Orion asked her tauntingly.

"Nah, the punishment for that crime is hourly dick kicks," Tory said with a smirk, but then her eyes slid to the sky and her amusement died just like that, her thoughts clearly on Darius again. "Does he know how to get here?" she asked in concern.

"We can message him," I said firmly, looking to Hamish. "Do you have an Atlas we can borrow?"

"Abso-tively," he said, nodding profusely. "But you'll need to come inside and make your star vows first. We have Atlases which have been enchanted to keep our location utterly butterly secret. The only ones who can share its location are the official Circle of Covert Keepers."

"Who are they?" I asked.

"They're very loyal royalists who may show others how to find The Burrows. Only a select few know of our location to ensure it can never be found by those who wish to harm us. Of course, you ladies will be welcomed into the Circle as will the Heirs if you so wish it," Hamish explained as we filed inside, following at our backs.

"Are we seriously going to join the C.O.C.Ks?" Tory hissed to me and a laugh erupted from my throat.

We arrived in a small entranceway with wooden floors and a mahogany grandfather clock dominating the space. Hamish moved around us as we all lined up and the front door swung shut at our backs, leaving us all enclosed in the small space.

"Make me one of the Circle too," Orion insisted and Hamish's eyes darted toward him before bouncing away again in dismissal and Seth snorted a laugh.

"Don't ignore him," I snarled, my hackles rising in an instant and Hamish looked to me in alarm, cupping his mouth with his hand.

"But my lady, he is *Power Shamed*," he whispered those two words in horror, barely able to speak them.

"Not to me he isn't," I growled.

"I-I-I-" Hamish stammered, trying to grapple with that.

"This'll make him look at me," Orion muttered then split his thumb open on his fang, turning his arm over and smearing blood across the inside of his forearm. The mark of the Zodiac Guild appeared like it was a living tattoo beneath his flesh, the silver sword etched with constellations and looking so ethereal it almost glowed.

Hamish let out a noise that sounded like the honk of a strangled goose then fell to his knees, his eyes rolling back into his head as he fainted and hit the floor in an awkward pile.

"Well that backfired," Orion deadpanned as I hurried forward with Tory and Geraldine to help him to his feet.

"By the stars' nipples," he murmured as he regained consciousness. "Pantaloons on the moon – oh gracious, forgive my language, my ladies. I have not seen the mark of the Zodiac Guild in many a year, and to see it worn by none other than a Power Shamed F-" He reared over and retched at those words. "Forgive me, a Power Shamed F-" He retched loudly again and Orion cursed under his breath while the Heirs all laughed.

"You there." Geraldine whipped around, pointing an accusing finger at Max who looked to her in surprise, his laughter choking out in an instant as he pointed a finger at himself in confusion. "Yes, you, you uncouth codpiece, get my father a chair this instant!"

He nodded several times, looking around for a chair, bumping into Caleb then running from the room and returning with three wooden stools in his arms a minute later.

He placed them down while Geraldine swatted him away and Hamish dropped onto one of them, dabbing at his brow as he regained his strength.

"We mustn't dilly dally any longer. We must get on with the star vows," Hamish insisted, beckoning me and Tory forward. He took one of our hands each then drew in a long breath and smiled at us. "Do you Tory and Darcy Vega swear upon the stars to never reveal the location of this place to Lionel Acrux or any of his loyal followers, and never speak of anyone you see here in its depths? And do you also swear to never grievously harm or kill a single person here in The Burrows?"

We both agreed and a clap of magic rang between us before the Heirs moved forward to make the promise next. When everyone had made the vows and Hamish had finally gotten through making the promises with Orion while he retched between his words and had to look out a window instead of directly at him, Hamish stood up again and guided us all towards the ornate grandfather clock.

It was twice my size in height and breadth, the thing looking like something out of a fairy tale with delicate carvings all over the wood and gilded details glimmering in the low light. As I looked closer at the golden dial, I realised it didn't just tell the time, it told the moon phases, the positions of the constellations in the sky and the phases of the two equinoxes too. A beautiful pendulum swung behind a glass window in the shape of the sun, the continual tick, tick, tick filling the room and seeming even louder up close.

"To enter, you must only speak your intentions towards the Vegas. The clock will detect the truth upon your soul," Hamish said dramatically. "No one of ill intent can ever breach our beloved safe haven."

Geraldine stepped up first, tilting her head back and speaking directly to the clockface. "I mean our true queens no harm." She stepped forward with encouragement from her father, opening the door in the clock and behind it was a dark passage lit by burning sconces on the walls. She stepped into it and the door snapped shut behind her instantly.

Tory went next, looking up at the clock with a cynical frown that said she wasn't convinced she needed to speak to a clock, but she did anyway. "I mean the Vegas no harm."

She opened the door then stepped through and I moved forward, repeating the words and heading after her.

A wide tunnel led away from us, carving a path beneath the earth which disappeared into the distance, lit with flaming torches, the walls carved from the earth itself. As I followed my sister into the cool tunnel, I instantly moved towards the nearest sconce, the fire feeding my magic reserves as we waited for the others to catch up to us.

When the Heirs arrived, they stood before us and I felt the weight of the words they'd just spoken sitting there in the dark, waiting for one of us to acknowledge them.

"I guess that proves it once and for all then," Caleb said with a lopsided grin, breaking the tension.

"That we're best friends?" Seth asked, bobbing on his toes as he looked between us excitedly.

"I never thought this would happen," Max said, scoring a hand over his short hair and smirking at us.

"Well, that's because you were a dastardly dogfish when you met the Vegas," Geraldine pointed out. "And I am not entirely convinced your dogfish ways are behind you yet, Maxy boy."

"Oh come on, Gerry, what more do I have to do to prove myself?" Max lamented.

"You could try being less of a troublesome trout, I suppose." She turned her back on him, heading off down the tunnel with a swing in her hips. But as everyone followed, I remained there, seeking out Orion who was barely visible where he stood in the darkest corner of the passage.

Hamish bustled past him, bowing low to me and calling out for me to follow him, but I found my feet rooted in place as the two of us were left behind.

"Waiting for me, Blue?" Orion asked with a hint of amusement in his voice.

"You look a little lonely over there in the shadows," I pointed out.

"I've always enjoyed the company of the shadows," he countered. "Besides, I'm a Vampire. I don't get lonely. Alone is what I do best."

"Well I guess I'll just walk by myself then," I said lightly and he shot to my side so fast it made my head spin, a smirk twisting up the corners of his mouth as he took hold of my arm.

"Turns out, I enjoy the company of your shadow more than any other," he said in a low voice that set my pulse racing. "So go ahead and walk away from me, Blue, but I'll be right behind you."

Neither of us moved, his fingers tightening on my skin and the heat of that single, innocent point of contact setting a volcano erupting in my body. This man was the most intoxicating thing I had ever known, the cinnamon scent of him like a drug lacing the air, making me so goddamn high I couldn't think straight.

"Thank you," I breathed. "For everything you did today. I'd be dead if it wasn't for you."

His eyes blazed with some dark emotion and I felt the very fabric of my soul crying out for me to move nearer to him.

"Are you okay?" I whispered, thinking of Clara. "Your sister…" Emotion burned the back of my throat at the idea of saying goodbye to Tory. How was Orion even still standing?

He hung his head, a crease settling on his brow as a heavy silence passed between us.

"Honestly, Blue, I thought I would shatter from losing her again. But

I...feel relieved." Guilt crossed his features and I held my breath as I waited for him to go on as he kept his eyes on the ground. "I mourned my sister a long time ago, and I saw the truth today. Her soul was trapped inside that shadow monster and now, well...now she's free. She's beyond the Veil where she belongs. She's with my father."

The conflict in his words made me raise a hand and take hold of his chin, gaining his attention so his gaze flicked up to meet mine.

"Does that make me heartless?" he asked, searching my eyes for the answer to a question that seemed far bigger than the one he'd voiced.

"No," I swore, seeing the age old grief in his eyes over the loss of his family, but there was acceptance there too, like a burden had finally been lifted from him. And I got it. As much as it terrified me to even consider having to live a life without my sister by my side, having to accept that she was suffering and aching to pass on would be so much worse. There had been hope for Clara while she was trapped in the claws of the Shadow Princess, but at least now she was free of that torment. She could be herself once more beyond the Veil and maybe she would find peace and happiness there too. "I understand."

"That's because you are far too forgiving of my sins," he murmured and his fingers travelled up my arm, spreading goosebumps tumbling out along my skin as he pushed my sleeve aside to unveil the black handprint mark left there by Lavinia's curse. But as he drew in a sharp breath, I looked down to find it was no longer there, my skin as smooth and untouched as if she had never laid a finger on me. Shock jarred within me as I stared at the impossibility staring back at me. How could it be gone? What did this mean?

Orion swore then picked me up by the waist, shooting us closer to a sconce and placing me down in the light to inspect the bare flesh with a franticness to his movements.

"It's gone," he growled, a note of hope humming in those two words, resounding right down to my bones.

I tried to reach within me for any feel of it, any trace of that dark power which Lavinia had forced beneath my skin, but there was nothing. No whisper of shadows, no clawing darkness trying to drag me down into its depths.

"Do you think...my Phoenix fought it off?" I asked, desperate for that to be true. I could feel the fiery creature within me burning right now. It was wide awake and so immensely powerful, that I was certain this really was possible. I'd seen what it was capable of. It had burned away the shadows from my body, so why not a shadow curse too?

Orion stared at me like I was a star fallen from the heavens, a creature so powerful that it was made of magic itself.

"Yeah...I think it did," he said, his faith in my abilities clear in his expression. "We don't know everything Phoenixes can do, and you have surprised me so many times that I'm certain you'll keep doing so. So yes, Blue, if you cannot feel it and there is no mark, then surely you're no longer cursed."

I released a sigh, an impossible heaviness lifting from my shoulders as happiness spilled into my chest like a river pouring into the sea.

"I'll talk to Tory about it tomorrow then," I decided as a grin drew my lips wide, not wanting her to worry while Darius was still missing.

Orion's dark eyes shifted from my arm to my face, relief washing over his features and a youthful smile breaking out on his lips, making the dimple in his right cheek pop. He shot forward, crushing me to the wall, his breaths mingling with mine as both our chests heaved from the proximity of one another.

"You're fucking extraordinary," he growled, the hardness of his muscles pinning me there and I wound my fingers into his shirt, drawing him closer, needing to just-

"Sorry, I, er-" Xavier cleared his throat and Orion stepped back as he turned to look at him as he came through the clock. "I was just doing my shoelaces, then everyone was gone, and I forgot the words everyone said. But I, um, figured it out so…"

"It's fine," I said, a little flushed as Orion glanced at me with a furious longing in his eyes, making liquid heat spill through my core. But I'd get him alone as soon as we had the chance. I had a lot I wanted to say to him, but I had a hell of a lot I wanted to do to him first.

We headed after the others, the tunnel dropping down steeply beneath my feet until it opened up into a wide cavern with more tunnels leading off of it in every direction. A soft green moss carpeted the floor and all around the walls were golden carved images of Lionel in his Dragon form being blasted by Pegasuses, Griffins, Manticores and Harpies. In one image, Tiberian Rats were climbing up his tail and biting him, and in another Sirens were drowning him in a lake alongside a myriad of water Shifters.

A laugh escaped me at it all as we hurried to catch the group who were being led down one of the tunnels with the words 'The Royal Quarters' carved above the arching entranceway and two crowns either side of it.

"You'll have to divide up into twos, I'm afraid," Hamish called back. "Each room has either a double-dilly bed or two silly-singles, and we are a little pushed for space until some of our earth Elementals finish digging out the fan-frilly-tastic new tunnels. But we set aside this tunnel just for you fine fellows so that you can have a little privacy."

I looked to my sister up ahead, then glanced at Orion. After everything that had happened at the battle, I knew I couldn't hold a grudge against him any longer. He still loved me and I loved him so fiercely it hurt. So all that was left was to voice those words and hope that we could mend the rift between us and build something more unbreakable than before.

"Now I'm sure you want to freshen up your long stockings and your under pits, so make your way into the royal bathhouses here. Left for the girls and right for the boys." Hamish pointed and we headed down the short stone passage which forked at the end. Dried blood stuck my clothes to my skin and I was desperate to wash away the scent of smoke and sand and death that clung to me too.

My gaze met Orion's as we were about to part ways, an urgent demand in his eyes stating that he didn't want to separate, but unless we wanted to remain filthy from battle, we had to. Our eyes remained locked until I turned into the girls' bathhouse and my lips parted at the enormous cavern filled with bubbling hot springs with palms growing between them, waterfalls tumbling down across the rocks and Faelights bobbing around in the air to light it all in an amber glow.

I pulled off my clothes and stepped under the flow of the nearest falls,

the hot rush of water like a godsend as I shut my eyes and just stood there in the heated stream. Tory climbed into one of the bubbling pools and swam beneath the surface, popping up on the other side as she rinsed her hair and groaned her relief.

"The plants are Washalilies," Geraldine exclaimed. "Just lather up a leaf like so. It even doubles as shampoo." She yanked a leaf off of what I'd thought had been a palm and started scrubbing it under her armpit. The leaf released a white lather and my eyebrows arched before I grabbed a leaf of my own from the nearest plant. The moment I rubbed it against my skin, a soft, honey-sweet lather built against it, and I worked it all over me before washing my hair and finally feeling Fae again.

When we were clean, I used air magic to dry off and found fresh clothes at the door to the bathhouse, dressing in grey sweatpants and a white tank top. Tory grabbed clothes without even really looking at them, not even bothering to dry her hair and ending up in a pair of sweatpants and a sweatshirt which were clearly meant for a guy about three times the size of her. I frowned at my sister and as Geraldine headed out of the room, I caught Tory's hand to stop her from following, seeing the worry in her expression.

"He'll be alright," I swore. "He's Darius Acrux."

She nodded, but her eyes burned with emotion and I wrapped her in my arms. "We can stay up until he gets here," I promised.

"You should stay with Orion." She pulled back, scrubbing at her eyes quickly before any tears dared to fall. "He just lost Clara, he needs you more than I do right now."

"I'm not leaving you alone," I said immediately.

"I want to be alone," she whispered, biting her lip. "I need to be, okay? I think if I'm alone I might be able to just…sense that he's alive. And then I'll be able to wait instead of leaving this place in search of him."

"Tor…" I breathed, hating the idea of not being with her tonight when she felt like this. And I could tell that there was more going on with her than just the worry over Darius. Lionel had had her at his mercy ever since he'd captured me and Orion, and I knew that she wasn't telling me the worst of what she'd been through in the last few days. But I also knew my sister and she would only open up if we were alone. "I need to be with you."

"You need to be with him," she insisted, squeezing my arm. "You've been apart too long, and you could have lost each other tonight. You love him, don't you?"

"I-" I started but Geraldine's voice cut me off as she shouted out beyond the bathhouse.

"You bat-eared blaggard!" she yelled, her voice followed by a loud thwack.

"Back off, Grus," Orion growled in response.

"You're standing out here dropping eaves on the true queens and I shall defend their privacy until my dying breath!"

We stepped out of the bathhouse, finding Geraldine hitting Orion with an eggplant she'd conjured, but it kept bouncing off of an air shield which surrounded him.

"I wasn't eavesdropping," Orion said as his eyes snapped to us. "I was just waiting for you."

21

His gaze bored into me and suddenly I felt too hot, the urge to move closer to him driving me wild.

The sound of splashing and laughter carried from the men's bathhouse and Tory and I stepped forward to look.

Caleb was speeding around in one of the pools with the gifts of his Order, turning the water into a whirlpool while Seth tried to escape from the middle. Max tried to blast Caleb with shots of water from up on a rock and Xavier cast glittering bubbles into his eyes.

"Boys!" Geraldine exclaimed, though a smile was dancing around her lips. "Their ding-dongles make them into such buffoons sometimes. This way, my ladies. You must be as tired as a sandgoose in the snow."

She led the way forward and Orion moved to my side, our fingers brushing and sending electric energy buzzing through my veins. I didn't look at him, but my breathing was becoming heavy and I knew there were a lot of words that needed to be spoken between us, but right now all I wanted to do was fall into his arms and find peace in them again.

Geraldine led us deeper into the sleeping quarters where oval wooden doors lined the walls and sconces lit the dark tunnel.

"The riffraff may pick any room to share with one other, I will be bunking in with Angelica tonight once she has appeared among the other rebels. But for you my queens, we shall of course be providing quarters worthy of royalty."

The sound of the other people were carrying to us now, heading this way led by Hamish's loud voice as he guided them to the bathhouse.

"Here we are." Geraldine threw a door open to her right which had the royal crest engraved on it, inspecting the space. There were two beds inside, each hung with flowers above the beds, a table set to one side with food and drinks waiting on it. "Is this suitable for you? Or shall I cast some more flowers across the walls? Shall I gild the beds? Or perhaps you would like me to ruffle your pillows and sing you a lullaby of old?"

"Where's Lance's room?" I asked, wanting him close after everything that had happened.

"Oh, erm…" Geraldine looked down the corridor just as Hamish strolled up to us with a wide smile on his face.

"How are the royal quarters?" he asked us loudly, not seeming to notice Orion at all as he swept his gaze right over him. "Is everything to your satisfaction?"

"We were just asking where Orion is staying," Tory asked, tilting her head to one side as Hamish instantly gagged.

"His…his…forgive me, my ladies but he is *shamed*. He should just sleep in the barn. Or perhaps the scullery-"

"The scullery?" I blanched, looking to Geraldine who was wringing her hands together. "What the hell are you talking about? I want him close to me here."

"Oh, erm, well, I…" Hamish looked at Orion then started to retch violently.

"Oh for the love of the stars, forget it, Hamish. Can you just tell us which room is for Darius?" Tory asked and Geraldine swung around with her eyes popping.

"Why of course, my lady Tory, you only need ask for anything in this place and it shall be yours."

Geraldine hurried along to the next room and threw the door open, narrowing her gaze at the space inside. "Is this one suitable?" She looked over our heads at Hamish who was biting down on his fist in an attempt to stop himself from throwing up and I could feel my temper fraying as Orion just looked down at his feet like he was just willing to accept this bullshit.

"That's perfect, Geraldine, thanks," Tory said, not even bothering to look into the room. "Do you need us to do anything else before we get some rest, or..."

"No, no. Fare morrow, my sweet queens. I shall see you in the morn," Hamish said hurriedly, glancing at Geraldine before turning away, though as he looked at Orion once more he heaved against his fist again before breaking into a run.

"Problem solved," Tory said as she waved Orion towards the room which she'd claimed on behalf of Darius before turning and making a move to leave. "I'll catch you in a bit, Darcy, I just need some time in my own mind." She stepped past us, glancing back at me and giving me a small smile in goodbye as I frowned, trying to decide if I should be forcing my company on her or just accepting her decision to walk away from me so that she could get her head straight.

"Hang on," Orion said, moving forward and taking something from his pocket. He held out the beautiful ruby necklace Darius had gifted to my sister and her eyes widened in surprise.

"I reclaimed it for you during the battle," he said and Tory took it from him possessively, squeezing it tight between her fingers.

"Thank you," she whispered, the fact that he'd saved it clearly meaning a lot to her.

My lips parted in surprise as she moved forward, giving him a one armed hug and a back pat before releasing him.

"Wait, if the bond was gone because my Ward had died, I'd still be marked," Orion said in realisation, pulling his sleeve up to reveal the bare patch of skin on his arm which had once held the Leo symbol for Darius. "Even in death, the bond doesn't die."

"Then I guess we just have to wait until he shows up with an explanation," she said, with a hopeful smile, but I saw it fall again as she backed up and slipped into the royal room.

Geraldine whipped around to look from me to Orion, smoothing down her light brown hair. "Well chestnuts in my nutsack, I am simply over the moon that you two are back together."

I cleared my throat, not looking at Orion. "We're not." Dammit, that didn't come out right.

"Oh," Geraldine gasped. "Forgive me for my presumption, my lady. Well perhaps it's for the best, hey? What will the rebels say of a true queen staying with a Power Shamed Fae – no offence, Orion."

"None taken," he gritted out. "Don't you have somewhere to be, Grus?"

Her eyes flicked from me to him then she nodded several times. "Oh forgive my nippy lips, they've run away with me! I shall bid you adieu and see you in the morrow. The butteriest of bagels will await you beyond your slumber, Darcy." She bowed then jogged off down the corridor and walked into one of the rooms, leaving us alone in the pressing silence.

I drifted towards the room meant for Darius and Orion, feeling my shadow following and as I raised my eyes to meet his gaze, he leaned closer, pressing his hand above my head on the doorframe.

"I'll see you later, Blue. You can have this room to yourself." His throat bobbed as his gaze moved to my mouth, his eyes full of the same burning hunger that rippled beneath my own skin.

He went to move away and I fisted my hand in his shirt, knocking the door wider behind me and pulling him inside.

"Are you really planning on staying somewhere else?" I asked, tugging him closer and making him smirk.

"I'll be wherever you want me to be, beautiful."

I released him, stepping back as the door swung shut behind him, my heart beating powerfully in my chest like the wings of my Order. I wanted this man with every fibre of my being and I was done wasting time apart. We'd proved how far we'd go for one another in battle, he'd bowed to me, he'd sworn his allegiance in every way a Fae could. But I wanted to show him that we were equals. That when we stood before each other and he saw a queen, I saw a king staring back at me.

I tugged my shirt over my head and tossed it away so my breasts were bared, and a growl escaped him as he stepped closer, capturing my waist and pulling me flush against him like our skin was desperate to touch. And as soon as his hands were on me, I realised there were no more walls, no more rules or laws keeping us apart anymore. It was just us and screw what anyone else in Solaria thought of that.

"Are you sure you wouldn't rather I share a room with someone else, Blue?" he asked, amusement glittering in his eyes.

There was only one place I wanted him to be tonight, and he damn well knew it. He just wanted me to spell it out. But this frantic energy between us was going to consume me whole if I didn't give into it soon.

"Shut up, Lance," I said breathily.

"So mouthy today." His fingers wound into my hair and he tugged, making my head drop back and exposing my neck to him.

"If you want blood, you can fight me for it," I taunted, flicking my fingers and casting a firm air shield against my throat like a second skin.

He smiled like a demon, his eyes sparking with the challenge. "Don't bait a Vampire unless you want to be hunted, Miss Vega."

"This isn't a classroom, Professor. If you want to teach me a lesson, you'd better do it with your hands."

"Fine by me." He shoved me down onto the bed, grabbing my hips and flipping me onto my front so fast that I bounced on the mattress. He yanked my pants down and his hand clapped hard against my ass, making me gasp, the sharp bite of pain giving way to pleasure as I moaned.

The door suddenly opened and I cursed as Orion yanked me to my feet and shoved me behind him while I tugged my freaking pants up.

"Woah, sorry. Didn't realise things were getting Fifty Shades of Blue in here," Seth laughed obnoxiously. "I mean, I did 'cause I heard you, but don't mind me. I've seen everything before and I mean eve-ry-thing. I once watched a guy ear-fuck a girl."

I glanced out from behind Orion who immediately grabbed my top from the floor with his Vampire speed and yanked it over my head to cover me up, leaving my arms pinned to my sides by the material. I pouted at him as I pushed my arms through the holes and narrowed my eyes on Seth.

"So you're just gonna continue breaking into every room I ever occupy without knocking, are you?" I asked and Seth grinned wolfishly.

"Nah, this is my room too, roomie." He walked straight past us and dove onto the double bed.

Orion immediately picked him up and threw him at the door like he weighed no more than a pitball, but Seth casually caught himself on a gust of air before he could collide with it.

"Get. Out," Orion commanded, but Seth ignored him, U-turning to the space beside the door and raising his hands as he wielded the earth to make himself a single bed out of stone and coating it in a thick layer of moss.

"Guess I'll take this bed then." He dropped down on it, testing the softness of the mossy mattress he'd created as he bounced lightly on its surface. "When I was on the moon, everything was so soft. Because we didn't really weigh much, see? It was like being in a bounce house at all times."

"You're not sharing a room with us," Orion snarled, stepping toward him as he squared his shoulders and I had to agree with him. I wanted some alone time with Orion after everything, but I was so exhausted from the battle I was struggling to summon the energy for this fight.

Seth turned his large eyes on me as he cast a fluffy pillow of moss in his arms and hugged it to his chest. "Max went with Xavier, so I got stuck with Caleb," he breathed, a plea in his eyes.

"So?" Orion snapped and Seth flicked a finger, casting a silencing bubble around me and him, cutting Orion out of the conversation.

"I'll get an awkward boner," he begged. "It happened the last time we slept together, but I got away with blaming it on his buttcrack feeling like a moon crater that time. I won't get away with that repeatedly, Darcy. He'll figure it out. And then it'll ruin our friendship. I can't lose him over this. Maybe I can get over him if I just have some time. I need some time. Please give me some time. I can't go to anyone else because you're the only one who knows. So when I heard you in here, I thought 'hey, my friend Darcy will take me in, she wouldn't turn me away.'" He looked so pathetic, and my heart was tugging so hard that I was already nodding my agreement.

Orion was working to break the silencing bubble, a look of savage anger on his face that said I was going to have a real challenge on my hands in convincing him to let Seth sleep here.

Seth turned his eyes on him too, a smirk lifting his lips. "Want me to keep making him jealous?"

"What do you mean *keep* making him jealous?" I asked in confusion then he barked a laugh and dropped the silencing bubble.

Orion bristled, taking a step between us and looking to me. "What were you talking about?" he demanded, a note of concern in his voice that made me frown.

I glanced at Seth behind him, finding him shaking his head fiercely and though I hated keeping this from Orion, it wasn't my secret to tell.

"Seth needs to stay," I said and Orion looked like I'd slapped him.

"Why?" he hissed, his fangs extending like he couldn't hold back the monster in him any longer.

"He's got some…issues with Caleb," I said carefully.

"You could always swap rooms with me, bro?" Seth suggested lightly. "Why don't you go stay with Cal? You could have some Vampy, bondy blood time or some shit. Me and Darcy will be fine here together. Alone. Just like we were all those months you were in prison."

Orion snapped around with a pulse of his Vampire speed and I caught his hand a second before he attacked, sensing it as he wielded the air around him, making my hair gust forward over my shoulders.

Seth grinned tauntingly at Orion, apparently in the mood to grant himself a death wish.

"Shut it, Seth," I hissed. "If you stay here, you can't be an asshole."

"But being an asshole is what I do," he whimpered as I worked to try and get Orion's narrowed eyes off of the Wolf goading him.

Orion finally turned his gaze on me and my heart fluttered at the sight of the wild animal I found looking back at me. He leaned down until he was nose to nose with me, my lungs ceasing to work as the scent of cinnamon wrapped around me and I was caged by his presence.

"I want you to myself, Blue," he said in a deep voice that sent a tremor rolling down my spine. "He can find somewhere else to stay."

"There aren't enough rooms to go around," Seth called. "And honestly, you might end up with a roommate anyway because smelly Wanda the Tiberian Rat is wandering around out there looking for someone to take her in. Hamish says she likes to make nesting material out of your underwear. At least with me, there's no chance of that. I'll just keep you guys entertained with tales of the moon. We can have movie nights and cuddle parties and-"

"No," Orion snapped, turning to him once more. "You think I'm gonna share breathing space with the guy who's been cosying up to my girl while I was gone?"

"Firstly, I wasn't your girl while you were gone. Because you were gone, duh." I prodded Orion in the side. "And secondly, if you suggest one more time that I hooked up with Seth, I'll unleash Tory's fist on your dick again."

Orion grunted, looking to Seth with narrowed eyes then back to me. "I wanna hear it from him."

I turned to Seth, gesturing for him to go right ahead while he spread himself out on the single bed and cupped his head in his hands.

"Well…that's not a straightforward answer, Lancey. Am I the sort of guy to fuck 'your girl'-" He air quoted the words "-given the chance? Of course I am."

Orion lunged forward a step and I dove in front of him to stop him from killing Seth, though I was half tempted to do it myself after that comment.

"Have I had visions in the past of her pinned beneath me, screaming my name? Definitely."

"Seth," I snarled, about to gag him with some conjured dirt as Orion shot around me in a blur of speed, shooting toward him with intent. He collided with an air shield Seth had cast around himself and he immediately started throwing his fists at it with a furious power.

"Would we make a beautiful couple that the whole of Solaria would celebrate instead of shudder at? Abso-fucking-lutely." Seth examined his nails as Orion fought to break his air shield.

"Seth!" I shouted, my anger rising. What the hell was he playing at?

"But did I fuck her in her bed, in every position I could think up including the Hungry Vampire, proving I could make her scream louder than you did? Well, that's debatable."

"There's no debate. We didn't have sex and we never would," I growled.

Orion's fist suddenly broke through the shield and he dove at Seth like a man possessed, his fangs exposed as he landed on top of him. He started punching him, his fists cracking against a tighter air shield around Seth who simply grinned widely.

"This is a weird way to ask for a threesome, but I'm game if you are," Seth taunted.

"For the love of god, stop it," I snapped, throwing out my hands and ripping Orion away from him with a whip of air and throwing him onto the bed behind me. "Seth, I'll make a freaking coat out of your fancy white Wolf fur if you don't stop winding him up. Tell him the truth or I'll kick your ass out of here myself."

"Alright, alright, we didn't fuck," Seth conceded and I looked to Orion, finding him pushing himself off the bed, his shoulders heaving with his ragged breaths. He caught my hand, tugging me against him with a protective growl and I gripped his chin, tilting his head down to make him look at me. His heart was thrashing and there was such a desperation about him at the mere thought of me being with someone else that it melted my anger with him. But screw him for not trusting my word on this.

"Yet," Seth whispered.

"Shut up," I barked as Orion stiffened, but I kept hold of his chin to keep him looking at me.

"He's trying to get a rise out of you," I said and he nodded, apparently unable to form a sentence beyond that. "He can stay for tonight then maybe we can find another room for him tomorrow."

"Or I murder him now and the problem resolves itself," he suggested in a deadly voice.

"I'm afraid you can't do that, bro," Seth chipped in. "Darcy and me are besties now. You wouldn't kill her bestie, would you? Imagine what that would do to her."

Orion's shoulders tensed but he remained looking at me, seeing the truth of that in my expression.

"Let it go," I begged and a decision darkened his eyes before he picked me up and shot into the bed, spooning the hell out of me as he clutched me against him, my face firmly aiming to the opposite side of the room from Seth as he yanked the covers over us.

I shifted the tiniest amount and he growled, his arms tightening around me and drawing me flush back against his body.

"Hey, Mr Psycho, I can't breathe." I prodded his arm and he slackened his grip a little.

Seth started regaling us with stories of his trip to the moon for the millionth time and Orion cast a silencing bubble around us to block him out.

"You need to calm down, Lance."

His breath was hot on my ear as he replied in a whisper that sent a shiver rolling down my spine. "I'm hungry and I now have to share my breathing space with the asshole who tried to destroy us after a battle where I almost lost you."

"Well, I can help with one of those things." I shifted my hair away from my neck and gripped the back of his head, drawing his mouth to my skin.

His fangs drove into a vein and he groaned the same moment a soft moan left my lips. The keen sting of the bite and the feel of his muscles folding around me sent a rush of heat between my thighs and I automatically ground my ass back against him, desire coursing through me. When he'd drunk enough, he drew his fangs from my neck, his breaths burning my cheek as the hard length of his cock drove into my ass. But I couldn't do anything about that with Seth in the room with us.

Orion released the silencing bubble and quiet reached us from Seth's bed, making me wonder if he'd fallen asleep already.

"Goodnight, Lance," I said breathlessly and he pressed his lips to the soft place behind my ear as his fingers ran over the bite to heal it.

"Goodnight, Blue."

"Goodnight, roomies," Seth whispered.

TORY

CHAPTER TWO

I stood out in the crisp winter air with my breath fogging before me and my wet hair dripping onto the oversized black hoody I was wearing.

Geraldine had caught sight of me slipping out of the sleeping quarters and had wailed something about the masculine clothes I'd put on not being fit for a queen. She'd rushed off, vowing to find me something more suitable for royalty and Max had chased after her, leaving the route to the exit free, then I'd headed straight towards it.

It had been a bit difficult to navigate my way through the throng of rebels who were all waiting to be allocated their own sleeping space in the tunnels to the south of The Burrows, but I'd managed to throw a little shadow over myself and keep my head ducked low as I slipped between them before finding my way back to the tunnel which led to the grandfather clock.

Of course there had been a group of five rebellion guards outside the farmhouse, but with a few choice words and a dark scowl, I'd managed to convince them to let me escape for a few minutes.

I'd been a prisoner for too damn long. My mind hadn't been fully my own, clear of shadows and bonds and the will of the fucking stars for so long that I'd almost forgotten what true silence sounded like.

I may have lied to the rebellion guards when I'd promised not to go beyond the fence which ringed the farmhouse where The Burrows were concealed, but I hadn't gone much further. The barn was still safely within the wards surrounding it to protect us and I really needed to be truly alone with my thoughts for just a few minutes.

I sighed as I took in the deep silence out here, leaning my back against the rough wood of the barn door and looking at the stunning view beyond. It was the dead of night, but the full moon was bright and cast the world in silver tones which made the sweeping mountain range look unearthly beautiful with its coating of pure white snow.

My feet were bare and the snow bit at the exposed skin, but a rush of

Phoenix fire coursing through my veins banished the sensation fast enough.

I blew out a deep breath, watching it fog and sail away as I focused on thoughts of Lionel and smirked to myself as I considered many colourful ideas for his agonising death without once feeling the urge to save him from that fate.

My fingers trailed over the smooth skin of my arm which had once been branded by the Aries mark that bound me to him, and I closed my eyes as I wondered for the millionth time how the hell it was possible that the Guardian bond had been broken.

And that wasn't the only bond that had been broken today either…

I hadn't let myself think about it much yet, but I knew I was in for a world of freaking out when I really accepted that the Star Crossed bond was gone too. The mirror in the bathhouse had been dimly lit, but even so, I'd stood staring at my newly green-again eyes for several long minutes. All the while my heart had raced a million miles a minute, but I'd refused to so much as consider the possibility that our curse could really be gone.

Because if I let myself believe that, only to find out it wasn't true, I wasn't sure I could survive it.

I needed it to be real. Needed to be able to touch and kiss and caress him as much as I wanted without a single thing standing between us. And yet the idea of that terrified me too. I'd let myself feel all the things for Darius Acrux which I'd always sworn I'd never allow myself to feel, and that had been fine when there was no real chance of us ever actually being together. But now… I was a barely functioning fuck up of a girl on my best days. I was snarky and abrasive, stubborn to the point of self-detriment and damn rude more often than not. I was the girl no one wanted. Unloved came easy to me. But Darius had made it more than clear to me that I wasn't the unwanted girl to him. In fact, if there really wasn't anything keeping us apart anymore then I was pretty certain he wouldn't want us to be apart ever again.

And the thought of that lit me up from the inside out and made me wanna dance naked in the rain, screaming that he was mine and cutting any bitch who might dare to glance his way… But it also scared the fuck out of me.

I didn't know how to be someone's everything. I was pretty sure I wasn't even my own everything. Without Darcy, I was just some jaded bitch who consistently fucked up and didn't apologise for it. And I couldn't shake the feeling that if there was nothing keeping Darius away from me anymore, he'd figure that out all too quickly and then he wouldn't want me at all. How was I supposed to accept that if I let myself fall for him any more deeply than I already had? How was I supposed to survive him if he finally drew back the curtain and realised the Fae hiding behind it was nothing but a scared, little girl with no clue how to be the woman he wanted me to be?

I took in another deep breath and closed my eyes as I tried to centre myself, forcing my mind away from the fire in my limbs which reminded me all too clearly of the Dragon I kept daydreaming about and allowing myself to drift in a little bit of nothing for a while as I tried to clear my thoughts.

But as the dark pressed in on me, it was impossible not to feel myself returning to that room on Christmas Eve where Lionel had strapped me to a chair and set his twisted pets against me.

Bile caught in my throat as I relived the feeling of Clara driving that blade into my stomach repeatedly, of my blood spilling hot and fast across my skin as my screams filled the air and Vard forced his way into my mind.

"Who do you love, Roxanya?"

Over and over again, those same words hissed into my ears as I thrashed and snarled and bled out all over the plush carpets of the room which should have belonged to my father. But this time I hadn't given up the answer they'd been trying to force from my lips. I hadn't said the words Lionel was trying to command with his torture as he watched my suffering with heat and lust in his eyes. He might have been getting off on my pain, but I'd refused to relinquish control of my heart to him.

"Who do you love, Roxanya?" Lionel demanded as Clara withdrew and the agony in my flesh threatened to consume me once again. But they wouldn't let me pass out. Any time I did, they just healed me and started again, feeding me potions to replenish the blood I'd lost and making sure that this cycle of horrors could go on and on indefinitely.

My head bobbed and Lionel caught my chin in his grasp, his nails biting into my flesh as my own blood slid across my skin and he forced me to look at him.

"I can make it stop," he purred, his gaze sliding down my body and drinking in the sight of my wounds, the cuts and burns which marked me and branded me as his plaything. But I wasn't. I was Roxanya Vega, daughter of the Savage King, sister of the most powerful and beautiful woman I'd ever known, child of the greatest Seer of all time. I wasn't born to bow to him. I was born to rise.

"I love him," I hissed between my teeth, ignoring the flare of fear which tried to ignite in my core as I thought of Darius, the son of this monster and the man who had stolen my shattered heart irrevocably. I didn't care how much Vard tried to force me to believe the worst of Darius. Because I'd seen the worst of him, the best of him and everything in between and he was my perfect match in every way. So they couldn't twist my mind or heart against him anymore and I was done with the lies, done with pretending I was weaker than I was. I'd broken free of their command and I wouldn't fall prey to their bullshit again.

Lionel growled, smoke spilling between his teeth as he bared them at me and acceptance finally dawned in his gaze.

"Love," he scoffed. "So be it. Keep your love for my defiant son if it means so much to you, sweet Roxanya. But know this; I will use your love to break you, I will take it and make it mine and create a tether around your throat with it which won't ever come loose. Today I will taste your heartbreak and you will watch as I enforce my dominance over you and the man you profess such feelings for. You will be the prize I hold above him and the threat which makes him compliant. And he shall be the same for you. I do not need your love to own you. I only need the object of your desire at my mercy."

I lurched forward suddenly, aiming my forehead to crack it against the bridge of his nose as I yanked against my restraints, but the fucking Guardian bond made me stop just short of actually doing it. Lionel jerked back, fury spilling across his features at me making him flinch, and the full force of his fist collided with my skull so hard that I lost my grip on reality and fell into the abyss.

I swallowed thickly against the memories, trying to ground myself in reality and the fact that I had truly escaped him this time. There was no Guardian bond tying me to him, no threat hanging over the heads of anyone I loved. Nothing at all to ever draw me back into his company, aside from the promise I had made to see him dead at my feet with my sister at my side.

I pushed my hands into the pockets of the enormous grey sweatpants I was wearing and ignored the shiver that ran down my spine from banishing my fire magic and just stood there, embracing the quiet calm of the place and focusing on the fact that we were safe. Free.

There was a hole in the left pocket of my sweatpants and I pushed a finger through it, running it over the scarred skin there as I tried not to relive the pain I'd felt as Lionel burned the tattoo from my flesh. Someone better trained than me could no doubt heal away the scars he'd left me with, but I hadn't looked for anyone to do that yet. I was fairly certain that healing it wouldn't fix the tattoo and I hated the idea of it being gone so much that I'd rather keep the scar and pretend it just lay beneath it.

"Is it totally conceited of me to hope you might be waiting for me?" Darius's voice called out from the dark and my eyes fluttered open.

"Yeah," I agreed on a breath as I drank in the sight of him standing before me in the half unbuttoned black shirt and smart trousers he'd worn to marry Mildred, my heart racing with the speed of a stallion and my throat thickening as I took in the very real man who was somehow standing a little way down the hill before me. "But I think I've always been waiting for you, so maybe you're right."

"Even when you hated me?" he murmured, stepping closer so that the light of the moon shone on his black hair. He kept coming, closing in on me and making that thrashing organ in my chest grow wings and beat them hard as it soared from nothing other than the sight of him. He closed in on me with his huge body and I had to tilt my chin up to look at him as the distance between us fell away.

"I still hate you," I lied, and a smile touched the corner of his lips before he stepped closer again, the air between us thickening with expectation.

"The bond is broken," he growled, stepping nearer still and making goosebumps speckle my skin with nothing more than his proximity.

His eyes were so dark that in the dim light I couldn't see any difference in them, but I needed to know if it really was true, so I twisted my fingers and cast a Faelight into existence beside him which flared and lit his features in an orange glow.

The light glinted off of his deep brown eyes and my breath caught as I hunted for the black ring surrounding his irises and found it missing.

Darius's gaze burned into mine as he devoured the sight of my clear, green eyes too and for the longest time we just stood staring at each other, trying to adjust to the fact that our fates had suddenly altered and all the things we'd been aching for were right here for the taking.

"How?" I whispered, afraid to break the silence as if I thought the stars might be listening, ready to steal this gift as fast as they'd offered it.

Darius hesitated for a beat too long, his brow pinching as he expelled a short breath which fogged the air between us. "Gabriel took me to an ancient palace that has long since been forgotten by our kind. There was old magic there and I convinced the stars to change their mind about the bonds," he said in a rough voice. "It looks like they agreed."

"Agreed to what?" I murmured, my heart beating so hard that I could barely make out the sound of my own voice over the tumultuous pounding.

Darius's brow lowered and he reached out to cup my cheek in his palm, sucking in a sharp breath as the heat of his skin met the freezing coldness of mine.

"Why are you so cold?" he demanded, pushing the warmth of his fire magic into my skin as a shiver, which had nothing to do with the temperature, ran through my body. My flesh hungered for him with the desperation of a soul who had been starving for his touch for far too long and my body reacted to his instantly, my spine arching, nipples hardening.

"Fire makes me think of you," I said.

"And that's…bad?" His voice was rough and his dark eyes seemed to look right into my soul as he demanded that answer from me and I was unable to deny him it.

"Only because I know I can't have you. Or *couldn't* have you, I guess…"

I glanced up at the quiet sky with the stars twinkling far overhead and my thrashing heart only picked up the pace as I realised they weren't doing a single thing to force us apart. No storms or earthquakes or Griffins flying by and taking a shit on top of us. Nothing.

"Darius," I breathed as he leaned forward, about to close the gap between our lips but my hand landed on his chest. "If you kiss me now, I don't think I'm ever going to be able to let you go again. So if this isn't it for you, if you can't handle my stubborn, selfish ass then please just walk away. Because I can't have you for this moment if I don't have you for every moment after it-"

"I'm yours, Roxy," he growled against my lips. "For every single second I have in this world, I'm all yours. And after that I'll still be yours, wherever I end up after I'm gone, I'll belong right here with you."

His mouth met mine and silenced any other objections I may have been about to make, and I melted into his kiss as his lips moved against mine.

A moan escaped me and his tongue pushed into my mouth, caressing mine as he kissed me slowly, savouring every second of it now that we could. The stars weren't going to force us apart, there was no reason for us to rush and the way he was kissing me said he had no intention of doing that.

I wound my arms tight around him and the Phoenix in me rose up to the surface, driving against his body in a demand which I followed without thought as the creature in me took control and dove beneath his skin, burning a path inside of him as it sought out the shadows and forced them out of him in a trail of blazing power which left us both panting in each other's arms.

"Holy shit, Roxy," Darius growled against my lips. "How-"

"I'm done letting Lionel or his shadow bitch or anyone else control us. They can keep their fucking shadows – we won't be tied to them by their damn power anymore."

Darius gazed down at me like he was seeing something in me for the first time and I raised my chin as he pushed his fingers into my hair and studied my face with a hungry, aching look.

"You're incredible," he said softly, drinking me in and making my skin tingle with the intensity of his gaze as he leaned forward to capture my lips with his once more, making my knees quake and butterflies erupt in my stomach.

"Let's head back inside," I murmured, pulling back just enough to look up at him and running my fingers over the rough stubble that coated his jaw. "The others have been freaking out over you and I can find some proper clothes and-"

"Gabriel will tell them I'm here," he said dismissively. "And I like what you're wearing just fine."

I breathed a laugh as I ran my hands up the front of his shirt and my fingers tangled in the dark material. I was wearing some shitty old man clothes, had wet hair and a bare face and was most definitely looking my worst, yet I got the impression he actually meant that.

But as he gazed at me intently, a lump rose in my throat and I tightened my hold on his shirt, remembering why he was wearing it.

"You and Mildred," I murmured, the thought of the two of them together after their wedding burning a line of bile down the back of my throat. "Did you…" I trailed off, unable to ask the question and knowing it was unfair of me to feel so cut up over the idea of him consummating their union. But fuck, I'd been a ball of anxiety ever since he'd left that chapel and I needed to know almost as badly as I didn't want to find out. I understood the pressure he'd been under, I knew the position Lionel had forced him into so I would find a way to get over it if he had, but the thought of it just made me want to burn the entire world down and rip Mildred's fucking face off.

"No," Darius growled, disgust flickering over his features. "And I wouldn't have even if Gabriel hadn't saved my ass. I had a plan to use an illusion to make her think she'd been fucked and then I was gonna just…well I have no fucking idea really, but it doesn't matter. I'm not married."

"You're not?" I frowned in confusion and he smirked at me as he shook his head slowly, reaching past me to shove the heavy beam locking the door behind me aside.

"No," he confirmed. "Thanks to your brother. But maybe we can get into that later? The point is, I'm not married, you're not bonded to my father, and we're no longer Star Crossed."

"Oh," I said, mentally berating myself for not coming up with something better to say in response to that.

"Yeah," he replied, pushing the door at my back open. "Oh. And just in case it wasn't clear, baby, I'm not going to be anyone's but yours. So maybe you and me should get hitched and I can show you what a real wedding night looks like?"

A crazed laugh slipped from me and I shook my head as I began to back up, hooking my fingers into his belt and tugging him into the barn after me.

"Can we just start out slow?" I asked, trying not to freak the fuck out at the idea of marrying him. "We can see if we can go a week without beating the crap out of each other and think about marriage in like twenty years or something?"

I expected him to laugh but his gaze darkened as he let me pull him inside the barn and for a moment, I could have sworn I saw pain registering on his features. But before I could focus on it, he pushed the door closed behind him and darkness fell around us as my Faelight was left outside.

"Whatever you want, Roxy," he growled and I gasped as his hands wound around my waist.

My pulse raced at the idea of that, but before I could get too caught up in the fantasy of a future with him, his grip on my waist tightened and he walked me backwards, his mouth against mine and his kiss so brutal it almost hurt. But it was the best kind of pain I could imagine.

My back collided with something and before I knew what was happening, he'd lifted me up and was perching me on a wooden platform scattered with stalks of straw as the scent of it rose up all around us.

There was a hole in the side of the barn behind me and the moonlight poured in through it, gilding us in silver and highlighting the strong lines of his cheekbones and jaw. He was so freaking gorgeous that it made my breath catch, like some mythological demigod come to shatter hearts and steal virgins from their homes. But this deity wasn't here to ruin me, he'd come to worship at my altar and the depth of the feelings in his dark eyes had my entire body trembling with a need I was certain could only ever be satisfied by him.

His fingers slid beneath the hem of my borrowed hoody and his skin burned hot against mine as he dragged it up and off of me, taking his damn time to reveal my body to him before tossing the black fabric aside.

A growl spilled from his lips as he found me bare beneath it, my nipples hard and chest heaving.

"You're more than I deserve, Roxy, but I'm not selfless enough to give you up," he said in a dark tone. "So I'm going to take my time with you tonight. I'm going to mark each and every inch of your flesh with my touch so that you can't even wash the feeling of me from your body."

"Big claims, big man," I taunted, my gaze trailing over his broad frame, drinking in the strong lines of his tattoos which peaked out from his collar and the firm cut of his muscles that pressed against his clothes. "You'd better make good on that promise."

Darius smiled darkly and I bit my bottom lip as we just looked at each other, bathing in the fact that we were alone and the stars weren't going to do a damn thing to stop us from being together. I wouldn't need to fight them with my magic or give any of my attention to anything other than him and I intended to brand his flesh with my touch just as surely as he had promised to do to me.

"Take it off," I commanded, narrowing my eyes at the remnants of the suit he was still wearing. "I don't wanna look at you wearing some outfit you were destined to marry another woman in."

His eyes flashed hungrily and I watched as he slowly began to unbutton his shirt, revealing his tattooed skin to me inch by inch.

I watched him with my heart in my throat, running my tongue over my bottom lip as he peeled his shirt open and shrugged it off of his broad shoulders, so I was left looking at the ink that decorated his skin as my whole body clenched with need.

I gave up on trying to be patient and leaned forward to grasp his belt, slipping the leather from the buckle and running my fingers over the tattoo that marked him as mine where it curled across his hip.

"Even if it had been a real wedding, you know that I will only ever belong to you, right?" Darius asked, watching me as I unbuttoned his fly and I paused as I pushed his trousers down to fall at his feet.

Some mocking jibe was on the tip of my tongue, some deflection or joke, anything at all to detract from the seriousness of his words which were so hard for me to accept, but as I looked up into his dark eyes, I found I couldn't speak the words.

Instead, I reached out slowly, laying my hand on the hard ridges of his abs and running it up his powerful body until it laid over his heart.

"Mine," I said roughly, possessively, meaning it with every ounce of my being.

Darius's lips curled up at the corners, a predatory light seeming to blossom in his eyes as he leaned down to kiss me, the heat of his mouth and force of that kiss stealing the breath from my lungs.

He kissed me like the world was ending and I was the only solid piece of it left in existence. The movements of his lips against mine were a desperate, primal claiming which demanded I be his now and forever, and I willingly gave in to that demand.

Darius's fingers hooked in the edge of my waistband and I moaned into his mouth as I lifted my ass to let him tug the baggy old sweats down. He didn't seem to even notice the masculine clothes, lack of makeup and general state of me. He was kissing me like I was the most beautiful creation on the planet, and I was nothing but a slave to his desire as he swept me up in it.

The sweatpants gave little resistance as he tugged them off and Darius groaned as he found me naked beneath them, running his hands around the curve of my ass as his thumbs circled over my hip bones.

But as his hand slid lower and the rough skin of the burn scar Lionel had left me with grazed against his thumb, he pulled back suddenly, his fingertips moving over the damaged flesh as a deep growl escaped him.

"I'm going to rip him apart piece by piece," he snarled ferociously, his fingers moving over the scar where my tattoo for him had been and the warm flood of healing magic fell from his palm to better mend the damage. "He showed me a recording of what he did to you. I can't stop replaying it in my head, over and over again, the endless sounds of your screams ringing in my skull, knowing he did that because of how much he knew I wanted you... I'll fucking destroy him for this, but I can't undo it and that kills me."

I watched him as smoke poured from his lips and his eyes shifted to Dragon slits while his muscles trembled with rage. He was a dangerous creature, violent, strong, ferocious. His father's son. A monster just like I'd always known he was from the very first moment I'd laid eyes on him. And if I was a smarter girl, maybe I should have been afraid. Maybe I should have taken the chance to run from him now that the Star Crossed bond wasn't making me pine for him. But there wasn't a single piece of me that wanted that anymore, and as Darius finished healing my skin and made a move to step away from me, I caught his wrist in my grasp and refused to let him leave.

"Roxy," he warned, his voice a growl that made a shiver race down my spine and set my hair standing on end.

"Darius," I growled right back, my fingers digging into his flesh as he tried to move away from me.

"Everything that man did to you," he began, his eyes dark with pain and hatred. "Especially everything since he realised how I felt about you, it's because of me-"

"No," I denied, glancing down at my thigh and tugging on his hand to make him touch me there again as I found the tattoo miraculously intact once more. The mark I'd chosen to give myself, showing the whole world how I felt, showing him how I felt, without needing the stars to grant me it or try to deny it. That was what counted. "Lionel is his own man. And you're yours. He might have tried to justify his cruelty by claiming it had something to do with keeping you in line, but that's bullshit, and we both know it. He did it because he's afraid of you, Darius. He knows you're the better man, he knows you're stronger than him and he knows that if he didn't use tricks and cruelty to control you that you'd destroy him. Don't ever let him make you feel like you're responsible for any of the things he's done."

"He made me in his image," he said darkly. "And I've proved more than once that I'm no better than him."

My hand cracked across his face before I'd even realised I intended to do it and Darius snarled as he turned the golden slits of his Dragon eyes onto me.

"You *are* better than him, Darius. And you might be a monster, but you're *my* monster now and I want you just the way you are."

We locked eyes for an endlessly long moment and suddenly his mouth was on mine again, the taste of smoke coating his tongue and the heat of the fire in his limbs enough to burn against my frozen skin.

I ran my hands up and over the broad slope of his shoulders, my fingers digging into his flesh as he loomed over me, dominating me with his huge body, his hands braced against the wooden platform either side of my hips.

My thighs parted as he stepped between them, my aching core desperate for more of him as he pressed closer and the hard ridge of his cock ground against my wet heat.

I grasped the back of his neck so tightly that I could feel my fingernails cutting into his skin and a growl of desire rumbled through his chest where it pressed to mine.

He dropped his boxers, kicking them away from us with his pants and catching hold of my knee as he hooked my leg around his waist, his solid cock grinding against me and making me whimper as it drove against my clit for a far too brief moment.

"I love you, Roxy," he growled, drawing back and cupping my face in his free hand, making me meet his gaze as his dick found my core and he slowly began to sink into me.

"I love you, Darius," I gasped in reply, my breath catching as the feeling of him stretching and filling me stole all of my focus.

A groan of pure pleasure escaped him as he took his sweet time filling me, his grip on my knee tightening as he held me exactly where he wanted me and sheathed every solid inch of his cock inside me.

Once he was fully seated within me, we fell still, our ragged breaths colouring the space between us, clouds of vapour emerging from our lips as the heat of our fire-touched skin met with the frigid air.

We stared at each other for several long seconds, drinking in the feeling of us being alone, together, united at long fucking last without a star in the sky lifting so much as a twinkly finger to try and part us.

And then he began to move.

I cried out as he rocked his hips, his cock driving into me in the most delicious way as my throbbing pussy squeezed tight around him, sending shockwaves of pleasure radiating through my body.

I remained upright, my nails digging into his shoulders as I clung to him and moved my hips in time with his, kissing him hard and demanding he give me all he had.

The wooden shelf I was perched on creaked and groaned beneath the savage thrusts of his hips and splinters drove into my ass as I clung to him, panting his name and begging for more.

Darius gripped my hair in his fist and yanked on it, forcing me to arch backwards in his hold and baring my tits to him so that his mouth could descend on one of my nipples as he continued to fuck me so hard I saw stars.

"More," I gasped, closing my eyes as he held me in that position, focusing on the feeling of him owning me as I drove my heels into his ass and my fingers raked down his chest.

Darius snarled at the challenge in my voice and he tugged on my hair and my knee simultaneously, forcing me to bend even further backwards until his dick was slamming into that magical fucking spot inside me which promised the most beautiful kind of oblivion and I was coming for him with a cry of ecstasy which almost drowned out the sound of shattering wood as the shelf I was perched on gave way.

"Fuck," Darius cursed as he fell on top of me amongst the broken boards and my back slammed down on a pile of straw which had been stacked there.

A laugh tumbled from my lips as he fought to push his weight off of me and I shoved his shoulder, encouraging him to roll onto his back as I moved to straddle him.

My smile widened as I looked down at him, bits of straw clinging to his sweat slicked abs like we were taking part in some kind of sweet romance fantasy and he'd just stolen my virtue in the barn while my daddy wasn't home.

"I love that fucking sound," he murmured, reaching up to pluck a piece of straw from my hair as I took his cock in my hand and began to slick my fingers up and down it.

"Yeah?" I asked, tipping my head to one side as I pushed up onto my knees, ignoring the prickle of the straw as it scratched against my skin and sinking down onto his huge dick once more, making him groan. "Well I love that fucking sound."

"Is that right?" His big hands gripped my ass and I let him guide my movements as I began to ride him, my pussy already aching for more even as the aftershocks of the pleasure he'd delivered to me still lingered in my flesh. "Well I love the sound of you coming on my dick, Roxy. I love feeling you squeeze me tight with that slick pussy of yours and cry out with a pleasure so raw I wanna fucking bottle it. I love it so much that I'm gonna get you to make that sound for me a hundred times before the sun rises today to make up for all the orgasms I didn't get to give you while we were cursed."

"A hundred?" I mocked, but my voice cut off with a gasp as he thrust his hips up hard and stole my goddamn breath. "Shit, you're so fucking big," I complained but the cocky look on his face let me know he didn't believe I was really complaining at all.

"Yeah, Roxy, a hundred times. I might as well aim for the stars, seeing as those bastards kept us apart all this time."

I laughed again, the noise an almost manic sound as I tried to take in this new reality where we could actually just be together as his thrusts got harder and his thirsty gaze moved to my tits as they bounced for him.

"Show me how you touched yourself when you were wishing I could do it," he growled, no doubt in his mind that I'd done just that, and I moaned instead of complaining as he continued to fuck me hard from below, refusing to let me dominate him despite my position on top of him.

I moved my hand to my clit and started working it for him like he wanted, my other hand teasing my nipple as his fingers dug into my ass and he fucked me even harder.

I was moaning again, the sound so loud I knew that the stars could hear every moment of this and the thought of overcoming their bullshit decision on our fate made me even hotter as I felt myself drawing closer to the edge.

Darius watched me with such clear desire that I couldn't look away from him for a single moment and as he commanded me to come for him, I did, pleasure radiating through me as my pussy tightened around his cock and begged him to join me in our release.

He groaned as he fought it, flipping us over once more and pinning me beneath him as he fucked me down into the pile of straw, his mouth claiming mine in a brutal kiss which swallowed my cries of pleasure as he chased his own release with a savage intensity which had every inch of my flesh coming alive for him.

I met every thrust of his hips with my own and when he finally came with a roar which betrayed his Order form, I couldn't help but shatter for him once more too.

My pussy throbbed and pulsed around him and he crushed me down onto the bed of straw as we fell apart in each other's arms, panting and shaking in the aftermath of it.

Darius rolled onto his side and tugged me with him so that I was laying over his chest, my head pressed to his heated skin as I listened to the heavy thump of his heart while we caught our breath.

"Nothing is going to tear us apart again now," I breathed into the silence, vowing it on the stars who had cursed us.

Darius hesitated before he replied and I turned my head to look up at him, feeling tension in his arms as they tightened around me.

"This is the only place I ever want to be," he said as he reached out to brush a lock of dark hair from my eyes. "Right here with you."

I smiled up at him, hardly able to believe that this was real. That I could feel so fucking happy so soon after feeling so damn helpless. But there was something about being in his arms which just made me feel like I was where I belonged at long last. And I wasn't planning on letting that feeling go any time soon.

"We should probably go inside and see the others," I said reluctantly but Darius shook his head as he turned to press me down onto my back in the straw again.

"I'm pretty sure I promised you a hundred orgasms and we're only up to three."

"I think it's physically impossible for me to have that many orgasms in a row," I joked but the look he gave was all insatiable lust and I got the feeling he really did plan on trying to make that happen.

"Only one way to find out, baby. So why don't you just lay back and let me feast on you until you're coming all over my face? Because once I'm done devouring you, I plan on living out every damn fantasy I've had about you since the moment we met. And believe me, there's a fucking lot of them to get through before dawn."

"Dawn?" I gasped as he pushed my thighs apart and lowered his mouth to my core, looking up at me with those dark eyes while he hovered just above my pussy, making me shiver with the desire for him to close that distance.

"Worried you can't keep up?" he taunted and I narrowed my eyes.

"I'm more worried that you can't," I tossed back before fisting my hand in his dark hair and pushing his head down so that he could make good on that promise and within moments I was writhing and panting beneath him once more as he brought me to ruin all over again.

LIONEL

CHAPTER THREE

Fury blossomed beneath my veins as I roared my rage to the heavens and released a blast of Dragon fire into the sky while clutching hold of the roof of the tallest tower in The Palace of Souls.

The stump of my right foreleg was bleeding across the tiles, my hopeless grief over the loss of it all consuming as I remained on the roof, stuck in my Order form like some newly Emerged whelp unable to control his fucking emotions. But this anger I felt was far beyond anything I'd ever experienced before.

That girl. That fucking offspring of the Savage King had done this to me through luck and timing alone. I couldn't fathom how she'd dared to betray me like this after all I'd done to bind her to me. But somehow, she had achieved the impossible and in that brief moment where I'd been slow to react to the sudden change in our bond, she'd struck at me with the speed and brutality of the beast who had fathered her.

I roared again, cursing the stars for letting me waste so many years building myself up to this point. It had taken me too long to claim my crown. They'd worked against me from the start, first stealing Clara into the embrace of the shadows without delivering their power to me like I'd been relying upon. Then tricking me into believing those fucking Vega girls had died as suckling infants as they should have.

And now, just as luck had finally begun to deliver all that I deserved and the crown lay upon my head at last, I was cursed with this insolence and test of my devotion to our great kingdom and my true purpose.

I roared again, my claws slicing into the tiles as I slipped, blood loss weakening me as I continued to bleed from the grotesque stump which I couldn't even bear to look at.

This loss was more grievous to me than the betrayal of my sons.

My hand. My fucking hand.

How was I supposed to cast my magic with the speed and power I was used to now? It would take years of training for me to match my previous skill with only one hand left to conjure with, and even then, I may not be able to match the other Councillors.

Everything I'd worked so hard to claim could be lost because of the return of two princesses who the world had been more than ready to forget.

I belched fire into the sky once more, the acid in my gut seeping through every inch of my being as I fought to contain this fury.

A sharp sting bit into my flesh and I whipped around, my body stiffening as the shadows within me seemed to throb and pulse with a command beyond my control or desire. A bout of dizziness almost sent me tumbling from my perch atop the tower just as the shift was forced on me suddenly by the darkness running through my veins as if it had a mind of its own.

I fell with a cry of fright, shadows whipping all around me as I shifted back into my Fae form and they encircled my entire body, slowing my fall before dumping me on my back on the cold concrete of the courtyard far below the tower.

A choked sound of pain escaped me as I fell on the stump of my arm, scrambling to push myself into a kneeling position as I looked up at the Shadow Princess before me. She was coated in a dress created entirely of darkness and her cruel eyes flickered with the Element which she ruled over. She no longer looked like Clara, she was a princess of darkness, the true woman behind the façade of the girl I'd thought had stood at my side. Her features were harder, her gaze sharper and the tilt of her chin suggesting she thought herself my equal rather than my subordinate. I didn't know what had happened to her in that battle, but this wasn't the creature I'd been controlling since her return to me.

"Don't snivel, Daddy," she sang, all trace of Clara banished from her as if my pet had never even been present within her at all. The bond between us was broken, just as the bond between the Vega girl had somehow been removed from my flesh too. Though I got the feeling this connection had been lost when Clara had taken leave of this body, not through any trick of the stars.

"I do not snivel," I snarled, forcing myself to my feet despite the way my head was spinning and slapping my left hand down over the stump of my right wrist as I pushed healing magic into it and stopped the bleeding, fusing skin over the wound and stealing away the pain. I could not grow a hand back like I could other limbs, it was one of the Cardinal rules of our magic. Any source of power could not be restored. Head, heart or hands. None could be returned if they were destroyed.

All the time I worked, the Shadow Princess watched me, her head cocked to one side and the shadows dancing all around her, caressing her skin and letting flashes of it be exposed so that I was gifted a view of her naked body beneath them.

"This is a disaster," I snarled, turning away from her and striding along the outer wall of The Palace of Souls as naked as the day I was born and looking for a target to aim my wrath at.

"Sire!" Jenkins called as he darted out of a door, my old butler ready and waiting with a robe for me like always. If there was a single Fae in this wretched kingdom who I held any kind of fondness for then it was him. And that was the only reason I didn't blast him apart to sate the bloodlust pounding through me and instead threw the robe over myself to cover my body.

"I need a full report on the fight and who was involved. I want names of every Fae who turned on their king and I will see heads roll for it. If you can't find the perpetrators then find me their mothers, brothers, sisters, children or their fucking pets. The executions will begin at dawn."

Jenkins bowed low and I strode on, my gaze scanning the dead bodies and the damage to the grounds as I went. This was unacceptable. I could not allow this kind of dissent in my kingdom and now the public were going to learn the price of crossing their king in the most public and gruesome ways I could imagine.

"What am I going to do without my hand?" I demanded of the stars, snarling up at them as they looked on without a fucking care as always.

It didn't matter anyway. I was the master of my own fate and the fate of the entire kingdom. So I would make the decision on how to proceed for all of us.

A prickle ran up my spine as the creature who had once shared a body with Clara followed me and I fought against the urge to look back at her, sensing the shift that had taken place here. For some reason, the girl who had been Guardian bonded to me was absent now and I got the feeling I was going to have to work hard to tighten my control on the shadow wielder that remained in her place. But I refused to balk at the change, refused to so much as acknowledge it as I continued to walk ahead of her, making her follow me and reminding her of who ruled here.

I would need to figure out this change in her and perhaps adapt my methods of control over her too, but if there was one thing I had learned during my rise to power then it was to make certain you never let anyone see you flinch.

So I would treat her as though nothing had changed while I figured this out and if luck stayed on my side then she would continue in the role I'd crafted for her without any need for me to tighten my hold on her.

A man let out a cry of fright as I strode closer to him, his wide eyes the only thing making it clear he wasn't a corpse as I observed the broken bones protruding from his body and concluded that he had likely fallen from a great height. But I didn't recognise him. And as his pleas for mercy reached my ears, I strode straight towards him, planting my bare foot on his throat and bearing my weight down as he began to thrash and fight beneath me.

I snarled as I watched him struggle uselessly against me, drinking in the terror in his eyes as he was forced to accept who the more powerful Fae was here, and my fury was tainted by a fleeting moment of victory as I watched the life spill from his gaze and sent him into damnation like the worthless cretin he was.

All the time, the Shadow Princess trailed behind me and I felt her curious gaze on my movements, assessing me and hunting for any signs of weakness.

No matter how hard I pushed for it, I couldn't feel any kind of bond with her now and my mind was spinning with what that could possibly mean. How had the Guardian bonds been thwarted? And now that she was no longer under my thrall, how difficult would it be to maintain control of her?

I stepped over a man who was covered in enough blood to make me assume he was already dead, but his hand snapped out as I made a move to pass him by, his fingers biting into my skin as he hissed a plea for help.

I sneered down at him, about to end his miserable life too, but recognition filled me before I could make the killing blow.

Vard coughed out a mouthful of blood, his skin pale, my Seer looking on the verge of death as he waited on my help.

I considered leaving him there to die. Or even taking his life myself.

He'd failed me tonight.

What use was a Seer who didn't manage to foresee such a devastating turn of events?

But as I raised my left hand with the intention of burning him to death, a whip of shadows yanked tight around my wrist and latched themselves on to the darkness which lurked within me, freezing me in place. My heart lurched in surprise which was quickly followed by rage as I realised what had just happened. What she'd just done.

"We might need him yet, Daddy," the Shadow Princess warned, her dark eyes meeting my furious gaze, the challenge in them making my hackles rise. I needed to rein her back in. Get her under my control again before she became a problem. But if that superior look in her eyes was anything to go by then I was willing to bet that forcing her beneath my heel here and now wouldn't be the smartest way to proceed. She was powerful in ways I couldn't claim to be and with my hand now lost to me, I was at a severe disadvantage. But I was no fool. And she was still standing by my side for some reason, so perhaps there was something simpler than violence which I could use to keep her in her place.

"As you wish, my love," I said to her in the same coddling tone I'd used to placate her while she was still bound to me through her connection to Clara. But there was nothing of that girl left in her now and as I looked upon the unfamiliar yet beautiful features of this new and unknown creature, I got the feeling she wouldn't be so easily pacified.

But she seemed to accept my words all the same, her power withdrawing as she returned control of my body to me and I shrugged off the hold of the shadows.

She inclined her head with a twisted smile and I reluctantly sent just enough healing magic into Vard's body to save him from the brink of death before turning away and storming back towards the palace.

I needed my fucking gold. And my throne. And my star damned crown.

Jenkins threw the doors to the palace wide as I strode past countless guards and FIB agents who were working to help or apprehend any survivors, ignoring them all as I headed straight towards the throne room.

The slap of my bare feet echoed through the huge hall as I headed straight for the seat of power where I'd been forced to bow to the Savage King far too fucking often in my youth. But I'd overthrown him in the end. Just like I would crush this pathetic uprising run by his untrained daughters and all the worthless Fae who had chosen to follow them in their hopeless quest to try and reclaim my crown.

"Where is Darius?!" I bellowed to no one in particular as Vard prostrated himself before the throne and the Shadow Princess began to slowly circle the room, brushing her fingers along the gilded cornices and seeming lost in her own world as the shadows trailed along behind her.

My gaze followed her movements as I assessed the changes in her, trying to figure out how best to tighten my grip on her now and wondering if Clara was gone for good or if I could coax that more compliant side of her back out again.

"I'll get him, my liege," Jenkins said. "He must still be consummating his wedding. Would you like me to bring his bride here too?"

I repressed a shudder at the thought of having to lay my eyes on the hideous girl I'd been forced to select as a bride for my Heir and jerked my head in a nod, knowing I needed to start thinking strategically. We needed to present a united front in the press. The Dragon King and his newly married Heir against an uprising caused by the Savage King's daughters.

I sneered at the memory of the other Heirs fighting against me tonight, but that would just have to be smoothed over. I would make the other Councillors denounce the three boys. I'd claim the Vega whore had been fucking all three of them for months with her poisoned pussy and that the insane one had been whispering curses in their ears with her imaginary crows until they believed in them too. The Spares would take their places in the line of succession, and I'd see them all hanged before this was done to make sure no loose ends remained.

I placed my golden crown upon my head and closed my eyes as I fought against the rage in my flesh, trying to figure this out. I could fix this. I'd gone up against worse odds than this in the past and won.

The Savage King and his stuck-up queen had died through my cunning and superiority and their offspring would soon suffer the same end. Once they were dead, there would be no one left alive who could match me or challenge me and I could rule in peace as I had intended from the start, making Solaria into the great and prosperous nation I knew it could be once Order supremacy was embraced the way it should be, and crossbreeding was finally abolished.

Minutes ticked by as I started working on my next move, waiting on the return of my son so that I could lace him into my plans more deeply.

"Sire!" a high-pitched voice made a shudder of irritation run through me and I looked up as Stella Orion burst through the door, her dark hair dishevelled. "Oh my love, I was so worried about you!"

She raced forward as if to throw herself into my arms and I flicked my fingers at her, stopping her short with a barrier of air magic.

"Was me fucking your daughter in place of you not message enough?" I snarled, my distaste for her desperation showing on my face, but I was done pandering to her delusions about me and I had far more pressing matters to address right now. I didn't need to waste time on this desperate woman.

"I don't know what you-"

"You were useful to me once, Stella, and I may have gotten a thrill from fucking you right under your husband's nose, but I long since grew tired of your over used cunt. And now I find myself tired of the sound of your voice too."

"I don't understand," she gasped, clutching at pearls which did not hang around her neck as her gaze darted to the beautiful woman who continued to circle the room like a predator on the hunt for blood, singing a strange and eerie tune under her breath. A frown of confusion pulled at Stella's features, and I realised she didn't know that her daughter was gone or what creature now stood in her place. And I had no more answers to how that had occurred than she did, so I wasn't in the mood to discuss it. Especially with the Shadow Princess listening in to every word and watching every move we made.

In fact, I was refusing to outwardly react to the change in the creature who held dominion over the shadows but in all truth, she was the main focus of my plotting now. I needed to bind her to me again, one way or another.

"You understand perfectly, Stella," I sneered. "So stop embarrassing yourself and prostrate yourself before your king as you should before I decide I prefer the idea of you dead."

Stella glanced at Vard who still remained bowed at my feet, his forehead pressed to the cold tiles and hands stretched out before him, clearly understanding how close I was to cleaning fucking house a lot better than she did.

"Where's Clara?" she breathed. "What happened here today? Why didn't you invite me to the wedding?"

"Did you not hear me, woman?" I spat.

Her bottom lip wobbled as she sank to her knees but as a growl escaped me, she quickly flattened herself before me alongside my other useless aid.

I toyed with the idea of ending her now despite her submission, wondering what use she even was to me anymore, but the sound of hurried feet drew my focus to the door once again.

"My King!" Jenkins cried, his voice filled with horror as he pushed his way into the room, dragging a breakfast cart along behind him with a hogtied, pig-ugly girl balanced on top of it.

"What is the meaning of this?" I demanded, shoving to my feet as I took in the sight of Darius's bride tied up and gagged with her beady eyes swivelling back and forth between my face and the stump where my hand should have been.

"I found her tied in the closet of the marital chambers. There is no sign of Darius. I thought you would wish to question her yourself," Jenkins explained, wringing his fingers together as he backed up and I stalked closer to the prize pig.

I ripped the gag from her mouth, the hair of her moustache brushing my fingers in the process and making my stomach turn with distaste.

"Speak," I commanded.

"I don't know what happened!" she wailed, fat tears leaking from her eyes as I left her hogtied on the breakfast cart. "I was so excited to marry my snookums. The last thing I remember, I was about to don my dress and the next thing I know I was tied in the closet all alone in the dark."

"This happened before the wedding?!" I boomed, my gaze snapping from her to Jenkins who shook his head helplessly. "Do you mean to tell me you didn't consummate the union?"

"I d-didn't even get to say my vows," she wept and a roar escaped me as I shoved the cart away from me, sending it crashing into the wall and knocking her off of it where she rolled away across the floor with a wail of fright.

"My own son was in on this! My only Heir!" I bellowed, my rage somehow growing as the beast in me begged for freedom once more and I tried to piece all of this together. How had he done this? How had they thwarted me in this??

I saw red as I strode away from her, my hunger for vengeance rearing up inside me like a tornado and threatening to consume every part of me.

"Get her out of my fucking sight!" I shouted, needing her gone before I did something foolish like killing one of the only pure-blooded female Dragons of her generation, and Jenkins caught hold of her bound ankles and began to drag her from the room on her stomach while she continued to sob.

I swear my vision actually clouded over as the depths of this fucking attack hit me and I realised I was left without the one thing I needed to secure my reign.

"What am I supposed to do without an Heir!?" I hollered at everyone and no one, the crystal chandelier above the throne rattling as my rage almost consumed me.

Darkness rose up all around me and in my fury it took me a moment to recognise the power of the shadows before the Shadow Princess stepped into my path and the might of her dark magic collided with me.

She hurled me back into the throne, pain splintering up my spine as curses poured from my lips and the entire room was shrouded in darkness.

Stella and Vard screamed as her power dug its way into their flesh, and she banished them from the room as they fled, slamming the doors behind them and striding up the steps to my throne as she closed in on me, her eyes flickering with darkness.

"Stop snivelling like some day old brat and raise your chin like a true king," she snarled, crooking one finger at me and using her control over the shadows which resided beneath my flesh to raise my right arm in her direction.

I cried out as pain burrowed through the ruined stump at the end of my arm, unable to fight back in any way as she wielded her magic against me and something grew from the stump with agonising slowness.

I gasped as I recognised fingers sprouting from within my own skin, their form fully built out of shadows which grew and grew until finally an entire hand sat there, formed from her dark power in place of the one I'd lost.

"There we go, much better," she said in delight, releasing her hold on me and I shoved to my feet instantly, towering over her and snatching her throat in my grasp, using my new hand and marvelling at the strength of it as I bared my teeth at her.

"What are you?" I demanded, my gaze roaming over her face as I drank her in, noting the strangeness, the power, the beauty.

"I am your queen," she replied, her voice hoarse from the strength of my grip on her. "A long, long time ago your ancestor promised to marry me and place me upon the throne of flames. Octavius Acrux promised me his hand in marriage. I am Lavinia Umbra and we made a deal which I expect his descendent to stick to. You owe me that, Daddy."

"That doesn't answer my question," I snarled, my mind scanning over my knowledge of my ancestors as I tried to place the man she spoke of, wondering how long she had been waiting for this so-called promise to be fulfilled and why it hadn't been originally upheld.

"I am the queen of my people. The leader of the shadow-born. Ruler of the power which has gifted me this eternal life. I am the woman who had her empire stolen and her fate sealed within the Shadow Realm for all too long. I am owed an Acrux King. You are *mine*." Her eyes blazed with the darkness of her power as I tightened my grip on her throat and she smiled manically as she looked up into my eyes without a trace of fear. "And you need a new Heir."

"What kind of Heir could a creature such as you birth me?" I scoffed, unable to believe that this thing could produce life in a womb filled with nothing but shadows.

"I will give you an Heir born of true power, with loyalty running in his veins as thickly as the shadows of his mother and the Dragon fire of his father."

"You can guarantee me a Dragon born child?" I demanded, my gaze falling over her body from her pale skin to her near black lips, watching the way the shadows moved around her like I was keeping my eye on a pit of vipers. But maybe this was it. The solution I needed. A way to bind her to me and bring her to heel. All good whores just needed a strong man to force them into submission after all and I couldn't say I had many objections to fucking her. She was beautiful even if she was filled with darkness.

"I can guarantee you a child more powerful than any born before him. He will be a Dragon with Elemental and shadow magic and he will rule in your stead the way you always dreamed your true Heir would. But only once you make me your queen."

I could taste the hunger in her for the power of my throne and I hesitated short of agreeing to this madness. Was I really going to grant this creature a throne?

Her hand snapped out and she locked my balls firmly in her grasp, a hiss escaping me as she glared into my eyes and despite the way my grip on her throat tightened, she didn't so much as flinch.

"I am owed an Acrux King," she warned, her eyes crazed and alight with wicked promises. "But if you won't make me your queen then I can just rip your manhood clean from your body and claim one of your sons instead. Rip, tear, pull, crush. So choose wisely, Daddy. For I am already a princess of the shadows, and I won't be denied what I am owed a second time."

I grunted in discomfort as she failed to remove her hand and jerked a nod of acceptance.

"I will make you my queen," I agreed and a smile lit her deadly lips as she released me like nothing had even happened. "But first we need to tighten our control over the kingdom."

Her gaze roamed over me as I squeezed her throat firmly and finally, she nodded, the shadows receding so that I could breathe a little easier, seeing I had her under my command once more.

"As you wish, My King. Let's get started then."

ORION

CHAPTER FOUR

I'd stayed up late into the night, hoping the sound of Darius's arrival would carry to me, but instead my ears only picked up faraway farts and the grunts of someone having sex a few doors down. Could have used a silencing bubble for the sake of the Vampires in the place, but did they? No fucking siree.

Eventually I'd fallen into exhaustion, holding onto Darcy and hating Seth with every atom in my body for ruining my night with her. Echoes of the battle kept clinging to me, holding me tight until I was suffocated by the horror of it all over again. I replayed Clara dying in my arms until it was scored into the inside of my skull. But I focused on the peace that found her as she left this world and reminded myself she was somewhere better now. And in a way, I really had saved her in the end, just not how I'd imagined. Her soul was free of Lavinia and no more torment would find her beyond the Veil. My sister was resting at long last, and for that I had to be grateful.

I stirred from a restless sleep and refused to open my eyes as I drew Darcy back against me, wondering if I could steal her away somewhere within these caverns to seize this girl as mine before she ever slipped from my grasp again.

I nuzzled into the hair brushing against my cheek, but frowned at the masculine scent carrying from it, wondering if it was those washalilies that lingered on her, and wanting to brand her with my own scent instead. My arms tightened on her and as I crawled deeper out of the haze of sleep, I realised she didn't feel right at all. She was too muscular, too large, and as my eyes snapped open and a growl rippled along my throat, I knew I'd be starting this day with a gruesome murder.

"Capella!" I barked, launching him away from me across the room and he slammed into the wall with a yelp, hitting the floor butt fucking naked as he scrambled to regain his senses.

"You broke my thucking nothe." He held a hand up to heal it as it pissed blood down onto his bare chest and I shot out of bed in a blur, tearing forward to finish the job of beating the hell out of him, but slamming into an air shield instead as he cast it between us.

"What the fuck were you doing in our bed?!" I snapped. "And where the hell is Blue?" I jerked around, hunting for her, but it was just me and the mutt. Which meant there'd be no witnesses when I ripped his spinal cord out and stuffed it up his ass.

"It was cold over there." Seth pointed at his own bed. "And there was a chilly breeze blowing in under the door."

"You're an air Elemental," I spat, stalking back and forth in front of his shield as I heaved breaths in and out, hungry for a fight.

"Yeah and I'm a Werewolf!" He got to his feet, wiping away the blood from his now healed nose on the back of his hand. "I need snuggles. Without snuggles, I get cold and lonely. And Darcy went to get breakfast, so your bear arms were going to waste, and I snuck in for a little hug time. I don't see what the big deal is." He grabbed some sweatpants from the floor, yanking them on.

"I don't snuggle," I snapped.

"Liar," he scoffed. "You snuggle with Darcy and Darius all the time. But where's my snuggles, Lance? Where's. My. Snuggles?"

"You're fucking insane," I hissed and he let out a whimper, stepping toward me with his eyes going all large and dog like. As if that would ever work on me.

A knock came at the door and I almost ignored it in favour of blasting Seth's air shield to bits and strangling him to death with my bare hands. But then Gabriel called out from beyond it, saying three words that made my heart leap into my throat.

"Darius is back."

My breath caught in my lungs and I spun around, shooting toward the door with my Order gifts and yanking it open, coming face to face with my Nebula Ally. He grinned, yanking me in for a hug and patting me on the back.

"Where is he?" I asked. "What happened?"

"He's been with Tory all night," he said.

"All night?" I barked, stepping back. "Why didn't you come to me sooner?"

"Trust me, you did not want to go and interrupt them. I had to keep myself busy all night just so I wasn't plagued by visions of my sister being railed by a fucking Acrux."

"By the moon, why would the stars show you that?" I grimaced.

"Because they're assholes who have a sick sense of humour, Orio. Now go see him before he gets mobbed by the Heirs. He's gonna be in the dining hall in two minutes. Go straight to the end of the corridor, first left and keep on until you get there."

"Did someone say Heirs?" Seth called behind me and I clapped Gabriel on the shoulder in thanks and shot away before the mutt could tag along.

I sped through the stone tunnels, shooting left and straight down through double wooden doors into an enormous cavern which was brimming with people. People who started to fall quiet as I came to a halt and they spotted me standing there in my sweatpants.

"Isn't that the Power Shamed professor who Dark Coerced a Vega?"

someone hissed.

"Why is he here?"

"He should be ashamed of himself."

"I'd rather die than be Power Shamed. I'd just slit my throat right there and then in court."

The hacking sound of someone retching drew my attention to Hamish whose eyes had found me. He doubled over, working hard not to throw up the oatmeal he'd been eating as his eyes watered and he twisted in his seat so that he didn't have to look at me. I clenched my jaw, trying to ignore the way everyone was turning their backs on me and pretending I didn't exist. This Power Shaming bullshit was something I hadn't had to deal with much yet, but down here it looked like I wasn't going to be able to escape it.

I spotted Blue sitting with Geraldine and a group of the A.S.S. members at the far end of the hall and her eyes found mine like a magnet. She rose from her seat, but I shook my head minutely, not wanting her to have to be seen with some Power Shamed Fae. It was making my blood chill. My life was wrecked beyond repair. I would never be seen as an equal in society ever again. Darcy and I were officially done. Because how could I ever really hope to date a Vega princess again? It would muddy her name, destroy the support she had for the throne. It was bad enough what they thought I'd done to her to earn my place in prison, but in ways this was even worse. Because I was a disgraced Fae and there was no fate more horrifying than that for my kind.

I momentarily forgot all about my ruined reputation when Darius said my name behind me.

I turned, finding him standing there with his arm slung around Tory's shoulders, his eyes as gleamingly brown as they had been before he'd been Star Crossed. My heart lifted as he drew Tory closer and not a single tremor rocked the earth, no sign of the heavens crying out to tear them apart. They were free of their bond, it was as clear as day, and I couldn't have been happier for them.

"What did you do?" I asked in astonishment, my hand going to the place where the Leo mark had been branded on my skin for so many years. It was gone. My shackles broken at long last, my life returned to me and no longer pledged to someone else. And the weight of that truth only hit me now as I saw the truth in his gaze, that he really had done this. Somehow, he'd broken the bonds.

"I prayed to the stars and they answered," he said with a smile brighter than I'd seen on his face in years. I'd almost forgotten he could smile like that, without the weight of a thousand burdens drawing it down.

"This makes no sense," I said in disbelief, shaking my head as I stepped closer, unsure where things lay between us now. I didn't know what we were without the bond, we'd been friends before it, but we'd changed so much over the years since then, what if we weren't as close anymore? What if this broke us?

I forced those fears from my head, shooting forward with a burst of speed and punching him in the gut. He doubled over as I barked a laugh, shoving him upright, tempted to do it again just to prove I could, and the smirk on his face said he was up for the fight.

But before we could break out into a full-on tussle, the Heirs appeared, descending on him and pulling him and Tory into their arms, crushing them in a tight hug circle while Seth howled his joy. They all started to echo it until the crowd in the room were cheering and I stared on, feeling out of place as my heart seemed to shrink two sizes.

"All rejoice! The true queens and the Heirs to the Celestial Council are united at last on the path of freedom and prosperity for us all!" Geraldine cried, her voice bouncing magically around the room and causing more and more people to cheer at the sight of my best friend as I was pushed away from him.

The crowd shoved past me, knocking me further back while keeping their eyes averted from me and my throat tightened. I stared at Darius over their heads while Max scruffed his hair and Caleb jumped up and down with Seth bouncing around them.

Darcy made it to them next with Geraldine in tow and they all hugged again, practically spinning around in circles as Geraldine started singing.

"Oh a great and merry day has come! The stars shine brightly on us all, us all," she sang and half the room joined her, apparently knowing this random song as she went on. "Oh now the gleaming moon has come! To glow upon us all, us all."

Seth howled louder and a chorus of howls carried up from a large group at the back of the hall who I recognised as the Oscuras. And if they were here-

"Must be sad having no friends." A hand landed on my shoulder and I turned, finding Leon Night there with his long golden hair and broad chest puffed out. He'd been in Gabriel's year at Aurora Academy and I'd played against him in Pitball a few times back when I'd been attending Zodiac, before he'd gone pro and ended up living the dream I'd always ached to live myself.

"I'll still be your friend, buddy," he said with a Lion's grin. "It must be lonely back here. All alone, without people."

"I'm fine," I muttered, my eyes falling on Darcy as Seth lifted her up on his shoulders and Tory was lifted up on Darius's a second later. My teeth ground in my mouth and I forced myself not to intervene as Darcy laughed, reaching out to hug her sister with happy tears in her eyes. Fuck, that girl deserved this. Both of them did. There'd been too much shit in their lives to wade through ever since I'd brought them to Solaria.

"I wouldn't be fine if *I* was Power Shamed," Leon said sadly. "I can't think of a worse fate actually. I'd rather be eaten by acid slugs, or chomped up and swallowed by a Bear Shifter, or dropped from a really, really, really, really-"

"I get it," I gritted out.

"Really high building," he finished with a sympathetic smile. "Oh shit, gotta go, dude. I put glimmer glue in Dante's poptarts." He darted away into the crowd and I saw Dante's huge form barrelling through the crowd as he tried to shout at Leon, but his lips were stuck together with a thick purple gloop so all he managed was a furious growl.

I watched Darcy until my eyes burned and I remembered to blink, slipping back into the shadows at the corner of the room. It was a relief to escape the disgusted glances that came my way, the backs turned on me and offering me insult upon insult as I was treated like a living plague. I tried not to care, but I did. Though I only had myself to blame for it. I'd known the fate

I was dealing myself when I'd sat on that stand in court and proclaimed myself a monster. And I was sharply aware of how little I could ever really be to Blue again because of it.

So long as she becomes the queen she is destined to be, it will be worth it.

Xavier and Catalina arrived for breakfast though she remained concealed within her fake identity and a new wave of laughs and sobs broke out as they hugged Darius. For a moment there was so much peace in the room, it was hard to remember that we were at the start of what would likely be a bloody war.

I edged around the side of the cavern as the songs and dancing finally came to an end, making a swift exit out the door and moving into the darkness of the tunnel, not really wanting to endure everyone treating me like I didn't exist and instead waiting in a dark alcove for someone to appear with a fresh coffee in hand. I'd shoot past them and steal it, then find the stores in this place to see if they had any of the ingredients I needed for the Zodiac Guild elixir. Then I could decide who might make good candidates to initiate into the Guild. I'd have to brew it from scratch again over the next six weeks and there were a few things I'd have to go and fetch myself, but it was something to focus on besides the feeling that now the bond was gone between me and Darius, he might not need me anymore.

Gabriel appeared walking down the corridor and I knew there was no point even trying to hide from him as his eyes moved immediately to me in the dark.

"That's no way to make friends, Orio," he taunted and I shrugged.

"I wasn't looking for friends," I said smoothly.

"Are you sure?" He gave me that twinkly Seer look that said he knew better than me, but he didn't. If Darius wasn't drawn to my company anymore then I'd Fae up and deal with it. Though even thinking that sent a dagger through my heart.

And what about Blue?

My gut tugged at the thought of her among the Heirs, laughing with Geraldine and her sister too. She looked like she was where she belonged at last and honestly, where did a Power Shamed loser fit into that?

"You're too hard on yourself," Gabriel growled, moving toward me and giving me a firm look.

"I didn't say anything." I folded my arms, hitching on my favourite give-no-fucks expression and he clucked his tongue at me like a mother hen.

"It's your aura. I can read you like a book," he said sternly. "But I can see you're not in the mood to talk about it, so why don't you go and do what you were planning to instead?"

I frowned. "I was planning something?"

He sighed like seeing everyone's futures was exhausting sometimes. "The Zodiac Guild elixir."

"Right, yeah. I'm gonna check the stores."

"I've already gathered what we need from the stores. Right now, you need to go and get the rothium grass from the Wasted Mountain."

"But I don't need to add that ingredient for weeks," I said in confusion.

"Trust me," he urged, moving to walk past me but I caught his arm, giving him an intent look.

"How did Darius do this?" I asked, stumped as to how he'd pulled this off.

"Honestly? I'm unsure. I cannot *see* the stars' decisions, so I don't know what conversation he had with them and he wasn't forthcoming when he emerged from the chamber where he made the deal. All he wanted was to reunite with all of you, so we made our way here." He frowned, glancing away and I sensed there was something more he wasn't telling me.

"What is it?" I demanded, my grip on him tightening.

He flashed me a smile, shaking his head. "Nothing, Orio. Just the Seer's curse. Too many fates, too many unanswered questions."

I nodded, letting him go, though I wasn't entirely convinced by that answer. Gabriel knew when not to tell me things though in case I swayed the course of fate, so I had to trust that whatever dark destiny was troubling him could be resolved so long as we followed his guidance. And as he'd encouraged me to go and find the rothium grass, I guessed I was going on a field trip.

Gabriel walked away into the dining hall and I put on a burst of Vampire speed, tearing into the bathhouse to wash, dress and latch my Phoenix sword to my hip before zooming through the dark corridors and making it back to the door in the clock that let me out into the farmhouse. I'd hunted Nymphs a few times on Wasted Mountain before with Darius, and I wasn't going to take any chances today.

I walked through the entrance hall, stepping outside into the icy wind and the four guards posted there looked to me with raised eyebrows.

"You can't leave without permission," one of them said, while the others glanced away from me, clearly trying to balance their duties with wanting to turn away from the Power Shamed Fae before them.

"Whose permission?" I growled in irritation.

"A Grus or a Vega's," he said, his upper lip curling in distaste at me. "Now get back inside, Power Shamed rat. Or there's some rope in the barn if you wanna off yourself."

"Good one, Jim," one of the guards said as the rest of his little buddies had a little chuckle at that, though they didn't turn to look at me again.

My fangs snapped out as I glared at this asshole who I was no doubt ten times stronger than, the beast in me raising its head and demanding I put him in his place. Part of being Power Shamed meant I wasn't legally allowed to challenge other Fae, but as I was already a fugitive and gave zero fucks about the law at this point, I didn't plan on abiding by the rules.

I shot forward, throwing out my fist, taking the savage route like I'd had to in Darkmore and catching the guy off guard as my knuckles connected with his smarmy face. He hit the snowy ground on his ass, his lip busted and dripping blood as he raised a hand to fight me off and the others all turned to look at last.

"You nothing *scum*, I'll have you cast out of The Burrows for that," Jim spat, blasting water magic at me, but as I'd predicted he wasn't anywhere near as strong as me and I froze it with a flick of my hand, the jet of water turning rock solid and slamming down onto his leg.

"Argh!" he wailed.

"What did you call him?" Darcy's voice made my heart jerk in my chest and I turned, finding her striding out of the farmhouse, her blue hair fluttering behind her and flames blazing in her eyes. Eyes which were locked on the piece of shit at my feet.

"M-my lady Gwendalina," Jim stammered, bowing his head like the dog he was. "I'm sure you're quite uncomfortable being in the presence of your abuser. We can remove him from The Burrows. It's no bother at all."

"I asked you a question," she growled, glaring down her nose at him and I swear I got a semi for her right there and then.

"I called him a-a nothing scum," Jim forced out.

"He is more than you will ever be," she hissed. "And if you speak to him like that again, I will have *you* cast out of The Burrows, do you understand me?"

"Y-yes, Lady Gwendalina."

"My name is Darcy," she snarled then grabbed my hand and stepped over him, towing me away from them while I stared at her with my pulse thrashing.

"You can't come with me," I said suddenly, realising Gabriel must have sent her here. "It's not safe for you to leave this place so soon. Lionel will have the world hunting for you."

She rounded on me with her gaze alight. "That sounded like an order."

"Maybe it was," I said, an edge to my voice.

"You don't get to make my decisions for me," she said, raising her chin as I stared down at her, the space between us alive with tension.

I sighed and we walked along, heading across the flat expanse outside the farmhouse until we made it over the magical boundary surrounding The Burrows.

"I'm just trying to protect you. I'm never going to stop doing that." I pulled her to a halt as she took a pouch of stardust from her pocket.

"Well Gabriel said you can't leave here without one of the true queens' approval." She arched a brow, taunting me and a growl rolled along my throat. Fucking Gabriel.

She turned away from me, tossing her hair. "I guess I'll see you when I get back then."

"You're asking for trouble," I warned, my cock twitching in my pants at her attitude. I wanted to rip through this tension between us and reclaim her, but I didn't know if I had the right to do that anymore. We may have loved each other, but there were still too many reasons not to be together, not least that I'd had my status stripped from me and would never be able to offer her anything she deserved.

"Maybe I am," she agreed, a dare in her eyes. She tiptoed up, so close her breath caressed my mouth and a hungry noise left me as I leaned forward to eat up the distance parting us.

I'd cut my heart out to claim that mouth alone.

"Think of the Wasted Mountain," she whispered before I could try and steal a kiss and the image of it filled my head a second before she threw a pinch of stardust over us.

We were torn away into the fabric between worlds, spinning through a beautiful sea of stars before my feet hit solid ground again and Darcy landed lightly beside me, no hint of a wobble in her steps. I kind of missed my clumsy little princess, but as she stepped forward onto the loose shingle at the base of the mountain, her foot slipped and my wish was granted.

"Stoney fuckwits," she cursed.

I shot forward to catch her with a grin, drawing her upright again and she glanced up at me with a tint of pink lining her cheeks.

"Well, who puts a load of shingle at the bottom of a freaking mountain?" she scoffed.

"Let's blame the stars." I smirked and a smile pulled at her mouth as she nodded.

We stood there half a second too long, still touching each other and lingering in the unspoken words between us which were starting to drive me to insanity. Then Darcy turned to look at the view waiting for us and I knew now wasn't the time to bring it up. It took me a beat longer to pull my eyes from her to take in the mountain towering up above us which had supposedly been blessed by a Vega prince long ago.

"So where's the rothium grass?" she questioned, walking toward a patch of greenery near an animal track.

"It could be anywhere on this mountain," I said with a frown. "It's not that. It's pink."

"Oh." She stood upright then pointed to the animal track. "I guess we'd better get looking then."

She ducked down the small path and I had to practically bend right over to fit along the overgrown track too where the thorny shrubs collided above the height of whatever creature had created this track. But as Darcy realised I was getting hooked on every thornbush we passed, she used her earth magic to part all the foliage around us, pressing it back so I could walk along without touching any of it.

We started climbing the winding track, hunting for the grass while my eyes occasionally strayed to Darcy's ass, and I had to force myself to focus. But she was the definition of distracting.

We searched around every rock and grassy knoll, but there was no sign of the colourful grass we were looking for.

"I bet it's right at the top," Darcy laughed, looking out over the incredible view as we crested a high ridge.

"Well at least I'll get to spend the whole day on this mountain with you," I murmured.

"What?" she called back, glancing over her shoulder with the light spilling over her shoulders in a glorious haze. She was so fucking beautiful, it was like the stars had plucked her from my most desperate fantasies.

I opened my mouth to answer but then a rasping, sucking rattle sounded somewhere to my right and I fell deathly still. I locked eyes with Darcy and drew the Phoenix sword from my hip, my muscles coiling in preparation of an attack.

Nymphs.

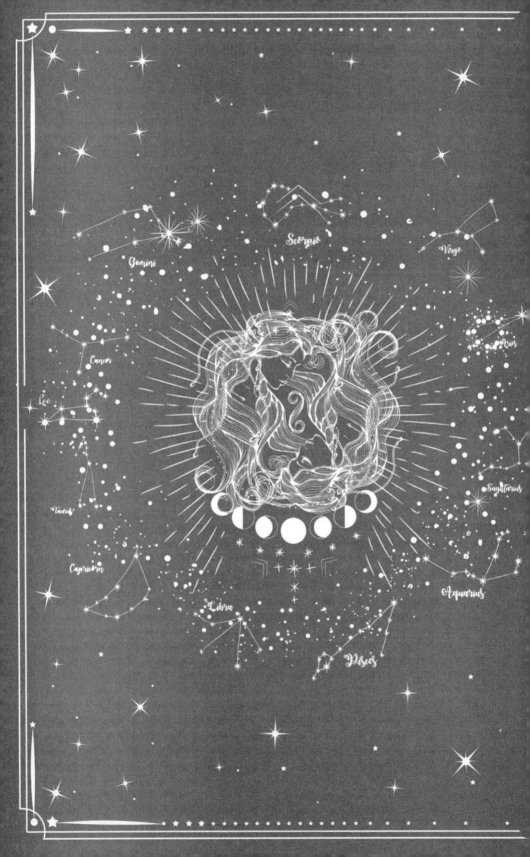

DARCY

CHAPTER FIVE

I raised my hands, Phoenix fire licking my fingertips as I listened for the creatures lurking out in the thick bushes running down the side of the mountain.

Orion braced for an attack, his head cocking to one side as he listened for their movements too.

I cast a silencing bubble around us, drawing it in tight so we wouldn't be heard as we moved back into the cover of the trees.

"How many?" I asked as adrenaline sped through my veins.

"Three," he said, his eyes darkening to nightshade.

"We've handled more," I said, a part of me excited for the fight. A part which was starting to feel as innate as breathing, and I knew it had everything to do with me embracing my inner Fae. We were born for challenges and the thrill of a battle, and I'd face our enemies now as surely as we'd faced them in that arena. Nothing would ever be as terrifying as that, kneeling on the ground certain I was going to watch the man I loved die. So I could take on any opponent now, I knew it in my bones. Maybe even Lionel fucking Acrux if he decided to show up at my door.

"You should use your speed to circle behind them," I suggested and Orion looked to me with a frown as another rattle shuddered through the air and I felt it cutting me off from my magic bit by bit.

"I'm not leaving you," he said simply, raising his sword and setting his gaze on the bushes ahead.

I gritted my teeth at his stubbornness, seeing that primal protectiveness in his eyes which made him act like a caveman.

"How many times do I have to tell you I don't need protecting?" I hissed.

"And how many times do I have to tell you, that I will protect you regardless?" he tossed back in his stern professor tone which just angered me even more.

"You're infuriating," I huffed.

"And you're cute when you're angry. Shall we air more facts about each other, Blue, or go and kill some Nymphs?" He gave me a devilish grin and I ran my tongue over my teeth.

Cute? I'll show him cute.

I raised my hands and blasted away the bushes before us with a blaze of red and blue Phoenix fire, revealing the three Nymphs as they ran up the hill toward us in their shifted forms, their hungry red eyes locked on us and their probes reaching for us as they came. They were like trees come to life, their skin made of a thick barky armour that was hard to penetrate, but certainly not impossible.

I started running to meet them, a storm of hellfire in my veins ready to be unleashed.

"It's a Vega!" one of the Nymphs cried in a voice that sounded like wood grinding against metal. "Don't kill her, take her to the king."

"Not before I get a taste of that magic," another one grunted and I released a blast of fire that took the form of wings, gliding towards them and knocking two of them onto their backs. The other one was faster, darting toward us and Orion shot past me in a blur of speed, swinging his sword as flames ignited along the length of it before he slammed it directly into the Nymph's chest. It died with a shriek, bursting into ash as I ran full pelt down the hill towards the other Nymphs who were scrambling to their feet.

Their rattles filled my ears and suddenly a clawing sense of darkness seemed to creep up in the back of my mind. Anger unlike anything I'd ever felt before rose in me and I coated my hands in flames as I dove at the closest Nymph, punching and punching in a wild, feral fury. Its probes tore down my back and a cry of pain left me a moment before I sent a fireball right into its chest, making it grow bigger beneath its ribs and watching as the beast turned to ash before me. A sick satisfaction rolled through me as the fire sizzled out against my palms and power thrummed headily through my veins.

Beyond it was the final Nymph, running straight for me and I raised my hands, my teeth bared as I prepared to take it on. I wanted to kill it for all the suffering my friends had faced, for the people who'd died at The Palace of Souls, for my father whose name had been ruined, whose magic had been stolen by these monsters. And I wanted to do it first hand, and feel it die because of me.

I let my wings burst from my back, raising up so I was on eye level with the enormous Nymph and lifted my hands, waiting for it to collide with me. But before it did, Orion shot into view, swinging his sword and beheading it with a furious blow that made his biceps bulge and the creature's black blood spray across his chest.

He hit the ground at the same time as the Nymph's head did, then it burst into ash and Orion looked up at me with a dark smile on his face.

Blood was running hot and thick down my back and my sweatshirt had been almost burned off of me by my wings, the scraps on my chest barely clinging there as the scent of death and embers hung around us.

I flew forward, landing in front of Orion as anger pulsed through me like a living thing.

"That was my kill," I snarled.

"You're bleeding and you weren't casting fire. I wasn't going to take the risk of it getting close to you like that other one did," he said, his tone hard.

"I'm not some damsel in distress who needs saving," I growled, pushing him in the chest which made his fangs snap out as he immediately moved closer. But then his eyes softened as he noticed the blood dripping onto the ground from my back.

"You're hurt." He reached out to heal me, but I slapped his hand away. "Why are you so angry with me?" he demanded and a dam of emotion shattered in my chest.

"I'm angry because I'm scared," I admitted in a rush of words. "Because if you keep trying to save me, maybe one day you'll put yourself between me and death and it will claim you from me." Terror coated the admission of my worst fear. "Or maybe you'll end up in Darkmore again because you make choices for us without consulting me and I'll lose you all over again."

"That's love, Blue," he said in earnest, capturing my wrists as I went to push him again, just wanting to let out some of this burning rage that was coiling through my body. "You've saved my ass countless times, you do it for me, but you can't bear that I do it in return. And you know why?"

I didn't answer, my teeth locking together as I fought to get my wrists out of his grip, but he just held them hard and placed my right palm against his thrashing heart.

"Because you've never let anyone love you but your sister. You don't trust the world and you have damn good reason for that, but I'm not your enemy. I know I've hurt you, but I did it because I love you in a way that's bigger than every galaxy in this universe. I was miserable before you showed up in my life, and now you've awoken a man in me who I actually fucking like, and I don't wanna lose him almost as much as I don't wanna lose you. So yeah, I'm going to put myself between you and death at every chance I get, and maybe that scares you, but it doesn't scare me, Blue. It gives me a purpose I've never had before, and I never want to let go of it."

"I can't watch you die," I said, my voice cracking and giving away my terror over that possibility. "I won't survive it, Lance. Swear to me you won't die."

We'd come so close to death in that arena, I'd almost seen his end and it was the most painful thing I'd ever faced. So now I wanted to be strong enough to take on the whole world and cast a wall of fire around him that no enemy could ever get through.

"I can't promise that, beautiful." He stepped closer, releasing my wrists and carving his thumb along the line of my cheekbone instead. "But I can promise that I'll try my hardest not to die just so long as you promise the same."

I nodded, leaning into his touch as a burning tear slid from my eye and he wiped it away before dropping his hand. And suddenly the barriers were falling between us and the animal in me was rearing up once more, wanting to draw him closer and equally wanting to punish him for all the pain he'd put me through. But how could I be angry when he'd done it all for me, and now he was Power Shamed and no one would even look him in the eye anymore? It was unbearable.

I let my Phoenix fire flare, rushing down my body and turning my clothes to cinders at my feet, my wings beating softly at my back as I looked up at Lance Orion and offered him everything I was with that single look. His throat bobbed as his gaze fell down me, taking in my hardening nipples and my burning, aching flesh which belonged solely to him. But before his eyes could travel any further south, I extinguished the flames clinging to my body and lunged up at him, my mouth colliding with his as I flapped my wings and rose several inches off the ground.

His hands went to my back, instantly healing the wounds there left by the Nymph and I moaned as he kissed me with deep and demanding strokes of his tongue. A flicker of anger seemed to rise inside me once again, bringing a wave of chaos with it. It consumed me so fully that I tore at Orion's back and a deep growl left me as it urged me to bite him, my teeth sinking into his lower lip.

Orion cursed in a way that said he liked it but I drew back, finding his lip bloody and my mouth wet with it. *Oh shit.*

His eyes danced with darkness and he suddenly grabbed me, hooking my thighs up around his hips and squeezing my ass hard as he ground me against the solid ridge of his cock through his pants. He sucked away the last of his blood on my lips and I figured going without him for so long had just made me a little feral. Totally normal to savage your super hot Vampire ex-boyfriend, right? Right.

My nails cut into his shoulders and I sent my flames gliding down all over his body, burning away his clothes without hurting him, not caring about anything but getting closer to him right then.

I raised my hips and the slickened head of his hard cock rutted against my pussy, making me gasp as he tugged me flush against him once more and guided my hips so I ground my arousal all over his shaft.

A whimper of need escaped me and he chuckled darkly as he stole another filthy kiss from my lips, leaving me shuddering in the anticipation of him laying his claim to me.

"Have me," I begged. "I was yours the first time you called me Blue."

He sighed like those words were a gift bestowed on him by the stars themselves and he drove himself inside me hard, my wings beating to steady myself as I cried out, my head tipping back and my hair bursting into flames of purest blue.

Orion groaned, his hands squeezing my ass harder as he guided my hips, using nothing but the strength in his arms to move my whole body up and down as he thrust into me again and again.

"Look at me," he commanded and I raised my head, my eyes hooded with desire as I watched his breaths fall heavily from his chest and the intensity of his gaze sent a flood of pleasure through my core. I gasped and moaned, gripping his shoulders for support while my wings continued to beat and keep us balanced.

It was so intense that I was already building to an impossible high, my clit grinding against his pubic bone with every thrust of his hips and arch of my back, the two of us becoming one perfect being of utter pleasure as his cock pounded against some deliciously sweet spot inside me.

I came in a slow, shuddering wave of pleasure that left me weak, my body moulding to his as our mouths met and he fucked me through every second of my orgasm, his tongue drinking in the taste of pleasure on my tongue.

Then before I could figure out which way was up again, he moved with a bolt of Vampire speed, dropping me to the ground and shooting around behind me. He shoved me to my hands and knees on the dry ground, placing one hand on my back as he knelt behind me and spanked me hard enough to make me cry out.

"Lance," I begged breathlessly, wanting more, needing it. I desired everything he had to offer. Pain, pleasure, it didn't matter so long as it was from him.

I let my wings fizzle away and embers sparked around us in the air as he slid his hand up my spine and caressed that incredible place between my shoulder blades, making me shiver for him.

"I've gone easy on you, Blue," he said, his hand moving down to stroke the stinging mark he'd left on my ass, but he made no move to heal it. "But I've seen you blossom into the strongest Fae I know right before my eyes. And I know you like this." He spanked me again, even harder than before, but this time clapping the back of my thigh and making something between a cry and moan leave me.

"So do you wanna find out why my Order is the best at fucking?" he asked cockily and I glanced back at him over my shoulder, his hair dishevelled and his eyes so full of lust it made my pussy throb with need.

"Yes," I panted, my skin tingling with the need for more of his touch while curiosity burned in my chest.

He smirked as he rose up on his knees, lining his beautiful cock up with my entrance once more and pushing every thick inch inside me in one head spinning thrust. I moaned his name, my eyes falling closed and he spanked me firmly on my ass as I got used to the huge size of him inside me.

"Look at me. I wanna see those stars bursting in your eyes when I make you come," he insisted and I did as he asked, watching him as he lowered his hand beneath me, finding my clit and the kiss of his water magic met sensitive skin, sending pleasure tearing through my body as his fingers started to move. Fast.

Omagod.

He used the gifts of his Order so his fingers were practically vibrating on my slickened clit and I could barely contain my next orgasm. My hips started rocking with the need for him to move inside me.

"Please," I panted.

"Brace yourself," he said with a hint of amusement in his voice and I did so a second before he started thrusting, his cock matching the pace of his fingers and leaving me unable to draw breath. It almost felt like he was vibrating inside me too as he pounded into me with impossible speed and my pussy gripped him tighter, making him growl in delight.

He fucked me harder and faster until I was coming all over his length with garbled noises leaving my lips and another orgasm already chasing the last, pleasure making me weak as my whole body trembled.

He gripped my hips to take complete control, holding me right where he wanted me as he drove himself in and out of my body, his cock rubbing my g-spot while his fingers worked some unholy magic on my over-sensitized clit.

"Again," he commanded.

"I can't," I gasped, sure I couldn't take anymore, but his hand smacked my ass in a way that sent another wave of pleasure skittering through my flesh.

"You can," he laughed and I moaned, proving his goddamn point as he showed me no mercy.

My knees chafed on the ground and my fingers clawed into the earth to stop myself from falling forward, taking everything he gave me with a plea for even more on my lips as I realised I wanted to reach the limit he was pushing me to.

As he somehow drew me into another earthshattering release and my pussy squeezed tightly around his shaft, he breathed a string of swear words then stilled deep inside me, filling me up and groaning through his own pleasure, his fingers digging bruisingly into my hips as he gave me every drop of himself. He slowly pumped himself in and out of me a few more times and I let my head fall to the dirt as the strength went out of my body.

He slid himself out of me, falling back onto the ground and I sat up, turning to look down at him in all his post fucked glory, his hair a mess of sweaty strands across his forehead and his muscles so tight as he panted that every one of his abs was perfectly defined. His eyes were on mine, a whole dark haven awaiting me there as a smile hooked up his lips.

"You burned all our clothes off," he said, then he started laughing and the sound was so infectious I immediately joined in.

"How are we going to get back into The Burrows without being seen?" I crawled to his side, laying down next to him and rolling onto my back to gaze up at the azure sky.

"You clearly didn't pay enough attention in that lesson, Miss Vega," he joked.

"What do you mean?" I looked at him with a frown.

"Vampire speed," he said. "I can move us as fast as the fucking wind. No one will see us."

I sucked on my lower lip, still tasting him on it and loving the way his touch had banished all the anger that had been burning in my chest.

"We still need to find the rothium grass," I said but he lifted a hand, pointing behind me and I turned, spotting some bright pink grass growing there beneath a bush.

"I think we already did."

I sighed, lending him the warmth of my Order as I lay against him, not wanting to leave this moment between us just yet.

"Are we...back together, Blue?" Orion asked after a while, making my heart squeeze with a thousand good feelings.

"I don't think we were ever really apart, Lance," I whispered and I turned my head to look at him, finding some hesitation in his eyes. But he blinked, banishing it, his gaze shining with happiness instead as he leaned forward to steal a kiss that laid a permanent claim on me. One that swore we'd never be parted again, that we'd fight for each other with the power of the moon on the tide, and no matter where each of us went in this world, the other would always follow.

CALEB

CHAPTER SIX

I'd spent another night tossing and turning, trying to convince myself to sleep while my brain turned over everything that had happened from the fight to us running for our motherfucking lives and abandoning everything in the name of rebellion against Lionel Acrux.

In fact, it wasn't just a rebellion. With us and the Vegas set against him, I could only conclude that what we'd all done on Christmas Day was declare civil war within Solaria and from now until the end of this we would be fighting to win.

Eventually, some time around dawn I'd passed out, wondering where the fuck Seth had gotten to again and taking up the entire bed in his absence as I fought to get some rest in this strange place.

A heavy thumping came at the door and I groaned, cursing whoever it was as they tried to wake me and calling out a choice insult or two as I dragged my pillow over my head.

"Cal?" Max's concerned voice reached me and I frowned as I felt the press of his worry on a tide of emotions that swept through the door.

"What is it?" I asked anxiously, pushing myself upright and reaching out with my magic to unlock the door.

Max shoved through it the moment he could and he strode into the room with an Atlas tight in his grasp. Hamish had given out untraceable ones to each of us earlier so we could keep up with the news outside of this place.

"Lionel has moved against our families already," he growled, holding the device out to me as my gut plummeted and fear for my Mom, Dad and siblings drove into my flesh.

My eyes widened as I read the article he'd given me which had been printed in the Celestial Times less than an hour ago.

A New Age for Solaria!
The Celestial Council have announced their support of three new Heirs to

take their places when the time for succession is upon us. Hadley Altair, Ellis Rigel and Athena Capella are now next in line after the shocking events which saw the original Heirs all turn from their life path and throw in with the unstable and untrustworthy Vega twins.

Reports have been running rife for months about the strange thrall the Vega girls used to capture the attention of the four boys who had once had such bright and promising futures ahead of them.

It is said that Gwendalina (Darcy) Vega has long since been using manipulation of the mind to convince those closest to her to believe in the ravens she falsely claims to see. Once convinced of the existence of such ravens, she uses that illusion to feed lies and delusions to those she seeks to control - just as the Phoenixes of old did a thousand years ago.

It was once well documented how tricksome and untrustworthy the Phoenix Order could be with their twisted gifts playing out in all kinds of horrendous and mind-altering ways.

Sadly, once the Phoenix power has been used to infect the mind of a victim, there is no hope for returning them to their former selves and unfortunately by the time it became clear that these girls were wielding their wicked magic against the Heirs of this kingdom, it was too late to save them. Not to mention it is too risky to ever consider allowing them into a position of power with their now tainted minds.

Reports of the sex magic that Roxanya (Tory) Vega has been using against the former Heirs have also been coming in thick and fast as it has recently been discovered that that too was a power the Phoenixes of legend once possessed.

Some of their kind hold a power over seduction and desire which is far more dangerous than even Incubus gifts. Once someone has lain with such a creature, they become bound to them. In using her body in such lewd and promiscuous acts, Roxanya has in fact been stealing pieces of the souls of the men she has had coital relations with and bound it to her will.

Many accounts have now emerged which prove that she has been having regular and some might say vulgar sexual relations with all four of the former Heirs, further working to place them all beneath her thrall and thus, the Vega twins have taken captive the minds and bodies of the boys we once hoped would help lead our kingdom.

But have heart! Our kingdom is not so easily knocked to its knees and in light of the disturbing acts which have taken place with the former Heirs, the Celestial Council and our king himself have all placed high hopes and faith behind their replacements.

A brighter dawn is coming. Though now it is feared that the rebel uprising caused by the daughters of the Savage King might put the lives of our loyal citizens at risk. But our king will work tirelessly to quell this small insurgence of power-hungry Fae who skulk in the shadows and don't dare to challenge him head on.

He will stop at nothing to assure the safety of his people, and may we all praise him for all he has done to protect us thus far.

He has already quelled many Nymph attacks as well as bringing the creatures to heel, saving us from the threat they once posed. Now, he will gladly rise to the challenge of protecting us all from this new and worrying *threat to our great nation.*

Beneath the article were a series of pictures, some of which had been kept from the press by our families before this moment. There were images of Darius and me dancing at the club with Tory all those months ago, some of me and her engaging in the hunt - even one of me bending her over a table in the Tarot classroom which was grainy and obviously taken by some perving asshole, but you could see the way her skirt was shoved up and my pants were half hanging off even if you couldn't see our faces.

Then there were images of her and Darius in various heated moments, a picture of her kissing Max when he'd caught her with his Siren Song and several of Seth with his arm slung around her and whispering something in her ear which in all likelihood had just been some kind of threat, but the way they'd been mixed in with the others helped to paint the picture they were trying to create of us being some kind of sex harem for her.

The images of us with Darcy had been just as carefully selected, some of us laughing with her at Pitball training or looking at her as if we were enamoured by her. There was even one of me on one knee before her with my head bowed which I was almost certain had been taken while I was tying my shoelace. There were a lot of her and Seth together, some of him going in and out of her room at the academy and even a few of her standing over him after she'd beaten his ass that time.

Then there was a full page spread with perfectly posed pictures of our siblings who had been selected to take our place like power claiming had fuck all to do with it and Lionel could just make a decision like that on a whim. My gaze scanned over my brother's face and I was certain I could see tension there as he posed for the shot, my throat bobbing as I wondered what Lionel had threatened him with to make him play along with this.

"Fuck," I breathed as I dropped the Atlas into my lap and looked up at Max as he scored a hand down his face.

"My dad wouldn't back Ellis for my position," he said. "Not unless he was forced to. He's always been firm in his support for me, and she's only got one fucking Element! Besides, she could no sooner take me down than fly herself to the fucking moon."

"Yeah, this reeks of that asshole with the crown," I agreed on a growl.

"We need to talk to the others. Seth is-"

"Seth is what?" Seth asked as he appeared, sticking his head around the door and grinning in at us.

"Show him," I grunted, shoving myself out of bed and hunting for some clothes.

I'd spent time wielding my earth magic in this space I'd been given to use as a bedroom, so I had a wardrobe, a proper bed, a mirror and even bedding which I'd spent a few hours casting from scratch by creating my own cotton. The mirror was just heated sand with a wooden frame and the rest of the furniture was made from wood too, grown into place with my magic. I'd even hung an everflame in a glass lamp above the bed and had made myself a carpet out of grass so soft it felt like silk beneath my bare feet. I wasn't the Terra Heir for nothing. Though as it stood, maybe I wasn't the Terra Heir at all.

I dropped my boxers and pulled on some fresh clothes, trying not to wrinkle my nose at the borrowed items and mentally planning to work on creating my own clothes the next time I had a few hours to kill. Either that or I wanted to go shopping. We were rebels, not fucking homeless people for fuck's sake.

I could feel eyes on me as I changed and I glanced over my shoulder, meeting Seth's gaze for a fraction of a second before he scooped up the Atlas and dropped onto my bed to read the article.

My skin prickled at the thought of catching him looking at me and I frowned as I wondered why I liked that so much. But as a mournful howl fell from his lips, I dragged my pants and shirt on and turned to him, my jaw clenching at the sound of his pain.

"It's a good thing," I said, moving to sit beside him and clasping his shoulder as Max dropped down on his other side.

"How is this a good thing?" Seth asked, his dark gaze whipping around to meet mine and I squeezed his shoulder tighter.

"Because they're playing along. I know my mom and she would never back Hadley over me unless he took me on and won. That's what true Fae do. They claim their fucking power, and there is no way in hell that she would just switch her preference to him unless she knew it was the only way that she could protect our family."

"He's right," Max agreed. "Think about it. Lionel will have threatened them and as it stands, with him having the shadows on his side and that shadow witch at his command, he is more powerful than our parents. If they didn't fall into line, then he could kill them."

"Then maybe they should run too?" Seth suggested. "They could all come here, join us and-"

"We need to find a way to contact them," I said decisively. "And we need Darius's opinion on this too. Where is he?"

"Fucking Tory Vega of course," Max said with a derisive snort. "I know you're not a Siren, but surely that amount of lust is enough for the rest of you to sense too?"

I breathed a laugh, shaking my head at him and getting to my feet.

"They can't just fuck all the damn time," I pointed out. "They're probably sleeping or some shit. Besides, they have to eat."

"We'll see." Max led the way to the door but as I went to follow him, I looked back and found Seth still sitting on my bed looking utterly dejected as he stared at the floor.

"Hey," I barked at him, shooting forward and gripping his hair in my fist, jerking on it to make him look up at me. "No pouting. We can figure this out."

Seth's eyes widened and he nodded slowly, his tongue wetting his lips and drawing my attention for a moment.

"Alright," he agreed, a smirk lifting the corner of his mouth. "But you didn't have to go all Dom on me."

"Oh please, you'd love it if I went all Dom on you," I tossed back, tugging on his hair a little harder and liking the way it felt to have him beneath me like that.

"Maybe I would," he replied and as my gaze met his, the joking lilt to our conversation slipped and I found my pulse picking up with that crazy idea.

I shifted a little closer to him, my gaze roaming over his face as he looked at me with something akin to vulnerability in his expression, like he was trying to tell me something without voicing it and I found myself really wanting to know what that was.

"Are you fuckers coming or what?" Max barked from outside and I released Seth's hair, barking a laugh as I stepped back and jerked my chin at him in a command for him to follow.

"I'll have to pencil in topping you for another time," I teased and Seth laughed a little manically.

"Yeah. Just tell me where and when and I'll make sure to bring the ball gag and the handcuffs."

I chuckled at the ridiculousness of that idea and Seth moved past me as we made it into the corridor, shoulder checking me hard enough to knock me into the damn wall.

"Asshole," I called after him and he flipped me off over his shoulder before jogging to catch Max and leaving me behind.

I followed them through the so called royal quarters and down the corridors dedicated to housing us, the roughly hewn tunnels made up of nothing more than the rock they'd been carved into with a series of everflames burning at intervals to light the way.

Max pulled up short by the door to Tory and Darius's room and knocked loudly as me and Seth moved to stand beside him.

There was a long pause, but no one responded from within the room and as I strained my ears, I couldn't hear a sound from inside it either.

"Are you sure they're here? Because if they are they're using a silencing bubble," I said and Max groaned.

"To drown out all the fucking sex noise," he said, giving us an 'I told you so' look.

"Well at least one of us is getting laid," Seth grumbled and I arched a brow at him in surprise.

"I thought you were too? You told me you weren't sharing a room with me because you were spending your nights getting your cock serviced by a secret lover."

Max snorted. "Yeah - probably his fucking hand, just like I am these days. You know Gerry still won't give me the time of day even after I became a star damned rebel?"

"Seth?" I pushed, frowning at him as he cut his gaze away from mine and moved towards the door to Darius's room, pressing his hand to it like he intended to bust the lock.

"A gentleman never tells," he replied, not looking at me as he focused on the door and I shot Max a confused look while he just shrugged, clearly more interested in his Geraldine drama than he was in Seth's night time antics.

I pursed my lips and dropped the questions. It wasn't like I gave a fuck who he was screwing anyway.

"Got it!" Seth announced and the door swung open a moment later, revealing Darius and Tory lying in bed together, but instead of finding them fucking like animals as we'd all been expecting, we found them holding each other.

Tory was nestled into the crook of Darius's arm, her eyes closed and breathing heavy as he trailed his fingertips along her spine, the sheets tugged over them enough to cover most of her body from us.

His gaze snapped to us, but in the brief moment before that, all I'd seen in his expression was this, deep, fulfilled kind of contentment as he'd been watching her, and it made the knot in my chest loosen to know that at least one good thing had come from this nightmare. The stars had finally been forced to reconsider and it looked like everything the two of them had suffered through had finally paid off.

Darius frowned at us, clearly less than impressed by the interruption as he flicked his fingers to disband the silencing bubble before tugging the sheet up around Tory more firmly to hide her body from our view.

"What is it?" he growled, his voice pitched low so as not to wake her as his muscles tensed in anticipation of a fight.

"Nothing life threatening," I reassured him before he could freak out.

"But we do need to talk," Max pressed. "And not all of us have sex on tap right now, so stop rubbing it in our faces and just come talk with us."

Darius rolled his eyes at the less than angry taunt and slowly shifted himself out of bed, drawing a murmur of protest from Tory as she sleepily reached for him.

"I thought I owed you a wake up blowjob?" she mumbled, catching his arm and making him pause.

"I will absolutely take you up on that later, baby. But right now, there are three assholes at the door," Darius replied, leaning down to press a kiss to her hair.

Tory rolled towards us and cracked her eyes open as Darius lurched forward to make sure the sheet remained over her tits to shield them from our view, a possessive growl escaping him as his Dragon peered out at us from within the depths of his eyes in a clear warning.

"Do the assholes just want him, or do I have to drag my ass out of bed too?" she asked us, scrubbing some sleep from one eye with a fist and yawning.

"Just the Dragon thanks, sweetheart," I confirmed and she nodded, grabbing a pillow and tugging it over her face in a clear dismissal.

"And this one claimed she didn't wanna be a princess," Seth scoffed, backing out of the room as Darius approached us wearing a pair of jeans and some sneakers, not bothering with a shirt.

It was cold down here beneath the ground in the middle of fuck knew where, but for those of us with fire magic it wasn't much of an issue.

Darius and Seth fell into step ahead of me and Max and my gaze roamed over the tattoo on my friend's back as I took in the Phoenix and Dragon which played at war with one another across his flesh. I'd always liked the image, but looking at it now hit different than it had before. Because instead of the heat of the battle which I'd always seen in the image, I found more of a dance in it now. Two predators who had met their match and fought for nothing more than the thrill of one another's company and the challenge they posed.

We headed down to the large cavern which had been set aside for meals and Seth picked out a spot in the centre of the circular space where a rough table and chairs had been hewn from the rocks. It looked exactly like every other table in the place, but I was guessing its location front and centre was what was drawing him to it, the circular layout of the domed cavern somewhat reminiscent of The Orb.

Before he could sit his ass down, I twisted my hand and sent magic spilling towards the stone bench, building a back for it from wood and leaves that wove together as they grew, then padding the whole thing with a layer of blood red roses with petals softer than silk until it resembled our usual couch.

Seth grinned broadly as he cast a silencing bubble around us then sank onto the newly modified chair and I took my spot beside him, nudging him with my elbow.

"I knew you couldn't cope without home comforts," I teased him and he shoved me back.

"Says the dude who has literally fully furnished his underground cave to make it look like it belongs in a five star hotel," Seth mocked.

"Well, no one said being a rebel had to mean living in squalor," I tossed back, shoving him again, but before we could fall into a full blown tussle, Max pushed us apart and sat down between us.

"Stop flirting with each other and focus on the problem here," he snapped, pushing a whole bucket load of serious energy at us to dampen the mood. It had only been a jibe, but why did I suddenly feel awkward?

Darius was reading over the article on the Atlas, ignoring all of us as he took in the latest bullshit to be tossed our way and I looked around hopefully as my stomach growled.

"The service in this place is a fucking joke," I muttered, looking between the rebels who were all gathered at various tables, each of them eating their own meals and drinking coffees, while none of them seemed inclined to bring any to us.

We drew a lot of looks, even after a few days down here and it was obvious that most of them didn't trust us one bit. But as we were powerful motherfuckers and the Vegas themselves had vouched for us, no one seemed inclined to voice their thoughts on whatever reasons they had to dislike us, so mostly we were left to our own devices.

"There is no service in here," Darius replied. "You're just an entitled prick who hasn't noticed that the food you've been eating has been brought to you by one of us for the last few meals instead of having it hand delivered by some lesser Fae like you're used to."

"Hold the fuck up," Seth said, shoving himself forward in his seat as I blanched at that suggestion. "Are you telling me that the food we've been eating is not only of a questionable quality but that there is no service here either?"

"No, asshole. They're rebels living in a fucking cave. There isn't any catering service, just like there's no laundry service or cleaning service or-"

"Are you telling me I'm supposed to just wear dirty clothes for however the fuck long I'm down here?" I interrupted, putting that shopping trip to the top of my damn list because that would be a fuck no. "I don't even have water magic."

"Well, I'll wash your clothes if you'll make my room all fancy with earth magic like you did with yours," Max offered and I nodded in agreement.

"Done."

"You guys are fucking princesses," Darius said, shaking his head as Seth continued to stare around in horror like he was expecting a waiter to appear from thin air at any moment.

"Oh so you don't want me and Seth to make your room all fancy?" I shot back. "Or do you just refer to it as a fuck palace now?"

Darius smirked and shrugged. "Alright fine. If you two assholes make the room nice for Roxy's benefit then I'll go find you something to eat."

"Pfft, like you don't want it nice for yourself," I replied. "That girl grew up in the mortal realm with no fucking money. She knows how to survive these conditions far better than you do and you know it."

"All the more reason for her not to have to suffer them again," Darius replied. "Now why don't you figure out what you wanna do about this situation with your families while I go find us some food."

"Alright," I agreed with a shrug like it was no big deal, but Seth practically sagged in his seat with a groan of relief and I couldn't deny that I was glad I wouldn't have to go figure out the food thing myself. I mean, if they had stuff to pick from then I'd be fine, but what if I was expected to actually cook something? Fuck that. I wasn't cut out for that kind of shit.

"So what are we going to do?" Max asked, swiping a hand down his face and relaxing back into his chair as he looked around the room like he was hunting for someone. Probably Grus. Man had it bad.

"I can meet with my mom," I said. "We have a plan in place for anything going to hell like this. There's a place where I can go and summon her. She left a crystal there which is linked to the stone in her wedding ring. No one knows about it besides me and her, so I know it'll be safe."

"Shit. Why didn't my dad think of something like that?" Max asked.

"Or my mom," Seth added with a huff.

"You don't have emergency plans set up with your families?" I asked in surprise and they both shook their heads at me. "Well I guess after everything that happened with her brother going missing she decided to take the safety of our family more seriously."

"Is it really safe for you to go though?" Seth asked, his brow pinching.

"My mom hasn't turned against me," I said firmly, knowing that in every fibre of my being. "She loves me and she would take the secret of that place to her grave. Besides…I need to be sure that my family are okay. I need them to be alright."

"She probably knows about our families too," Max added and Seth looked to me hopefully.

"Yeah," I agreed. "They're all in the same situation so she should know how they are."

"Though if Lionel wants to bump off my evil stepmother I won't be complaining," Max added, making me smirk.

"I'll head off once we eat then," I said and we all glanced around in hopes of seeing Darius returning with a huge tray of food for us, but instead found Geraldine striding into the room in a tight red and blue jumpsuit with 'A.S.S. Forever' printed over her tits. She was holding an enormous plate piled high with buttery bagels and another filled with every kind of topping anyone might ever dream of putting on one.

"Make way for the breakfast of the true queens!" she cried, striding towards us and making my damn stomach grumble as the scent of those delicious creations wafted over us.

"Oh fuck yes," Seth groaned, pushing to his feet as Geraldine swerved us and placed her bounty down on the table next to ours.

She set to work decorating the table the way I had our couch, creating two chairs large enough to arguably be called thrones and setting them at either end of the long stone table she'd selected then covering the table in flowers and laying the food out on top of them.

Several other A.S.S. clubbers hurried over with a pitcher of orange juice and a large cafetière filled with fresh coffee before placing plates, mugs and glasses down too.

"How come the Vegas get table service?" Seth whined, dismissing the silencing bubble that surrounded us so that Geraldine could hear him.

"Do you mean to ask why the true and glorious monarchs of our fair and noble land deserve the mightiest of breakfasts to sup upon before the start of their day of training in the quest to conquer the dastardly Dragoon?" Geraldine scoffed loudly. "I think the answer to that most foolish of questions is more than clear, even to a lowly mutt, a bothersome barracuda and a sharp toothed Sally such as you rapscallions."

"Come on, Gerry, give us a couple of those bagels," Max tried, getting up and moving towards her. "You know the Vegas can't possibly eat all of-"

"Avast!" Geraldine cried, flinging her arm out and damn near smacking Max in the face as she pointed across the room to the tunnel which Darcy and Tory were emerging from, appearing less than thrilled at the fact that everyone was now looking at them. Darcy was dressed in a white shirt and a pair of faded blue jeans, but Tory had just thrown on one of Darius's shirts and a pair of thick socks, looking pretty pissed about being the centre of attention. "What's this? Two shining stars come down to grace us with their beauty? Two flawless gems, blessing us with their attendance? Two most beauteous-"

"Stop, Geraldine," Tory begged, slipping through the crowd with her sister. "I'll go on a fucking hunger strike if I'm forced to endure this kind of welcome every time I come looking for food."

"You heard my lady!" Geraldine roared. "Avert your gazes and return to your business!"

Tory cringed and Darcy blushed furiously as they made it to the table and everyone in the room pointedly looked anywhere but at them.

"Good morrow, fine ladies!" Hamish called as he bustled his way across the room with a bowl of fresh fruit in his arms and my stomach rumbled as I looked at the fucking feast that had been laid out for the Vegas. "How are you on this wondrous day-ahhh!"

His greeting turned to a cry of horror as Orion shot into the room and dropped into the chair beside Darcy just as she took her seat in one of the thrones Geraldine had created for them and our former Cardinal Magic professor scowled back at him.

"My lady, are you certain you wish to dine with a Power Shamed cretin such as...such as..."

Hamish seemed to gag over the idea of speaking Orion's name and I couldn't help but bark a laugh at his expense.

"I want him here," Darcy said firmly. "He's my boyfriend."

Hamish paled at that and Seth bounced up and down in his seat as Tory grinned at them. Orion glanced at Darcy with some objection in his eyes as Hamish broke out in a sweat.

"Thanks to me," Seth said excitedly.

"What's that supposed to mean?" Orion demanded, narrowing his gaze on him, his hand straying towards a pineapple in a fruit bowl on the table.

Seth mimed zipping his lips and throwing away the key as Orion's hand closed around the pineapple in a threat. Darcy laid a hand on his arm, drawing it away from his weapon of choice and Orion's eyes slowly slid to her instead, the death threat in them melting.

"This conversation isn't over," Orion warned Seth, but he just shrugged and I tried to catch his eye, unsure what his game was and why I wasn't in on it.

"Remember how I said it's best if we keep our relationship between the people we know, considering my position in society," Orion said to Darcy in a low growl.

"Yep, and remember how I said I didn't care what people thought of me for dating you?" Darcy tossed back with a firm look and they fell into a glare off that pretty much put them at a stalemate.

Hamish cleared his throat. "Forgive my doodads, my lady, but the shamed Fae makes a fair point." He grimaced as he swallowed like bile was rising in his throat then continued on. "It is best it remains a secret until you inevitably go your separate ways in life."

Orion's shoulders stiffened as pain crossed his features, but he said nothing and I had to admit I felt kinda sorry for the asshole.

"We're not going to go our separate ways," Darcy hissed and Hamish bowed his head in deference.

He managed to reign in his silent retches as he looked to Orion in horror then turned away from him, drawing my attention to Darius and his mom as I spotted them at the far side of the room, smiling together and even laughing. She still had her disguise in place so that no one would be able to recognise her, but if anyone paid attention then surely they'd notice how much time she spent with Darius and Xavier. They could figure it out if they were smart enough.

I watched as Hamish headed over to them, placing the back of a hand to his brow as he pointed at Orion in dismay, and Catalina patted his arm sympathetically.

Darius withdrew from their interaction, heading our way with a plate in hand and I perked up at the arrival of our food.

"This is the best I could manage," Darius said, dropping the plate of toast down on the table before us and making Seth gasp in horror.

"Why is there only butter on it?" I asked.

"And why isn't the butter all the way to the edges?" Seth added.

"Do I smell burning?" Max asked, picking up a slice and turning it over to reveal the black underside.

"I've never tried to make toast with my magic before, alright?" Darius grumbled. "Would you rather I'd just brought you uncooked bread?"

"Than this horror show?" Seth said, clutching his imaginary pearls. "Yes I would."

Tory laughed at us as we all picked up a less than desirable looking slice of toast, before taking a big bite of the butteriest bagel I ever saw and groaning in pleasure as she ate it.

Darius turned away from us and moved to pour her a mug of coffee, making it how she liked and placing it down beside her plate before leaning in to press a kiss to her hair.

He made a move to back away and return to us, but she caught hold of his belt and tugged him back again, scooting out of her own seat and nudging him into it before dropping onto his lap with a grin.

"Hey, how is that fair?" Seth demanded while Max continued to try and catch Geraldine's eye as she got to work placing toppings on bagels, singing a tune which seemed to be about a troublesome tuna who ended up baked in a fish pie.

"He worked up a big appetite last night," Tory replied, smirking at us as Darius's hand landed on her thigh just below the hem of the oversized shirt she was wearing. "And he needs to keep his energy up if he plans on keeping up with me again tonight."

Darius leaned in and murmured something in her ear which I chose not to listen in on as it managed to bring a blush to her cheeks and she slapped his chest in mock anger before biting her lip and saying 'maybe.'

"Oh so all we have to do to earn our way onto the tasty table is give a Vega a bunch of orgasms then, is it?" Seth demanded, like that was some kind of challenge.

"Well technically I have given a Vega a load of-" I began but Darius cut me off with a snarl.

"Do not finish that sentence, Caleb," he barked. "Or I swear to fuck, I'll cut your dick off and toss it in the tray with those chipolatas over there."

"Oooh, there's chipolatas?" Seth asked hungrily, looking around and I raised my hands in surrender, letting my joke fall away.

Probably best not to goad the Dragon over the fact that me and his girl had history.

"Come on, Darcy," Seth whimpered, turning the puppy dog eyes on her as he failed to spot any miniature sausages. "We just got bad news about our families, and we're stuck in this strange place and nobody here likes us and we're really, really hungry but we don't know how to fend for ourselves like common people and now we're going to starve to death and-"

"Will you shut up if there's a bagel in your mouth?" Darcy shot at him and he mimed zipping his lips again, nodding profusely and making me laugh. "Fine. Then the three of you can join us - but only so long as you keep playing nice. One dickish piece of behaviour and you're back to burnt toast at the losers' table."

Tory laughed at her sister's joke, but I resisted the urge to protest that assessment of our current social standing in favour of eating a decent breakfast.

We dropped down opposite Orion and Geraldine, listening while Orion filled us in on how he was getting on with brewing his fancy potion.

Seth's arm kept brushing mine as we ate, and I allowed his Wolfy ways, even nudging him back from time to time, enjoying giving him that little bit of pack reassurance even if I shouldn't have really needed it myself. But I was away from my family like he was, cut off and in this strange place, so it made sense for our honorary Alpha pack to draw closer to one another while we were getting used to the changes here.

Once we'd finished eating, I filled Geraldine in on my plan to go get some information from my mom and despite her warnings about me 'taking the utmost of care out in the wild beyond,' as she seemed to be referring to the normal world, she got her dad to agree to me going. Not that they could have stopped me, but it made sense for me to at least seek permission before I went even if it was only to keep the peace.

Seth followed me up into the farmhouse which hid the entrance to The Burrows and he walked with me out into the snowy landscape which surrounded the hidden sanctuary until we made it to the magical border which kept the place hidden.

"Why don't I come with you?" he suggested, clearly worried about me heading out there alone but I shook my head.

"It's not worth risking you as well," I said firmly. "I'll be there and back before you know it."

"I'll wait right here," he swore, folding his arms against the cold and making it clear he wouldn't be swayed from that choice.

"Okay," I agreed, flicking my hand at a spot beside him and casting a fire into existence to keep him warm while I was gone.

Seth lunged at me as I made a move to cross the barrier, yanking me into his arms and squeezing me tight as the rich, earthy scent of him enveloped my senses and I breathed in deeply.

"Stay safe," he growled fiercely. "I love you."

"I love you too, man," I said on a breath of laughter, patting his back as he tensed up in my hold. "I love every fucking one of you. And I'll be just fine. You'll see." I leaned back and clasped his face in my hands, pushing fire magic into his skin to warm him up as he gave me a lingering look which made my throat bob.

"Stop looking at me like you think you might never see me again," I teased, trying to break the tension but it only seemed to build higher.

"If I never saw you again I think I'd just cut my heart clean from my chest rather than live on in that agony," he breathed and I frowned at him as I felt the intensity of those words.

"I'll be back," I swore and he nodded, stepping back forcefully and making my hands fall from his face.

I gave him one, last reassuring smile, then stepped through the crackling energy of the magical barrier which was in place to protect us here, before tugging a pouch of stardust from my pocket and tossing it over my head.

The snow filled mountain scape was whipped away as I was torn from my position in the world and the stars spun me through their hold before depositing me where I desired.

I landed smoothly despite my footing being uneven, my gifts lending themselves to a quick correction of my balance as I found myself in a sun baked desert.

I glanced around warily, squinting against the onslaught of light from the bright blue sky and blazing sun as I held the stardust ready just in case there was any kind of magical detection system here which would alert the FIB to my presence. It was highly unlikely. My mom wouldn't give up this location even under torture but with Lionel's talent for Dark Coercion I couldn't rule anything out.

After a few minutes it was clear that there was no one here besides the buzzards circling high above and the sand surrounding me, so I strode forward. This place was quite literally in the middle of nowhere. It was just a random spot in the centre of the Kerdian Desert with nothing but sand and wasteland for miles all around it. Hell, we weren't even in Solaria anymore. This came under the rule of the southern kingdom of Voldrakia where the Vegas' mother had been born - not that anyone made any use of this endless expanse of nothing.

I couldn't see what I was searching for, but I knew it was here, buried beneath the sand and waiting for me, the stardust having brought me to the right place beyond a doubt.

I lifted my hands and took hold of the sand surrounding me with my earth magic, hunting through it until I felt the pulse of my mother's magic which protected this place then shifting the sand aside until a large, black boulder was revealed beneath it.

I stepped up to it, placing my palm flat against it and bypassing all of the spells cast upon it, which would send anyone other than me or her scurrying away from this place long before they got close enough to touch the stone like this.

I pushed my magic into the rock, summoning the treasure buried within it and drawing out the gem hidden there until it sat shimmering in my hand.

I glanced around once more before pushing a flare of magic into the white opal gemstone, letting it read my magical signature and knowing it would alert my mom to my whereabouts.

I prepared myself for a long wait, not knowing what she might need to do to set up a cover story for her absence, but she appeared in a flash of stardust barely a heartbeat later, her arms flying around me as a relieved sob spilled from her lips.

"Oh my darling boy, I've been so worried," she gasped, her head buried in my shoulder as I wound my arms around her in her grey dress. She looked like she'd been doing something official if her outfit was anything to go by and I got the feeling I had far more reason to be worried about her than the other way around.

"I'm fine, Mom. How about you guys?" I asked, concern lacing my voice for my family.

"Making the best of it," she said, the anger in her tone clear as she drew back and wiped the tears from her face. My mother was a loving woman and she wasn't afraid of her emotions, but she knew how to lock them down when she had to for her job and I could see that professional facade slipping over her now. "Don't tell me anything about where you are. Just tell me the other boys are okay so that I can pass the message along to Tiberius and Antonia."

"Yeah, we're all good, Mom. I swear, you don't need to worry. The Vegas are safe as well."

She nodded, relief spilling through her eyes which were the exact same navy shade as my own.

"Good. I only have a few moments - I'm in a Council meeting with the so-called king and I just excused myself to the bathroom."

"What the fuck, Mom?" I exclaimed, fear of them catching her out making my heart race.

"It's fine. Much easier to slip out from under his nose than to try and do anything when I'm at the house. He has spies on all of us and though I'm confident I could bypass them if necessary, it is far simpler to do it this way. Now, take this." She handed me a small journal bound in brown leather and I flipped it open, frowning at the empty pages.

"It's linked to my scribing stone. Whatever I write on my stone will disappear from my end and reappear in this. We will pass you whatever information we can."

"Why not just join us?" I begged but she was already shaking her head.

"We have to be close to him. You need people working against him from the inside and we'd never manage to get everyone out anyway. He will come for anyone we love or even just *like* if we try to turn from him. So far, in his arrogance he believes we are all content to serve him as we did the Savage King. We can let him go on believing that while you gather the strength you need to face him."

"But what if he uses a Cyclops on you or Dark Coerces you or something even more powerful?" I hissed, clutching her hand like she might be about to leave me already.

"I'm not afraid of Lionel Acrux," she scoffed. "He may have cheated his way into gaining command over the shadows, but he isn't any more powerful than me. In fact, he's barely an echo of the man his brother would have been if he'd come into his power instead of dying the way he did."

Everyone knew the rumours about the apparent accident that had seen Lionel's older brother Radcliff into an early grave, and there had long since been suspicions that Lionel was the one who was truly responsible for killing his brother off so that he could take his place without ever having to face him like Fae. His father had crushed the rumours at the time, but if the Lionel we now knew was anything to go by, then I was willing to bet that Radcliff's death was nothing beyond cold blooded murder.

"Are you certain?" I asked, unwilling to let her go even though I could see her mind was set on this and there was never any changing it once she got like that.

"Yes, Caleb, don't worry yourself about me. Just keep hold of that ledger and we will figure out the rest as we go along. Now unless you want them all to think I'm taking the world's longest shit, I need to go."

I breathed a laugh and let her pull me into a tight embrace once more.

"Keep the gemstone with you. Activate it if you get any information which leads you to believe my life is in danger or if Antonia or Tiberius' lives are at risk then activate it to warn me of that too. Just press your power into it once if it's my life that is in danger, twice in a row if it's Antonia's family and three times for Tiberius. If you do it four times then we will know that we all need to run. I'll make sure we have plans in place if it comes to that."

"I don't know how long it will be until I see you again," I breathed, crushing her in my embrace and almost feeling like the little boy who used to crawl into bed with her when she got home late from a Council meeting, even though I was now more than a foot taller than her.

"I'm always in your heart, Caleb. And you're always in mine." She pressed a kiss to my cheek, squeezing me one last time before stepping back and disappearing in a swirl of stardust.

My gut clenched as I watched her go, knowing she was heading back into the lap of that psychopath and fearing that I might have just seen my mother for the final time. Our parents were the closest Fae in the whole of Solaria to his level of power. They were the most obvious threat surrounding him. And maybe for now he cared enough about public opinion to try and force them into line rather than just killing them off, but long term? I didn't trust him one fucking bit. Which really just meant we needed to work even harder to bring him down as fast as possible.

I drew in a deep breath, took my own stardust from my pocket and left the desert behind as I fell into the embrace of the stars.

I landed back in the cold, snowy landscape which housed The Burrows, glancing around once more as I failed to spot the farmhouse or anything to let anyone know that the rebel stronghold was right beneath my feet. The illusions around this place were strong and I was certain I wouldn't have found it at all if I didn't already know its position and hadn't been granted the right to enter.

I started walking, my eyes set on a distant snow-covered mountain as I went until I met the resistance of the magical barrier flaring against my senses. I ground my teeth as the power of the magic tore through me and the next moment the farmhouse and barn appeared alongside a ring of worn-out snow which had been trampled along the edge of the barrier.

I frowned at the set of footprints which were ground right down to the mud before the sound of a wolfish bark made me spin just in time to get pounced on by a big ass white Wolf.

Seth knocked me to the ground, making an oomph leave me and I laughed as I fell beneath him in the snow and he ran the pad of his tongue right up the centre of my face.

"Gah!" I batted him away and his excitable yips turned into laughter as he shifted back, straddling me and grinning widely.

"Dude, I've been pacing since the moment you left," he began. "I'm so fucking hyped up it's untrue. I don't think I've ever been so glad to see your gorgeous face before."

"Oh yeah? Just how grateful are you to find me alive and well?" I asked, my gaze trailing over his neck and landing on the thump of his pulse beneath his skin.

"I see how it is - you only want me for my blood," he huffed, leaning back and giving me a clear look at his abs, not to mention his cock which was out and pretty much half mast. Then again, he always seemed to be hard these days so I was starting to think it must be a Wolf thing. He was used to getting laid a whole hell of a lot with his pack after all so maybe his body had grown used to the demand of satisfying so many of them.

"Are you staring at my dick?" Seth asked, tilting his head as he looked down at me and I snapped my gaze back to his face.

"More like the artery in your thigh," I replied quickly though that wasn't entirely true.

"Oh yeah? Well maybe if you can overpower me then you can bite me there," he teased and my grin turned feral as I felt the bloodlust powering through my veins.

"Promise?" I demanded.

"Cross my heart and hope to die," he replied before shoving himself off of me and taking off fast towards the barn, his bare ass on full display in the pale light of the day.

I tried to shoot after him but found myself rooted to the ground by earth magic I hadn't even noticed him wielding.

A curse spilled from my lips as I severed the roots which were clinging to my shirt and jeans before lunging to my feet and taking chase.

Seth cast a blizzard of air magic back at me as he raced for the barn, almost knocking me on my ass before I managed to shoot aside, speeding around to the other side of him so fast that he couldn't change the direction of the wind in time to stop my advance.

He darted into the barn and I chased right behind him, scenting blood in the air and losing control of the beast inside me as I slammed into his back and whirled him around, throwing him against the rotting wooden wall of the barn.

Seth swore and threw a punch at me but I dove below his strike, dropping to my knees before him, grabbing hold of his leg and yanking it aside a second before driving my fangs into the thick vein at the top of his thigh.

"Sweet, holy, mother of…*fuck,*" Seth gasped, his fingers taking hold of my hair and dragging me closer as I kept a tight grip on his leg with my right hand and splayed my palm against his firm abs to hold him in place with my left.

The rush of blood I got from that throbbing pulse point was enough to make a growl of pure pleasure escape me as I swallowed greedily, the mixture of his blood and the adrenaline rush from the hunt getting me hard as I flexed my fingers against the firm ridges of his six pack.

"Cal…by the stars, Cal, this is so fucking…I can't…holy shit," Seth garbled and I felt the brush of his cock against my cheek as he got hard too, his fingers still tightly fisted in my hair as my pulse spiked and I froze for a moment, realising exactly where I was biting him and what this might seem like.

But…he was pulling me closer, not pushing me away. And even though I probably should have been pulling back myself, that was the last thing I wanted.

My heart began to race as I sucked on his thigh again, an insane idea occurring to me as my dick chafed against the fabric of my boxers with a need I wasn't sure I wanted to put a name to and I slowly began to shift my hand down Seth's abs.

"Caleb, are you sure you want to-" Seth groaned as I sucked harder on his thigh, drawing even more of his delicious blood into my mouth and no doubt making him light-headed as I took more than I knew I should. But I couldn't help myself. I was becoming addicted to the taste of him and I couldn't help but be a glutton when it came to feeding from him like this.

I growled in warning as he shifted his weight and he cursed as his cock scraped across my cheek in a demand I felt echoed in my own body. A demand I was starting to seriously think about answering.

A wet drip landed on my cheek and I flinched minutely before a second drip fell on my skin right next to it.

"What the fuck is that?" Seth hissed before a yelp of alarm spilled from his lips and he shoved me back with enough force to make me respond.

I jerked my fangs free of his leg, tilting my head back to look up at him, unsure what I was even going to say or do-

A wet splatter hit my face once more as I found him staring at the roof above us and a curse spilled from my lips as I spotted a body hanging from the rafters. Or what remained of a body anyway. And as I squinted, using my heightened vision to see through the darkness, I spotted the body parts of other victims, whole pieces of them strewn everywhere.

Blood and gore filled the space above our heads and the wide open mouth of a Fae caught in an endless scream stared down at us from above.

"Holy fuck, what the hell did that?" I swore, scrambling to my feet and training my senses on everything around us as I tried to make sure nothing was about to leap out at us from the shadows.

"I think that's the group of rebels who should have been on guard out here," Seth said, his hand latching around my arm as he drew me back towards the exit, a shield of air forming around us just in case. "Can you hear anything nearby?"

I strained my hearing to the best of my ability, but if there was anything here it was either concealed within a silencing bubble or it was neither moving nor breathing. Fear crept along my skin at the thought of our enemies being so close to my friends.

"Nothing," I confirmed, hunting the shadows for any signs of movement and finding nothing there either.

"We should tell the others," Seth said urgently and I nodded, letting him draw me back towards the exit and leaving the bloodbath behind as my gut knotted and frayed.

"Come on. We need to make sure the others are alright. Are you certain no one passed you while you were waiting for me?" I demanded, my skin prickling with tension as I kept my senses trained on everything that surrounded us.

"I'm pretty sure," Seth said, looking around too, tilting his head to one side as he no doubt used his Order gifts to survey the surrounding area just like I was. "But I was running and focused on you. I guess there's a chance that someone fast could have gotten past me. I wasn't exactly on high alert."

I nodded. "Then we need to make sure everyone is safe," I said, fear twisting through me as I grabbed Seth and hoisted him onto my back before shooting towards the farmhouse to find the others.

I had no idea how a bunch of guards could have been massacred without anyone noticing a damn thing, but we needed to figure out what the fuck had happened here.

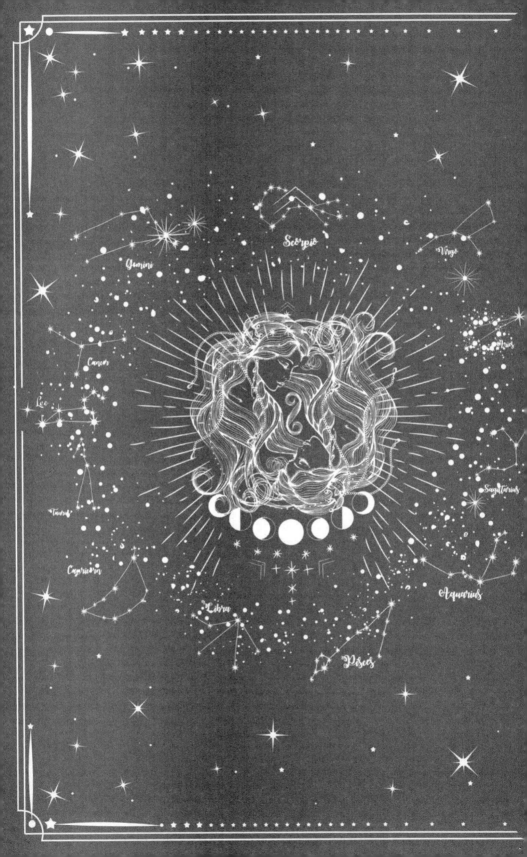

DARCY

CHAPTER SEVEN

I lazed on a chair built into the rocks, leaning back against Orion's bare chest as I watched Xavier, Max and Geraldine playing catch with a ball of water in one of the bubbling pools. Geraldine had decided that the girls' bathhouse within the royal quarters was required for relaxation for me and Tory this morning - despite my protests – but it was hard to keep complaining when Orion ran his fingers repeatedly through my hair and I practically started purring like a Lion Shifter with how content I was.

Tory and Darius had gone back to their room to 'fetch something' and hadn't returned yet, so I decided not to think about why that was. I was kind of regretting letting Seth stay with me and Orion considering we now had nowhere to get any privacy. Despite this place seeming to have endless tunnels, it also seemed to have endless Fae too, and when we'd snuck off to try and have some alone time last night, only Orion's Vampire ears had saved us from being caught by a couple of Oscura Wolves out on a run in their shifted forms. He'd yanked my panties up so fast I swear I could still feel the wedgie then he'd shot us away into the dark so no one saw us.

"Is there any way I can contact someone who's not part of the rebellion, Geraldine?" Xavier asked with a frown on his brow.

"Who, my dear Xavier?" she asked, her large breasts bouncing in the tiny green bikini she wore which was dotted with little Cerberuses.

"Sofia," he said, his cheeks pinking a little as Max tossed him the ball of water and he caught it before throwing it to Geraldine.

"Oh, sweet Sofia, our glittery gallopy friend," Geraldine sighed. "But no, Xavier, we cannot make contact unless it is of utmost urgency. Merely speaking with her could put her at risk of Cyclops interrogation."

Xavier hung his head and my attention was snagged as Darius and Tory walked into the room. She was wearing a red bikini which matched my blue one in every way, the surface a mimicry of snakeskin. Geraldine had let Tory pick out a few items for one of the supplies runs yesterday but we still didn't have a huge amount of clothes to work with.

I waved to her and she jogged over, her hand locked in Darius's as she pulled him along, his black and gold swim shorts the only thing he wore and I couldn't help but smirk at their matching tattoos. My sister had gone freaking soft on that Dragon even if she had chosen to display it in a badass way instead of a soppy one.

Orion shifted beneath me as Tory dropped down onto the lounger beside ours and Darius looked to him as he remained standing.

"Hey, brother," he said, a look of uncertainty in his eyes for a second.

"Hey," Orion said, clearing his throat and I sensed an awkwardness between them which made me shift in my seat. What was going on?

Tory didn't seem to notice, picking up a towel folded on the end of her lounger and dropping it over her face. "Wake me up for lunch. I need to catch up on some sleep."

I breathed a laugh, looking to Darius as he lingered there, his eyes on Orion then flicking to the others in the pool.

"That's not how you play water ball," he said with a scoff and he walked over to them, casting a huge water ball in his palm which was spinning and spitting water everywhere. He launched it at Xavier and it slammed into his face, knocking him clean out of the pool and tumbling across the floor.

"Ah, you asshole!" Xavier leapt up, creating an equally fierce water ball in his hand and throwing it hard at his brother.

Darius tried to duck, but it hit him in the chest and sent him stumbling backwards a few steps.

Max burst out laughing and they all fell into a violent game which Geraldine started taking very seriously, casting explosive water balls that sent everyone running in different directions as she roared like an Amazonian warrior.

"Wanna play?" I asked Orion keenly as I sat up, grinning at the game as I prepared to join in.

"Nah...you go," he said and I glanced back at him with a frown.

"What's up?" I asked, sensing something sad in his expression and his eyes trailed to Darius again before back to me.

"I-" he started, but he was instantly cut off by the arrival of the other two Heirs.

"Murder!" Seth shouted and I spun to face them, finding him on Caleb's back butt ass naked and wide eyed.

Caleb had blood smeared along his cheek and for a moment, a smile pulled at my mouth as I expected some prank, but their expressions made me get to my feet.

"Whatever do you mean?" Geraldine demanded.

"Some guards have been ripped to pieces out in the barn," Caleb said seriously, letting Seth down.

"Fuck." Orion was on his feet in an instant and I hurried over to wake Tory who was dead to the world already.

"Whasappening?" she slurred as I pulled her upright, my heart starting to beat unevenly.

"Some guards have been killed," I said and her lips parted in surprise.

"We must fetch my father at once!" Geraldine announced, climbing out of the pool and dripping water everywhere as she ran for the door.

"Everyone should get their weapons," I said urgently, the fear of our enemies being here creeping under my skin.

"Wait here," Orion growled before shooting off out of the bathhouse and barely a few seconds passed before he returned with everyone's Phoenix weapons in hand, handing them out as well as slapping a pair of sweatpants into Seth's chest for him to cover up with.

"Oh wow, thanks friend," he said before pulling them on.

"I'm doing everyone else a favour, not you," Orion muttered.

"Because of how intimidating my mega cock is," Seth agreed with a serious nod which had Caleb turning to look at his dick for a moment before glancing away again like he hadn't meant to look at all. "Sorry to make you feel inferior."

Orion snarled but ignored him as we all hurried out of the bathhouse in the direction Geraldine had headed.

Darius and Orion fell back to walk beside me and Tory, and my hand brushed my sister's as we shared a worried glance.

As we made it to the tunnel that led to the farmhouse, we found it thronging with frantic people.

"What's happened?!" someone cried.

"Is King Lionel here?" another shouted in panic.

"He's not the fucking king," Tory growled irritably.

"Keep your flans on a low heat!" Hamish called out from somewhere up ahead. "We shall get to the bottom of this post haste."

We pushed through the crowd and I looked up at Orion who could see over most people ahead of us.

"What's going on?" I asked and he looked at me with a frown.

"Looks like Hamish is heading outside with a group of Fae," he said, taking my arm and pulling me closer like he thought I might be attacked at any second.

As the crowd noticed us coming, they created a path to allow us through and we made it to the front, waiting for Hamish to return while Geraldine spoke to Catalina in a low voice. When he finally came back from the farmhouse, his face was pale with worry and my pulse became more rapid.

"There has been an incident," Hamish called out, using magic to send his voice echoing throughout the entire Burrows. "Cyclops Interrogation will commence immediately. Please return to your rooms and wait to be summoned."

"Can we help?" I asked, stepping toward him.

"No, my lady Darcy," he said. "Please return to your room. We will find the culprit swiftly."

"You don't think it's to do with Lionel?" Tory asked, her right hand tightening into a fist as Catalina's spine straightened at his name.

"As of yet, there is no sign of further attack," Hamish said. "But we will be most vigilant, of course." He wafted us away and Geraldine looked to us with tears in her eyes.

"My ladies, do forgive me. I would never bring you to a place of danger and bloodshed intentionally," she croaked a sob.

"It's not your fault," I said softly but she just covered her face and wailed while Orion took hold of my arm, pulling me away.

We were carried along with the crowd back to the royal quarters and I chewed my lip anxiously as the others started splitting away into their rooms. I caught hold of Tory before she could go, wrapping her in a tight hug.

"It's not him, Tor," I said and she nodded.

"If it is, I'll take his other fucking hand," she growled and the strength in her voice brought a smile to my lips.

"We'll cut his legs off too and throw him in a river to drown," I agreed as we parted.

Darius nodded to us and pulled her across the hall in the direction of the room they'd made theirs since his return. I hadn't actually mentioned anything to Tory about the fact that she'd jumped straight into living with her new boyfriend. I was semi sure she would freak out if it was pointed out to her, and I didn't want her sending him off to find another room because she was afraid of jumping in too deep too fast. This whole thing had been a long time coming and I was just happy to see her smiling so much.

We walked into our room with Seth close behind me and the door swung shut behind us, the sound of worried voices still carrying from down the halls.

"Um, Darcy?" Seth whispered, pulling on my sleeve as Orion headed to the closet to grab some clothes.

"Yeah?" I asked.

"I know this isn't exactly the time, but…" He cast a silencing bubble around us and my curiosity piqued. "Before we found those bodies in the barn, me and Cal were in there and I was naked, and he was on his knees and he totally got down and dirty with my boner."

"What?" I gasped. "He did?"

"Well…no, but his cheek did. And his ear a bit."

"What are you talking about?" I frowned, not wanting to judge but like, was that some sort of kinky shit I'd never heard of? Because a cock to the ear didn't sound particularly fun for anyone.

"He was biting me," he said, bobbing on his toes. "He bit me right here." He tugged his sweatpants down to show me the mark, but unveiled his dick in the same movement and a freight train seemed to run him over a second later.

Orion slammed him into the wall behind me and I whipped around with a gasp as he choked Seth with one hand while Seth's pants fell fully down to his ankles and he blinked back at him innocently.

"What the fuck do you think you're doing?" Orion barked and in the next second, Seth blasted him away with a hurricane of air, sending him flying into the opposite wall, causing a crack to rip up the centre of it.

Orion hit the ground running, but Seth kept blasting a huge storm of air at him to keep him back, turning to me with a casual grin as he pulled up his pants with his free hand.

"Anyway, my boner was right there while he was biting me and I swear he flirted with it a little. His hand was moving down my abs and everything," he said giddily and I glanced at Orion, unsure if I should continue with this conversation while he was battling to get to us with a satanic look on his face. But Seth kept going anyway, casting a silencing bubble around Orion as he started hurling abuse at him so that he could tell the rest of his story.

"So I've had a really good idea of how to make my next move," he said, looking like he could barely contain it. "I'm gonna play gay chicken with him."

"Gay chicken?" I frowned.

"Yeah, because Cal is competitive, see? He can't ever bear to lose. So I'll just dare him to go gay for me and he won't be able to back down on the dare because he'd have to admit defeat by doing so. Then he'll go full gay and we'll get gayer and gayer together until one day we're married and it's ten years down the line and he's still so committed to the dare with our fourteen children who often ask why Daddy C always goes to those strip bars at the weekends with the booby ladies and-"

"That's a terrible idea," I cut over him and he looked crestfallen, like he'd really thought he'd cracked it this time. I took pity on him, resting a hand on his shoulder with a sigh. "Just tell him the truth, Seth."

He frowned, twiddling his thumbs. "What if you ask him if he likes me while I hide under a barrel nearby? And then if he says he's not into me, I can jump out and say it's a prank." He had to focus for a second as Orion's air magic started to cut through his own and his expression tensed.

"I'll talk to him if you want, but he changed the subject every time I tried to bring it up before," I said sadly.

"I know, but that's because you two need more bonding time. Hang out with him, be his new bestie, and he'll talk to you." His eyes gleamed like two giant pennies and I nodded my agreement. Dammit, he was too cute when he gave me the puppy eyes.

"Fine, but you have to stop winding Orion up. And could you like, be his friend? He says he doesn't need any more friends, but I see him watching you guys when you're all having fun and it kinda breaks my heart because he just stands back, alone..." I said with a frown. "I think he needs you guys more than he'd ever admit."

"Yeah, it's so sad isn't it? The way he stares at us when we're playing together," he said with a whine in his throat. "Poor, sad little Lance Orion. With his washed up dreams, two careers down the drain, now he's Power Shamed and outcast for life..."

"That's enough," I growled in warning, and he nodded seriously.

"We'll be best friends soon, Darcy. I promise." He hooked his pinky around mine. "But right now, I'm gonna release him and run for my life, so if you could dive into the way, that'd be great, babe." He winked then dropped the storm holding Orion back, whipping the door open with his air magic and flying out of it on a cloud at high speed, his chuckle carrying back to us.

Orion shot after him in a blur of speed, but I cast a net of vines to catch him, yanking him back and throwing him onto the bed.

He snarled, practically spitting venom as he shoved the net off of himself and worked to get up. But I pounced on him like a cat, straddling his lap and pressing my mouth to his with a smile as I ground down over the ridge of his cock through his pants.

"I know what you're doing, Blue," he warned as his hand latched around the Imperial Star hanging on a chain around my throat, pulling it tight enough to make my heart race as I sank my tongue between his lips.

"I know what I'm doing too," I teased and he cursed as I rocked my hips again.

I forgot all about the distraction as he used two fingers to push my little bikini bottoms aside and sank them into me with a growl in his throat. It might not have been good timing, but as we had to wait here for our interrogation anyway and death seemed to lurk around every corner in our lives these days, I was going to steal a moment with my man and fuck him breathless.

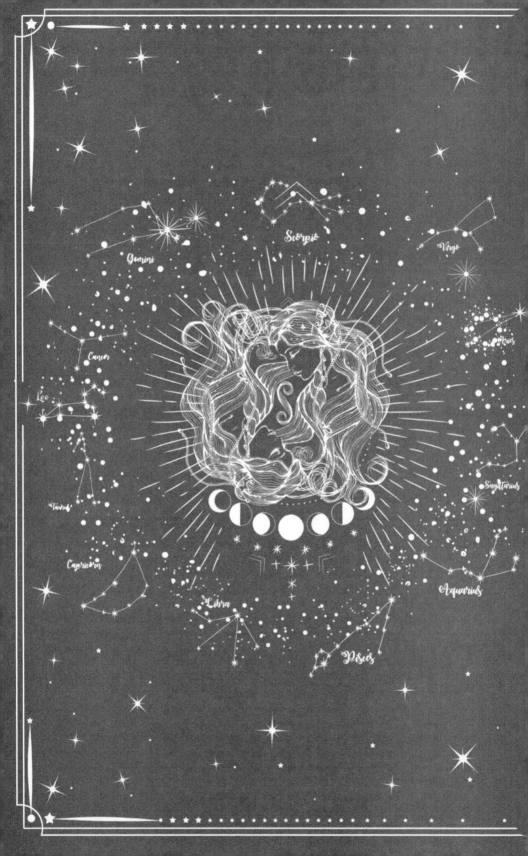

TORY

CHAPTER EIGHT

I shoved Darius back against our bedroom door, kissing him hard and moving my hands to his waistband as my heart thundered to a panicked rhythm and I worked really damn hard to keep the violent memories of being at the mercy of monsters out of my head.

"Roxy," Darius growled against my lips, pulling back and breaking our kiss but I just moved my mouth to his neck and started kissing my way down it as I yanked his shorts down. *"Roxy,"* he said with more protest to his tone, his hands moving to my arms as he tried to nudge me back but I ignored him again, dropping to my knees in front of him.

"I want you to fuck my mouth, Darius," I replied, looking up at him as I pushed my hand into his shorts and he released a Dragon's growl as I took his solid length into my grip and licked my lips in anticipation.

"By the stars," Darius groaned in frustration, cursing as he reached down and caught my wrist before I could tease him anymore and pulling me to my feet again with his hold on it.

"What?" I snapped as he fixed me in a glare and I reached for his cock again, but he had already tugged his shorts back up and was shaking his head at me.

"Tell me about it," he insisted. "I saw that look in your eyes when Hamish said there would be a Cyclops interrogation and I know that Vard-"

I yanked out of his grip as a knot of tension formed in my stomach and memories of what I'd suffered through the night before his wedding coated my tongue with acid as they tried to creep in again.

"I have my Phoenix back again now," I replied, trying to shrug it off as I turned away from him and moved towards the bed, snatching one of his shirts from it and pulling it on over my bikini, trying not to feel the sting of rejection at him pushing me away. The black fabric swamped me but I felt better like that, hiding myself beneath it like I was wrapped in a security blanket. "No one can get into my head if I don't want them there."

"That doesn't make it any easier on you," he insisted. "I know what they did to you. I know how the idea of anyone else getting into your head must make you feel."

"It's fine," I said, my pulse thumping against my eardrums as I remembered the sickly, cloying feeling of that fucking creep crawling around inside my head, of all the things he'd tried to make me believe and the fear he'd tangled up with all the good memories I had of the man in this room.

"It isn't," he snapped, moving up behind me and gripping my arm as he pulled me around. My heart leapt at the contact and fire burst to life in my fist as he made me look at him, the echoes of the fear they'd tried to make me feel for him lingering in my skin for several seconds before I forced them away.

"You can talk to me about it," Darius insisted, his hand curling around my cheek as my breaths came faster and I closed my eyes as I tried to fight off the memories. But they wouldn't leave me be. And suddenly it didn't feel like his hand was on my cheek, it felt like Lionel's as he'd forced my gaze up to meet his while I panted through the agony of my flesh and sat chained before him with my skin slicked in my own blood.

"Don't touch me," I snarled, jerking back and feeling the fire race up my arms to coat my body, coming to my aid the way it couldn't that night.

My back hit the wall and I was vaguely aware of someone calling my name but all I could feel was the heat of the fire magic which raged against my skin while my Phoenix was buried away and pain of a knife sliding between my ribs.

A hand locked around my throat, taking the burns from my fire as he continued to shout my name and suddenly the sound of a door bursting open crashed through the screaming in my skull. Except it wasn't in my skull and as I peeled my eyes open, I found myself curled up in a ball on the floor with Darius leaning over me, his eyes blazing with concern.

"It's alright, little Vega," Max said softly, his hand slipping into mine, his skin cool with the touch of his water magic and an offer of escape in his deep eyes which I accepted wholeheartedly as I fought to stop myself from thrashing against the wall.

Another hand took my free one and I turned to discover my sister there, finding peace in her gaze as she squeezed me tight, the fire unable to burn her at all as I continued to blaze between them.

"Come on," Max said, his voice filled with the allure of his kind as he pulled me away from the panic and helped me bind those memories with hate and rage instead. Because I refused to cower in fear from the motherfuckers who had done that to me. They'd drugged and immobilised me to do it, and it was clear that they wouldn't have stood a chance of penetrating my defences if I'd had access to my Phoenix.

I let that hatred and desire for vengeance rise in me until I was fit to burst with it then let Max encourage those flames to simmer instead of blaze, drawing me back to the moment we were in and offering me a sense of peace and calm which I took hold of greedily, releasing a long breath as the fire consuming me finally guttered out.

Darius slid his hand from my throat up and into my hair, his gaze wary as he took in my reaction to him, and I had to fight against the tears which pricked the backs of my eyes. His skin was stained with soot and his shorts had been burned from his skin in places, but he'd already healed away any burns I'd given him so at least I didn't have to dive into the guilt I'd have felt over those.

"I know it wasn't you," I swore to him and he nodded, leaning in to press a kiss to my hair while Max let the calming sensation of his magic run through me and my pulse finally began to settle.

"It was because of me though," he replied, drawing back and releasing me as I frowned at him.

"I don't believe that," I replied firmly and Darcy slipped closer to me, winding her arm around my shoulders while still keeping hold of my hand.

"We all know this comes down to Lionel and his followers," she said firmly. "Don't let him get between the happiness you two have found together out of some bullshit sense of guilt, Darius."

A sad kind of smile tugged at his lips as he pushed to his feet before us. "The shrew has bite."

"You know I do," she confirmed. "And I'll prove it if you even consider pulling away from this now. Tory needs you. So get that self loathing shit out of your eyes and be the man she needs you to be."

"Ouch," Max muttered, throwing a smirk up at Darius as he nodded in acceptance.

"Alright, alright. But I'm not going to let any fucking Cyclops near you, Roxy. I'll tell Hamish he can just take your word over these murders unless he wants me committing a new one."

I snorted a laugh and the corner of his lips lifted as he tugged off his ruined shorts and tossed them aside before using water magic to clean his skin. Darcy and Max looked away, clearly not interest in seeing him naked, but I kept my gaze fixed on him. It was kinda like watching my own personal strip show and I bit my lip as I watched the way his wet abs glistened as he scrubbed at his skin.

The cold sensation of a bucket of ice being dumped on my libido fell over me and I cut Max a glare as he shrugged innocently.

"You need to stay calm for a bit," he said by way of explanation. "No eye fucking the Dragon."

Darius threw me a look filled with promises for later then pulled on a fresh shirt and a pair of jeans and moved to the door. "Look after her, Darcy," he said before he left and Darcy clucked her tongue at him.

"I think your boyfriend needs reminding of his place on your favourite person list," she muttered.

"Oh he knows," I promised her. "A couple more orgasms and he might even make the top ten."

Max chuckled darkly as he released my hand and I looked to him as we both waited to see if I'd hold it together on my own. But this wasn't our first rodeo and we were pretty in sync now, so I wasn't surprised when my heart rate stayed low and nothing but hatred and a desire for vengeance filled me when I thought of Lionel, Vard and the Shadow Princess.

"Thank you," I murmured and he gave me an easy smile, though I could see the tension around his eyes which hadn't been there before from the weight of taking on my fear and pain.

"Any time, little Vega." He got up and headed from the room, a strangled sob from beyond the door letting me know that Geraldine was hanging around out there as he emerged.

"Oh you salty sealion," she praised. "You have a true heart of gold beneath that barnacle encrusted exterior, don't you, Maxy?"

"Err...yeah?" he replied, his tone seeming brighter already.

"Come let me fix you some snacks to rebuild your fortitude," she offered and the sound of them heading away together drifted down the corridor until we were finally left alone.

"What are the chances that there's someone down here who doesn't know about my freak out?" I asked in a low voice and Darcy looked away from me as she made a show of thinking about that.

"Well...you didn't have a silencing bubble up so Lance and Caleb definitely heard and Seth was the one who ran to get me even though I was already on my way, and obviously Geraldine heard so..."

"Let's hope it was just our group then," I muttered though I wasn't really embarrassed about it. I would happily challenge any fucker who thought less of me for losing my shit to spend a night in the company of my tormentors, let alone the amount of time I'd endured them, and come out peachy on the other side.

"We could always spread rumours of a ghoul in the tunnels if it comes to it," she agreed, squeezing me tight and I knew she was hurting over what I'd been through.

"I'm here now," I reminded her, though maybe I was reminding myself too. "Free." I pointed at the clear patch of skin on my arm where the Aries brand had once marked it and a real smile lit her lips as she nodded.

"Thanks to Darius," she agreed, looking towards the door for a moment before frowning as she turned back to me. "Has he told you exactly what happened to make the stars release you from the bonds?"

"He just said he begged them to break them and they listened," I replied, unable to hide the smile that came to my lips at that. "I guess we were overdue a turn in our luck."

"Hell yeah we are," she agreed but her brow furrowed and I tilted my head as I realised she was holding something back.

"What is it?" I asked.

"Hopefully nothing," she replied quickly.

"But?"

Darcy blew out a breath, making a lock of deep blue hair flutter before her and she sighed. "The Shadow Princess tried to place a curse on me during the battle."

"What?" I gasped, pushing away from the wall and sitting up so that I could look at her directly. She started explaining all about how the real Shadow Princess was called Lavinia and that she'd possessed Clara's body. She told me about how Orion had had to drive a blade into his sister's body to free her soul and that the shadow bitch had remained in her place. But I couldn't get my mind off of the word 'curse'.

"What did she do to you?" I demanded in fear.

"Honestly, I think it's fine," she said quickly. "There was a mark on my arm here when she left the curse." She rolled her sleeve up to show me her arm, but there wasn't so much as a freckle out of place. "But it disappeared again and Lance and I think my Phoenix has burned it out of me."

"Really?" I asked dubiously, gripping her arm and turning it back and forth to inspect it more closely, but there was nothing to see.

"Really," she swore. "I feel absolutely fine and our Phoenixes have burned a whole lot of crap out of our bodies, so it makes sense that it would work to protect me from this too."

I nodded slowly, relief filling me.

"And you definitely feel okay?" I confirmed, annoyed at myself for not asking her more about the battle sooner, but honestly, I'd just been glad to steal a little respite from the horrors of that day.

"Yeah. I feel great. I hope that bitch is off crying herself to sleep somewhere because her dumb curse didn't take root in me," she joked and I grinned.

"That's because you're a total badass," I replied knowingly.

"Well that makes two of us," she said.

"Wanna go find some snacks to steal and watch some trash TV with me while we wait for Hamish to finish up the interrogations?" I offered and her smile widened.

"There'd better be chocolate down in these tunnels."

"If there's not, what even is the point of living?" I lamented and she laughed.

"I can see the headlines now, the Vega twins die in joint chocolate-related suicide," she said and I chuckled.

"I think our bigger concern around here is a sneaky white Wolf stealing all of our chocolate away," I added, narrowing my eyes on the door in case Seth was already lingering close by at the mere mention of snacks.

"Then we'd better go and get our hands on it first, Tor, because I swear to god, I'll summon an army of fleas to take dog boy down if he takes our chocolate."

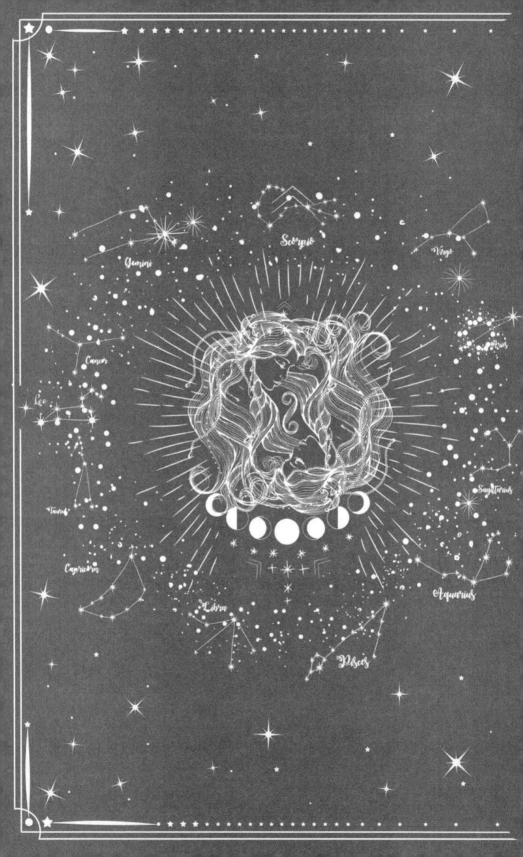

DARCY

CHAPTER NINE

Darius ended up getting both me and Tory out of the interrogation, and I was glad to have some alone time with my sister after everything that had happened lately. We ate our way through two massive chocolate bars as we talked shit and reminisced about old times, then I helped her stash a few bars in her room for later, knowing Seth would sniff them out if I took them anywhere near my room.

The interrogation showed up nothing. No culprit. Which either meant the guilty party had trained their mind well enough to hide the truth from a Cyclops which was damn difficult, or they weren't here and had probably broken through the boundaries to kill those men. I wasn't sure which of those thoughts unsettled me most, but both led to countless unanswered questions that set me on edge.

I sat between Orion and Tory in the dining hall, the Heirs sharing our table along with Geraldine and Xavier as we discussed the endless theories we had about the murderer. And the thing that left me the most terrified was the theory that this had something to do with the 'man with the painted smile' from Gabriel's prophecy.

We hadn't been able to talk to our brother all day since he'd helped out with the interrogations, trying to *see* anything from the people being questioned. But now as I caught his eye across the hall where he sat with his family, he stood up and came over to join us, taking a seat beside Geraldine opposite us. I spotted Justin Masters looking wistfully over at her from a table full of royalists, picking at a bagel.

"Any news?" Darius asked instantly, the tension in his posture speaking of his concern over this situation.

Tory absentmindedly stroked his arm beside him, turning to our brother for the answer we were all anxious for.

Gabriel shook his head, lines of stress forming around his silver ringed grey eyes. "Nothing. But I'm hopeful that means this incident is nothing to do with you. Perhaps someone here had a feud with the guards, so it's something I cannot *see* because it does not affect those I care for. But on the other hand…"

"What?" I breathed as Orion's hand dropped to my knee under the table and squeezed reassuringly.

"It could be that this is linked to the Nymphs somehow as I cannot predict their moves and the shadows hide them from me. But the attacks seemed more savage than their usual style," Gabriel said thoughtfully. "We can't rule it out. But if this was Nymphs, then they have somehow breached the magical boundary protecting this place. And that seems highly unlikely…"

"Could Nymphs be here already?" Tory asked slowly, glancing at other people around the room in suspicion. "We didn't know Diego was a Nymph and we saw him at school every day."

"How can we tell a Nymph from a Fae when they aren't shifted?" Max asked, narrowing his eyes at everyone around us like they could all be our enemies in disguise.

"You can't," Orion said simply.

"I totally can," Darius said cockily. "It's in their eyes."

"Bullshit, you always think that, but it isn't true," Orion tossed back. "How'd you miss Diego if you can tell the difference?"

"I always knew there was something off with that hat kid," Darius said with a shrug.

My heart tugged over Diego and I thought of his hat which was now stashed in the nightstand in our room. Maybe there were more answers there waiting for us within it…maybe I should try to see into the soul web again.

"I still don't get how he passed the stars' test at The Reckoning," Max said with a head shake.

"I should have known he was a Nymph when I tasted his blood that time. Shame their blood isn't black when they're in their Fae-like form or I would have noticed." Orion grimaced at the memory. "I just figured he'd Emerge as one of my least favoured Orders."

"Like Heptian Toads?" Caleb asked with a knowing nod.

"Yeah and Grieven Slugs," Orion said, miming a retch while Caleb laughed.

"Have you ever tried a Polar Bear Shifter though? They taste like a snow cone," Caleb said excitedly.

"Well, nothing tastes as good as a Vega," Orion said tauntingly and Caleb bared his fangs as they locked eyes.

"Yeah? Try hunting the most powerful Werewolf in Solaria," Caleb said with a smirk and Orion bared his fangs at him.

"I'd rather drink a Toad's blood than drink from him again," Orion sneered as Caleb locked his arm around Seth and Seth's eyebrows shot up as he looked at him.

My heart pulled at the sight of all that gleaming hope in his eyes, but there was nothing to suggest Caleb wasn't just getting protective over his Source. Hell, I really hoped for Seth's sake it was more than that though. My fluffy Wolf friend might have been an asshole in the past, but he had such a squishy heart these days and I really wanted to see him happy.

"Bullshit," Caleb snarled. "I bet you've checked out his veins plenty of times since we got here."

"Why would I be interested in the blood of a mutt? I've got a Vega princess as my Source," Orion said proudly.

"Are Power Shamed Fae even allowed to legally have Sources?" Caleb asked airily, pushing a hand into his blonde curls and flexing as he tightened his grip on Seth. Orion stiffened as though he'd been struck and I could see a war breaking out in his eyes.

"Don't call him that," I hissed.

"Don't worry about it, beautiful. He'll be tasting his own blood in a second." Orion rose from his seat and Caleb stood too, both of them posturing for a fight.

"For the love of Hyacinth the first! Do sit down you pompous, sharp-toothed velociraptors!" Geraldine banged her fist on the table. "We have a murderer in our midst, and the game is afoot. We must solve this mystery before one of our own is found butchered in the night. Or would you rather we have this discussion while picking up the pieces of our beloved Xavier, because let us be unduly honest, he is quite the target with his sweet innocence and gentle soul."

"Hey," Xavier protested around a mouthful of lasagne. "I'm not innocent."

"On a completely unrelated side note," Orion addressed him as he and Caleb fell back into their seats. "I need the blood of a virgin for the Zodiac Guild elixir, do you mind if I grab some from you after dinner?"

Xavier spluttered his way through swallowing, his cheeks turning bright red. "I'm not a virgin."

Darius boomed a laugh and Tory smacked him while the rest of the Heirs cracked up and Geraldine doubled over, wheezing as she held her side.

"Oh my great aunt Gweneth on a merry-go-round, I needed that laugh during this sombre eve, dear Xavier. Thank you," Geraldine said, wiping tears from under her eyes.

"I'm not joking," Xavier balked. "I've had plenty of…sex."

"With who?" Darius demanded, leaning back in his seat and folding his arms.

"Girls," Xavier blurted. "Lots of girls. I've had girls on their knees while I rut my…horn on their swollen…parts."

"Oh dude, please go fuck someone, it's painful to hear you talk about something you've never done." Caleb pointed to another table where a group of girls sat together and Xavier's shoulders stiffened.

"I'm not a virgin," he insisted, his cheeks getting somehow redder.

"It's okay, man." Seth leaned across the table toward him, lowering his voice. "How about I teach you some stuff? Ease you into it with a nice orgy, huh? I could get five or six of those hot Oscura Wolves over there to fuck you sideways."

"Five or six…" Xavier visibly gulped.

"Not everyone's first time is a fucking orgy, Seth," Max laughed.

"Well, it should be," Seth insisted. "Then you can work up to the one-on-one stuff later. If there's five other people fucking around you, you can learn on the job, pick up tips from the best fuckers while they guide your hips. It's like a swimming lesson."

Everyone laughed, even Orion, but he quickly caught himself, flattening his smile into a glare at Seth like he was offended that the Wolf had made him laugh.

"Can we move on from talking about my little brother having an orgy?" Darius asked.

"I actually wanted to apologise to you, Gabriel," I said, biting my lip in concern as I caught my brother's eye.

"About what? Oh," he said as he *saw* the answer and nodded. "About the fact that the house I painstakingly built with earth magic for my family was badly damaged by Lionel Acrux when he captured you?"

"Yeah…that," I said sadly.

"Yeah, sorry Noxy," Orion added.

"I'm hardly going to blame you for that," Gabriel said, waving a hand. "Anyway, I've already *seen* a new wing I'm going to add with an indoor swimming pool. So no harm done."

Relief rushed through me, though I still planned on paying for that damage and I'd get him a big ass hamper full of all kinds of his favourite stuff too when this war was over.

"What else have you *seen* about the war?" Darius cut in. "I don't wanna stay in this hole in the ground forever. When can we strike at my father?"

"I'm waiting to *see* an opportunity," Gabriel promised. "You know I'll tell you as soon as one arises. Just be ready at all times, because with the Shadow Princess blocking most of my visions of Lionel, I may only get a small window to *see* a way to get him, and we may have to act on it fast." He rose from his seat, heading back to his table and placing a kiss on his wife's lips before taking the little baby boy from her arms and snuggling him against his chest. I'd not had nearly enough cuddles with my nephew yet, but I decided that was definitely on the agenda for me this evening.

Orion followed my gaze and pinched me softly to get my attention onto him. "You want one of those?" he murmured, darkness entering his eyes.

"One day," I said, reaching up to brush my thumb over the dimple in his right cheek and picturing how cute it would look on a tiny little baby. He shifted back from my touch and my heart crushed at that action, frowning as he turned away from me.

"Don't you?" I asked.

He took my hand beneath the table, squeezing and the contact sent a tremor of pure heat through my body, but he didn't answer me.

"Is that a no?" I pressed, realising how much I wanted that in the future as the idea of him not wanting it was presented to me.

"My shame would be passed on to any child we had," he said tightly, his quiet voice just for me and I opened my mouth to say that was ridiculous, but was cut off by someone shouting.

"Cooweeee!" the shockingly familiar voice made my vagina ziplock itself and I twisted around in my seat in alarm, spotting Professor Washer sashaying through the wooden doors with two large suitcases levitating along behind him. He wore a velour purple tracksuit, the top half unzipped to reveal his tanned, waxed chest and the bottoms looking two sizes too small as they clung to his muscular thighs and - more horrifyingly – the bulge between his legs.

"Oh for the love of fuck," Orion said under his breath as Washer instantly spotted us and started making a beeline for our table. As he got closer, he noticed Orion sitting beside me and gasped, pointing a quivering finger at him.

"Miss Vega, stand aside! That man is a fugitive. He addled your mind, he made you do terrible, terrible things to him and he did dirty, filthy things all over your body. I read the report back to back to back, every last detail committed to memory so I would know how best to help you recover."

"That's it," I spat, jumping out of my seat and climbing onto the table. But I didn't know the spell to make my voice louder, so I faltered and looked to Orion. "Can you cast the loud voicey spell on me?"

"Why?" he asked anxiously, glancing around at the rebels.

I looked to Seth instead, beckoning him closer. "Can you do it?"

"Sure, babe."

"Don't." Orion rose from his seat, but Seth was already reaching up, brushing his fingers over my throat and a cool magic caressed it before I started shouting.

"Lance Orion is not a criminal!" Everyone in the room winced. Oh shit, I did not need to shout while the voicey spell thing was on me.

"Darcy, stop," Orion commanded, but I ignored him.

I cleared my throat and the sound of that echoed painfully around the room while Hamish started retching in the corner at the mere mention of my boyfriend's name. And I was so fucking done with it.

"He lied to the court to protect me because he knew I'd lose my place at Zodiac Academy. So stop treating him like he's a monster. He didn't hurt me or abuse me or cast any kind of spell on me." I looked down at Orion, but he didn't smile, he reached for me frantically, trying to pull me off the table.

"Please, Blue," he begged.

I danced out of his way. He deserved the world to recognise who he was, to see the sacrifices he'd made for Darius, for me, for the kingdom. So I wasn't just going to sit here and let people pretend like he didn't exist.

"So stop shaming him!" I cried, but the only answer was an awkward, echoing silence.

Tory was gazing up at me, sucking her lip as she clapped to try and get the crowd started, but they didn't follow her lead even when she elbowed Darius and he gave a couple of pitying slow claps too.

"Not a fucking slow clap, asshole," Tory hissed.

"Either kind of clap is awkward as fuck," Darius muttered back and my skin prickled as the distant sound of Hamish retching reached me.

"Get down," Orion growled, his eyes flaring at me and my cheeks blazed as I didn't get his backing in this.

"Get up here with me," I countered. "Tell them the truth."

He shook his head and Tory and Darius shared a glance while Geraldine pulled at her hair and looked around the room in alarm.

"All praise the eloquent way my lady speaks!" she cried suddenly. "How passionate her plea is, how heartfelt and…beautifully put. She glimmers like a starstone on a moonbeam with her passion and prose!"

Several people clapped at that which was worse because now they were just applauding the way I'd said it, not the words I'd spoken at all.

Muttering was starting to break out and Seth whined in discomfort for me, the sound making my skin burn with embarrassment.

I climbed back down from the table, sinking into my seat and Orion reached for my hand under the table, but I snatched it away, unable to believe he hadn't fought his corner, hadn't stood up there with me and shown the world who he truly was.

Everyone in the room hurriedly turned their backs on him again, and my throat thickened.

"Why won't you tell them the truth?" I whispered to Orion and he looked to me with confliction in his eyes.

"Because it will make no difference. I'm sorry, Blue."

Those words chipped at my heart and I stared down at my hands in my lap, feeling like a complete idiot for being left hanging like that in front of the whole room.

Washer drifted closer, trying to use his Siren gifts to get a feed on my emotions.

"Well if you have any concerns and need to get things off your breast – er chest, my dear, do come to me," Washer purred and Orion snarled.

"She won't be coming anywhere near you, Brian," he hissed and Washer forced his eyes onto him.

"Now, now, I didn't want to cause a hullabaloo. In fact, I come bearing gifts." He turned, gesturing to the large suitcases behind him. "I have brought all of the Vegas' things from the academy. I've up and quit, see? The academy has gone totally downhill and if I'm being entirely honest, I'm fairly sure Elaine was planning to have me murdered, so here we are." He beamed at me and Tory. "Oh and I have an extra surprise for you! I handwashed all of your little knickies and knackies so they'll be silky fresh for your royal behinds."

"You did what?" Tory snapped.

"Please tell me a knickie and a knackie isn't what I think it is," I murmured.

"You really must take better care of your delicates, girls. G-strings and thongs can get a teeny weenie bit frayed if they aren't rubbed down regularly with a good soap. I use a gentle foamy white soap that I make myself, I'll give you a sample sometime. I call it Washer's essence." He winked.

"What the fuck are you saying?" Darius growled, smoke pluming between his teeth and I grabbed Orion's arm to stop him from getting out of his seat, though maybe letting him go psycho Vamp on Washer's ass alongside Darius wasn't the worst idea.

"I'm saying it's a secret recipe, silly boy. Cheery chow!" He headed away towards Catalina and Hamish, embracing them and his ass wiggled back and forth with each hug.

Ergh, great, I thought I'd seen the last of that creeper.

I noticed everyone was still working hard to keep their eyes away from Orion and my shoulders fell with dejection. "I don't understand why they won't stop this Power Shaming shit."

"Because Power Shaming is more than law, Blue," Orion said, his eyes falling from mine, showing me he was ashamed of it too, and that broke me more than anything. My anger with him melted a little because I could see that this was something I didn't really understand, but it still hurt me. "It's cultural and people don't want to be associated with it. And it isn't something that can be undone. I am grateful for what you were trying to do, beautiful, but commanding the world to acknowledge me won't work."

I sighed, hating this crap. What was the point of being a 'true queen' if they weren't going to listen on something that mattered this much to me?

"Yeah, just you sitting at our table is bringing us down like a thousand cool points," Seth said with a sigh. "But that's okay, bro, we wanna be your friend, don't we Cal?" He elbowed him and Caleb glanced at Orion with a hint of a growl on his lips.

"No thanks," he muttered as Orion straightened at the challenge in his eyes.

I knew their Order drove them to competitiveness, but I guessed I'd just never spent so much time around the two of them together to realise how deeply that instinct ran.

"I am torn in two, my lady Darcy," Geraldine said to me. "By my loyalty to you and my instinct to shun your Orry man until he is no more than a ghost of a shadow in my periphery. But I can overcome any obstacle for you, my queen."

"Thank you, Geraldine," I said and she rose from her seat, walking around to Orion and hugging him from behind, making him stiffen like he'd just been struck with a whip. "I see you Lance Azriel Orion. My eyes are wide open and there you are like a crisp apple balancing upon the bosoms of the stars."

"Thanks," he forced out. "I mean, not about me being a tit apple, but the other part." He awkwardly patted her hand while subtly trying to unlatch her arms from him and she hurried back to her seat with a choked sob leaving her.

"Would it help if I dick punched anyone who ignored you?" Tory offered and I laughed.

"Is that your answer to everything, little savage?" Orion asked her with a smirk and she thought on it for a second.

"Most things, yeah," she agreed and Darius frowned at her.

"How come you've never dick punched me then?" He almost sounded like he felt left out and she made a show of curling her fingers into a fist in front of his junk.

"Are you sure you wanna cash in on all the dick punches you're owed?" she asked teasingly.

"Dick punch time," Seth breathed, taking out his Atlas and pressing record.

"She'll send your dick into orbit if she gives you what you're owed," Max pointed out to Darius, trying to casually take Geraldine's hand beside him but she jabbed him away from her with a fork.

"What are you doing encroaching on my personal feeding space you Larry lobster?" she demanded of him, jabbing him harder with the fork and making him curse and yank his hand well out of the way.

We finished our meals and spent the rest of the evening discussing who the murderer might be, only to circle back around to the same conclusions. It could be anyone, so we had to keep our wits about us, cast security spells on our doors and always travel around the place in pairs. Surrounded by my friends, I wasn't nearly as afraid as perhaps I should have been. I was among the most powerful Fae in Solaria, and if anyone could take on some sneak lurking in these tunnels, it was us.

When we left the dining hall, I invited everyone back to our room to try out Diego's hat again. Caleb frowned around at our room as we arrived, immediately starting to decorate it with moss on the walls and glittering silver streaks through the ceiling. I smiled at the beautiful magic as I helped cast some chairs and a sofa out of rock with Tory, and Seth coated them all in thick moss before everyone sat down.

Darius cast a few everflames to warm the space and I sat crossed legged on the bed beside one while Orion dropped down at my side. Caleb and Seth dropped onto the sofa while the others took the chairs. I looked to Orion then started telling them everything we'd learned about Lavinia including the visions we'd *seen*, the things we'd learned within the hat before and everyone listened with rapt attention. Then I grabbed Diego's hat out of the nightstand, knowing it was time to look for more answers, to see what other secrets this held.

I found myself just staring at it with my heart crushing and grief tearing up the inside of my throat. My eyes blurred with tears as I missed my friend and thought of the sacrifice he'd made for us in the woods when he'd tried to take on Lavinia.

Silence fell in the room and Geraldine sniffed loudly.

"Our dear, hatted friend," she croaked. "He will not be forgotten. I shall write a ditty about his soul-weaved hat and his dear abuela, and we shall sing it to the stars so loud that he shall hear it beyond the Veil."

I nodded, smiling sadly at Geraldine before turning to my sister who gave me an encouraging look.

"We need to all hold hands so you'll see the memories too," I explained.

Seth grabbed Caleb's hand and Max took hold of his other one before snaring Geraldine's hand too, and we connected the circle with Xavier, Tory and Darius.

"Are you sure we should be messing with this soul hat thing?" Tory glanced at the hat nervously and I knew she was worried about the feel of the shadows again.

"It's okay, baby. I got you," Darius said and she looked at him with the fire of her Order lighting up her eyes, making me feel all fuzzy for them as she nodded her agreement.

"Everyone ready then?" I asked and everyone assented, making my heart race with anticipation of what we might see. We'd talked about Diego countless times before, but none of us had answers about him. Was he an anomaly? The only Nymph with a good soul? Or were there more like him out there?

I took Orion's hand then pulled on the hat with the other before reaching for Tory's hand beside me. As her fingers met mine, I was yanked away into the darkness of the shadows, tumbling into their depths while feeling the presence of everyone following me into it.

A gasp hitched in my throat as the white cloud of the soul web appeared before us and I felt Diego reaching for me from within it.

Fingers curled around my arm though I couldn't see anyone there, but then his presence moved closer and his voice echoed around me and I felt Tory being drawn nearer to him too.

"It's time to know the truth, amigas."

He pulled us into the web and I braced myself for what was going to happen as I fell deep into the past, drawn into a long lost memory as my eyes opened and by instinct I knew whose memory this was. It was Diego's.

I held a little blue Pegasus toy between my finger and thumb, making it fly in front of me as I knelt in the mud around the back of my house. I'd found the toy washed up at the edge of the river down in the woods and though I knew I should have given it to Mamá, I also knew she'd throw it away if I did. She hated anything to do with the Fae, but I secretly wanted to know more about them. Everything about them.

I wondered about the kid who'd owned this little Pegasus, if they knew what they'd Emerge as one day. What would it feel like when they had their power Awakened? Did the stars shine on them and make them feel all good inside?

Mamá didn't like the stars. She said they'd cursed our kind and that was why we never had much money or food. My stomach growled in hopes of a meal that might not come tonight, but I was used to that, and while I was looking at this little blue winged horse in front of my eyes, I didn't feel much of anything except the imaginary life I was dreaming up for myself.

What would it be like to fly?

To have a herd, and magic in my veins, and gifts from the stars?

Would the stars like me if I was Fae? Would I get to walk along the streets in the daylight instead of having to hide away all the time?

Suddenly a strong hand latched around the back of my neck, yanking me to my feet while another snatched the little Pegasus from my fingers. I was thrown against the wall and I stared at my Uncle Alejandro as he sneered at the toy in his hand in disgust, my pulse thumping furiously in my ears.

"What is this?" he spat, but I couldn't get an answer out, fear making me choke. "Answer me, Diego."

"J-just a toy," I spluttered.

"Was my nephew playing in the mud dreaming of being Fae?" he snapped and I shook my head several times, feeling every drop of blood in my face draining away.

He clucked his tongue then let fire bloom in his palm to surround the little Pegasus and something possessed me to lunge forward with a cry, reaching for it and burning my fingertips as I tried to save it. But Alejandro knocked me back with his other hand and I watched as the Pegasus turned to blue gloop which he let fall onto the grass with a hiss.

"Be thankful your madre didn't find you with it," he said, stepping closer and adjusting the bright red scarf around his neck as he scrutinised me, running a hand over his short, dark curls. "How old are you now? Eight?"

"Ten," I whispered, wishing he'd go away, but the look in his eyes filled me with dread because I could see he was far from done with me.

"Old enough," he said under his breath with a decisive nod. "Come. I have a job you can help me with." He shoved me ahead of him, striding after me and my mouth dried out in fear as he corralled me towards his car.

When he opened the door and shoved me onto the backseat, mi abuela came hurrying down the porch steps of the house, her old legs carrying her towards me as panic ringed her eyes.

"Alejandro, where are you taking him?" she demanded.

"It's time he became one of us. The boy has gone soft," my uncle

explained, getting in the car and locking the doors.

Mi abuela tried the handle of the back door, looking to me in alarm as she shook her head frantically. "He's just a baby!"

Her fear made my palms sweat and a ball rise in my throat as Alejandro started the car, driving down the track into the woods.

"Wait!" she cried as she was left behind, but he didn't listen and my hands began to shake as Alejandro drove deeper into the dark forest that bordered our land.

"U-uncle Alejandro?" I stammered. "I-I'd like to go back now."

"There's no going back. You need to become a true Nymph. You need to let her influence in, then maybe you'll become someone this family can be proud of."

I fell quiet, thinking on that. I did want my family to be proud of me. I always seemed to disappoint Mamá and Alejandro didn't like me much at all. Mi padre never really paid me any attention, but maybe he would if I could make him proud.

The car bumped along the track and the darkness thickened around us, blocking out nearly all of the daylight as we headed in the direction of Alejandro's work shed. I wasn't allowed out here, but I'd come and had a look one time. Just once. Because I'd heard a scratching, clinking sound I didn't like coming from his shed and I'd run away and never, ever come into the forest again.

Now we were heading toward it once more, I remembered those sounds and terror twisted up my insides. I didn't want to go to his work shed. I didn't want to see what was in there.

The track soon started climbing the hill that led to the shed and the trees thinned out towards the top of it, revealing a wide open space where the wooden structure stood, just a shadow under the dying sun. The door handle was made of bone, a skull etched into it with two hollow eyes that whispered of the monsters which lurked beyond that door.

Alejandro stepped out of the car, yanking the door open beside me, but I didn't move. I couldn't. I was frozen and scared and I just wanted to go home to the arms of mi abuela.

"Out," Alejandro barked, but I shook my head in a fierce refusal.

He reached into the car, fisting his hand in my shirt and dragging me out of the car, giving me no choice as he hauled me along toward the shed.

"Please," I tried, my voice so small it barely carried anywhere at all. "I don't want to go in there."

The rattle of chains sounded from within it and a groan carried from inside that made a tremor run down my spine.

Alejandro locked a hand over my shoulder, ignoring my pleas as he led me to the door and unlocked it by pressing his palm to the surface. He pushed the door inwards and darkness greeted us along with a sound like a whimper.

I squinted into the dark, my lips parting at seeing a teenage girl there, bound and chained, but then my stomach turned and I tried to run as I saw the two bloody stumps where her hands should have been.

But my uncle kept a tight hold of me, shoving me into the shed and making me stumble to my knees in front of her. She was gagged, her eyes fearful and large, and blonde hair was matted around her shoulders.

I scrambled backwards to escape, hitting Alejandro's legs as he swung the door shut behind us and switched on the light. The single bulb above us cast her face in harsh shadows, but I could see her green eyes more clearly now and the panic in them made me want to run and never stop running.

Alejandro stepped past me, walking to the back of the shed where a line of tools were hanging on the wall, and my stomach started to churn as I noticed the countless dried patches of blood across the concrete floor telling me this girl wasn't the first to have come here.

"I want you to shift your right hand into a probe, Diego," Alejandro instructed casually, like we weren't in some horror show murder shed and I managed to get to my feet and make it to the door, jiggling the handle only to find it locked tight.

I turned, my back flush to the wood as I stared down at the girl on the floor as she begged for mercy against her gag. I wanted to find the key that would free her, let her out of this shed. But mostly I just wanted to run and run and run until my feet were bleeding and I couldn't get any more distance between me and my terrifying uncle.

"Do as I say, Diego," he snapped and I did, looking down at my right hand as it shook and shifting it into the long, wood-like probes of my kind. I'd been able to shift since I was five, and I knew what my probes were for. Mamá had told me that one day, if I didn't use them, I'd start to get sick. So sick, that eventually I'd die. Though sometimes it seemed like she wanted that to happen.

"You don't want to be Fae, sobrino," Alejandro said in a dark tone. "You want their power though, like all our kind do. And it is yours to take. We are their hunters, we are higher on the food chain, and we'll rise again one day and take our rightful place in this world as their rulers, you mark my words. The Shadow Princess will ensure it is so."

"I don't want to hurt anybody," I forced out around my heavy tongue as the girl on the floor started to thrash like an animal in a trap. I didn't like this. I didn't like any of it. I just wanted to go home and never come back.

Alejandro turned around, revealing a sharp looking knife in his hand which he pointed at me. "Press your probes to her heart."

I shook my head and he strode forward, slashing the blade across the girl's cheek and making her scream against her gag as her blood splashed to the floor.

"I will make you watch me slice her apart piece by piece if you hesitate another moment, Diego," he said with a sick look in his eyes that made me sure he meant that. And I was so afraid of that happening that I stumbled forward, holding out my arm.

Alejandro smiled cruelly as he took hold of my wrist and placed the tips of my probes to her heart. I immediately felt it, that deep source of power within this creature. This Fae. And my pulse began to slow as some instinct burned in me to take it. I was hungry. So, so hungry for this power that it made me ache inside.

"That's it," Alejandro purred, gripping my wrist tighter as my probes cut into her flesh and she screamed against her gag.

But the second I saw blood, I shook off the feeling of that instinct, fighting it away and trying to draw my hand back.

"No, I don't want to," I begged as the girl groaned in agony. "I don't want to hurt her."

Tears slid down my cheeks as Alejandro's grip became bruising and in the next second, he'd slashed the blade across her throat and hot, wet blood splattered me, making me blink in complete shock.

"She's dead regardless," he hissed. *"Take her power or I will cut your throat next."* He drew my probes tight against her flesh once more as she started to choke on her own blood and I squeezed my eyes shut as my probes cut into her skin, driving in deeper and deeper.

I don't want to, I don't want to, I don't want to.

"That's it," Alejandro purred excitedly. *"Do you feel the connection to her power? She is not the most powerful Fae, but when you are stronger you may wish to replace her magic with that of another. You cannot accumulate power from multiple Fae, Diego, but you may exchange it when you are ready to claim the Element of a more gifted Fae."*

I resisted for as long as I could but then a strange whispering started up in my head, the soft caress of a woman's voice. "Take it, Diego. The Fae have wronged you. Take it and join us."

There was something so alluring about the voice that I couldn't help but listen to it. My probes sank into the muscle of her heart and I gasped as magic rushed up my arm, pouring into me in wave after wave. I trembled at the feel of it tumbling into my veins and winding around my own heart, burying in deep and taking root there.

For a second I forgot all else as I drowned in the amazing feeling of all that power filling me up, but as the rush of it settled within me, my eyes cracked open and I found the girl dead, staring lifelessly at me with so much accusation in her eyes that it broke something in me.

I yanked my hand away, shifting it back to normal and backing up as the horror of what I'd done fell on me.

There was so much blood, I could smell it everywhere, and it was all I could do not to retch as my spine hit the door.

Alejandro moved to open it with a satisfied smile on his lips and I stumbled out onto the grass, scrambling away from him as I sucked down lungfuls of cool air. And suddenly something else was rearing up in me, dark shadows pooling through my skin as they wound their way inside of me and connected me to the darkness of their nature by this violent act and the power of some deity seemed to tug on the strings of my heart, taking hold of me as surely as if she was a part of me. And as she spoke to me again, I knew this was the Shadow Princess my family had told me of. "You are one of us now."

I was pulled out of the memory, shock jarring my heart as I processed the horrors I'd just witnessed, but I barely had any time to recover before I was cast back into Diego's memories and saw him walking up to the gates of Zodiac Academy beside his uncle, a darkness about him that he'd lacked as a kid.

"Repeat your instructions back to me," my uncle commanded and I nodded as he cast a silencing bubble around us. It was one of the few basic spells he could manage along with locks and the rough hold he had over his

stolen Elements.

"*I'll learn everything I can about harnessing Fae magic and feed all the information back to you and Mamá,*" *I said, nerves warring in me over this task. What if I was caught the second I walked in there? I'd be killed and there was no chance my mamá, mi padre or Alejandro would try and save me. The moment I walked through the gates of Zodiac Academy, I was on my own. And yet...I didn't care. Since mi abuela had died, all I'd wanted was to get away from my family, and the only dream I'd had my whole life was being a part of the Fae world. So I'd agreed to this loco plan because it was a chance at seeing the Fae world from the inside. She'd knitted me the hat I wore now which connected me to the web of souls and had added extra protective spells which helped keep the shadows from crawling too deep into my mind. It was the only thing that made me feel like myself, so I rarely took it off. When I did, I could hear the Shadow Princess whispering in my head and I was afraid of how easy it was to fall under her command.*

"*And?*" *Alejandro growled. The next part was the most frightening, this whole thing planned so last minute that I wasn't even remotely prepared for it.*

"*If the Vegas are discovered and brought to the academy, I must get close to them and find a way to deliver them to you and Mamá,*" *I said, that particular part sending my heart into overdrive. They were the Vegas, the strongest Fae in the whole kingdom. How was I ever going to pull this off?*

"*And if you fail to do so?*" *Alejandro prompted with a dark look that made me feel miniscule.*

"*You'll kill me,*" *I rasped.*

"*Yes. Slowly,*" *he said the word like he was devouring it. I'd seen the monstrous things this man was capable of over the years and I never wanted to be at his mercy. "And no one will miss you, because you will be nothing but a failure. This is your one chance to make your mother proud. Lionel Acrux has paid your tuition and you would be wise not to squander this opportunity he has offered you.*"

I nodded, wringing my hands together as I felt the pressure of this task like a noose around my neck.

"*But if you succeed, Diego, you will be deemed worthy among our family,*" *he said with a pointed look. "So do not disappoint us.*"

"*I won't,*" *I breathed, though how I was going to pull this off I had no idea.*

Alejandro left me at the gate and I found myself being swept along with other students here for their Awakening. I glanced back to see him shrinking into the distance and felt the shackles of the home I'd been a slave to my whole life loosening just a little. As I took in the huge, gothic buildings of this elite Fae school, my jaw slackened in awe. It was fantastico, more beautiful than anything I'd ever seen and despite the weight of the burden on my shoulders, excitement trickled into my blood, and I wondered if I might just be lucky enough to claim an inch of freedom here. For a little while at least.

We eventually arrived in a huge meadow that stretched away before me under the stars. I looked up at the sky which seemed clearer than I'd ever seen it, the swirling blue and pink path of the Milky Way streaking through the heavens above, built of countless gleaming stars.

As everyone formed a circle at the centre of the meadow, two girls and a tall man appeared out of nowhere, making my heart jolt violently, realising a second later that they must have used stardust to travel by. Everyone started staring and muttering the girls' names, confirming they were the Vega twins and my gaze latched onto them, my heart beating fiercely beneath my ribs. They seemed a little lost as the guy directed them to join the circle and I glanced between their perfectly mirrored features as they stood side by side, a sense of dread sliding over me as I knew what would happen to them if I succeeded in my plan.

The professor at the centre of the circle started chanting to the stars and I tipped my head back to look up at them, my hands shaking a little with the pressure of what I had to do next. I rarely used my air Element since I'd stolen it all those years ago, but Alejandro had forced me to practise with it to ensure I could fake my own Awakening. And as Professor Zenith called out for the air Element to arise, I cast air from my fingertips, making the grass rustle around me like it was for everyone else and I didn't breathe again until she announced we were air Elementals without so much as a suspicious glance my way.

I dropped my head, setting my gaze on my fate once more as the shadows stirred beneath my skin. These two girls had to die or else I would die instead, and I was just thankful I wouldn't be the one to strike the killing blows.

I was pulled out of the memory and shock descended on me. Diego had been planning to hand us over to his uncle and mother? I didn't even have time to get my head around that before I fell back into another one of his memories, finding myself in a dark woodland.

I crept through the trees of The Wailing Wood, hunting the ground for what I needed to restore my magic. After I'd stolen the magic from that butchered Fae years ago, I'd been bound to her power in the way her Order had been bound to it. My uncle had told me she had been a Cerberus, so to recharge my magic I had to do what she had done and feast on Aconite – or as some called it, Wolfsbane. I'd heard it grew out here in the woods and now I could feel the well of my magic hollowing out, I needed to find some and recharge it fast.

There were other Orders out here, Fae in their shifted form lumbering through the darkness around me, but none came too close as I continued my search, delving deeper into the trees and using the light on my Atlas to hunt the ground.

At last, I lit up the purple flowers I was looking for and I crouched down, turning off the light on my Atlas and stuffing bunches of them into my pockets. I ate some of them too, chewing through the flowers and stems, loving the taste of what should have been a deadly poisonous plant as it recharged my well of magic.

Then when I'd gathered as much of it as I could, I stood up and started making my way back to the path.

The crash of some large beast sounded somewhere behind me and a tremor ran through me at the power of the Fae in this place. It thrilled me and equally terrified me, because I knew all of them would turn on me, rip me to pieces if they discovered what I was.

As I made it back to the edge of the path, I spotted a girl walking along it in the dark. Alone.

She had blue tipped hair and my pulse increased as I thought of the task I'd been given here. I could creep up behind her, shift into my Nymph form and overpower her. Maybe no one would see. Maybe I could subdue her long enough to get her off campus and call my uncle and my mother to come for her.

I chewed the inside of my cheek anxiously as I followed her, staying in the trees just off the path and trying to force myself to focus. I could do it.

I thought of the Fae I'd killed in Alejandro's shed, her hands cut off and terror filling her gaze. It made my stomach churn and it wasn't the last Fae I'd seen like that despite how much I wished it could have been. Alejandro liked to play with the ones he caught and he'd made me watch enough times to break something in me. But I'd never spoken to those Fae, never seen them before their bloody ends. This was different. I'd sat beside Darcy in class. She'd been nice to me. She even seemed to like me a little.

My hands shook and I tugged on the corner of my hat as I drew on the strength of my abuela, though she'd likely hate me now for what I was becoming.

I followed Darcy, debating what I was going to do, thinking of the bloody death that awaited me instead if I didn't capture her and her sister. But I hadn't been here for hardly any time at all, there was still so much of the Fae world I wanted to see. And getting hold of the Vegas wasn't my only task anyway, I was supposed to feed information back to my family about what I learned in classes on how to wield my magic. So...why act tonight?

A twig cracked under my foot and I swallowed a curse, ducking behind a tree as Darcy swung around to look in my direction. Mierda.

When she started moving again, I scurried across the path, trying to keep quiet as I ran into the trees on the other side of it. I slipped deeper into the shadows, deciding to go back to Aer Tower and deal with this another day. It was too soon anyway. Far too soon.

The memory changed fast and I found myself in Andromeda's Place in Tucana the first time we'd visited the bar with Diego and Sofia.

"Washer is a total perve," Sofia whispered then giggled and the sound made a grin pull at my mouth. She was something else, this chica. She shone when she was happy, and even whinnied sometimes. I was fascinated with her and her Order and sometimes I couldn't tear my eyes away from her.

"Is that why we have to wear bathing suits that barely cover our asses in his class?" Darcy asked and I looked at her.

"I'd bet on it, chica," I laughed, nudging her in the ribs, the sound all too genuine.

I was facing a real big problem with my plan now that I'd successfully gotten closer to the Vegas twins. I was not only starting to like them more than I wanted to admit, but I was also liking this life way too much. I was so free. I could do anything I wanted. I had my own room, my own space, and yeah sometimes the teachers could be hijo de putas – especially the one who was currently sitting at the bar looking like a smarmy pendejo – but despite that, it was still the best place I'd ever been in my life. And maybe it wasn't a coincidence that I hadn't made any moves against the Vegas yet, but that ended today. And as much as my smiles were real for every moment I'd spent with them tonight so far, dread was creeping up on me like a plague. Because Alejandro and my mamá were getting impatient, and they wanted me to make a move against them.

We ate our way through our meal and I checked my Atlas subtly under the table while the others chatted, my gut knotting with dread at the message there from my uncle.

Alejandro:
I'm growing impatient. How much longer?

I tapped out a reply, trying to keep my breaths calm and steady.

Diego:
Maybe tonight isn't the right night.

Alejandro:
It's the perfect night. Do not fail me, or you will regret it.

My hands shook and bile rose in my throat as I pushed my Atlas back into my pocket and tugged at my hat, wishing I could speak with mi abuela right now and ask for her guidance. But I was on my own tonight and the fear of what Alejandro would do to me made me push down the guilt writhing in my gut and commit to the plan I'd put in place.

"Shots!" I announced, rising from my seat and working to still my shaking hands.

"Yes!" Sofia cried and the twins laughed as I strode away to the bar, trying to get my mind in the right place for this.

For a moment, I let the shadows slide deeper under my skin, allowing them to lull away my anxiety and focusing on what I had to do.

I ordered the shots at the bar, glancing over at Professor Orion as he cosied up to some woman opposite him. He seemed distracted by something as the shots were laid before me and I slid the vile of powdered knotroot from inside my jacket, quickly sprinkling some of it into two of the drinks.

My throat nearly closed up as I shoved it back into my pocket, throwing Orion a fearful glance, but finding him staring across the room. And as I followed his gaze to Darcy Vega, I grimaced and gathered up the drinks.

I may have loved living among the Fae but there was one kind I didn't like at all, and it was the Vampires. They used others as blood bags, stealing what they needed, and in all honesty, it reminded me of my own kind. I'd seen what Nymphs could do, and if I could trade away that part of me to be any kind of Fae, I would. Except a Vampire.

I headed back to the table, frowning as I found Geraldine Grus in my seat and heat skidded up the back of my neck. I held the shots out of her reach as she tried to grab one, my pulse hammering as I worked to keep control of this situation. I felt sick, but all I could think about was Alejandro gutting me if I didn't pull this off and the fear of that was enough to make me stay on this path.

"Isn't that your gang out there?" I asked Geraldine, nodding to the window and she gasped.

"Oh sweet raisin bran!" She gathered up her badges and leapt out of her seat before curtsying to the Vegas. "Your majesties, forgive me but I must go."

"You're forgiven," Tory said lightly.

"I can be back in one hour!" Geraldine exclaimed. "Then we can all go dancing together." She ran out of the restaurant, leaving me with one less obstacle, but I didn't even hear the girls' next words as my pulse blared in my ears so loud it drowned out all else. I hated myself for what I'd become, for what would happen because of my actions tonight. But I was a pathetic coward too, because I didn't want to die.

I dropped into my seat with a sigh. "Who needs a drink?"

I was about to pass the two spiked shots to the twins when Sofia swooped down, grabbing one of them and swallowing it whole.

Santa mierda!

Before I could get hold of the other one, she got her hands on that too, drinking the rest and sending a flash of panic right through me.

"Sofia!" I gasped in horror.

I was suddenly yanked out of the memory and thrown into another one so fast it made my head spin.

"What have you done?!" Alejandro roared, his hand tightening on my throat as he crushed me back against my car at the side of the road. Sofia was asleep in the back of it, passed out from the knotroot she'd swallowed. My uncle had nearly driven me off the road on my way back to Zodiac Academy and now I knew I was fucked. Deader than dead. He wouldn't forgive me for this failure.

"It was an a-accident," I stuttered in terror. "Sofia drank the knotroot."

"There's another nest of Nymphs vying for the Vegas' magic in Tucana tonight, Diego," he spat. "If they get to the Vegas before us and claim their magic, I will make you pay severely. I want all four Elements to be mine." A manic glint entered his gaze.

Alejandro's eyes slid over my shoulder as he looked down into the back seat of the car and I tried to shift protectively in front of Sofia. Please don't wake up.

"You can't kill her," I blurted and he looked at me with a mocking sneer.

"And why not? Do you really think you can claim her from me?" he laughed coldly, wetting his lips.

"If she dies, it'll blow my cover. I was the last person seen with her," I said frantically, knowing that if I didn't sell him this, he was going to kill her, and I just couldn't let that happen.

He considered that, a crease of irritation forming on his brow. "Well perhaps I'm tired of waiting for you to prove your usefulness. You've fucked up at the first hurdle, why should I even let you return to the academy?"

"I'll have another chance. And I've only been there a short time, I can learn all the spells so you can wield your magic better. That's important too,

isn't it?" I asked, trying to keep the hint of begging out of my voice as his fingers sharpened to probes around my neck and started to dig in.

"Hm," he grunted then yanked his hand back, curling it into a fist and driving it hard into my stomach in a winding blow instead.

I doubled over, clutching my side with a groan of pain as Alejandro backed up.

"Go," he barked and I got into the car, trying to start it with fumbling fingers. "You'll bring them to me soon, Diego."

I nodded, getting the car going and tearing off down the road with panic in my chest.

What the hell was I going to do?

Holy shit, Diego had tried to spike our drinks that night so he could hand us to his psycho uncle? I felt for my sister's presence and drew her closer as shock and anger tore through me, but then I was falling again, diving deep into another memory.

"Falling Star wants to meet," Darcy told us and Sofia bobbed up and down in excitement.

My heart clenched as Darcy moved to walk away and my hand shot out to grab hold of her. "Wait, is this a good idea? It might not be safe."

I didn't know who this Falling Star person was but if they were dangerous, I couldn't let the twins go to him. I was trying to make myself believe that that was because their deaths by any other hand than my family's would equal my own, but it was more than that. More than I dared to admit. I was starting to like them. And as I looked to Sofia, I realised I was becoming protective of this little friendship circle we'd formed. I didn't want things to change when they had been good for the first time in my life.

"It's fine," Darcy promised. "Falling Star has helped us. Why would they hurt us?"

I shared a concerned look with Sofia and Tory rolled her eyes and walked away. "It's happening, Diego. Get over it."

I frowned as Darcy gave me an apologetic shrug and the two of them headed off together towards the library.

"Hey Sofia – you're looking as hot as a rainbow on a cloud, baby," Tyler Corbin called, walking over to us with swagger in his step.

I didn't like Tyler. Mostly because he had everything I'd ever wanted and he didn't even care. I'd watched him shift into a Pegasus and fly with Sofia, the two of them the most beautiful thing I'd ever seen. And I'd wished so hard that I could just trade lives with him and fly through the clouds with her at my side instead.

Sofia blushed and I watched her flutter her lashes at him with my throat tight. "You should go say hi," I forced out and she arched a brow at me.

"Are you sure?" she asked and I nodded stiffly, watching as she trotted over to talk to him and they walked away towards the dance. I hated to do that, but I needed to go after the twins and make sure I wasn't seen.

When I was certain no one was paying me any attention, I crept towards the library, slipping inside and hurrying silently through the stacks as I followed the sound of Tory and Darcy's footsteps.

As I made it to the iron stairway at the back, I kicked off my shoes and picked them up as I ran silently up the metal steps to the wide balcony that overlooked the bookshelves below.

I hugged the shadows up there as I sought out the twins in the stacks beneath me, my heart beating a mile a minute as my gaze landed on them standing there with Professor Astrum.

"I'm sorry for not revealing myself sooner," he said in his rasping tone and my lips parted in shock. This guy was Falling Star?

He started speaking about the Savage King and I pulled my Atlas from my pocket, angling it at them and pressing record, sure this conversation was incredibly important. And as I listened, shock rolled through me as he accused Lionel Acrux of leading the Nymphs into the Savage King's palace to murder their parents. My uncle had been working with him for years though he never told me much about their alliance, I had to admit this guy's suspicions sounded spot on to me. But if he was pointing fingers at our kind, what else did he know? What if he was onto me? He could have been warning the girls about me for all I knew.

But I relaxed as I realised that he was way off base when he started accusing Darius Acrux and Professor Orion of controlling our kind during the recent Nymph attacks. That had had nothing to do with them. The Nymphs were coming out of hiding more often recently because the Shadow Princess had been calling out to us louder and louder to do her bidding.

My panic started to rise as I listened and I feared being discovered here so I hurried back to the stairs, jogging silently down them and moving between the stacks towards the exit.

A creak sounded as my foot pressed down on an old floorboard and my heart galloped harder as I ran faster, remaining as silent as I could before making it outside and darting around the side of the building to hide.

I pushed my feet into my shoes, clinging to the shadows as I kept moving, trying to decide what to do. And I knew I only had one choice.

I brought up my uncle's number, forwarding him the video and leaning back against the wall as I waited for a reply. It came a minute later as he called me, and I answered in a whisper.

"Hello."

"Good work, Diego. You are proving of some use at last," he growled. "I need you to use the amulet I gave you tonight. Place it in the ground at the eastern fence and meet me there when I message you."

"Okay, what are you going to do?" I asked, fear lacing my words at the idea of my uncle coming here, but the line went dead.

I sighed, pushing my Atlas back into my pocket and adjusting my hat over my ears as I decided to head back to Aer Tower to fetch the amulet before I went to the party. And as I stared up at the darkening sky, I wondered if the stars truly hated me like my mother believed they did.

The memory changed to later that night, and I was thrown back into Diego's body as he slipped out of The Orb and started running towards the eastern fence.

Adrenaline fuelled my limbs as I ran as fast as I could across campus, my smart jacket flapping out behind me as I tore along the dark paths and tried not to panic about what my uncle planned to do tonight.

As I made it to the fence, he stepped into view among the trees beyond it with my mamá at his side, the two of them wearing all black apart from the knitwear my abuela had gifted them.

"Hurry up," my mamá snapped and Alejandro pointed to the ground at my feet.

I took the amulet from my inside pocket, pushing it into the ground and feeling the dark magic imbued within it. It snaked out into the dirt and the magical boundary in front of them crackled and shrouded in shadow. The two of them stepped through it and Alejandro used the heat of his fire magic to bend the bars so he and my mamá could climb through the fence onto campus.

My breaths came unevenly as I stared at them, fearing what they were going to do now and knowing that I was responsible for it. But as Alejandro stepped closer, his upper lip peeling back as he looked at me, I knew I'd had no other choice. He grabbed the back of my neck, swinging me around and shoving me ahead of him.

"Take me to Astrum," he snarled.

"That old man's been avoiding his fate far too long," Mamá purred excitedly and a shiver of dread ran down my spine.

"What do you mean?" I asked, looking to her and her eyes dripped over me in disdain.

"He's old enough to know," Alejandro said as he shared a look with his sister.

"He worked at the palace when we killed the royals," Mamá said with a twisted smile on her lips that made my stomach knot with dread.

"You...what?" I breathed, sure they were just messing with me.

"Where do you think I got all of my power, idiota?" Alejandro smirked, playing with flames in his palms and making my throat tighten. "I'm the strongest Nymph in Solaria."

"That's because you didn't share," Mamá sniped at him. "Though the queen tasted oh so sweet when she died. I can't say I'd have wanted to miss that." She grinned evilly and I found my feet unable to move any further as I stared at them, realising what they were saying.

"You killed the Vegas' parents?" I rasped.

"Yes," Alejandro said with pride in his voice. "Thanks to Lionel Acrux."

"He loved watching them kick and scratch us as our friends held them down for us, didn't he?" Mamá said, the image making bile rise in my throat. "I think he enjoys death more than you, Alejandro."

"No one enjoys it more than me," he said darkly, grabbing my arm and shoving me along again. "But look at your son, he can't even stomach the thought of blood."

"He's the spitting image of Miguel in every way," Mamá said in disgust, but I didn't know how I could resemble a man who rarely spoke and seemed to be void of all emotion.

My legs felt numb as I kept walking towards The Orb where I'd last seen Astrum, wondering if there was some way I could alert everyone to the Nymphs being on campus without unveiling myself. I could deal with them just like that, my troubles gone forever, and I could stay in this world pretending to *be Fae for as long as I could get away with it.*

"I want my hands on a Vega tonight," Mamá said greedily as she quickened her pace. "Let's be done with it, Alejandro."

"I don't want them to die here," he purred. "Let's take them home. At least one of them."

I thought of the girl in that shed again and slowed my pace, unable to bear the idea of seeing the twins in that vile place.

"You won't get close to them. There's too many Fae around," I tried. "Even Professor Astrum will be hard to get alone."

Alejandro swung towards me fast, his hand fisting in my shirt as he held raging flames an inch away from my face and I saw a demon staring back at me in his eyes. "Those sound like the words of a coward," he snarled. "I am hungry for a kill tonight, sobrino, and if it is not a Fae then perhaps it will be you. And perhaps I will make it a long, agonising game too."

I shook my head, frantically trying to push his hand off of me as my mamá watched with a cold detachment in her gaze. Terror clawed through my insides as I stared at the hatred in my uncle's eyes and I wanted to vanish so I didn't have to face it.

"Okay, okay," I blurted and he let go of me, pointing me ahead of them and I stumbled on, my breaths coming raggedly as I led them towards The Orb.

As we approached the golden building, I spotted Professor Astrum standing out on the lawn in front of it, looking up at the stars with his eyes closed like he was somehow speaking with them.

I glanced at my uncle and Mamá in fear as they locked him in their sights like their next meal and I wanted to call out to him to run.

There was no one else around, the party still thriving inside The Orb, but no students were hanging around outside. I didn't understand why Professor Astrum was just standing there like that, but as he opened his eyes and lowered his head to look toward us, he spoke.

"Ah, of course," he sighed, nodding. "I couldn't see my death, only the darkness that awaited me beyond this night. But now it makes sense."

Alejandro and Mamá advanced on him and I scurried after them with a plea that died on my lips as my uncle called out to him.

"Where are your pretty stars to protect you tonight, Seer?" he said mockingly.

"The stars await me." He checked the watch on his wrist, nodding with a solemn look in his eyes as Alejandro and Mamá closed in on him on both sides.

I stopped walking, my eyes darting to The Orb and back as I wondered if I should try and run for help. If I could make it there and alert the faculty to their presence then maybe they'd be caught, maybe they'd kill them and I'd be free at last.

Astrum's eyes fell on me and a frown knitted his brows as realisation crossed his features. I'd been so caught up in fear, I hadn't even thought to hide from him before I exposed myself.

He looked to the stars again, murmuring something to them and his eyes widened as his eyes fell on me with understanding.

Alejandro kicked out the backs of his knees and Astrum fell to the ground, no hint of magic flashing in his hands as he seemed to accept this fate. But I wanted him to fight, to rise up and attack the monsters who stood either side of him. More than that, I wanted to fight them myself, to make a stand and refuse to follow their orders any longer.

Instead, I found myself frozen in terror and unable to do anything but watch as my mamá laughed coldly and shifted her hands into Nymph probes. She stepped forward with intent as her rattle filled the air and locked down Astrum's magic, combining with the sound of Alejandro's until he was weakened before them, though it was clear he'd had no intention of fighting this.

Mamá drove her probes into his chest and Astrum tipped his head back with a smile pulling at his lips as he mouthed the names of the Vega king and queen like he could somehow see them before him.

Alejandro let my mamá torture him for several seconds before shoving her aside and driving his own probes into Astrum's chest in a brutal blow that sent blood splattering across the ground. I knew they weren't planning to take his magic, I'd seen them do this before, getting high on connecting with a Fae's magic source without ever actually exchanging it for the Elements they'd already claimed for themselves.

Astrum never moved his eyes from the sky and Alejandro growled in anger as he didn't get the reaction he wanted. And as Astrum slumped backwards onto the ground, Alejandro unleashed a furious fire from his veins, burning him as he grinned at the carnage he caused, the huge flames heating my cheeks as I stumbled back and watched the fire twist higher and higher, burning Astrum's body away to nothing beneath him.

Mamá spat into the flames and my eyes darted to the path as a pitchy scream sounded beyond the blazing fire that blocked us from view. Alejandro grabbed Mamá's arm and the two of them ran, tearing past me and nearly knocking me over as they made their escape before they were spotted.

I stood in shock, trying to gather my wits as more and more students poured out of The Orb and I circled around to join them, hugging the shadows so I wouldn't be seen.

My mouth was too dry and the scent of death hung everywhere as I pushed into the crowd and melded with the panicked students.

"Move aside!" Professor Orion's voice carried above them and he came barrelling through the crowd with Darcy and Tory on his heels. Darcy's hair had been sheared off and Tory's eyes were alight with some horror, making my gut tighten. What had happened to them?

"Who is it?" a boy muttered beyond me.

"Do you think it was a Nymph?" another girl whispered and panic rose in me like an oncoming storm.

I had to throw them off, I had to make them think it was something else.

"What the hell is that?" Darcy whispered in fear as she squinted at the raging flames.

"I've only ever seen Dragon Fire burn like that," I said loud enough for my voice to carry, latching onto what Astrum had told the twins and casting shade on Darius in the hopes that no suspicion would fall on me or my kind. Because I knew a terrible fate awaited me if I gave my family away, and maybe my uncle was right. Maybe I was a coward.

I could feel Diego's panic wrapping around me from that night and I didn't know what to think as I was cast forward into the future. I started to see moments blurring together, Diego letting the Nymphs onto campus the day they'd attacked at the Pitball pitch, him tossing the vile of knotroot out the window into the bushes at the base of Aer Tower to hide it from the FIB raids, his anger as Orion had broken the box gifted to him by his grandmother, his embarrassment as Orion had exposed his secret crush on Sofia to the agents around him. I saw the night he let his uncle onto campus and I fought with him in the astronomy tower, but I also saw Diego willing me to kill the man who'd tormented him, praying I was strong enough to destroy him.

And then I was thrown into another memory of Alejandro choking him in the woods at the edge of campus, his vision going dark as his uncle demanded he work harder to deliver me and my sister to him. I could feel Diego's fear tearing up the inside of me and his absolute longing to shed himself of his family, his Nymph form, and be Fae like his friends, like us. The people he was truly starting to love and care for in ways that he had never felt for anyone.

Then I was in Diego's room, watching as he pulled his hat off, leaving it on the desk as he tugged down his sleeves to cover bruises his uncle had left on him, and the next minute I was in the woods with him, his hand taking hold of mine as he we headed to the Fairy Fair together. Without his hat, the shadows slithered deeper beneath his flesh and the Shadow Princess purred evil commands in his ear. He found it easier to be colder, to draw me in and try to get closer to me as his uncle had asked. It was why he'd kissed me, why he'd tried to flirt with me, but all the while he'd been hurting over Sofia dating Tyler, knowing she would never choose him instead. And he believed in his soul it was because he wasn't Fae.

The shadows had burrowed deep within him during the Fairy Fair and he'd almost lost his mind to them, the Shadow Princess calling to his soul and filling him with rage against Fae kind. It was the reason he'd snapped at me, called me a whore. He'd let his mind sink so deep into the shadows that it had nearly consumed him whole. And the moment he pulled it back on later that night, I felt his remorse, his pain. And I felt the beating he'd taken from Alejandro for failing him once more too.

I suddenly crashed into another memory on the night of The Reckoning, looking up at the stars through Diego's eyes with terror making his bones quake.

A glimmering number three hung above my head, a mark of how poorly I'd done so far, but now The Reckoning would be the final deciding factor and I was certain I was about to be either sent home for good or exposed by the stars for what I was.

I glanced over at the Vegas, guilt eating me up over how I'd behaved at the Fairy Fair, sure I'd ruined our friendship, though I didn't know why I even cared. I'd tried to hurt them last night, tried to do what Alejandro had demanded of me and bring them to him at last. But even while embracing the shadows, I'd failed. And now I felt the weight of what I was becoming like my heart was turning black within my chest. I was growing sick of this game and I was so tired of being a traitor to the girls I'd come to really care about. But what kind of friend was I? They'd hate me if they knew the truth. And now it had all come to nothing, because I couldn't lie to the stars. They'd see me for what I was – if they'd even bother to judge me at all.

Principal Nova directed us to all make a circle in the meadow and join hands like we had at the Awakening, and I waited with bated breath for the axe of fate to fall on my neck.

As Zenith called out to the stars, I looked up at the gleaming pinpricks of light and a shudder ran through me before the entire sky seemed to twist in a vortex. Suddenly I was standing in a chamber of darkness, seeming to float there as if I weighed nothing, as if I was nothing. And for a second it was a relief to feel like the world was over, and no more was going to be asked of me.

I wondered if this would be it for me, a void where no stars existed, no powerful beings bothering to turn their gaze on someone as worthless as me.

But then a whisper filled my head which sounded like it was woven from the fabric of the universe itself.

"Imposter," it breathed. "We see you, son of the shadow born. And it is time to face The Reckoning."

I swallowed hard, wondering if they'd punish me now, kill me maybe. And perhaps that was better than going back to a life where I would be made a monster again and again.

"A great burden rests heavily upon you, and a path of dark and light lays before your feet. So which will you choose?"

"I can...choose?" I asked in surprise.

"All creatures of the stars may choose."

"But I'm not Fae," I said thickly, shaking my head.

"You are a child of cruelty and misfortune, but you are still our child."

"I don't understand. Please, tell me what do. How can I protect the Vegas without ending up dead for it?" I begged.

"Death is your greatest fear."

"Yes," I croaked.

"What is it you are afraid of, son of the shadow born?"

"To be nothing," I breathed. "To disappear and never have known anything good."

"Do you know nothing good?" the stars asked and the darkness lifted, showing a vision of me laughing with my friends, the smile on my face so unfamiliar to me that I reached up to touch my own lips.

The vision faded away again and tears pricked my eyes. "I have to bring them to my uncle," I half sobbed. "If I don't, he'll – he'll-"

The vision changed before me, showing me that fate, me chained in that dark shed in the woods, my hands cut off and Alejandro standing above me with a blade in his grip and a sinister smile on his lips. I screamed, trying to block it out, but no matter if my eyes were closed or not, it was all I could see.

"Please – stop – stop!" I cried and the vision faded once more, leaving me in the pressing darkness. But I preferred that to the visions of the stars.

"I don't want to see anymore," I whispered.

"What does a Fae do when their back is against the wall, son of the shadow born?"

"I don't know," I rasped.

"What does a Fae do when their back is against the wall, son of the *shadow born?"*

"I don't know - I'm not Fae!" I shouted, my voice ripped raw as the pain of those words tore through me. "But I wish I was," I murmured, a tear running down my cheek.

"A Fae faces their fears," the stars whispered.

I hung my head.

"What does a Fae do when their back is against the wall, son of the shadow born?"

"They fight," I said softly, knowing that was the answer but still knowing I wasn't one of them.

"What does a Fae do with their heart?" the stars asked and I frowned at that question, thinking on it.

"They love," I decided.

"And what will a Fae do to be worthy of their place in Solaria?"

I frowned, the answer coming to me easily and falling from my lips. "Anything."

"You have passed our tests." The stars released me from their grip and I could hardly believe that I was being let go, that I was deemed worthy to stay at Zodiac Academy. It made no sense, and yet it was the best thing I had ever experienced. And for a moment, I could almost feel what it was like to be Fae.

I was yanked back out of the memory and more zoomed in front of my eyes from one to the next. I saw Diego struggling with his conscience, saw him face Alejandro time and again and meet his wrath.

I saw him spiking Tory's drink in The Orb, his attempt to take her to his uncle, then felt his relief when Darius intervened and he once more faced Alejandro's punishments. But now he seemed to prefer it, finding strength in his actions by deciding to take the pain instead of truly fulfilling any of his uncle's wishes.

I watched him smile and laugh with his friends and enjoy every single second of his time at Zodiac Academy, and I saw him grow stronger right before my eyes, more than I'd ever even noticed when he'd been right there in front of me.

I fell into another memory which made my heart lurch with fear because I knew what was coming as I walked in his shoes, shedding his clothes and hanging his hat on a branch in the woods that bordered Stella's property.

I shifted into my Nymph form and felt the tug of the Shadow Princess's power rolling through my veins as I was called to battle. "Time to fight. Time to kill. Come to my aid."

Alejandro and Mamá crashed through the woodland close by as they fought against Darcy and some of the Heirs.

The shadows beckoned me into them deeper and deeper, but I wouldn't go. Not tonight. Not when Darcy and Tory were in trouble. Mi abuela had told me that I was strong enough to fight against the will of the Shadow Princess if I only believed it was so, and tonight I'd finally found that strength in me, refusing to be a pawn to that creature any longer.

I may have been sent to Zodiac to capture them, but I was done playing my uncle's game. And now when they were in danger, I wasn't going to let them down. They'd been loyal to me and I would be loyal to them in return, even if it meant my uncle saw what I was. I had friends now. They'd help me. They'd accepted my connection to the shadows, so maybe they could accept that I was a Nymph too. Because I was done lying, done betraying them.

And I'd stand beside them tonight and fight like the Fae I wished I could be, and pray they could forgive me when they learned the truth.

"I don't know who you are, but you're not Clara Orion. You're just a hollow thing full of shadow and death," Darcy spat as I crept up behind the Shadow Princess, feeling the stars turning their gaze towards me.

"So which would you rather I give you, Darcy Vega? Shadow or death?" the Shadow Princess flexed her fingers and Darcy's eyes widened as she prepared to shield. I knew in that moment she was going to act too late to protect herself.

I lunged forward, ramming my probes into the Shadow Princess's back with a bellow of defiance and lifting her off the ground as I raised my arm. My lungs laboured and victory rushed through me as this golden moment gilded every one of my veins and made me feel like a god as I finally made a move against the monsters I'd been enslaved to my entire life.

Darcy cast a fireball to finish the bitch off, but the Shadow Princess twisted around to avoid it, forcing me to drop her as she gripped the shadows within me and I growled in frustration as she hit the ground on her knees.

Before Darcy could strike at her again, the Shadow Princess shot away with a burst of Vampire speed.

I looked to Darcy, triumph pounding through me, but it was quickly followed by uncertainty as she raised her hands at me, a frown pulling at her brow as she tried to work out if I was her enemy or not.

I took a step back, bowing my head to one of the true queens, because of course that was what she and her sister were. I'd seen them blossom into the most incredibly powerful Fae and I'd happily kneel at their feet and serve them in any way they wanted. They may not have known it, but they'd given me a family, a home, and I would repay them for that in any way I possibly could.

The Shadow Princess suddenly leapt onto my back and I was too slow to act as she reached around and drove a blade into my chest.

The shock of the strike made me roar, but the sound died as she drove that knife into my chest over and over until pain was all I could feel as I tumbled to the ground in a heap, blood washing over my body and making me dizzy.

It had all happened so fast, and I was finding it impossible to draw in any breath as I felt the stars press closer.

"Son of the shadow born, do you remember what Fae do with their fears?" the stars whispered to me as terror wound its way around my thrashing heart.

"You dare attack your princess?" the Shadow Princess snarled as she stood over me and I nodded, the answer to the stars' question now so blindingly clear.

I do dare. Because Fae face their fears. And I'm almost as afraid of you as I am afraid to die.

Darcy released a flare of Phoenix fire at her, but the Shadow Princess darted out of its way and blackness curtained my vision for a moment as I lost *consciousness.*

When I woke, the shift had fallen over me, so I lay there naked in the mud with blood pouring down my chest and death calling my name. I could see the stars through the trees, shining so bright it almost seemed like day.

"Diego?" Darcy gasped, dropping down beside me as horror lined her features. She rested her hands over my chest, trying to heal the wounds, but I knew it was far too late. And there was so much more I needed to say. But one thing more than any other.

"I'm so s-sorry, Darcy," I forced out, needing her to hear it though knowing there wasn't enough time to explain why.

"I don't understand," she sobbed, still working to stop the flow of blood, but I was already falling away. "Max!" she screamed, turning to him but I clutched her arm, desperate for her not leave when I was only moments from death.

"Fae magic can't heal me," I whispered.

"How can you...how are you here?" she croaked, tears running down her cheeks and I hated to see her crying over me. But it reminded me that she cared, that someone really cared. And I had meant something on this earth in a world where I should have meant nothing.

"I'm not your enemy," I swore, needing her to know that and she took hold of my hand, squeezing tightly and making my fear lessen just a little. My heart was slowing and the stars above me were whispering of my end, so I had to give her the key to everything I knew, things that could help her defeat my uncle, my mamá, even Lionel Acrux. "You'll see... you need to...take my hat." I coughed and blood rose in my throat, the taste of it everywhere, but the pain was turning to a cold numbness now.

Darcy wiped the blood from my lips, pain written into her features as she tried to keep me here. And it felt so, so good to be wanted like that. To know that I would be missed.

"Just hold on," she begged. "There must be something I can do."

I shook my head slightly, understanding what the stars were asking of me now. I had to face my fear, and this was it. I just hoped there was something waiting for me in death beyond darkness, I hoped there was a place for me among the stars.

"I just wanted to be useful. Did I do okay? Was I good friend?" I asked as a tear rolled from my eye as I knew I'd never see Sofia again, or Tory, or Geraldine. The friends who had given me a life I had always dreamed of having.

"You're the best friend, Diego," Darcy promised and before death could steal me away, happiness spilled into every inch of my being and for a single second, I felt like a Fae who was dying a worthy death for his friend. His queen.

And as her face faded from view, and I slipped away somewhere far warmer and safer, I felt mi abuela's hand taking hold of mine and drawing me into her arms, her voice so familiar and comforting as she held me. "I am so very proud of you, Diego."

I was forced out of the shadows of the hat, finding my face wet with tears as Orion pulled me onto his lap and I let myself cry against his shoulder at reliving that awful goodbye once more.

Geraldine wailed behind me, sobbing Diego's name as Orion stroked his hand up and down my back.

It was so much to take in and I didn't know whether to even be angry with him at all for the things he'd done, because in the end he'd given his life to save me and he'd made his choice to tell us the truth, he'd just never gotten the chance.

When I finally looked around, I found the Heirs and Xavier deep in thought and Tory wiped tears from under her eyes.

Orion tugged the hat off of my head, tossing it onto the bed and kissing my wet cheek as I pulled myself together at last, the grief in my chest a tight pinch which wouldn't go away.

"The hat kid's name was Diego? I swear it was Darnell," Darius murmured to Tory and she punched him in the arm with a muttered curse about him being an asshole.

"He will not have died in vain," Geraldine said, rising to her feet and sniffing loudly as she reined in her tears. "We shall avenge his brave soul and destroy the wicked witch who laid him in the ground."

I nodded my agreement, looking to my sister as she reached out to squeeze my arm and I saw the need for revenge in her eyes as keenly as it lived in me.

"Her life is marked," I growled. "As is Alejandro's."

"For our mother and father too," Tory growled.

"We'll send them into death screaming for mercy, and tear our parents' Elements free of their veins," I hissed.

Geraldine kissed her fist and held it to her chest. "For the true queens!"

ORION

CHAPTER TEN

"So Nymphs can be…good?" Xavier questioned, resting his elbows on his knees as he looked to Darcy like she held the answer to that. But we'd all seen what we'd seen.

I hadn't liked Diego much, but I'd come around to him a little when I'd had a glimpse of the shitty upbringing he'd had. It was difficult to let go of my inner instincts which were raging over what he could have done. He'd tried to drug the Vegas, even *had* drugged Tory and could have done fuck knows what to her if Darius hadn't stepped in. He'd been planning on bringing them to his psychotic mother and uncle, so how could I forgive that?

He may have been threatened into it, but it still made my fangs prickle as I looked at the two girls who'd come into this world with too many enemies to count. Even one of their friends had been plotting against them.

"Good is a strong word," Darius growled. "He fucked with the twins, and he could have killed them." He gripped Tory's hand, his knuckles turning white as he held onto her and smoke seeped between his teeth. "If I hadn't intervened that night when he'd managed to drug Roxy in The Orb then she would be dead right now."

"I knew I shouldn't have been that shit faced that night. I can handle my damn drink," Tory muttered. "But then I woke up in your room and I was more concerned about what I might have done with you than I was on figuring out why I'd been so wasted."

"I should have questioned it more," Darius sighed, his eyes flickering with fire.

"So should I," Tory said. "But I just got caught up in all that shit between us and my nightmares-"

"Nightmares I gave you," Darius replied, his brow pinching as he looked at her, his guilt over the way he'd treated her plain on his face as she raised her chin and looked right back at him, not giving him a free pass but not making any more of it either.

"Well, I don't fear drowning anymore," she replied, expelling a heavy breath. "My nightmares have a much clearer face these days. But I should have realised what Diego had done back then. Maybe things would have been different if I had."

Darcy reached for her, shaking her head as she took her hand.

"He was forced into it," Darcy said and I shifted in my seat as I looked at her. She was so fucking everything to me, and despite understanding that, all I could think about was her lying in a grave because of Diego and it awoke a monster in me, one more violent than any criminal I'd met in Darkmore.

Protectiveness was clawing at my chest and I was finding it very difficult to see beyond Diego putting that fucking knotroot in Darcy and her sister's drinks. Even if he had been threatened. Even if I could understand why he'd done it. I was still pretty sure I would have murdered him if he was standing before me now for the threat he'd posed to my girl.

"You should know better than most what it's like to do things you didn't want to because you were threatened into them," Tory said, arching a brow at Darius and he ran his tongue across his teeth.

"Touché," he muttered and Seth, Caleb and Max all shared a look.

"I never liked his hat," Seth said thoughtfully. "Now I get why. I must have been sensing its evilness."

Caleb gave him a hollow look. "Bullshit, you didn't sense shit."

"I did!" Seth insisted. "That hat was always giving me the heebies."

"I never even paid attention to the kid," Max said with a frown. "If I had, maybe I might have gotten a good read on him. He just had a really forgettable face, you know? Like one minute he was there then it was like…I'd totally forgotten he even existed. Like even now, I can picture his hat so much clearer than his face. But also that could be because the hat is right there." He pointed to the hat as he squinted in concentration like he was trying to remember what Diego had looked like.

"Maybe it was a Nymph power," Seth suggested mysteriously. "Maybe he made us all forget he was there so he could try and probe us in the night."

"You lot are always so busy playing kings of the world that I bet you couldn't name ninety percent of the students you go to school with," I said dryly and the Heirs considered that before conceding with a nod.

"Good point," Seth said. "I once had a girl suck me off seven nights in a row. She had my name tattooed on the back of her neck, made me a mix tape with every single one of my favourite songs on it and I just called her Blowie the whole time because I couldn't remember her name. To her face, guys. To her face."

"That's because you're an asshole," Caleb laughed.

"I'm no good with names," Seth said innocently.

"Last night you listed every single one of the team players in the entire Solarian Pitball League and their star signs," Max reminded him.

"Because you bet me ten auras I couldn't do it," Seth said with a shrug.

"So you can magically remember hundreds of names for ten auras?" Max questioned.

"I can do endless things for ten auras, Max," Seth said with a cocky grin. "I could do a triple standing backflip with no air magic for ten auras."

"Ha," Max laughed, folding his arms. "Go on then."

"We're getting off topic," I interjected in frustration before Seth could get up to try to prove himself. "The point is, we may have to acknowledge that Nymphs aren't inherently evil."

Darius scrubbed a hand over his face. "I've killed so many Nymphs, man."

"We all have," I said darkly.

"And they've all meant us harm," Max said with a firm nod. "I can feel their intentions. We've never killed one that hasn't meant to kill us. I'd have noticed if they had been forced into it."

"Thank god," Darcy whispered, rubbing her eyes and I realised she looked drained as hell. I hoped that hat hadn't fucked with her because I'd personally go diving into it again to choke out Diego's soul if it had. "But what are we supposed to do now? How does this change things?"

"Maybe it doesn't," Tory said. "Maybe Diego was different. The shadows were obviously trying to turn him evil and he had his hat to help fight against them. But I've never seen another Nymph wearing a hat, so it makes sense to think they're all corrupted."

"But if it's the shadows that are corrupting them then doesn't that suggest that they wouldn't be inherently evil without the shadows?" Darius suggested and I shifted in my seat uncomfortably at that idea.

"Poor, poor Diego," Geraldine sighed, hanging her head.

Silence fell between us as no one had a definitive answer to what we'd just witnessed. And as Darcy rubbed her eyes again and her face paled, I knew she needed to rest.

"I think I'm all hatted out," she murmured and I leaned over to kiss her temple.

"You're hatigued," I joked and she chuckled at me, making my heart lift before her smile fell away again, her eyes darkening as her thoughts no doubt drifted back to Diego.

It wasn't long before everyone started heading out the door, Xavier and the Heirs muttering about the Nymphs as Geraldine half tore Max's shirt off of him to use it to wipe her damp eyes.

I stood and plucked the hat from the bed, stuffing it into my back pocket to make sure Blue didn't get any ideas about putting it on again tonight. She was leaning on Tory, looking about ready to fall asleep and I could tell they wanted a moment together as they exchanged a twin look.

"I'll catch you in a bit, baby," Darius said as he noticed too, kissing Tory before heading to the door after the others, glancing back over his shoulder and catching my eye.

I took a step toward him on instinct but Seth's hands latched around him from behind, yanking him out into the corridor so the door closed between us.

I ran my tongue over my lengthening fangs, the urge to cut the mutt down to size rising up in me. But then I looked at Blue again, seeing the exhaustion in her and I forgot about everything else but her. I shot to her side, eyeing her paling features a second before she stumbled into my chest like she was about to pass out. I caught hold of her waist in alarm, clutching her against me as I searched her expression.

"Oops," she said through a yawn.

"What's wrong?" I demanded as Tory took hold of her sister's hand.

"Nothing, I'm just tired. It must have been the hat," Darcy said, her voice weak and an echo of exhaustion in her deep green gaze.

"You look dead on your feet," Tory said in concern, pulling Darcy towards the bed. "You should lie down."

Darcy nodded, going willingly and crawling over the bed before curling up like a cat by the pillows. Her eyes fluttered closed as Tory lay beside her and dropped an arm around her sister.

Darcy smiled contentedly, her hand raising to rest on Tory's arm and my fears washed away, knowing there was no place better for her than with her other half.

"I'll let you get some rest," I said and Darcy hummed her agreement as I walked to the door.

"Love you," she whispered before I left and I glanced back at her, my world brightening at those two small words.

"I love you more, beautiful." I stepped out of the room, shutting the door behind me and finding Darius playing around with the Heirs and Xavier, though it looked like Geraldine had taken off.

Caleb was zooming around them all in high speed circles while they did their best to try and land a punch on him, all of them chuckling like idiots. But as I watched, I found myself transfixed by their unbreakable bond with one another.

I was about to slip away, figuring I'd track down Noxy and see if he wanted to hang out for a bit when Seth caught sight of me and let out a bark of excitement.

"Lance, come play!" he called, but I just folded my arms in answer to that.

Caleb shot past Seth, slapping him hard enough to make his head wheel sideways and Xavier whinnied a laugh. Seth chased after him, trying to land a hit in retaliation but Caleb was moving like the wind and started slapping him with every circle he completed, riling Seth up into a frenzy as he tried harder to catch him, though he never resorted to using magic.

"Orion's too boring to play," Max said dismissively, a goading smile on his lips.

"Why would I play a game I could win in five seconds flat?" I responded and he sniggered.

"Prove it then," Max encouraged and I almost stepped forward but then I glanced at Darius again.

He looked like he wanted to say something, but no words left his mouth and doubts crawled through me as I wondered if he wanted to spend some alone time with his friends. Maybe he felt too awkward telling me to fuck off. Maybe he couldn't stand to be around the guy he'd been forced to spend the past few years with, who he'd cuddled in bed with night after night without him ever truly wanting that. Maybe I was always going to be a reminder of his father's control over him, and we'd keep drifting apart until we were strangers.

The mere thought of that made my gut tug and I searched for the words that might make it right, but came up short. He'd been unwillingly bound to me for so many years, I had to give him the space he'd been denied without complaint. He deserved that much. Though being away from him was honestly starting to feel painful in a way that had nothing to do with magical bonds. I just fucking missed him.

Caleb yanked on Seth's hair on his next circuit of the Heirs and Seth growled, lunging forward to catch him but colliding hard with Xavier instead. Glitter cascaded everywhere from Xavier's hair as he was knocked to the ground and Caleb swept by again, slapping Seth in the face, his right cheek now a bright pink colour as Max roared a laugh.

"Come and catch me then, Cal!" Seth cried, leaping to his feet and running into Caleb's room, slamming the door shut before Caleb could get through so he crashed into it instead.

Caleb swore then shoved into the room and Max and Xavier ran after them as Seth howled a challenge.

I was left alone with Darius in the corridor and the silence rang in my ears like a bell chiming out a death toll for our friendship.

I cleared my throat, taking a step backwards as he glanced after his friends, figuring I'd make this easier for him and get out of here.

"I'll er…catch you later?" I said and Darius frowned, stepping toward me as I prepared to leave.

I lingered there for a second, wanting to say so many things and yet finding my voice locked up in my throat.

I turned to leave, but he spoke my name in a way that seemed laced with a thousand hopes and regrets. "Lance?"

I turned back, my eyebrows rising as the space between us seemed to shrink a little. "Yeah?"

"You know it wasn't all fake, right?" he asked, his eyes burning with the flames of his Order.

My heart sank, because I knew what was coming. The apology, the acknowledgement that yes, we had been friends in some ways, but not like he was with the Heirs. He'd want space, time to get used to a life without our bond, but with those things would come distance. And I just didn't know if we'd recover from it.

"Yeah, I know," I said on a sigh. "But I also know that I'm a reminder of your father's chains now. So enjoy your freedom, Darius. Really. You deserve time with people whose company isn't forced upon you. I swear I don't begrudge you it."

Hurt flashed across his eyes as he took another step toward me. "Is that what you really think, brother?"

"Don't you?" I asked, my fear over the answer to that spinning a razor-sharp web inside my chest.

He shook his head, moving closer still and part of me – a really fucking big part – wanted to wrap my arms around him like the bond was still driving us together. It wasn't some magical force guiding it this time though, it was the purest kind of friendship, and love for a man I had shared my hardest days with.

"Come on, Darius!" Max called from Caleb's bedroom, but Darius didn't turn his gaze from mine.

"They're waiting for you," I muttered, but Darius only stepped closer to me.

"I think I'm gonna take a nap," he said, giving me a pointed look. Those words so damn familiar to me from all the years we'd been bonded, and they had always meant one thing before now.

"Oh yeah?" I questioned, frowning uncertainly at the implication in his words. *Did he want what I think he wanted?*

He nodded, stepping past me and heading toward his room further up the corridor. I watched him go and as he made it there, he looked back at me, inclining his head towards the door in an offering. A smile quirked up my lips that he immediately mirrored, and I started walking after him, quickening my pace as he pushed through the door and I followed.

He dropped onto the large bed at the heart of the room, scooping some gold jewellery off of his nightstand and starting to put on the large bangles, chunky necklaces and rings as I kicked my shoes off.

"Are you sure?" I asked and he nodded again, making my grin widen further before I dove onto the bed to join him.

He lunged at me, trying to wrestle me into being the little spoon, but I didn't have to do his damn bidding anymore so I fought back and the two of us wrestled like Wolf pups, starting to laugh as we threw a few playful punches too.

We eventually settled on laying side by side, our heads resting on the same pillow as the piece of my soul which had been missing finally settled back into place.

I could see the peace in his eyes as we looked at each other and happiness caressed my heart over having my friend back. Entirely on our own terms.

"Is this weird?" he asked.

"Definitely," I confirmed. "Maybe we've both got a few pack animals in our ancestry."

"Yeah, let's go with that," Darius said on a bark of laughter.

"Don't tell Seth that though," I warned. "He's been trying to force hugs on me and I refuse to give in."

"Ha, the day you cuddle Seth will be the day my father hands over the throne with a nice little bow on it."

"Maybe you could remind him of that, because dog boy seems to enjoy my company far too much for my liking," I said with a grimace and Darius snorted, reaching out to tussle my hair.

"Maybe you should cut him some slack," he suggested.

"Why?" I snarled instantly, my hackles rising. "He fucked with me and Darcy when we were hiding our relationship, he could have easily been the one to give us away. And even though I know it wasn't him, I'm still not convinced he never would have outed us purely for his own sick amusement."

"Yeah, he's an asshole, but he wouldn't have sold you out. He just likes playing god sometimes. He gets high on power, like pretty much all of our kind. And look, I'm not saying what he did is forgivable. But what he's done since might be enough to make up for it."

"And what's that?" I demanded.

"You know all those photos and shit he sent you of him and Gw-" I bared my fangs at him and he changed direction mid-word, "-*Darcy?* They were a game to make you jealous so that you'd fight for her. He's been boasting about it ever since you two made up. He thinks he can take all the credit for your entire ongoing relationship. I'm surprised he hasn't told you himself yet."

I narrowed my gaze, hunting for the lie, but it looked like Darius really believed that.

"Bullshit," I hissed. "And even if that was true, you think I'd thank him for it? For fucking with my head, for making me think he – that he and her-" A snarl ripped from my throat as I was unable to contain the utter, murderous rage I felt over the mere idea of them together.

"Well, it worked, didn't it?" Darius raised an eyebrow, the smirk on his lips telling me exactly whose side he was on.

"How long have you known about this?" I asked in a suspicious tone, my eyes sharpening on my best friend.

"Since you asked me to find out if there was anything going on between the two of them." He shrugged innocently.

A beat of angry silence passed then I lunged at him and we fell into another furious fight for dominance. I used my Vampire strength to slam him down onto the mattress beneath me by the throat and he threw a punch into my ribs that forced the air from my lungs, a big ass smile still on his face.

"You asshole," I snapped, but his smile broke into a laugh and I realised how fucking happy he was at long last. The strength went out of me and I let him go, falling back down beside him instead. "Fuck you," I said lightly as he continued to laugh, and a grin tugged at my mouth which I gave up on trying to hold back.

My laughter joined his and I soaked in the peace in this room that seemed so impossibly unreal after all we'd been through. Hell, things might not have been perfect with Lionel still ruling the world and society falling apart piece by piece under his command, but in this haven beneath the ground I was in the company of my best friends in the world and the star damned love of my life, so I wasn't gonna complain. I'd spent too long living in the shadows in my mind, and it was time I stepped into the sunlight for as long as I could.

"So you played me, huh?" I elbowed Darius as he rolled onto his side to look at me.

"Seth played you. I just let him," he said innocently. "So are you gonna thank his ass or spank it?"

"I'll ram a fucking pineapple up it," I muttered.

"He's a good guy," Darius pushed and I tsked. "Alright, he's a bit of a sadist, but he's got a good heart. Better than most actually. It just doesn't always seem that way."

"Well, I'm never gonna be in the mood to go mining for his heart of gold, Darius. I've got enough friends. Especially now I have you back," I said stubbornly, unwilling to change my opinion on the mutt.

"You didn't lose me," he scoffed.

"I thought I did for a minute there," I murmured. "You and the Heirs, I...I'll never be that for you. But I'll be here. Always. Whenever you need me."

He frowned. "I'll always be here for you too, Lance. And you're not that different from the Heirs, you know, you just dislike them too much to let yourself see it."

"They're a bunch of entitled pricks," I said dismissively, shaking my head.

"So am I." Darius grinned. "But you like me just fine." He pinched my cheek and I smacked his hand away, though I guessed he had a point.

My hand fell on something cool and hard on the bed and I looked down, finding the silver coin there which was concealing my father's diary. It must have fallen out of my pocket, so I picked it up, examining it and pushing the concealment spell off of it so that the leatherbound book appeared in my hand.

"When's the full moon?" I wondered aloud and Darius grabbed the golden clock off of his nightstand which had the moon phases curving along the bottom of the clock face.

"Tonight," he said, looking to the diary. "You wanna read it again?"

"Yeah," I said decisively. I'd been memorising the power words for the Imperial Star the last time I'd been able to read it, but there were plenty I still hadn't committed to memory. I really had to start teaching them to the twins as soon as possible in case they ever got the chance to use it. We had to be ready - though I could tell by the look on Darius's face that he wasn't exactly happy about my new role as the Guild Master. And I didn't wanna leave things unsaid between us even if he had claimed he didn't want to fight over this before.

"So…are you still planning on challenging Lionel?" I asked and Darius nodded firmly, his eyes flaring with the passion of that task. The sole thing we'd been working towards year after year, and I was still firmly in his corner when it came to defeating his psychotic father. Only, I could see a different way to do it now.

"Of course," he growled passionately, smoke seeping between his teeth. "As soon as Gabriel *sees* a chance to strike at him, I will challenge him and I will win."

"And you'll take his throne?" I asked, an edge to my voice because I knew what that could lead to next.

"The Heirs and I will figure it out from there," he said, not meeting my gaze. "They'll either challenge their parents or their parents will step aside and we'll form a new Council. One that will succeed in bringing peace to Solaria."

"And what about the twins?" I asked in a growl and his eyes bored into mine as his jaw ticked.

"I'm Fae, Lance. What would you have me do? Bow down like some weakling after all my father has done to us?"

"Weakling?" I snarled. "Is that what you think of me?"

"So you've really bowed to them then?" he asked in shock like he didn't already know. But what did he expect? I was the Master of the Zodiac Guild. I was in love with a Vega princess.

"I knelt for Darcy in the arena," I admitted, staring him straight in the eye. "She is my queen, whether that be by the choice of the stars or a fate carved by my own hand. I was always meant to kneel for her."

"And Roxy is my queen too. But she is not Solaria's," Darius said, raising his chin, stubbornness filling his expression and my jaw tightened as I felt us standing on two sides of an uncrossable chasm.

"Rule with them," I pleaded.

"This isn't some fairy tale where the lost princesses show up and magically make everything better in the world, Lance," he replied. "Think of it logically. Even now, they know barely anything of our world. They couldn't pinpoint most Solarian cities on a map. They don't know the laws of old, they don't know the intricacies of the Orders' needs, they don't have a lifetime of knowledge that a ruler requires to rule well. Like me and the Heirs do."

"So teach them," I demanded. "I'll teach them too. Between you and I, we could prepare them for that role."

"I'm not saying we won't give them the chance to learn those things, but the truth is, it would take years for them to fully grasp even half of what has been drummed into the other Heirs and I since we were born. I'm not thinking of the throne, or my own personal power, I'm thinking of Solaria. And returning our kingdom to the rule of the Vega line makes no sense if they're not the best choice to lead our people to peace and prosperity. You know the plans the other Heirs and I have to make changes for the better in this kingdom. Would you have us throw away everything we've worked for our entire lives just because the line of succession states they should wear a pretty crown and we shouldn't?"

"I'm asking you to put your knowledge to use. Teach the Vegas so that they can sit on the throne, and sit at their side as their guidance on the Council."

"The Heirs need the power to make real change in Solaria, they can't be shackled in their decisions by the rule of a monarch. And no matter how well meaning the Vegas might be as queens, the fact is, they don't know enough to make those decisions. They aren't prepared to make the kinds of calls that will have to be made to force the change that needs to happen, and the Celestial Council can't be forced into submission over decisions that will affect millions of lives by girls whose ignorance makes them incapable of understanding the issues fully," he hissed determinedly, his eyes shifting to reptilian slits. "My father has taken the kingdom hostage, he has taken my entire life hostage, he took *you* hostage for years as well, not to mention what he did to Roxy. And I will make him pay for every single one of his crimes and take the throne from him so he will see that he created his own downfall in me."

I reached out to rest a hand on his arm, understanding this need in him. I really fucking did, but the throne didn't have to be the prize for his revenge plot. He could have all of that still and guide the Vegas, it was the better way.

"Is there something else to this?" I asked, frowning at him as his eyes burned with the intensity of his desire to end Lionel's reign.

Darius cut his gaze away from mine, frowning slightly as he shook his head, seemingly frustrated with me because I didn't share his opinion on the Vegas taking the crown. But yes, I knew what he was saying and yes, they absolutely needed further education to rule this kingdom properly, but it seemed to me that if the Heirs just found a way to reform the Celestial Council as it was intended, supporting the monarchy instead of resisting it, then maybe they could find a way to make it work that would be better for everyone.

"I can't bow to them, Lance. Not while I know they aren't the better choice for our kingdom. It's not about vanity or ego or any of that crap. Hell, there's a good chance I won't even survive this war to see how this plays out. But in the event of my death, I want Xavier to take my place, not the Vegas, because he also understands everything required to rule which they just don't."

"You forget that your father was the one to teach you a lot of those lessons," I murmured and he nodded his head in acceptance of that.

"I believe I have proved that I'm my own man now. I stand apart from his cruelty and have learned first-hand the damage that kind of leadership can cause. But if you truly believe that I am too like him to claim this place then say it," he challenged and I shook my head in a clear denial of that.

"You have dark in you, Darius, but you are not your father. You know my faith in you has never wavered. I only want you to consider uniting to rule beneath the Vegas."

"I know. But all the while I know they aren't the better choice for Solaria, I can't consider that as an option."

I squeezed his arm where I still held him, letting him know I understood that even if I didn't hold the same opinion. He released a slow breath in recognition of my feelings on the matter too.

He slowly reached up to grip my hand where it was pressed to his arm, giving me a nod that showed me this would not break us. We were divided but not apart. And I was relieved to find that nothing could shake the foundations of our friendship.

I sighed, resting my head on the pillow as he did the same, the familiar thump of his heartbeat reminding me of the countless naps we'd taken together. And as we lay there in silence, I could feel myself falling into the peace of sleep, and I let myself drift away with my brother at my side, realising that we were bonded regardless of Lionel's power chaining us together. We would always have each other's backs, and I knew now that nothing would ever change that.

"Ohmagod," Darcy's voice carried to me, but I couldn't quite stir out of sleep to find her. "This is too cute."

"Shh, you'll wake them and I need to get a photo so that I can mock them tirelessly with it," Tory whispered.

"They're cuddling," Darcy whisper-squealed and Tory shushed her again but started suppressing a laugh.

"It's called a man hug," Darius said, his voice gruff from sleep and I cracked my eyes open, finding we'd shifted close together and were tangled in a ridiculous cuddle.

"I guess old habits die hard," I tried.

A whoosh of air made my eyes snap sideways and I found Darcy leaping toward me with a grin on her face. I was glad to see she was feeling better, the light in her eyes making a knot loosen in my chest.

I caught her before she collided with me, forcing her between Darius and I and drawing her flush against me as I shut my eyes again. Tory hit the bed next and Darius caught hold of her, shoving her in beside her sister and the two of us closed ranks so they were crushed between us.

Darcy wriggled to try and get free, but I held her tighter and tugged her ear between my teeth. "Stay," I commanded.

"Was that an order?" She jabbed an elbow back into my chest and I grinned as her laughter filled up the room.

"Do you need another dick punch, Lance?" Tory asked and I opened my eyes again, scruffing her hair and messing it up royally as Darius held her down so she couldn't escape.

"Nooo, don't dick punch him. You'll break it and I need it," Darcy complained, making me chuckle darkly.

"How about if I break it, you can break Darius's in return," Tory offered conversationally and I swear my cock tried to run and take shelter from this heartless dick hunter.

"Hey," Darius barked as the two of them hooked their little fingers together to make the deal.

I grabbed Blue's arm as Darius grabbed Tory's, yanking their hands apart before they could doom our dicks for all the stars to see.

"Ooh! Are we having a cuddle party?!" Seth cried as the door flew open and he came bounding in like a puppy looking for its master.

"No," I snapped a second before he dove onto the bed and started nuzzling everyone. Including me. Which was not going to go unpunished.

"Argh." I fought to get him away from my face as he rubbed his head against mine, but before I could throw him across the room like a pitball destined for a pit, two more massive bodies slammed down on top of us and the girls squealed.

Max and Caleb laughed, squashing us between them as Seth howled his enjoyment.

"Giggle hug," Max announced, pushing the feeling of amusement over all of us until we were all laughing. But I shoved my mental shields up to block him out and growled as Seth's stubble scraped against my face.

I cursed as I held onto Darcy then yanked her out of the pile and pulled her off the bed, returning the diary to its coin appearance before pushing it into my pocket and glancing at the time.

"The full moon's up," I whispered to her as her laughter fell away. "Come outside with me."

She smiled seductively and my hand closed around the drawstrings of her sweatpants, yanking her closer to me by them as dark thoughts entered my head. Me and her. Outside. Alone. No one would see us together, I'd make sure of that. And once I had her in my grasp, I'd build a wall of ice around us and keep her trapped there until I was buried inside her with her body wrapped around mine and a plea of mercy on her lips.

"The moon?" Seth leapt to his feet as Max stopped pushing amusement into everyone. "I want to see the moon – I'm coming!"

"Yeah, I could use some fresh air too," Max agreed.

Fuck no.

"Same, this room smells like a bonfire. Darius has been sleep smoking again," Caleb said, pointing to the haze of smoke swirling up by the ceiling.

"I love it when he does that." Tory kissed Darius and he immediately released a small plume of smoke against her lips as she grinned.

"No," I said simply, grabbing Darcy, throwing her over my shoulder and shooting out the door at high speed.

I tore through the tunnels, making my way to the exit before planting Darcy down in front of me and smirking at her. She didn't smile back, pursing her lips instead.

"That was rude," she said but I stalked closer to her, pushing her hair over her shoulder and knotting my fingers in it.

"And?" I leaned in close, teasing her lower lip between my teeth, but she pressed a hand to my chest and stepped back.

"*And* you could try getting along with them," she suggested.

I shot behind her, locking my hand over her throat and tilting her head sideways to expose her neck to my fangs.

"Mmm. Or I could drink your sunshine-sweet blood then find somewhere private to fuck you breathless." My fangs hit a tight air shield over her skin and a growl left my throat. "Playing hard to get, Blue?"

My instincts rose as my hunger for her increased and I scored my thumb along the length of her neck as I hunted for weaknesses in her defences, but fuck she was getting good at her casts these days.

"Maybe I'll give you a sip if you promise to play nice with the Heirs," she offered with a teasing lilt to her voice. But if she thought she could play games with me and win, she was about to find out what it was like to go up against a man whose name was defined by the constellation of the Hunter.

"I don't do nice," I warned as I released her throat and started to circle her instead, my eyes narrowed on my beautiful, delicious looking prey. The game was too enticing to resist, and so long as she didn't run and I didn't chase, I wasn't breaking the Vampire Code. I knew how to control myself, but I also knew how to work at the very edges of my leash too.

"You do with me," she pointed out.

"Nice?" I laughed, showing enough teeth that she knew I was nothing but an animal right now. "Am I nice to you, Blue? Do I kiss you nicely? Do I fuck you nicely? Do I spank you nicely?" I slowed to a halt behind her, clasping a handful of her ass in my hand and leaning down to speak in her ear. "Or do I kiss you like our tongues are made of fire and ice? Do I fuck you like the world is ending and you're the goddess of my salvation? Do I spank you hard enough for you to feel it everywhere? So you know exactly who owns you."

She spun away from me, lust rising up from the seven sins in her eyes.

"I can't be owned," she said, a dare burning in her gaze like she wanted me to prove she could be.

"Well I can," I said, hounding after as I tipped my head down, shadows sliding over me as I turned my back to the closest sconce. "I can be owned and shackled and made into a slave for you, beautiful. But I'm not the kind who does as he's told. I'm the kind who seeks out the secret desires in your eyes and feeds them to you piece by piece. I'm your most corrupt wants brought to life and it's my fucking calling to sate you, Blue."

Her ass hit the door that led to the farmhouse and I rested my hand above her head, caging her there as I tasted my lower lip, wishing it was hers. Her gaze was hooded and her chest was rising and falling with her quickening breaths, but I wanted her breathing even faster and gasping my name like it could deliver her redemption. Having to stay away from her in front of the rebels was exhausting, and with Seth sharing our room it was rare to get her alone. But now I had her, I didn't plan on letting her go until dawn.

"Let's go outside," I said, my voice nothing but sex as my eyes fell to that perfect mouth which I was about to do unspeakable things to.

"I love the moon and the moon loves me," Seth sang somewhere behind us and I could have put my fist through the wall there and then. Was there no privacy in this fucking place? "Oh hey moon friends, shall we go see the moon together? Everyone else will be here soon. They said something about giving you two space, but I was like 'why did they invite us along if they need space?'"

"We didn't invite you along," I said irritably.

"That's a weird thing to say to your moon friend, moon friend," Seth said, a teasing smirk on his face.

Darcy leaned sideways to look past me, but I didn't move even when she pressed a hand to my chest to try and make me.

"We're not moon friends," I gritted out.

"Well, that seems like an awfully moon friend thing to say, Lance," Seth said lightly. I was sure he was trying to wind me up and by the stars was it working.

"Stop saying moon friends," I snarled.

"What's a moon friend?" Darcy asked curiously.

"It's not a thing," I growled.

"Er, it absolutely is a thing. And I'd know, as I've been to the moon," Seth said cockily.

"Really?" I deadpanned, rounding on him. "I hadn't heard."

"Yeah, I went last summer. Cal got me a ticket. And while I was there, there was this really good-looking crater which whispered my name and-"

"I know," I snapped, not wanting to hear this fucking story for the thousandth time.

"But you said-" he started.

"I was being sarcastic," I hissed and he barked a laugh.

"Oh Lance, you are *so* jealous of me going to the moon. Shit, they wouldn't let a Power Shamed Fae on the moon, would they? Or maybe they would but then they'd leave you there so you wouldn't make people uncomfortable here on earth anymore..." he said thoughtfully and my scowl deepened. "Nah, they wouldn't disrespect the moon like that actually."

Darcy caught my hand, tugging me through the door before I decided to break the mutt's neck.

As he followed us, I tried to figure out if it was worth turning back and waiting another whole month for the full moon to rise again so that we could do this without Seth. But dammit, I couldn't come up with a good enough reason to do that.

The feel of the magical protection spells trickled over me as we stepped out of the clock that concealed the entrance to The Burrows then we headed to the door of the farmhouse.

I tried to pointedly ignore Seth as he rehashed more of his stories from the moon, but it was impossible. The only thing stopping me from shutting him up for good was Darcy's hand squeezing mine and the looks she kept throwing me that said killing the Wolf would not go down well.

As we made it outside and the guards appeared ahead of us, I tugged my hand from Darcy's and dropped back a few steps behind the two of them while she threw me a frown over her shoulder. *Get used to it, beautiful. I'm not bringing you down with me.*

"Princess Darcy. My name is Barney Von Bonderville, and I am at your service. Please, let me walk you away from that Power Shamed vermin." The nearest guard bowed his head before throwing me a sickened look.

147

Anger poisoned my blood but I fell back a little more, hugging the shadows in front of the farmhouse as Seth and Darcy moved into the glow of the guards' Faelights. I despised having to keep myself in check every time someone threw insults my way, but if I went around breaking the bones of everyone who spoke about me like that, the whole rebellion would be in peril.

"He's not vermin," Darcy snarled at him and he bowed lower. I fucking adored her for standing up for me like that, but I really had to get her to stop. They were going to start questioning her sanity if she kept it up.

"Forgive me. How can I assist you?" Barney asked.

"Just make sure we're not disturbed," she said sharply and the guards all moved back as she swept past them, glancing over her shoulder when she realised I wasn't right behind her.

Her eyes found mine immediately even though I was sure I could barely be seen here in the dark, but Blue always had a way of seeking me out.

"Lance, walk beside me," she commanded, her chin high and far be it from me to ignore an order from my queen. I shot to her side, walking with her across the thick snow, though my heightened hearing didn't miss the muttered words between the guards, and I suddenly questioned my choice to move so close to her while we were still in sight. If they told the rest of the rebels and people got wind of us being a couple, Darcy could lose their support, and I couldn't bear to be responsible for that.

"Why does she keep that washout felon around?" Barney Von fucking Dickweed said.

"He must be of some use to her, but let's hope that doesn't last much longer."

"Yeah, she'll discard him soon enough. Then he'll melt into the background of society where he belongs."

My spine prickled at those words, the urge in me to fight back and show them the measure of my strength surging up in me like a tsunami. I'd technically been stripped of that right. I wasn't allowed to challenge a Fae to a fight because of my status and though I didn't give a shit about breaking the law, I didn't think those assholes would be beyond having me locked up for it. Darcy and Tory may have held the power around here, but it was too deeply ingrained in our kind to let go of my shaming after it had been made so public, so official.

Even if the Vegas could one day take the throne and pardon me of my crimes, the damage was already done. I would never be seen as worthy for a Vega Princess. But all the while she wanted me, I'd keep coming to her in secret, keep offering all of myself for as long as she'd have me. But deep down, I knew that if she eventually took a seat on the throne beside her sister, she would have to think of heirs to that throne. And a Power Shamed Fae could not provide legitimate ones. No Fae in this land would acknowledge them as such even if Darcy ordered it, it was our way. So who was I to take that away from her? To place that burden on her children? I'd never seen myself as a father, but with her, well, anything was possible with her.

My gaze locked on Seth over the top of Darcy's head as we walked across the snow, following a Faelight that Darcy had cast as we headed towards the boundary.

"Darius had something interesting to say about you, mutt," I said and he looked to me with intrigue.

"Was it about the nipple thing? Because I can teach it to you if you both want to try it?" he asked excitedly.

"Ew." Darcy wrinkled her nose at him. "What nipple thing?"

"Do not answer that," I growled as Seth opened his mouth. I had zero desire to hear about him and the weird sex shit he got up to in his free time.

"So what was it then?" Seth asked, looking even more curious.

"Apparently you've been goading me, making me jealous when it came to Darcy so I'd try and get her back." I fixed him with a sharp glare and a smile broke across his face as Blue looked to him for an answer to that too.

Seth pushed a hand into his long dark hair, smirking like an asshole. "I can't confirm or deny my secret mastermind plans."

"Well let's put it this way. Either you sent me photos of yourself with her just to try and piss me off, or you really did try to get with her and you're currently walking your final steps towards your bloody grave." I smiled like a demon, locking an arm around Darcy's waist and pulling her against me as we moved out of sight of the guards.

"Seth?" she pushed as he glanced between us, mulling over his answer.

"Okay, the truth is, I played you like a horny little piano who hadn't had her keys touched for a decade," Seth said, his smile wide and cocky and punchable.

"Are you kidding me?" Darcy growled, fire sparking in her hair as she tried to lurch toward him, but I kept hold of her, my sights fixed on the Wolf who had messed with us in every way he could think up.

"Why?" I asked in a measured tone, deciding how I was going to approach this. I could be a reasonable kind of guy. If the definition of reasonable was stringing this Heir up in a tree and beating him like a pinata until his guts bled out.

"Don't be angry," he begged with a whine in his throat, looking at Darcy more than me. "I know how protective assholes work. Lance was getting all gives-upsy because he thought it was the right thing to do. He's a noble assbag, you see? So I had to give him a nudge by making him think I'd spread you out in my bed and fucked you raw like a good little Beta."

My fangs lengthened at the mere idea of that and I shot toward him, slamming into an air shield the same moment a violent earthquake knocked me to the ground.

"See?" Seth said innocently, giving Darcy the big eyes. "He's so easily riled up. He's like a gorilla-sized chihuahua."

I snarled, slamming my hand to his air shield and freezing it solid before throwing my fist against it hard enough to shatter a hole in it. He yelped as I grabbed his ankle and froze that too, his legs going as stiff as boards under my power before he toppled forward, smashing through the ice and landing on top of me.

"Stop it," Darcy gasped, rolling Seth off of me so he hit the ground on his back, his legs still frozen together and as rigid as a ruler.

I got to my feet, dusting the snow off my ass as Seth used air magic to rise onto his feet like some kind of awkward scarecrow.

"Well, that's thanks for you. If it wasn't for me, you wouldn't even be back together." He rocked back and forth as the air magic kept him upright, his frozen boots just touching the ground.

"If it wasn't for you, we wouldn't have gone through hell thinking you were gonna tell people about us," I snapped.

"I was never going to do that." He rolled his eyes and folded his arms, rocking side to side and back and forth. "You're so dramatic, Lance."

"Oh *I'm* dramatic?" I scoffed. "Everything about your ridiculous plan was dramatic."

"Which is why we'll make such good friends when you stop holding onto these silly grudges. You know what people say about grudges? It's like taking killblaze and expecting your enemy to get high and kill themselves. But I'm never going to get high and kill myself, Lance. I'm going to be here always, as your friend. Just give into it, bro. It's inevitable. Like you and Darcy were inevitable."

"That's kinda cute," Darcy said, looking to me with her eyelashes fluttering.

"No." I pointed at her. "Don't you fall for that shit. He acts like he's a puppy when he wants something, but he's still the savage Wolf who cut your hair off, Blue. I'm never going to forget what it felt like finding you on the floor in the wake of his cruelty."

"Come on, I've done way worse than that to my friends and they still love me. I once locked Max in a room full of Manticore farts for three hours – and let me tell you, it was some chore getting those Manticore farts in there. At least Darcy could grow her hair back with a simple potion, Max still has Manticore fart flashbacks to this day. He can't even be near a Manticore without feeling queasy. And you sped up that whole hair growth process anyway, didn't you, Professor Professional?" He gave me a pointed look. "Darcy told me you helped her get her hands on that potion. That wasn't very Fae of you, sir, was it? You go all mortal for this girl, and I get it now. She's your moon flower. Rare, with muscular petals and curly golden hair you just wanna grip in your fist while you make him - *her* smile-"

"What are you talking about?" I balked.

"The point is, she's special." He looked at Darcy with a doggish grin. "She and Tory are something else. And all the shit we did to them? Well, call me an asshole, but I think it made them bloom."

"I mean, I'm never gonna thank you for that, but I think you fucked yourselves over." Darcy shrugged. "We told you we never wanted the throne, but then you pushed and pushed us and made us want it more than you can even imagine."

"You would've wanted it anyway eventually," he said, a challenge in his eyes now. "But I like a little competition, babe, I'll be more than happy to beat your ass when it comes to it."

"We'll see," Darcy tossed back and I frowned at the way they were looking at each other, seeing their friendship properly for the first time since I'd come back into Darcy's life. And shit, it looked familiar. Like the sort of bond I felt with Gabriel.

My gaze slid onto Seth as I chewed the inside of my cheek, knowing I was never going to like this guy, but perhaps I could be civil for now. For Blue's sake.

I flicked my fingers, melting the ice binding his legs together and his eyebrows arched as he lowered himself to the ground and shook them out to get the feeling back in them.

"Did we just become true moon friends?" he asked with hope shining in his eyes.

"Absolutely not." I turned my back on him, heading away across the snow and looking up at the moon as I slid the coin from my pocket and let it expand back into my father's diary.

A whinny caught my ear and I spotted Xavier flying up above us, circling in the sparse clouds that hung like cotton wool in the dark sky. A smile twitched the corner of my lips up as he did a cartwheel then a barrel roll through the air, lilac glitter catching the light of the moon as it cascaded from his mane through the air.

I stuck two fingers in my mouth, whistling to get his attention and he neighed in greeting as he sailed down towards the ground and landed lightly before me. I reached out to rub his nose and he snorted happily before he trotted into my personal space and dropped his chin over my shoulder in a horsey hug.

"Hey Xavier." I patted his shoulder, noting the Pegobag on his back and as he shifted into his Fae form, he slid it off and grabbed some clothes out of it, pulling on sweatpants and a shirt as he shivered in the cold.

"What are you doing out here?" he asked as Darcy and Seth joined us. I held up the diary and he released a little snort of curiosity. "Can I join you?"

"Sure, so long as you give me some blood." I grinned and he sighed, his shoulders dropping.

"Fine, but don't tell anyone about me being a you-know-what," he said under his breath.

"Alright, man," I agreed. "But I mean, everyone knows."

"Yeah, eveeeeryone," Seth jumped in. "I told eight people just this afternoon and they're talkers, Xavier, real talkers. I'd say they told at least another three people each so that's…" He started counting his fingers and Darcy smacked his hands back down to stop him.

"It's nothing to be ashamed of," she said and Xavier looked to her with hope in his eyes.

"Really?" he glanced at me then back to her. "Are you still one?" he whispered hopefully and I roared a laugh.

"Oh, um…" she said, biting her lip before breaking a laugh too, her eyes meeting mine as I gave her a filthy smile.

"Alright, I get it," Xavier muttered, his ears pinking as he pursed his lips at us.

Seth started laughing too which made it immediately not funny anymore as he caught my gaze and nodded along. My smile stuttered out as I glowered at him instead, catching hold of Blue's arm and tugging her against me.

"Darcy's legs are more spreadable than peanut butter when it comes to you, amiright Lance?" Seth waggled his eyebrows at me, and I bared my fangs at him in response.

"Shut it, Seth," Darcy growled and for a moment she went feral in my arms as she swiped at him like an angry tiger.

I looked down at her in surprise, finding her features twisted in a snarl and I smirked at my pocket sized monster as I held onto her. Though maybe I should have let her go full savage on the mutt.

"Woah there, babe, do you want me to shift so you can chase my furry tail?" Seth wiggled his ass at her as she swiped at him again and I figured fuck it and released her. She leapt on him with a growl and I folded my arms as I watched her go wild, blasting him to the ground with a gust of air that made him yelp like a pup. He used a vine to uproot her and she slammed down onto her back in the snow before he leapt on her with a yip of excitement, smooshing a whole fistful of snow into her face.

"*Hey*," I barked as Xavier stared on in surprise, but my girl immediately gathered a large ball of snow with her magic, suspending it over him for one second before dropping it onto his head like a hat and shaping it into a cock with a laugh, constructing a pair of balls over his face too.

His muffled cry came from within the snow as he rolled off of her and clawed at the snow cock to break it away from his face.

I grinned at his panicked struggle, leaning down to help Darcy to her feet and placing a kiss against her cool cheek.

"Nicely done," I said, unable to help praising her like we were in a lesson back at Zodiac. I was half tempted to give her some House points for that cast too.

She stumbled against me for a second, blinking hard and I frowned as I ran my fingers through her hair to dislodge the snow clinging to it.

"Are you okay?" Xavier asked, stepping closer under Darcy's Faelight which was still hovering above us, flickering a little as if her magic was waning.

"She's a monster," Seth lamented as he got to his feet, gasping down air before grinning like a maniac. "It's fucking awesome."

Darcy smiled and my concern ebbed away as heat rose from her skin and steam coiled up around her hair to melt the last of the snow from her body.

A blur and a whoosh caught my attention, my head snapping around a second before Caleb arrived with Darius on his back and Max and Tory balancing precariously on each of his outstretched arms.

"Told you I could carry you all at once," Caleb said with a cocky grin as he placed them all down on their feet.

"You nearly broke my leg when you hit that wall, dude," Tory said as she set a fire burning in her hands to warm them up.

"Keyword *nearly*," Caleb said and Seth chuckled.

Darius punched Caleb in the kidney with a challenging grin. "You break her leg, I'll break your pretty face."

"You always were so jealous of my pretty face. Any excuse to get rid of the competition, right Darius?" Caleb taunted and Darius shoved him, but Caleb's light-footedness meant he just danced around him and took to Seth's side.

"Gerry said she's gonna come meet us," Max said as he looked down at his Atlas, his eyes glittering hopefully as he glanced over his shoulder like she might appear at any moment.

"When are you going to ask her out, man?" Caleb asked.

"I've asked her out fifty times," Max said in anguish. "She just starts calling me a silly seabass or some shit and then descends into some sort of sea language I just don't get, but it makes me so damn hard I can't even concentrate anymore."

Tory and Darcy shared a twin look then started laughing.

"What?" Max demanded. "Do you two know something about this fish language that I don't?"

"No idea, dude," Tory said through a grin. "It's fucking hilarious though."

"She seems to like fish, so I think it's affectionate," Darcy offered thoughtfully and Max's face brightened at that.

"I know she wants me, I just don't know if she wants me, wants me, you know?" Max sighed.

"You could try asking her?" I suggested.

"Yeah, taking advice from a guy who fucked a student, went to prison for it and is now Power Shamed doesn't seem like the best idea, thanks all the same though, man," Max said casually and I clenched my jaw.

"Don't be an asshole," Darius growled, but I didn't give a fuck. I'd lose about as much sleep over the Heirs disliking me as I would if I'd taken ten sleeping drafts and laid down on a fluffy little cloud.

"Maybe you should try the Capella smoulduction," Seth suggested.

"And what the fuck is that?" Max asked, narrowing his eyes at him.

"I'd bet both of my hands he just made it up," I said.

"No way, it's my power move," Seth insisted. "Half smoulder, half seduction. C'mere, Cal, lemme show them how it works." He tugged on Caleb's shirt, dragging him into his personal space and everyone watched them with rapt attention.

"What are you doing?" Caleb muttered under his breath.

"You'll see," Seth said, leaning close so they were nose to nose then dropping his gaze to Caleb's mouth. Seth wet his lips, desire pooling in his eyes as his hand ran down the plane of Caleb's chest, his gaze never faltering from his friend's.

I suddenly felt like I was watching something private and glanced at Darcy as her eyes darted between the two of them with intrigue.

Caleb's hand fell to Seth's waist for the briefest second, almost like he was going to tug him closer before he shoved him back a step and carved that same hand through his hair, laughing a little.

"Fuck off, man, that shit might work on your pack, but not me," he said dismissively and I swear Seth let out a small whine.

What the hell was that about? *Oh right, I don't give a fuck.*

"Shall we do the book thingy now?" Darcy suggested excitedly, looking up at me and everyone's attention followed.

"Wait for me, dear Burrow buddies!" Geraldine's voice sounded across the snow as she came gliding towards us upon a sheet of ice she'd cast beneath her feet, sliding gracefully to a halt beside Max, her light brown hair fluttering around her shoulders in the breeze.

I twirled my finger through the air and a wall of ice shot up surrounding us to give us some privacy. Darius cast a fire burning on the ground between us and the place immediately warmed, though I kept the ice hard and compact around our group so it didn't melt.

Caleb started making mossy seats around the place and I fought the urge to roll my eyes. Did he have to make everywhere into a damn palace for himself?

I took a seat all the same and opened my father's diary on my lap as the rays of the moon fell over us from above.

We sat there for over an hour as I listed out all the power words for the Imperial Star and Geraldine made note of the things it could do on a piece of star damned papyrus she'd cast with her earth magic, using a pen made of bark and some organic ink she'd conjured too.

Tory and Darcy repeated each word as I spoke it, though it was clear the Heirs were memorising them too as time went on, their faces full of concentration. And I hoped that didn't mean they were getting ideas about using the star if they ever claimed the throne. It was meant for the Vegas, and I could feel the Zodiac Guild brand itching beneath the skin of my forearm at the idea of someone else wielding its power.

I reached the final empty page of the diary and I ran my thumb over the blank paper, trying to feel out any lasting sensation of my father there, sad that this was the end of his notes for me.

Geraldine rolled up the papyrus and cast a strong wooden case for it before sliding it inside and sealing it up tight.

"Righty-ho, that was a true and wonderous night. But my cockles are tired and I must say fair the well so that I might go and tend my Lady Petunia before the night is out."

"Why can't I tend your Petunia?" Max pouted and Geraldine smacked him around the head with the wooden case.

"Because you are fiddlesome flatfish, that's why Maxy boy. Perhaps if you gave more thought to your nolly then you could water my lawn until the day is done." She walked up to the ice wall, carving a door in it and stepping out into the night.

"What's a nolly?" Max muttered, a hopeless frown pulling at his brow but no one had an answer for him.

"Is that a star sign?" Darcy asked suddenly as she leaned close to me and the scent of strawberries carried from her like the sweetest temptation.

"Hm?" I asked, too distracted by her full lips and large eyes to do anything but stare at her. She tapped the page my thumb was still on and I looked down, finding two small Gemini symbols had appeared at the top of the paper.

"What the fuck…" I breathed.

She brushed her finger over one of the symbols, a light suddenly burning from within it. "Holy shit. Tory, get over here," she urged.

Tory moved to my other side and Darcy guided her hand down onto the other symbol, making it illuminate too and suddenly light spilled out all across the otherwise blank page, revealing star sign after star sign, all of them forming a zodiac ring surrounding the image of a rising sun.

The details were beautiful, delicate lines joining the signs together and hand drawn images of the constellations surrounding the circle. Beyond them were drawings of precious gemstones which were linked to each of the star signs. I'd taught classes on this, how these gemstones could enhance the gifts of each sign when used in various magical practices, but something about these specific stones gave a ring of power to the image which made the hairs along the back of my neck stand to attention.

A handwritten note was revealed below it from my father and my gut tugged at finding another connection to him, feeling him so close in that moment that it was like he was looking over my shoulder.

"What is it?" Darius asked and I read the words aloud as everyone perked up to listen.

"Six were found and six were lost. These are the stones of the original twelve. All must be united to restore balance to the kingdom and reform the Zodiac Guild. Find the six we recovered within the Chalice of Flames."

"What does that mean?" Tory asked curiously as I cut my thumb open on my fang and reached into the air before me, carving my fingers through the moonlight and summoning the chalice to my fingertips. I drew it from the very atmosphere and the others watched in awe as the beautiful silver cup caught the light of the moon.

Latin words inscribed on its side in beautiful calligraphy captured my attention.

Ego meum sanguinem confirmo in Vega regali acie.

"I pledge my blood to the Vega royal line," I translated.

My father had spoken of these words earlier in his diary; when it was time to initiate new members to the Guild, they had to speak them, and I had to admit it gave me a thrill to think of reforming it.

I examined the warm metal carefully, hunting for any sign of gemstones inlaid within its gleaming surface, but there was nothing there.

Darcy took the cup from my hand, tipping it over to look at the bottom and suddenly six beautiful gemstones cascaded out of the cup onto the snow at my feet.

"Ooh, so shiny," she breathed, leaning down to pick up a fat diamond as Darius let out a growl of possessiveness, rushing forward to gather up some of the others as he knelt in the snow.

"Those are not yours, Darius." Tory grabbed them from him, but he had that wild glint in his eyes which he always got around treasure, trying to prise them back out of her fingers.

"I'll look after them," he said firmly. "Give them to me."

Xavier whinnied a laugh as Darius tried to get the diamond from Darcy's fist and I swooped down to take hold of it myself, holding it above his head to examine it in the firelight.

"The diamond is aligned with Aries," I said as Darius tried to grab it from me.

I tossed it into the air, making him drop the others as he tried to catch it and I plucked those up from the snow as he fell on the diamond.

"Moonstone for Gemini," I said, running my thumb over the beautiful opalescent rock in my palm. All of them were the same oval shape and size, as wide as my thumb and perfectly smooth. I could feel the weight of the power in these stones, all of them more pristine than any I had ever seen.

"What's this one?" Darcy asked as she pointed to a dark red stone and Xavier, Seth, Caleb and Max all stood up to get a better look.

"Ruby for Cancer," I said as Darius rounded on me again, his eyes locking on the gems in my palm.

"Give them to me," he commanded, but the Heirs caught hold of his shoulders to keep him back, his fist still locked tight around the diamond.

"These aren't yours, they belong to the Guild," Tory said with a grin. "So unless you wanna sign up, you can't play with them."

"Never," Darius hissed.

I rolled the light green gemstone over in my hand next. "That's Peridot for-"

"Leo," Darius finished in a snarl. "My star sign. My gemstone. *Mine*."

"Calm down, bro," Xavier tried, but Darius was in a Dragon treasure frenzy, his eyes flashing gold and smoke spilling from his mouth.

Tory handed me the one she'd managed to get hold of the final of the six, and Darcy's eyes lit up at the sight of the incredible blue sapphire.

"This is for Virgo," I said, the light of the moon making the gem glitter beautifully.

"I'll keep them safe," Darius insisted.

"Can I see the diamond?" Tory asked, holding out her hand but Darius's fist only tightened around it.

The Heirs wrestled him down onto his back and Seth sat on his chest while Caleb used his Vampire strength to prise his fingers apart.

"No!" Darius snarled as Max snagged it and tossed it to me.

"Bad Dragon," Tory teased but Darius just fought harder to escape the others who were having a whole lot of trouble restraining him.

I slid all six of them back into the chalice and guided the cup back into the moonlight, the whole thing disappearing just before a Dragon collided with me.

I fell off my seat, hitting my back on the ground as Darius clawed at my hands in desperation.

"Bring them back," he ordered, his eyes bright gold and narrowed to slits.

"Nah, I'm good." I smiled mockingly and he growled deep in his chest in frustration. "But let me know if you change your mind on becoming a Guild member. I'm gonna be recruiting soon. Maybe I could make you the keeper of the stones if you do."

"Asshole," he muttered as he got up, but I could see the tension leaving his posture now that the gemstones were out of sight.

I pushed myself upright, picking up the diary which was on Darcy's lap and finding the page blank again where the zodiac circle had been.

"I guess we need to find the rest of these…"

"And how are we gonna do that?" Tory questioned with a frown.

"Hm…gemstones like that are very rare. There must be some record of them," I said thoughtfully. "But unfortunately, the book I need to tell us more is in my office back at Zodiac Academy. I have a tome called Stones of the Sky that lists all known powerful stones in Solaria dating back over two thousand years."

"Of course you do," Darcy said with a teasing smile and I grinned at her.

"Well it's no good to us there," Caleb sighed. "How are we gonna get it?"

"I'll ask Gabriel in the morning," I said. "Maybe there's another version we can get hold of…though that was a particularly rare edition my father gave me. If he wanted me to find these stones, maybe there was a reason he gave me that book."

"Do you really think we need some random gems? What's the Guild good for anyway?" Max asked. "Seems like a load of old traditional bullshit to me. And it's not like the Vegas are gonna rule anymore anyway."

Tory swung a punch into his arm. "You sure about that, big man?"

He grinned in reply, letting water slip between his fingers in a challenge as he faced her.

"We can find out here and now if you're looking to get your ass beat?" he offered and the look in Tory's eyes said she was damn tempted by that.

"Lance's dad wouldn't have gone to all this effort to make sure he knew about this stuff if it wasn't important," Darcy said, drawing everyone's attention back to the matter at hand and I nodded my agreement.

"Fine, we'll find the mystical rocks or whatever. But right now, I'm sleepy," Seth said through a yawn.

"Here." Xavier stepped toward me suddenly, slitting his thumb open with a blade of ice in his palm. "You need the blood for the elixir, right?" he mumbled and I smiled in thanks, creating a small vile of ice in my palm and collecting what I needed from him before sealing it over and putting it in my pocket.

I melted the wall of ice around us and we started heading back to The Burrows as I fell into contemplative silence over how I might get hold of that book. It wasn't like we could go marching back onto campus to get it. It was about the most dangerous place for us in Solaria right now short of the false king's throne room.

I fell to the back of the group as the guards greeted us, keeping enough of a distance from the twins that I didn't cast any kind of shame on them with my presence. The guards glanced at me all the same, their noses wrinkling and more quiet words passing between them as they cut me down to size.

I'd known being Power Shamed would suck, but this was even worse than I'd imagined. It was like I had a constant brand on my forehead marking me as infectious, and I didn't know how I was going to stand a lifetime of it. Especially as all I had wanted for so long was to claim Darcy publicly as mine, but now I was forced to keep that secret all over again. It was insufferable, and I knew she wasn't happy about it either. There just wasn't another option.

When we returned to the tunnels and made it back to the royal quarters, Darcy looked back to find me, a need blazing in her eyes that I wanted to fulfil.

The others said goodnight as she dropped behind them and by the time she reached my side, we were alone and the air was thick with want.

"Stop keeping your distance from me around the rebels," she said, a crease forming between her eyes as I cocked my head to one side.

"It's for the best, beautiful," I replied as I glanced over my shoulder to make sure no one was there watching us.

She caught my hand, towing me into the royal quarters and down the side passage that led to the private bathhouses before drawing me to a halt.

"What have I told you about making decisions that are for my best interest?" she said sternly as the darkness swallowed us up, the flicker of firelight from the sconce at the far end of the tunnel only just about reaching us.

"I'm Power Shamed, Blue, I don't think you're understanding the magnitude of what that means," I said seriously.

"And I don't think you're understanding the fact that I don't care what it means. I'll fight to make everyone see how worthy you are. I'll make them all forget this stupid title placed upon you," she said fiercely and I fucking loved her for that.

"It's not that simple." I toyed with a lock of her hair, loving the way the dark blue colour glittered deeply in the firelight.

Lust was making my thoughts hazy as I stared at this captivating being before me, wanting her in every way, always.

"Yes, it is," she insisted. "You're my equal. The man I'm in love with. And I won't let you keep acting like you're some lesser Fae now. In fact, I want to prove how much I think of you…"

She ran her hand down my chest, sucking her lower lip before slowly sinking down to her knees on the hard stone floor, making my pulse go through the fucking roof.

"No. Get up, Blue," I growled, leaning down to pull her up but she knocked my hands away, a dangerous fire flaring in her eyes.

"I will kneel for you as you would kneel for me. You're my king and I'll rub my knees raw for you until you're sated," she said powerfully and I was suddenly so hard for her I could barely stand it.

She squeezed my cock through my sweatpants, her eyes on mine as I rested one hand on the wall behind her and gave in to her desires. I was only fucking Fae after all and with those words on her lips and the way her large green eyes were drinking me in, I was undone. Totally, fucking shattered into broken glass for her.

She tugged my pants down, freeing the full length of me and leaning forward to run her tongue up the underside of my cock. I groaned with the need for more as she teased me with that weaponised tongue, up and down before taking me into her hand and sucking the tip of my twitching head between her lips.

"Blue," I sighed, my free hand falling to her hair as she took me in deeper, her mouth hot, wet and perfect around me as she started to pump the base of my cock.

I swore as she flicked her tongue over the head of my length in a way that had me groaning and wanting to stay in this moment for as long as I could.

"So fucking beautiful," I growled, my breaths coming heavier as her hand glided up and down my shaft in firm, tight strokes that were begging me to fall apart for her already. "Look at me, Blue."

Her eyes flicked up to meet mine and I braced myself more forcefully on the wall as she ruled me with that single look. Her lips were reddened and glistening as my fingers pushed through her hair and I took over from her, driving my hips forward to fuck that perfect mouth.

My fangs snapped out as she took me deeper and deeper into her throat, moaning like she loved every second of pleasing me, and that sound alone sent another rush of blood to my cock as I fought off the inevitable release she was demanding of me.

Her eyes remained on mine, the flames of her Order burning at the edges of them as her tongue glided along the underside of my cock once more.

My muscles grew taut and a lock of hair fell into my eyes as I stared down at her, transfixed by this creature who owned me right down to the worthless dust that made up my soul.

Her hand slid around to squeeze my ass, her nails biting into my flesh as her eyes blazed with a command for me to come. And I was too far fucking gone to even try and hold off any longer.

I thrust deep into her mouth, holding her where I wanted her as I finished with a growl, pleasure ripping through me like an earthquake.

She swallowed every drop of me and licked and sucked her way along my cock as I shuddered through the aftershock of my absolute ruin.

Then I dragged her to her feet, pushed her against the wall and sank my tongue between those gifted lips, tasting myself on her and getting high on having her do that to me. She was everything. The brightest fucking star that existed in the universe and for some unknown reason she wanted *me*.

I tugged my sweatpants up with one hand, kissing her deep and slow, my hand still locked tight in her hair as her hot tongue chased mine and a soft moan spilled from her mouth into my own.

"You have me leashed and collared, Darcy Vega. I'll always be close by, watching you from the dark for as long as you'll have me there." I kissed the corner of her mouth, my fangs grazing her lip as the hunger in me grew sharper.

She raised her hand, casting a razor blade of ice between her fingers and slicing it down her thumb. I fell on it ravenously, sucking her thumb into my mouth as she watched me with hooded eyes, the taste of her blood like ecstasy on my tongue.

"You are meant for the sunlight, Lance Orion. So you'll stand with me in it or else we'll stay in the dark together," she said hotly and I met her gaze, the taste of that very sunlight she spoke of on my tongue now. She was my destiny, and there was no two ways about that. I would follow her so far into the light that I'd go blind, or so deep into the dark that I'd be lost forever.

"Is that an order, my queen?" I asked, a taunt in my voice as I slid my hand into her sweatpants, finding her pussy soaking and bare for me.

Before she could answer that, I drove two fingers inside her and she tipped her head back with a moan that made me grow hard again already. And I knew I'd spend every hour left of this night either inside her or tasting her, because she didn't get to make me come without me returning the favour tenfold.

"Yes," she gasped breathlessly as I fucked her with my hand and watched her crumble for me. "That's a goddamn order, my king."

"Do the angry words of the day, sir!" Seth cried as he bounced up and down in his seat. "It's not the same without the angry words of the day."

I looked around the classroom Caleb, Seth and the twins had created for our daily lessons in a cavern off of the royal quarters.

There were other classrooms set up in the main part of The Burrows for other young Fae who were living here to use for their education too, but this class was special. For one, it was mine, and secondly, it had a very small circle of students who I was determined to educate to the best of my ability with every spare hour we could find. Washer was teaching classes of his own, and there were volunteers among the rebels too to ensure none of the youth were missing out on their education, but I didn't let him interfere with this group unless they specifically needed water Elemental training.

Though it had been constructed hastily, the classroom was a stunning example of the power of earth magic. Each desk had been personally made for the Fae who used it, their names and Elements engraved into the petrified grey wood that had been grown into shape and then hardened to stone. The walls were tall and a domed roof hung far above our heads, a silvery pool of water suspended there with pale Faelights hanging inside it to give the illusion of sunlight in our underground hideaway.

The dirt walls had been coated with pale grey tiles, each decorated with little zodiac symbols or carvings of Fae in various Order forms. There was a space at the back of the room for physical lessons and an arena that had been cordoned off with vines which sat within a magical shield to keep any wayward magic contained within it.

There was also a glittering pool of water in one corner and a roaring fire which sat behind my desk as well as a flourishing green area full of flowers for earth lessons, and lastly a corner filled with windmills and ribbons that spun in a magical breeze.

This wasn't the only part of The Burrows that was getting a makeover either, with so many earth Elementals trapped underground with little to do with their time, the place was becoming an underground palace which the Heirs seemed to feel much more at home in.

Caleb and Tory had taken charge of the last few supply runs and now everyone in our group was dressed like fucking kings and queens. I wasn't exactly complaining either. Darcy had put in an order with them for skimpy underwear which I enjoyed peeling off with my teeth or ripping to shreds whenever I got the opportunity. She held a mini funeral for the remnants of them most mornings with a tiny pout on her face, tossing the bits in the trash, but I wasn't going to mourn the fuckers when I enjoyed destroying them so much.

I glanced through my notes for today's class. I was teaching them everything I knew, ensuring none of them missed out on their education while we were stuck down here in The Burrows waiting for a chance to attack Lionel.

Between teaching classes of his own, Gabriel spent time in the amplifying chamber we'd worked together to build, trying to *see* paths forward not only to get to Lionel, but to find the gemstones my father had wanted me to acquire. But with each passing week, we were all going a little bit more insane over waiting for opportunities.

Being stuck down here was suffocating, no matter how much work was going in to making the place look beautiful and if it wasn't for Gabriel's constant assurance that venturing out of here to fight Lionel would end in our destruction, I was sure we all would have done it already.

"For the hundredth time, it is not a real classroom and you do not have to call me sir," I said in exasperation, pressing my fingers into my eyes for a moment.

Tory was sitting on Darius's desk with his hand inching higher and higher up her skirt as she stroked his hair while Max, Xavier and Caleb were throwing an ice ball between them at the back of the class. Darcy was chewing on a pencil, eye-fucking me to no end which was distracting as hell while Seth kept talking incessantly and asking questions that had nothing to do with the lesson. Geraldine was the only one paying rapt attention, sitting with her back ramrod straight and her Atlas in hand as she listened.

"Right, that's enough!" I barked and they all stilled.

I hadn't wanted to do this. I'd been trying to teach them without going full professor, that part of my life well and truly in the past. But this was getting ridiculous.

"Miss Vega, get your ass in your own seat." I sent a blast of air at Tory, sending her flying down into the chair beside Darius, making her lips pop open in surprise. "Rigel, Acrux and Altair, if you throw one more fucking ice ball in my classroom, I will blast you through the wall and you can forget about coming back here to learn a single thing." I caught their ice ball with a whip of air, sending it flying into the door so it smashed into a thousand pieces, and the three of them slowly sank down into their seats in shock.

"What would happen if a Fae with a big Order form swallowed three people then shifted back into their Fae form? Do you think they'd die? I think they might die," Seth mused aloud. "Actually, I know some annoying people we could send as bait to Lionel, then when he eats them, we could shoot an Order Suppressant dart up his ass and bang. Dead Dragon. Annoying people eaten. Win – win."

"Capella, if you ask another pointless question this lesson, I will force feed you three people in your Werewolf form and we'll put your theory to the test," I snarled, stealing the air from his lungs as he opened his mouth to respond.

"So hot," Darcy said under her breath as she watched me, shifting in her seat as desire filled her eyes.

"Miss Vega, if you keep looking at me like that, I will bring you up here, bend you over my desk and spank you in front of everyone. Is that what you want?" I demanded, trying to ignore the way my cock was twitching for her.

She considered that for a second then glanced at her sister and shook her head, her cheeks pinking as she sat back in her seat and withdrew the pencil from her lips.

Silence fell and I looked around the quiet classroom with my eyebrows arching. *Well holy fucking shit, I guess that did it.*

I turned to the chalkboard that had been made for me by Geraldine, writing across it in bold, capitalised letters before striking a fierce underline beneath it.

YOU CANNOT DEFEAT LIONEL ACRUX IF YOU CAN'T EVEN DO

BASIC FUCKING SPELLS.

I twisted around to glare at them all and Geraldine started jotting down what I'd written.

"You've already lost a bunch of time to Highspell's bullshit classes, are you going to waste any more of it?" I demanded and they all shook their heads at me like obedient little mice. *Perfect.* "Right then." I turned back to the board, writing today's objective there. "Aura detection is imperative when facing your enemies. It can be very subtle, and in the current circumstances, considering the murders that have been committed, it is more important than ever that we be vigilant. Auras can give away a Fae's true intentions."

"I'm a Siren, though. I can detect people's emotions easily, I don't need aura training," Max said dismissively and Geraldine twisted around in her seat.

"Auras are different to emotions, you stagnant stingray," she said and he pouted.

"Correct," I agreed. "You may be able to detect emotion, Rigel, but if your enemies have strong emotional shields from you or if they are simply enjoying doing bad deeds, how will you be able to detect them any clearer than someone enjoying their dinner? Auras are more effective in reading a person's intentions. It is a more subtle, and far more difficult skill to perfect, yet it can give a more accurate read on someone's character."

"If you're so good at it, then why haven't you found the murderer yet, sir?" Caleb asked, his eyes shooting over to Seth beside him who was fighting to feed himself air through the block I'd cast on his throat.

He was half keeled over the table and I flicked my fingers to release him from choking so he started gasping down air.

"There's hundreds of people in The Burrows and most of them want absolutely nothing to do with me, Altair," I gritted out. "If I can train you all in this well, then perhaps one of you will have more success than me in finding the culprit."

They finally all gave me their full attention as I started explaining the intricacies of detecting auras. But before I could get them trying it out on each other, the door burst open and Hamish walked in with a handkerchief held to his mouth.

"Lance Orion, I need to speak with y-" He retched into the handkerchief and I released a weary sigh. "You," he forced out, then waved his hand, clearly casting an illusion over me as my face dropped into a scowl.

"Why did you make him look like a lamp?" Darcy growled as Hamish moved toward me through the room.

"It's just a Milly-modicom easier to address an inanimate object than him, my lady," Hamish gushed.

"I find I can get used to it if I focus on a point just over his shoulder, Papa," Geraldine said while my hands curled into fists.

"What do you want, Hamish?" I growled and he reared over, clutching his stomach as he retched, making irritation flare through me.

The Heirs cracked up as Hamish dabbed the corners of his mouth with his handkerchief like a little bit of vomit had come up that time.

"Sorry, it's the shame, you see?" Hamish muttered. "It's quite potent."

"Well let's have this conversation at double the speed then, yeah?" I pushed, wanting this over with as Hamish nodded, apparently unable to look at me even in lamp form, the bulb flickering as I spoke.

"We need to discuss you being the Master of the Zodiac Guild." He dry retched several times before he was able to continue. "I am here to offer myself in substitution for that role. It will cause quite the hullabaloo and billabalong if we ask our most loyal royalists to join the Guild under the management of a Power Sha-" He retched. "A Power Sha-" He retched again and I carved a hand down my face in exasperation.

"Enough, Hamish," I said. "My position isn't one just chosen by me, it was by my father and the stars too. I can't do what you're asking of me. Destiny decided this. I can't change it."

"He's the rightful Guild Master anyway," Darcy said firmly and Hamish looked at her as he wiped a line of sweat from his brow.

"But what will become of the gallant Guild? How will it ever be reformed? No one will sign up to it under the rule of a shamed Sharleen," he said in horror, then fell to his knees and gripped Darcy's hand. "Please, my lady, think of the children."

"What children? And Orion is the right person for the job, it was his fate. Why can't you all let go of this stupid Power Shamed crap?" she demanded and Hamish buckled forward, retching like a cat with a hairball lodged firmly in its throat, his back arching and bowing as he heaved up nothing but air and the Heirs burst out laughing.

"Oh sweet, sensitive daddipops." Geraldine jumped from her seat, helping him upright and he swayed a little as she guided him to the door. "We shall overcome this titanic task. There must be a way to see past his...*shame*," she whispered the last word and Hamish battled with another retch as she led him out the door.

I folded my arms, flicking my fingers to dispel the illusion he'd put on me while a gnawing sensation in my gut told me maybe Hamish was right. No one was ever going to respect me as the Guild Master. How was I supposed rebuild it when most of the people in this place wouldn't even look at me?

The Guild elixir would be ready tonight and I didn't even have a single member in mind to initiate, because the Heirs certainly weren't going to pledge themselves to the Vegas and between Geraldine and her father, I wasn't sure they could bear to join up while I was in charge either.

Fuck.

I met Blue's gaze and she calmed some of my worries with that single look. Her belief in me was iron clad, but that didn't change the truth of the situation. I'd lost the respect of nearly every Fae in Solaria, so how was I supposed to resurrect an ancient royal society for the Vegas?

Maybe Hamish was right, maybe it would be better if I was able to pass on the baton. But I was bound to this role now, there was nothing I could do about it. And as I brushed my fingers over my inner forearm where the Guild mark was hidden, I couldn't help but feel protective of the role anyway.

My father had wanted this for me, the twins' mother had seen me standing in this place, but had I taken a wrong turn on the path of fate somewhere? Had they not foreseen me becoming Power Shamed in all of this? Or had they always expected me to pass on the role to someone more worthy?

I turned back to the board, writing out a few notes on auras as chatter broke out among everyone. My heart sank into the depths of my chest because

I couldn't help but feel like I was letting Blue and her sister down, and worst of all, it made me fear I really was as useless as the world now believed I was.

DARIUS

CHAPTER ELEVEN

I lay with Roxy in my arms, her dark hair spilling across my chest and her breathing heavy. There was a smile playing around her lips and every now and then she released a breathy kind of sigh.

I'd hardly slept myself. In fact, at this point I was using so many alertness spells and drinking so many wakeful potions which I'd convinced one of the rebels to brew for me that I barely slept at all. I just didn't want to waste a moment of the time I had on sleep.

Eight weeks had already passed, and I felt like I'd barely stolen a fraction of the future I wished I could claim with her. I'd let that time slip by like grains of sand running through an hourglass and I knew I really needed to start making preparations for what would have to happen after my bargain with the stars ran out.

I'd already been spending any spare time I had with Xavier, helping him hone his magic so that he would be ready to step into my position on the Council once my time ran out, though he just thought I wanted to help him get stronger for the war.

The ache in my chest over the reality of my fate wasn't even about all the things I would lose and wouldn't have the chance to experience. It was about this girl who owned my heart and the future she wouldn't get to live out with me. About my brother and the Heirs and Lance and the pain my loss would cause them. That was where the guilt stemmed. Yet still I hadn't spoken a word of the deal I'd made with any of them.

Perhaps at heart I was a coward. But that wasn't why I was hiding this truth from them. I needed them to focus on the chances we would get to strike at my father and those who followed him. And I knew if this came to light, they'd all want to work on finding a way to twist my fate just as they had when they were determined to see our Star Crossed bond fall.

But this wasn't like that. I'd struck this deal of my own free will. I'd given my life for hers and her sister's because I knew that they were far more deserving of life than I was anyway. I may have hated my father and was working against him with all I had, but at heart I was always going to be the creature he'd created. But this girl in my arms was so much more than that. Worth so much more than me.

Roxy shifted a little, rolling onto her back and biting that full bottom lip of hers as a soft moan escaped her again and my cock hardened at the sound. She was as insatiable as I was and this freedom we'd claimed to own each other in the way we chose had torn down any final barriers that had been there between us.

Every night we fucked like animals then fell into each other's arms panting and grinning and telling each other stories about every little thing we could think of. I wanted to know all there was to know about her and the places she'd grown up in, the bond between her and her sister and everything she'd been through, and she was just as interested in getting to know me. Neither of us held back, we didn't shield the ugly truth of the things we'd survived and there was a freedom and a beauty in that. For so long, my secrets hadn't even been mine to share. My father had locked them away inside me with his Dark Coercion so that I couldn't tell a soul even if I'd wanted to.

Roxy never looked at me with pity when I recounted the times he'd beaten me or the cruel lessons he'd forced me to learn. Instead, her eyes would flare with this unending hatred for my father and a lust for his death that made my heart thrash with the knowledge that she cared for me so deeply.

And when she explained about the way she'd lived, how she'd learned to steal to ensure the survival of her and her sister, I didn't show her any pity either. Only pride in the strength and fortitude she'd found to survive and rise up through the shitty fate they'd been dealt to become the powerful woman she was now.

She hardly even had any nightmares these days, seeming to have finally found peace in her sleep as she lay curled in my arms and only seeking Max out for help for a few moments here and there. I knew there was no instant fix to the scars my father had left on her memories, but she had so much good in her life now that it seemed like she was able to at least live in that feeling now, no longer plagued by the things she'd endured. They'd just made her harder, stronger and more like the Fae queen she'd been born to be.

Roxy moaned again, a single phrase spilling from her lips which made it more than clear what she was dreaming about and brought a cocky grin to my lips.

"More, Darius."

And I wasn't going to deny my girl when she asked so nicely.

I pressed a kiss to her neck which had goosebumps erupting across her skin and her spine arching against the bed, her firm nipples making me groan as I moved my mouth lower in need of them.

I ran my hand down her bare side, finding the tattoo she'd gotten to link herself to me and caressing the skin there before sucking her nipple into my mouth and making her moan a little louder.

I swear her skin tasted like fucking cotton candy, so sweet and intoxicating I could never get enough of it. She began to writhe beneath me, but as I glanced up I found her eyes still closed while she continued to dance the line of sleep and wakefulness. And to be fair to her, I'd worked really hard at exhausting her last night so she could probably do with the sleep more than she needed another orgasm. A good man might have left her to rest. But I was never going to pretend I was a good man when it came to her.

I shifted to kneel between her legs, pushing her thighs wide and looking down at her body with so much lust and need pulsing through me that I knew even if I had an entire lifetime of loving her, it would never be enough. But I didn't have a lifetime. I had ten more months. So I would have to fit as much love and lust and pleasure into that time as I could while aiming to wipe my father from this world and leaving it safe for her to live in after I was gone.

I wondered if she would find someone else after me, my gaze running to the priceless ruby pendant she wore around her neck and a possessive snarl building in my body at the mere thought of anyone else ever touching her again.

Perhaps I should have wanted her to find love when I was gone. But I wasn't a man built to be selfless and the mere thought of it sent a wild kind of fury burning through my limbs alongside a hungry desire to spend this year claiming her so thoroughly that I knew no other man would ever be able to live up to the memory of me.

Selfish? Yeah. But fuck it. She was mine.

I dropped down between her thighs, that unfair anger still burning hot through my flesh as I pushed her legs wide and ran my tongue straight up the centre of her wet pussy, a hungry growl erupting from me at the taste of her as I found her so turned on already.

I sucked her clit into my mouth and Roxy gasped as she woke fully, a curse leaving her lips as I sucked hard before going back to licking her with the hunger of a starving man.

I was furious at the mere thought of someone else even thinking about touching her and the beast in me was rising to the surface of my skin demanding I claim her fully and remind her of who she belonged to now.

Roxy moaned loudly, bucking her hips against me as I licked and sucked at her, fucking my face while she ran her hands over her tits and teased her nipples to gain even more pleasure.

I growled against her sweet pussy, driving two fingers into her as she moaned for me and making her come with just a few thrusts of my hand.

Her spine arched and she cried out beautifully as her wet pussy clamped tight around my fingers and I continued to lick her clit until she stopped pulsing around me, making her pleasure linger for as long as I could.

The moment she dropped back against the mattress, I caught hold of her hips and flipped her over, claiming this moment of weakness while her body was spent to dominate her before she fought me for control again.

I gripped her round ass in my hands, squeezing her flesh and groaning as I drove my cock into that slick pussy of hers, keeping her flattened against the bed as I did so and growling her name as I felt the perfect tightness of her surrounding my shaft.

I fucked her hard, forcing her body down beneath mine as her cries of pleasure filled the room and the bed slammed into the wall so hard that I could hear the wood creaking in protest.

I pressed my chest to her back, kissing and biting her neck as her hands fisted in the sheets and she cursed me out between the thrusts of my hips.

"Mine," I snarled in her ear as she fought to push back against me, the curve of her ass feeling so good as I drove into her that I couldn't help but push a hand between us and press my fingers against her other opening.

"Jesus," she gasped which I'd long since figured out meant 'hell yes' in her language and I grinned as I pushed my fingers into her ass and fucked her pussy even harder with my solid cock.

Roxy came hard and fast, her body taking hold of mine and forcing a roar of pleasure from my lips as I spilled myself deep inside her and bit down on her shoulder in a dominating move that was born of the beast in me. I couldn't fucking stop myself when I was around her, she made my animal rise up and pay attention, and it needed to maintain its hold over her just as desperately as I did.

I pulled out of her and fell onto the bed beside her, dragging her into my arms and grinning as she tried to scowl at me.

"Asshole," she muttered, reaching out to run her fingers along my jaw and making my smile widen, which was bound to only incite her more.

"I can't help it," I protested, knowing she was objecting to the dominating thing, but I'd also figured out that as much as she protested to me doing that to her, she also came so much harder whenever I did. Roxy may not have been submissive by nature but she sure as hell liked it when I managed to force her beneath me while we fucked.

"You'll pay for that," she said, her lips twitching with amusement which I knew meant she was already thinking up how best to turn the tables on me next time. She'd managed to distract me enough to tie me up with her earth magic more than once now so that she could take charge and ride me instead of me pushing her down beneath me, but I couldn't say I had any real objections to that kind of punishment.

"I get possessive sometimes." I shrugged, gripping her ass in one hand and tugging her closer so that I could kiss those full lips and taste her some more.

"What was it this time?" she teased. "Did you see me smiling at some other guy again?"

I scoffed like that was ridiculous even though I had kinda gone all Alpha on her and dragged her into a side tunnel to fuck her against a wall after I'd seen her laughing with that rebel asshole with the dimples last week. But that wasn't the point.

"Dragons are all about treasure," I explained and she tilted her head to the side as she looked at me, her dark hair falling to brush against my arm and revealing the teeth marks I'd left on her shoulder when I'd gone full animal and bitten her.

"Yeah, I noticed the huge chest of it taking up half of our room," she teased. "Not to mention the fact that I wake up with gold coins stuck to my ass every other day." She reached over and plucked a coin from the mattress behind me to prove my point and I smirked at her.

"The most important thing to my kind is finding the most valuable treasure you can imagine and then hoarding it away to protect and keep safe away from any and every threat to it. And you, Roxanya Vega, are more important to me than all the gold and jewels in the entire world combined. I'd go without them for the rest of my days if it meant I got to steal a moment in your arms with you looking at me the way you are right now. There is nothing I wouldn't do to keep you safe and to make sure you stay mine. I want to possess you with all the greed and wrath of the monster in me and I want to own you with the desire of a thousand Dragons guarding a priceless treasure, but more than all of that, I just want to love you like this. Endlessly and brutally and possessively. Now that you're mine, I won't give you up for anything."

"Not even the throne?" she teased, the one remaining point of tension between us raising its head while I shook mine.

"You'll make a stunning Councillor's wife," I teased and she punched me in the pec hard enough to bruise. "Ow," I complained as she gave me a look that warned the next one would be harder.

"*You'll* make a gorgeous king consort," she tossed back. "You know, pretty, good in the sack...silent."

A laugh burst from my lips and I dove at her, wrestling her down beneath me as she fought like an alley cat, a squeal of laughter leaving her even as she tried to kick me in the damn balls.

But before we could fall any further into the trap of each other's arms, a terrified scream echoed through the tunnel outside our room and we both fell still.

"Darcy," Roxy gasped even though it hadn't sounded at all like her sister screaming.

But after Cal and Seth had discovered those dead guards weeks ago, we'd all been worried about the people we loved down here.

I rolled off of her, tossing her a pair of jeans and a black sweater before pulling a grey tracksuit on and grabbing some sneakers.

We were out the door and hurrying along in a tide of bodies within moments and Roxy called out in relief as we spotted her sister's blue hair in the group ahead of us. Lance was with her and he caught her arm, tugging her to a halt so that we could catch up to them.

Roxy hurried forward and grabbed Darcy's hand, the two of them exchanging relieved looks and muttered reassurances as I moved to stand beside them.

"What's going on?" I asked, looking to Lance as he strained his ears to listen for some more information.

"I think another body has been found," he said in a dark tone, meeting my eye with the same fear in his gaze as I felt in my soul.

If someone was somehow striking at the rebels down here, then it was more than clear to both of us who their real targets would be and the girls standing between us were it. But we'd made vows upon the stars when we'd entered The Burrows and anyone who came here had to swear they meant them no harm. So maybe we were wrong, but something in my gut told me we weren't. I just didn't know how they were pulling it off without Hamish feeling the vows break.

Dragon fire flickered through me at the thought of anyone trying to hurt the twins and I placed an arm around Roxy's shoulders, tugging her close to my side as I narrowed my eyes at the people swarming past us.

"We should go see who it was," Darcy said urgently, taking Roxy's hand and tugging her into a jog as she slipped out of my grip instantly.

"Tory too, huh?" Lance muttered as we fell into step, hurrying to keep up with them as we strode down the huge tunnel. The earth Elementals had been hard at work here too and the walls were all lined with grey stone now, a decorative, vaulted ceiling making the tunnels feel less oppressive and plenty of water and fire features decorating the walls. "Darcy refuses to let me protect her as much as I want to."

"That's because they're stubborn as all hell," I grumbled, smirking as Roxy heard me and flipped me off over her shoulder.

"Yeah. Remind me why we're with them again," Lance teased but as the two of us continued to jog along behind them like a pair of whipped little guard dogs while blatantly checking them out, the answer to that question seemed kind of pointless.

We made it to the dining cavern before finding a huge crowd bottlenecked at the entrance to the tunnel which led down to the communal bathhouses.

"Make way for the true queens!" Geraldine bellowed, a doggish bark following her demand which had the rest of the rebels leaping to attention and backing out of the tunnel to let the Vegas pass.

We kept close behind them and I tensed briefly as another Vampire shot up behind us, relaxing as I recognised Cal when he fell into step beside me and let Seth drop down from his back.

"Have you seen Max, Xavier and my mom this morning?" I asked them anxiously, glancing around to look for the people I loved in hopes of spotting one of them.

"Yeah, I had to borrow some toothpaste from Max earlier and Xavier was in the room with him," Caleb said, his gaze fixed on the tunnel ahead of us as we walked down it at a fast pace.

"And I saw your mom a few minutes ago making food with Hamish in the kitchens," Seth added. "She called me a naughty pup and chased me out of the room when I tried to steal some cookies. They let the Vegas have anything they want though, so my only snack avenue is through them. At least Tory likes to leave them out for me to find."

He looked a little salty about the situation and I snorted in amusement. I'd never realised my mom had an interest in cooking, but she'd been throwing herself into it wholeheartedly since we'd been here, helping to make all of the meals for the rebels while Hamish hung around her, murmuring sweet praises and stealing kisses from her whenever he thought no one was paying attention.

I wanted to protest against the idea of my mom hooking up with a damn Grus, but she just looked so fucking happy whenever I saw her with him that it was impossible for me to make any kind of issue about them being together. She deserved something good and someone to really care for her like that after spending years shackled to my father.

Lance exchanged a relieved look with me at the knowledge that the people closest to us were okay just before we turned the corner into one of the men's bathhouses and the stench of death hit us hard.

There were lumps of flesh and gore strewn all over the place, pieces of a destroyed body splattered up the walls and a severed head with terror filling his dead eyes lay floating in the middle of the central pool.

"Oh, for the love of the bulbous and everlasting moon!" Geraldine cried.

"What the hell could have done that?" Darcy muttered, her nose wrinkling in disgust as she looked at the remains of the body.

"Plenty of Fae could do that in their Order form," Seth piped up. "Like Dragons or Manticores, or Lions or Bears or Wolves or-"

"A Vampire could do it easily," Caleb added and Seth nodded thoughtfully. "Can anyone see tooth marks? Or claw marks? Someone pass me that arm."

"I'm not touching some gross severed arm, dude," Roxy replied with a shudder.

"No one touch anything!" Geraldine cried. "We must conduct a full investigation."

"Oh my god, I think I know who it is," Darcy breathed, stepping closer to the pool of water as she peered in at the floating head which was slowly circling in the current of the water. "Isn't that the guard who was on duty outside when we went to Wasted Mountain, Lance? Barney Von something?"

"Oh yeah," he agreed as he moved closer to get a look. "That guy was a dick."

Geraldine gasped as she whirled towards him in outrage, but before she could say anything in protest to describing the dead guy as a dick, one of the rebels wailed in recognition.

"Noooo, not Barney Von Bonderville!" The girl rushed forward and started sobbing, and I exchanged a look with the others before we all wordlessly retreated, heading out into the tunnel and hurrying away.

We made our way to the dining hall and I looked up at the vaulted ceiling which had piercing golden stalactites decorating it, the glint of all that gold always tugging on the attention my inner Dragon in the way The Orb once had.

A waterfall tumbled down the back of the cavern into a gleaming pool where a stone seating area was built and symbols of the star signs decorated the wall around it, lit up in gleaming blue Faelights. The pool was full of auras that people had tossed in, making wishes on the stars to win us favour in the war, and I'd seen a few precious crystals in there too which had caught my eye. It was tempting to scoop some of the coins out too, but I guessed it would be a dick move to steal people's wishes.

The tables were made of stone, most of them circular except the large rectangular one in the middle built for the 'true queens' and their entourage. There was a statue of a Phoenix bird beyond it, its wings outstretched and its beak open as if it were releasing a cry, a fire burning at its base and even more coin offerings had been tossed into those flames.

The floor glittered with constellations, marked out across the stone with gleaming jewels and to the right of the room, the wall was painted with an intricate map of Solaria that some of the more artistic Fae were still working on, every corner of our kingdom accounted for from the Polar Capital right down to the Neptian Sea.

The cavern was alive with hushed whispers and suspicious gazes as everyone in the room looked between each other, wondering if the person beside them might just be a killer and I gritted my jaw against the tension. As if we needed something else to worry about while we were trying to prepare to take my father on. Every day there were new laws and announcements which put more and more Fae at risk, and the rebels had been working tirelessly to relocate Tiberian Rats, Sphinxes and Minotaurs as his Nymphs closed in on them.

The Burrows were being expanded daily to house all the new refugees, meaning Seth, Caleb, Geraldine and the twins were spending a lot of their time wielding their earth magic to create a deeper and deeper labyrinth down here to house all of them.

Eugene Dipper had taken full command of the Tiberian Rats and their quarters had been made up of tiny tunnels which no one aside from them could enter in their shifted forms, insisting none of them minded shifting for sleep so that they could take up less space. The only problem was that the Rats required a lot of nesting material and for some unknown reason they had a strong preference for underwear which meant it was going missing from the laundry caverns every damn time any of it was sent to be washed.

The others moved towards the centre of the cavern and I started after them, but a hand grasped my elbow before I could take more than a few steps and I turned to find Gabriel Nox holding my arm and scowling at me. He was shirtless with his wings on display as usual and I arched an eyebrow at him, letting him know I wasn't all that pleased to be stopped by him.

"We need to have a word," he said firmly before turning and grinning in Roxy's direction just before she twisted around to look back for me. He gave her a friendly little wave, making her smile brightly in return like she thought the two of us were doing some cute brother and boyfriend bonding thing or some shit before she turned away again, and he turned a glare on me once more.

"Did you just bullshit my girl?" I asked him and he leaned closer to me, still giving me a death glare.

"Maybe you shouldn't be throwing stones from your glass house, Darius," he hissed.

"What's that supposed to mean?" I asked.

"You tell me - you're the one who doesn't seem to have a future past Christmas Day."

My heart lurched and I gritted my jaw, glancing over towards Caleb and Lance to make sure they hadn't heard him with their Vampire gifts while wondering if there was any way this asshole really had any idea about the deal I'd made with the stars, or if he was just fishing. I could admit that I'd been avoiding him as much as possible since we'd made it back to the group here too, not wanting him to look into my future, but I guessed it was so entwined with Roxy's now that it was impossible for him to miss it. Either way, I didn't want any of the others listening in on this, so I cast a silencing bubble around us and jerked my chin towards an empty passage to our right before ducking into it.

"You don't know what you're talking about," I growled, closing in on him and trying to make him back off with the threat in my posture, but he only looked me in the eyes and sneered.

"I think we both know I do. So tell me, asshole, what deal did you make with the stars to break the bonds placed on you and my sister?" he demanded like he had a right to know my business.

I wanted to punch him in his stupid face. I never had liked this prick.

He was always giggling with Lance over their little private jokes or acting so self-assured because he had the damn Sight. Though I had to admit that he'd saved my ass when it came to Mildred, and if he hadn't taken me to that star damned cave then Roxy and Darcy could well be dead right now.

I turned away from him, stalking a few paces into the dark as I swiped a hand down my face and tried to banish the anger born of my Dragon and think rationally about this. He had The Sight. And even if we weren't close, my connection to Roxy clearly meant enough to him to give him a view of my life, and he'd obviously already figured out that my future ended pretty fucking sharpish on Christmas Day in ten months' time.

The reality of him having *seen* that hit me like a punch to the gut. Yeah, I'd known it was coming. I wasn't a fucking idiot. But I'd also been trying to live for the moment, enjoy the love and life I'd only just begun to sample a taste of since my far too recent liberation from my father's control. It had been eight weeks already, but it didn't feel like that. It felt like a blink of an eye and barely a taste of everything I'd always dreamed I might be able to claim for myself. A year was never going to be enough, but now I could see that it was going to be so brief that it broke me.

I turned back to Gabriel, pain tearing into my chest as I forced myself to face the truth and own up to this.

"They were going to die," I told him, my voice cracking a little as I remembered the visions I'd been forced to endure. "The stars told me their fates and showed me how that fight would play out if I didn't act. Either Roxy or her sister or maybe even both of them would have died just like you told me they would if I didn't make that deal."

"What deal?" he asked, his posture rigid like he was preparing for a blow that he already knew was coming.

I stared at him for several long seconds, knowing the moment I gave voice to this truth that it would become real. I'd lose control of it. Cast it into reality and be forced to deal with whatever came of it if I did.

The words fell from my lips in a rush which left me aching with grief as they escaped me. Because I may have been terrified to lose Roxy when I'd made that deal, I may have been more than willing to trade my life for hers because of how strongly I felt for her. But I hadn't yet experienced what truly getting to love her and be loved by her would feel like. And this bliss which I had stolen for us was rushing to an inevitable end that would only cause her more pain. The one thing I'd sworn never to do again.

"I traded my life for theirs. I get one year to prove to her that I can give her the world then the stars will tear it away from her when they call me into their embrace."

Gabriel's jaw dropped and I could tell he hadn't been able to foresee those words leaving my mouth. Hell, I hadn't even known I was going to tell him until they'd forced their way free. But there it was. The ugly, honest truth of it and now it was cutting him open just as it was carving into me.

"This will destroy her," he breathed, the pain in his eyes on behalf of the girl I loved enough to crack something inside me.

"I know," I choked out, feeling the raw brutality of that truth as I spoke it. "I'm weak. I know I should have stayed away from her. I should have spent this year trying to make her fall out of love with me so that it would hurt less when the time came but I…I'm nothing without her, Gabriel. She's the only girl who ever looked at me and saw the man worth loving within my skin. She didn't see my position or my power or my wealth. She saw *me* and she made me become a better man for her. She's every fantasy I've ever had and every dream I ever dared give thought to, but she's even better than that because she's real. I can't give her up. I might as well drive a blade through my heart right now if I have to."

"Oh fuck," Gabriel exhaled, his eyes glazing with The Sight as he shook his head slowly like he was trying to deny the fate laid out in front of me, but I knew he couldn't. The power of the stars had been so immense in that place that I knew there was no denying them in this. I'd made my bargain with them. There was no changing the price. "I'm sorry, Darius…I can't see any other future for you…"

Gabriel's face crumpled in pain like he was already *seeing* the future that left Roxy with, and in that one look I knew that this would do more harm to her than any of the awful things I'd subjected her to in the past. I'd given my life for hers, but I was the one getting off lightly in that trade.

"I had to do it," I muttered. "I couldn't let her die."

Gabriel nodded hopelessly before stepping forward and pulling me into a tight embrace. It was so unexpected that I only froze, unsure what the hell to make of that from a man who had made it so clear he disliked me since the moment we'd first met.

"Please don't tell the others," I begged. "I know what they'll do. They'll want to focus on changing this fate, on making some other bargain and trying to save me despite it being hopeless. We need to concentrate on killing my father and destroying the Nymphs, not to mention that Shadow bitch he has working with him. They can't waste this time on me. What if it costs them more lives than mine by stalling?"

Gabriel drew back and frowned at me, but he nodded slowly. "You're right," he said, clearly *seeing* that future too. "They'll turn their focus onto saving you over destroying him, and…"

"And there's no hope for me regardless, is there?" I demanded, almost wishing he'd tell me I was wrong, though I already knew he wouldn't.

"I'm sorry, Darius," he replied, shaking his head. "I promise I will keep looking into your future to *see* if any way presents itself, but…"

"Yeah," I said bitterly, trying not to think of all the things I ached to live for beyond that ultimatum. It didn't matter now anyway. I had to concentrate on what I could do with the time I had.

"What does this mean about your intentions for the throne?" Gabriel asked me and I released a long breath.

"I don't know anymore. I was born to rule but now I'm fated to die. But my opinion still stands true that the Vegas don't know enough about running this kingdom to just claim the throne and do it. They know little to nothing of the way our political system is run, and they may be powerful but they aren't knowledgeable in all the things they would need to be so they could rule successfully. All I ever wanted was for our kingdom to be run better than it has been in the past. And I'm yet to be convinced that two mortal-raised girls could do a better job of it than my brothers who have been taught the ways of our world since the moment of their birth. We have endless plans for how we would help improve Solaria and the lives of its people. I doubt the Vegas even know where to begin."

"So you'd have Xavier take your place on the Council?" Gabriel asked, not giving his own opinion on my thoughts on the subject of the throne, though I had to assume he was all for his sisters claiming it. But surely he could *see* what that future would bring to our kingdom, so maybe he was the right person to ask for advice on it.

"Yes," I agreed. "In truth, I've been spending what time I can with him helping him to strengthen his magical abilities. He was already given the same lessons in politics and ruling that I had as a child, and he is a better man than I am anyway."

Gabriel nodded. "I can see that future as a possibility. The kingdom run by the other Heirs and your younger brother. But it is one of many futures open to us at the moment and the way to almost all of them are paved in death. The most likely path right now is that your father will wipe all of us out given time and his brutal reign will continue."

"It won't," I snarled furiously. "If there is one thing I am determined to achieve before my death then it is to see that bastard's head torn from his traitorous body."

Gabriel opened his mouth to respond but he fell deadly still instead, his eyes darting back and forth as he *saw* something which was beyond my comprehension and the stars fed him some vision.

"We have to go," he gasped as he came to again and the fear in his voice made my heart race.

"What is it? Has he found us? Are we under attack?" I demanded.

"Not here. Not us. He's claiming that the Pegasus herd your brother was a part of are linked to the rebels and has ordered a cull-"

"A what?" I barked, fire flaring through my limbs as my Dragon reared its head in anticipation of a fight.

"You need to find your brother. You and Xavier alone. If you leave now, you have a chance to beat him to the academy - but Darius, every second you waste could mean another life lost. You must hurry."

"Where is he?" I asked, knowing I had to trust him on this or face the cost in blood which he had already foreseen.

"He's with your mom and Hamish outside the kitchens. It's hard for me to *see* much of what will happen at the academy, but I know that if you can save the Pegasus herd and get Lance's dark magic equipment our future looks brighter."

"Got it," I said, shoving past him, his final words chasing after me as I broke into a sprint.

"Run, Darius! Fate is shifting with every passing second!"

XAVIER

CHAPTER TWELVE

Chaos was breaking out in The Burrows over the death of another rebel and my heart galloped like thundering hooves as I hurried through the masses looking for my family. My mom came into view, her form hidden by a perfect concealment spell which made her look like a plain woman, her dark hair pulled into a ponytail, but her eyes were just the same deep brown colour as always.

She stood at Hamish's side as he directed the rebels back to their rooms, a glimmer of panic in his eyes that unsettled me. There were no leads on the murderer, and now they'd struck again, I was starting to fear who would be next.

I made it to my mom and she clasped my hand, pulling me close and her familiar scent coiled around me as I embraced her. I was taller than her these days and she melded against me easily, resting her head against my shoulder.

"Are you alright?" she whispered with worry coating her words.

"I'm fine, what about Darius?"

"He's okay," she swore, gripping me tighter for a moment before releasing me, looking up at me like she wanted to draw me away somewhere to safety. But I wasn't a baby anymore, and I'd spent too many years locked up and unable to fight my own battles. If there was a threat in this place, I'd damn well be facing it alongside the people I loved.

I let out a soft whinny as Hamish clapped a hand to my back and leaned closer.

"Not to worry your Wendy about it, my boy," he promised, giving me something of a fatherly look – or as close to one as I could imagine anyway. My father had certainly never looked at me like that.

"I just don't understand how there can be a killer down here," I said, stamping my foot in anger. "We have some of the most powerful Fae in Solaria in these tunnels hunting for them, why hasn't Gabriel *seen* anything? Why aren't the Cyclopses able to give us answers?"

Hamish shook his head in dismay and I could see the pressure he was under as he ran a hand across his bald head and down over his mutton chops. "It's quite the carp of a conundrum, dear Xavier. But rest assured, we will find the wicked willy who lurks down here and see that they face the wrath of the stars."

I nodded, though my gut was still in knots as I stepped back, wishing there was more I could do to help.

"Xavier!" Darius's booming voice carried over the frantic chatter of the rebels and I spotted him muscling through the crowd to get to us. Mom pulled him into a hug, checking him over as Hamish blocked the crowd's view to us with his large body, giving them a moment of privacy.

"What's going on?" I asked, seeing some dark thought in my brother's eyes.

"I need your help with something." He gripped my arm, nodding to Mom and Hamish in goodbye as he guided me away through the masses.

"What is it?" I asked, but he didn't answer, instead quickening his pace until I was forced to trot at his side as he jogged down a narrower tunnel that led towards the exit of The Burrows.

He flicked a silencing bubble up around us, glancing at me as we made it to the clock and slipped out into the farmhouse. "Gabriel's had a vision," he said in a low voice.

"What vision?" I demanded anxiously, sensing something was wrong as we hurried out into the freezing air where snow was falling thick and fast upon the guards.

"You need permission from the Vegas to leave the-" one of the guards started, but Darius knocked him to the ground with a blast of water, baring his teeth at the others as they exchanged nervous glances.

We jogged past them as they started to regroup, and Darius pulled a pouch of stardust from his pocket as we headed straight for the boundary. The second we stepped through it, he threw a pinch of it over our heads and I had no more time to ask where we were going as the two of us were dragged into the stars, sending us wheeling through a glittering galaxy of light before we were transported onto soft ground between two thick bushes.

I looked around in surprise as I spotted the outer fence to Zodiac Academy, a glimpse of Earth Territory beyond the bars looking back at me.

"What the hell are we doing here?" I hissed in alarm.

"Listen," Darius growled, stepping closer to me as a cloud of urgency fell over him. "Gabriel has foreseen your herd being killed today; they're being denounced as traitors. We have barely any time to get them out. And I have no doubt Father will have made a new boundary around Zodiac to alert him of us returning here. The moment we step past this fence, he'll know where we are." A whinny of fear escaped me as I thought of Sofia, even fucking Tyler, and Darius clapped a hand over my mouth to silence it. "Your herd is going to die if we don't hurry. We don't have time to waste. Can you do this, brother?"

I nodded, my fear giving way to determination as I thought of the Pegasuses who had welcomed me into my wings, who'd accepted me even though many of them feared my father. And as my mind settled on Sofia with her gentle soul and all the words that had passed between us over the months I'd been stuck at Acrux Manor, I knew I would do anything to save her today.

She had been my salvation and so I would be hers.

"Let's go," I growled, my voice taking on the roughened edge of a Dragon for a moment and Darius nodded, clapping my shoulder and leading the way to the fence.

He stepped through one of the bars which was nothing but an illusion and I followed him, feeling the magic of a powerful detection spell running over me. I recognised the touch of my father's power and a shudder ran through me. He'd know. And he'd be coming here right now to claim us. I realised I'd rather die than return to his captivity.

The two of us broke into a sprint, tearing across the grounds as Darius cast powerful concealment spells around us to give us the best chance of evading Father for as long as fucking possible.

"Where would they be?" Darius called to me as we ran down a steep bank and through a cluster of trees. There were no students so far from the centre of campus, but it wouldn't be long before we came across someone.

I mentally calculated what day it was in my head, trying to remember my school schedule and a gasp snagged in my throat.

"They'll be at Order Enhancement together," I said, veering left as the path forked and Darius fell into step with me as I led him towards the hills in the eastern side of Earth Territory.

"No doubt Father has chosen this moment precisely then," Darius bit out. "If they're all together then they are more easily destroyed together."

A snort of rage left me as I quickened my pace, the two of us moving as fast as we could on two legs in the direction of my herd.

A deafening, terrifyingly familiar roar cut through the air like a thunderclap and I caught Darius's eye in fear. Father was here.

"You get them out of here. I'll distract him." Darius tossed me the pouch of stardust and I fumbled the catch as he started pulling his clothes off.

"Wait!" I cried in panic for my brother, but he turned away from me, leaping off of the path and shifting into his enormous golden Dragon form, answering my father's roar with a roar of his own. "Darius – be careful!" I begged as he took off into the sky with two powerful wing beats, his shadow swallowing me up for a moment before he soared away across campus with a stream of hellfire spilling from his lips.

My breaths came more frantically as I turned down another path and the sight of the eastern hills came into view. I spotted my herd there, pulling off their clothes as they prepared for the shift, though some of them were pointing to the sky, clearly having caught sight of Darius, perhaps my father too. The echo of two roars filled the air and as I started running up the nearest hill, I threw a look back over my shoulder to search the sky for them.

Father was chasing Darius through the clouds, their wing tips carving through the white as my brother pulled up hard and disappeared into the heavens.

The enormous jade beast that was my father followed with fire pouring from his lungs and my heart beat wildly as he disappeared into the clouds too and their silhouettes were lit up in a blaze of orange firelight.

"Sofia!" I yelled, turning to look for her as I ran toward my herd, waving a hand to try and capture their attention.

I couldn't spot her among them, but Tyler turned, his shirt in his hand

and his hair messed up from pulling it off.

"Xavier?" he balked, his blue eyes widening in surprise as the rest of my herd spotted me tearing toward them.

"Mr Acrux?" Professor Clippard gasped, jogging down the hill a little to meet me. "What in Solaria are you do-" His voice was cut off as a torrent of fire carved through the clouds above and my father's monstrous head broke through them, his jaws wide as he burned my professor alive, his wail dying almost instantly as his blackened body crumpled into an ashy pile.

Screams broke out and terror made my heart nearly burst as I forced my legs to keep moving towards my herd.

Father dove from the clouds, his gaze set on me as his jaws widened once more, a furious hate in his gaze that made my stomach lurch. I threw out my hands with a yell of anger, a vortex of fire and water twisting away from me in an impossibly powerful blast that slammed into his face, knocking him off course with a roar of fury.

He was so low, I fell to the ground to avoid the swing of his tail as he sailed over me, but I forced myself back to my feet instantly, racing toward the Pegasuses up on the hill.

Darius plummeted from the clouds, sending a stream of fire towards our father which lit up the whole world in a deep red glow. He forced Father away from us, giving us another chance to run as I made it to the herd.

"Follow me! Lionel has come to kill you all!" I cried as Tyler stared at me in wide eyed shock before he shifted into his large silver form with a neigh that commanded everyone to listen.

They all shifted fast while I frantically looked between them all. I still couldn't spot Sofia, but she had to be here, where else would she be?

I grabbed Tyler's clothes in my fist, snatching a handful of his mane and swinging my leg over his back before he could stop me. He reared up in anger, but I locked my knees around his sides, refusing to let go.

"I'll throw the stardust over the herd the second we get past the boundary," I barked and he whinnied furiously, but didn't try and throw me off again.

Tyler cantered forward and took off into the sky as everyone around me flapped their wings, chasing his tail as he flew as fast as he could towards the outer boundary.

A roar of anger told me my father had seen us, but I didn't look back even when a fireball went flying overhead, tumbling down to the ground and blasting a hole in the grassy mounds of Terra House.

My heart jerked as I looked around at the herd, desperate to find Sofia there but I still couldn't spot her.

Students were screaming on campus now, running for cover and looking up at us in shock as we flew overhead.

We tore over the boundary so fast that I was nearly knocked from Tyler's back with the force of the magic which rushed over me.

"Fly above the herd!" I barked at Tyler and he did as I commanded, twisting around and soaring over the Pegasuses as I tossed stardust over them, willing it to take them to The Burrows, and they disappeared in the glittering air with neighs that begged us to follow.

But as the last of them were transported away to safety, I knew for certain that Sofia hadn't been among them.

"Where is she?!" I cried, yanking on Tyler's mane to force his head around and I found panic shining in his eyes.

He twisted back towards the boundary and I held on tight as he flew back through it and I took in the furious battle taking place between my brother and father in the sky. Darius outpaced him again and again, but there were deep claw marks along his side and his leg was charred with the mark of a burn. Lionel wasn't fairing much better, his snout bleeding and his tail cut to ribbons, but neither seemed to be slowing down.

A shadow in my periphery made my head snap around and a gasp got caged in my throat as I spotted the Shadow Princess rising up on a tower of swirling shadow, hunting for prey.

"Land," I hissed at Tyler and he dropped from the sky like a stone, his hooves hitting the ground in The Wailing Wood and I prayed she hadn't seen us.

I slipped from his back, gazing up through the trees and pressing a finger to my lips as shadows rippled across the sky and she sailed upon it like the wings of death. Tyler pressed closer to me as we hugged the darkness beneath the trees, and I held my breath as she floated by overhead.

"Shift," I whispered to Tyler and he did so, pulling on his clothes as I passed them to him and running a hand through his hair.

"What the fuck's going on?" he hissed as he cast a silencing bubble around us.

"My father's decided our herd are traitors. He came here to kill you all," I said, my throat desperately dry. "We have to get Sofia out of here."

Tyler nodded seriously, pointing off through the trees. "She's in detention in Jupiter Hall with Highspell."

"Fuck," I cursed. "That bitch will hand her straight over to him."

Tyler took his Atlas out, shooting Sofia a text and I leaned over his shoulder to see what he wrote.

Tyler:
Lionel's here. I'm coming to get you.

Sofia:
Highspell locked me in Orion's office. I'm trying to get the door open.

Tyler:
Hang tight, baby.

He stuffed his Atlas back in his pocket and took off through the trees. I kept pace with him, our arms rubbing as our united cause set a fire burning in my veins.

The roar and crash of the Dragon fight above echoed further away in the distance and I prayed my brother was strong enough to hold him off a little longer.

Tyler cast concealment spells around us and I aided him as best I could with my limited magical knowledge, but between Darius and Orion's lessons, I was getting better and better at them, at least enough to keep the shadows hugging us as we moved and I just had to hope that would be enough.

Darius

CHAPTER THIRTEEN

I roared furiously as I wheeled through the air, swinging around to meet my father in a clash of claws and hatred as I snapped my jaws and lunged for his throat, fully giving in to the power of the beast which shared my flesh.

Father bellowed a challenge right back as he rushed to meet me, beating his jade green wings hard as he came at me with the claws of his front feet extended towards me, making my eyes widen in surprise as I took in the shadow foot he had in place of the one Roxy had cut from his body.

I snarled ferociously, hating the fact that he'd clearly found a way around the loss, though I still loved the sight of the damage Roxy had done to him. He seemed more hesitant to use his new limb and I used that hesitation to my advantage as I swept left, snapping my wings in tight against my body and diving at his flank fast, my teeth locking on the spine of his wing as we collided.

Lionel roared in pain as I ripped into his wing with my powerful jaws, his blood running hot and fast across my tongue and making the beast in me bellow with thoughts of victory as we plummeted towards the ground.

His teeth sank into my rear leg as I continued to tear at his wing and I kicked out hard, my claws raking down his chest and splitting the green scales which lined his body, spilling blood which fell to the treetops beneath us just before we slammed into them.

We crashed through the canopy, his body taking the brunt of the hit as I remained on top of him and I kicked again, managing to dislodge his teeth from my skin just as we hit the ground.

A tremendous boom sounded throughout the woodland we'd landed in and several trees were sent crashing to the dirt as we continued to fight with teeth and claws and I managed to plant my feet against his side. I reared back, his wing still clamped in my jaws and a roar of pain blossomed from his lips as I tore at the limb, damn near ripping it free of his back as I used all of my strength to destroy it.

My father shifted before I could finish the task, his much smaller Fae body falling between my claws before I could crush him beneath my foot as blood poured down his back and he escaped the destruction I would have wreaked on his Dragon.

I twisted my head fast, roaring at him as he used his air magic to sweep himself away from me and I sent the full force of my Dragon fire tearing after him.

He threw his hands up with a yell of defiance, shielding himself from the power of my attack and forcing me to shift too as he threw a spear of shadow and fire racing for my heart.

I landed on my feet and threw a dome of ice up before me, blasting water at him and gritting my teeth as his attack struck my shield.

"You had so much potential, Darius," he called bitterly. "You could have been magnificent. But you have your mother's weak heart in you."

"The only weaknesses I possess were gifted to me by you," I growled, bracing against his strike again.

"I'll soon beat those thoughts out of you, boy," he called back as I threw a mixture of fire and ice crashing down on him from above, feeling the strength of my attack rattling against his air shield as he fought to maintain it.

"You have nothing to hold over me anymore, Father," I sneered. "Which means I won't ever be taking a beating from you again. In fact, I fully intend to rip your throat out before this day is done and end this fucking war for good."

I dropped my shields suddenly, sprinting towards him with a battle cry which turned into a roar as I shifted mid stride, leaping forward in my enormous golden Dragon form and blasting his shield with an inferno of fire.

My father's eyes widened in alarm as he fought to hold his shield up against me and I slammed my weight down on top of it, slashing with claws and fury as I continued to fight.

His magic burned out and his shield shattered, forcing him to shift in the same breath, his jade green scales taking the brunt of my power as he slashed at me with the claws of his shadow foot.

I roared in agony as he caught me in my side, the shadows burning me from the inside out as they sank beneath my flesh and dug into the deepest recesses of my being.

I threw my weight into him, knocking him to the ground beneath me as my superior strength and size allowed me the advantage then I lunged forward, my teeth closing on his throat as blood spilled between my jaws.

Father kicked and thrashed beneath me, a shriek of pain escaping him as I shook my head, my teeth ripping through scales and skin as I fought to end this. End him. And every terrible thing he'd forced me and the people I loved to suffer through played on repeat inside my skull.

I wanted him to bleed for them, to burn for them and fucking die for them.

I'd finally proven which of us was the stronger Fae, the better Dragon and now I would rip his conniving, vindictive skull from his neck and set the whole of Solaria free from his tyrannical reign.

But before I could lose myself in the glow of this win, a scream of fury reached my ears and a blast of power slammed into my side, enveloping me in shadow and throwing me away from my father with the force of a tornado as

I smashed through the trees with a roar of pain.

I hit the ground hard, tucking my wings tight to my sides as my claws cut into the dirt and I fought to stop myself from rolling, turning to face my new opponent as Lavinia came to stand before my father's bleeding body.

"Tut, tut, naughty boy," she purred, raising her hands and grinning at me with bloodstained teeth as shadows pooled all around her. "I can't let you take my king from me. Unless you're offering to fill his role instead?"

I braced my feet in the dirt and roared at her, sending a plume of my Dragon fire blasting over her and setting the forest ablaze all around her as the shadows rose up in a cloud and shot into the treetops above me.

My fire burned out and I tipped my head back, looking up just in time to see her diving from the trees above me with a wild cry and a look of glee in her eyes.

I whipped around, trying to snap her in my jaws but she managed to shift aside, landing on my back between my wings and slamming her fists into my scales, driving spears of shadows right through me and making me bellow in agony.

I shifted fast, rolling away from her as we fell to the burning floor of the forest and throwing my hands out as I blasted her with fire magic.

She sent the shadows whipping towards me to counter my attack and the moment our power collided, I flicked my fingers and sent blades of ice flying at her back, hoping to impale her on them while her focus was on my fire.

But before the blades got close to striking her, more shadows sprang up to intercept them, hurling them aside as she laughed and cast her power at me with even more force.

I cursed as the entire weight of her control on the dark Element collided with my magic, obliterating my fire and almost striking me before I managed to throw a shield of ice up between us.

I grunted as the weight of the shadows bore down on my magic, channelling all I had into maintaining the shield while having nothing spare to use against her.

The wound on my side was bleeding heavily and I cursed as I was forced back several steps by the might of her power.

I drew on all of my strength, building everything I had into one mighty strike as I coated my fist in flames and channelled all of my power into it, relying on this one savage blast to take her out as I braced myself and prepared to drop my shield.

The moment I let it fall, the shadows slammed into me and I released the fury of my power, throwing everything I had left into the blow as I willed my flames to devour her and I was thrown away through the burning trees by the tainted power of her shadows.

I hit my back hard as I slammed into a thick trunk, pain echoing through my body from the wound my father had given me and making me curse as I fell to the ground, the last of my magic shivering in my fingertips as I found myself tapped out and bleeding on the forest floor.

"Is that all you've got, son of the Dragons?" Lavinia called through the trees and I hissed in pain as I forced myself to my feet again, hating the fact that she'd stood so easily against my attack and knowing in my soul that I had the shadows to thank for that. Her connection to the Shadow Realm made her power endless and with mine tapped out, I was nothing but prey waiting for her to find me.

I wanted to keep up our fight, but with my magic waning and her dark power seeming eternal, I knew I was out of luck with that.

Shadows coiled between the trees before me like snakes slithering across the undergrowth in hunt of something to devour and I spat at my feet before turning from them and taking off into the sky, shifting into my Dragon form with a roar which dared her to follow me.

If I was going to have to run from here then there were things I needed to salvage before I left.

Lavina took chase as I flew away into the sky and I snarled as I pushed myself on faster, heading for the clouds to gain some cover and hoping she'd keep chasing me into them to give Xavier a better chance to escape.

I may have been out of magic, but I had Dragon fire, wrath and claws on my side. So we'd soon find out how well she fared against that.

XAVIER

CHAPTER FOURTEEN

We made it to the edge of The Wailing Wood without being noticed, but the long stretch of open ground between here and Jupiter Hall made my throat tighten. Especially when I spotted the Shadow Princess sailing above The Orb in the distance on a cloud of darkness, looking to the clouds and seeming to hunt for something within them.

"How fast can you run?" I asked Tyler.

"Fast enough to outrun that shady bitch," he said determinedly.

"Shit, we're really doing this, aren't we?" I said, shedding my clothes as I stared up at the Shadow Princess, preparing to shift.

"What's the matter, Xavier? Scared?" Tyler taunted and I snorted indignantly.

"Never," I said fiercely and we looked to the sky as the Shadow Princess turned her back our way, giving us a tiny window of opportunity.

"Race you there." He winked, leaping forward and shifting and I shifted in the same instant, the two of us staying on the ground as we galloped as fast as we possibly could towards Jupiter Hall.

I didn't dare look at Lavinia, my gaze firmly fixed on the entrance ahead of us as our hooves slammed into the grass. I was fuelled by the need to reach Sofia, to get her the hell out of here and to the safety of The Burrows.

Somehow, impossibly, we made it inside and we both shifted back into our Fae forms, naked and panting as we looked around the atrium.

All was quiet, and after a few more seconds I figured we had to chance that no teachers were close and we ran across the tiles and up the stairs in the direction of Orion's old office.

I made it to the door first, pressing both of my hands to it and bringing a colossal amount of earth magic to my fingertips.

"Stand back, Sofia!" I called.

"Xavier?" she gasped, excitement and fear lacing her tone.

"I'm here," I said then blasted the door with my power, obliterating it so the whole thing exploded across the room in a hundred pieces.

I ran into the space and Sofia collided with me, wrapping her arms around me as I rested my chin on her golden hair and crushed her to me.

"Are you alright?" I asked as Tyler closed in on her from the other side, nuzzling against her head and I didn't even have it in me to try and shove him away. I was just relieved to have her in my arms again, her sweet scent filling me up and making me never want to let go.

My eyes met Tyler's over her head and I saw that very same need in him that lived in me, and for a second I was trapped in his gaze too, so fucking relieved that he hadn't died at my father's hands even though I disliked him ninety nine percent of the time.

I released Sofia, frowning as I took in the ash smearing her cheeks. Her brow furrowed then she stepped back and pointed to a pile of burning books on the floor with guilt in her eyes, a bunch more lined up beside it, clearly taken from Orion's cupboard.

"Highspell made me burn them in preparation for the 'new age'," she spat bitterly. "She had me burn the ones on Phoenixes first."

My heart tugged, knowing how Orion treasured his books and I suddenly remembered that he needed one in particular to help him discover more about the zodiac gemstones. I grabbed an empty satchel hanging on a hook by the door and stuffed the remaining books into it, my heart humming with joy as I found the Stones of the Sky tome among them. I slung the bag over my shoulder just as a high-pitched shriek sounded out in the corridor.

"Miss Cygnus!" Highspell yelled. "You have been summoned to a Nebular Inquisition Centre by the king himself!"

The clip of high heels sounded our way and Tyler shifted into his Pegasus form while I blasted through the spells keeping the window intact with as much power as I could put into the blow. Glass flew outwards in every direction, leaving it wide open and I tossed Sofia up onto Tyler's back before following her onto him and wrapping my arms around her waist.

"Stop!" Highspell wailed, running towards us with her arms outstretched, but Tyler lifted his tail and farted a spurt of glitter in her face before leaping through the open window and freefalling, her ice cast missing us by inches as the deadly blades flew overhead.

Tyler's wings snapped out, catching us before we hit the ground and my stomach lurched as he wheeled upright again, racing for the sky.

My gaze hooked on Darius as he plummeted through the air above Ignis House, shifting as he did so and crashing through the window that led into his old room. A whinny of terror left me as Lavinia landed on the roof, tendrils of shadow ripping through the coloured glass and sending massive pieces of it smashing to the ground. A plume of fire burst from Darius's room, blazing along Lavinia's flesh and making her shriek as she raised up on a tower of shadow, leaving a shimmering trail of glass in her wake.

Darius leapt back out of the remains of the window with a bag in his hand, shifting into his golden Dragon form once more and catching the bag between his teeth. I had no fucking idea what he'd just risked his neck for but as he sailed towards us and jerked his head in an order for us to flee, Tyler put on a burst of speed towards the boundary.

I held the stardust ready in one hand while keeping Sofia locked against me with the other, my eyes pinned on Lavinia over my shoulder as she chased after Darius, shadows spewing from her hands as utter rage flared in her black eyes.

I neighed in encouragement to Tyler and he flew somehow faster towards the fence that marked our freedom. But my brother apparently wasn't done risking his neck as he swung away from us, flying fast and furiously towards the parking lot a hundred yards away.

"Darius!" I cried to him in panic as Lavinia veered after him with a murderous intent in her gaze.

But Darius was faster, his talons tearing away the roof of the lot and latching around a pristine super bike while huge lumps of masonry smashed down on the beautiful cars there. He was moving again before Lavinia could get close enough to strike at him, swinging back towards us with the motorcycle clutched in his talons and a flare of victory in his gaze.

But the Shadow Princess descended on him like a plague from above, coils of shadow wrapped around her arms and pulsing with an eerie energy. Huge pillars of smoke whipped out from her, trying to catch hold of Darius and I whinnied in horror, throwing out a palm and slicing through one of them with a torrent of water as it exploded from me.

The whips tried to bind Darius in their grasp and for a second, I saw my brother's death looming as Lavinia closed in on him.

"Faster!" I roared at my brother and he twisted sharply, slicing through the shadows, a decision in his eyes as Lavinia turned her full power towards us and the entire sky turned black with her terrifying power.

Tyler lurched aside to avoid a blast of her shadows and Sofia screamed as she tumbled from his back, bursting through her clothes into her pink Pegasus form a moment later and tearing along beneath us as my heart bunched with fear for her.

She flew hard, gaining height and whinnying in alarm as Lavinia shot a spear of shadows right at her, forcing her to wheel overhead as I cried out in alarm.

"Shift back!" I roared, my voice thick with the commanding tone of a Dom and she did so instantly, tumbling through the sky and falling right towards us as the shadows missed her by mere inches.

I reached for her as Tyler whinnied in fright, snatching her into my arms and holding her close, my cheeks heating at the feel of her naked flesh pressing against mine as she stared at me in wide eyed gratitude and surprise.

"Go!" Sofia cried in panic and I felt the heat of Darius's breath at my back just as we made it over the boundary, the magic tingling against my skin a heartbeat before I threw the stardust, making sure I tossed enough backwards to reach my brother.

We were torn away into the ether, my head spinning as we seemed to spiral out of control for a moment before we were spat out in a sky full of snowflakes with silence reigning in every direction.

Darius roared his relief, picking up speed to fly beside us, his golden eye turning on me as he checked I was alright, and a laugh of complete relief fell from my lungs.

"Holy shit, Xavier." Sofia turned her head to look back at me, her short, blonde hair flying out around her in the wind and her eyes full of awe.

I leaned forward, wanting to kiss her, the urge burning in me brighter than the sun, but as I lowered my head, Tyler flapped his wings hard, bumping me up on his back and making my mouth collide with her eye instead, ruining the moment entirely.

Fucking Tyler.

Tyler whinnied a laugh and I scowled at him as Sofia turned to look back at the view, her cheeks a little pink as we followed Darius down to land on the snowy ground where he'd laid the motorcycle and bag beside him, the rest of my herd looking on in shock as we arrived, clearly unable to locate The Burrows and wondering why the fuck I'd brought them to this desolate place in the middle of nowhere.

I jumped off of Tyler's back after Sofia, relief rushing over me as I looked at the Pegasus herd, taking a head count and feeling almost certain that they were all there.

Darius shifted back into his Fae form the same moment Tyler did, and my hand slid smoothly around Sofia's, not wanting to let her go after how close we'd just come to death.

"What is this place?" Sofia breathed, shivering in the cold before using her fire Element to heat herself through, and I worked hard not to glance down at her tits which were on full display.

"It's a haven for the rebels," I explained. "You'll have to stay here now."

Tyler smiled widely, excitement flashing in his eyes. "Hell yes, we're on the run, baby." He grabbed hold of Sofia, pulling her from my hold, but as Darius caught my eye I found another reason to be angry.

I wheeled on him, pointing at the motorcycle he'd risked his neck for. "What the fuck were you playing at? You could have been killed for that thing."

Darius was breathless from how hard he'd pushed himself in the fight against my father and my gaze fell on a bloody wound at his side, his hand pressed to it, a grimace crossing his lips as he opened his mouth to answer then collapsed to the ground in the snow instead.

"Darius!" I yelled in fright, running forward and falling to my knees beside him. I didn't know how to heal yet, but I placed my hands against the wound all the same, my fingers slipping in the blood as panic took root in me and I willed my magic to do something to help.

"I got you, bro." Tyler dropped down beside me and rolled Darius onto his side, placing his hands against the wound. My shoulders trembled as Tyler worked to heal him, his brow furrowing as he struggled and the claw marks gouged into Darius's side began to knit over achingly slowly.

"Why isn't it working?" I demanded and Tyler shook his head helplessly.

"It's taking more magic than it should. I don't understand-"

"Shadow wound," Darius grunted, a noise of relief leaving me as he began to stir, his eyes cracking open as he looked up at me. "It will take a lot more power to heal it."

I nodded my understanding, slapping my hand to Tyler's shoulder and pressing my power towards him, urging it to meld with his.

Tyler's eyes widened in surprise as he realised what I was offering but it didn't take him long to drop his barriers, our magic rushing together in a vibrant burst of power which stole my breath and made him groan with pleasure.

"Fuck, you're so powerful," he gasped, staring at me in surprise as he felt the full weight of my magic.

"Not as powerful as me," Darius muttered, unable to help himself even while he was bleeding out on the ground.

"True," I admitted because of course that was the first thing our father had checked when my magic had been Awakened and he was right. I wasn't as powerful as my older brother as far as power levels went. "But I have three Elements," I taunted and Darius chuckled, though it turned into a curse of pain.

Tyler quickly tugged on my magic, using it to boost his own as he continued to heal Darius and the wound slowly stitched over more.

"That will do," Darius said after another few minutes, despite the fact that the wound was still bleeding. "Lance will need to finish it. But I'm good enough for now."

"Really?" I asked as I clutched his arm, squeezing tight as the panic of losing him ebbed away. I wouldn't survive that. I needed my brother more than anything. He was my rock.

"Good enough," he confirmed but it looked as though it still hurt like a bitch. At least the colour had returned to his face.

"Don't scare me like that," I hissed, punching him in the arm and he frowned for a moment before pushing himself up to sit in front of me.

"Thanks Tyler," he murmured and Tyler shrugged like it was nothing, rising to his feet and beckoning Sofia over.

Fuck, he annoyed the hell out of me, but he'd just saved my brother and now I was grateful to him too.

"You know you'd be fine without me, right?" he said and a whinny of pain escaped me as I shook my head.

"No, I wouldn't," I said. "How can you say that? I'd be lost without you, Darius."

"You're stronger than that," he pushed, gripping the back of my neck and pulling me forward so our foreheads rested together. "You're the good Acrux. Father didn't corrupt you."

"You're not corrupted," I growled. "You're the best person I know."

He laughed dryly, letting me go. "Did you hit your head back there?"

"You've done bad things, Darius, but that doesn't make you a bad person," I insisted and he frowned, shaking his head at me.

"Bad deeds are what make bad people," he said, pushing himself to his feet and pulling me up with him.

"No," I disagreed. "The reason for doing bad things are what defines a person. And you've never done one bad thing without trying to do it for a good reason."

He sighed, looking like he was going to keep arguing but then he gave in and slung an arm over my shoulders. "Fine, but don't go putting 'here lies a saint' on my tombstone. Make sure it's honest. Like, 'here lies an absolute legend'."

I shoved his arm off of me, shooting him a glare. "That's not funny, Darius."

He rolled his eyes, walking over to pick up the bag he'd gotten from

Ignis House, sitting it on top of the motorcycle and wheeling it towards The Burrows.

"What's in the bag?" I asked curiously as I walked with him after the Pegasus herd.

"I grabbed Orion's dark magic equipment and I owe the twins some stuff they left in the mortal realm," he said, his brows pulling together, then he jerked his chin at the satchel hanging at my side. "What did you get?"

"Orion's books," I said, grinning smugly and flipping the bag open, rifling through the tomes I'd saved. I pulled out a hardback with a cover that looked like it was encrusted with multicoloured gemstones, reading the title on the spine. *Stones of the Sky.*

"This is the one he wanted, right?" I asked Darius hopefully, waving it under his nose and my brother broke a grin before scruffing my hair.

"Well done, asshole," he said affectionately, though I didn't miss the way he pressed a hand to the wound on his side once more. "He's gonna turn into a kid when he sees those. I bet you fifty auras he says 'oh my stars!' like a boy on Christmas morning."

I laughed, shaking his hand in agreement of that deal as we headed inside, leading the herd with us and allowing them to pass through the magical barrier.

The guards cried out in surprise as they spotted us, one of them announcing that he was going to get Hamish so that he could perform the vow with the new refugees and allow them into The Burrows.

My attention fell on Sofia up ahead as Tyler guided her along, the two of them whispering to one another, but as her gaze turned to meet mine, my stomach rippled with heat and I found myself smirking stupidly at her. It was so damn good to see her again, and now she was here, I knew I had to Fae up and tell her how I felt. It was horrifying to think she could have died today, and I didn't want to waste a single second longer keeping the truth from her. Sure, it might blow up in my face. She might pick Tyler outright, but at least I'd know where I stood then.

I just needed to make the right gesture first. Make sure I was the best Pegasus for her possible, and I was pretty sure I knew what I had to do to ensure that.

Darius rolled the bike into the farmhouse, keeping the bag over his shoulder and I was relieved to shut the cold air out at last and feel the presence of my father finally leaving my body.

"Darius!" Orion's voice carried to us, a whoosh of air and a blur of movement signalling his arrival a second before he crashed into my brother and the two of them went sprawling over the ground. "Where the hell did you go?"

Darius started explaining as Orion checked him over for wounds, frowning at the bloody injury on his side and pressing his hand to it with a snarl of frustration, muttering something about him not feeling it before they exchanged a look which ended in them laughing.

I watched as he healed the wound, his jaw gritting as he concentrated on it and Darius muttered an explanation about our father having a new shadow hand which made my gut knot with tension. Of course the asshole couldn't just have been left with a useless stump which made it easier for us to face him when the time came. No. Now he had a shadow hand more powerful than the one he'd lost. I swear the fucking stars were laughing at us for believing we'd gotten that small victory.

Orion finally managed to heal the wound, though it left a set of pink lines on the side of his body which he said would need further heeling to remove entirely and I sighed my relief as Darius stood once more.

There were still other cuts and bruises marking his skin but as Orion sagged a little, it was clear he'd used all of his magic on the shadow wound.

"Anyone wanna offer up a vein?" he asked, looking over to the herd but Darius shook his head.

"The rest is superficial. I can do it myself once I get back to my gold."

Orion frowned like he wasn't really okay with that but nodded his agreement before shooting off and getting him some jeans at such a speed that he was back before I'd blinked. Darius pulled them on and Tyler and Sofia pouted, still butt naked.

"No clothes for us?" I grumbled and Orion threw me an apologetic look, carving a hand down the back of his neck.

"Sorry, it was an old Guardian bond habit," he muttered. "I can go get some…"

"It's fine," Sofia said. "Let's just get inside."

I lost the battle of trying not to stare at Sofia, my gaze falling to her perfectly round tits and the gleaming vajazzle that glittered around her pussy. Shit, she was so beautiful. I didn't know what to do with myself, and every time I looked their way, I kept getting an eyeful of Tyler's fancy fucking dick like it was trying to catch my eye. Gah.

I forced myself to look at Orion instead of them, remembering the books I had with me and clutching to that excuse to stop staring like a virgin.

"I got you these." I flipped open the satchel again, offering him the book on gemstones first and Orion's jaw went slack as he took the book from my hand, turning it over gently like it was the most precious thing in the world.

"Oh my stars," he gasped, grabbing the bag from me and rifling through the books with a youthful smile on his face. I snorted a laugh as Darius gave me a pointed look, realising I'd just lost myself fifty auras, but the look on Orion's face was definitely worth it.

"I'm afraid Highspell had some of your other ones burned," I said with a frown and I immediately regretted saying that as Orion looked like I'd just told him I'd murdered his puppy.

"Burned them?" he rasped and I nodded, offering him an apologetic look as he hugged the bag of books to his chest like he didn't want them to hear what had happened to their friends.

"Sorry, man." Darius rested a hand to Orion's shoulder and he growled.

"I'll murder that fake-faced witch," he snarled, his fangs on show as he held onto his books even tighter and I was pretty sure he was making that promise to them. Dude would definitely kill in revenge for those books.

"I got this for you though," Darius said, taking a large wooden chest from his bag and handing it over, making Orion grin again.

"All my equipment?" he asked excitedly and Darius nodded.

Orion gave the chest a shake and it rattled like there was something heavy inside it.

"You got the bones too?" he asked and Darius gave him a dark smile, glancing over his shoulder and tossing a silencing bubble around the three of us before answering as he took hold of the bike's handlebars and started pushing it towards the entrance to the tunnels just as Hamish opened the door hidden behind the clock and stepped out.

"Well I didn't spend all those years learning to wield dark magic against Father to just forget about it when the time finally came to take him down."

Orion nodded eagerly. "We can restart your lessons soon then."

"Welcome fine fellows and gentle Fae!" Hamish called eagerly and Darius dropped the silencing bubble. "Step forth to make your vows and we will get you all set up inside in no time."

Tyler strode forward with a snort of warning at the other Pegasuses who all parted to let him go first, and he led Sofia over with him so that they could make their vows.

Darius continued past them. Guiding the bike into the tunnel and leading the way into the impressive corridor which almost felt like it belonged in a manor house instead of beneath the ground with its vaulted ceiling and pale grey walls.

We started walking deeper into The Burrows together and I realised how quiet it was. "Is there another sweep taking place to try and find the killer?" I asked in a low tone.

"He's got the Cyclopses working in force again," Orion said with a nod, a line of worry on his brow. "But if they don't find something soon, I think we'll have to take this into our own hands." Him and Darius shared a dark look which told me exactly what kind of plan they had for getting information out of people and I released a nervous little whinny.

"Have you got any suspects in mind?" Darius asked him as he cast a silencing bubble around us.

"Well, we're trusting the Cyclopses to find the truth. Who better than one of them to hide their involvement?" Orion suggested and a shiver of trepidation darted down my spine.

"You really think it could be one of them?" I asked, shuddering at the memory of the last interrogation and the invasive feeling of the Cyclops pushing into my memories.

"Seems like a decent place to start," Orion said and Darius nodded.

"I'm not going to rest until this is dealt with," Darius growled.

"Then let's pay them a visit," Orion said.

"I'll catch up with you. I'm going to see Roxy first," Darius said and Orion nodded his goodbye, heading down a side tunnel and melding into the dark like a shadow given life. I was more than happy to leave him to that twisted task.

I slowed my pace, waiting for the herd to catch up as they made their vows and we were soon leading them deeper into the impressive labyrinth of tunnels that had been created down here to hide the rebels.

There was an unsettled energy passing between everyone, little shivers running through the herd who followed behind us and I brushed my hands over them on instinct to calm them.

My heart twisted over Professor Clippard's death, and my hate for my father grew a little sharper as I worked to reassure the members of my Order who he'd planned to kill today.

I trotted over to Tyler and Sofia and she immediately pulled me closer with a soft neigh leaving her lips. My pulse shot up as her naked curves were pressed to my body and my dick jumped to attention which she definitely fucking felt. She didn't pull away though and I couldn't help but trail my fingers over the sensitive place between her shoulder blades, making her whinny softly as she shivered for me.

I simply ignored Tyler's narrow eyed look at me as I held her tight, trying to muscle his arm off of her, but he didn't let go. My hand grazed his and heat washed out over my skin from the contact.

"Thanks for everything, buddy," Tyler said in an overly friendly way as I released Sofia and I wished I had some damn pants because I was half masting and it was not something I could hide. "We can take it from here."

"Don't be an asshole," Sofia said, stamping her foot and Tyler snorted indignantly, looking over at me again. "He saved our lives today." Sofia's light blue eyes glittered and my chest swelled with pride. "Is there some way we can talk to our families? I don't have my Atlas."

"Hamish can get messages delivered to families. But you won't be able to contact them directly. He'll give you an Atlas, but it can only be used for the private network we have in the Burrows," I said and she frowned, her worry over her family clear. "I'll get Hamish to come see you today," I promised.

Tyler nodded, his cocky mask slipping for a second to reveal his worry over his own family and I knew I had to do this for them.

"Are Tory and Darcy here?" Sofia asked hopefully.

"Yeah, come on. They'll be excited to see you." I led the way forward as they followed and Darius swung his leg over the bike, starting the engine and riding it down the tunnel, the roar of the engine echoing off of the walls.

It finally dawned on me how close they'd all come to death today, a pit of dread opening up in my stomach. If we'd acted any slower, if Gabriel hadn't *seen* it coming…

My breaths came unevenly at the idea of losing Sofia, and even fucking Tyler. He may have been an asshole, but the thought of him dying in my father's fire made terror pull at my heart. Now my herd was here, I had to protect them. And I'd make sure my psychotic flesh and blood never got near them again.

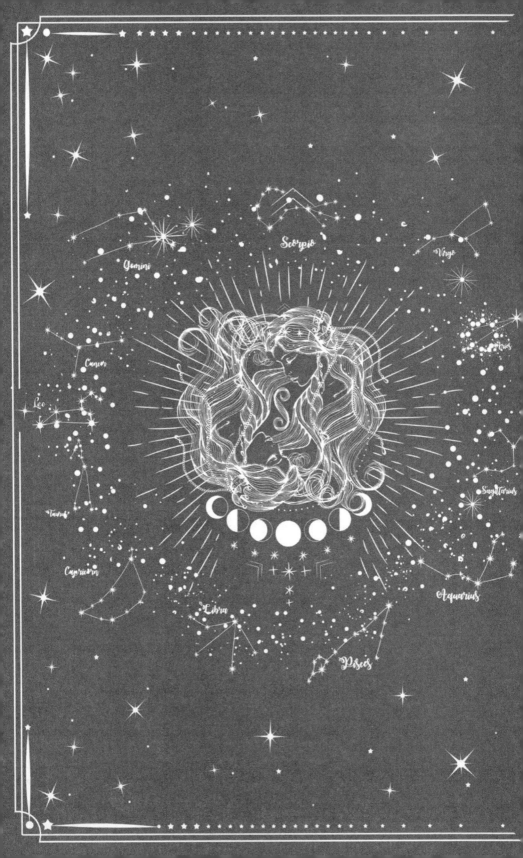

TORY

CHAPTER FIFTEEN

I paced up and down inside the dining hall of The Burrows, looking between the large clock on the wall and the tunnel which led up to the farmhouse as I waited for Darius and Xavier to appear. I didn't even know how long it would take them to fly here from the academy or how far away it was, but I also didn't know how much stardust they'd had with them and whether it was enough to transport the entire herd, so I had no idea how long I might be waiting and Gabriel just kept telling me to be patient. But fuck patient.

"He'll be okay," Darcy reassured me, coming to stand at my side and taking my hand to squeeze it. The rest of the rebels had been sent back to their rooms while investigations were being carried out over the latest murder, but I'd refused to be confined to my room so I was waiting here instead – though I would have chosen to be outside if I'd gotten any real say in it.

I glanced at Gabriel, wondering if he might have *seen* anything else to make that guess a little more certain.

"So long as Darius doesn't lose his head to rage, he should arrive back safely. But it's hard for me to *see* too much of what has been happening – probably because the shadows are somehow involved. There are futures open to us which show him returning, so there's a good chance," he said cryptically, barely reassuring me at all, because since when had Darius Acrux ever been any good at not losing his head?

"I can't bear it if anything happens to him," I muttered, allowing myself that single moment of love-struck weakness as I bit down on my bottom lip and tried to remind myself of just how fucking strong that man was.

"Darius may be a lot of things, but he would literally move heaven and earth to be with you," Gabriel said. "I'm sure he's doing everything within his power to return to you quickly."

I clucked my tongue, knowing that was the truth while still unable to shift the sense of unease from my gut.

"I feel like everything we're doing here is taking too long," I said.

"We fought to get free of Lionel, stole a hand from him, managed to gain the Imperial Star and kept it from him and yet here we are, sitting around in some cave network, taking magic lessons in between helping make more caves to house a thousand refugees instead of just finishing this."

"It's not the time," Gabriel said, the sigh in his voice letting me know that it was infuriating him too but also confirming that nothing had changed.

"I just want him dead at my feet," I snarled. "Is that too much to ask? For my boyfriend's father to just bleed out painfully at my goddamn feet?"

"Wow, you get really bloodthirsty when you're worried," Darcy teased.

"I'm not worried," I replied, "I'm fucking angry, I'm gonna beat his scaly ass when he gets back here for running off without me like that."

Gabriel chuckled like he wasn't opposed to the idea of that at all and I grinned at him.

"Here," Seth's voice came from behind me and I turned to find him standing there, holding out a cupcake with a large letter B iced on top of it. "You look like a girl who needs some comfort food."

"In the form of a cupcake with a random letter B on it?" I questioned, arching an eyebrow at him.

"Yeah. No doubt you'll need to keep your energy up for all the angry sex you and Darius will be having later on."

"Keep the sexual references about my sisters to times when I'm not within earshot, yeah?" Gabriel suggested with a grimace. "It's bad enough that the stars show me flashes of that shit without me having to listen to conversations about it too."

Seth had a devilish look on his face like he'd just been challenged and I rolled my eyes at him, half looking forward to watching Gabriel use The Sight to beat him in the little game I could see brewing in his beady eyes.

"Where did you even get that from?" Darcy asked, pointing at the cake.

"It was just sitting there for anyone to take in the kitchens!" Seth replied with a grin.

"So why the B?" I asked, still not reaching for the cake which he continued to hold out to me.

"I didn't know you'd be so fussy about the letter I chose. You could have had your pick really. Maybe I should have given you the T."

"There was a T?" I asked.

"Yeah. There were a bunch and each one had a letter on it which spelled out 'Happy Birthday Brodie' in this yummy blue icing." Seth grinned and my brow dropped.

"So you stole someone's birthday cakes?" Darcy asked him, looking somewhere between amused and horrified.

"No, not all of them. Just the Hs and the Bs and the Ps...to be honest I did take *almost* all of them, but I left the last three - the icing just wasn't up to the standard of this one and I wasn't gonna eat a substandard cupcake."

I eyed the blue icing smeared to the right of his mouth and laughed as I realised what he was saying. "So you stole someone's cupcakes on their birthday, and the only ones you left behind spell out the word 'die' right after another guy has been randomly found dead? You're a fucking psycho."

Gabriel laughed with me as Seth frowned and Darcy slapped a hand over her mouth like she was trying really hard not to find that funny even though it totally was.

"Are we having cake?" Caleb asked as he shot into position in our group, his arm dropping around my shoulders as he gave me a little squeeze and I quickly accepted the cake from Seth.

"Mine," I taunted, taking a big bite from it and making him grin at the challenge before he shot towards Seth, grabbed his jaw and held him still so that he could lick the icing from the edge of his lips.

"By the stars, Cal," Seth gasped as Caleb just chuckled and pushed his jaw further back before sinking his teeth into his neck.

Seth's hand moved to grip the back of Caleb's neck as he fed, drawing him closer with a Wolfish growl which sounded all kinds of hot. I exchanged a look with Darcy as Caleb continued to feed, his entire body pressed flush to Seth's for several long seconds before he finally pulled back with a rueful grin.

"You're getting sloppy, man," he teased. "What kind of hunt was that?"

"I got distracted by being an amazing friend," Seth protested, his gaze on Caleb as he reached out to heal the bite on his neck before sucking the last of the blood from his thumb.

"Yeah well, some might think you're getting sloppy. Or that you actually *want* me to bite you."

"Pfft." Seth shoved him harder than could really be called playful, his cheeks pinking a little. "I just like having someone to wrestle with who can actually match me, that's all."

"Well then next time, maybe you should try fighting back instead of making it so damn easy for me." Caleb grinned then shot away from us, leaving Seth standing there staring after him.

He snapped around to face us again, pushing his fingers through his long, dark hair, his gaze fixing on my sister.

"Darcy, I need a super urgent word with you about the state of these rocks," he said suddenly.

"Rocks?" I asked in confusion as Seth nodded.

"Yep. It can't wait. And I need some comfort food," he added, reaching out to snatch my half eaten cupcake from my hand.

"Hey!" I barked at him, but he was already shoving the entire thing into his mouth and dragging Darcy away from us while she gave me an apologetic smile. "What the fuck was that about?"

"I don't know and I don't want to know," Gabriel replied. "I don't wanna find out any more about what goes on in that Wolf's head than I already do."

Before I could reply, he jerked his chin towards the corridor which led back to the surface and I gasped as I spun to face it.

All of my worries flashed through my mind as I held my breath in anticipation of their arrival. I knew that Gabriel had told them they had to go alone, but that didn't mean I had to like it and I was going to be giving Darius a piece of my mind just as soon as I made sure he was okay.

Before I could freak myself out even more, a clamour of noise announced the arrival of a group further up the tunnel and my lungs collapsed on themselves as I blew out a relieved breath and ran forward to meet Darius and Xavier.

The roar of a motorbike engine made my eyes widen and I stared in shock as Darius burst from the darkness of the tunnel riding on the back of the limited edition super bike he'd bought me while an entire herd of Pegasuses ran along behind him butt naked and in their Fae forms.

I spotted Xavier running at the front of the herd and as I scoured the group, I caught sight of Tyler and Sofia right behind him, my heart lifting with joy at seeing them again.

Darius sped straight towards me on my bike, the wheels skidding on the stone floor of the dining hall as he yanked it around and pulled up right in front of me.

I took in the blood staining the right side of his face and marking his entire side half a beat before he dragged me into his arms and kissed me so hard he stole the breath from my lungs.

I broke for him, falling apart and kissing him back as the scattered pieces of my soul reformed and burned for him so fiercely that it felt like my entire body must have been glowing.

His tongue pushed into my mouth and he growled possessively as the scent of smoke, cedar and man enveloped me and I felt the furious pounding of his heart against my chest, letting me know how close he'd come to a much worse fate.

I shoved him back suddenly, my fist snapping out and driving into his chest – which actually hurt like a bitch because his stupid muscles were rock solid so it was kinda like punching a wall. "Don't fucking worry me like that," I snarled before turning away and moving to greet my friends.

"Roxy!" Darius called after me, but I just flipped him off over my shoulder and kept walking.

Geraldine came rushing over to the herd with a mountain of clothes floating along behind her on a gust of air magic.

"Never fear, Grussy is here!" she called by way of welcome, clicking her fingers at a group of rebels who had followed her here so that they could help hand out the clothes to the Pegasus herd.

I spotted Catalina embracing Xavier while he crushed her in his arms, blood staining his skin and making my gut clench with the knowledge of the danger they'd been in.

Sofia squealed as she spotted me approaching and I threw my arms around her, squeezing her tight despite the fact that she was butt naked.

"Shit, I've missed you," I breathed as she crushed me in her hold and let out a choked kind of laugh.

"Zodiac hasn't been the same since you all left," she replied just as another set of arms joined our hug and I was smashed between her and Tyler as he wrapped himself around me from behind.

"That had better not be your balls pushing up against my ass," I warned him, though I was grinning, unable to really summon the strength to get angry while the relief over them being here and being okay filled me.

"My balls belong firmly to the girl on the other side of this hug sandwich," Tyler replied. "So don't worry about it, Princess."

I snorted at the use of my title and let them squeeze me for a moment longer before the interruption of a pissed off Dragon snarling behind us drew my attention.

"Oh, Tyler there's probably something you should know about me and Darius-" I began a beat before Tyler was ripped away from me with the force of a Dragon Shifter in beast mode and I whipped around to find him sprawled on the floor several feet away. Darius was stalking closer to him with death burning in his eyes.

"Where did the black rings in your eyes go?" Tyler asked as he stared up at Darius from the ground, his gaze shifting to find my eyes and a gasp escaping him as realisation hit. "No fucking way! How did you guys-"

He was cut off as Darius lunged at him, but I managed to flick an air shield up between them before he could attack and I stepped forward to grip his arm, tugging on it to force him to take notice of me.

"Hey dude, the only balls I have any interest in are yours, even if they aren't going to be getting anywhere near me for the foreseeable future due to the stunt you just pulled by running off on me like that," I snapped.

Darius ignored me, smoke spilling between his lips as he glared down at Tyler who raised his hands innocently from his position butt ass naked on the floor.

"I get it man, she's your girl. Even if that makes no star damned sense after the whole Star Crossed thing. But whatever. Message received. No more naked hugs no matter how emotionally provocative the reunion is," Tyler promised and Sofia stepped from foot to foot anxiously as she watched.

Darius still looked intent on murder, so I reached out and gripped his jaw in my hand, forcing his gaze around to meet mine.

"I'm guessing you're all tapped out?" I asked him, the irritation in my voice pretty clear over the fact that he'd let himself end up vulnerable like that. No doubt he had damn good reason for it, but right now I was pissed at him for risking himself without having me there to watch his back, so I wasn't going to be reasonable.

Darius grunted some kind of affirmative response that didn't contain words and I tightened my grip on his jaw in warning, my fingernails biting into his skin just enough to make him take note of how serious I was being.

"Then I think instead of attacking my friends, you should be getting cleaned up and piling gold all over yourself to replenish, don't you? I'll come find you once I've made sure Sofia and Tyler are settled in. We need to talk about your macho bullshit."

"Don't give me the 'we need to talk' crap, Roxy. I'm not some house pet for you to train up. And if I wanna beat the crap out of this asshole for touching my girl with his cock out then I'll fucking do it," he replied.

I stepped closer, tilting my mouth up towards his without quite getting close enough to kiss him as I spoke in a low tone. "Well unluckily for you, Darius, I have plenty of magic in reserve and I'm putting myself between you and Tyler, so unless you think you can take me on without a drop of magic in your veins, I suggest you go on back to your room before I beat your ass in front of all of these lovely people."

Darius growled, leaning in to me and taking hold of the side of my neck, his thumb slipping around to caress my pulse point which pounded as he drew me closer by the hold on my throat.

"You should know better than to threaten a Dragon, Roxy," he said, his words brushing against my ear as he moved his mouth so close to my flesh that it made a shiver of energy pass down my spine. "I might just have to remind you why that is."

"Bring it on, asshole, I'm not afraid of you." I tilted my chin up, making no attempt to remove his hand from my throat and bathing in that pissed off Alpha energy he was exuding all over me as I stood my ground and dared him to do his damn worst.

Darius tightened his grip the smallest amount, drawing closer to me and speaking low into my ear, making my whole body spark with the energy I only ever experienced when I was riling up this particular beast. "You're lucky I like it so much when you call me names, baby."

He released me suddenly, brushing past me and leaving me hanging in the abruptly empty air which rushed in to try and fill the void his aura had left behind.

I rolled my eyes at his back, trying to maintain the illusion that I was utterly unaffected by that monster of mine and no doubt failing miserably as I practically drooled all over the floor and stared at his ass in those jeans while he walked away.

I dropped the air shield which had been protecting Tyler and offered him a hand up as he released a low whistle.

"I'm gonna need access to an Atlas and info on the FaeBook group you all run in here - what did you call it? Rebels Forever? Down with the King? Let's stick it up his Dragon Ass? Tell me it's something catchy."

"I dunno, dude, there hasn't been a whole lot of social anything going on here so far as I know. It's a closed system so we can only share FaeBook posts and messages with other people in The Burrows on our Atlases. I spend most of my time training with Orion and the Heirs so-"

"Back the fuck up, you have the Power Shamed professor here? Hashtag did they do it in detention. Hashtag did she get spanked by the Vampire tank-"

"No hashtags," I said firmly, reaching out to place a hand over his mouth and looking around to find Darcy with Sofia and Xavier as they all embraced and she got caught in her own naked hug sandwich.

Instead of arguing with me, Tyler followed my line of sight then snorted angrily, stomping his foot as I withdrew my hand.

"Oh for fuck's sake, he's already trotting in on my girl," he grumbled, his eyes narrowing on Xavier. "Look at him. He's clearly been working out this whole freaking time. He's all, 'hey, Sofia, look at my tight ass and washboard abs and did you know I could totally bench press you beneath a rainbow?' Gah."

Tyler took off at a fast pace and I breathed a laugh as I fell into step with him and we approached the others.

"Hey Xavier!" Tyler called out with a bright smile as the hugging ended and I exchanged a grin with Darcy over having Sofia here with us, safe from the monster who was currently ruling our kingdom.

"Oh, hey man," Xavier replied, his gaze roaming over Tyler in that assessing man way before hesitating on his dick which I had to admit had been trying to catch my eye too. Not that I had the slightest bit of interest in Tyler's cock, but it was super sparkly and covered in gems and shit so it kinda drew the eye. "I'm so glad we managed to save you."

"You were so brave," Sofia said, batting her lashes up at Xavier and biting down on her bottom lip.

"Can you put some clothes on?" I interrupted, holding a hand out to shield my eyes from my boyfriend's brother's dick which was casually on display in front of me.

"Oh, I'm so sorry his plain Jane dick is offending you, Tory," Tyler said dead seriously, turning and grabbing some sweatpants from the floating pile behind Geraldine with a whip of earth magic. He handed a tracksuit to Sofia who pulled it on as he and Xavier got dressed and Darcy tried not to laugh while the two male Pegasuses seemed to race to be the first to get their clothes on.

Tyler won by about half a second and Xavier stomped his foot like a three-year-old who had just been told he couldn't have any candy.

"I was just telling Sofia that we can make up a room for her and Tyler along in the royal quarters," Darcy said as we all silently agreed not to discuss the racing. "There's one going spare since…" She glanced at Xavier then over to Catalina and cleared her throat uncomfortably.

"You mean since Catalina started sneaking into Hamish's room every night instead of sleeping in her own?" I asked, making Xavier wrinkle his nose.

"She thinks me and Darius haven't figured that out," he muttered, glancing over at his mom who was helping Hamish hand clothes out to the rest of the herd since he'd arrived. "And I don't think she will admit it if you asked her, so maybe they'll just have to get a room in the new tunnels." His gaze moved to Sofia and I could tell he didn't really want her to be that far away - The Burrows were getting so damn big now and there were so many refugees here that the latest sections of them were literally a couple of miles away beneath the ground. There were additional bathhouses and kitchens which were being run by the people who lived in those areas too, and if they ended up down there, we weren't likely to see a whole lot of them.

"I'll deal with Catalina. You guys show them around and I'll catch you up once it's sorted."

Xavier gave me a look which said he seriously doubted that would work and I just offered a cocky grin in reply before heading over to talk to his mom who was just finishing up with the last of the herd.

"Beautifully done, Kitty," Hamish murmured, his hand brushing against the small of her back as she turned a bright smile on him, and I swear I could feel the happiness pouring off of her.

"Sorry to interrupt," I said, moving closer so that they spotted me and they flinched apart like I might not have noticed that whole exchange.

"Oh gooseberries on a gander bush, you gave me quite the heebee jeebies there, My Queen," Hamish breathed, pressing a hand to his chest as I smiled at him.

"Because you thought you were being all subtle with your sweet nothings as you whispered them to each other?" I teased and Hamish honest to shit blushed while Catalina's full lips popped open.

She really was a beautiful woman, and that was so much more apparent now that she was here, dressed in simple dresses which flattered her figure without flaunting it, her long, dark hair free of its perfectly polished up-dos and instead threaded with tiny flowers which she'd placed there with her earth magic. She still had her illusion in place, but Orion had taught us to see through simple ones like hers last week. And because I already knew the illusion was there, it didn't take much effort on my part to see the real her.

Her smiles were no longer plastic but shone with actual happiness and she was finally able to spend time with her sons and shower them with the love they'd been missing from her for so long. She even extended that maternal love to me and Darcy whenever the opportunity for it arose, as well as Lance and even Geraldine too. It was like she'd been bursting with a love that had been all trapped and tied up inside her for so long that now that it was free, she couldn't help but dole it out to everyone as often as she could. And though I found it hard to express, I freaking loved her playing mom with me. She'd even styled my hair for me a couple of times and it had made my heart feel all light and fluttery even though I hadn't known how to tell her that. But I kinda got the feeling she knew, because she'd been missing that kind of affection for so long herself that she just recognised it easily in others.

"Do the boys know?" she asked, glancing around for them but Darius was long gone and Xavier was pretending not to have even noticed us talking.

"Everyone knows," I deadpanned and Hamish threw a hand to his forehead.

"Oh by the love of the stars, I have tarnished your good name, my lady," he gasped.

"I'm pretty sure Lionel tarnished my name a long time ago when he started lending me to his friends for political advantages," she muttered bitterly and I frowned at the thought of that.

"Well Lionel is currently still learning to jerk off with his left hand, so let's hope he can't even satisfy himself these days," I growled and Hamish gasped again.

"Oh my!"

Catalina breathed a laugh though, so I just owned it. I had made it clear on plenty of occasions that I really wasn't princess material anyway and my blunt tongue was the least of it.

"Well, point is, Xavier would fucking love it if Sofia could get a room close to his because he's got that whole Dom thing going on with her. I think he really needs to be around some of his herd again too after being cooped up here without a Pegasus in sight for the last few months. So I was hoping they could have your room, seeing as you spend your nights with your new boy toy anyway-"

"Sweet heavens, forgive me," Hamish whimpered and I arched a brow at him in surprise. Fae weren't generally prudish about this kind of thing, but he looked like he was hoping the ground might open up and swallow him to rescue him from this conversation.

"What's the big deal?" I asked.

"Hammy believes that fornication outside of marriage is all well and good until love is involved. And since we umm...said the L word, he feels like we should really be married if we are going to continue to be...physical." Catalina honest to shit blushed and if that wasn't just the cutest thing in the world then I didn't know what was.

"So...do you want to get married?" I asked, unsure if that was what she was saying or if she was saying she'd refused.

"Well, technically as I didn't really die, my marriage to Lionel still binds me. So if I tried to marry again, the bond wouldn't form and the stars

208

would reject it. You can marry multiple partners in a polyamorous union, but in this kind of situation the stars would know I am being dishonest." Catalina's lips turned down sadly and Hamish tugged her to his side, placing a kiss to her head.

"I only wish to honour you as my bride, my love, don't think for one moment that I think any less of you because of your miserable union to that cad," he murmured.

"What would it take to divorce you from the lizard king?" I asked, wondering if we could find some way around this.

"A Fae marriage can be dissolved by law - but in that case we would have to file paperwork which he would be notified of, therefore informing him that I was still alive. I have considered it. We are safe here after all, but-"

"I won't allow my Kitty to come under the notice of that menace once again, unless she is truly ready to do so," Hamish growled protectively, a doggishness to his tone which spoke of his Order form.

"What else then?" I asked.

"Death," she breathed then shrugged.

"So, the Savage King didn't have the power to dissolve marriages?" I asked, thinking of the power the old mortal kings used to have and feeling like I'd heard something about them being able to do that. Then again, maybe I was wrong. History had never been my best subject.

"My lady…I think perhaps he did," Hamish gasped, looking at me with hope in his eyes.

"Then his daughters might be able to do it?" I suggested, the corner of my lips lifting as Catalina stared at me with barely contained excitement.

"Perhaps! Oh fish on a Ferris wheel, do you think you could?" Hamish gushed.

"I dunno, what would we have to do?" I asked, glancing around and waving Darcy and Geraldine over to join us from where they'd been standing talking to Gabriel.

"Gabriel said it will work," Darcy said as the others turned to look to her too. "With no further explanation."

"Any chance he told you what we need to do?" I asked, a grin filling my face as I realised that this was actually happening.

"He just said we should combine our magic, call out to the stars and tell them it is so. Whatever the hell that means." She shrugged.

"What in tarnation is going on, my ladies?" Geraldine asked, looking between me and her dad who still held Catalina close.

"Their royal majesties are going to attempt to untether my dearest Kitty from the clutches of that uncouth usurper to the throne," Hamish said excitedly. "He will free her from her bonds and make her available to woo in the most natural of ways!"

"In English?" Darcy asked me as Geraldine burst into tears.

"We're gonna try and give Catalina a star divorce," I explained and Darcy smiled widely.

"Okay then. Let's do it." She reached for my hand and I took hers, pushing my magic up to the surface of my skin to meet with hers and waiting for her to drop the barriers dividing us.

Darcy frowned for a moment and I cocked my head as I looked at her in confusion while I waited for her to power share with me. I'd never had to wait like this with her before, our magic always desperate to collide and combine so the pause was more than a little odd.

"Is everything okay?" I muttered as she gritted her teeth.

"Yeah. I'm just feeling a little tired today," she said in frustration just as her magic slammed into mine and I gasped at the collision, getting used to feeling the might of all that power as one.

I tipped my head back to look up in the direction of the stars beyond the cavern roof, unsure if I actually had to say the words or what they wanted from us, but as soon as I thought about wanting the marriage between Catalina and Lionel dissolved, I felt the presence of the stars all around us.

I sucked in a sharp breath as the whispers of the eternal beings slipped through the air and seemed to brush through my hair like soft fingers, exchanging a look with my sister as we both held our intentions clearly in our minds and like a sudden downpour of rain upon my cheeks, I felt the magical bond which we were trying to affect fall apart.

The stars seemed amused by the relief that tumbled through my chest and the next thing I knew, they were retreating, leaving us alone once more and turning their attention elsewhere as I focused on pulling my magic back and separating it from Darcy's.

I released her hand and she stumbled as she withdrew, managing to keep her feet at the last second and laughing at herself as she muttered an apology.

"Did it work?" Geraldine cried, drawing my attention to her wide eyes and clasped hands as she waited desperately for the news.

Hamish and Catalina were holding hands, looking to us hopefully too and I couldn't help but grin as I nodded.

"You're free," I told Catalina and Hamish howled like a dog baying for blood as he swept her into his arms and dipped her back like they were finishing up some old Hollywood movie as he kissed her deeply and Geraldine started sobbing.

When they finally broke apart, Hamish dropped to one knee and pulled a sapphire ring box from his back pocket, flipping the lid open and presenting a ring with a rose quartz crystal the size of a freaking egg to Catalina as he got all choked up and found himself unable to even ask the question.

"Yes!" she cried, lunging for him and kissing him so hard that they fell back onto the floor, the ring crushed somewhere between them as we backed up and laughed, trying not to get knocked over by their exuberant display.

"The wedding shall occur on the new moon to give it the most wondersome of blessings!" Geraldine announced, taking off running without another word, her arms flapping in the air as she barked excitedly.

"Isn't the new moon in like two days?" Darcy asked me, grinning as we backed away a little more while Hamish and Catalina continued to make out like a couple of horny teenagers.

"If anyone can pull off the wedding of the century in two days it's Geraldine Grus," I replied as we started heading for the royal quarters.

"So how much shit are you going to give Darius for running off on you like that?" Darcy teased, knowing me all too well.

I smirked, shrugging innocently. "Only as much as he can handle.

Besides, I get the horrible impression that he's been deluding himself into believing I've gone soft since we got together properly. I think he needs reminding of exactly who he's dedicating himself to."

"Well just warn me if world war three is going to break out down here because I get the feeling you've met your match in that one, and I'm a little worried you'll bring the roof of this place down on all of us if you really get into it."

I laughed, not disagreeing because she knew me well enough to know that would be bullshit.

We went our separate ways as we made it to the royal quarters where we could hear Geraldine sobbing and gushing about the news to anyone and everyone, and I peeled off to go find my Dragon and give him hell for scaring me like that.

I strode up the corridor quickly, reaching our room and disabling the magical locks to pull the door wide.

My heart did that insane skittering thing as my eyes fell on him and I stilled, taking in the sight of him lying in the heart of a heap of treasure, chains around his neck, rings on his fingers and a couple of crowns perched lazily on his head, tilting to one side.

His chest was still bare, and blood stained his inked skin from several wounds which he still hadn't healed, and I guessed that was down to him lacking in magic. I frowned as I spotted a set of four raised pink scars on his side, my throat bobbing as I remembered the wound Clara had given me when she'd tried to drag me into the shadow realm, and a thousand questions about what the fuck had happened at the academy rushed to my lips, halting there as I gave myself a moment to process this rush of emotion.

I was furious and terrified and the depths of my feeling for this beautiful nightmare of mine was pressing down on me so hard that I couldn't fucking breathe.

Darius's eyes were closed and his breathing heavy and as I stood there, I found my irritation sliding into relief at having him back.

He was okay. Here. Mine.

That was all that really counted. Besides, he'd helped rescue Sofia, Tyler and the rest of their herd so I couldn't really justify staying angry over that.

Shit. Maybe I was *going soft.*

I closed the door quietly behind me, locking it again and casting a silencing bubble around myself so that I wouldn't disturb him as I moved further into the room. The space felt weirdly like home despite the fact that it was just a cave beneath the ground. But since Darius had gotten Caleb to create furniture and little home comforts around the space and formed a hearth in the corner which always held a roaring flame, I couldn't help but like it here. There were little white flowers decorating the rock walls, a soft carpet of moss on the floor and a tiny waterfall which tumbled down the far wall in an endless trickle too and somehow it just felt like it was…ours. Our own little slice of peace away from the world outside.

I drew closer to Darius, tilting my head as I looked at him, drinking in this rare sight of his features fully relaxed in sleep as he just lay there, the monster in him dormant and the man so achingly beautiful I couldn't tear my eyes away.

I couldn't remember the last time I'd caught him sleeping. He always held me in his arms while I drifted off then inevitably woke me up every morning with his mouth either on my lips or on some other part of my body if I was particularly lucky.

Then we'd get up, head to the surface for our run which consisted of endless laps around the protected area above ground before getting breakfast together - where he made sure to grab me a coffee every single day. But amongst all that, I never really caught him sleeping, and now that I had, I was starting to realise how odd that was. Did he always sleep this little? I'd never had the chance to find that out before we came here, but it seemed strange that he literally never fell asleep before me or woke after.

I climbed up onto the bed, my silencing bubble hiding the sound of the treasure shifting about all around me and the few coins which tumbled to the floor as I made my way onto his lap.

Darius murmured something in his sleep, his hands shifting to my thighs as he drew me a little closer and I let the silencing bubble fall away.

But his grip was loose, his breathing still deep and there was a furrow in his brow which made my heart tug.

I reached out gently, my fingers caressing the tattoo he'd gotten for me where it curved over his left hip and disappeared beneath the waistband of his jeans. My eyes drifted over the words as I sought them out. *There is only her.*

Fuck, I loved this man.

I pushed my hands up his chest, healing magic building in my palms as I went and I sent it into him, seeking out the cuts and bruises, healing the wound to the side of his head where blood clotted against his temple and finding a cracked rib which I promptly fused back into place too.

I wasn't even sure I wanted to know what the hell he'd survived while he'd been away from me.

It took a fair bit of magic and a lot of concentration, but with the fire raging behind me, it was replenishing almost as fast as I was wearing it down.

A sigh escaped my lips as I finished and I realised my eyes had fallen shut in concentration. I opened them again, finding Darius's gaze locked on mine as I did, his grip on my thighs tightening enough to make me feel like he was holding onto me just as much as I was holding onto him in that moment.

"Shit, I didn't mean to fall asleep," he said with a frown, looking genuinely pissed off about the fact and I breathed a laugh as I reached out to run my fingers along his jaw, loving the bite of his stubble against my skin.

"Are you apologising for sleeping?" I teased, but it didn't lessen the unease in his dark eyes.

"I just don't want to miss anything," he said, swiping a hand over his face and releasing a flash of magic which looked like a beam of pure sunlight. It sank into his skin, making his eyes blaze more intensely as he dropped his hand back to my thigh, his fingers moving over my pants where my tattoo lay against my skin.

"What was that?" I asked, cocking my head to one side curiously because he didn't even look tired anymore, his gaze intense and raking over me like he was afraid I might disappear if he looked away.

"Just a spell to give me energy and keep me awake," he said dismissively.

"I didn't have the magic to do it when I got here and my eyes must have fallen shut…"

"What's so bad about falling asleep?" I asked, moving my fingers down from his jaw to his neck and over the pattern of flames that curled across his shoulder and onto his chest, seeking out the letters he had hidden within them. The blood, dirt and smoke from the fight he'd taken part in still clung to his skin, but I didn't make any attempt to wash it off, liking him like this, seeing the raw truth of him on the outside too.

Darius only watched me for the longest time, not answering my question and letting the seconds drag until I thought he wasn't going to reply before finally he did.

"I wish we could just stay here like this forever," he murmured, his voice low and rough like he was trying not to tarnish the silence with his words. "Make time stand still beyond that door and live in this moment eternally."

"That's not living," I replied, the corner of my lips lifting as I shifted over his hips, feeling the hard length of his cock pressing against me in a demand.

"So what is?" he asked, like a starving man begging for scraps and my heart hurt as I looked down at him, hating the scars which Lionel had placed upon him inside and out.

"Taking hold of every moment and making it count," I replied. "A life well lived should be full of adventure and danger and passion."

"Sounds like every moment we spend together then," he replied, his hands moving to my waist and pushing the hem of my shirt up a little as I nodded, his heated skin brushing against mine in the most delicious way.

"I guess we have it pretty perfect then," I agreed. "You wanna tell me what's in the bag?"

Darius glanced down to the bag he'd brought back with him where it sat beside the bed and released a slow breath.

"Don't be pissed at me."

"That seems unlikely."

"You're infuriating," he accused. "You don't even know why I'm asking you not to get angry."

"The fact that you have to ask that has already warned me that you've screwed up, so I reserve my right to flip out," I replied with a shrug which made him growl.

"Fine. You remember when me and the other Heirs went to the mortal realm to beat the shit out of your ex?"

"How can I forget? The sight of you beating him bloody was basically my favourite porno for about six months."

"Seriously?"

"Well I couldn't have you at the time so I got pretty good at satisfying myself. The inspiration was appreciated," I teased.

"Savage girl," he said, his voice full of heat.

"There was a point to this story," I pushed as his hand moved towards my waistband and he fell still with a sigh.

"Alright. So after we'd finished teaching him and his punk friends a lesson, we decided to go see the place where you'd been living before you came to the academy."

I fell still as I took that in, my gaze slipping to the bag again and the edge of a well worn sweater jogging my memories.

"Oh."

"We weren't trying to pry into your business," he said, his hand moving to grasp my chin as he got me to turn and look at him. "We were just going to take some photos of us there or whatever. We thought you'd find it funny. We didn't really expect it to be so..."

I fought against the shame I felt at the idea of the four richest assholes in the whole of Solaria stepping into the shitty apartment we'd been shacked up in, and forced myself to hold his eye.

"So you brought our stuff back for us?" I asked.

"It made me realise why you'd been so upset by me burning your clothes off that first night. Why so little money had meant so much to you-"

"It wasn't a little bit of money," I bit out. "It was fucking everything we had."

"Roxy-" Darius began but I cut him off as I sighed, forcing myself to let it go. We were past all of this now anyway. And if I was being totally honest with myself, I was glad he'd seen it, because I could tell he really did understand now, and I wasn't sure he ever would have if he hadn't gone there himself.

"It's okay," I said. "Thank you for saving it for us."

"That's it?" he asked suspiciously.

"I'm not totally unreasonable," I pointed out and he arched a brow like that wasn't true.

"And I'm not a hot headed asshole," he replied, making me laugh.

"What happened while you were gone?" I asked, my fingertips moving to the four pink scars on his side and he looked down at them as I traced the raised ridges. "What's this?"

"Lavinia gifted my father a shadow hand to replace the one you took from him," Darius replied darkly and I growled angrily at that revelation.

"Oh, fuck him," I snapped angrily. "He's such a fucking dick. Why couldn't he just be off crying over his lost hand and feeling sorry for himself in a hole somewhere? I bet he was so fucking smug about it too."

"He didn't look so smug when I was tearing him open with tooth and claw. He got lucky with this one." Darius's hand landed over mine on his scars. "But I fucking had him, Roxy. I was so close to ripping his miserable head off."

I smiled at the fire in his eyes even though I knew there was a but coming.

"Lavinia?" I guessed and he nodded.

"Yeah. The UnFae piece of shit had her save his ass again," he grunted.

"Well, let's hope he's off licking his wounds and having nightmares over the way you beat his ass," I said, trying to focus on the positives because that really was something. If we could only get Lavinia out of the fucking picture then maybe we could win this war and end Lionel's reign for good.

"I really did." He smiled savagely and I fucking loved that bloodthirsty look in his dark eyes.

"Are you going to show me how to heal this then?" I asked, shifting my fingers over his scars. "Because when I was healing your other wounds this one didn't respond the same way."

"You just have to use a lot more power," he sighed. "The shadows taint the wound and make it resist Fae magic. But I'm fine. I'll do it myself once I'm replenished." He ran his fingers through the gold he was sitting on and I shook my head.

"No chance of that," I said, looking into his eyes as I pushed my magic into his skin and worked to continue the healing process on the scars. They resisted like he'd said and I frowned as I forced more and more magic into him, the fire at my back topping up my magic as I used it and slowly, the scars smoothed out until there was nothing left of them at all and I was left trembling a little from the exertion of using so much magic at once.

Darius pushed himself up so that he was sitting beneath me, his lips brushing mine as he looked me in the eyes and tightened his hold on my waist.

"I still don't deserve you," he said. "But I love you with all my wretched heart has to offer and I'm going to keep proving that to you with every moment gifted to me on this earth until my dying breath. So no, Roxy, I don't want to sleep. Because I refuse to waste a single second that I've been gifted with you. I want to claim each and every one and work to make them good enough for you."

My heart lodged in my throat at the sincerity of those words and as he kissed me with a soft and unyielding form of possessiveness, I felt like my entire being was falling apart for him.

His tongue pressed between my lips and I moaned softly, unbuckling his belt with shaking fingers as I tried to accept the weight of his love despite my natural inclination to feel unworthy of it. Because when Darius Acrux looked at me like I was his entire world, it felt like a whole lot of pressure for a jaded, guarded girl to live up to and yet his faith in my worth was so fierce that it was impossible to deny.

We peeled each other's clothes off with slow, intense, and deliberate moves, which had my chest heaving between the kisses which locked us together and threatened to drown me.

Darius held me like I was the most precious thing he'd ever owned and as I sank down onto the hard length of his cock, our magic spilled between our skin, merging together and stealing my breath completely.

The feeling of being possessed by Darius, body, heart, magic and soul consumed me as his dick sank in inch by delicious inch until I was finally filled by him in every way.

Our kiss broke and we fell still as we looked at each other, every part of us united as one while his power and body took hold of me, and I willingly fell prey to his demands while claiming him right back in return.

When we started moving, every single fragment of my soul came alive for him and as he drove me into a climax which stole the air from my lungs and dominated every fibre of my flesh, I knew there was never going to be any turning back from this. From us.

Darius Acrux had taken full ownership of my heart. And I was claiming his right back in return.

GERALDINE

CHAPTER SIXTEEN

"**H**oly guacamole, what a magnificent day to marry into a family of Dragoons!" I cried as I flung my bedding asunder, smacking a rather startled looking Angelica in the face with it as I leapt out of bed as bare as the day I'd been born, breasts bouncing and Lady Petunia airing in the wind of this most joyous of days. Honestly, sometimes that girl looked like she needed a good shake in a basil bush to banish the dander from her ears. "Well don't just sit there gawping, you nilly Nelly, we have much to do and only eighteen hours to do it. Don your heavy duty attire, my dear - tonight will be a night to remember. Nothing on heaven nor earth will be able to set these most mighty of plans adrift. So avast, my hot-blooded reptilian friend for we haven't the time for your waffling!"

I yanked the door open and strode out into the corridor, almost knocking straight into the slippery salmon himself as I hurried towards a bath to soak my begonias in anticipation of the day.

"Oh Maxy boy, do watch where you're drooling or someone will slip," I chided, reaching out to shut his gaping jaw with a sharp tap of my index finger before taking off at a fast pace.

"Where the fuck are your clothes?" he spluttered, scrambling after me like a snake on its belly, once again drawn close by my feminine wiles.

"I have no time for garments on a morning such as this," I replied, wondering if he intended on following me about endlessly and if I could make use of his brawn for hanging decorations if he did.

"Everyone has time for fucking garments, Gerry. People are gonna see your tits if you keep walking around out here like this and then I'm gonna have to kill them and there will be a whole clean up issue and-"

I stopped abruptly, whirling around so that he crashed straight into me as he failed to notice my halt in time to stop himself. He grasped the ample curve of my backdoor to stop himself from falling and I rightfully punched him in the nose, knocking him back once more.

"Do not lay a hand on my personage until after the nuptials, you salacious squid," I cried, wafting him back as I cast a leaf over each of my nipples and a petunia to bloom over Lady Petunia to stop his constant gandering. "I haven't the time to spare on watering the lawn until then."

"I wasn't trying to grope you, I almost fell on my ass when you stopped like that," he barked. "And I was going to say...wait a minute did you just say not until after the nuptials? Like you're down to hook up after then?"

"It is a wedding, is it not?" I asked him, unsure if he'd hit his head on my bouncing Bettys and gotten a concussion when we collided. "What kind of wedding would it be if the bridesmaid didn't end up with an eel in her secret Cecil by the end of the night?"

"In your...where the fuck is a secret Cecil?" he asked, frowning at the leaves which concealed my lady nips like they weren't to his satisfaction, and I rolled my eyes at his constant ignorance of the female form. Honestly, without my training I wasn't sure he'd even know a poppet hole from an under globe.

"Well, if you can't figure it out then maybe I should find someone who can." I threw my hands up in despair and turned away from him, giving him a full look at the orifice in question as I took off at a fierce pace, already losing too much time to this bothersome barracuda.

"You can't keep wandering about dressed like that!" Max yelled after me, but I just waved him off and kept going, heading to the bathhouse to douse my petunia and freshen my fanny.

"Make way!" I bellowed, breaking into a sprint as I made it to the cavern which held the royal baths and a few early risers shrieked in alarm as they were forced to leap aside as I took a running jump and swan dove into the pool.

I arose from the water like a swan shedding its grey down and emerging all in white feathers at long last. I grasped a washalilie and scrubbed my flesh like a heathen, scouring every nook and cranny in record sped before dousing myself with a cold wash of icy water magic and leaping from the pool once more, a petunia and two green leaves floating away across the water behind me as I strode back out of the bathhouse and headed for my room.

The antagonising anaconda was waiting for me in the corridor as anticipated and I sighed dramatically, shrouding myself in moss to cover my body before he could chastise me any further.

"Do make yourself useful if you plan on shadowing me and dry my hair for me," I called over my shoulder as I passed him by, not giving him the opportunity to start blathering on.

"You know, you're kinda moody today, Gerry," he pointed out as a gust of warm air spun around me and dried me out so thoroughly that I could have practically started a fire by rubbing my thighs together.

"Well, if I could get the preparations done in good time then that would alleviate a lot of my tension, but the list is endless, and time is ticking away." I pushed back into my room and let the door swing closed in his face before dismissing the magic which covered my bountiful body and pulling on a pair of denim dungarees and a white t-shirt.

Angelica was thankfully out of bed, getting herself dressed for the day and I double checked with her that she had everything under control for the wedding meal which we would sup on after the nuptials.

I drilled her eight times over the details to make certain she had them all in hand so that I could be assured that not so much as a buttery bagel would be left aside, and I finally allowed her to finish putting her bra on once I was satisfied.

I turned and whipped the door open again, meaning to head straight for the venue to start on the decorations but instead finding myself in the middle of a standoff at the meat market as both Maxy boy and dear Justin stood glaring at each other beyond my door.

"Oh, what fresh hell is this?" I demanded, placing my hands on my hips as I waited for an answer to my question.

"I came to offer you my assistance today, my sweet Grussy," Justin said, straightening out the tweed jacket he was wearing and offering his cheek to the obnoxious Heir to his left.

"Well I was here first and I'm pretty sure she wants someone with the kind of magical skills that are actually useful for putting on a wedding - you're only good for burning things. Unless you were planning on helping out in the kitchens?"

"Marvellous, it would seem you have found a solution without any need for my intervention," I said, clapping my hands together firmly. "Justin, you may assist Angelica in the kitchens, and I shall take the bothersome barracuda up to assist me with the decorations."

I pushed my way between them, damn near choking on the testosterone which filled the corridor while Max smirked provocatively, and Justin pouted like the little sea slug he could so often be. Honestly, that fellow needed a jolly good slap with a sardine from time to time.

"Have you thought any more about allowing me to be your date for the wedding?" Justin asked as he hurried to fall into step at my side and I huffed in frustration.

"I have told you; this is an exclusive event. We don't want every Tom, Dick and Justin in attendance. Only the personally invited guests of both my papa and his sweet love, Lady Catalina are going to be in attendance and as neither of them have requested your presence, it will not be required."

"Wait." Justin grasped my arm and jerked me to a halt just as we reached the dining cavern and I whipped around to look at him with a sigh of frustration. Honestly, sometimes he had the temper of a toddler with a toothache. "Surely as your fiancé, my invitation is guaranteed. Hamish will be my father-in-law soon so-"

A snarl like a beast from a cavern of sin filled the air and a rush of wind wiffled through my hair a moment before Justin was hurled back and pinned to the closest wall with a crack which said something had likely broken. Probably his ego, but it was hard to be certain.

Max strode between us like a peacock with his tail in full bloom and bared his teeth at Justin as he came to stand before him, wielding the air to hold him against the wall.

"Don't put your hands on her," he warned, going all Alpha and feral and I could admit that it got my waters flowing to see him releasing the kraken on the man who was destined to whisk me away from his arms. "She told you

you're not invited so get the fucking hint or I'll put you in your place."

"My place is by her side," Justin snarled, his quaffed blonde hair a flip and a flop of mess which spilled into his eyes. "You're the one who is forgetting your position in all of this. Why are you even here anyway? You're not loyal to the Vegas."

"I'm loyal to Solaria," Max replied, releasing Justin from the air magic which had him pinned to the wall as I bit my lip and gave myself a moment to watch the shenanigans unfold. "But if you have a problem with me then I'm always down for a fight with you."

Fire flared to life in Justin's palms and Max gave a cocky little smirk not unlike the one he'd gifted me on an occasion or two when he was plundering my sea cave.

My heart pitter pattered like a herd of stampeding Minotaurs, and I fanned myself a little as the fight broke out in earnest, a fireball smashing into a blast of water which caused a huge cloud of steam to engulf all three of us as the two of them leapt at each other.

Fists and magic flew, and I indulged in the little thrill of being fought over like I was a slab of meat laid out for them to chew on before turning and striding away, emerging from the cloud of steam like a gorilla from the mist.

A loyal A.S.S. member awaited me by the exit with my buttery bagels in hand and I thanked him kindly, reminding him of the importance of making sure that my ladies had a breakfast fit for queens this morning as always before heading along the tunnel which led to the farmhouse.

Cries and the sounds of the continued fight followed me, and a smug little smile tugged at my lips which had Lady Petunia all of a flutter. It wasn't very ladylike of me to enjoy the ruffians fighting for my attention the way they were, but I couldn't help but appreciate the mental picture of Maxy boy pounding sweet Justin's adoring little woodlouse face into the floor.

It wasn't that I particularly disliked my husband to be or anything like that. But I just knew that dithering with his dallywhacker was never going to come close to dancing with the dolphin, and that made me a little forlorn. If only Maxy boy could see the error of his ways, bend the knee, take up some soulful hobbies like knitting and make himself into a suitable alternative, I might even have indulged in the fantasy of ending the arrangement that had been made between Justin and I, and prancing off into the sea foam with him. Daddy wouldn't mind. He only wanted me to be happy. Not that that mattered, for I had given my word to do this, and I was nothing if not a lady of my word, my dear, sweet, utterly dead Mama had taught me that. Besides, the only thing which would ensure my happiness would be seeing the Vega queens upon the throne and having a husband at my side who took as much joy in that fate as I.

I sighed regretfully at the knowledge that my slippery salmon could never be that man, and turned my attention to the task at hand as I climbed the tunnel which led up into the farmhouse and exited into the brusque morning air.

March was upon us now and there were some signs of spring on the wind, though the snow still hadn't melted from this northerly outreach. But birdsong carried from the forest and a daffodil or two were poking their heads up in anticipation of a bountiful bloom.

I looked around, casting my eyes towards the spot I had selected on the far side of the space within the magical barrier where the mountains fell away and the view beyond was most beauteous, and a shriek of pure delight escaped me as I took it in.

I strode across the frosty ground, feeling out around me with my earth magic as I went, relishing the fullness of my power after I'd spent last night beneath the moon gathering aconite.

The sound of pounding feet drew my attention and I looked around, finding my lady Tory running along the edge of the magical barrier which kept us all safe and shrieking in delight as none other than the dastardly Dragoon chased after her in a clear attempt to capture her in his arms. It filled my heart with starlight to see her smile like that and I glowed even brighter as he tackled her to the ground and she managed to knee him in the man biscuits as they fell.

The sweet sound of a Dragon cursing the damage to his prized treasure filled the air and I sighed as her laughter followed. Now he only needed to bend the knee, rescind his claim to the Celestial Council and live ever on as her devoted house husband, rearing the next generation of Vega princes and princesses for the throne while she took over the kingdom alongside her sister as the stars intended.

I turned my attention to the task at hand and dropped to one knee as I began to craft the wedding venue with my earth magic, first erecting a pergola grown from the ground itself on a dais raised up to face the stars, before moving on to the seating which I arranged in two neat rows behind it. There were only to be eight guests here to witness this most joyous of events. Daddy had requested that the Vegas and I be present while Catalina wanted her sons and the other Heirs here. There had been mention of one Power Shamed ex professor attending too, but when poor Daddy swooned and almost busted his head open on a rock, it had been decided that it was best he stay away with his shame in case it tainted the magic of their union.

Heavy footsteps drew my attention to my back, and I turned my head as I finished constructing the frame of my design and found Maxy boy approaching, his shirt half burnt off and one eyebrow singed, but a cocky swagger to his movements let me know he'd given Justin a jolly good pummelling.

"You left," he accused, moving to stand behind me and I pushed to my feet too.

"I have work to do, as you well know," I chastised him, reaching out to slap his chest, my hand meeting with the firm muscle of his pec and lingering against his deliciously dark skin. "But tell me, did he scream like a salamander in a cesspit?"

Max chuckled cruelly, leaning in and dominating me with that big aura of his as his mouth dropped to my ear.

"I made him beg for his momma and piss his pants for good measure," he growled, taking my fingers in his and using his gifts to offer up a view of the memory.

A shiver tracked down my spine as I allowed it, my lips curling up in amusement as he showed me the moment he'd overwhelmed Justin with his brutish power and had thrust a wave of terror into him with his Siren gifts, causing him to weep and beg and indeed wet himself.

"Oh you are a bad, bad, barracuda, aren't you?" I murmured, my hand

221

sliding down his chest and tracing the firm ridges of his abs as he groaned softly at my touch.

"I don't like that fucker trying to steal you from me," he said, owning his devotion even though we both knew that it could lead us nowhere.

"He cannot steal that which is not claimed," I replied with a sigh, drawing my hand away and looking to all the work I had yet to do, but of course he wouldn't be so easily perturbed.

"I *have* claimed you, Gerry. You're just too blind to see it."

I raised my eyes to his again, frowning at the brash audacity of his tone and stamping down the little jig Lady Petunia was trying to start up in my undergarments.

"I don't have time for philandering today," I began, but he was already following my gaze and nodding.

"Alright. If you need to concentrate on making this all pretty and sparkly and shit, then you've got the perfect man for the job at your side. I can do things with water magic that would blow your insane little mind, Gerry."

Max took my hand and I looked down at our interlocked fingers in surprise as I felt his magic pressing against the barrier of mine in offering.

"And if you wanna make something truly amazing then we should really work on it together," he added, a dare in his tone and a twinkle in his eye.

This dastardly dogfish would be the death of me one of these days.

Yet despite every reason I had to mistrust a troublesome Heir, I found my magic rushing towards that point of contact he held, the power within me buzzing with the scandalous idea of merging with his.

"This is practically blasphemy," I murmured, not pulling away.

"Oh come on, Gerry. It isn't like it's the first thing I've ever put inside you."

I barked a laugh at his jest and nodded in agreement. "Alright then, let us tangle our tentacles once again, Maxy boy. I want to see what you've got."

His grin widened and I pushed my barriers aside, finding it far easier to do so than I should have with a cad like him. Our magic merged and oh, what a merger it was!

I gasped at the rush of his power beneath my skin, near panting with the flush of water and air which crashed through my body, meeting my own magic and combining with it in a furious wave. My power over earth grounded us but the might of our combined water darn near swept me away on a tide of bliss I never wanted to come back from.

"Oh wet begonias on a Sunday morn," I moaned, soaking in the feeling of him filling me.

"Yeah," Max panted, his eyes alight with the thrill of me being inside him too. "What you said."

I chuckled loudly, the mirth in me bursting forth and making him smile too as I turned my attention to the work at hand and we began creating the wedding venue of dreams.

"Tonight will be a night to remember," I cooed as we worked and Max drew closer to me, slipping his arms around my waist so that he could increase the contact between us, and I found myself not protesting the move in the slightest.

"Yeah, Gerry. It'll be perfect," he promised and by golly, I believed he actually meant to make it so.

We finished our work with barely a moment to spare, the elegant pergola where the union would take place dressed in millions of tiny starflowers which blossomed only beneath the light of the stars which would be out at any moment as the sun had already dipped beneath the horizon.

Everything sparkled with the most delicate touch of frost, each snowflake individually crafted to hold the initials H and C intertwined in eternal love which made my giddy heart glow with adoration.

Above the seats which had been created from the pure white wood hung a swathe of lilac and pink flowers in every variety, each of them frost tipped and glimmering even in the low light of the rising moon.

"Oh what a joyous and most magnanimous evening," I gasped, my wet Wandas getting the better of me as a sob choked its way free of my lips and tears sprung from my eyes.

A solid arm wound its way around my shoulders, and I fell apart as I allowed the slippery salmon of my heart to draw me closer to him, burying my face in his chest and breathing in his raw man scent like it was a balm to my senses.

"You've done an amazing job here, Gerry," he said, touching a soft kiss to my hair which made me gasp and cry some more.

"You know full well that without the addition of your magic it would be a mere husk of the beauty it is now," I chided, and he chuckled softly.

"Well, I might have leant you the magic to get the job done but this is all you. Your dad will be thrilled."

"You think so?" I asked, tilting my head back to look at him and he reached out to brush the tears from my cheeks with a soft smile which crept into my heart and unfurled there.

Oh, what a shame it was that he was such a slanderous sardine.

"I know so," he swore, his gaze dropping to my mouth and making me think he might just steal a kiss, but instead he cleared his throat and drew back. "You don't have long to get yourself dressed, Gerry. I'd hate to make you late for this after you worked so hard to pull it together."

"Oh good galaxies, you're right!" I cried, looking up at the moon and gauging the time from it. "I only have a few moments to prepare myself!"

I spun away from my fabulous flounder and took off post haste, racing back down into The Burrows and sprinting at full speed to my chamber where my ladies were due to meet with me.

The corridors were busy but I dropped my head low, squared my shoulders and bellowed a warning for all to move aside as I charged through the crowd, knocking any lollygaggers to their posteriors as I raced by.

I flung open the door to my room and gasped in delight as I found the two Vega princesses looking every bit the queens they were in the stunning taffeta gowns I'd had made especially for the occasion for them.

Tory's nose was wrinkled as she looked at the layers upon layers of moss green skirt which ruffled out around her endlessly and I pushed my way through them as I moved to grasp her chin and raise her gaze to meet mine.

"Do not doubt the beauty you exude, my fair queen. I assure you that you wear this stunning gown and it does not wear you - so fear not!"

"Err, that wasn't what I was-"

"They're really something, Geraldine, thank you," Darcy cut in, giving me a wide smile with so many teeth that they glittered like stars. I had selected her the same gown in a vibrant orange colour which really complimented the blue of her hair and I darn near started sobbing again as I looked between them.

"I don't think we'll fit through the door though," Tory added. "Maybe if I just cut a few layers off…"

I burst out laughing at her jest, swimming through the swathes of their skirts as I headed to claim my own blush pink gown in the very same style as theirs.

"I know that I am but a lowly servant to the crown," I said as I stripped down and stepped into my dress, unable to look at them as I spoke these words. "But I cannot explain the honour I feel in matching you ladies in our attire on this most special of occasions. I never had any siblings, but I know the love I feel for the two of you must equal what I would have felt for sisters of my very own."

"Aww, shit, don't go getting all soppy on me or I'll end up wearing the damn hat too," Tory teased as she waded through the confines of her dress and managed to wrap her arms around me just as Darcy did the same from the other side.

"We're so lucky to have you, Geraldine," she added, making my unworthy heart burst into a million pieces and scatter themselves among the stars to glow on in eternal happiness in the heavens.

"Oh, my ladies," I gasped. "If Lionel Acrux himself were to show up here and kill me this very night, I would die content and endlessly happy in the company of those kind words and the love I hold in my heart for you."

"Jesus, Geraldine, you can't say shit like that," Tory said, swatting my arm to chastise me. "That's like tempting fate. You might as well have said something like 'nothing could possibly go wrong now' or 'I had a feeling everything was going to be okay.'"

Darcy laughed. "Yeah, don't go tempting the stars to turn on us, they already have enough fun screwing with us without needing any encouragement. I swear a couple of the sparkly shits gave me and Lance an evil look when we went for a walk outside last night."

"I apologise," I giggled. But I knew not a thing would go wrong tonight. This union was already blessed before it had begun, now we just had to get to the part where they said 'I do.'

I made it fully into my dress and my queens helped me to apply my makeup as best they could while we all worked around the confines of our dresses until finally, the three of us stood ready before the mirror, admiring ourselves.

The orange, pink and green fabric of our dresses all fought for dominance as we tried to squeeze close to one another to admire ourselves, and I giggled at our three little heads popping out from a tide of taffeta like a colourful Cerberus, and it was so endlessly glorious that I almost cried again.

"We look…wow," Tory said, her eyes raking over all of us in the reflection as she found herself too gobsmacked to even smile.

"Yeah," Darcy breathed, equally flat mouthed. "Wow."

"Wow indeed!" I gushed and we all fell into fits of giggles as we slipped our feet into our stilettos and headed for the door.

"Fuck it," Tory said, throwing a final look at the mirror before pulling the door wide and leading the way out. "Let's go watch a wedding."

I cupped my hands around my mouth as we began along the tunnel, crying out for everyone to move aside for the passage of the true queens so loud that my voice echoed throughout the entire network of underground chambers and tunnels. And move they did. People gasped and pointed, eyes widening. Some of them turned utterly giddy at the sight of my majesties looking so thoroughly royal that they found themselves in a state of nervous giggles.

"This might be the best day of my life," I choked out as we continued our parade through the caverns and headed towards my father's new destiny.

"That's great, Geraldine," Darcy said, placing a hand on my shoulder as we made it up into the farmhouse and the whispers and praise of the crowds were left behind us.

I led the way out into the night, gasping with joy at the starflowers coming into bloom all over the pergola where the union was to take place.

The Heirs and Xavier had already arrived, each of them looking dashing in black tuxes and their eyes all widened as they turned to watch our approach.

"By the bat shit crazy stars," Seth gasped in delight, his eyes widening as he drank in the visage which was my ladies and me. "Do you know you all look like-"

Caleb slapped a hand over his mouth before he could finish that no doubt crass compliment and I giggled coyly as I drank in the sight of so much well packaged man meat.

"Looking…stunning, girls," Caleb said and by golly he did look stunned.

Tory snorted in that unladylike and yet utterly endearing way of hers which gave away her pleasure at them all appreciating our attire so much, and I couldn't help but flutter my eyelashes at Maxy boy who seemed to have lost the power of speech.

We moved to take our seats and Darius and Xavier stepped forward to help us spread them apart a little to make room for the voluminous skirts of our gowns.

"You like?" Tory asked, giving her devilish Dragon a smile worthy of launching a thousand vessels as he looked her up and down.

"Fuck me, Roxy, I know I really am in love if I can see you in that gown and still want you just as fiercely as ever," Darius muttered as he helped her into her seat, and I practically glowed at seeing him swoon over her in her finery.

"Well try to control yourself," she whispered back. "It would be a crying shame if it was burnt to cinders by your fire magic while you were trying to get me out of it."

Darcy laughed and I hid my own chuckle beneath my hand. They really were the most well matched of mates. Even if they weren't actually mates at all now…I frowned as I thought on that, looking up to the heavens and wondering if they would offer up a fresh chance at an Elysian Mate bond for the two of them so that they could accept it with all of their hearts now. Surely they deserved that much.

Before I could muse on that too long, footsteps announced Papa's arrival and I squealed as I leapt to my feet, flinging my arms out wide and accidentally smacking Xavier in the eye as I did so.

"Ow!" he cursed, stumbling back a step and I whirled to him with an apology.

"I am so sorry, my dear brother, but fear not - I brought you a gift in honour of us becoming siblings which I'm certain will take the sting away!" I reached down to lift the skirts of my gown, rustling and rummaging until I found the two gifts I had gotten my new brothers and I darn near squealed again, wondering what they'd gotten me in return.

"Brother?" Xavier muttered, glancing at Darius like he was so overwhelmed by my new claim on him that he had no words for his emotions.

Darius gave me a look which was so full of sibling love that he couldn't even manage to make his face react to it, the blank, utter shock concealing the jubilation which I just knew was hiding beneath the surface.

"Perhaps save the gifts you got me for later?" I suggested, fanning my eyes as they threatened to spill over. "I think I'll end up all of a dither if I open them now."

"Gifts?" Xavier asked and bless his cotton socks, he was so overwhelmed with emotion that it appeared he'd forgotten what was even going on here.

Darius opened his mouth, but Tory had a sudden knee spasm which caused her to kick him in the shin and he grunted in pain as he looked to her instead.

"Perhaps just save it for the morning, yeah? You don't want Geraldine to cry her makeup off," she said pointedly.

"Oh yes, the morning sounds perfect," Darcy agreed, nodding profusely. The sweet little lamb was clearly on utter tenterhooks for the celebration and could hardly contain herself.

"Yes," I agreed frantically. "Let's save it for the morn when I can fully fall apart without it impacting on this fine day."

I handed over the gifts I had gotten for my new brothers and they both thanked me with frowns of curiosity and anticipation lining their brows.

I watched with rapt attention as Xavier unwrapped his, revealing the bushel of seven utterly perfect carrots alongside the poem I had written for him, and his smile lit up the darn moon.

"This is…so great," he said, already salivating over the feast I had prepared for him and by golly I fell apart at the onslaught of emotion I felt pouring from him and flung myself into his arms with a sob, clutching him to my bosom and swearing to love him in all the ways a big sister should. He was so lost for words that he could only pat my back and nod along, but I could feel the connection between us forming into a solid and unbreakable bond which I knew would remain in place until our dying days.

"You got me a gold coin?" Darius asked and I turned my attention to him, nodding through my tears as I pointed to it.

"I had it engraved with this date upon it," I gushed - the day we became a family.

Darius smirked at me, shaking his head like he was just lost for words.

"Can I see?" Darcy asked, reaching out towards it but he growled, his fist snapping closed over it before he pushed it into his pocket, muttering *'mine'* like the treasure hoarding Dragoon he was.

I turned and hurried over to Papa as I noticed him shuffling from foot to foot, nervously smoothing down his moustache as he kept glancing over his shoulder down the short and empty aisle. He was wearing a dashing, powder blue suit with ruffles galore and a blush pink kerchief poked out of one pocket to match my dress.

"What do you always tell me when I get myself in a kerfuffle?" I barked at him.

"Chin up, chest out and don't let them see you blubber," he replied sternly, trying to take his own advice as he straightened his spine and I nodded firmly, stepping forward to straighten his bowtie as Darius and Xavier strode away from us to collect the bride.

I was all of a film-flam as I stood there like a pelican who'd lost his fish and as a warm hand caught my arm, I allowed Max to draw me away and return me to my seat.

Darcy took my hand as I sat between her and her sister, my heart racing along like a penguin on land, trying to escape a polar bear - awkward and bumbling yet determined all the same.

Music sprung to life as Catalina's arrival triggered the magical spell I'd set on the place, and I shrieked like a banshee as my excitement got the better of me and I spun to look upon the bride who would soon become my step-mama.

My thoughts turned to my own mama who I'd lost so many moons ago, and my heart let out a tiny sob as I missed her. For a moment, I could have sworn I heard a whisper upon the spring breeze and the caress of my beloved Mama's hand down my cheek, causing a tear to slide smoothly from my eye and drip from my chin as I was filled with reassurance. I was sure she was here in some form, peering out from beyond the veil to watch my cherished Papa find happiness once more.

Catalina walked between her two sons, her smile as radiant as the first sunbeam of the dawn, her skin as effervescent as the pool of Anu which was rumoured to hold the key to eternal life, her pale pink, hand sewn wedding dress demure and dazzling at once, hugging her figure and yet looking regal and elegant too.

I was so caught up in squealing with excitement and staring on in endless love and adoration for my father as she reached him that I utterly forgot that I was supposed to be silent for the procession.

I clapped my hand over my mouth to stifle my cries of joy and Darcy muttered a curse as she shook out the fingers I'd been crushing in my excitement.

My eyes watered as they spoke their vows to one another, the purity of their smiles and honesty of their love shining so brightly that it was impossible to look away from it as they chose one another and bound themselves into a life of love and commitment for the rest of time.

It was as beautiful as a boomsday bunny in a bonnet on a buttery bagel. And as the stars granted their request and bound them to one another, I leapt up and screamed for all the world to hear, pouncing on the two of them and crushing them against my bosom as I sobbed in purest, sweetest joy.

SETH

CHAPTER SEVENTEEN

I ran through the tunnels with my tongue hanging out the side of my mouth and a bottle of bourbon locked in my fist. I was excited as hell as I raced away from the cavern where the wedding had descended into a messy party since Hamish and Catalina had gone to bed.

Everyone else had gotten drunk as fuck, but not me. My shoulder bumped off the wall and I stumbled sideways, hitting the opposite wall. Oh who was I kidding? I was as drunk as a mouse in a tiny house and I had plans. Big, big plans.

I made it to our room door, shoving it open and finding Orion on the bed with his shiny little gemstone book open on his bare chest, a hopeful glint in his eyes. But then his face fell as he realised it was me, not Darcy and I smirked, swaggering into the room and holding the bottle of bourbon behind my back.

"Everyone's having fun," I announced.

"Great," he said flatly.

"But you're here all alone like a lonely llama." I moved to the bed, crawling onto it as I kept the bourbon behind me and his eyes narrowed.

"I was, but now a dog has come to annoy me," he said.

"Lemme see," I urged, reaching for his book but he whipped it off his chest and put it in the nightstand drawer with a burst of Vampire speed.

I hadn't listened much when he'd told us about what he'd learned in his glittery gemstone book earlier, I'd had my eyes trained on a chocolate bar sticking out of Tory Vega's pocket. A chocolate bar that was now stashed under my pillow. It was cute how she kept playing this snack hunt game with me. Sometimes she hid the snacks so well, it was almost like she didn't want me to find them. But I always did.

"What do you want, Seth?" he growled and I held out the bourbon to him with a tempting grin.

"I brought you a gift."

"Is it laced with poison?" he asked suspiciously and I pursed my lips.

I tipped my head back and howled sadly that he'd think that about his moon friend, but he lurched forward, slapping a hand to my mouth to stop me.

"What's wrong with you? Go back to the party." He shoved me away and I hit the floor, clambering back onto the bed and pawing at him while offering him the bourbon.

"Darcy asked me to come get you," I lied. This was my surprise to Darcy, because I was going to butter her up tonight and get her to put the feelers out on Cal. It was the perfect crime. But she was always the most butterable when Orion was around. Plus, maybe this would be a good bonding exercise for us.

"She did?" he asked, his eyes brightening and I nodded, waving the bourbon at him. "But you have to catch up because everyone else is drunk off their tits."

He slowly accepted the bourbon, twisting off the cap and sniffing it.

"Come on, if I drugged you Darcy would neuter me," I said. "It's just a gift."

He gave me a narrowed eyed look before taking a sip of the bourbon and I smiled Wolfishly.

"Can I tell you a secret?" I whispered, leaning forward to rest my chin on his shoulder.

"No," he said bluntly, sipping more of the bourbon as he tried to jolt me off of him, but my chin was staying right there on that meaty muscle bit.

"It's a good one," I whispered. "One that could ruin me."

He frowned, observing me as he swallowed another mouthful of bourbon, intrigue glittering in his dark eyes. "Oh yeah?"

"Yeah. But if I give you this power, Lance Orion, you have to be my friend," I said, prodding him in the dimple. "B to the double F. Got it?"

"Sure," he said lightly, and though the echo of my sober brain said he was probably playing me like a whore of a flute, drunk brain said it was green lights all ahead.

"I'm in love with my best friend," I breathed my most terrifying secret.

"Darius?" he balked.

"No." I swatted him.

"Max?"

"No!"

"Darcy?" he growled dangerously.

"No," I snarled through my teeth. "Forget it." I shoved off of the bed, but I paused as he said the name that unravelled me like he was pulling on a thread of my soul.

"Caleb?" he asked, his voice softening ever so slightly.

"Yeah," I rasped, wheeling around again with a whimper in my throat. "I love him and he'll never love me back because he's not – because he doesn't like – because I have a massive – and he has an equally big – and – *oh*." I flopped down onto the bed, burying my face in Orion's chest and he growled in warning, shoving me back.

I looked up at him, finding his fangs on show and I pointed at them. "Wait - you have fangs! So you must have the answer I've been looking for. Does drinking blood turn you on? Like, say you drank from an ugly leprechaun but he tasted like a rainbow, would you get a hard on? Or do you have to find your blood bags hot to get hard? You have to tell me, Lance, how do you get hard?!"

A movement in my periphery made my head snap sideways and I spotted Justin Masters looking in at us with wide eyes through the open door with his lips parted in shock.

"How much did you hear?!" I bellowed, ready to slice his ears off and make threats to every single member of his family so he never spoke a word of this.

He backed up several steps, fear crossing his features.

"J-just you asking Professor Orion how he gets hard," he spluttered and I breathed a sigh of relief, hurrying to the door and slamming it in his face.

"Thank the stars," I said heavily.

"Oh yes," Orion said sarcastically as he glowered at me. "Thank the stars."

I wheeled around, casting a silencing bubble and leaping back onto the bed as Orion chugged more of the bourbon. It was almost like he wanted to be drunk to endure my company, but it couldn't be that. I was a delight.

"So?" I demanded. "Do you get hard for Darcy's blood or is it because it's Darcy's blood that it makes you hard? Have you ever gotten hard just off of blood? I need to know, Lance. Stop holding out on me."

He sighed, lowering the bottle and giving me an exasperated look. "Fine," he huffed. "Yes, I've gotten hard from powerful blood before."

"Before Darcy?" I asked and he nodded, not meeting my eye as he clearly didn't want to discuss this. But discuss this he would.

"Whose blood was it? Did you fuck them? Or was it an uggo? Or did you fuck an uggo?"

"It was Darius, alright?" he snapped and my lips parted.

"Oh my stars…you fucked Darius. That explains everything."

"No I didn't!" he balked. "His blood turned me on, that's all."

"Right." I winked. "It's okay, Lance. We're in a sharing circle here. You can tell me the truth. Did you do the downward Werewolf with him? Or did you let him ride your Milky Way?"

"We did not fuck," he snarled and I sighed.

"So why are you telling me you did?" I asked.

"I didn't," he said in disbelief.

"Okay, okay, so you're saying you got hard for your best friend and you *didn't* stick it in him?" I asked, needing to clarify this because he just wasn't making any sense.

"I got hard for his blood. And anyway, that was when we were Guardian bonded, it was different," he said with a frown. "It has no bearing on how Caleb feels about you."

"Hm…so you're saying I should Guardian bond Cal to me, then I'd be irresistible to him?"

"No, that's not what I said."

"Uhuh, but let's say I could figure out how to do that-"

"Seth," he hissed and I sighed.

"Yeah, yeah, I wouldn't actually do it. You know what I could do though…"

"Tell him the truth?" he suggested and I waved a hand dismissively at that.

"Don't be ridiculous, now you're sounding like Darcy."

"So telling him the truth is ridiculous but Guardian bonding your best friend to you so that he might be more tempted to fuck you isn't?"

"Exactly." I nodded. "You see, Lance, I'm trying to find an angle where I don't have to tell him, but I still get to have him. And especially a solution where I don't have to take any responsibility for it all going wrong if he rejects me."

He shook his head at me. "Have you ever Faed up and owned your own shit, Seth Capella?"

I thought on that, frowning at my new friend as I slipped the bottle of bourbon from his hand and took a long sip. "Is that a rhetorical question?"

"No."

"Hmm, seems like it is. Shall we go to the party now?" I sprang off the bed and headed to the door, but turned back to him before I exited, vulnerability spilling through me. "You won't tell anyone I told you that, right? Especially not Cal. If he finds out and he doesn't like me back, I'll lose him. And I can't lose him. I'm so fucking scared to lose him."

He frowned, pushing to his feet and pulling on a t-shirt before swiping the bottle of bourbon from my hand, keeping me in suspense as he hung this secret over my head like an axe. "As much as you deserve to have that bomb go off in your face, I'm not going to stoop as low as you have in the past."

"Hey, I never told anyone about you and Darcy," I countered. "Not even the Heirs. I just liked messing with you."

He kicked on some sneakers and shot to my side in a blur, a cruel smile lifting his lips. "And how confident are you that I don't like playing my own games, Capella?"

I chuckled darkly, liking this psycho side of him. It reminded me of me. And me was awesome. "Go right ahead. But I have a secret weapon now. Darcy's my bestie. So bring it on."

He flashed his fangs at me then opened the door and I dove on his back before he could shoot away from me, his Vampire speed nearly giving me whiplash as he took off at the same moment. I howled loudly in excitement, holding on tight as he cursed, tearing along in the direction of the cavern where the rest of our friends were partying.

He slammed to a halt so hard that I went flying over his shoulder, my howl turning to a yelp as I hit the stone floor and bounced along it, catching myself on a gust of air a second too late. He laughed obnoxiously and I couldn't help but join in as I shoved to my feet and gave him a challenging glare.

"Oh, you wanna play rough with me, do you Lancey?" I ran at him with a battle cry tearing from my throat but he shot out of the way, darting through the door into the party and I twisted on my heels to follow him, immediately losing interest in the game as I spotted Caleb up on the table between everyone with his shirt off and five beers levitating over his head upside down. His mouth was wide as Max guided the liquid to his lips and he chugged it. Half of it missed, running down his naked chest and my cock rose like the sun at dawn as I stared at his glistening abs and the flex of his throat as he swallowed again and again. STAY by The Kid LAROI and Justin Bieber played from someone's Atlas and it instantly became my favourite song of all time.

Fuck...me.

"Lance!" Darcy squealed, leaping from her chair amidst a mass of orange taffeta and he caught her out of the air, crushing her to his chest and looking down at her endlessly ugly dress in amusement.

It was just our group of friends here, which was my favourite place in the world because they were my real pack. I didn't need daily blowjobs, creampies and ball tickling to keep me content. I mean, sure, I'd have thrown those things into the mix with Cal if I could have, but as it was, I was going one hundred percent celibate these days – which for a Werewolf was a big ass deal. I didn't even jerk off that much because I only ever ended up thinking of my best friend and feeling guilty for being so obsessed with him. So I was down to like twice a day.

"Hey beautiful, what in the ever loving fuck is this?" Orion asked, plucking at the bright material as she laughed into his chest.

"My dress," Darcy's voice came out muffled against his shirt.

"It's a radiant gown for a queen of Solaria!" Geraldine cried.

"And there was me thinking a pumpkin had puked on her," Orion said with a smirk and Geraldine smacked the table in anger.

"You have no taste at all, Lance Orion. You would have her dress like a common beansprout."

"She can dress in whatever the fuck she likes so long as I'm the one tearing her out of it later." He gave Darcy a wicked smile and Tory tossed an empty beer bottle at his head. His hand snapped out, catching it at the last second as he turned his grin on her. "Problem?"

"You're being gross with my sister," she complained.

"Says the girl with her hand an inch away from my best friend's cock." Orion gestured to where Tory's hand laid on Darius's thigh.

"Agreed," Xavier said as he swigged on a sparkly bottle of something called Bacarroti Ice.

"Touché," Tory said, leaning back in her seat.

"If you keep ripping me out of my clothes, I'm gonna have none left," Darcy chastised Orion, though her eyes sparkled like she didn't mind all that much.

"That's precisely my intention," he joked and Darcy laughed, the two of them unable to stop staring at each other. It was cute, and I wasn't jealous at *all* of having that kind of unwavering bond with someone. Sigh, who was I kidding?

My eyes flicked back to Caleb as he dropped his head to look at me and beer spilled over his hair from another couple of bottles Max had sent up there, washing down onto his shoulder as he wiped his mouth with the back of his hand. Which was the least of his problems considering he was fucking drenched now. But by the stars, I wouldn't have minded cleaning him up with my tongue.

"Seth Capella!" Geraldine cried from where she was sitting beside Max. "You missed your turn, now you will double dog dare someone to do something extra dastardly."

A smirk hooked up the corner of my mouth as I strode toward the table and plucked a beer out of a large bucket of ice Max had cast earlier. The white tablecloth was filthy from drinks that had been spilled all over it, but the rest of the place was still pretty well intact, twinkling Faelights strung all across the ceiling and beautiful ice and flower decorations everywhere. It was so pretty it made me wanna puke. In a good way though.

Orion grabbed a seat next to Darius, pulling Darcy onto his lap as Tory climbed over Darius to hug her sister, looking drunk as hell as she nuzzled her like a cat. She sure wasn't huggy when she was sober. She'd throat punched me the last time I tried to snuggle her, but I wondered if now was a good time to try and get that snuggle…

"Well, what's it to be, Capella?" Geraldine demanded and I sucked on my lower lip as I looked up at Caleb, taking a moment to sip some of my beer as I decided on the dare. Cal seemed happy to remain up there as Max flicked a finger and let the empty beer bottles plonk down onto the table behind him. My mind raced as I tried to come up with a dare that might help me figure out if Cal was into me or not. And my little drunk mind had just the idea.

"Alright, I dare everyone to sink a bottle of beer. The last one to finish has to kiss me." I grinned widely, looking Caleb right in the eye as his lips parted for a second then he shrugged like it meant nothing. And maybe it did, but also, maybe it didn't.

"Roxy isn't playing," Darius announced with a growl in the back of his Dragony throat.

"Or Darcy," Orion chimed in and I looked over at them with a chuckle.

"You guys just want me all to yourselves, huh?" I taunted and Darius flipped me the finger while Orion gave me a hollow look, though I could tell the bourbon was having an effect on him now, his angry little eyes not quite as bloodthirsty as usual.

"Gerry can't play either," Max said, but Geraldine conjured a turnip in her hand and whacked him round the ear with it.

"Nonsense, Maxy boy!" she cried. "I will not be excused from a game of daring and wit. I shall beat this beast head on."

Max shot me a look that said if I dared lay my mouth on her he'd cut my tongue out, but Geraldine Grus was definitely not my target in this game.

"Come on then," Caleb said, jumping down from the table and landing in front of me with a sideways grin. He plucked a bottle of beer from the ice cooler and clinked it against mine, never breaking eye contact with me and my heart raced to a dangerous, hungry tune. "Game on."

Max, Geraldine, Darius, Xavier and Orion grabbed fresh beers and I smiled around at them, my heart thumping harder as I wondered how this was gonna play out. If Cal secretly wanted me, surely he'd drink slow and lose the game, right? This had to work.

"Ready…set…go!" I cried and they all started drinking their beers as fast as they could.

Max kept side-eyeing Geraldine, drinking slower so he was always a bit behind her, and my jaw ground as I prayed I wasn't gonna have to kiss him just so he could save Gerry from my edible lips. I mean, he was hot and I'd definitely get off on it a little, but his wasn't the mouth I wanted to claim that kiss from.

Orion and Darius raced through their drinks in two seconds flat and Xavier seemed well on his way through his too as I let my eyes slide to Cal. He had at least half the bottle left and as his eyes met mine, my pulse drummed to a furious tune, hope filling me up and calling me lucky.

Geraldine finished hers with a gasp for air and Max followed her, leaving it down to Xavier and Caleb.

"Wow, how bad would it be if we had to kiss, right?" I said to Caleb, chuckling nervously. "So bad, right?"

"Done!" Xavier announced and my heart took off and flew to the moon, doing fifty cartwheels around it before crashing into a crater to make a home there.

It's happening.

It's on.

It's going down to Tucana town.

Caleb finished his drink half a second later, lowering the bottle from his wet lips and our friends started laughing and cheering us on like this was one big, fat joke. But it secretly wasn't a joke. It was what I'd wanted for so fucking long and now he was stepping closer to me with his eyes on my mouth and I couldn't breathe as I stepped toward him too.

"Come on then, sweetheart. Gimme a kiss," Caleb said cockily, fisting a hand in my shirt and drawing me so close to him that I could taste the beer on his lips already.

His smile was for the game, but his navy eyes were deadly serious and they were devouring me just like I was aching to devour him. Or at least, that's what I wanted to believe. That there was a deeper reason for him finishing last and surely once we'd kissed, I'd know for certain. I'd be able to feel it without ever having to ask him. And he'd feel it too and then, and then-

"Wait, wait, wait," Max called, as Caleb's smile fell and his eyes bored into mine with a want in them that I felt right down to the centre of my being. "Xavier didn't finish his."

"You're such a snitch, man," Xavier complained and Caleb turned to look at them, leaving me staring at him with my jaw grinding as his fingers tightened in my shirt.

"Well you shouldn't be a little cheat," Max tossed back and I forced myself to look, my gut plummeting as I saw the bottle of beer which had half an inch of liquid left in the bottom of it.

Max shook it as proof that Xavier hadn't finished the game and my heart was speared on my own misery.

"No," I breathed and Caleb's eyes snapped back to me, but I forced myself to step away, his fingers still knotted in my shirt like he couldn't let go.

But then he did and he slapped on a bright smile, a laugh leaving him like he was relieved.

"Well thank fuck for that," Caleb said and maybe it was just a lie, but it didn't feel like one. It felt like a knife driving right into my chest and carving out my heart.

Xavier shoved out of his seat with a sigh, striding towards me and suddenly I was faced with kissing Darius's goddamn little brother and Caleb was walking away to sit down beside Max.

No. Fucking no. It wasn't fair. This wasn't how it was supposed to go.

Xavier looked to me with a frown and I grabbed the back of his neck, yanking him against me with a growl and kissing him with so much bite that

he whinnied in protest. Then I shoved him away from me and drained my beer in one before throwing myself down onto the chair beside Orion and Darcy.

Darcy looked at me with pity in her eyes as the game continued on, but I slapped a fake ass smile on my face as I pretended my heart hadn't just been kicked and stamped on. That I didn't feel like I'd been rejected. Because I hadn't, but somehow, I had.

"My turn!" Geraldine cried, pointing a finger at Orion. "You sir have gotten away with this game far too easily."

"I literally just got here," he said as he swigged from his bourbon bottle.

"Precisely," she said. "So I dare you to wear all the A.S.S. regalia I can carry from my room to here for the rest of the night and right through breakfast tomorrow as well."

Orion wrinkled his nose while Darcy and Tory burst out laughing, nodding excitedly as he groaned and gave in.

"Alright," he agreed. "Bring it here then."

"Come salmon man, I need your bulky arms to assist me." Geraldine hopped up, pulling Max after her who seemed more than willing to follow as he stared at her ass, though how he could see anything through the miles of pink taffeta covering it, I had no idea.

Caleb glanced over at me as he grabbed himself another beer and I pushed my fingers into my hair, pretending I was as chilled as a cucumber on ice when inside I was dying.

"I can't believe you bit me, man. Is that how you always kiss people?" Xavier dabbed at his swollen bottom lip.

"Ah shit, did I just steal your rough kiss V-card?" I asked. "Or was it your first kiss V-card?" I gasped in horror.

"Dude," Darius growled at me and I shrugged innocently.

"What? He shouldn't have cheated if he didn't wanna be mouth fucked. I can't help it if it was his first time."

"Seth," Darius hissed. "I've already had to watch you kiss my fucking brother like he was one of your little Wolf pack Betas, can we stop talking about it now?"

"Alright, alright," I said, backing down and looking to Xavier whose cheeks were pinking. "Sorry, man. If you need some cherry popping pointers though I'm all ears."

"Who's popping Xavier's cherry?" Tyler stepped into the room with Sofia under his arm and Xavier swore beneath his breath.

"Look who we found in the hallway!" Geraldine exclaimed as she came prancing back into the cavern with Max trailing after her, his arms full of A.S.S. merchandise.

Tyler smirked at Xavier as he grabbed a couple of beers, passing one to Sofia as they moved to sit with him.

"What happened to your lip?" Sofia asked, reaching out to heal it and Xavier's blush deepened.

"Seth bit it," he murmured.

"It was weird," Tory said thoughtfully. "It was such an angry kiss, like he was trying to rip Xavier's mouth off."

Caleb's eyes slid to me as I fought to keep my smile hitched in place.

"Says the girl who kisses Darius like she's trying to eat his whole face,"

I tossed at her.

"I do not," she protested as Darius boomed a laugh.

"Circling back to Xavier's cherry," Tyler said lightly, his eyes glinting maliciously at Xavier. "Still a virgin then, are you buddy?"

"Fuck off," Xavier growled. "I'm not a virgin."

"It is quite alright for the moon to not yet have shone upon your delicate lampoon, Xavier," Geraldine said as she walked over to Orion and started directing him to dress in the A.S.S. gear. Apparently he'd had enough bourbon to slide into it willingly too.

"The moon *has* shone on my – I mean, I don't have a delicate lampoon," Xavier spluttered.

"It is a plain lampoon though, isn't it?" Tyler taunted. "Not a gemstone in sight."

"There's nothing wrong with that," Sofia insisted, elbowing Tyler in the ribs.

"Rhinestones turn you on though, don't they baby?" Tyler said with a smirk and Sofia blushed. "What did you say about mine? That they make your pussy sparkle."

"Well yeah, but that doesn't mean everyone has to get them," she protested.

Darcy slipped off of her chair, helping Orion change into a jumpsuit which was silver with A.S.S. embroidered across the back and over the crotch. Geraldine hung an A.S.S. medallion around his neck before pinning on an A.S.S. badge then pulling on an A.S.S. beret over his head too. Darcy wrapped a fanny pack around his waist and belted it in place while he downed more bourbon and the rest of us started laughing at him. He looked fucking ridiculous, especially when Geraldine slapped some flashing neon stickers all over him and Tory reached up to stick one on each of his cheeks.

"Happy now?" Orion asked as a stupid smile pulled at his mouth.

"Yep, and I'll be even happier when you show up to breakfast in this stuff," Darcy said through a laugh. "You look so freaking cute."

"No one looks at me anyway, beautiful," he reminded her.

"They will now," Darius muttered, looking caught between amusement and irritation over his friend being dressed up as a Vega supporter, though it was a bit late for that. Orion had gone full royalist and he didn't even pretend otherwise, though I reckoned when he sobered up tomorrow, he was gonna regret agreeing to this dare.

"My turn," Orion said with a feral smile, pinning Geraldine in his sights as he dropped back into his seat. "You have to sing that awful fucking away, away, away song but do it as if you love the Heirs, not the Vegas."

"You krout of a lout," Geraldine gasped, falling to her knees at the twins' feet and shaking her head. "I would never besmirch the name of my fair ladies."

"It's just a game, Geraldine," Tory said.

"We really don't mind," Darcy promised as she dropped onto Orion's lap. "I actually really, really wanna hear it."

Geraldine released a strangled noise then nodded, slowly rising to her feet and lifting her chin up as she started singing. And while everyone was distracted by her wincing her way through the song with our names in place of the Vegas', I subtly cast a silencing bubble around Darcy and Orion, leaning closer to them.

"He doesn't want me," I groaned and Orion jerked away as he realised I was right by his ear.

Darcy frowned, patting my head. "You don't know that."

"Hey, let me innnn," Tory poked her sister as she scooted her chair past Darius to join us and Darcy looked to me with a hopeful plea in her eyes.

"She won't tell anyone," she said and I whimpered.

"You swear?" I asked and Darcy nodded.

"I pinky promise. Plus she knows Caleb pretty well, so maybe she can help?"

She did know Caleb pretty well. She even knew his dick pretty well. In fact, she could probably tell me all the things he liked doing in the bedroom and give me some idea as to how big of a deal her tits and vajooza had been in the equation. I mean, what were the chances that he'd enjoyed getting her to wear men's clothes and put on a gruff voice while he bent her over and called her Bernard from time to time? Sure, I was totally down with him liking the tits and stuff some of the time because it wasn't like I hated them myself, but if he'd gotten her to do the whole Bernard thing at least a few times then I'd have a glimmer of hope that he was at least cock curious. That didn't even seem all that unlikely.

I flicked my fingers to let Tory into the bubble and she glanced between us all, leaning on her sister.

"Are we telling secrets?" she whispered conspiratorially. "Do you have a secret, Lance?"

He considered that then nodded. "Actually, I do. I have a secret about Gabriel, but I can't ever tell anyone. It's so fucking funny though." He started laughing to himself about it and the twins immediately pounced on him.

"What is it?" Darcy demanded as Tory brandished her beer bottle at him.

"Tell us," Tory pleaded. "It's a girl's right to have dirt on her brother."

"Come on, Lance," Darcy begged, giving him the big eyes. "Gabriel let me fall in a puddle the other day even though he totally *saw* it coming, and he laughed like a dick so now I want revenge."

"I can't," he said, shaking his head. "I swore I'd never tell. You'll have to try and get it out of him."

"If you tell us then I'll…" Darcy leaned forward and whispered something in his ear that made him growl and I bounced in my seat.

"Did she say she'll let you do her in every door? Front and back? In whatever order you like – you won't even have to knock?" I asked and Darcy swung around and punched me in the arm, making Orion smile satisfactorily.

"What's your secret, Seth?" Tory's eyes flipped onto me again and I sighed, glancing over at Caleb who was still distracted by Geraldine as Tyler recorded her singing the song and Sofia laughed her ass off.

"It's Caleb," I mumbled under my breath.

"What?" Tory leaned in closer.

"It's Caleb," I repeated louder.

"What about him?" she asked and I tossed another look his way before blurting the truth. I was too drunk to have any kind of filter now anyway.

"I love him. I'm in love with my best friend and I'm a stupid fucking loser because he will never love me back and every time I think he might feel something for me too, I realise I'm just kidding myself, but I also keep holding onto the teeny, tiny possibility that maybe I'm not imagining things. But then stupid horse boys have to go around not finishing their beers and stealing kisses meant for hot Vampires and here we are Tory. Here we fucking are."

"Woah," she breathed, exchanging a look with Darcy. "You like Caleb?" she asked in shock.

"Yeah," I said tightly, flopping forward to bury my face in Orion's shoulder and he tried to nudge me away, but I clung on tight. "I think it started longer ago than I like to admit, because there was this one time in the Shimmering Springs where we started a threesome with a girl but then she left and we kissed a little, but he denies it ever happened, so maybe I'm crazy. But I think I need to find out for good, you know?"

"So ask him," Darcy pressed and I lifted my head, turning to look at her and grabbing her cheeks between my hands.

"No. I won't," I said stubbornly. "I can't face the rejection. I can't look him in the eye when he turns me down and says I've been imagining this whole thing. I won't do it, Darcy. I *won't*."

Orion grabbed my arms, yanking my hands off of his girlfriend's face and baring his fangs at me, but I jerked free and grabbed hold of Tory's face instead.

"Tell me you have ideas. You didn't tell Darius you liked him for ages. You danced all around it beautifully. How did you figure out he liked you without actually admitting you liked him back? I need to know, Tory. How did you evade telling him the truth for so long, because I need your skills."

"Well…maybe if we'd been honest with each other from the start, we wouldn't have wasted so much time," she said, her lips pushing out as I squished her cheeks.

I let go of her with a sigh of annoyance. "Useless. I need a solid plan where Caleb has to kiss me without knowing he wants me to kiss him, so I can get a read on his dicktuation while we're cock to cock and then I'll know. I'll just know. And I had the perfect plan, but Xavier had to go and cock block me. Again."

"Again?" Tory asked excitedly, but then Caleb dragged a chair over and dropped down beside me.

"What are you lot talking about?" he asked and I dropped the silencing bubble as my heart thundered up into my throat.

"Lance has got a mysterious ball rash," I blurted the first thing that came into my head and Orion shot me a death glare, his lips parting to contradict me and his fist rising like he was going to punch me.

Darcy caught hold of his wrist, giving him a subtly imploring look as she pushed it back down to his side and - whipped asshole that he was - he gave in.

Tory snort laughed as Caleb's eyebrows arched. "Oh…shit, sorry bro," he said awkwardly and if looks could kill, Orion's gaze would have incinerated my brains by now.

"We were just discussing his best options, but if he doesn't get it treated soon, I think they're gonna fall off," I said sadly, patting Orion's arm and

Darcy shook her head slightly at him in a clear warning not to murder me.

"Have you seen them?" Caleb whispered to me in alarm and I nodded seriously.

"Yeah, it's not good. They're like two purple pears just hanging there, ready to fall from a doomed dick tree," I said sadly.

Orion lunged for me and I moved fast, leaping out of my seat and dragging Caleb away with me as Darcy intercepted, sinking her tongue between his lips. He resisted for a few more seconds before she shamelessly ground down on him and he gave in. He'd probably thank me tomorrow, it looked like the guy was gonna get laid as fuck tonight. Yeah, he'd definitely be grateful for this come morning. Besides, what was a little ball rash rumour between friends?

I dropped down beside Xavier across the table, putting a healthy amount of distance between me and my potential murderer as Cal sat down beside me.

"There's nothing wrong with a plain Jane D," Tyler was saying as he slung an arm around the back of Sofia's chair, looking over her to Xavier. "I mean, some people might say a perfect dijazzle is the mark of a true Dom, but you're just a Sub, so what does it matter?"

Xavier stamped his foot, glaring at him with a challenge in his eyes and I slid my hand into a bowl of chips on the table, slowly bringing them to my mouth and crunching through them as I watched this play out.

"I could be a Dom," Xavier said firmly. "And I will be."

Sofia glanced up at him through her lashes, then back to Tyler as she bit her lip like she couldn't decide which of them had her more intrigued. "You don't have to do anything you're not comfortable with, Xavier," she said.

"Yeah, Xavier," Tyler said through a bright smile. "But if it bothers you, why don't we do a poll to find out what's more popular among our kind?" He took his Atlas out of his pocket, twirling it in his hand. "But we'd get the best response if we had a couple of photos for people to compare."

"Oh my stars, you mean with dick pics?" Sofia breathed.

"Yep. Only if Xavier isn't too chicken shit," Tyler said, looking to him.

"Fine by me," Xavier said instantly, puffing his chest out and I shoved a few more chips into my mouth. This was gold.

Tyler stood up and I shared a look of amusement with Cal as he pulled out his waistband and snapped a photo of his cock before passing the Atlas to Xavier. Xavier immediately got up, pulling out the waistband of his own trousers and taking a picture before handing the Atlas back to Tyler.

I glanced over at Darius, sure he'd go apeshit if he realised his brother was about to post his junk all over social media, but he was distracted by Tory as she fed him chocolates from a box. A box I assumed she wanted me to come and steal from her. *The snack game is on.*

"Um, Xavier," Caleb said. "That's not a good idea."

Xavier ignored him as Tyler started furiously typing out the FaeBook post and Caleb looked over at Darius, clearly torn on what to do.

"Posted," Tyler announced, stuffing his Atlas back into his pocket and smirking at Xavier. "It's my peen versus yours, dude. May the best cock win."

I snatched my Atlas from my pocket, curious as hell over this post and opening up FaeBook as Cal leaned closer to read over my shoulder, his manly scent rolling under my nose and making me want to get even nearer to him.

Tyler Corbin:

One, two, three, four, did someone declare a peen war? Because we're about to VIOLATE someone's newsfeed with a #cock-off. It's no secret that Xavier Acrux has been vying for the position as Dom of MY herd, so may the best wang win.

Close your eyes and imagine this, you're walking through a wild and untamed meadow, your nips brushing the grass fronds and a Lunar Eclipse hanging above you in the sky, drawing you towards a #perfectpecker. What do you come across as your wishes are fulfilled? Is it a #decorateddong that glitters in the moonlight, a cocktacular masterpiece which stands tall and proud, adorned with #prickpearls and #trousersnaketreasures?

Or is it a #boringboner without a single shiny thing on its plain ding-a-ling?

Comment below to vote for the sheen of a #gemlesspeen or the glory of a #gildedschlong in the ultimate #battleofthedicks.

Oceanis Deason:

Oh my stars, I'll take a spangly wangle all day and night, but the size of that unadorned leviathon is making my waters tingle #whychoose #sparklecock #hardandlongisneverwrong

Bianca Movileanu:

Is that a peenasaurus rex I see? Perhaps it would like to come plunder my treasure trove to find the missing gold? #tojeweliscool #studsforthestud

Stephen Mulgrew:

I'm all for a simple peen, and that mammoth of a man marrow is something else! #keepthepeenclean #letmeseethoseveinsofglory

Justin Battles:

I need some gleam on my peen #glitterisfitter #jazzyjizzer

Telisha Mortensen:

So long as it's hairy this munching Mindy is always down #thehairierthebetter #everymanhoodneedsamane

Lucy Burfoot:

Oh my stars! I have a #glammerpuss that could match your #lustrouslovestick if you want some inspiration for a dijazzle, Xavier! #razzledazzlethatD #gilditdontgeldit

I barked a laugh as Caleb started chuckling in my ear and I turned my head, finding him so close to me it made me ache. I swallowed the lump rising in my throat as he met my gaze for a second and I realised how wholly, desperately in love with him I was as his dark blue eyes swallowed me up.

"If you were going to deepthroat one of those bad boys which would you pick?" I asked him super subtly.

Cal frowned as he looked at the images again before shaking his head. "Between my best friend's baby brother or risking my life through choking to death on a loose dick gem? Pass," he replied with a laugh and I huffed because he hadn't outright objected to the D just these particular Ds, but what if there was another D in the mix? What then??

I considered taking a dick pic and sending it to him, but even my drunk brain could see that that was a little much, so I let the idea go along with my hopes and dreams for finding an answer to that question. Unless I challenged every guy in the room to a 'who has the best cock' competition and made Cal judge it. But what if I didn't win? No, I couldn't do it to myself. Not when I was going up against Darius's talented mega dong and Orion's jumbo secret sausage which I heard was so gifted it granted wishes. And then there was Max's Siren slammer that could probably turn on everyone in this room the moment you looked it in the eye. Dammit, there had to be a better way.

Caleb sat back in his seat, falling into a conversation with Max as I continued to steal glances at him. And when his hand dropped to his side and brushed my leg, I swear a thousand bolts of electricity awoke every nerve ending in my body. He didn't move it either, his fingers barely touching me and yet I could feel them as if he was dragging them over every square inch of my skin. And I realised how hopelessly fucked I was. Because I'd fallen too deep, too fast, and now there was no going back. I was on a collision course with Caleb Altair, and I feared what was going to happen if I ever let a word of this slip out. Because I was sure it would equal our absolute ruin.

LIONEL

CHAPTER EIGHTEEN

I strode down the long corridor in the FIB interrogation suite with agents trailing at my spine and an air of cautious respect surrounding me which I had to admit I liked the taste of.

Too long had these rebels thwarted me. Too long had I been playing cat and mouse in a game where the mice found hiding all too easy. Too long had I suffered the intolerable taste of failure upon my tongue. But at last, that was over.

Agent Hoskins kept his head bowed respectfully as he led me to the room where the prisoner was being held and pulled the door wide for me. I stepped through without a word, Vard close on my heels with his black cloak sweeping the floor behind him.

"This is her?" Vard questioned, taking in the bloody, broken woman who sat with her hands cuffed at her spine - likely the only thing keeping her upright on the chair.

"I want every filthy rebel secret torn from her mind before the execution."

"Yes, My King," Vard simpered, licking his pale lips as his red shadow eye swirled with darkness in its socket and he drew his hood down to reveal his lank hair.

The woman whimpered and I was torn between a sneer and a smile as she lifted her terrified gaze to meet mine.

I moved to perch my ass on the edge of the interrogation table before her as Vard took the empty chair intended for an investigating officer and sat before her, watching, waiting, ready to strike on my command.

I took my Atlas from my pocket and opened the most recent article this woman had published about me, a thrill dancing through my veins at finally cornering this thorn in my side and knowing I would be tugging it free permanently before the day was done.

"The Rise of the False King," I read, anger bubbling beneath the surface of my skin as my fire magic licked a path around my body. "By Felicity

Corbin."

Felicity raised her chin at the sound of her name, her swollen features conveying contempt and disrespect even after hours of the most punishing questioning the FIB could offer. Still that defiant spark flared in her eyes as if she really believed she were a true Fae. Like her defiance in the face of my might meant anything to me at all.

I skipped a lot of the waffling trite she'd published in her rag of a newspaper and cut to the pieces which would see her burn.

"The self proclaimed 'most powerful man in Solaria' has done little to claim his crown upon his own merits, instead, his use of the shadows and dark magic have been the true claimants to his power. Without the aid of these dark and twisted additions to his magic, he is in fact no more powerful than the rest of the Celestial Council and never will be. Worse still, the power he is wielding has been outlawed since long before he ever sat his unworthy ass upon the throne, and this alone should nullify his claim and see him sent to Darkmore Penitentiary to rot." I looked up at her over the grossly provocative bullshit she'd published about me time and again, wondering how much longer it would take her to break.

The interrogation had turned up nothing of interest. So far as the FIB could tell, she didn't know where the rebels were hiding, but I knew she had firm links to them. Her royalist drivel and repetitive sniffling over the treatment of her kind and that of the other traitorous Orders made it more than clear where her loyalties lay, and she would soon suffer the consequences of that devotion. But I had to admit I was a little surprised to see the defiance still burning in her eyes as she looked at me with disdain.

"The true queens will rise," she hissed, her split lip spilling blood down her chin. "When they ascend fully into their power, they will come for you. They will tear their father's crown from your brow and rip you from the throne, showing the whole of Solaria what a small man you truly are."

I backhanded her so hard I damn near knocked her from her chair, the crack of breaking bone lighting the air as she fell dangling from the seat, only her bound hands holding her to it where it was bolted to the floor.

"Do it, Vard," I growled, shoving myself upright so that I towered over her at my full height, letting her see how big this small man was. "And make it hurt."

Vard's smile widened as he leaned forward, reaching out to grab a handful of Felicity's tawny hair and forcing her upright in her seat, making her meet his gaze as he shifted. I watched as his deep red shadow eye merged with his normal one, the swirling darkness within that bulbous orb making Felicity tremble as he forced her gaze to lock with his.

He dragged her into the depraved depths of his mind with a twisted smile on his scarred face and her screams filled the air as he began tearing each and every secret from the recesses of her brain. But as he scraped everything he could from her worthless head, leaving her mind scarred beyond repair, I knew she was going to offer me nothing. Which made her a waste of perfectly adequate oxygen.

I pushed Vard aside when I was done waiting, setting a fire at her feet which licked around the base of her chair and scalded her legs. Her head fell back as a cry of anguish left her and I smiled, rising up on a gust of air to make sure I was the only thing she could see.

"Do I look like a small man now?" I asked, leaning in close to taste her fear, coaxing the flames higher as they began to burn and char and consume.

She trembled violently as she held back another scream, but through the fear and pain in her eyes rose another wave of rebellion. "You are nothing but a parasite living in the house of the true queens. And when they kill you, long may they reign."

I spat a snarl, raising my hand so my fire raised with it, and the wretched waif screamed her last screams as it ravaged her.

I kept my eyes on her, watching the skin melt from her bones and the pained sobs die in her throat as she was devoured in my fire, my gaze snagging on a locket which hung around her neck.

When she was nothing but ash and bone, I doused the flames and took hold of the golden chain, yanking hard enough to decapitate her charred head from her body and turning the locket over in my palm, claiming my new treasure. It was of high quality, but an arrangement of diamonds in the front of in the shape of a Pegasus marred it. I ran my thumb across it, melting the surface of the gold to dislodge the gems and letting them fall into my jacket pocket.

Then I cracked open the locket and found a photograph of a boy who I assumed was Felicity's son; he was around the same age as my Heir with silver glitter in his hair.

I sneered, pressing my thumb to the photograph to burn it to cinders before dropping the necklace into my pocket and turning to Vard. "Was there anything else in her possession?"

"Just a pouch of stardust, my Lord," he said. "It seems she has been evading the FIB for quite some time by moving from location to location with her herd."

"How dare they use a Dragon-made creation to defy their king," I spat, striding past him out the door with a decree firmly in mind as he scurried along at my heels. "Inform the press that a new law will be announced this afternoon. I am prohibiting all Orders from carrying stardust except Dragons or those with a permit from the king. Anyone found in possession of it will be charged with treason."

"Yes, sire," Vard said. "A wonderful choice, My King."

I strode out of the FIB headquarters, fastening my coat as the wind whipped around me and a throng of photographers rushed forward to intercept me. A ring of FIB agents kept them back, but I paused a moment on the steps, letting them take their pictures as my chest swelled and a satisfied smile filled my face.

"Another traitor has been dealt with," I called, pride in my voice as a barrage of photographs were taken and questions were thrown my way which I had no interest in answering. I'd have a statement drawn up tonight and-

A loud splat made me look down as something wet hit the ground at my feet and I sneered at the pile of shit which had exploded across my shoes.

"My Lord," Vard gasped, grabbing my arm but I shoved him away from me with a snarl just as a huge and foul smelling turd slapped down onto his shoulder and chunks of it splattered across my chest.

"Argh," I growled, my head snapping up to look toward the sky where

it had come from, finding a familiar looking lilac haired girl sitting on the back of a Griffin as she held up its tail and another huge pile of faeces came tumbling towards me. I tried to wield air to stop it from striking me, but I was still within the no magic wards which surrounded the FIB headquarters so I was helpless to stop it as it slapped across my entire face and I staggered backwards in disgust and outrage.

I wiped it from my eyes, the substance already beginning to burn and itch as I set my enemies in my sights with a roar of fury.

"All hail the king of the turds!" she cried.

"Seize them!" I bellowed as the FIB hurried to get themselves in order, but the girl was already throwing stardust over herself and the Griffin she was riding, disappearing into the ether as a roar tore from my lungs.

I turned to the press, finding a hundred cameras going off in my face as I tried to wipe the shit from my eyes, the burn intensifying.

I hurried towards my car, barking at Vard to keep up as my driver opened the door for me and I leapt onto the backseat, ripping my coat off of my back and wiping at my eyes.

"Oh Daddy, how embarrassing," Lavinia said from somewhere beside me and I snapped around to find her as smoke billowed from my nose. "What if she'd tried to kill you, you'd be deader than dead and I would be a lonely queen." She laughed and I locked her hand around her throat, silencing her.

"Do not mock me." I snarled in warning. "No one can cast within a hundred yards of the FIB headquarters. She couldn't have fucking touched me with anything lethal."

I felt my shadow hand rising, latching around my own throat and tightening hard enough to cut off all of my air. Panic rose in me as I fought to regain control of the hand she had gifted me, trying to force my own will into it and finding it unresponsive as it continued to work against me, following her command instead of mine. *No.*

"Do not speak to me in that tone," she hissed, a crazed look entering her gaze that spoke of the power she held.

Shadows spilled out all around the car and I fought to blast them away from me with the Element of air, but her power was too great. She bound me in shadow, forcing me down onto the seat and climbing on top of me as she smiled like a demon.

I struggled for air, anger flaring hotter and hotter inside me. How dare she wield her power against me? She was nothing without me. *Nothing!*

"Poor angry little Daddy," she purred, gripping my shirt and ripping it open with a sharp pull that sent the buttons scattering everywhere. She let me breathe again and I growled, thrashing against her hold.

"How dare you?" I snarled. "Release me this instant and grovel to your king!"

She laughed wildly, scratching my chest hard enough to tear open the skin as she wielded my shadow hand against me once more, making me slap my own face hard enough to bruise, bringing the taste of blood to my tongue.

"Silly boy, you're all mine. Mine, mine, mine. My Acrux King," she said with a wild gleam in her eye and I fought harder to get free, fearing her power as she crushed me within it and held me at her mercy. This was unacceptable. I had to exert my will over her, show her who her master was.

"You will obey your king!" I roared as she bounced up and down on top of me.

"Um, sire?" Vard asked meekly from the front of the car.

"What?" I spat.

"It seems there's going to be a protest against your claim to the throne in the city of Nostria this afternoon," he said, his eyes glazing with his vision. "If we head there now, we can round the rebels up before it begins." He didn't look directly at me, clearly pretending not to see the situation Lavinia had me in as he fixed his gaze on the rear window.

Her grip suddenly lessened and I was able to sit up, eyeing my shadow hand with trepidation at how much power she wielded over me. I had to get her back under my control and as she slithered into the footwell and started wetting her lips in preparation for my cock, I was glad to see her submissive side returning.

"Take me home," I commanded as I tried to ignore the blazing itch in my eyes or the way the scent of shit still lingered on me. "But I will not capture them Vard. Any rebel I get my hands on today will die."

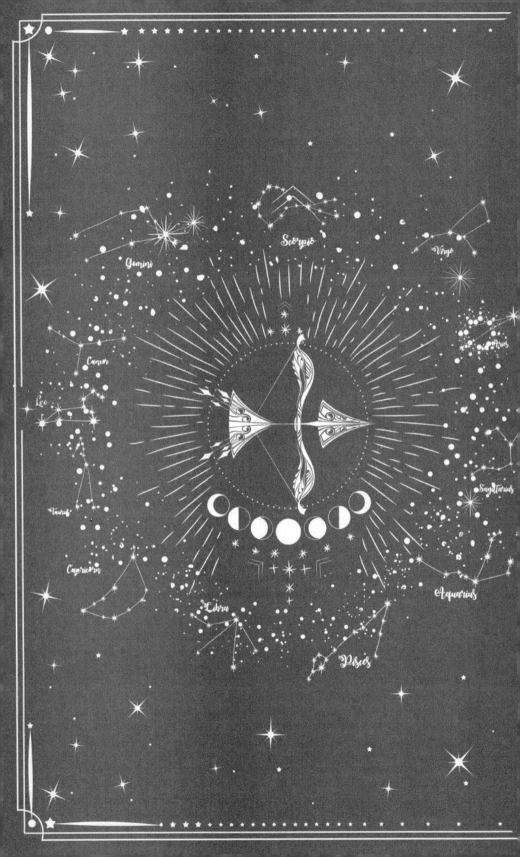

XAVIER

CHAPTER NINETEEN

I scrolled through the comments from countless Pegasuses on Tyler's FaeBook post which declared a decorated dong was better, though at least enough people had commented on the size of my cock not to entirely destroy my confidence. It wasn't like I wanted a plain dick. In fact, I'd had plans to decorate the hell out of it not that long ago, but then there'd been a battle and I'd come here, and there hadn't exactly been time to think about how I was going to go about getting my dick dijazzled.

I sighed, heading down to the dining hall and stuffing my Atlas in my pocket, sick of looking at Tyler's beautiful dick online. Sofia had gone back to his room last night, and I once again was left feeling like I was failing at this whole Pegasus thing. My instincts wouldn't quit though, they demanded I seize position as Dom of the herd and claimed Sofia as my own. And that was exactly what I planned on doing. But I couldn't do it with a bare dick, that was for sure.

No, I needed to up my dick's game, give it a makeover that crowned it as the king of the cocks. That'd show Tyler. He'd tremble at the sight of my dazzling D and then we'd see who the herd wanted to follow. Then we'd see...

I noticed a guy up ahead who I'd seen tattooing Fae in the dining hall and I trailed after him now, his silky black hair pulled into a topknot and the loose fitting tank top he wore showing off the endless Disney tattoos covering his arms. He was a big guy, his muscular arms tanned and looking strong enough to crush someone's skull, and he had an air of terrifying about him which was enough to make me hesitate in my approach, though I refused to let it put me off entirely. He might just have been my dick's only hope after all.

I picked up my pace, clearing my throat to try and get his attention, but he didn't look back.

"Um, excuse me?" I asked, and he glanced around with a frown before continuing on as if he hadn't noticed me smiling politely and waiting for him to reply.

I trotted to catch him, moving to his side and trying to keep up with his fierce pace.

"You do tattoos, right?" I asked him and he glanced at me with narrowed eyes.

"Maybe," he muttered. "You want one?"

"No…I actually want some piercings. Do you do those too?" I asked hopefully and his gaze roamed down me in an assessing way.

"Aren't you the Acrux kid?"

"Yeah," I said, lifting my chin. "And?"

He observed me a beat longer then shrugged. "What do you want, your ears pierced?" He chuckled at the idea of that and heat ran up the back of my neck as I prepared to ask him for what I really wanted.

"No. I want my…you know." I jerked my head to gesture towards my dick and the guy frowned.

"What?" he asked in confusion.

"You know…my…" I lowered my voice to a whisper. "Dick pierced."

He bellowed a laugh and the heat in my neck travelled to my cheeks as I tried to front this out.

"Well can you do it, or not?" I hissed.

He ran his thumb over the knuckles of his right hand thoughtfully then shook his head. "I *can* do it, but I won't."

"Why?" I stamped my foot and his eyebrow arched at me.

"Because I don't want to." He tried to quicken his pace, but I caught his arm, tugging to make him look at me again, which he did, and the death glare I received was enough to make me release him, though I still forged on with my request.

"Come on, I'll pay you. And I'll do something for you in return too. What do you want?" I asked and he thought on that.

"Anything I want?" he confirmed and I nodded.

"Anything," I agreed and he thought on that for a minute.

"Do you know Gabriel Nox?" he asked.

"Yeah, what about him?"

"Well he's an old friend of mine, and he likes to use his Sight to get one up on me. Like the other morning, he told me he foresaw me choking on the last pancake if I ate it. But then *he* went and ate it, so I know his game. He played me like a fucking fool."

"Okay…and what do you want me to do about that?"

"I want a little revenge," he said with a grin. "But I can't get him back myself because he'll be watching for me. But he's not gonna be watching for you…"

"So you want me to do what exactly?" I frowned.

"I don't wanna know a single thing about what you do, or else he'll *see* it coming. But I want you to prank him so fucking good he'll never mess with me again."

"You know he could literally *see* this conversation right now though, don't you?" I said, aware that I had about as much chance of pranking Gabriel Nox as I had of shifting into a Dragon like my good ol' daddy had always wanted.

"Nah, he's busy right now," he said with a knowing smirk. "So have we got a deal?" He offered me his inked hand.

"Dick piercing first?" I confirmed and he nodded, so I slid my palm into his and a flash of power rang between us as we made the deal. I had no idea how I was gonna fulfil my end of that bargain, but I'd give it a shot.

"Alright, I'll get what I need. You know where the Oscura Clan are housed?"

I nodded my agreement because yeah, everyone knew where the pack of cutthroat Werewolves had taken up residence – you could hear them howling, partying or fucking at all hours of the day and night unless the silencing bubbles were maintained at all times, and Rosalie and Dante Oscura arrived at the dining hall with their enormous pack in tow every morning drawing plenty of attention. I'd even been down there with the Heirs and the twins to party with them a couple of times and it had been seriously good fun.

"Just before you get to their quarters there are a series of rooms for me and my family. I use the first on the left for my work. Meet me there in ten minutes."

I nodded, bounding away with an excited neigh as I headed in that direction. I grabbed an apple and a couple of carrots as I passed by the buffet, thankful no one I knew was around as I walked down the twisting tunnels which led towards the Oscura Clan's territory.

Inside the room the tattooist had directed me to was a small lounge area with a few couches and chairs that looked like they'd been made from woven moss.

I chomped my way through my apple with an excited whinny before starting on my carrots, putting my feet up on the wooden coffee table as I waited for my new friend to arrive. When he appeared with a box in his arms, I sat upright in my seat, swallowing a mouthful of my carrot.

"I didn't get your name?" I asked brightly.

"Carson," he said, placing the box down on the table and flipping the lid open.

I gasped, leaning forward as I took in the terrifying-looking needle inside which sat beside a tattoo gun.

"Alright, let's get this over with. Pants off, lay back on the couch," Carson directed and a little tremor of nerves ran through me before I dropped my pants alongside my boxers and laid down on the mossy cushions, leaving my 'Horn and Raised' t-shirt and rainbow socks in place.

"What about the piercings?" I asked. "Don't I need to pick something?"

"Pick whatever you want," he said. "I'm an earth Elemental. I can make metal and gemstones however you like. Just give me an idea of what you're going for here. A Prince Faebert?"

I shook my head, knowing exactly what I wanted. "A Jacob's Ladder," I said with no hint of doubt in my voice. "A rainbow one."

He stared at me with his dark green eyes shining with mirth. "You sure about that? The whole fucking cock?"

"Yup," I said with a nod. "The whole thing. Top to bottom, front and back, as glittery and shiny as you can make it."

He scrubbed a hand over the stubble on his jaw, then took out the large needle from the box. "Well it's gonna hurt like a motherfucker."

"Can't you heal it as you do it?" I whinnied in protest.

"Nah, not my style. I'll heal it after." He smirked cruelly, shoving my legs aside as he sat beside me on the couch and roughly took hold of my cock, making me neigh in alarm. "Ready? On three."

I nodded nervously as he lined the needle up with my shaft, and I suppressed another whinny as he prepared to spear my freaking dick with it.

"Three." He pierced the needle through the skin and I neighed so loud the roof trembled.

"Ahhhhhh!"

"You can come out from under the pillow now," Carson said and I felt his healing magic running along my cock at long fucking last. Why? Why oh fucking why had he done it without numbing my star damned dick first? I'd begged for him to do it, promised him gold and riches beyond his wildest dreams, but he'd continued to insist it was his process, leaving me in agony the whole way through.

I released a heavy breath as the pain finally ebbed away and I pushed the pillow off my head, feeling like I was about to witness a horror show, my dick carved to pieces, served up like sushi on my lap. Why had I trusted a random stranger to stab it with a fucking needle? Had I lost my mind? He could have butchered it, ruined it beyond repair.

I kept my eyes on the rocky ceiling of the cavern, afraid to look and discover what fate had befallen my precious cock. Because I was somehow sure I'd made a terrible, terrible mistake. But when I'd tried to escape halfway through the slaughter of my manhood, Carson had held me down and said I could always change my mind after he was done. But could I? Would healing magic ever repair my dick if he'd mutilated it?

"I took a bit of creative liberty," Carson said. "Come on, look at it, asshole. If you hate it, I'll take them out."

I inhaled deeply, praying he really could fix this if I needed him to, saying a silent prayer to the stars as I made myself look down.

The breath got trapped in my chest as I took in the absolute perfection staring back at me. A ladder of interconnecting bars ran up the length of my shaft with the most beautiful gemstones I'd ever seen painting out the colours of the rainbow along them. A bar had been run through the very head of my cock too with a diamond on each end of it and as I took hold of my dick, I felt that same interlacing network of bars running all up the underside of it too.

"Oh my stars," I breathed, running my thumb over each gleaming stone that adorned my cock, knowing without a shadow of a doubt that I officially had the best dijazzle in the whole of Solaria. This was the work of a cock piercing god, a dick decorating deity.

"Well?" Carson grunted and I looked up at him, gratitude sweeping through me in waves.

I lunged at him, wrapping my arms around his shoulders and he went stiff in my hold, grumbling something about his life being riddled with over-friendly people before patting me awkwardly on the back.

"So you like it?"

"I love it." I pulled away from him, leaping to my feet and hurrying over to a lamp to examine it better in the light. It glittered like a thousand suns lived within it and a neigh of pure joy left me. "How can I repay you for this? I can get you gold, as much as you like."

"Just mess with Gabriel and we're square," he said, a slight grin pulling at his lips and I nodded, sure I'd find a way to do it because I owed this guy so damn much.

I had to show Sofia and Tyler right now. I had to rub it in Tyler's face that I had the best fucking cock in the world.

I burst out laughing, casting a thick raincloud around my naked ass and junk before sprinting from the room, tearing through the dining hall and running towards their room as I shot left and right down the tunnels, skidding along on my rainbow socks every time I took a turn.

When I made it to their room, I shoved the door open without knocking, letting the cloud dissolve to expose my entire cock which was now hard with how excited I was, showing off every sparkling stone in all its glory. "Ha! Look at my cock now, Tyler!"

But Tyler and Sofia weren't alone. Tory and Darcy were there, patting Tyler on the shoulder while Sofia was curled up in his lap and all the Heirs stood beyond them. Orion was fucking there too and it only got worse, because apparently Hamish, my mom, Geraldine and her fucking A.S.S. friends Angelica and Justin had joined whatever this intense-looking meeting was about too.

"Tyler's mom died, Xavier," Sofia said in horror as she looked up at me, her eyes full of tears as Tyler looked over at me through a haze of distress on his face.

And my cock just remained standing there, slowly starting to deflate as this entire shit show played out and I took the starring role.

"By the light of an unholy moon!" Geraldine cried, shielding her eyes. "What a time to unveil your Long Sherman!"

"Xavier," Darius hissed. "Cover the fuck up."

"Here, baby boy." Mom grabbed some sweatpants from the bed, tossing them to me and I scrambled into them, nearly falling on my ass as everyone looked at me and my cheeks burned as hot as the sun.

No.

Why was this happening?

Why?!

The shame of what I'd done made my mind slow to catch up with the magnitude of this situation, but as Tyler buried his face in Sofia's neck and everyone else started discussing what could be done to strike back against Lionel, I realised she hadn't just died. My father had killed her. And I'd burst into Tyler's room with my cock out only minutes after he'd heard the news.

"I'm sorry," I blurted, hurrying over to Tyler as embarrassment, horror and sadness washed over me in heavy waves. "I'm so sorry. I didn't know."

"Let's give them some space," Darcy said softly, tears in her eyes as she looked at Tyler and she reached out to take Tory's hand.

Everyone started filing out of the room and my brother tried to guide me out with them, but I dug my heels in, shaking my head at him. I had to say something, do something. I couldn't just walk away after what I'd done. I needed to be there for my herd.

Darius let go of me and as the door clicked shut, I stepped closer to Tyler as Sofia ran her hands over his back in soothing circles.

"What can I do?" I rasped.

"There's nothing you can do," Tyler said hollowly and a whinny of distress left me.

I climbed onto the bed with them, needing to offer my comfort, to be close to my kind as I felt their suffering tangling with the air in this room. I wrapped my arms around them both and Tyler looked up, his reddened eyes meeting mine. There was rivalry between us still, but as he let out a soft snort, I could tell he was happy to put it aside right now, as I was. And he leaned against me as I nuzzled the side of his head, the sweet scent of Sofia melding with his richer aroma.

Our heads all fell together and we remained in silence as the weight of Tyler's grief crashed down on us all like a sword on our backs. And my hate for my father grew to an almost tangible thing, begging to be sated.

He'd struck a blow at my herd and I felt bound to drive my horn into his heart and make him bleed in penance for this. But for now, all I could do was offer all the comfort I had to give and pray this didn't break Tyler. Because he may have been my rival, but I realised he'd become more than that to me too. I cared about him in a way I didn't really understand, and our fight for dominance wasn't ever going to change that. He was a part of the family I'd found for myself, my herd, and I embraced that connection to him like I had embraced my own Order. And that was something my father could never take from us.

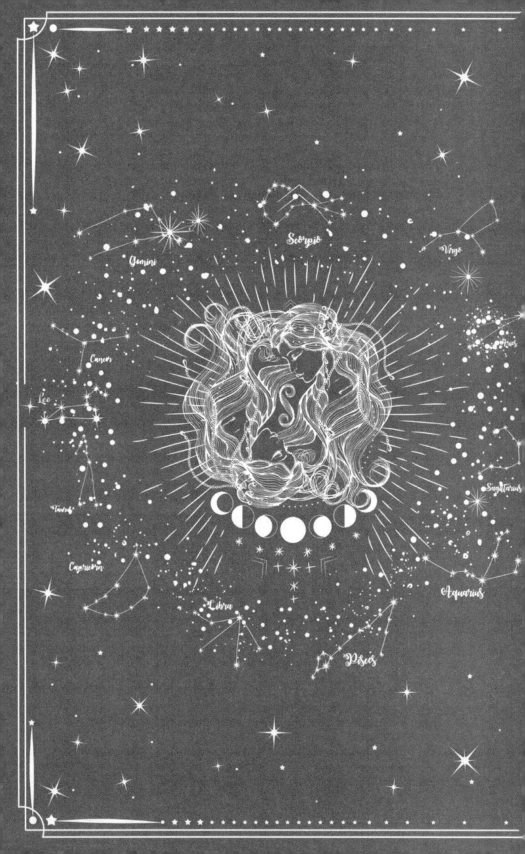

TORY

CHAPTER TWENTY

I sat in Darius's lap, my forehead pressed to his as our heavy breaths mingled. I smirked to myself as I tried to summon the energy to dry us out after I'd managed to distract him enough to freeze him to a chair before climbing into his lap and taking control as I rode him to a climax that had made my fucking head spin while the heat of his Dragon worked to melt the ice away. Safe to say, it had been hot as hell and we'd both ended up drenched by the time he fought his way free and was coming inside me with a growl that made my entire body shiver with pleasure.

His magic was still thrumming within my skin and I rested my hands on his chest, feeling the solid thump of his heartbeat as his hands lingered on my waist and we remained there, enjoying the feeling of being so connected to each other.

It had been almost a month since Darius and Xavier had rescued the Pegasus herd from the academy, and since then a lot of time had been taken up with rescuing more of their kind from Nebular Inquisition Centres and using tip offs we'd received to stop Lionel's persecution of their kind.

Gabriel and his family had been working to test the extent of Vard's Sight, showing up at rallies and press conferences to try and strike small blows at Lionel that tested Vard's abilities. They couldn't hit very hard considering Lionel never went anywhere in public without having protective spells around him or anti-magic zones forged by the FIB, but the newspapers were filled with images of the false king covered in Griffin shit, splattered with Victoria sponge cake and even covered in glue that was mixed with Pegasus glitter. I wasn't entirely sure what Gabriel was learning about Vard's abilities, but whatever it was, it was sure as shit funny to see Lionel's day ruined time and again for the sake of it.

Darius and I were meant to be meeting the others in Darcy's room to discuss what to do about striking back at Lionel, but then Darius had slapped my ass and told me he couldn't wait to own it later and I'd seen that domineering Alpha glint in his eye, so I'd been forced to remind him who was in charge in this relationship. And that was me.

"Sometimes I wish the Savage King had never died," he murmured, almost to himself as he kept me close. "I think about how different everything would have been if he'd managed to stop my father before this all happened. How much longer I would have had with you…"

I sighed, shifting my fingers up to his jaw and tilting his chin so that he looked at me.

"We have all the time we want now," I said. "The past is done. We can't change it, so why think about it?"

His brow pinched and he slid his hands up my spine until he was caressing my shoulder blades where my wings lay dormant beneath my skin, making me arch my back and moan softly in pleasure.

"Roxy, on Christmas Day, when I thought-"

A banging sounded at the door and I turned my head to look towards it as Max called out to us.

"I'm taking this break in the rampant lust to mean you've stopped fucking and are just doing the cuddling shit – so stop making us all wait for you and get your asses in here so we can figure out how to do this."

I breathed a laugh, unable to even feel bad about making them wait as the man in my arms tightened his grip on me and I looked back to him. We'd had to wait a long damn time for this taste of happiness so I was going to savour it as often as I could.

"Give us ten minutes," I called.

"No," Max snapped. "Darius will be good to go again in five. Then it'll be a whole other round of us watching the damn walls rattle while Gerry tells us tales about the gardeners who have watered her fucking lawn, and I swear to the moon I will go on a killing spree if she brings up a single fucker other than me."

"It's super weird that you know how long it will take me to get hard again, asshole," Darius called back, a laugh colouring his voice.

"It's super awkward for me to be feeling so much lust all of the time too, but you two literally never stop, so here we are."

I laughed as Max's footsteps moved away from the door and Darius cocked his head at me.

"He's wrong anyway," he said, shifting his hips beneath me so that I was left with no illusions as to how hard he already was, and I bit my lip at the temptation in his dark eyes.

"You were saying something about Christmas," I said, trying to keep my damn head because we really were running late at this point.

"Forget it," he said, shaking his head slightly. "It was only about how fucking amazing you looked when I saw you waiting for me at the end of that aisle. I know it wasn't ever meant to be our wedding day, but I've spent years knowing I was going to be married off to that hag Mildred and I can't tell you how many times I fantasised about it being a girl like you."

"Like me?" I teased but he didn't smile back at my playful tone, only pushed up until his lips were brushing mine and my breath was catching in my throat.

"No. Not *like* you. It *was* you. Even before I ever laid eyes on you, it was you, Roxy. Only ever you."

He kissed me and I fell for him. Not in the way I already had, but in this utterly captivating, moment of clarity kind of way which let me know right down to the roots of my soul that it was always going to be him for me too. This was it now. Me and him, bound together in a way that we didn't need the stars to grant us, because it was ours and we'd chosen it, fought for it and won it with blood, pain and heartache and no mate bond gifted to us by the heavens could ever compare to that. I didn't want silver rings in my eyes. I only wanted this man before me and the knowledge that we were the ones who had fought to claim one another without needing any help or guidance from any celestial beings. Because it was ours. And no one could claim it but us.

I pulled back reluctantly, tasting him on my lips and letting our magic coil together in a mixture of fire and air that dried us out and left my hair looking a lot less recently fucked.

Darius pushed to his feet, lifting me as easily as if I weighed nothing and striding across the room as I wrapped my arms around his neck and let my gaze run over the strong features of his face, the dark stubble lining his jaw, the frown which never seemed to entirely abandon him.

He placed me down beside the wardrobe that Caleb had built for us and pulled on a white t-shirt and some black sweatpants, then took some clothes out for me. I smirked at him as he dropped to one knee and dragged a pair of black panties up my thighs, dressing me with a dangerous look in his eyes that promised he'd be the one undressing me again soon enough.

He helped me into a pair of stonewashed jeans next, standing slowly and tugging them over the curve of my ass before buttoning them for me, tugging me forward a step by the waistband so that he could steal a kiss.

I moaned into his mouth as his hands caressed my breasts as he kissed me, tugging on my nipples just enough to make me ache before breaking our lips apart and pulling a long sleeved green crop top down over my head.

"I know what you're doing," I accused, looking up at him as he carefully pulled my long, dark hair out of the collar of my shirt.

"What's that?" he rumbled, his lips brushing my ear.

"You're trying to get me worked up so that you can force me beneath you again later on and you can go all Alpha on me."

"Don't pretend you don't like it, Roxy. You always come the hardest when I have you pinned beneath me."

He moved back before I could punch him, his deep laughter making me want to smile and battling against my desire to beat his big head in with my shoe. I decided on a nice midpoint and flipped him off instead, kicking my high-top sneakers on and striding out of the room ahead of him.

Darius only seemed more amused by my bratty behaviour, and I made a mental note to stop letting him get away with his shit with me so easily. But it was a lot harder to stay mad at him than it used be these days thanks to all the freaking orgasms he gave me. I'd literally been yelling at him, calling him a lizard asshole with an ego the size of one of Jupiter's moons the other day, and he'd told me to keep insulting him while dropping to his knees and pushing his head beneath my skirt where he proceeded to make me forget why I'd even been angry with him in the first place. I was sure that I'd remember at some point and give him hell for it again, but as of now I was still blinded by the memory of that orgasm and couldn't recall for the life of me why I'd been intent on calling him every name under the sun.

I pulled open the door to Darcy and Orion's room and my twin looked around at me, rolling her eyes dramatically while I just shrugged like I was as innocent as pie and slipped into the room, taking a seat beside Caleb who was perched on the couch alone.

He gave me a smile, shifting his posture and dropping his arm along the back of my seat as the others all greeted us or muttered less than subtle commentary on how long we'd made them wait.

"I'd say I'm sorry, but I'm not," Darius said with a shrug as he took a seat on the other side of the room to me beside Orion, his gaze flicking from me to Caleb as he growled a little warning which I was guessing was aimed at the arm which lay over the back of my seat.

Caleb ignored him, the corner of his lips lifting in amusement as he looked to me instead of the Dragon asshole. "We've just been discussing the issue we have with the Nymphs being tainted by the shadows," he explained, pointing to Diego's hat which Seth was currently sniffing while he sat cross legged on the bed. "Because if your little knitwear loving friend wasn't an evil, mindless creature when his hat was helping him stay grounded, then it makes sense that the shadows are at least in part to blame for the Nymphs all acting so psycho all the damn time."

"They're still the bad guys though," Max added, drawing my attention to him where he sat beside Geraldine. "Whatever way you cut it, they get their magic by stealing ours and they do so by killing us."

"Oh of course your simple little sausage of a mind would see it as so," Geraldine chastised. "But our dear Diego didn't probe anyone while he was at the academy. He didn't slip so much as a digit into any orifice of mine and I was in his company on many an occasion."

"You were literally attacked by a fucking Nymph the night he tried to drug the twins," Max said in outrage and Geraldine sighed loudly while Orion swiped a hand down his face like he was praying to the stars to give him strength.

"In that vision we saw of Diego getting his powers from that Fae girl Alejandro had locked in his murder shed, he felt the shadows and heard the call of the Shadow Princess for the first time. So what if him using his probes like that was kinda like us using our Order gifts for the first time? So it awakened that side of him and his connection to the shadows which gave her a way in?" I suggested.

Orion nodded thoughtfully, leaning forward and tapping his finger against the book which was laying there, the spine of it encrusted with what looked like emeralds. "Over the last few years while me and Darius have been out hunting the Nymphs, we have noticed them gathering dark objects – the kinds of things that could easily be linked to the shadows. Diego mentioned his family treating the Shadow Princess like she was some kind of deity, so what if they were answering her calls, using those objects to help link themselves to the shadows more firmly so they could hear her better? It would have brought them closer to the creature they'd chosen to worship while allowing her to gain greater influence over them at the same time as she tried to find a way to cross back into the Fae realm."

"There has to be more to it than them just linking up a few dark objects to one another," Darius said. "The few times we caught them with something like that they'd always been carrying it. So what if they were trying to take them somewhere?"

"So how can we figure out where they were taking them?" Darcy asked, twirling a lock of dark blue hair around her finger.

"By golly, I think I know," Geraldine gushed, raising her hand like we were in class and she had an answer to offer up to the teacher. Orion fell back into his professor role without even seeming to notice and pointed at her, giving her permission to speak. "We catch one of the dastardly Daniels and our very own bothersome barracuda uses his gifts to take a root around in its Nymphy noggin!" She looked to Max with an excited expression and he raised a brow.

"You want me to interrogate a Nymph?" he asked, looking kind of excited by the challenge in that suggestion.

"That could work," Seth said keenly, pushing himself up and bouncing on the bed a little. "You could go full Siren on its woody little ass and dig all of their secrets right out of its brain."

"That didn't go so well when our parents tried to interrogate one," Caleb pointed out, shifting forward in his seat so that his knee knocked against mine and Darius growled at him in warning again.

"That is because your parents, much like the four of you, have no finesse," Geraldine cried. "You don't catch a trout on a hook and expect it to lead you back to its lair. You slide a slippery worm down its blowhole and tickle its tentacles until it's offering you its secrets as willingly as a wildebeest."

"Trouts don't have blowholes or tentacles," Max muttered in confusion and Geraldine groaned dramatically, throwing the back of her hand over her eyes and almost hitting him in the face with her elbow.

"Heavens save me from the linear minds of men!" she cried.

"I think what Grus is saying is that you should get the Nymph under your thrall before it even realises you're there," Orion translated as I laughed. "So that rather than trying to probe anyone or attempting to hide its secrets, it just wants to offer them up to you."

"It won't hurt them, right?" Darcy asked in concern, and bless my fucking sister for her sweet soul. I mean, she'd killed a bunch of Nymphs - like, a whole *bunch* – but I knew since seeing Diego's side of things she was worried about attacking someone innocent. And I guessed she had a point.

"It won't, beautiful," Orion said, looking at her like he'd just fallen for her a bit harder.

"You're gonna have to seduce a Nymph," I said, barking a laugh and pointing at Max who scowled at me.

"Fuck off," he growled. "I'm not doing that."

"You don't think you can?" Darius taunted and Max bristled.

"I could seduce you away from Tory if I had a fucking mind to, asshole. Don't doubt my power."

"Prove it," I said.

"You want me to seduce Darius?" Max teased and I glanced over at my big Dragon boyfriend, wondering if my jealousy could take a backseat long enough for me to enjoy watching that show before my gaze fell on Seth who was still bouncing about like a puppy on the bed behind him.

"Nah. I've got a better idea," I said. "You should make Seth and Cal hook up instead."

Seth's lips popped open and he gave me half a death glare mixed with half an I love you glare while I just smirked at my master plan. Subtle? Not so much, but genius all the same.

"Too easy," Max said dismissively, waving me off and ruining my master plan as Caleb straightened in his seat beside me.

"So are you gonna get us the information we need or what?" Orion asked, cutting through our game with his bossy professor tone.

"Is it information or Nymphormation?" I asked, barking a laugh at my own joke and Darcy fell apart with me while the others just looked at us like we'd cracked. "That was fucking funny," I grumbled when none of them joined in.

"It wasn't, babe," Seth said, shaking his head at me like I was some poor pathetic soul. "You're not the funny one. Just try and stick in your snarky, bitchy lane, yeah? It suits you better."

I opened my mouth to protest that, but Darius turned and punched him in the arm before I could. "Don't tell her she can't be funny, dickhead," he warned like my own personal dark knight.

"Well tell me this, Darius," Seth said seriously, looking him square in the eye. "Did. You. Laugh?"

Silence followed as Darius glanced at me, knowing full well he hadn't laughed, and I tried to look pissed off over that fact as the others all fell apart. Caleb broke first, shoving me playfully as I tried to hold out on my indignation over what had been a perfectly valid joke, but I gave in as Seth leapt on top of us and I found myself at the bottom of a dog pile a moment later.

I felt Darius leaping onto the pile as the air was driven from my lungs and I kicked and punched before he managed to drag the others off of me and toss them on their asses, stealing the spot Caleb had been sitting in and tugging me into his lap.

"Papa has been getting regular reports on Nymph movements and he has the locations of several known ragamuffins who the false king has given lodgings to near The Palace of Souls. We could sneak up on one of them like two geese looking for a gander," Geraldine suggested, her eyes bright.

"Maybe you should go without Grus," Orion suggested as Max got to his feet, seeming more willing to do it now that Geraldine was up for tagging along with him. "So that you can keep your mind on the task of seducing the Nymph instead of her."

"Oh good gracious, you're right, oh shameful one," Geraldine cooed, instantly dropping back into her seat. "Papa will give you their location and I will stay here so as not to distract you from your gallant work."

"Great," Max grunted, heading towards the door. "Anyone wanna come with me then or am I just going alone?"

"Fine, I'll come," Darius said, getting up and placing me back in my own seat, while keeping a hand on my shoulder like he was planning on forcing me to stay behind, but I wasn't really interested in sneaking up on Nymphs and watching Max do his thing, so he needn't have worried about that.

"You boys have fun," I called as Seth and Caleb got up too, the four of them exchanging grins at the thought of their little hunting trip.

"You coming, Lance?" Darius asked as they made it to the door, but he shook his head.

"I think I found something in this book earlier, but I need a bit more time to make sense of it so I'll finish that," Orion replied, his grabby little hands already curling around the gemstone book possessively and I couldn't help but grin at him for being such a geek.

"You're too cute." Darcy kissed him on the cheek and he smirked at her.

"I think I'm gonna go for a swim and have a nap then," I announced, looking between the girls. "Wanna join?"

"I'm in," Darcy agreed as Lance opened the book and stuck his nose into it, seeming to have forgotten we were here already.

"Well ruffle my feathers, I can't say no to some girl time with my queens," Geraldine gasped and I grinned as we walked to the door.

"I'll text Sofia and Angelica," Darcy said, taking out her Atlas and I smiled, peace washing over me as we headed down the corridor.

This place might have been a temporary reality away from the war raging up above us in Solaria, but it was a haven I was damn happy to enjoy for as long as I could. Because down here with my sister, Darius and my friends, it was as if time had stopped and everything was so perfect I just wanted to press pause and stay here forever.

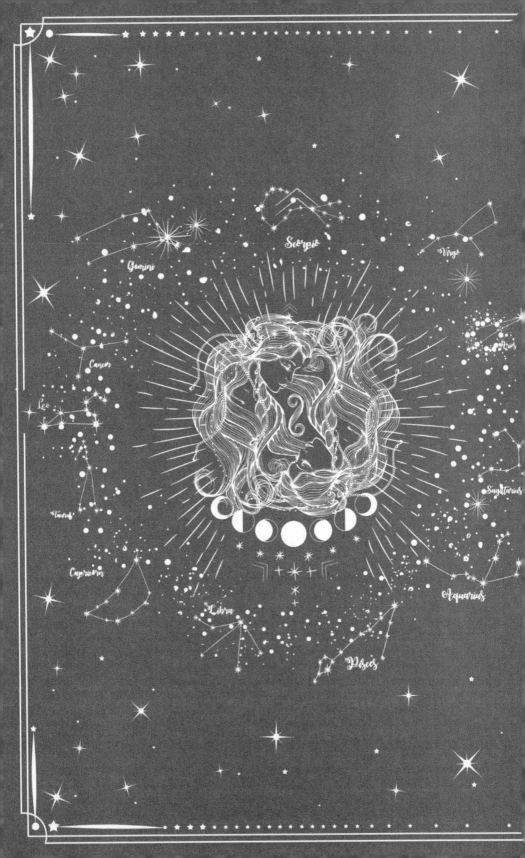

DARCY

CHAPTER TWENTY ONE

I twirled the Imperial Star between my fingers as I lazed in one of the bubbling pools in the bathhouse, sighing contentedly and daydreaming about going for a fly later on today with Tory and Gabriel. We sometimes cast rings of fire in the air and raced through them, the three of us tossing spells at each other to try and throw each other off. It was a game of dirty tactics and all of us ended up in fits of laughter by the end of it, and none of us had any idea of who had won the most rounds by the time we trailed inside – though Gabriel always insisted he had *seen* that it was him.

I was getting well used to his little pranks with his Sight, and it was damn hard to get one up on him, but Tory and I were managing it more often by learning to act unpredictably around him. We'd even managed to cast an illusion on his shirt once after he'd been out flying, and when he'd put his wings away and pulled it on, the words Crabby Gabby had illuminated on the back of it. He'd worn it halfway through dinner before he'd figured it out and cursed us, promising to deliver vengeance swiftly. It was almost impossible to remember a time before he'd come into my life, and I wanted to make up for all the years we'd lost.

Tory lazed beside me while Angelica, Sofia and Geraldine sat in the bubbling tub opposite me.

"How's Tyler, Sofia?" I asked with a tug in my chest over his mom.

"He's okay, I mean…he's not really. But he puts on a brave face," she said with a sad whinny in her throat. "Xavier's been amazing. He brings Tyler anything he needs and makes sure he doesn't have to want for anything. But it's also made me realise, well…" she sighed.

"What is it my sweet Sofia?" Geraldine urged as tears gleamed in Sofia's eyes, glitter sparkling within them.

"I don't want Tyler and Xavier to go back to fighting. When the three of us are together, we find this kind of peace which reminds me of home," she whispered. "And I know Tyler feels it too even though he won't admit it.

We're a herd, and it feels right to just enjoy that."

"Are you still hot for Xavier or is it just a Pegasus Dom thing?" Tory asked.

Pink glittery tears spilled down her cheeks into the water. "I'm in love with them both," she admitted on a breath like she'd been holding those words inside for who knew how long. "And it kills me every time they've fought before now. Just being able to spend time with them without them snapping at each other feels so good. I don't want it to end." She clapped a hand to her mouth at what she'd said. "I don't mean I don't want Tyler's pain to end. I didn't mean it like that."

"Of course you didn't," I said, moving across the pool to hug her and Geraldine and Angelica fell in around us, squeezing us tight then Tory joined a beat later, patting Sofia's head before we pulled away again.

Sofia drew in a breath, wiping away her tears. "I just want peace in my herd. And I know things are still unbalanced, I can feel it. But while Xavier's playing Sub to appease Tyler, things are at least amicable. And by the stars, sometimes when the two of them are pressed in on either side of me at night, I can't help but think what it would be like to claim them as my stallions. Both of them."

"Go Sofia," Tory said with a grin and Sofia cracked a laugh.

"That's pretty common in Pegasus herds anyway, right?" Angelica asked.

Sofia nodded with a small sniff. "Yeah, but not with Doms. A Dom could bond with two or more Subs easily enough, but Tyler and Xavier are both so strong headed, they're never going to find a balance together. With them, it has to be one or the other."

"If I may interject with my two tuppence," Geraldine said, leaning back against the side of the tub as we all looked to her. "A Ron Johnson or four between the bedsheets is all well and good for pickling your baguette, but when it comes to matters of the heart, a platoon of Long Shermans would never be satisfactory. So do Tyler and Xavier rock your underboats as well as showering your cockles in fresh whelks? Do they make your Lady Petunia do the ding-dang-tango *and* button your damsen?"

"I'm not sure what you're saying Geraldine," Sofia said apologetically.

"I don't know how to put it any clearer, my little pink Pegafriend," Geraldine said in frustration.

"Are they both good for your heart?" I translated, pretty sure that was what Geraldine was getting at.

"I think they could be," Sofia said forlornly. "But I'm so torn between them. How will I ever pick?"

"Maybe you could toss a coin?" Angelica suggested and Geraldine splashed her.

"Hobgoblins," she admonished her. "The fate of Sofia's dear petunia and cockles cannot rest upon the flip of a hapless coin. No, she must forge through the black and stormy night of these emotions, ride the waves like a unicorn from the nevermore and come to the shores of her chosen Ron Johnson with a stout heart and her choice solidified in iron."

"Hi everyone."

We turned at the gentle voice and I spotted Catalina walking into the room with a plate of cookies in her hand. She was dressed in a high necked black swimsuit and Hamish came lumbering in after her in a pair of bright pink trunks, his large body as hairy as a wolverine.

"Don't mind if we join you for a bit, do you? I brought snacks," Catalina said and we all scooted over in the pool as the two of them got in.

Catalina sat to my left and Hamish sat beyond her as they handed out cookies and I groaned at the delicious food as I took a big bite out of one.

"These are my sister Brenda's recipe," Hamish said as he placed the tray down on the side of the pool. "She taught my Gerrykins how to make her bagels when she was just a pup, didn't she poppet?"

My heart tugged with longing at the thought of growing up with a family like Geraldine's, the warmth of such love surrounding our home.

"That she did, Papa. Every Christmas we would make themed bagels too. Cinnamon and eggnog, brandy and spice, oh – I cannot wait to do it again, I shall bake us up a bagel bounty."

"Do you have any Christmas traditions, Angelica?" Hamish asked her and she nodded.

"My mom always gets us to lay out on the roof and stargaze. We cuddle up in blankets at midnight on Christmas Eve each year with a glass of mulled wine. It's my favourite thing in the world," she cooed and my heart tugged even sharper as I shared a glance with Tory, seeing the same ache in her eyes.

"Me and my family always go Carol singing," Sofia said, her face lighting up. "We put on these massive silly Christmas pyjamas in our Pegasus forms. Half the fun is trying to get into them while we're shifted, and all of us fall about laughing our asses off. The one who gets into them last has to wear a silly hat too which has the word Pegadunce on it," she giggled. "We fly from house to house in our neighbourhood, shift back into our Fae forms with these baggy clothes hanging off of us and sing to all our neighbours."

"Oh what fun! I shall have to join you in this merriment one year," Geraldine cried.

"Do you have any family traditions?" Angelica looked to Tory and I and quiet fell as we glanced at each other.

"Um…" I chewed my lip awkwardly.

"Christmas isn't really our thing," Tory said, trying to deflect.

"Halibut! You must have some tradition," Geraldine pressed and they all looked to us eagerly while my stomach knotted and heat rose in my skin.

"Well we have a snowball fight," I said.

"Of course you do!" Geraldine cried. "And what else, do you snuggle around the fire afterwards and cosy up with a cup of hot nosh and open your presents?"

"We didn't really have presents," I said awkwardly.

"No presents?" Sofia gasped and Tory became overly interested in her nails as everyone kept staring at us.

"We had each other," I tried, but then they just all looked a whole lot sadder for us.

"But you must have had a kind and bubbly foster mother? And a sweet-toothed foster sister with a fondness for warm hugs?" Geraldine asked, looking desperate for that to be true and I realised why we'd never brought these things up with her before. We'd told her a few bits and pieces of our past, but she'd be devastated to know how bad it had really been.

"We didn't have anyone," Tory said bluntly and I felt those words ringing around the empty space inside my chest.

"It was us. Just us," I said, sharing a look with Tory and she smiled half-heartedly back at me.

Catalina suddenly touched my arm and I looked to her, finding her face taut with emotion. "You deserved better."

My heart turned to mush at the way she was looking at me lately. She was so naturally motherly that she pulled us all beneath her wings with barely any effort at all. And I yearned so deeply for that part of me to be fulfilled that it was easy to let her, and to allow myself to bathe in the affection from her that we had never known from our own mom.

"Maybe this year we could create some new traditions?" Catalina suggested, her eyes brightening as she looked between me and Tory hopefully. "There were so many I wanted to have with my boys over the years, but Lionel never allowed it…" She blew out a harsh breath. "The point is, that both of you as well as my boys, Lance and me missed out on a lot of things, but that's no reason to keep missing them. Can you think of anything you might like to do?"

"I wouldn't hate a Christmas Eve drag race," Tory said, her lips quirking in amusement. "I could get Darius a new bike every year and give it to him early just to beat his ass in a race right in time for the festivities."

"Oh and we could all attend!" Catalina said enthusiastically. "We could knit family sweaters each year and wear them to the race and bake festive goodies to eat while we watch."

"I've always wondered how you make mince pies," I said with a shrug, kinda liking the idea of learning.

"And I've always liked eating mince pies," Tory added, making me laugh.

"We could go for a flight on New Year's Day?" I suggested. "Lance could ride Darius and we could invite Gabriel's family too?"

"Gerry and I could run beneath you, howling you on," Hamish added enthusiastically but Catalina shook her head.

"No. You should ride on me," she said, her cheeks colouring as she voiced the idea.

"Upon the back of a Dragon?" Hamish gasped. "My lady, what a scandal we shall cause."

"Lionel will roll in his grave," Catalina replied wickedly, and we all laughed hopefully at the idea of him being dead.

"What else?" I asked excitedly, my grin widening at the thought of taking part in some huge family Christmas like that.

"We could grow our own tree and garlands," Catalina added, her excitement clear too.

"And deck the halls with all the festive fangles!" Geraldine added. "Bake flamberbam cookies, hang naffly mistletoe, build gingerbread igloos, lay traps for elves, pickle a gherkin, wash some homeless fellows, dance upon a gooseberry, do the naked jive, place a prickly pinecone between our fanny cheeks in a Christmas Pine Cleansing, befriend a bad-tempered owl, tie bows in the shoelaces of Fae who have forgotten how and-"

"Take it down a notch, poppet, you're losing your noggin again," Hamish interrupted as Geraldine kept going without drawing breath, her face reddening more and more as she went on. "You don't want me to tell Santa's elves you got too exuberant again now, do you?"

"No Papa," she agreed, slapping a hand to her mouth and sagging back in the water.

Ohmagod, she still believes in Santa.

"That all sounds great," Tory said, breathing a laugh. "It would be really nice to be able to just enjoy a Christmas like the ones we might have had if Lionel hadn't stolen our family from us."

"I would be honoured if you considered me a part of your family," Catalina said, tears shining in her eyes and my heart swelled at the thought of that. Of how much we might all be able to claim with one another once we were done fighting this war.

"I would love that," I murmured and Tory took my hand beneath the water, letting me know that she agreed with that too.

"You deserved to know your sweet mother and your gallant father," Hamish said brusquely, rage colouring his cheeks. "Oh what I would give to see them again. Your father and I studied together at Zodiac Academy, you know? He was a pioneer of a man, always shooting for the moon. I was a senior when he started, but good golly, he wowed me like a candy to a crow. We bonded when we were on the Pitball team together, see?"

"You were friends?" I breathed, latching onto the connection to my flesh and blood keenly.

"Indeed we were," Hamish confirmed, smiling at some memory I wish I could pluck from his head and see for myself.

"What was he like?" Tory asked, shifting closer to me and Hamish rested his arms back on the sides of the tub.

"Oh he was a cad of course, every Lilith and June swooned at his feet. But he had the mark of a true king even then. His power was unlike anything I had ever seen, his casts so beautiful, it often brought a tear to my eye. And though his popularity was faultless, he was always humble. He liked his private time, he liked to draw too. His art was more wonderful than a lambent moon on a hillside."

My breath caught at that fact. I hadn't drawn in a long time now, but it was something I used to love, and hearing that my father had loved it too made me want to start another piece. It was something I'd always done in the past to escape reality, but since coming to Solaria, I hadn't exactly needed that outlet when the whole world was constantly exciting.

"What else?" Tory pushed and Hamish started regaling us with stories of our dad on the Pitball team, the Earthbacker, which made Geraldine squeal as that was her position. I got lost in the sea of stories that painted a picture of the man I'd never know in my mind, my longing to meet him so fierce, it opened an old wound in my chest.

I had always wondered what it would be like to have a father, the concept so alien to me it was hard to even picture Hail as being that to me. And as I laid my head back against the side and new images were built up in my mind of him, I felt a little closer to the man I'd never really know. And hoped one day when I walked beyond the Veil, he'd be waiting there for me with the same passion and love in his heart that Hamish described him to have. I just wished death didn't have to be the first time we'd meet.

After a while, Hamish and Catalina left and Angelica headed off to go and see her boyfriend, a heavy sort of silence falling over the rest of us.

Geraldine dabbed at her eyes. "Your dear father would have been blazing with pride like the sun in the height of summer for you, my queens."

Before I could answer that, a head popped up from the water that made us all scream in terror.

"Cooweee! Only me," Washer said as he stood fully out of the water to reveal his waxed chest as his cyan Siren scales shifted from his skin and vanished. "I've been taking a dip down in the depths of the pool in my Siren form. Nothing to get your panties in a twist about."

"Have you been down there this whole time?" Tory gasped as I kicked away from him, his leg brushing mine and making my insides writhe.

"Yes, it goes much, much deeper than you'd think down there. I lay right on the bottom and did my hip thrusts," he chuckled, looking between us and I dropped lower under the water as his gaze dripped over me.

"Get out of here," I snarled.

"Yes, you crusty old crabbit, this is the royal quarters!" Geraldine snapped. "How did you even get into the true queens' bathhouse?"

"I have my ways," Washer purred, climbing up out of the pool and starting to do some lunges in the tiny speedos he was wearing. "I just gave the wards a little thrust and a hip drive and they came loose for me. It's much wetter in here. And I like it wet."

"Get. Out," Tory growled, pointing at the door.

"Fine, fine," he sighed, lunging his way out the door as his speedos slid up his asscrack and I shuddered.

"I shall reinforce the wards, my ladies. Forgive me," Geraldine said, her head falling forward. "I have failed you."

"It's not your fault he's a total creep," I said and Geraldine nodded sadly.

"Alas, creeps will be creeps. But I shall reinforce it all the same, never fear." She leapt from the water, hurrying to the door and starting to cast the wards that only allowed certain people through them. "Be gone foul blaggard! And keep your crack of dawn for a faraway sunrise!"

CALEB

CHAPTER TWENTY TWO

The stardust spat us out on Moon Street before one of the most desirable properties in the city, just a stone's throw away from the grounds which surrounded The Palace of Souls.

It had once been owned by a lot of the most politically influential families in the kingdom, but not anymore. Lionel had taken possession of this run of houses, alongside several others in the city, and had gifted them to the Nymphs to use in the name of this so-called peace he'd brokered with them.

The house was starkly white with imposing walls that cast dark shadows across the road, fronted with a porch held up by impressive pillars that were shaped like the Orders. From Minotaurs to fierce looking Medusas and Harpies, the masonry was so skilled and beautiful, the pillars almost looked alive.

Spring birds twittered in the nearby trees and I relished the warmer feeling of the air with the shift in seasons fully upon us.

My skin prickled as I looked down the street, the illusion spells we'd worked together to cast shimmering against my skin as they bounced the morning light off of us and directed all attention away from our position.

Darius took the lead as he jogged up the steps of the grand town house and the three of us stayed close to him as he headed up to the door, pressing his hand to the wood to check for magical locks.

Seth's shoulder knocked against mine and I glanced at him, the illusion allowing us to see one another even though no one else would be able to, so I could drink in the excited look in his earthy eyes.

"Ready?" I teased and he grinned wider, magic crackling at his fingertips as he practically buzzed with energy.

"I'm just so ready to start fighting back properly," he replied with a Wolf's snarl on his lips. "And this feels like the beginning of it, doesn't it?"

"Yeah, I guess," I agreed.

"We should do something wild to celebrate if this goes well," he said. "Like throw a party or go base jumping, or cage fighting, or karaoke or something. What would you do if you could do anything at all to celebrate?" he asked, knocking his arm against me again and making my muscles tighten at the contact in the most exhilarating way.

"I need to hunt," I said instantly, my gaze moving to his neck as I lost myself in the fantasy of my mouth against his skin and the hot rush of his blood between my lips as I pinned his body beneath mine. "And I need to get laid," I added without thinking.

Seth's brows shot up and he blinked at me a couple of times as I realised what I'd just said and I laughed it off, shaking my head to clear it of the desire I was feeling for his blood just as Darius declared there were no magical locks or wards on the place. That wasn't surprising really. Even Lionel wasn't dumb enough to start teaching the Nymphs how to harness their magic and cast spells like that which could so easily be used against our kind.

"Okay, I'm gonna make sure everyone inside is asleep before we break in," Max said. "We don't want them to sense our magic and be on alert before we even get close enough for me to manipulate one. You guys should make sure your mental shields are up or you'll find yourselves snoring too."

I nodded along with the others, tightening my hold on my barriers, though they didn't really need any reinforcing. I'd been keeping them locked up tight recently anyway, my thoughts too scattered and my emotions too confusing for me to want him picking up on them. I didn't need the drama involved with his questions if he detected some of the shit I had running through my head, especially when some of it could pose a threat to the balance we all maintained between the four of us.

I glanced down the street, this area pretty familiar to me seeing as it wasn't too far from my family home. My mom had contacted me a few times through the journal to say they were alright, and she'd been letting us know Lionel's schedule so we always knew his movements. Not that it helped us a whole lot considering the entourage of Dragons he often travelled with, the FIB who attended his events in force, and the Shadow Princess hounding his every move. But Gabriel had a team who was working to push his defences at public events and figure out how easy it was for Vard to detect our movements.

I felt the brush of Max's power against my shields, and I couldn't help but yawn despite the strength I held against his gifts as he worked to take down anyone close enough to sense us while we were here.

I glanced around at the empty street as he worked, wondering how long we could risk hanging around here before one of the Nymphs felt our power and raised the alarm. Best we worked fast to avoid that.

Max nodded as he finished and Darius gripped the door handle, melting it and the lock in his grasp before pushing it wide so that the four of us could step inside.

We dropped the illusions the moment the door was closed behind us and I shot away from the others, pulling my twin Phoenix fire daggers into my grip. I raced in and out of every room in the house to check how many Nymphs we were dealing with, only discovering one in the kitchen, slumped over the counter and fast asleep beside the stove.

I skidded to a halt before the others who had only made it a few steps into the house and gave them a cocky grin as I stowed my weapons away once more and pushed my fingers into my blonde curls to tame them.

"He's in the kitchen and he's a big fucker. The rest of the house is clear," I announced, earning myself a grin from Seth and a nod from Darius.

Max strode past me in the direction I'd indicated, pushing his gifts out before him and sending a sense of peace and trust vibrating through the air as his navy blue scales crept across his skin to peek out from the edges of his clothes.

We fell into step behind him, keeping close as he headed into the kitchen and approached the Nymph who was still sleeping in his Fae-like form spread out across the kitchen counter.

My heart began to race as we closed in on this creature which was the enemy of our kind and yet looked so like us in this form that it was hard to even comprehend how dangerous it could be.

Max reached out to place a hand on the Nymph's arm and I stepped closer, touching Max's shoulder so that I could see what memories he was coaxing from the Nymph too.

Seth caught my hand just as I was tugged into the mind of our enemy and I curled my fingers around his, holding on tight.

Darkness shifted around us as Max worked to sort through the memories and I caught glimpses of a life lived by this creature with locations and faces shifting all around me so fast that it was impossible to fully distinguish them from each other until one jerked to a halt before us and I found myself watching it play out.

A Nymph in shifted form was stalking through the trees of a dark forest with patches of snow on the ground, his hand clamped tight around something red which caught in the dappled light spilling between the trees.

The creature whose mind we were currently trespassing in walked behind the other Nymph, listening to whispers which seemed to come from within his own mind as they urged him further up the sloping path.

The taint of the shadows coated my tongue and I was half aware of Seth whimpering at the feel of it and Darius stiffening in recognition where he held onto Max's other arm.

"Feed it to me. Make me stronger," the Shadow Princess breathed into the mind of the Nymphs and they upped their pace, passing through thicker and thicker woodland before stepping out into a huge clearing where a pyramid of onyx stone arched up towards the heavens.

The vision flickered around us and I watched a new memory unfold as the Nymph laid the red and gold platter onto a huge altar which seemed to be carved from the pitch black stone which made up the pyramid we were now standing within.

There were carvings all over the altar of a woman who I recognised as that shadow bitch Lionel kept by his side as she took part in various battles and sexual acts.

As the Nymph set the platter down, the entire room began to hum with a dark and rampant energy and the space above the altar pulsed and flexed, darkness seeming to form of its own accord as the shadows slipped through a rift into our realm and the demands of the Shadow Princess grew louder within the mind of the Nymph.

There were other items laid out on the altar, each of them connected to the rift which flickered in the space above it by a tendril of shadow which

277

tainted the air and made bile rise in the back of my throat.

"Where is this?" Max's voice echoed through the space, his tone laced with a seductive kind of lilt which made me want to answer him even though I didn't have an answer to give.

The Nymph fell prey to his demands and more images flashed before us, moving so fast that I couldn't keep track as he showed us how he had gotten to this place and where it was located in the far east of our kingdom.

"How many Fae have you killed?" Max asked next and I gritted my jaw as I was gifted memories of him working alongside other Nymphs as they broke into the houses of innocent Fae, butchering them and sinking their probes into the chest of men, women and children alike. I could feel their hunger, their need for that power like it was written into their souls.

There were more of those memories, more and more until rage was boiling through my blood as I felt the cruelty and violence in the creature so viscerally that it filled me with rage and the desire to wipe him and all who were like him from the face of the earth.

The vision shattered abruptly and I flinched as I was snapped out of it, finding myself back in the kitchen as blood splattered my face and made me suck in a sharp breath of surprise.

Seth was still gripping my hand tightly and Max looked just as shocked as I felt as we all looked up at Darius who was standing beside the severed head of the Nymph with his blood covered axe in hand and a snarl on his face that reminded me of his father for a moment.

"We need to destroy that altar," he said firmly, taking a pouch of stardust from his pocket.

He threw it over the four of us before we could say anything else and we were whipped through the embrace of the stars and deposited back outside the magical barrier which hid The Burrows within seconds.

"I felt that death like it was my own, asshole," Max snapped, throwing a fist at Darius's face and catching him in the jaw.

"It needed to die," Darius growled back, dropping his axe and throwing a punch in return.

"Not while I was inside its fucking head!" Max yelled angrily, launching himself at Darius and Seth tugged me back a step before they could plough into us.

I turned to look at him, finding blood sprayed across his face too and I reached out to wipe some of it from his cheek with my thumb.

"Turns out we've still got a bunch of Nymphs to kill after all," I said with a grin and the smile he gave me in return made my breath catch in my throat.

"Shall we beat them inside to deliver the news then?" he suggested, glancing at Darius and Max as they continued to wrestle among the spring flowers and I nodded, shooting forward and sweeping him off of his feet as we raced back inside to find the others.

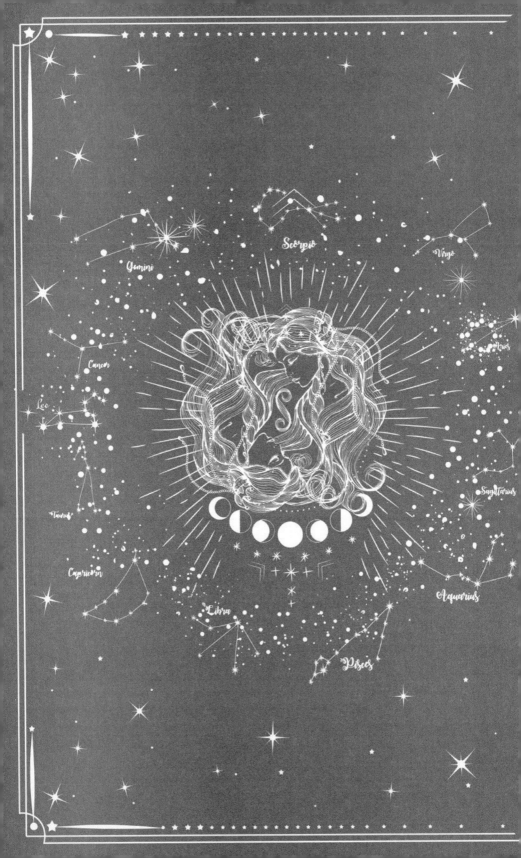

TORY

CHAPTER TWENTY THREE

"We'll cause a distraction."

I looked up at the sound of Gabriel's voice as it drew me out of my nap where I lay on the edge of the lounger in the bathhouse. It was so warm and steamy in here that I couldn't help but try to recover a few minutes of rest to catch up on the sleep Darius was so insistent on stealing from me - and even the frizzy hair was going to be worth the nap time.

"Why do we need a distraction?" Darcy asked from her position lounging at the edge of the warm water where she was watching Geraldine float across the surface in a giant mermaid shell she'd fashioned for herself out of earth magic. Sofia was lazing in the pool beyond her, her eyes closed as she relaxed.

"I don't know – whatever it is, is hidden from me by the shadows so I won't be much help with it, but I've already *seen* me and my family hitting a Nebular Inquisition Centre tonight so Lionel and his shadow bitch will be after us instead of you." Gabriel tipped us a salute as he turned and left as quickly as he'd appeared, clearly decided on his fate and knowing that it wouldn't involve us.

"Be careful!" I called after him and he chuckled as he headed back out into the corridor before calling back to us.

"You should head back to see Orion – the Heirs will return at any moment and Darius is all worked up wanting to go kill things," he said.

"So what's new?" I replied.

His laughter carried away from us and I forced my sleepy ass to sit up as the others got out of the pool, Geraldine paddling her seashell to shore while singing a ditty about a salacious salmon.

They got dressed and dried off and we headed back to Orion and Darcy's room, Sofia peeling away to go find Xavier and Tyler as they had plans to fly with the herd in the clouds this afternoon.

I followed Darcy inside with Geraldine and found Orion sitting cross legged in the middle of the bed, his hair looking like he'd run his fingers through it a hundred times and his nose so deep in the pages of that book on rocks that he could probably taste the glue that bound it.

"Shit dude, you look like you've been cheating on my sister with that hardback," I teased and he looked up at us with a grin as he laid the book down in front of him.

"Do I need to break her spine?" Darcy teased as he shoved his messed up hair out of his eyes with a deep laugh.

"I think I've found something," he said, beckoning us closer and pointing to a piece of text which was absolutely not written in English. "Look here, it talks about the twelve Zodiac Guild stones."

"Golly gosh nuts," Geraldine breathed.

"Oooh," Darcy cooed, moving to sit on the bed with him as I dropped into a chair. "What does it say about them?"

"Not a lot," Orion sighed. "It's only this small passage really. But it implies that the stones were once held by the heads of twelve powerful families, each of which represented a single star sign. Then I remembered a passage I'd read in this book-" He turned and grabbed one of the many books which lay on the bed behind him and flipped through the pages of the dusty tome as carefully as he could before holding a handwritten page out for us to see. "This is an account of prophecies which were foretold in the last few hundred years which may or may not have come to pass – basically any prophecy that a Seer of note was gifted from the stars which wasn't about events in their lifetime. I went through a stage of being obsessed with finding old prophecies and figuring out what they'd been referring to and whether or not it came to pass as a boy, so-"

"We get it, you had books for friends as a kid. But why does that equal you looking like you might make a mess of your pants at any moment?" I interrupted, seeing a whole series of reminiscence about his childhood reading habits in my future if I didn't get him back on track. Darcy looked like she was into his lust for books, and I was kinda wanting to step out of the room before they descended into some sort of book orgy that I seriously didn't want to have any awareness of.

"Right, yeah, so this is a prophecy which is almost four hundred years old and it says; 'Reuniting the stones of the Zodiac Guild will mark the dawn of a new reign.'"

Orion looked between my sister and I with a wide grin and Geraldine shrieked before throwing a hand to her forehead and collapsing in a heap.

"Holy shit, Geraldine!" I cried, diving out of my chair and rolling her over as I pushed healing magic into her body, wondering what the hell had just happened.

"Are you okay?" Darcy asked in concern as she leaned in close too and Geraldine began to murmur something beneath her breath.

"The time is nigh, the time is nigh, the time is nigh…"

"What?" I asked, looking to Orion in alarm as he stood over us. But before I could freak out and start wondering if she was having a vision of her own, Geraldine leapt to her feet and thrust her arms into the air, an explosion of noise bursting from her throat as she cast that voice amplification spell thing on herself and made her words echo throughout the entire Burrows.

"THE TIME IS NIGH!"

"Jesus!" I clapped my hands over my ears and Darcy winced violently as Geraldine burst into tears, thankfully ending the spell before dropping to her knees before us.

"We must reunite the stones and mark the dawn of your reign, my queens," she gasped between sobs and my frantic heartbeat finally began to calm as I realised she was just having an A.S.S. episode.

"You scared the crap out of us, Geraldine," Darcy scolded as Orion shook his head and moved back to his precious books.

"So where are the rest of the stones?" I asked, looking to him and wondering if there could be any merit to a prophecy from hundreds of years ago.

"Lost. Have been for generations," Orion sighed. "I found records in some other books which refer to them by various names and I'm almost certain that they are in fact all referring to the same set of twelve stones. The most well known being The Gems of Lariom which were rumoured to be the prized possession of a Dragon called Hermiod hundreds of years ago. He loved them more than life itself and the stars cursed him to lose them for prizing them above all else. It's a children's story which I never really gave much credit to, but if there are some tendrils of truth in it then maybe we could track them down..."

"Has anyone ever tried to find them before now?" Darcy asked, drifting closer to him to get a better look at the book of rocks while I dropped into my seat once more.

"Oh, countless Fae have tried, your highness," Geraldine said, managing to peel herself off of the floor as she moved to look at the books as well. "The Gems of Lariom are a much sought after treasure which no Fae has ever proven really exist at all. And yet many still have taken up the hunt. It is said to be the most hopeless endeavour ever to be undertaken in Solaria. The hunt for the stones is called the endless expanse, the pointless quest, the life of the fool, the most idiotic of journeys, the hope of the madman, the-"

"We get it, Geraldine," Orion growled. "But maybe it just wasn't the right time until now – we found six of them already after all."

The door opened behind us before she could respond and the Heirs strode into the room, Max sporting a bloody nose while Darius's lip was split open.

"What happened?" I asked, shoving to my feet as my gaze locked on the sight of those injuries and the blood which was splattered over all of them too.

"Don't worry, babe," Seth said casually. "Darius just decapitated a Nymph then Max started a fight with him after we got back because he didn't appreciate the way he handled it. No biggie."

"Oh." I dropped back into my seat again and Darius scowled at me for how quickly my concern fell away, but he was clearly fine so I wasn't going to fuss over him like some mother hen.

"You killed it?" Darcy breathed.

"It was evil, little Vega," Max promised. "We saw what it had done to our kind."

Darcy's shoulders dropped in relief and I had to admit I was relieved too. If there *were* happy little Nymph friends out there, I didn't want Darius going around decapitating them, but if he killed one or two who liked to spend their free time murdering innocent Fae then who was I to judge?

"Aren't you gonna come running over to heal me, baby?" Darius taunted me.

"Fat chance of that. Don't get into fights with your friends if you can't handle the fallout," I scoffed. "Besides, I wanna hear what you guys found out from the Nymph."

"Yeah, tell us what you discovered," Orion encouraged, moving to sit on the bed before leaping up again as he almost placed his ass on one of the books.

"Are you okay, man?" Caleb asked him, cocking his head to one side. "Is that ball rash still causing you problems?"

"What? No," Orion snapped, shooting a death glare at Seth who just shrugged innocently.

"Oh dear, not a rash on your John Ronalds!" Geraldine cried. "I can make you a special ointment for that. Allow me to ask my papa if he still has a store of wartslime and-"

"I have it under control, thank you, Geraldine," Orion snarled and I sniggered as he shot Seth another look that promised him a slow and brutal death. Darcy and I glanced at each other, nearly cracking up further before Orion's gaze slid onto us, and his demon professor eyes had the eerie effect of making our laughs die in our throats. Dude was gifted at the bossy teaching shit even if he never had liked his old job. "Let's just hear what the four of you found out."

"There's a rift between the Fae and Shadow Realms which is feeding Lavinia power and the Nymphs have been helping her bolster it with those dark artifacts," Darius explained, picking up an Atlas from the table and opening up a map of Solaria before zooming in on a section of deep forest to the far east of the kingdom and pointing at it. "There's a temple or something there containing it and it looked like the place was crawling with Nymphs."

"Question is, how do we close a rift between the realms?" Seth asked as he dropped into a seat opposite me.

"With dark magic," Orion replied in a serious tone. "But it won't be simple to achieve."

"Who cares about simple?" I asked. "I wanna know if it's doable or not."

"I think it will weaken Lavinia if we can manage it," Darius added. "We definitely got the impression that the artifacts alongside the rift were increasing her power. That was before she crossed into our realm, but it makes sense that it would be helping her draw the shadows through to our realm too."

"The vision we saw of Lavinia showed the Vega queen banishing her to the Shadow Realm and closing the rift to cut off the remaining Nymphs from the power of it," Darcy added thoughtfully. "So maybe closing this one would weaken them again."

"There are bound to be countless Nymphs there," Orion protested, leaning in close to look at the map which Darius had pulled up on his Atlas. "Fuck knows how many they'd leave guarding something that important, but it's not going to be easy."

"Well nothing ever is for us, is it?" I shrugged, earning myself one of those blazing looks from my Dragon which spelled out just how much he hated the way we'd begun with each other.

The corner of my lips twitched in amusement as he frowned at me though, because I might have fucking hated him once and it might have been a whole lot easier on the two of us if we'd just been upfront over our feelings and attraction to one another to begin with, or even if he'd gone against his father's wishes when it came to me, but that wasn't our story. And I wasn't certain I would love him this desperately if it had been. The way we came together might not have been a pretty little fairy tale filled with sonnets and roses, but it was raw, brutal, real. Ours. And I'd felt every damn moment of it along the way.

"Maybe we should just hit them hard," Darcy suggested. "We have an entire army here waiting to strike - why not bring them out in force and show Lionel what we're capable of?"

"We don't have the stardust for that," Max pointed out. "With Lionel restricting access to it, we're going to be hard pressed to even make sure we have enough to keep using it ourselves."

"We can handle it," Caleb said with a cocky shrug. "We can take out a few Nymphs."

"Hell yeah we can," Seth agreed. "We're the Phoen Dream, Bitchy Flame Eyes, Wolfman, Bitey C, Fish Fury, Dragzilla, Professor Shame and Batty Betty."

"Don't start with that shit again," Darius groaned as Geraldine chuckled loudly at the name he'd gifted her and my smile widened at mine. I still kept getting caught off guard by seeing him acting so damn normal around his friends, that utter asshole facade slipping just enough to let the light in when he was surrounded by people he trusted.

"Oh fuck off," Orion growled. "If I have to have a shit nickname, at least don't bring my damn shame into it."

"Aw, look at you wanting a cute nickname from Seth," Darcy teased him and Orion sighed as Seth immediately dove on the opportunity to play with him.

"It's hard not to bring your shame into when it's looking me right in the eye, Lance," Seth said airily. "You should just own it, make a shame club with shamed friends who go on shameful adventures."

"Or I could cut your hair off and strangle you with it, how about that?" Orion tossed back.

"Wow, Professor Shame is grumpy today," Seth muttered and Darcy flicked a finger, casting a perfect shot of water right up his nose.

"Ah!" he yelped.

"Don't bring shame into it," Darcy insisted.

"Fine," Seth sighed. "I'll think up something else, but we'll use Professor Shame as a placeholder for now."

"We should consult with Gabriel about this altar," Darius said, steering us back to the task at hand.

"Gabriel can't help us with this," I said, pursing my lips. "But he said him and his family are going to keep Lionel and Lavinia distracted for us. So

I think the best thing we can do is strike at them out of the blue and hit as hard as we can."

"Her majesty is right," Geraldine agreed with a solemn nod. "We must drive ourselves deep within their darkest recesses, slam down hard upon whatever cranny and crevice we can thrust through, pound them down beneath us and leave them begging for absolution."

"Yeah, what Gerry said, let's pound them until they can't take no more," Max agreed with a grin as Geraldine gasped.

"Do not be so vulgar you stupendous sea urchin!" Geraldine cried, back handing him around the head so hard that he almost head butted the table in front of him.

"If this rift is feeding Lavinia more control over their shadows, they will be guarding it furiously," Orion warned. "I seriously doubt we will be able to just force our way in there. Besides, if we linger too long Lionel will likely show up and we still aren't ready to take him down."

"And he'll probably bring the Dragon Guild with him," Darius muttered.

"Well if Gabriel is busting into one of his Inquisition Centres that should buy us some time at least," I said and Orion nodded as he thought on that.

"Why don't we just play to our strengths then?" Seth suggested.

"Which are?" Darcy asked curiously.

"Well, you may not have noticed, babe, but I can be a bit of a showboater when the occasion calls for it."

"The occasion never calls for it and yet you do it incessantly," Orion pointed out and Darius snorted in amusement.

"I beg to differ," Seth said, raising his chin. "Like right now for instance, the occasion most certainly calls. If we were to attack them outwardly, maybe snatch a few of their friends and tie them to stakes, leave them screaming for their little buddies to hear, then the Nymphs would all come running to help them."

"Then what?" I asked, trying to understand how us drawing the lot of them to us would make getting to that rift any easier.

"Then Cal shoots round the back while they're distracted and blows their rift to smithereens before they even realise he's there," Seth said simply, grinning at Caleb who seemed to like the sound of that idea.

"Yeah, I could play hero if you need me to," Caleb agreed, pushing his fingers through his blonde curls in that flirtatious way he always did as his gaze lingered on Seth's.

"You can't blow the rift up," Orion growled, shaking his head. "It is a tear in the fabric which separates our realms and unlike the bridge we leave open to the mortal realm, this one is dangerous. We need it sealed so that the shadows can't slip through anymore. If we do it wrong then we could end up making it bigger and gifting Lavinia and the Nymphs more power instead of taking it from them."

"And you're saying I can't manage that?" Caleb asked, quirking a brow at him.

"I'm saying it will take dark magic and a whole lot of concentration and even then, I'm not certain it can be done. The rift will be incredibly volatile, one wrong move and we could tear it wider, releasing more shadows upon our realm instead of sealing them away. And fuck knows what will happen to all of us then," Orion replied tersely.

"Well if anyone can manage it, it's you, Lance," Darius pointed out and we all turned to look at our former professor as he frowned.

"It will be dangerous," he said and Darcy's throat bobbed as she looked at him.

"Everything is dangerous these days, dude," I pointed out and he nodded in reluctant agreement.

"I'm guessing it will require the use of a binding needle to do it which is a seriously dark artifact which none of you have been trained to handle," Orion added thoughtfully.

"This is the kind of blow we need to strike against them," Darius said firmly. "So I say we do it. I can lead the charge to distract the Nymphs and draw them out of the temple. But if you're going to need to concentrate while you work to mend the rift then you can't go alone. You'll need to bring someone you can trust to watch your back."

"I'll go with you," Darcy offered instantly, but Orion shook his head.

"I'm guessing getting in there without being noticed will be seriously difficult. I'm going to need to move at my top speed and I can't do that while carrying someone. It's better if I go alone, Blue."

"Or bring the strongest Vampire in Solaria with you," Caleb interjected, his chin tilted up in a challenge as the two of them faced off. "I can watch your ass and deal with any threats that might come at us while barely breaking a sweat."

"Fuck yeah you can," Seth chuckled, his eyes alight as Orion simmered, a refusal brewing in his gaze.

Darcy reached out to grasp Orion's arm, giving him a stern look. "If you can't risk carrying someone then Caleb is your only choice. He's powerful and you can trust him. So what's the problem?"

"Yeah, all you have to do is ask me nicely and I'll come protect you for sure, Lance," Caleb said, smiling sweetly, though the effect was ruined by the sight of his fangs peeking out.

Orion growled, clearly unimpressed by the idea and I arched a brow at the two of them, feeling weirdly like I was watching a wildlife show where two predators had just stumbled upon each other at the edge of their territories and were about to fight to the death to claim pissing rights on the closest tree.

"Oo-ee, is it me or is it getting all kinds of hot in here?" Geraldine asked loudly, fanning her face as the two Vampires glared at one another in clear dislike. "I swear all of this testosterone is going to impregnate one of the ladies here present if you boys don't find a way to dial it down a notch."

"Yeah, suck it up, boys. The plan is already decided," I said, flexing my fingers and letting Phoenix flames ignite along the surface of them as the thought of the fight got my veins buzzing. "Me and Darcy are gonna lead the group as we distract the Nymphs and draw them out of the temple. You two just need to sneak in while we keep them busy and fix the shadow hole with that fancy needle thingamabob. Simple."

"You're not leading shit, Roxy," Darius growled, reaching out to grip my arm and tugging me closer to him as his pupils shifted to reptilian slits in warning. "You've only been on a handful of Nymph raids before. So I'm not gonna let you risk your neck trying to prove you can do something which you clearly haven't got the first idea about."

"Oh, there he is," I said, leaning down and placing my hands on the arms of Darius's chair as I looked at the darkness in him and prepared to stoke it with flames. "The asshole who still thinks he's more deserving of our throne than the Heirs who were born to sit on it."

"And there *she* is," he replied in a low voice, our unending argument making the air crackle between us as we poked it awake once more. "The little girl who thinks placing a crown upon her head will make her capable of running a kingdom she knows nothing about."

"Shall we do rock, paper, scissors to decide who will lead the charge?" Seth stage whispered. "It just seems like that stare off will go on all day if not and we have Nymphs to kill…"

Caleb barked a laugh and Max snorted too, but I just held Darius's gaze and waited to see if I would find any flicker of doubt in his big ego, but all that looked back at me was a Dragon who was once again certain he knew best. Gah, sometimes I wanted to kick him in the dick even more than I wanted to use it for the fun things.

"Darius is right," Orion said behind me and I forced my gaze around to look at him. "He is the most experienced among you when it comes to fighting the Nymphs. He should lead you."

"Oh should he now?" Darcy asked with narrowed eyes, but before our argument could escalate, Geraldine leapt to her feet and upended the table, forcing all of us to scramble away from it - though Darius just stayed right there in his seat with his legs spread in his big balls pose without even fucking flinching.

"Ladies, let us prepare to leave - I have a gift for you to wear into battle and we have no time to waste on flimflamming with these uncouth ruffians. I suggest we all meet up in the barn post haste and the rest of you go and retrieve your weapons from your rooms - we cannot just sit around here lollygagging while Nymphs await their deaths at our fair and star bound hands."

I opened my mouth to protest, but Geraldine snatched hold of mine and Darcy's wrists and promptly dragged us from the room, leaving the Heirs and Orion staring after us in shock.

Damn that girl knew how to make an exit.

"I wasn't done telling Darius where to get off," I grumbled as I was towed along at what was arguably a run.

"I know, my lady," Geraldine said, casting a look over her shoulder before hurrying on, not once loosening her grip on me or my sister. "But that is the problem. Your dear Dragoon is blinded by his unfortunate upbringing, a need to prove himself worthy of his position and your love, his Leo pride, the stubbornness of Mars itself and not to mention the most desperate desire of his heart to keep you safe. There will be no reasoning with him, and I thought it prudent to save you the wasted breath. Big men like to talk the talk and bluster on about how powerful and right they are - but you gals and I know the truth."

"What truth?" Darcy asked as we were pulled into Geraldine's room.

"That a woman holds so much more power than any man could ever hope to. We are stalwart and true of heart, we love fiercely and protect ferociously, we are kind when kindness is due and stubborn when the right thing must be done and best of all - we are not blinded by the whims of a

Long Sherman flapping between our thighs. And though Lady Petunia and her counterparts may have their attentions turned every now and again, we still hold the power that men can never hope to. So let the Dragoon believe he is in charge if it makes his manhood feel bigger-"

"It doesn't need to be any damn bigger," I muttered and Darcy laughed. "TMI, Tor."

"I'm just saying." I shrugged and Geraldine giggled girlishly.

"Oh do tell, my lady - I must say I have had my curiosities over the size of a Dragon's dongle berry - they are so very large after all. And I may have perused its impressive size once or twice when he has been in the nip from Shifting, but I haven't ever seen it in its fullest, most excited glory if you catch my meaning. So is it in proportion to his impressive physique?"

I smirked and shrugged. "For Darius it sure as fuck is - but not for all Dragons."

"Oh sweet mercy, you don't mean to say-"

"Relax, Lionel never put his stumpy cock near me, but I saw him slamming it into Clara enough times while I was all shadow freak to understand why he's got so much damn rage in him. It looks like a mushroom that got half decapitated."

Darcy burst out laughing and Geraldine howled so loud I was pretty sure some dust dislodged from the roof to scatter down on us.

"Well I shall have to get you to regale me with tales of being jolly rodgered by your scaly side piece later, my lady. Not to mention an account or two of how bossy your chompy blood badger gets in the rose bush too, Darcy dear. I've heard a rumour or ten about how a Vampire's speed may be wielded within the rutting sack, and those fitted slacks he wore for classes told quite the story of his colossal man bulge. I will even give you an account of my latest soiree with the slippery seabass himself-"

"Wait," Darcy interrupted. "You and Max hooked up again?"

I perked up at that little titbit and Geraldine sighed dramatically as she opened a chest at the foot of her bed. "Yes...well I do seem to be developing a taste for his dingberry, I will admit. Alas, I fear it will only end in heartache though."

"Why do you say that?" I asked, wondering if she really believed Hamish would hold her to the dumb arranged marriage thing if she decided she didn't want to go through with it. He certainly didn't seem like the type to want to do anything that would make his daughter unhappy.

"Never mind that now," Geraldine said dismissively, standing suddenly and whirling towards us with a grin so big it was damn near blinding as she held out two large bundles wrapped in cloth. "The queen herself, your mother, left these in the possession of my father and asked him to keep them safe until the day came when they were needed. It has been many years, but he never once questioned that she knew what she had been doing when she entrusted him with their safety and this very morn, he told me that he felt it in his waters. And his waters are never wrong. It is time. They are yours."

I frowned a little as I felt the weight of the bundle and moved to place it on her bed, exchanging a look with Darcy as we both untied the ribbons securing the white cloth in place. The knots were firm and the thing was bound tightly but when I finally unwrapped the fabric, I gasped as my gaze fell on the gift from our mother.

My lips parted as I stared at the beautiful armour that awaited me within the package. The metal was a bronze colour which looked as if it had been dipped in oil, swirls of red and blue imbued in every inch of it and a pulse seemed to emanate from the metal itself before I even laid a hand on it.

"This armour was crafted for the queens of old. Your ancestors from times gone past who shared your heritage and held your Order forms," Geraldine breathed reverently. "It has the fire of the Phoenix living within it, utterly unbreakable and untarnishable."

A small note lay on top of the stunning breastplate and I swallowed a lump in my throat as I reached for it with shaking fingers, the name Roxanya written in the swirling script I'd come to recognise as my mother's handwriting.

Fly fast and true, sweet girl. Secrets wait beneath the ground, search fearlessly and they shall be found.

I arched a brow at what I had to assume was some kind of prophecy, holding my note out for Darcy to read as she showed me hers.

When darkness steps closer, lean into the light. The strongest of weapons is forged in the flame, hold your breath and fight through the pain.

"That sounds about as uplifting as ever," I muttered, wondering why the damn stars had to be so freaking cryptic all the time.

"I guess we just have to remember what it says and pay attention to any clues which might help us understand it," Darcy replied with a shrug, biting her lip nervously.

"I'll give it a try but honestly, none of these things ever make a blind bit of sense to me until it's too damn late."

"Get dressed, my queens, it is no time to dilly dally," Geraldine barked suddenly as she leapt to her feet, flapping her arms at us and making me jump half out of my freaking skin.

"Jesus, Geraldine, don't do that," I growled, giving in to her demands and changing into the admittedly badass looking armour.

The breastplate which was clearly designed to be worn by a woman, laced together at my sides with a material which almost seemed like leather but was somehow tougher and more supple, creating a layer of softness against my skin within the metal. The pants were made with a mixture of the leathery fabric and metal panels which slid over each other to allow my legs to move freely while still protecting them and I couldn't help but admit how comfortable the armour was despite its weight.

There were boots which were made of the same supple material and there were braces for my arms, though the upper part of my back was left bare, my shoulder blades free to allow my wings room to materialise.

Thankfully there wasn't a helmet, because I was pretty certain I would have had to draw the line there. I was already feeling kinda weird putting this shit on and was wondering how offended Geraldine might be if I just switched back into my own clothes, though as I caught sight of us in the mirror, I quickly dismissed that idea.

"Well shit," I muttered, looking between Darcy and myself in the reflection as my heart paced and my palms grew slick. "We look like we're doing one hell of a cosplay."

Darcy snorted in amusement, tilting her head and nodding. "Comic Con here we come," she agreed, grinning with me as I turned around to look at the back of it.

"Nonsense!" Geraldine cried. "This is no costume you have donned to play dress up! This is the armour of your kind, forged in the fire of the Phoenixes themselves - they are the garments worn by the warrior queens who sired your line many a moon ago. So hold your head high in preparation for wearing your crowns because the day will soon come for you to finish this attire with those shining tiaras and when you sit upon the throne, all in Solaria will rejoice and know that the true queens have finally returned!"

Geraldine dropped to her knees with a sob, prostrating herself before us and murmuring about what a joyous day this was as I gave the armour another look in the mirror, wondering if it really would be able to withstand the full force of our flames when we shifted.

"We do look kinda regal," I admitted, a smirk on my lips as Darcy grinned.

"And our mom wanted us to wear it," she said with an ache in her eyes, her fingers trailing over the beautiful armour. "Do you think she *saw* us wearing this?"

"Maybe," I whispered.

"I definitely won't complain about being able to fully shift without having to focus on not burning my clothes off," she said in realisation.

"There is that," I agreed, pinching the leathery material of the undershirt between my fingers and wondering if it really would survive my Phoenix flames. It seemed unlikely, but if this had belonged to our ancestors then I guessed it must have been put to the test more than once.

We were so distracted looking at our own outfits that we hardly even noticed Geraldine pulling on her own armour which gleamed like freaking sunlight and covered her from head to toe, making her look like a knight due at King Arthur's table and suddenly our own outfits didn't seem that ridiculous at all. Her breastplate was moulded to accommodate her large chest and narrowed to triangular points on both boobs.

"Oh I feel better now," I said, looking to her and exchanging a grin with Darcy.

"Yeah, no one will notice us while you're dressed up like that," Darcy agreed, as Geraldine lifted her flail into her hand and gave it a few test swings.

"Balderdash. I am but a lowly worm beneath the notice of a crow. But I am a worm who will stand firm between you and death my ladies, no matter the cost."

"Err, thanks?" Darcy said and I shrugged, unsure what the response to a proclamation like that should be either.

"Let's have less death talk, yeah?" I suggested. "We're just gonna go there, barbecue a bunch of Nymphs while Orion and Caleb fix the rift and be right back here in time for buttery bagels at dawn."

"And they shall be the butteriest of bagels indeed," Geraldine crowed. "The Flail of Unending Celestial Karma shall see it so."

291

We headed for the door and Geraldine rushed forward, casting a concealment spell around us so that shadows clung to us as we headed out into the corridor, and she muttered something about this mission staying between the eight of us until it was completed.

I didn't complain. I was all for keeping my new look under wraps for now because no matter what Geraldine insisted about it being 'all the rage' for Phoenixes back in the day, I wasn't convinced that thousand-year-old fashion ensembles really met with today's standards.

My plan of keeping the sight of us in our armour on the down low ended spectacularly though when we stepped out of the farmhouse above The Burrows and found Tyler Corbin waiting for us with a camera which flashed in our faces.

"Your choice, princesses," he said, backing up quickly as I cut him a glare. "I can use that candid shot or you can go pose over there by that set Geraldine created for you."

I looked over to the far side of the barn where he was pointing and found a huge boulder standing amongst a field of blood red flowers with petals which kept coming loose in an unnatural breeze and fluttering all around the area above the rock. I was glad to see a hint of light back in his eyes again. He had hardly left his room for two weeks after his mom had been murdered, but eventually he'd braved the world again and I could see a hardness in him now that hadn't been there before.

"When did you even do this?" Darcy asked as Geraldine squealed in excitement and ushered us over to her stage.

I was seriously tempted to let Tyler run with his candid crap but one look at the god awful face I was pulling in it as he let me see it set my mind against that. I also considered just blasting his camera apart so that he couldn't take any more photos but as I caught a glimmer of defiance in his gaze, I realised that this was about a whole lot more for him than just posting some FaeBook post.

"You're taking over The Daily Solaria?" I asked, realisation dawning as he nodded.

"My mom died determined to get the truth into the hands of the people of Solaria. She didn't back down no matter how much Lionel threatened her and she remained brave and true to her beliefs until her dying breath. That paper was more than just her job. It's her legacy. And no matter how hard Lionel may try and block me from continuing, he won't be able to stop me. There are tech guys here who know how to circumvent every block he has in place and can make sure our articles still get out into the hands of the public. I want to do it for her. I want to prove that he can't stop the truth from getting out there."

I sighed, unable to deny the truth to his words and acknowledged the fact that I would be a total asshole if I denied his request now as I nodded.

"Then we wanna help however we can," Darcy said firmly, looking at him with flames dancing in her eyes.

"Okay, let's take a few quick shots and you can run a story on us taking out a bunch of Nymphs just as soon as we're all back here safe and out of Lionel's reach again," I agreed.

Geraldine let out her pterodactyl screech, damn near giving me a heart attack as we moved to stand on the rock, posing for a few overly dramatic shots while I tried not to roll my eyes at the posturing crap and made myself remember that we needed to get our side of this out there. Lionel was working hard to discredit us at every turn. We needed the people of Solaria to know that we were still fighting and that we fully planned to reclaim our kingdom from that beast of a man.

The Heirs and Orion arrived as we were finishing up, Seth wolf whistling at us while Max made a joke about us looking hot before Geraldine sucker punched him in the gut and told him to put his tongue away.

Darius seemed to have forgotten that we were in the middle of an argument as he came to stand before me where we still stood on our posing rock, his hand reaching out to brush my thigh as he looked up at me.

"You look ready for battle," he murmured, his gaze trailing over the armour and his brow furrowing with concern.

"Yeah?" I asked, my gaze slipping down the leather jacket he wore, taking note of the russet colour and the scent of smoke which clung to his skin. His muscles were tight with tension and the Dragon in his eyes was peering back out at me keenly. His battle axe was held tight in his free hand and I could feel the call of the flames which lived in it like they were hungry for this too. "Well you look ready to kill."

"Damn straight I am," he growled, his grip on me tightening protectively. "Are you going to be good and do as you're told while we're out there?"

I stepped forward, dropping down from the rock so that we were chest to chest and I was looking up at him as usual. I might have liked the idea of making Darius Acrux bow for me, but I was quite happy pitting my shadow against his too. He might have been bigger than me, but that didn't mean shit when it came down to our strength. And I was just as strong as him plus some.

"Oh, silly boy," I said, tiptoeing up to speak in his ear. "You wouldn't like me if I was a good girl."

Darius growled, making a move to grab me but finding his arms bound to his sides by the vines I'd cast while he was distracted by my closeness, and I smirked at him as I sidestepped and headed after the others who were waiting to exit through the barrier.

I looked over at my sister, finding Orion circling her like a wolf as he examined her armour with a heated look in his eyes. She bit her lip as he came back around to stand before her and I snapped my fingers to gain their attention before he could pounce on her.

"Promise me you'll make sure your sister behaves, Blue," Orion muttered to Darcy as I closed in on them. "Just do what Darius says and stay safe while we're out there."

"Don't worry," Darcy agreed easily, glancing at me and twinunicating the fact that neither of us would be blindly taking orders from my boyfriend tonight. "I won't let Tory out of my sight," she promised and Orion nodded in relief, taking her hand and squeezing her fingers as we stepped through the barrier and into the dark field beyond it.

"As soon as we get there, we move," Orion said, looking between our group as we gathered close to each other, and we all nodded our agreement.

"Let us raise our batons to the stars and fight in the name of justice for the prosperity of our great kingdom and the true queens who are destined to rule over it!" Geraldine cried as she took the stardust from a pouch she had stashed in her cleavage.

"I don't think we all agreed to fight for-" Seth began but Geraldine threw the stardust in his face to stop his protests and we were whipped away into the grip of the heavens as the sound of my laughter spilled out around us.

We landed somewhere deep in a forest where huge evergreen trees towered over our heads and rain rushed down to soak us the moment we landed. My feet sank a good inch into the mud and the cold of the place met with the sound of falling rain as it lashed against me.

"Nice," I muttered, glancing up at the clouds which I could barely see above the thick canopy of trees just as thunder crashed overhead.

"It should give us some good cover at least," Max said, shifting just as I looked his way so that his navy scales crept over his skin and a shiver of pleasure danced along his flesh from the kiss of the rain.

"Of course the Siren is loving the weather," Caleb scoffed and a smile touched my lips as we all took off into the trees.

"It's this way," Darius said, jerking his chin. "I can practically taste their foul scent on the wind."

He strode to the front of the group, walking with such purpose that I had to assume he really did know what he was talking about. I moved forward to walk beside him, sniffing the air and smelling nothing but rain and moss.

"Did you just shift your nose or something, dude?" I asked him and he shot me a look which confirmed he'd tapped into his Dragon gifts.

"Don't call me dude," he growled and dammit if I didn't like it when he growled.

"Why not?"

"Because I'm not your fucking dude. I'm the guy who makes you come so hard you can hardly breathe, let alone see straight. I'm the one who makes your heart race every damn time you look at me because you know I'll never stop hungering for you the way I do, and I'll never get enough of you or be able to love you with any more passion than I possess right now. And I'm the guy who you'll have to answer to if you do anything against my orders tonight - which believe me will hurt at least as much as you'll enjoy it. Got it?"

"Got it. Not my fucking dude," I teased and he growled again.

Yeah, he'd pretty much just given me every excuse I needed to misbehave even if I hadn't been fully planning on it just for the fact that I wasn't his to control anyway.

I felt a silencing bubble slip over my skin and looked around to find Orion and Caleb both staring out into the trees to our right where the ground sloped upwards.

"I think there's two of them coming this way - probably a patrol or something," Orion said and all of us tensed.

"Three actually," Caleb disagreed and after another brief pause, Orion nodded.

"Sounds like the perfect number to use for our bait," Seth said excitedly.

"Then I think it's time we got to work," Geraldine said darkly and I found myself smiling as the need for a fight surged through my veins.

It had been too damn long since we'd struck a real blow in this war, and I was ready to get back to the fight.

Max

CHAPTER TWENTY FOUR

The rain kissed my skin where it splashed against my scales along my arms and neck as we took off into the trees and I tugged my bow from my back, loading an arrow into it as I focused on my water magic and formed a connection with the Element.

I could feel the moisture saturating the air, the rush of droplets falling from the sky, crashing through the pine trees and soaking into the ground at our feet. This was my domain and it made little rivers of pleasure run through my skin.

With a little more effort, I linked my focus onto the air surrounding us too, closing my eyes for a moment as I focused on the patterns the two Elements created as they fell against boulders, trees and the Fae surrounding me.

I kept walking with my eyes closed, using my link to my Elements to map out the area surrounding me as I pushed my awareness out from my body, building up a far greater vision of the forest which surrounded us than I could see with my eyes in the dark and the rain.

Our group moved quietly as we headed up the hill, Cal and Orion walking either side of Darius as they used their Vampire gifts to listen for the Nymphs, but I got a lock on them first.

At the top of the hill, a ridge formed along the edge of a clearing in the forest, hard rocks cutting though the saturated ground and forming a void of awareness in my mind. And standing on that ridge, moving together were three towering figures, each of them shifted into their Nymph form and prowling along the outskirts of the clearing like beasts guarding their home.

"They're about a hundred yards up there," I said, pointing as I fell still and the others took my lead, falling in around me.

I pushed my awareness out further, hunting for more figures lurking in the dark of the trees and finding them, group by group, either patrolling the edges of the forest which surrounded that clearing or gathered closer to the centre of it.

I pushed my awareness that way, chasing the rain and wind as it hammered down on a huge, stone structure which kept them both out and formed a point of darkness in my mind which had to be the reason for them all gathering here.

"There's a huge structure in a clearing through the trees beyond them," I said, breaking my connection to the Elements and opening my eyes so that I could look around at my friends. "I'm guessing that's the temple where they're keeping the altar and that the rift is inside it too."

"Oh you are a devilishly devious dolphin on occasion, aren't you?" Gerry purred as she looked at me, her flail casually balanced against her shoulder, the spiked ball hanging from the end of it swinging slowly back and forth. I had been going to protest to the dolphin comment, but I got distracted drinking in the sight of her in that armour and before I could form some kind of response, Darcy spoke.

"Sounds like the earth Elementals have got this one," she said, a dangerous glint in her eyes as she flexed her fingers in anticipation.

"Me and Caleb will circle through the trees so that we're in position as soon as you draw them out," Orion said, his eyes lingering on Darcy like he didn't want to leave her and Seth shifted closer, slinging his arm around her shoulders.

"Don't worry, Lancey, I've got your girl," he said confidently, though as his gaze flicked to Caleb, I detected a hint of concern in his emotions. It was quickly tempered by his usual confidence though and I knew he had total faith in Cal being able to pull this off. Still, these games we all played were dangerous now and I couldn't help but worry for my friends when we headed out into the fight like this.

"You take your fucking paws off of her," Orion snarled, stepping forward, but Darius slapped a hand to his chest and pushed him back a step.

"Seth, stop being a dick and Lance, stop letting him bait you. We've all got more important things to focus on," he said firmly.

"Well, the earth Elementals do, anyway," Tory replied, taunting him with every move she made as she began to back away in the direction of the Nymphs. I swear that girl had a death wish when it came to riling the Dragon in him, then again, Darius probably needed someone who would bite back whenever he got too Alpha. "You and Max should probably just stay here and watch our backs. Wouldn't want there to be any chance of anyone sneaking up on us while we get the job done now, would you?"

Darius growled as Darcy smirked, shrugging Seth's arm off of her shoulders and stepping forward to kiss Orion hard, grasping his shirt and tugging him close for a moment before shoving him back a step firmly.

"Don't die," she commanded and the corner of his lips twitched in amusement.

"Yes, My Queen," he replied and the other Heirs and I all tensed at that casual term of endearment, but Orion just ignored us, jerking his chin towards the trees to our left in an order to Caleb before shooting off into the dark.

"Stay safe," Cal said to all of us, his eyes lingering on Seth for a beat before he shot away too.

I cut my gaze to Seth who cleared his throat and turned away from me, his mental shields slamming up as tight as a duck's asshole all of a sudden and making me narrow my eyes in suspicion.

"Onward, my ladies, let us begin this most noble of tasks!" Geraldine strode away after Tory, swinging her flail and decapitating a sapling as she went. I just stared at her ass in her chainmail and wondered why the hell I was so obsessed with an insane royalist like her. But I couldn't freaking help it.

"We're coming with you," Darius growled, hurrying forward to catch up to Tory who just shrugged innocently like she didn't mind either way, but I caught enough of her emotions to get the feeling she was up to something and as Darcy looked her way, I sensed the same troublemaking emotions coming from her.

Damn Vega twins were going to be the death of all of us if they didn't just accept their place soon, this power struggle between us was going to keep building in intensity until then though. I just hoped that when it came down to it and we had to face off with them for real, that we could all maintain this semblance of peace we'd managed to form once it was done.

Then again, power always did tend to corrupt even the best of things. My own mother had been murdered for it, so I should know.

We crept through the trees, climbing up towards the ridge and my heart began to pound powerfully as we drew closer and closer to the Nymphs who I could still sense up ahead with my water magic.

The darkness of the trees pressed in thickly and the rain continued to mask any sound aside from the crash of it falling through the canopy and the rumble of thunder which accompanied it from somewhere far above us.

The twins moved ahead as we drew closer to the place where the Nymphs were waiting, Geraldine and Seth spreading out either side of them as I held back a little with Darius.

I glanced at my friend as he stood rigidly beside a huge redwood, his grip tight on his axe and his eyes glued to Tory's back as he watched her creeping further up the hill.

"She's got this," I murmured, my gaze scanning across Gerry and Seth too as they slipped into the shadows to surround our quarry.

"I know," he replied, his tone heavy. "But it doesn't make it any easier watching her walk into danger."

"She doesn't strike me as the type who would appreciate you clinging to her side though."

"She's not. But I won't be giving her much choice once this really kicks off."

"You really love her, don't you?" I asked, tasting the intensity of that feeling on his skin and soaking it in with a shiver of pleasure.

"She's everything," he replied simply and I damn near grinned at the shift in his emotions. Darius had had so much dark, so much pain and angst thrown at him in his lifetime. And though those emotions weren't totally banished now, I could feel the love, hope and joy which surrounded him these days so clearly that it made my fucking soul lighter just to know about it.

A sharp gust of wind crashed into us, just hard enough to feel unnatural without knocking us from our feet, signalling the others being in position.

"Get ready," Darius murmured and I raised my bow as he lifted his axe, willing the Phoenix fire within it to ignite so that the brightness of the flames cut through the dark of the woods.

I squinted against the onslaught of light and a shriek of alarm came from the top of the ridge as the Nymphs spotted the flames.

I set my feet and held my ground as they came for us, the sound of their huge bodies crashing through the undergrowth setting my nerves on edge and adrenaline pounding through me in anticipation of a fight.

I tugged the bow taut as the Nymphs burst through the trees, the three of them racing straight towards us, the booming rattle of their magic-stealing power slamming into me and locking down my connection to my Elements as I tightened my hold on my bow and took aim at the front runner of the pack.

Darius tensed beside me, readying his axe to swing, but before either of us could be forced into action, vines shot out from all around the Nymphs and they fell to the ground with their arms and legs tied and dirt filling their mouths to halt the use of their rattles.

Seth howled in triumph from somewhere out in the trees as the Nymphs thrashed in their trap and the Vegas dropped from the sky, using air magic to lower themselves down to land beside the creatures which hungered for our deaths.

"Max?" Darcy called and I stepped forward, still holding my bow ready as I closed in on the Nymphs who were kicking and thrashing on the ground before us.

My gaze flicked around for any sign of Gerry, but she was nowhere to be seen. My gut churned as I forced my mind away from that concern and stepped closer to the bound Nymphs.

I reached out towards them with my gifts, hunting their emotions and searching for any sign that they might not just be the mindless, evil creatures we had always assumed they were before finding out the truth about Diego.

I set my attention on the closest Nymph, sensing nothing but hatred and violent intentions from him as he set his deep red eyes on me and thrashed against his binds. The others were the same, nothing but malice and hatred oozing from them, making it simple enough for me to continue with this plan without guilt.

"Nothing," I said, looking to the others and taking a step away from the creatures who still fought to get free. "They're our enemies through and through."

"Good. That makes this easier then," Darius said, striding forward and kicking the one closest to him. "Let's get this fight started."

I looked up at the sound of footsteps through the trees and relief spilled through me as Gerry burst out from behind a bush, her flail in hand and her chin high as she panted heavily.

"I have checked the perimeter, my queens, all is clear for us to proceed."

"Good. Let's string up some Nymphs and see how loud they scream when they have Phoenix fire tickling their feet," Tory said, that same demonic gleam in her eyes that Darius got so often, reminding me once again of how weirdly perfect they were for one another even as they continued to play this little power trip game while we worked.

Seth and Darcy quickly grew thick wooden stakes up from the dirt before Geraldine strapped the Nymphs to them and we all moved to take up our positions hiding in the trees, far enough from the creatures to be safe from the worst of their rattles once they came.

Tory, Darcy and Darius each flicked a flame to life at the foot of one of the stakes and Geraldine removed the gags of dirt from the Nymphs' mouths so that they could scream for help as we'd planned.

Adrenaline spiked through my limbs as I held myself aloft in the tree canopy on a gust of air and I used my gifts to build a wall of utter terror at the entrance to the clearing for the Nymphs to pass through when they arrived. They might have been able to fight back against our Elemental magic easily enough, but they had no idea what they were going up against when they came face to face with the monsters which lay within us. We were the most powerful of our Orders in the entire kingdom, and we were ready to play.

ORION

CHAPTER TWENTY FIVE

Caleb and I were crouched on the branch of a huge pine, gazing over the ridge of the hill to where a black stone pyramid rose from between the trees like a cursed mountain. Endless stairs ran up the closest side of the temple and Nymphs were crowded on them in droves. But as pain-filled shrieks carried through the air from behind us, the Nymphs surged towards them as one.

We remained in the shadow of the tree canopy, not moving a single muscle as the Nymphs charged beneath us through the undergrowth and my grip tightened on the hilt of the Phoenix sword at my hip. Those assholes were heading right towards the girl I loved. But as I thought of Blue, I remembered the monstrous flames of destruction she was capable of casting with her Phoenix fire. That girl could bring about an apocalypse on this world, and I knew in my heart that she could defend herself. She was a force of nature, a fucking hurricane. And between her, Tory, Darius and the others, I knew they could handle this. The Nymphs were running towards some of the most powerful Fae to ever walk this earth, and it was just a shame I wasn't going to be there to join the fight.

I shared a look with Caleb as the last of the Nymphs scurried beneath us, their heavy footfalls fading into the distance and they left the temple without a single guard on its steps. A competitive smile curled my lips and a challenge flared in his eyes as he nodded in answer to the question in my mind.

We leapt out of the tree we'd been using as a hiding place and shot forward at the same moment, sprinting toward the temple with the full force of our gifts, my feet barely touching the ground with how fast I was moving. The air whipped against my face and the tension of an oncoming war hung everywhere around me.

We made it to the black steps of the temple, my shoulder slamming into Caleb's as we turned onto them and raced up the stairs at a furious speed. We were both fighting to prove our speed, our rivalry flaring between us as we ran so fast it made my skull rattle and my heart rush to keep up.

The world was a blur of grey as I set my gaze on the ominous opening at the top of the pyramid and pushed myself to my absolute limits. A wild thrill fell through me as we made it to the entrance, speeding into the darkness inside, immediately swallowed whole.

We rushed down a sloping floor and the gravelly voices of Nymphs carried up from within the belly of the pyramid below us. As we hit the bottom of the ramp, I took in the droves of Nymphs before us with my heart jack-hammering.

We didn't slow, we couldn't. If we missed a single step, we'd be spotted so we sped towards the open doors at the end dark room with all we had. The Nymphs turned as they felt us pass and realised we were there, but we were too quick to be caught, their rattles crackling in my ears as they battled to lock our magic down.

Their shrieks sounded out as they took chase and I weaved left and right to avoid them while Caleb did the same on my other side. We shot through the door together beyond our enemies and a whoop left my lips. The two of us turned as one, slamming it closed and bracing it with a combination of my ice magic and Caleb's earth, but I didn't know how long it would hold once the Nymphs caught up.

We ran on into the dark, sprinting through winding passages where cobwebs hung on the walls and the scent of dust hit the back of my throat.

When we finally arrived in a large chamber, we slowed down and a prickle ran down my spine, our feet skidding on the slick stone as the energy around us shifted.

I cast a Faelight into the air and took in the sight before us as we fell still.

A huge stone altar stood at the heart of the chamber, old bloodstains caked into the stone and the top of it covered with artifacts. Jewels, necklaces, precious stones, all of them humming with some dark power that made it harder to breathe in here.

The altar itself and the walls were covered in ancient-looking carvings depicting stories of the Nymphs, a lot of them featuring a woman who looked suspiciously like Lavinia, but I couldn't decipher their meaning, especially as I was distracted by the most suffocating thing in this space.

Above the altar was a rift cut into the air, like a doorway into absolute nothingness. Inside were the shadows, swirling and pulsing like they were hungry to be set free and as I took step closer, I felt them calling to me like I'd cut myself with a draining dagger and they were begging me to submit to their power.

Caleb moved forward too, clearly tempted toward them and for a moment I wondered what it would be like to simply walk through that deadly gateway and fall into their complete embrace.

"What is it?" Caleb breathed, sounding in awe as he reached the altar and his fingers grazed against a black-hilted dagger.

He sighed, picking it up and twisting it between his fingers, his eyes growing hooded as he immediately turned it against his own arm and a twisted smile spread across his face.

The lull of the shadows was so strong that I nearly let him do it, but then

I felt the echo of my father's hand on my shoulder, his warnings about dark magic. I had to find the good to hold onto, had to keep the light in my mind so no darkness could creep in.

I thought of the moment I'd pulled Darcy beneath the water in the Acrux swimming pool and stolen the kiss I'd been craving for so fucking long I'd almost been driven mad with want. And then of her showing up at my door in a storm, her hair freshly dyed, every piece of her soaking wet and the word 'blue' on her lips. She was my ruin and my making at once. She had offered herself to me in that moment, though I had staked a secret claim on her long before then. But that had been the night it become a reality.

With her at the forefront of my mind, I dragged myself out of the pressing stupor, shooting forward and knocking the blade from Caleb's hand.

He blinked, looking up at me with rage in his eyes, but as he met my gaze, his shoulders dropped a little and he blinked out of the trance.

"Fuck, did I nearly slit my star damned wrists?" he cursed, pushing a hand into his blonde curls as he stared at the dagger on the floor in disgust. "I'm too pretty to die in some ugly shadow cave."

"You must not cut yourself in this place," I said urgently, eyeing the rift with concern as I felt the certainty of those words passing my lips. "That fucking thing will rip the soul clean out of your body to be devoured within it if you do. Focus your mind and resist it - you need to think of something good."

"Like what?" he snapped, the shadows clearly still affecting him as he gazed longingly at the rift again, moving toward it with intent.

I grabbed his arm, forcing him back a step and keeping a firm hold of him.

"Caleb," I snarled. "Think of the best memory you have and hold onto it with everything you've got."

"What are you talking about?" he muttered, trying to pull free again, his eyes falling back to the blade, but I clung on, getting up in his face so he had to look at me instead of that portal or the weapon it wanted him to wield against himself. Though I wasn't much use to him considering he hated me.

"Think of the Heirs," I tried. "Of Darius, Max, Seth."

His eyes softened as I said that last name and the tension rolled out of his posture.

"Think of Seth," I latched onto the change in him and he nodded, slowly relaxing and taking a step away from the rift.

"Have you got a good memory to hold onto?" I asked, not wanting to let go of him in case he decided to use his speed to dive into that portal headfirst.

"Yeah, yeah, Tinkerbell," he muttered. "I've got my happy fucking memory. You can let go of me now." He shoved me away and I bared my fangs at him in irritation, only causing him to bare his back at me, the rivalry between us flaring up. But we didn't have time for that shit, we needed to close the portal and get the hell out of here.

"This place is tainted by the Shadow Princess," I said thickly, looking to the rift which must have been cut directly into the Shadow Realm.

A Nymph shriek made us both whip around in the direction of the exit and we shot forward, working together to shut the doors and Caleb picked up a huge wooden pole beside it, slotting it into place through a latch to lock it.

The door shuddered as a weight of Nymphs collided against it and Caleb used his earth magic to seal the door more thoroughly, hissing a curse.

"Hurry up then, asshole," he said. "I'll keep this door shut, you close that fucking shadow portal."

"On it," I growled, striding towards the swirling rift in the air and taking the enchanted binding needle from my pocket which would help me seal it up. But the immensity of the power in this place said it was going to take a lot from me.

I'd manage it somehow though. Because this felt like striking right at the heart of Lavinia herself, the bitch who'd killed my sister, who'd tried to curse Blue. And though I didn't understand exactly what this place was used for, it was clear some sort of offerings had been placed here for the Shadow Princess over the years. The dark power in those artifacts on the altar were no doubt feeding power into the Shadow Realm and on to the shadow bitch herself.

"Hi Lavinia." I smirked at the dark portal, raising my hands as I prepared to start the spell which would cut her off from this pool of power. "I just came here to say fuck you."

DARIUS

CHAPTER TWENTY SIX

More Nymphs than we possibly could have anticipated spilled from the trees, each of them in their shifted forms and screaming with the full force of their rattles as they ran between the thick trunks to come to the aid of their brethren.

We'd formed a ring surrounding the clearing, each of us in the trees above them as we waited for the carnage to descend, but there were so many of them that it was impossible to stick to our plan of picking them off from above.

Max swept between the trees to my right, firing his bow and arrow as he used his air magic to keep himself aloft, fighting to maintain a hold on his Elemental magic, but remaining high enough above them to lessen the effects of their rattles.

The twins swept across the clearing ahead of me, Phoenix fire pouring from their hands as they created a giant blazing X which cut through the ground and set fire to it, effectively dividing the Nymphs as they were forced to retreat from the flames and several of them were destroyed by their power.

"Stay close to me!" I bellowed, my eyes on Roxy as she tore across the clearing in her fully shifted form, fire gilding the armour Geraldine had given her and her hair a blaze of scarlet flames.

"Try to keep up, asshole!" she called back and I snarled, my grip on my axe tightening as I looked down into the clearing below, shooting more magic down at the Nymphs from my perch in the treetops.

But as Roxy and her sister beat their wings and launched themselves further away from me with the clear intention to keep going instead of following my orders, I gritted my teeth and leapt from my perch with my axe raised.

I roared a challenge as I landed on a Nymph who had been charging between the trees beneath me, colliding with it and cleaving my axe down upon its head just as I felt the sharp slice of its probes against my side.

I had no room to shift here with the trees packed so tightly, so I took off on foot, my flaming axe burning in the darkness as I ran to meet my next opponent, my gaze flicking between the Nymph and the two Phoenixes who were speeding away between the trees ahead of me.

I lost sight of them entirely as I met my foe, swinging my axe with a savage cry and taking out its leg as it lunged for me. The thing fell like the tree it resembled and I pounced on it the moment it hit the ground, bringing about its ruin with the weapon I'd been gifted from the sister of the woman I loved.

The fight descended quickly into chaos and bloodshed from there and I lost all sight of Roxy and her sister as I gave myself to the fray.

I swung my axe with such brutality that my arms ached and each strike of my weapon against bone or woody flesh reverberated through my body like the toll of a death march.

A howl burst through the trees at my back and Seth leapt over me in his enormous white Wolf form, taking a Nymph to the ground with his flaming metal claws and sinking his teeth deep into the creature's throat as it snarled and kicked beneath him.

I wrenched my axe from the chest of my latest kill, a violent snarl passing my lips as smoke spilled between them and the urge to shift tugged at me incessantly, my inner animal aching to join the fight.

An arrow shot past my head so close that I felt the heat of the flames as they passed me by. I swung around to watch it find a home in the eye of one of the creatures a beat before a solid weight collided with me and sent me crashing down onto the forest floor.

I managed to roll as I fell, my fist cracking against the bark-like flesh of my opponent as it drove its weight down on me and its rattle sounded so loudly that my limbs damn near locked up with the power of it.

The magic inside me was frozen, my axe knocked aside as my muscles contracted against the alien feeling of the Nymph's power taking hold of mine. I snarled in fury as the Nymph stabbed at me with its probes, jerking aside to avoid the blow which hit the leaves beside my head instead.

It struck at me again and again as I thrashed from side to side, evading the strike of those sharpened probes repeatedly as I drove my fist into its side and fought to get out from beneath it.

The Nymph screamed in my face, more of its foul power slamming into me and stealing my fucking breath from my lungs as I was incapacitated by it, the slice of pain in my chest breaking through the numbness in my mind to whisper promises of my death as agony broke through me.

But as I tried to take hold of my Dragon and shift to save myself, the Nymph screamed in pain and burst into flames above me, its body scattering into a mess of ash and embers which dispersed to reveal the blazing girl behind it as she raised her chin at me in greeting.

"Get up, asshole," Roxy snapped like saving my ass had pissed her off and I shoved to my feet, fighting to access my magic so that I could heal the bleeding wound in my chest as I scooped my axe up off of the ground.

"Get back in the air," I barked at her, my heart thrashing as she turned that feral gaze on a trio of Nymphs who had just spotted us between the trees.

Roxy glanced at me, the corner of her lips twitching in amusement as I felt the shadow of my own smirk in reply.

"So fucking bossy," she commented before beating her wings hard and taking off like I'd commanded.

But instead of flying for the safety of the sky where she could continue to fire long range attacks down on our enemies like I'd commanded her and Darcy to do throughout this, she flew across the forest floor, barely an inch from the ground and sailed straight for them.

"Roxy!" I roared, taking chase on foot, my axe raised above my shoulder and poised to kill as the desire to protect her merged with the hunger of the monster in me, and I looked those Nymphs in the eyes and promised them their ruin at my hand.

I charged after her, the heat of her flames warming the air I ran through and the pure blaze of her red and blue fire damn near blinding me as I chased after it.

Roxy released a battle cry of her own as she made it within striking distance of the Nymphs and the blast of power which escaped her nearly put me on my ass as a heatwave crashed over me and burned the rain from the sky for several seconds with its intensity.

Fire poured from her in a torrent, engulfing the three Nymphs within it and by the time I'd made it to them, I merely burst through the burning ash which was all that remained of their bodies and watched her as she finally turned towards the sky and raced up out of my reach.

More Nymphs were closing in on us and I turned, meaning to head back towards the creatures we had left tied to the stakes in the centre of our trap, but finding an enormous Nymph stepping out of the trees blocking my way.

The sound of a Tarzan yodel drew my attention to my left and I glanced that way just in time to spot Geraldine swinging between the trees on a thick vine, her flaming flail aimed with brutal precision as she bore down on a Nymph with a yell of, "Not today you nilly nodger!"

The huge Nymph released a rattle so powerful that I felt it down to my toes and my magic was locked down hard once more, but I smiled as I slowly swung my axe back and forth in my grip, striding towards it between the trees while the rain pattered down on my head.

I was a man at home in the thick of the fight, and I was ready to prove my mettle against every dark souled creature here.

CALEB

CHAPTER TWENTY SEVEN

Orion cursed as he worked to close the rift and I gritted my teeth as I struggled to maintain the hold I had on the doors, digging in deep with my earth magic while Nymphs howled and set off their fucking death rattles right outside it.

It hadn't taken them nearly long enough to break through the first door we'd sealed, and I suspected the proximity of the shadow rift was working them up into a frenzy. It was clear why they were so affected by it too. Even now, as I fought with all I had to hold the door, binding it with rocks and vines against the strikes of the Nymphs on the far side of it, I still felt the pull of that dark and tainted magic.

It was like the brush of a hand down my spine, the whisper of a lover in my ear and the call of a Siren even more powerful than Max who was aching to lure me to paradise.

The tendrils of darkness reached for me much like they were reaching for the dark objects which lined the altar, and I had no doubt that other Fae had come here before me and fallen into the trap of their call. More than one of the dark items were weapons, ready and waiting to be used to spill the blood of the sacrifices which had clearly been brought here time and again if the scent of blood and stains on the stone were anything to go by.

With the doors shut, the space in here was almost entirely black, barely a hint of daylight finding its way in through the tiny cracks which lined the edges of the door, the Faelight Orion had cast the only brightness in the whole space.

I gritted my teeth and fought to hold the door as another tremor rocked through it.

"How's it going?" I yelled over my shoulder, my fingers curling into fists as the door was pounded with even more force and the whole temple seemed to rattle with the strike, dust falling from the roof and scattering in my hair.

"Better when I'm not distracted," Orion grunted like the asshole he was and I shook my head, wondering why I'd expected anything more from him as I slammed my hand against the wooden door and upped the flow of magic coursing through my veins.

"Well, if we aren't done, I'll have to seal us in fully," I muttered, drawing a deep breath in through my mouth before closing my eyes and releasing a blast of potent earth magic as I pressed my palms against the door and took hold of the essence of it, forcing my will to change its soul to stone instead of wood and solidifying the entire thing while the Nymphs continued to shriek in fury outside it.

I sealed the door entirely, strengthening and thickening it until a slab of impenetrable granite stood between us and the monsters who'd come for us, effectively locking us in this place while making sure they stayed out.

I turned back to face Orion, lighting a fire in my palm so that I could see more of what he was doing and my breath caught in my lungs as my gaze fell upon the rift instead.

It was pulsing and writhing now, a desperate kind of energy building in it as it almost seemed to be trying to pull away from Orion as he worked to stitch the fabric of the fucking realms back together like he was sewing an easter bonnet for a damn parade.

As my gaze caught on the twisting vortex of darkness, I felt a sharp tug in my chest and before I knew what was happening, I was shooting forward, my thighs crashing against the edge of the altar as I snatched a wicked black dagger into my grasp and a groan of pleasure escaped my lips.

Shadows crept across my skin, whispering promises of untold fulfilment as I tipped my head back and groaned again, the caress of a thousand fingertips roaming all over my flesh, undoing every piece of me and promising me more power than I had ever even dreamed of owning.

Orion shouted something and I heard a single name amongst the words he spat my way, a name which had me shaking my head in an attempt to clear it, remembering the feeling of warm hands against my flesh and blood on my lips.

I clung on to that feeling with all I had, closing my eyes for a brief moment and severing the tie the shadows had tried to leash me with before I snapped them open again, looking down at the dagger in my hand and snarling as I realised the fucking shadows had almost snared me.

I called on my fire magic, igniting the hottest flames I could summon in my fist and working to destroy the blade in my hand, melting the metal and making the shadows hiss and spit angrily.

I threw the melted lump of metal away from me and the air above the altar seemed to vibrate as the shadows howled in protest, making my gaze fall to the myriad of other dark objects which were scattered across the altar.

I leapt up over the altar, turning my back on the rift as Orion cursed and fought to seal it, his arms trembling with the effort of forcing the thing shut as he continued to stitch the divide between this realm and the next.

I grabbed the edge of the stone altar, and with a combination of my earth magic and Vampire strength, I ripped the stone table from its setting and sent every dark item scattering across the floor away from the rift. The shadows screamed and wailed even louder, the sound threatening to make my ears bleed as I gritted my teeth against it and threw my hands out, blasting every one of the objects with my most potent fire and destroying as many of them as I could manage.

I felt the lash of the shadows against my back and braced against the sting and bite of pleasure they offered, fixing my mind on all the best memories I could muster and planting myself firmly within this realm where the true owners of my joy and love existed.

A panicked curse made me snap around and I found Orion gripping onto the edge of the broken altar, his eyes wide and fearful as his gaze met with mine. Something seemed to tug him towards the last slither of the rift which was still gaping open as the needle hung loose in his fingertips and blood dripped from his other hand, a small prick on his finger causing droplets of deepest red to run through open air towards the rift which hummed and groaned with a violent power that I knew would devour our entire realm if only it got the chance.

"What do I do?" I demanded as I shot towards him in a panic, grabbing his arm and trying to pull him away from the rift as it howled louder, more and more of his blood racing towards it.

I tried to push healing magic into his flesh so that I could block off the connection to his blood, but the moment I began to build it in my palm, Orion roared a refusal.

"Don't meld your magic with mine or you'll be doomed too," he snarled, knocking me against the broken altar as pain and pleasure flashed in his gaze in equal measures. "When my grip fails, it will consume me," he gasped. "You have to find a way to close it. You need to cut Lavinia off from-"

"Don't start talking like you're already dead, asshole. Is it your magic that it's caught you by?" I asked frantically.

Orion grunted a confirmation, his face drawn in pain which I knew had nothing to do with whatever the fuck the shadows were doing to him and everything to do with what he thought he was about to lose if he was ripped from this life.

"Once it burns through all of my magic it will drag my soul after it," he ground out. "You need to run, you need to-"

I shot towards him with a snarl, my fangs snapping out as I got my answer and I collided with his back, locking an arm around his chest and fisting his hair with my other hand before yanking his head to the side and driving my teeth deep into his throat.

Orion snarled furiously, the outrage he felt at me biting him more than clear in the rigidity of his posture as I drew in a mouthful of his blood and swallowed greedily.

The moment the power of his magic swept over my tongue, his ability to use it was locked down and his connection to the shadows via it was severed.

He stumbled a step as his link to the rift was destroyed but I held him up as I drank deeply, savouring the intoxicating taste of his blood while keeping my fangs buried in his neck so that the connection couldn't reform.

Orion struggled for a moment before seeming to realise the chance I was giving him and raising the needle once again, driving the point of it into the edge of the rift and growling with the effort of using his leaden limbs to force it through the divide.

I kept drinking while he finished his work, the entire chamber we stood in rattling and shaking as the rift fought against its destruction until the very last moment.

A deep and heavy silence fell as the rift was finally sewn shut, the pressure in the chamber dropping so suddenly that my ears popped.

Orion dropped the needle, sagging against me as I found myself caught in the bloodlust, unable to pull back like I should have done as I continued to feast on his blood.

This wasn't what our kind did. It went against the Vampire Code.

But he was one hell of a powerful Vampire and I couldn't deny the thrill I was getting from owning him blood and bone like this.

I growled as I sucked harder and Orion growled right back, his hands taking hold of my arm where I still held him and lifting my wrist in a flash of speed. My heart lurched with realisation, but I wasn't fast enough to stop him before his fangs slid into my wrist and a snarl of victory rumbled through him.

Shock rolled through my core as he began to drink, my Elements locking down inside me and my heart thrashing at what we were doing.

This was beyond taboo. The Code had been drawn up in part to stop this very thing. Since the height of the blood ages almost two thousand years ago, the practice of forming covens had been discarded as a part of the pact formed to end the bloody hatred between Vampires and other Fae. It was ancient history now, but back then, our kind had built covens by doing this very thing, feeding from one another and forming a bond which linked them closely and made it easier for them to hunt in packs. For years, Vampire covens had roamed the land, killing other Fae with abandon and using their combined ferocity as a unit to spread terror far and wide. It hadn't been long before other Fae had started hunting our kind, killing them to stop the bloodshed and coming damn close to wiping us out.

But then a deal had been struck. The last remaining Vampires had created the Code and the practice of forming covens had been disbanded along with promises being made by our kind not to indulge in the hunt so that our bloodlust would be kept in check.

To this day, our Order were bound by that code and it was our responsibility to follow it or face the consequences of losing control of the bloodlust if we didn't.

The flow of our combined magic swimming from my body into his then back to mine again was making my head rush and my pulse spike.

I could feel the power of that connection building between the two of us until the beasts we were seemed to merge into one, the surge of power and bloodlust combining into a heady mix that only those of our kind could fully appreciate.

My blood heated and buzzed in my veins, an ancient magic warring beneath my skin and his, changing our natures as we found a unity which had never seemed possible between the two of us before that moment, a deep and unshakable respect and bond growing in us as we became something so much more than we had been before.

We both drew our fangs from each other's flesh at the same moment, stumbling apart and turning to stare at one another with heaving chests, bloodstained lips and thrashing hearts.

"Oh shit," Orion breathed in shock and I nodded because I felt it too.

"We don't have time for this," I panted, trying to get my head straight while the rush of what we'd just become made my skin itch and my muscles tingle with the need for the hunt.

Orion nodded, licking his lips and giving me a hungry look which told me I clearly tasted as good as he did. But I couldn't let myself get caught up in the fact that I'd just crossed that most taboo of lines with him.

"Then let's open this place up so the twins can destroy what's left here," Orion said firmly, lifting his gaze to the roof above our heads and bringing a smirk to my lips as I realised what he was planning.

"Earth and Air combined would do a better job," I pointed out, offering him my hand and he only hesitated for half a second before slapping his palm into mine, the rush of our magic colliding instantly as our barriers fell away as if they'd never even existed in the first place.

"Looks like I trust you now, sanguis frater," he said, offering me a dark smile which made my fangs prickle.

"Seems so," I said, returning his smile as we both raised our hands and used our combined magic to blast the roof from the temple with an explosion so immense, I swear the entire forest trembled beneath the force of it.

We sped out after the lumps of shattered rock while the dust still billowed and lumps of it still sped through the air, Orion lifting us on a gust of air magic while I made the rocks we landed on as soft as a mattress and we shot away together so fast that not even the stars could see us as we ran.

DARCY

CHAPTER TWENTY EIGHT

A violent tremor rocked the ground at my feet, knocking two Nymphs down before me as I beat my wings, taking off so I didn't fall too and hovering there as I tried to figure out where it had come from.

I looked over to Tory, finding her finishing off one of our enemies with a blast of Phoenix fire that turned them to ash, looking like a warrior princess as fire roared around her and glinted off of her armour.

The Nymphs beneath me started to rise and I lifted my hands as my upper lip peeled back, anger twisting through me like a tornado. It frightened me how savage I felt today, like a beast had awoken in me and was determined to make every one of these monsters suffer for all the Fae they'd killed.

But before I could unleash the unholy fury that lived within my veins a blur shot past me, a glint of silver swiping across their throats and slitting open their bark-like skin. Orion wheeled around, stabbing them both in the heart in quick succession and they burst to ash before him. He turned to me, a lopsided grin on his lips and I smiled in relief at him returning.

"Those were my kills, Professor," I growled in mock anger, dropping down to land lightly in front of him.

"Then why did they die by my sword, Miss Vega?" he teased.

A Nymph charged through the trees behind him and I gasped, releasing a furious wave of fire from my palm over his shoulder. It slammed into the creature's chest, knocking it to the ground where it died with a shriek, blackened ash dancing on the air around us as it went out of this world.

Darius and Tory whooped as they took down a giant Nymph to our right and two arrows whistled through the air in quick succession from Max's bow, killing another two in an instant.

Seth was in his Wolf form, tearing at Nymphs with the fiery gauntlets, his tail wagging as he ran and Caleb leapt onto his back, using his twin daggers to slash at any Nymph that got too close them.

Geraldine was beyond Max, swinging her flail with violent blows as her hips bobbed and swayed with every strike she landed like she was performing some sort of murder dance.

Orion grabbed me suddenly shooting me over to stand beside my sister and Darius, casting an air shield around us to buy us a moment from the onslaught of the battle.

"You two need to get to the temple," Orion urged me and Tory. "There's an altar there full of dark artifacts that needs to be destroyed. Caleb started the job but your Phoenix fire should be able to finish it."

I shared an excited look with my sister as we nodded and Orion dropped the air shield, twisting around and driving his sword into the chest of a Nymph while Darius leapt up and swung his axe, beheading another beast so ash burst out around us. The two of them laughed with the thrill of the fight, staying close to one another as Tory and I took off into the sky, our wings beating harder and flaring with fire as we made it above the treeline.

The rain poured down on us as I spotted the temple looming up from the trees ahead, and we put on a burst of speed. For a heartbeat the fire along my wings flickered out and my breath snagged as I was almost sure my wings were about to fall away, panic crashing through my chest.

They reignited in the next moment and I glanced at Tory ahead of me, glad she hadn't noticed as I steadied my thrashing heartbeat and kept flying. I guessed my magic was running low, though I didn't know why my Phoenix felt so heavy as I drew it back to the surface of my flesh.

The mist that clung to the edges of the forest made it seem like we were approaching the edge of the world as we circled down over the temple, and my gaze hooked on a swarm of Nymphs as they reached the steps and started sprinting up them towards the blasted open top.

The desperation with which they moved made me certain they were coming for the artifacts laying amongst the fallen bricks and Tory hovered opposite me as we came to a halt above it and raised our hands. A sinister energy rolled through my limbs as I prepared to destroy every one of those dark items and steal them away from Lavinia and her monstrous Nymph army.

"Together?" Tory offered and I grinned, placing one hand in hers and letting my barriers down so that our magic could rush together.

Except that wasn't what happened. My magic stuttered like the flickering flame of a candle in the wind and the fire along my wings stuttered out too.

"Darcy?" Tory asked in alarm as I willed my magic toward her, clenching my teeth as I pulled on the threads of power within me which seemed to be snapping and fraying one by one.

"Hang on," I growled, panic and determination colliding inside me. I didn't know what was happening, but I had to fight it, I had to find the strength I knew lived within me.

The Nymphs were almost at the summit of the temple and I cursed as I fought to take charge of my power and send it towards my sister.

My Phoenix shuddered back to life and a breath of relief left me as our fire coursed together in a never-ending wave. There was no time to question what had happened as Tory looked to me in concern. We had to finish this.

The Nymphs were scrambling across the fallen masonry to try and reach the altar and we couldn't spare another second as we released our power down on them like a spear of fiery death. The wings of a beautiful red and blue bird rushed out from us, plummeting through the sky in a blaze of unbelievable power before it collided with the top of the temple.

The Nymphs shrieked because it didn't just consume the altar, it consumed the entire temple, the fire rippling down it like high speed lava and devouring everything in its wake and I gasped at the immensity of our Order gifts.

The Nymphs tried to flee but they were too slow, caught in the flaming wave of death as it rolled out to the very bottom of the temple and the whole thing started to collapse.

Bricks tumbled as the temple trembled and fell beneath our power, shattering and burning.

But before I could celebrate, rage clawed its way up through my insides and a black cloud descended on me, pulling on my power and tearing it from my grasp.

I fought back with a snarl, frightened of what had a hold of me as my fire flickered out once more and Tory looked at me with my name on her lips and fear in her eyes.

I fought with the chaotic, hungry thing dragging my flames into its hold and suddenly my power burst from me in an explosion that slammed out of my body and into my sister's, sending me and Tory flying apart like a shockwave had struck us.

My ears rang and pain flashed up my arms and chest. A scream fell from my lungs as I cried my sister's name, and she was blasted away from me with such force that it made my heart still in my chest.

I caught sight of her as she fell, her flames extinguishing as she was launched far away from me by the blast, tumbling from the sky with a cry of terror and I was gripped with fear and horror over what I'd just done.

But the blackness was rising within me once more and as I threw out my hands to cast air magic, nothing came out.

I was falling two hundred feet through the air and I suddenly felt so terrifyingly mortal as my wings dissolved and a few bronze feathers scattered around me on the breeze, racing up towards the storm clouds above me as I fell so fast that I was certain this was my end.

I thought of Lavinia, of her marking me, and her wicked eyes as she placed her curse on me, and suddenly the darkness was sweeping in too fast for me to do anything about it. I was blacking out and the trees were rushing up towards me above the sharp rocks of the ground, and all I could think of was my sister, of Lance, of my brother. Because there was nothing I could do to save myself and I wasn't even going to get to say goodbye.

The darkness claimed me fully and fear surrounded my heart. I was only half aware of the scream still tearing from my throat.

A force collided with me and suddenly I was rolling, held by strong arms against a hard chest, Orion's body caging me so I didn't feel the impact of the ground as we tumbled across it and he saved me from my end.

But even stronger than the arms which held me, was the monstrous thing keeping me in its grasp within my body, so fiercely that I couldn't escape it. It was a desperately starved thing and it wanted my power more than anything in this world.

"I've got you, Blue," Orion growled, his voice laced with fear, and I tried to claw my way up out of the darkness to get to him, but I couldn't find my way back.

We'd stopped rolling, but he didn't let me go and terror drowned me as hot, wet blood fell against my cheek.

My head was swirling with a pressing, clawing mist and rage was filling every part of my soul.

I started to thrash, trying to seek out my Phoenix, but I couldn't reach it. It was buried so deep within me, it was like it wasn't there at all. And that terrified me more than anything.

Laughter tangled with the air, a cruel and high pitched voice I'd know anywhere now. Because it haunted my nightmares since that day in the arena at The Palace of Souls.

"Lavinia's coming!" Max cried. "We have to go!"

I tried to mouth my sister's name, but nothing came out as I slid deep down into the dark again, losing my grip on consciousness.

For a second two black eyes seemed to glare back at me from inside my mind, like I was looking directly into the soul of the Shadow Princess and she had me in her grasp, her fist squeezing my heart and her laughter still ringing in my skull.

I couldn't get free, I couldn't do anything but drown deeper and deeper in the shadows which seemed to live within my flesh. Yet they didn't feel like they used to; it was as if they were hiding in my soul, lurking out of sight, but still so present that I could hardly draw breath.

Anger rose up in me again and I clawed at whoever had hold of me, a growl on my lips as I tried to get free, trying to remember what I was fighting my way towards. But then it came back to me, riding on a wave of terror.

Tory.

My sister.

Where is she?

"Go!" Seth cried, panic breaking out around me, though I couldn't see any of it.

My head spun and my whole centre of gravity seemed to shift, making me realise I was travelling through stardust and panic began to swell within me. Because I couldn't feel my twin. I couldn't find her. She wasn't here.

"Tor?" I managed to bend my tongue around the word, but it came out as a whisper.

"Wake up, beautiful. Look at me," Orion begged, healing magic slipping from his skin into mine, but he couldn't heal this tearing sensation inside me. It was like a chasm opening up in the centre of my body, dragging me into it. No…not my body, my power, my Phoenix.

No, no, no.

My head spun and the rage took over again as I fought with the arms that held me, needing to get away, to get back to myself, to Tory. But I couldn't find anything but more darkness.

I dragged at the well of power where my magic resided, but it was hardly there at all. As if my power was running away down a drain and this time no fire in Solaria could restore it.

And through all the blackness, I thought of my twin again, because I couldn't feel her. And I needed to know she was here, that she was okay after what I'd done.

"Open your eyes, Blue," Orion commanded and I held on to him as I lay on my back, recognising him again as I felt the warmth of his body pressing down on mine.

Seth whined close by and Geraldine wailed in terror.

"My queen!" she cried. "Please look upon the face of your lover! Come back to us!"

Somehow, impossibly, I managed to do as Orion asked, my eyes cracking open and two achingly familiar dark eyes staring back at me. Blood ran down his cheek from a wound on his temple and panic washed through my chest.

"You're hurt," I rasped, then Caleb was there, his fingers pressing to Orion's head as healing magic glowed beneath his palm.

"Thank you, sanguis frater," Orion said to him and Caleb nodded, but I was too dazed to ask what that meant.

Orion's head fell forward as a heavy breath of relief left him, his lips pressing to my forehead.

"Tory," I rasped and Darius's head snapped around to look for her where he knelt beside me, his hands banded around my wrists like he'd been working to pin me down.

Orion lifted his head, turning as well and two painfully silent seconds passed where I knew in the foundations of my being that she wasn't here.

Something collided with Darius, taking him to the ground as two large black wings flexed up from the shoulders of his attacker and Geraldine screamed like a banshee.

I gasped as Orion dragged me out of the way and I stared at Gabriel as he smacked Darius over the head with a yellow sleeping crystal, making him fall unconscious at his feet. But as Gabriel went to stand up, Darius rose like the dead behind him with a snarl on his lips and bloodlust in his eyes. Gabriel fell on him again, hitting him with the crystal over and over until Darius fell still at last.

We all gaped at him in horror as Gabriel stood up, his inked chest bare as his wings folded behind him and an apology formed in his eyes.

"Gabriel's turned evil!" Max roared and Caleb lunged at my brother, throwing a punch at his jaw which he avoided with a flash of movement, letting me know he must have *seen* it coming as Seth ran forward with a snarl.

Gabriel shoved Seth back with a blast of water, standing his ground in front of Darius's prone body as we all stared at him in shock.

"What are you doing?" I gasped.

"He was going to go back for Tory," he said gravely, his eyes rippling with regret. "But he'll die if he goes. I've *seen* it."

The Heirs all exchanged a look as they fell still, and horror weaved through my chest like a serpent at what he was saying.

"But she's alone back there," I said in alarm, trying to fight my way free of Orion's grip, but my body was still weak and his arms were like iron.

I had to go back for her, I had to make sure she was safe.

"She can survive this," my brother promised. "We have to wait for her to return, Darcy. If anyone goes back to try and help her, it will only make things worse."

"No," I spat, fighting harder as a vicious animal rose up in me and I knew I'd do anything to get my sister back. I could take on Lavinia, I could take on all of them for her. I would leave a trail of death and destruction in my wake, but she would be safe and well at the end of it.

"Blue, listen to him," Orion commanded, but I wouldn't. She was my other half. And she was alone back there among our enemies. I'd done that, I'd hurt her, and who knew what had happened to her after she'd been blasted from the sky? There hadn't been anyone there waiting to catch her like Orion had done for me.

I thrashed harder, but Gabriel gave me a sad look as he stepped forward and placed the sleeping crystal to my head.

"I'm sorry, but you have to trust me," he said as the weight of the crystal's power fell over me and between that and the exhaustion already gripping my body, I drifted away into the dark.

But within it, I found no peace. Only a violent, endless rage that stole away the very essence of who I was and drowned me in its cruelty. And somehow, I knew that it was never going to let me go.

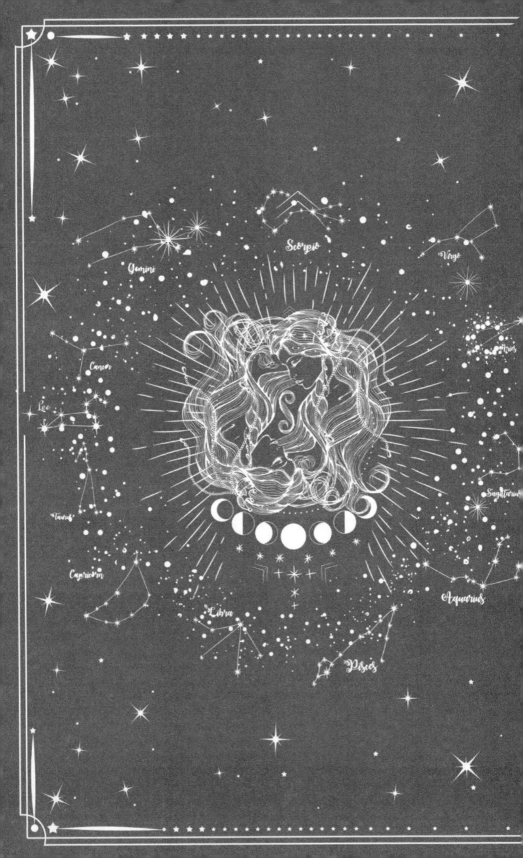

TORY

CHAPTER TWENTY NINE

I'd hit the ground on my back with the force of a fucking freight train, my skull rattling and wings crushed to my spine beneath me, blacking out from the pain of the impact with the mocking stars looking down on me the last thing I'd seen.

"Wake up."

I felt the brush of ethereal fingers grazing against my cheek and a groan escaped me as I clawed my way towards consciousness and the agony of my injuries rushed in to claim me.

Long stalks of grass stroked against my cheeks as the pounding rain continued to batter me and the scent of it drew me out of the void of my mind.

I was alone, vulnerable and dressed in an agony that burned brighter than the fire of my Phoenix.

I flexed my fingers, moving them to press against my side just beneath the base of the metal breastplate where I could access a sliver of skin, and I drove healing magic into my body, thanking the stars and our continued magical lessons for the fact that I knew how to heal broken bones now.

I sucked a shuddering breath between my teeth, working to remove the pain from my body first before shifting my attention to seeking out the injuries themselves and healing those. My broken wings had taken the brunt of my fall and I closed my eyes to concentrate as I mended the breaks in them before moving on to heal the rest of my body too.

When it was done, I blinked my eyes open, squinting up at the dark clouds which continued to spill water down on top of me endlessly, making me shiver as I felt the cold which had sunk into my bones while I'd been out of it.

A flick of my fingers cast a shield over me to keep the rain off and I called on my fire Element to dry me out and banish the chill from my body as I tentatively sat up to try and get my bearings.

I'd landed on a small hill which was coated in grass and peeked out from between the trees to the far side of the clearing which held the destroyed remains of the temple. I glanced down at the ground I was sitting on, finding a perfect silhouette of my body and wings burned into the stalks from my landing and my gut knotted as I thought about what had happened.

We'd only been power sharing, so why the fuck had our magic exploded instead of merging the way it always did?

The sound of heavy footsteps approaching chilled my blood and drew my attention from that thought. I looked around into the trees, noticing a group of huge figures moving between them, closing in on my position.

I couldn't hear the sounds of battle anymore and one glance at the sky told me there wasn't a Phoenix or Dragon flying past either, and I frowned as I tried to figure out where the hell they all were.

The haunting rattle of a Nymph drove beneath my skin like splinters, worming their way towards my magic and working to lock it down.

I looked around towards the smoking remains of the temple and found more and more of the creatures moving among the wreckage, far more of them than I had realised were here, and as the figures in the trees turned my way, I found myself vastly outnumbered and alone, like a sitting duck just waiting to be devoured.

The Fae in me wanted to stand and fight, but as a figure clouded in shadow shot across the cloud-hugged moon and I recognised Lavinia on the hunt, I got the horrible feeling that this fight was weighted too heavily against me.

The Nymphs released that god awful rattle again and as I felt their power sliding into my bones, I made the snap decision to hide, driving my fingers into the earth either side of me and harnessing my earth magic so that I sank into the dirt.

I created a pocket of air all around me, banishing my wings to make it easier for my body to slide beneath the ground and willing the grass to grow lush and thick above me to cover the evidence of where I'd been.

With my connection to the earth, I could feel the heavy vibrations of the group of Nymphs drawing closer and my breaths feathered in and out as adrenaline scored a path right through me as the power of their rattle drove into me again.

I had no idea if the creatures could sense my magic or were able to tell that their power was taking effect on a Fae nearby, but I wasn't gonna stay here and find out by letting them cut me off from my magic so that they could pluck me from the ground like a daisy and devour me whole.

I ground my jaw as I worked to cling on to my power and started driving myself down, further beneath the ground and away from the hunting Nymphs, burying myself alive and delving into the dark.

I was so focused on feeling for their approach that I only noticed the space beneath me opening up as I fell through the roof of the tunnel below me.

A scream caught in my throat as my stomach lurched and I threw my hands out wide, catching myself with air magic before I could hit the floor and illuminating a Faelight as I landed on my feet, looking around for enemies as dirt cascaded down on me from above.

The tunnel I was in was carved from the same black stone as the temple had been, though I was nowhere near the wreckage of that place, so I was guessing this was either connected to it from afar or its own structure built alongside it.

I cast an amplification spell and held my breath as I listened for the sound of anyone else drawing close to me, but I didn't detect anyone other than the Nymphs who were now walking through the clearing I'd been laying in just a few moments ago.

Once I was confident that I wasn't about to bump into a Nymph down here, I let myself look around at the dark tunnel, taking in the unlit sconces which lined the walls and the carvings which marked the black stone.

I walked closer to one of them, spotting an image of a woman who looked a whole lot like Lionel's Shadow freak as she cut her own flesh open with a sharp blade. I glanced at the image beside it, finding her now bleeding tendrils of smoke, winding their way from her body and into the hands of a Nymph who kneeled before her.

I arched a brow as I kept walking, seeing the Nymphs accepting the smoke which I was now guessing was actually meant to be the shadows before they got to their feet and grouped themselves together into an army.

I ran my fingers along the ridges of the carvings in the black stone as I took in the scenes of battle which finally culminated in a lot of celebrating Nymphs and a shadow bitch sitting on a throne with a crown on her psycho head.

I was hoping that whole scenario had been wishful thinking by the artist rather than some kind of prophecy, but I was willing to fight the stars themselves if it was the latter, because there was no fucking way I'd let that future come to pass while I still drew breath.

My boots echoed against the hard floor as I moved further along the empty tunnel and I cast a silencing bubble just in case anyone happened to get close enough to hear me before looking up at the roof and wondering what the hell I was supposed to do now.

Stardust would have been nice, but we'd split it between our group and I hadn't been carrying any - not least because my Phoenix fire might well have destroyed it if I'd tried. So here I was, stuck in some Nymph tunnel with no idea where the others could be and an uneasy feeling that something had gone horribly wrong.

There had been no sign of any of them when I woke and no sounds of battle either, so what did that mean? They wouldn't have just left me here, but I equally couldn't accept any version of reality where they'd been beaten or taken captive. So what the hell was going on?

Before I could get too caught up in that question, the brush of fingers against the back of my hand made me jolt in surprise and I whirled around, Phoenix fire igniting in my fist as I prepared to fight. But there was no one there.

"Come," the ethereal voice which had woken me before demanded and I stiffed in alarm, my gaze scouring the empty corridor as my senses prickled and I fought to figure out what the fuck was happening.

But before I could go all Phoenix on this place and just blast everything around me to shit in hopes of striking the invisible entity in the room too, I spotted a glimmer of something golden hidden between the stones near the foot of the passageway.

I knelt down, my fingernail catching in the little metal thing as I tugged it free of its hiding place and a tiny golden charm in the shape of a Hydra fell into my palm.

Energy rushed along my skin like a kiss of recognition and I straightened, frowning as silver footsteps appeared on the dark stone at the far end of the tunnel and I stilled, realisation finally finding me.

"Mom?" I breathed into the quiet, feeling like a fucking idiot for saying it aloud, but now that I wasn't jumping at shadows, I was sure it was her. Or the memory of her at least.

"Come," she repeated, the voice sounding further away now in the direction of the footsteps.

I swallowed a lump in my throat as I wished for Darcy to be here with me too before taking off after the ghost of my mother with the charm held tight in my fist.

The tunnel continued on along several corridors, short staircases leading me further beneath the ground and getting me turned around before I found myself in a wide chamber with a dark aura about it which made me hesitate on the threshold.

"You need to see," my mother's voice echoed around the open space and I stepped into the room, my gaze shifting over the chains which hung from the wall and the wooden chest which sat closed in the corner of the room, hiding fuck knew what.

But as I took another step forward, the room seemed to shift before my eyes and my gut swooped like I was falling as the black walls melted away and I found myself outside The Palace of Souls, watching as my parents strode up the steps and into the throne room, the sound of a cheering crowd following them in from outside.

"There," Hail Vega said heavily, waving a hand to push the door closed at his back and drawing my mom closer to him as she smiled brightly.

"Didn't I tell you they would accept me?" she teased and he smiled back down at her, grabbing her by the waist and drawing her body flush with his.

"Of course they will," he growled. "I am their king. They accept whatever I tell them to."

He leaned down to kiss her hard and I belatedly took in the white dress she wore and the crown which was balanced in her hair. I'd seen images of the two of them wearing these exact outfits when reading reports on the unexpected royal wedding.

Hail had returned from his trip to the southern kingdom of Voldrakia with a foreign princess on his arm and had married her that very day, sending the entire kingdom into an uproar. There had been some backlash from the family of the man she'd been betrothed to in her home kingdom, but Hail had threatened war and the issue had been resolved through some political alliances and the exchange of a substitute bride for him from our own kingdom.

Hail dropped his mouth to claim a kiss from the woman he had fallen so irrevocably in love with and I drank in the sight of them together, happiness clinging to every inch of them as she drew him closer for several lingering moments before pulling back.

"They'll come looking for us if we don't approach them ourselves," she sighed and he growled in frustration.

"Heavens save me from the inconvenience of politics. Let's get the rest of this over with then, so I can have you to myself," he rumbled, taking her hand and leading her through the palace to a large room full of guests where my gaze fell on the Celestial Councillors and my throat tightened as Lionel greeted them warmly, offering exuberant congratulations.

I shifted closer, wanting to overhear what they were saying, but my attention was drawn to a group of men and women who stood to the side of the room, each of them wearing a royal blue cloak and looking over to my parents with interest.

One particular member of the group stood out to me, and I stiffened as I recognised Vard. The oily Cyclops hadn't had the mop of long hair back then or even the scar on his face, but my heart thrashed harder as I took in the sight of him so close to my family.

"Rain!" one of the cloaked women in his group suddenly cried and a few moments later rain began to pebble the windows.

"I could have told you that a week ago," my mother laughed, glancing up at her new husband with love in her eyes as his attention was drawn to the robed people.

"We haven't had any great Seers emerge in our kingdom since my father's man Narbord died eight years ago," Hail said, his eyes sweeping over the group with slight distaste. "So I was forced to create a group of individuals who had enough of The Sight to be relevant, hoping that the minds of the many would amount to the mind of one."

"And do they?" Merissa teased, a knowing glint in her eyes.

"There isn't one among them who can even sit in the Royal Seer's chair," he muttered irritably. "Though perhaps that was because it had been waiting for you, just as I was."

Vard's head snapped around and he looked at my mother with a whole lot more interest than he had initially.

"The new queen has The Sight?" he asked curiously, though I could tell how threatened he and the rest of his group of less talented Seers felt about that.

"She does indeed," Hail purred, drawing his new bride closer to his side. "She can *see* better than anyone I've ever known."

The Seers broke into muttered conversation over that, their attention fixed on the new queen who answered their questions politely with a soft smile on her face.

Merissa straightened suddenly, her hand snapping out to catch an apple which had been aimed at Hail's face and Lionel barked a laugh, clapping loudly as everyone whirled to look at him.

"My King, I think you truly have found a gem to treasure here," he cried, looking like he was honest to shit happy, though I knew enough of him after spending months trapped in his company to recognise that dangerous, conniving look in his eyes. "I aimed the fruit at you while she was distracted and yet she still *saw* it coming! She is a true Seer indeed and her love for you must be fierce for her to sense threats against you so easily."

People around the room broke into applause at Lionel's lead and Hail grinned as he tugged his new bride closer, lifting her chin with his fingertips and looking deep into her eyes.

"Yes, she truly is something special," he said, kissing her in front of all of them to more applause but my attention flicked between Vard and Lionel, both of whom didn't look the least bit happy about the arrival of the new queen.

I opened my mouth, wanting to ask what else had happened, but the vision was already shifting, showing me the first time Merissa sat on the Seer's chair, her official elevation to the position of Royal Seer and various occasions where she'd seen something that Vard and the others hadn't even caught a whiff of. Time and again, Vard's jaw tightened with frustration and he continually offered up predictions which had varying levels of accuracy to them.

Over time, Hail met with the other Seers less and less, often not even informing them of the predictions Merissa made as his interest in their visions lessened to the point of him hardly consulting them at all.

Vard had come to him on more than one occasion, begging to be allowed to use the Royal Seer's Chamber so that his own visions could be more accurate, but he was denied.

I was thrown into another vision then, finding myself inside that very room as my mother sat on the chair, her eyes glazed with a vision and my father standing over her.

"Well?" he asked, his brow furrowed with concern as she came to, her eyes brightening as she shook her head.

"Nothing today, my love," she confirmed and his anxiety fell away with a sigh.

"I swear bringing you back here has changed everything for me," he said, moving close to her and falling to his knees before her. "I should reward you for that."

My mom giggled as he closed in on her, hitching her skirt up while leaning forward to kiss her neck and I wrinkled my nose, wondering why the fuck I was being gifted a vision of my parents getting it on and feeling a little sorry for Gabriel as I failed to find a way out of it.

My father growled hungrily, yanking on the top of her dress and ripping the material as I turned away sharply, not needing to see another moment of that as he dropped his mouth to her breast and she moaned loudly.

I turned to the door, clapping my hands over my ears and wondering if I could walk through it in a vision to escape this hell just as it burst open.

"My King, I really must insist that I be given use of-" Vard cut himself off abruptly as he realised what he'd just walked in on, and I turned to look back at my parents as a ferocious roar escaped Hail Vega which made the fucking walls tremble.

I expected to find him in his shifted form but instead I gasped as a knife was flung at me, the glint of sun steel flashing ominously as it sailed right through me and sliced across Vard's face.

Blood splattered against the wall and Vard howled in agony as he dropped to the ground, clutching at his ruined eye as blood poured freely from it.

"You dare to lay your eyes on my wife's body?" Hail bellowed, launching himself towards the bleeding, sobbing man on the floor with murder in his gaze and my mom cried out in alarm behind him.

She caught his arm, throwing a hand towards Vard, capturing him in magical vines which dragged him out of the room.

"You can't kill a member of the royal court without a trial!" she yelled, her fingers biting into my father's arm as she fought to contain his rage and I could see the essence of the monster in him shifting restlessly behind his eyes as he worked to look at her. "That isn't the king you want to be anymore. Remember what you asked of me? You want me to help you see a way back to the light."

"No man can lay his eyes upon your flesh and live to speak of it," he snarled, taking hold of her face between his hands and gazing down at her like she was the most precious thing in all the world to her. "I won't stand for it. You know that."

"I do," she breathed, holding her ground beneath his rage and not flinching once, that fire in her making my heart swell with pride as I watched her with this beast she'd chosen to love and saw the purity of that bond between them. She was his light and he was her dark. They balanced each other, but only when they worked for that unity as they were clearly trying to do now.

Hail looked fit to burst with fury as he yelled for the guards to take Vard out of his sight, but the vision shifted before they could arrive and I found myself watching as Merissa woke suddenly in the night, a vision drawing her from her husband's bed with an urgency which saw her racing from their room and diving out of a window into the night.

I relished the experience of flying alongside her as she shifted into her Harpy form, her wings beating hard as she flew straight to the amphitheatre where Darcy and Orion had been forced to fight the Nymphs at Christmas.

I chased after her as she landed lightly, running past the bodies of two dead guards and hurrying down to the cells which held prisoners in the darkness, though none of them seemed to notice her running past them.

She skidded to a halt outside a cell which stood open, a curse escaping her as she frowned, trying to force a vision into existence.

"How are you hiding from me?" she hissed, her frustration clear as she worked to get a vision which would lead her to the man who had escaped the royal dungeon.

Her head snapped up suddenly and she took a pinch of stardust from her pocket, tossing it over her head and yanking me along with her through the stars as she was whipped away through them.

I sucked in a surprised breath as we landed in the exact forest that I had been fighting in alongside my friends just a short while ago.

I followed my mom as she crept through the trees towards the pyramid shaped temple in the heart of the forest where she spotted Vard hurrying towards it, words pouring from his lips which she couldn't understand any better than I could and a draining dagger in his hand which hummed with the dark power I'd come to know all too well.

A shriek approached as Vard closed in on the temple and two Nymphs appeared at the top of the steps we'd not long destroyed, making Vard jerk to a halt in alarm.

He turned to run but four more of the creatures had appeared at his back and he found himself surrounded.

"I've come to beg mercy of the Shadow Princess," he called loudly. "I've felt her presence in my work with this blade and I wish to offer myself up as her humble servant. I have the gift of The Sight and was a member of the Savage King's court until he did this to me."

Vard trembled as the Nymphs closed in on him and I glanced at my mom, finding her ready with a pinch of stardust between her fingers, but she stayed where she was, watching, waiting.

A man strode out of the temple next, my blood chilling as I recognised Diego's uncle Alejandro with his black curling hair, thin moustache and dark, forbidding aura.

"Wait," he called, raising a hand as the Nymphs closed in on Vard and causing them to fall still. "The Shadow Princess has use for him."

Alejandro beckoned Vard forward with a single finger and the Nymphs at his back all corralled him up the steps, sending him scuttling forward with a whimper of fear that made me think he might have been second guessing this decision to come here.

I waited in the dark with my mom as they disappeared inside, turning my attention on her and slowly circling her as I drank in the sight of her face. Looking at her opened up an ache in me which I had long since fought to ignore, but it was impossible to do so while I was here, staring at the woman who had loved me and Darcy so much that she allowed her own life to be forfeited for the chance to keep us safe.

There was a lot of her in the two of us, and my heart pounded at each small similarity I found between her face and ours or Gabriel's. She was a memory of a life we should have been gifted the chance to live, but it had been stolen from us and the hurt I felt over that would never truly go away.

Lionel Acrux had a hell of a lot to answer for.

Merissa's gaze shifted suddenly and I found her eyes on mine, a gasp escaping her as she looked at me and a soft 'oh,' leaving her lips as she reached out as if to touch my cheek.

"Can you see me?" I asked shakily as the ghost of her hand skimmed the line of my jaw and I felt the faintest echo of that touch.

"You need to *see* this, don't you?" she asked and I wasn't certain she could hear me or even that she was really talking to me, but as my brow pinched she took off, passing straight through me as if I wasn't there at all and making the fragile pieces of my heart shatter with the love I ached to feel from her.

I turned to watch as she ran towards the temple, drawing the darkness tight around herself and hiding so thoroughly that I couldn't even see her myself, only knowing where she was headed through pure instinct.

I took off after her, hounding her up the steps and into the temple where screams echoed out to us and my mom followed the sound of them, slipping down dark corridors and stone steps until she reached a room where the screams were so loud that they made my skull rattle.

She hesitated by the doorway, looking in to offer me the opportunity to *see* this too, knowing she couldn't get a vision about this place while the shadows clung so closely to it and instead viewing it with her own eyes so that she could offer up this memory.

The sounds of agony coming from that room made me want to turn away, but I didn't, understanding the risk she'd taken to witness this for us. Whatever she saw in there had to be important and I needed to know what it was.

I stepped forward, moving to stand in the doorway and falling still as I spotted Vard, stripped to the waist and chained to a stone table as he begged and panted. Alejandro stood over him with a bloody blade in hand and my stomach writhed as he shifted to one side, revealing the bleeding mess of Vard's face and I couldn't help but wince as he tossed a destroyed eyeball aside, letting it hit the floor with a wet slap.

"I'm begging you to let me meet with the Shadow Princess!" Vard wailed and Alejandro laughed cruelly in reply.

"No one meets with our god," he spat. "But you came to the right place if you wish to serve her."

He whistled sharply and a Nymph strode from the corner of the room in his shifted form, his huge, tree-like body sending a wave of fear through me as I watched him drop to his knees before Alejandro and look up at him with all the mindless adoration of a true zealot.

Alejandro raised his blade once more as he closed in on the creature, murmuring words beneath his breath which sounded like a prayer or perhaps something more sinister. My breath got caught in my lungs as he grabbed hold of the Nymph's throat and drove the blade into his eye socket.

The creature stiffed, a cry of pain coming from it, but it didn't try to fight as Alejandro kept going, carving the Nymph's blood red eye from its face and plucking it out to lay it in his palm.

Bile coated my tongue as I watched the eyeball start to twitch and writhe in Alejandro's hand which he held aloft as he continued to chant and pray, the words making every hair on my body stand on end as I felt the rush of the shadows racing into the room.

Darkness swept towards the Nymph's eye and as Alejandro continued to call on the power of the Shadow Princess, the thing began to twitch more violently, until suddenly it sprung clean out of his hand and landed on Vard's chest with a wet and bloody thump.

"Fucking hell," I gasped as I watched the thing filling with more and more tendrils of darkness as it began to wriggle its way up Vard's chest like some sort of fucked up worm and made its way to his face before lodging itself in the empty eye socket which awaited it there.

Vard screamed bloody murder as the shadow eye attached itself to his body and I had to fight the urge to heave as Alejandro watched with a cruel and malicious smile on his face.

"Ask and you shall receive," he purred, watching as Vard thrashed and screamed against his restraints and the darkness of the shadows took a grip on his soul.

A clamour of noise drew my attention to the corridor behind me and fear sent a shiver through my limbs as I turned at the sound of countless Nymphs coming this way, looking to my mom in alarm as I tried to figure out how the fuck she'd escaped this place of horrors. But she answered my question simply enough as she tossed the stardust she'd been holding over her head, vanishing in an instant and dragging me along with her as the vision faded away.

"I saw Hail's death if I ever took him to that place." Her voice echoed

around me as I came back to myself and I shuddered at the thought of that.

I landed back in my body inside the tunnel beneath the mountain, suddenly recognising this as the room where Vard had gotten his gross Nymph shadow eye. It made so much fucking sense to me now. How he'd been able to *see* the shadows, why the deep red colour of it had always unsettled me so damn much. He had a fucking Nymph's eye in his face and no one had ever questioned it. Or maybe they had, and I was just late to the party. Lionel almost certainly knew and he had clearly been trading for power from Lavinia since he'd been gifted that thing.

Was it the reason they'd managed to work around my mom's visions? Had this moment been the deciding factor in their fate? One scorned asshole throwing a bitch fit because someone came along and did his job better than him?

Pain radiated through my chest at the thought of that. Of how something so small had become so important. My father had been angry and perhaps overly harsh, but the monster he'd created in Vard with his actions had to have been beyond all possibilities to predict.

I blew out a breath, looking around at the dark space while my chest tightened with anxiety for my friends.

I needed to get out of here. I needed to get back to them and figure out what the hell had happened to them.

I wasn't going to give too much thought on what the hell had gone down between me and Darcy when our power had collided, but there was a heaviness in my soul and a fear for my other half which lingered there, waiting to emerge the moment it got the chance and leaving me with the desperate desire to be reunited with her so that I could make certain she was okay.

I headed back the way I'd come, following a long passageway and feeling out ahead of me with my connection to my magic to make sure I wasn't about to meet any surprise guests down here in the dark.

The passage turned and I found myself at the foot of a long stairway, the brush of fresh air against my cheeks making me think I must have found my way back to the surface.

I made sure my concealment spells and silencing bubble were firm around me and began to climb, jogging up the steps quickly in hunt of the fresh air I could feel billowing around me.

I wanted out of this dank series of tunnels and I needed to get back to my friends.

At the top of the steps, I found myself in a stone arch which was cut into the side of the hill, overlooking the now destroyed temple below where I could make out a large figure moving among the rubble.

My blood chilled at the sight of the Nymph and I hesitated just inside the doorway as I looked out at them through the sheeting rain, hunting for any sign of Darcy or Darius or any one of the people I'd come here with. But there was nothing.

My mind began to turn with a plan to get closer to the destruction down there, to hunt for them and figure out where they were, but I flinched at the sound of Lavinia's voice and I shrank back into the shadows instead.

"Come out, come out, wherever you are…I want a taste of rebel blood tonight."

I spotted her as she landed amongst the rubble in the valley below, a shriek of fury escaping her as she yelled at her Nymphs to search harder and find her some prey.

Hope swelled in my chest as I took in her frustration, and I was struck with the certainty that she hadn't found them after all. But then where were they?

It was hard to believe that they would have left here without me, but maybe they hadn't had a choice. Maybe they thought I was dead. The explosion of power which had collided between me and Darcy had been enough to hurl me far from her and any of the others, and I had no idea how long I'd been lying in the grass unconscious either.

A tugging sensation in my gut made me turn and look to the north, a feeling of need filling me as I squinted into the storm and was hit with the desire to fly that way, sensing my mother's presence once again like there was more she wanted to show me.

I'd never felt her like this outside of the palace before and I wasn't certain if it was the golden trinket in my hand or the head injury I'd received that was causing it, but I was going to have to hope it was the trinket.

I glanced down at the little Hydra charm in my hand before tightening my fist around it and turning my back on Lavinia and the destruction we'd left here, choosing to have a little faith for once in my damn life and calling my wings into existence.

I was careful to keep the flames of my Phoenix at bay as I took off, holding the darkness around me with a concealment spell and using the storm to hide my progress through the sky as I tore away from this place and its foul memories.

I hurried through the rumbling storm clouds, flying higher and higher as the freezing water coated my skin and armour, making goosebumps pepper my flesh and my hair stick to my cheeks.

The clouds were thick and freezing cold as I flew into them, the thrum of electricity present all around me and making memories of my torture at Lionel's hands rise to the surface of my mind. He had taken a special interest in watching me scream beneath the strike of the lightning which he kept trapped in those jars. Even this faint tingle of that power had me back in that room, back at his mercy and trapped in my own mind.

I fought to shake off those memories, trying to cling to the lessons Max had been giving me in compartmentalising and deep breathing. But I really wasn't a meditation kind of girl, so I worked on my favourite coping mechanism instead as I failed to find that calm place inside me which always seemed to elude me too easily. Revenge. My desire for cold, hard, revenge was what was going to get me through those flashbacks. I gave myself over to thoughts of all the ways I dreamed of making Lionel, Lavinia and Vard pay for what they'd done to me and countless others besides.

And while I indulged in fantasies about carving them up and burning them in Phoenix fire, I burst through the barrier of the storm clouds and made it up to the peace above them where only the stars could see me as I flew on.

I let the sensation I was getting from the Hydra charm guide me as I flew on, filling my body with the heat of my fire magic as I went and leaving the chill of the storm behind alongside the shadow bitch who was mourning her poor lost rift.

I wasn't sure how long I flew for, but by the time I felt the urge to descend from the sky, dawn was lightening the horizon and my wings were aching with fatigue.

I dropped down through the clouds which were now white and hazy, the storm left long behind alongside the forest and I found myself gliding over a huge, flat plane which was covered in grass and wild flowers tipped with morning dew.

The charm in my fist almost seemed to heat the further I flew until eventually I spotted a stone circle standing in the centre of an otherwise open expanse of grass.

I cast a detection spell to hunt for anyone who might be hiding themselves here, but found nothing to suggest that I wasn't alone as I dropped from the sky and landed softly in the centre of the ring of stones.

I looked around at the enormous lumps of rock, wondering if an earth Elemental had cast them into existence here because there was no sign of any other stones about the place.

The charm in my fist heated further as I stood there and as I opened my hand to look at it, I found myself tugged into another vision, this one of my father as well as my mother, with Lionel and the other Celestial Councillors all standing close by and watching as the king stood in the centre of this stone circle.

"Have they destroyed the Nymphs who created this?" Seth's mother Antonia asked and I looked to see what she was referring to, noticing the crackle in the air at the centre of the stone circle as I did so.

"The FIB are on the hunt," King Hail replied, moving forward and placing a hand in his pocket as he scowled at the rift.

"How many of these things have you discovered?" Tiberius Rigel asked as he stepped closer to inspect the rift, the taint of dark magic coating the air surrounding it and clearly making all of them wary.

"Enough to be concerned," the king replied. "I think we need to focus our efforts on hunting the Nymphs down and annihilating their foul race once and for all."

"They've grown too good at hiding over the years," Melinda Altair murmured. "But if you can deal with these rifts as you say then perhaps it's not such a concern."

"The Nymphs will always be a concern," my mother replied.

"How would you know when you can't even *see* them?" Lionel asked in a teasing tone.

"I've *seen* enough of the future to know they could cause all kinds of problems for our kind if nothing is done to stop them," she replied.

"Perhaps we are looking at this the wrong way," Lionel murmured, stepping into the stone circle alongside the king and reaching his hand out towards the rift, causing shadows to coil out and brush against his fingers. "If we could figure out a way to harness them then imagine the power they could provide."

My father laughed loudly, knocking Lionel aside with his shoulder, the force enough to make him fall against one of the huge stones as he strode forward.

"Azriel, explain to Lord Acrux why that is a terrible idea," the king said in a condescending tone which I could tell riled Lionel to no end while the other Celestial Councillors all seemed amused by his rebuke.

A man I hadn't even noticed stepped out from behind one of the largest stones, pushing a pair of golden glasses up his nose which hummed with enough magic to let me know they were doing far more than enhancing his vision. He had dark, messy hair and a pale complexion, his clothes expensive but worn without much care like he only dressed so well to suit appearances. He seemed slightly irritated to have been drawn away from whatever he'd been studying, and I couldn't help but feel a little amused as I noted that similarity to his son.

"The shadows aren't a toy to play with or lay claim to," he said, taking his glasses off and tucking them into his breast pocket. "They are a living, feeling embodiment of their realm. You could never hope to wield them the way you wield Elemental magic no matter how much effort you went to to contain them. Their power is corruptive, mighty and endless. Each shadow is connected to the next no matter how you may try to divide them, and only death would lay in the fate of anyone fool enough to try and take ownership of them for themselves."

"You would think being among the most powerful Fae of our generation would be enough for you," Tiberius teased and Lionel laughed along.

"Well, one can never have too much power," he replied with a laugh.

That hungry look never left his gaze as he kept it trained on the rift, like a starving creature aching for a taste of life.

"Knowledge is power, so I can admit I agree with that," Azriel replied and Lionel gave him an assessing look, but said nothing further.

"Stand back," my father commanded and everyone else retreated from the circle as he held his hand out and Azriel Orion summoned a staff from the fabric of the air at his side, a stunning stone set in the top of it which hummed with so much power that I could practically feel every Fae in attendance salivating over it. The Imperial Star glowed brighter as the king grasped the staff and I sucked in a breath along with everyone else as he drove the base of the golden staff into the ground and spoke a word which echoed around my skull and out of existence.

"Suturi!"

His voice boomed across the plain in every direction, flattening the stalks of grass with the power of that one command and with a flash of blue light, the Imperial Star took hold of the rift to the Shadow Realm and closed it for good.

"Let's head back to the palace," Hail commanded as he finished his work, handing the sceptre back to Azriel who promptly returned it to wherever the hell he'd found it in the first place and it winked out of sight.

The Councillors and Azriel all vanished in a flash of stardust, but Merissa stepped forward, reaching out to cup the king's jaw in her hand.

"How many of these have you found now?" she asked and he sighed heavily, looking into her eyes as she tried to get a reading from him and allowing her to see all the rifts he'd discovered and closed so far.

I was gifted a view of what she *saw* too, flashes of different landscapes and locations flickering before me, some with altars like the rift we'd just destroyed, others located in remote locations that seemed utterly inaccessible, each of them allowing a little of the shadows to slip through the gap and into our realm.

"No doubt there are countless more I am yet to discover too," he murmured, his gaze filling with concern. "I fear what they will mean for Solaria if we don't manage to seal them all again. There is a great power in the Shadow Realm which is trying to push through to our side and with these rifts open, it has a way to slip through."

"Then we will find them all and you can seal them up again," she vowed and he nodded.

"That is what I intend to do."

Hail tossed the stardust and the vision faded as they were drawn away, the light shifting around me as I found myself back in reality, standing in a ring of stones which held no evidence of a rift ever having been here at all.

But his words hung heavily in my ears and I couldn't help but look up to the stars and wonder if he had managed to do that or not. Because if one rift had been missed in his hunt then I had the sinking suspicion that there would be more that had gone unaccounted for, each of them feeding power through from the Shadow Realm for Lavinia to make use of. So now the only question left was, how the hell were we supposed to find them?

I flexed my wings, looking around and trying to get my bearings as I cast the homing spell Orion had taught us to help us find The Burrows if we ever ended up in a situation like this. I cast healing and energising magic into my limbs to soothe the ache of the long flight I'd already taken part in then launched myself into the sky once more.

The rifts may have been a problem, but at least now I knew more about them. So we were just going to have to figure out how to track them down and close them too because I had the feeling that if we managed that, we'd soon find ourselves on a level playing field with the so-called Shadow Princess. And once that was the case, all bets were going to be well and truly off.

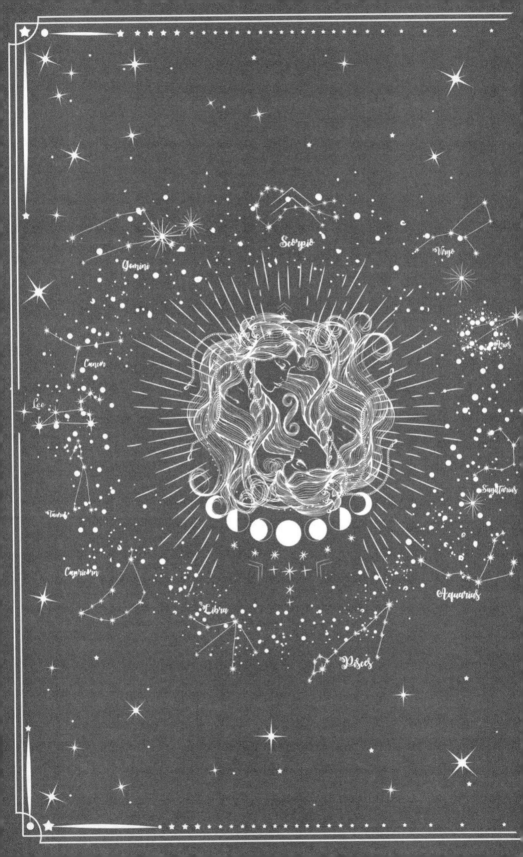

DARCY

CHAPTER THIRTY

I woke to the sound of banging which seemed to rattle all around the inside of my skull. On instinct, I reached for my magic to protect me and was endlessly relieved when it came to me from the darkness, though my Phoenix was slower to respond.

I forced my eyes open as I pieced together everything that had happened and panic descended on me fast, realising I was now in mine and Orion's room.

"Tory," I gasped, shoving out of the soft bed and finding Darius in the room with me, throwing his flame covered fists at the door over and over again. But the door shimmered with the might of magic that echoed all the way around the room, clearly stopping him from breaking through.

I was dressed in a soft pair of blue pyjamas with frilly bows on the cuffs and collar, making me instantly certain they were Geraldine's and I had to assume she had changed me out of my armour while I was sleeping.

"What's going on?" I hurried toward Darius, but as I made it to him, weakness pressed down on me and my knees hit the floor.

No, get up. Fight for her. Find Tory.

Darius suddenly took hold of my arm, pulling me to my feet with worry in his eyes and cradling me in his strong arms carefully. "Are you alright?"

"I don't know," I admitted, tugging free of his grip with determination burning through my soul. "But it doesn't matter. We have to get out of here. We have to get back to Tory."

He nodded, though his eyes lingered on me with concern written into his strong features as I turned to the door and placed my hands against it, encouraging my earth Element to rise. It came heavily, like it was being dragged out of a sinkhole and I growled determinedly as I forced it to obey my command.

I blasted the door with the force of an earthquake, trying to break it off at its hinges, but the forcefield cast around it wouldn't give.

"Lance!" I shouted. "Are you out there?"

"I'm here, Blue," he replied darkly. "Don't ask me to let you out. Gabriel instructed us to do this."

"Good, then I know whose head to rip off first when I get free," I snarled as Darius moved to my side, pressing his own magic into the door again as we worked to break it open together.

"It's for the best, Darcy," Gabriel's voice carried to me next. "Do you really think I'd do anything that put either of you in danger?"

"So she's not in danger?" I asked, hope spiralling through my chest.

"Well…" His hesitation made me snarl and Darius's fist collided with the door again, a Dragon roar leaving him.

"Let us out!" I yelled.

"You'll regret this. All of you," Darius spat like an animal.

"When have I ever led you astray?" Gabriel asked calmly, and I wanted to punch him for that relaxed tone of his.

I knew he wouldn't put Tory in direct danger, but she was still alone out there. And as tough as she was, it wouldn't matter if Lavinia teamed up against her with a Nymph army.

"Please," I begged. "Please let me go to her."

"You need to rest," Orion growled like a bossy asshole.

"What I need is my sister," I snarled.

"Are you feeling okay?" Lance asked like I hadn't just snapped at him.

"I'm fine," I ground out.

"She collapsed again," Darius said and I shot him a glare that marked him as a traitor.

He shrugged, showing me exactly where his loyalty lay and I punched him in the arm.

"You and your sister are violent women," he muttered, though not like he had an issue with it.

I turned back to the door, anger swirling in me like a raging vortex. "You have no right to hold us here!"

"Trust Gabriel," Orion urged.

"No," I hissed, venom bleeding through my veins as a wild and violent creature rose up in me, ready to destroy the entire world for my other half.

Darius pummelled the door again, falling into a frenzy as he fought to get us out and I helped him for as long as I could before weakness rolled over me once more.

I was suddenly falling and Darius scooped me up in his arms before I hit the floor, moving to the bed and laying me down on it as he sat beside me, guiding healing magic into my flesh.

"I've got you, little shrew," he murmured reassuringly, a soft, teddy bear of a Dragon peering down at me instead of a raging animal as I felt the truth of that statement.

"What's wrong with me?" I whispered in fear, not wanting to voice it to anyone else but him. I didn't want Orion or my brother to think I couldn't look after myself. Not when Tory needed me, and I needed to convince them to let me go to her.

Darius frowned, feeling my forehead for a temperature then dropping his hand. "Maybe you're sick," he said weakly, but I shook my head, knowing what this was deep down, but I was terrified of admitting it.

"What is it?" he asked, clearly seeing something in my expression that gave my fears away. "No bullshit, shrew."

I swallowed thickly, dragging the words up from the depths of my chest and letting them out. "Lavinia's curse."

The door opened and Orion shot into the room, passing through the forcefield as if it was nothing as he sped to my side. Darius charged at the door, slamming into the magic cast over it and crashing down onto the floor with a grunt.

Gabriel stepped over him, hurrying to my side and both he and Orion leaned over me, clearly having heard what I'd said. Orion gripped my face in his hands and examined my eyes, hunting for something that confirmed or denied it, but I wasn't sure what he found.

"You're not cursed, Blue," he said in a way that told me how absolutely terrified he was that I could be. Like saying those words would stop it from being true.

I rested my hands over his with an echo of pain in my heart. "But what if I am?"

His features twisted and I stared at this dark and forbidding man who would do anything to protect me from this fate.

"Then I will sell my soul to save you," he growled, the power of those words falling into a pit of terror inside me. Because I didn't want him to pay any price for me. He'd already given up his whole world for me, I wouldn't let him do it again.

"No," I said through my teeth. "We'll figure this out together."

He nodded, though the dark promise in his eyes told me of the sacrifice he was willing to make for me, and it left me unsettled.

"All of us will," Gabriel agreed and I looked over at him as Orion released me, finding a line of worry on my brother's brow. "Every curse has a way to be broken," he added heavily and I frowned, desperately hoping there was a simple way out of this. But when had we ever been so lucky as that?

"Can you see anything that could help us?" I asked.

"If Lavinia did this, then she is the key to undoing it," Gabriel said solemnly. "I cannot *see* her or this curse."

"What of Blue's fate?" Orion growled, gripping his friend's arm tight as he forced Gabriel to look at him. "You must be able to *see* if she lives through this. What do you *see*, brother?" he begged.

Gabriel swallowed, pain crossing his eyes. "Orio, you have to understand, we're in a war. I *see* all of you die so regularly that I can hardly stand it. There are so many fates, I cannot predict any of your futures for certain." His eyes trailed to Darius as he joined us again, looking at me with his jaw grinding.

"What if we kill Lavinia?" Darius suggested and I nodded, liking that idea. I'd head to her now and drive a spear of ice through her chest if I could.

"Curses are not often as simple as that," Orion said thickly, his gaze never leaving mine like he was desperate for an answer to present itself in my eyes.

"True," Gabriel agreed with a sigh then his eyes glazed for a moment and we all stared at him in silence, waiting for him to reveal something that could help. He reached for my hand when he came back to us, squeezing tight. "I can *see* that you and Lance will visit the Library of the Lost, I cannot *see* a lot of the books you will read or what you will find within them, but I am sure that means those books contain knowledge on the shadows."

"I'm not going anywhere until my sister is safe," I said stubbornly and Gabriel nodded slowly, his eyes glazing again then a relieved breath fell from his chest.

"She will be back very soon," he said finally and a weight fell from me like the whole sky had been resting on my shoulders.

Gabriel's posture loosened and I realised how awful it must be to *see* everyone you love dying around you in visions, *seeing* their end a thousand times and only being able to nudge them away from death where possible. It sounded like hell.

"You're sure?" Darius asked, a crease of anxiety between his eyes.

"Yes," Gabriel promised. "The fate is set."

"Thank fuck for that." Orion swiped a hand down his face then dropped onto the bed beside me with his jaw ticking. "Tell me everything you can about how you feel, Blue. I need to know as much as possible so I can help search for the right books in that library."

I nodded, shame inching into to me at what I was about to say. Because suddenly I didn't want the world to know what I feared was happening to me. It made me weak, and Fae were the exact opposite of that. But I couldn't keep this from everyone, I had to fight it, had to find a way to stop it, and I couldn't do it alone.

"It's like there's a chasm inside me," I said tightly, placing a hand against my chest where I felt it. "And out of it spills rage and anger and hate. But it takes from me too. It sucks away my magic, feeding on it like some hungry animal, and…" I choked on my next words, the fear they caused swallowing me into a void. "It wants to take my Phoenix too. When I power shared with Tory, it was like that rage took over and power exploded from me as I tried to fight back. But then as I was falling, I couldn't sense any of my magic at all. I felt…" Tears burned my eyes, but I didn't let them spill over as dread burst through my chest.

"What, Blue?" Orion asked, my own fear mirrored back to me in his eyes.

"Mortal," I whispered and I swear everyone in the room flinched.

"That's not possible," Orion rejected the idea instantly, but Darius looked to Gabriel, seeking the answer from him as I did the same.

Gabriel shook his head, staring at me in disbelief. "I wouldn't be able to *see* your fate at all if you lost your magic," he rasped. "It wouldn't be like the shadows, it simply wouldn't occur to my mind at all."

"But it's not possible," Orion insisted, rising to his feet as his fangs snapped out, looking to aim his anger somewhere, but there was no one to blame in this room. He grabbed Gabriel, dragging him closer to me. "Look at her fate more closely, you must *see* an answer. There must be one you can find."

"I will look," Gabriel swore to him, to me.

They all started discussing what to do and my breaths came heavier as the sound of their voices bounced off my ears and I brought my knees to my chest, hugging them tight. I couldn't become mortal, I couldn't go back to the life I'd come from. The fear crept up on me so fast, I could hardly stand it. A tide of memories drowned me as I recalled living in poverty in a world I'd never once felt I belonged in. Of nights wrapped around my sister, my twin the only comfort in a world so dark it had always been so hard to find the light. And it was worse than even that, because if I had to return there, I would have to go alone. And if I had no magic in my veins, I could never come back to Solaria. And the people I loved would rarely be able to visit or over time, they'd get sick. I'd have to be away from them all, my sister, Orion, Gabriel, all of my friends...

I knew I was getting ahead of myself, that right here and now that fate wasn't yet set. But how long did I have? What if my magic was gone tomorrow for good and I started getting weak from being in the Fae world? What if the only option was for me to leave Solaria, to have to abandon my friends and family to a war I would never get the chance to fight in again? It was unthinkable. Unbearable.

I took a slow breath, forcing myself not to panic. I was Darcy Vega. I didn't worry about the bad, I always focused on the good. And I had to do that now, because if I didn't, I'd be engulfed by this terror and it would never let me go.

Nothing permanent had happened yet, and I was surrounded by people who could help me find the answer. I had the best Seer in Solaria for a brother and the smartest professor for a boyfriend.

"What's going on?" Tory's voice snapped me out of my own thoughts and I gasped, leaping up and running to her as she stepped into the room. I slammed into her, hugging her tight as tears welled in my eyes. "I'm so sorry. It was all my fault."

"It's alright." She squeezed me against her and my heart slowed a little at being reunited with my twin.

Darius grabbed her from my arms, kissing her hair and growling protectively. She had to half fight her way free of his arms to get to me again. "What happened?"

"Nothing I couldn't handle," she said firmly, looking to me in concern as Gabriel moved to hug her too. "What's going on? Why is everyone looking so anxious?"

I took a breath and told her the truth, but raised my chin in defiance of it.

"I'm cursed," I said, those words seeming to fill up the whole room and my sister started shaking her head in immediate refusal.

"No, you said you fought it off. You said your Phoenix dealt with it," she said firmly like she was willing it to be true.

"I was wrong," I said, my heart hurting more for her than myself because I could see fear taking hold of her and I hated to be the reason for it.

Orion moved to my side, his arm sliding around my shoulders. "We'll leave immediately for the library." He looked to my sister. "I'll find an answer to this," he swore and Tory's throat bobbed as she tried to place her faith in him.

I looked up at Orion and a frown pinched my brow as I spotted two silvery pin prick marks on his neck. "What's that?" I reached up, tracing my fingers over them.

"Caleb and I…" He cleared his throat, looking to Gabriel who gave him a knowing look. "We drank from each other back at the altar, and accidentally formed a sort of…Vampire Coven. It's something which is against the Vampire Code because it drives our instinct to hunt. He's my blood brother now, my sanguis frater. It's a bond that has made us form an alliance and ended our rivalry."

"Bond?" I growled the word, thinking of the Guardian bond which had caused him such suffering, but he shook his head.

"This bond requires nothing of me, it only provides me a sort of kinship with Caleb," he explained.

"It's more than that," Darius said, his eyebrows raised in surprise. "You'll be worse with him than you are with your precious Noxy."

"Fuck off, he's not worse with anyone than me," Gabriel growled, then pointed us to the door. "Come, let's go. If you leave now, you'll be back before nightfall…unless, oh shit, never mind." He scrubbed at his eyes. "Just hurry up, alright?" he said a little sharply and we nodded quickly.

I hurried to the wardrobe and grabbed a black skirt and fitted white sweater out of it with some underwear, changing behind the door and pushing my feet into some knee high flat boots, then I followed Gabriel out the room with the others.

Tory kept to my side, throwing me anxious glances and I shrugged out of Orion's hold as I took her hand instead. "Please don't look at me like that. I can't bear it."

She nodded, glancing away and I squeezed her fingers to get her attention again. "What happened to you back there? Were you in danger?"

"A little," she admitted. "But actually, I…*saw* our mother." She took a little charm from her pocket, showing it to me and I admired the tiny Hydra in surprise.

"You did?" I asked, an ache in my chest over missing out on that.

Tory started explaining everything she'd *seen* and the others gathered closer too as we listened. When she told us about what Vard had done and the vile ritual he'd gone through to get his shadow eye, a shudder of disgust ran through me.

"Why do you think she showed you that?" Gabriel asked her as Tory examined the Hydra charm.

"I don't know, but I think it's important."

We fell in to thoughtful silence as we headed outside The Burrows and before we exited, Darius moved forward and hugged me, making my eyebrows shoot up.

"I'm gonna go tell the others about all this, little shrew. I want you to know you have a weight of Dragon gold to buy any cure in this world that you need, and the full wrath of my Order to help you find an answer to this curse."

He released me and I looked up at him with my heart bunching up in my throat. "Thank you, Darius."

He nodded, looking to Orion and clapping his shoulder as a look passed between them and Gabriel that promised they'd tear the world apart for an answer to this curse. Then Darius kissed my sister goodbye and he jogged off down the passages.

"At least I don't have to be there when Geraldine finds out," I said to

Tory, releasing a little laugh but Tory didn't smile.

"You always smile even when it's raining," she said, her eyes glittering with tears.

"I like the rain," I pointed out, but when she looked at me like her heart was breaking, I hugged her tight. "I swear this will pass, just like every other rainstorm, we'll find a way through it together."

She nodded against my shoulder. "I'll fight every single rain drop if I have to. One by one, I'll cut them out of the air."

"I know you will," I said, loving how much my sister loved me.

We all headed outside together and Orion kept his arm locked around my shoulders, his expression fitting for a witch hunt as he led me after Gabriel while Tory walked on my other side.

My brother turned to me as we made it beyond the boundary, tugging me out of Orion's hold to give me a bone-crushing hug. "A friend of mine will meet you there. She'll help you find what you need."

I nodded against his shoulder, gripping him tight and he stepped back with a frown, looking to Orion over my shoulder. "Look after her, Orio," he warned.

"Always, Noxy," Orion growled.

"Are you sure you don't want me to come with you?" Tory asked anxiously as she dragged me into her own fierce hug.

"I'll look after her," Orion answered for me.

"You need to rest," I told her, giving her a tight smile. "We'll be back soon."

"We'll be back when we have a way to break the curse," Orion corrected me and Tory swung a finger towards his face.

"You find an answer, Lance Orion, or I'll make you regret it. Do your nerd thing and find a way to fix this," she commanded and Orion held out his hand to her.

"I swear I'll do everything within my power to break the curse," he promised and Tory slapped her palm into his before I could stop her, a flare of magic igniting between them as the deal was struck.

"You don't need to make deals on the stars," I said anxiously.

"Don't worry, he's not at risk of breaking the deal, Darcy. Look at him. He'd find a way to lasso the sun out of the sky and bring ruin on us all if it saved you from Lavinia's curse," Tory said, smiling darkly at him.

"That's the problem," I muttered, but no one listened to me as Orion grabbed my hand and Gabriel took a pouch of stardust from his pocket. I knew we couldn't spare it, but the look on his face said we were going to use it whether I liked it or not. And I looked between these three powerful members of my family, my heart warming at having them around me, the bond between us so strong I knew nothing would ever break it.

"She's waiting for you," Gabriel said then took a pinch of stardust from a pouch and passed the half empty bag to Orion.

Gabriel blew the stardust over us, guiding us to our destination as we tumbled away into a sparkling sea of light.

We landed under a dark, cloudy sky, standing before a wide black lake with a small island in the middle of it. The ground was green and lush and as I gazed around, I realised we were on the rolling moors of a place that reminded me of photographs I'd once seen of Ireland. A heavy mist swept across the land, the chill in the air cutting right down to my bones, and I willed fire magic into my veins, offering it to Orion too through the point where our palms connected.

A series of rocky steps were cut into the ground beneath our feet, leading down to the lake's edge and disappearing into the perfectly still water.

"Princess Darcy?" a soft female voice came from behind us and we both turned, finding a pretty woman there with short cropped hair and dark skin. She wore a denim dress with a book tucked into a pocket on the front of it, a Skylarks Pitball team pin on her chest.

"Hi," I said, still struggling to get used to being addressed like that.

"I'm Laini," she said, dropping into a curtsy, her eyes falling to the ground before darting back up to look at me. "You're very beautiful."

"Oh…thanks," I said awkwardly, tucking a lock of blue hair behind my ear.

"We need access to the Library of the Lost," Orion said abruptly and Laini's eyes shifted to the brooding guardian at my side.

"You're Lance Orion," she whispered and Orion sighed.

"Let's skip the retching and the disgust at my Power Shaming," he growled. "We need to get into the library."

"Oh, I'm not disgusted by you. I mean, the shaming does make my stomach turn a bit, but I can push through it," she said brightly. "A few of us are quite in awe of you here actually."

"What? Why?" he balked and I smiled in surprise.

"Me and my friends figured it out," she said with a hint of pride in her voice. "For starters, I don't believe a single word of the drivel printed in The Celestial Times. So I did my own digging, I read every article about the court case and have spoken with Gabriel and his wife too. I know what you did for one of the Vega Princesses." She pointed to me. "She wouldn't be standing beside you now if what everyone else believes is true."

Relief washed through me and I immediately liked this girl as she looked to Orion with the admiration he deserved.

"Thank you. I wish more people would realise that," I said heavily and she nodded sadly.

"I mean, most people here don't get it. But I'll introduce you to the ones who do," she said brightly.

"How many are there who feel the same as you?" I asked hopefully.

"Um, four. Including me," she said.

"Well stars be damned, my fate will surely turn by midnight with that kind of backing," Orion said dryly and I jabbed him in the side.

"Would you like to go inside now?" she asked, ignoring his tone and I looked around, unsure what she meant by that.

"Yes," Orion growled in frustration at being kept waiting, his manners apparently left behind with his smiles.

She stepped past us, heading down the steps towards the dark lake and I frowned in confusion.

As she reached the bottom of the steps, I gasped as she walked straight onto the water and a narrow stone bridge rose from beneath the lake. I walked after her and Orion stayed at my back as we crossed over the water, ripples spreading out across the surface from the emergence of the bridge.

We made it to the island at the centre of the lake and as Laini led us onto the mossy ground, I realised we were standing inside an ancient zodiac wheel. The star signs were all carved into the ground around us and as Laini dropped down to a crouch and brushed some moss aside from something at the centre of the circle, I saw a sun symbol etched there. She placed her hand against it and golden light shone under her palm a second before a heavy thunk sounded beneath our feet.

The zodiac wheel dropped a few inches and my stomach swooped before the wheel beneath us started sailing down into the ground with us standing on top of it.

The moment we made it beneath the ground, another stone wheel slid into place above us, sealing the entrance and we were plunged into total darkness.

We continued to descend, a rumbling sound carrying around us and vibrating through my bones. Suddenly the darkness evaporated and all words abandoned me as I took in the crystal clear bubble we were inside, giving us a view out into the lake. But down here it wasn't dark at all, it was full of dancing light and as a cluster of lights rushed past us, I realised they were fish. Silver, glowing fish that left gleaming trails in their wake.

I pressed my hand to the wall of the bubble, the surface like softened plastic, moulding to my hand as I pushed against it, but it didn't give.

"It gets better," Laini said excitedly. "Just you wait."

We finally descended beneath the bottom of the lake, leaving the sandy bed behind along with the stunning fish which danced above our heads, and blackness surrounded us once more as we continued to plummet through the earth.

The darkness lifted and light spilled over us once more, a breath becoming trapped in my throat as we descended into a cavernous place the size of two cathedrals combined.

The beauty of this library seemed otherworldly, the walls were darkest grey and arching overhead in magnificent struts. On the four walls of the gigantic room were beautiful stone faces of women, each representing the Elements.

The one for earth was draped in moss and ivy, flowers blooming in her eyes and across her lips; the face for water had her mouth agape and a waterfall spilled from her lips all the way down to a glistening pool at the bottom of the library that sparked with light; the face carved into the rock for fire had eyes that were burning in brightest blue and streams of lava swirled within the cracks of the stone; lastly, the one for air was coated in white fluffy clouds and though her hair was carved of stone it somehow seemed to move and shift in a magical wind. Around each of them were stairways leading to bookcases built into the walls and tunnels led into the deeper passages of the library beyond them.

Below us, endless bookcases spiralled together, made of wood and stone and glass. There were bridges passing over the pool beneath the face of the water Elemental, each of them holding smaller bookcases which Fae were perusing.

The zodiac wheel beneath our feet landed at the heart of the cavern and

I stared around in amazement at the place. Laini strode away into some of the stacks, guiding us along as I took in the incredible surroundings, not wanting to blink in case I missed something.

Butterflies danced in the air ahead of us, their wings tipped gold and leaving trails of light behind them like the fish had up in the lake. I looked around for Orion's reaction, knowing how much he adored books and expecting to find a look of glee in his eyes, but there was only darkness there as we walked, and I was sure that had everything to do with the curse.

I took hold of his hand to reassure him, but he didn't look my way, intent on following Laini as we passed between the ancient looking books on either side of us.

"We need to see any texts you have on the shadows, or dark magic," Orion said, his eyes boring into the back of her head.

Laini glanced back at him with a nod. "Of course," she agreed. "But come see my friends first, they're dying to meet you."

Orion looked ready to argue, but I tugged on his hand, giving him a look that told him to bite his tongue. They didn't know I was cursed, and I sure as hell didn't want to tell them either. We could spare a few minutes to say hello.

We rounded the stacks, arriving in a section where tables were laid out and Fae were sitting around reading. A girl with dark hair jumped up from her seat with a honk. My eyes widened in surprise at the noise and she quickly flattened herself to the floor to bow to me.

"That's Brittny," Laini announced just as another girl came running towards us with blue streaked hair. "This is Kandice." The girl bowed low to me, her eyes darting towards Orion.

"This is so exciting," Kandice squealed. "Can I get you a beverage? Perhaps a snack? Or a foot rub? Brittny is great at them, aren't you Brittny?"

Brittny opened her mouth to speak but a loud honk came out instead and she clapped a hand to her mouth, her cheeks reddening with embarrassment.

"She's a moose shifter. She has a nervous honk," Laini explained. "This is Eugene."

"Hello." A slim man rose from his seat, a shock of white hair on his head and a look of admiration in his eyes.

"I know you," I said in realisation. "You've been staying at The Burrows. You're the High Buck, erm, thingy, right?"

"That's right. High Buck of the Solarian Mischief of Tiberian Rats. It's a pleasure to meet you properly, Princess."

"And you. What are you doing here?" I asked.

"I've been staying at the library for a few weeks now to help find new ways of travel to replace stardust. Some of the old legends speak of something called vaporgation where you could turn yourself into gas form and have an air Elemental blast you away across the land at high speed," Eugene squeaked.

"We love trying to prove old legends true," Brittny said excitedly.

"Unfortunately, we think vaporgation might have had serious side effects like peeling a few layers of your skin off and making your fingernails rot," Kandice said with a frown.

"Oh," I said with a grimace.

"Are we quite done with the introductions?" Orion drawled.

"The princess saviour is looking at us," Kandice breathed and Brittny honked nervously as the two of them blushed.

"Wait, if you like proving legends, there's actually one we need some information on," I said in realisation and Eugene squeaked, an exhilarated look in his eyes.

"What legend? We would be honoured to assist you," he said, practically brimming with pride at the idea and I flicked up a silencing bubble around us.

"We're looking for The Gems of Lariom," I revealed, deciding to trust these people, though Orion glanced at me like he wasn't sure if we should. I was pretty damn good at reading people though, and Gabriel would have said something if he'd *seen* anything shady about them.

"Oooh, that's my favourite legend!" Brittny cried and Eugene scurried over to a bookshelf, grabbing a book from it which was twice the size of his head and wheezing as he carried it over, laying it down on a table with a heavy thud.

"We'll get right on it, my lady," Eugene squeaked. "This is a record of all the books on legends in the library." He flicked fast through the worn pages then stopped on one and pointed to the title at the top above a seemingly endless list of books. *Texts on The Gems of Lariom.* "We'll get looking through all of these, your highness, and if we get even a whiff of their locations, we'll let you know immediately."

"Not all of them," Orion cut in, giving in to my desire to set them this task. "We need information on the gems for Libra, Scorpio, Sagittarius, Capricorn, Aquarius and Pisces."

"Okie cokie karaoke." Eugene beamed and Orion nodded stiffly, turning to Laini.

"We're here for an urgent matter. Take us to the section on dark magic, we can't waste anymore time," he said brusquely, his patience clearly at its limit.

"Please," I added.

Laini nodded quickly, muttering an apology before jerking her head in an offer for us to follow. Kandice waved goodbye to us and I thanked her and her friends for their help as Orion caught my hand and towed me along after Laini.

"The dark magic section is in the labyrinths," Laini said, leading us through a stone archway and into another section of the library.

This place was massive. Everywhere I looked there were more books, more shelves, more beauty. We passed over a small bridge above a trickling stream then approached a large door which was as black as iron and bolted shut. Laini pressed her hand to the centre of it and magic sparked out from beneath her palm, shimmering across the door and making the bolt slide back with a loud clunk.

The doors parted before us and a huge man stepped forward from the darkness. His head was transformed into that of a bull with huge horns curling up from it and his humanoid body was huge, towering over me with dark brown fur covering his skin. The Minotaur bowed to me and Laini gestured for us to join him.

"Arnold will take you to the dark magic section. Don't ever leave his side or you'll get lost down in here and we'll never find you. Only the

Minotaurs know the way around this section. It's how we protect the most dangerous knowledge in this library."

We moved forward to join Arnold and he released a deep moo before turning and leading us away into the dark. We hurried to keep pace with him as the sound of the door shutting behind us sent an echoing boom out around into the tunnels ahead of us.

My pulse flickered and I immediately cast a Faelight to guide away the shadows. Arnold apparently had no trouble seeing down here, but he made no objections to the Faelight I'd cast as he quickened his pace and turned down a narrow passage that pressed in on us on both sides.

The air chilled the further we walked, and the ground slipped away beneath my feet as we descended deeper into the Earth, and as my fingers brushed the wall, I felt the damp against its surface.

The passages turned left and right sharply as we walked through the labyrinth, my sense of direction lost already. Arnold never slowed his pace and sometimes he turned so fast that Orion would shoot us forward with his Vampire speed to ensure we didn't fall behind. Eventually, one of the passages opened up into a dark cavern that made my heart beat faster.

The roof domed above us and below us the entire floor fell away into an abyss that was terrifying to behold. We stood so close to the edge that I knew if someone turned too sharply out of that tunnel, they'd plummet straight to their death into the shadowy chasm below.

A narrow platform extended across it and a lectern made of some dark metal stood at its centre. Upon it was a white book, its pages open and blank. Arnold turned and gestured for me to approach the book out on that deadly looking platform and my eyebrows arched.

"What is this?" Orion asked.

Arnold's eyes flashed to him then back to me before falling to the ground. "I cannot address him, my lady."

A growl rolled up my throat, but we didn't have time to waste trying to exonerate Orion's name to some random Minotaur. And one look at Arnold told me it wasn't even worth trying.

"Then tell me," I asked.

Arnold nodded, an apology in his eyes as he turned his massive body towards me, shifting so that his back was to Orion as if even looking at him caused physical pain. "The book is a gateway to all the dark books we keep here. You need only ask it what it is you're looking for, and the book will present you with everything you might need."

"What if we don't know what we're looking for?" Orion growled.

Arnold's eyes shot to him then back to me again, a sweat breaking out on his cow brow.

"Tell me," I said in frustration and Arnold nodded.

"You must try to be as accurate as you can when thinking of what it is you need, my lady. If there is something you require but cannot find, then I will try to help you as best I can. When you are finished here ring the bell and I will come to collect you – or you may ring it if you need my assistance." He pointed above my head and I turned, finding a bronze bell hanging above the entranceway with a long rope dangling from it.

A bell sounded off in the distance and Arnold mooed loudly in answer before charging off into the tunnels, the sound of his hooves clopping across the stone floor carrying back to us as he went.

"Well thank fuck he's gone," Orion muttered, striding straight out onto the platform towards the ominous looking book.

I followed him, glancing down at the terrifying drop below, even the knowledge that I had air magic somehow not comforting me. I wondered how deep that hole was, if it fell away into the pit of the Earth, and my stomach twisted at the thought.

I joined Orion out on the platform, gazing down at the white book. Up close, it was clear the book's cover was made of some white glass, and as Orion tracked his thumb along it, one look at his expression told me how valuable the substance was.

Orion scrolled through the blank pages before looking to me. "You'd better ask it, Blue," he prompted, stepping aside so that I could stand even closer to the book. "Think of all the symptoms you can."

I took in a slow breath, focusing on the blank page before me and conjuring up every dark feeling that had clung to my soul when I'd fallen from the sky back at the temple. As I held onto those awful feelings, I formed a question in my mind, grasping it tight before speaking it aloud. "Which shadow curses could steal away Fae magic?"

Dark ink blossomed across the pages like rain spilling from the sky and staining the book with words. A list of curses gathered on the page with a single paragraph written beneath each one.

Orion shifted closer to read them, glancing at me in the corner of his eye.

"Does any of this seem familiar?" he asked anxiously.

I read through each of them, from a curse which caused your skin to decay, to another that ate at your bones from the inside until you were unable to walk. But the loss of magic seemed like a by-product to these curses, something that happened in the final stages before the Fae inevitably died.

"No," I said. "It's none of these." It was a damn relief too, because some of this shit sounded like a gory ass horror movie.

"Then ask it again," Orion pressed. "Be more specific."

I nodded, trying to think of a new question that would help me gain my answer. "What kind of shadow curse could fill me with rage and make me unable to use my magic?"

The page became blank once more until new ink started spreading across it, but there was less this time. I shook my head at what appeared, the text detailing the anatomy of some shadow beast, a dark plant which could grow roots within you and turn you inside out, and a shadow worm which could burrow into your skull and drive you insane.

"We're missing something," I said to Orion, looking up at him as a crease formed on my brow. He reached out to cup my cheek, a burning intensity in his eyes.

"You can do this, Blue. We'll stay here until you do this."

A shiver ran through me as I nodded, turning my gaze back to the book and starting to ask it question after question, hunting for the answer we so desperately sought.

"Let's be more general," I said after an hour of trying and failing to find what we needed. Orion nodded his agreement, his hair dishevelled from how many times he'd run his fingers through it.

"How can the shadows affect Fae magic?" I asked.

A whole page appeared before us and I frowned in intrigue, leaning closer to read the text.

The scholar Hanson Edgelight hypothesised that the Nymphs once lived in harmony with the Fae. Although he was widely mocked for the opinions he held, and many of his theories were disapproved, this one held a ring of truth to it.

It has long been known that there was a time when Nymphs and Fae did not collide in the way they do now. However, many of the texts from these times have since been lost. Edgelight claimed that he had found evidence of a village of Nymphs hidden in the cloud forest of Serendipity who were living independent of Fae society. He claimed he had visited this village but would not give out its location for fear of the Celestial Council moving to attack the Nymphs who resided there.

This one photograph survived his accounts after he burned the evidence when a group of Nymph hunters came to his door, seeking the village. The charred remains of this photograph show Edgelight standing before a Nymph with their hands clasped together in what appears to be a peaceful interaction.

If a village like this really did exist, it would bring into question everything we know about their kind. Nymphs can only survive by feeding off of Fae magic once they have awakened their own shadow power. So if a Nymph village really does exist away from our kind, then we can only assume they are either hunting Fae and Edgelight was unaware of this, or they have found some way to survive without us.

Today, the FIB handle the Nymphs to keep society safe from their attacks, but if we are to believe Edgelight's theory, and take this photograph as evidence of a peaceful Nymph population living somewhere in Solaria, then we would have to also question the morality behind killing their kind.

"It's not possible, is it?" I asked Orion and he ran his tongue over his fangs thoughtfully.

"Anything is possible, though this seems unlikely."

"Maybe it's worth exploring though, right? If there *are* Nymphs out there who don't need to steal magic to survive, then maybe they can teach other Nymphs how to live that way," I said hopefully.

Orion nodded slowly, though he didn't seem convinced by the idea. "Let's keep looking for information on the curse, Blue."

"Perhaps we're coming at the curse from the wrong angle," I sighed and he cocked his head.

"What angle do you think we should be coming at it from?"

"Maybe we should be looking at the power of my Phoenix. Maybe there's a spell or gift I have that could help me, instead of trying to find the exact curse which I'm bound to."

Orion's eyes brightened at that idea and he turned from the platform, striding back towards the bell and ringing it hard. "Good idea," he said.

Arnold's moos sounded off in the tunnels as he answered the call and came charging our way, the sound of his hooves pounding along the passages towards us.

"I'm not just a pretty face," I teased and Orion's lips quirked up ever so slightly before falling flat again. Perhaps the worst part of this curse was seeing how it was affecting everyone around me already, and I knew in my heart that I would do anything and everything to ensure that I broke it for their sakes as much as my own.

Arnold arrived with a snort and a foot stamp, bowing to me once more. "My lady, how can I help you?"

"Do you have any books on Phoenixes?" I asked.

"My queen, we have books on everything."

"Then take us to them, Arnold," Orion said impatiently, no hint of friendliness in his voice.

Arnold pretended he wasn't there, looking to me for direction and I huffed in frustration.

"Take us to them," I said firmly and he snorted happily before turning and guiding us away into the dark caverns once more.

We followed at a fierce pace, jogging to keep up with him as Orion kept hold of my hand in case we had to speed forward to catch up.

We wound deeper into the labyrinth, and even as I tried to count the turns, something about this place had my mind completely in a haze, like it was designed not to let me remember the way.

A lurch of panic rose in me at the idea of being lost down here with no way out, and I trotted faster at Arnold's heels.

He turned into another cavern and the flare of a fire brushed against my cheeks as I took in a huge stone goblet at the heart of the room burning with a bright red and blue fire.

Arnold turned to me with a bright smile pulling at his lips. "Over a thousand years ago, the Phoenixes visited here. They set this fire burning in the Goblet of Eternal Flames and it has never died. Your ancestors, Princess Vega, they are the ones who set it alight." He pointed to it grandly and I stepped closer to it, feeling my magic reserves swell under its immense power.

Orion remained behind me as I reached out, pushing my hands into the flame and feeling the kiss of the past against my skin, part of me wishing I could reach right through these flames and touch the ones who'd lit it. Some piece of me belonged within this fire, and I felt the most aching sense of belonging as I stood in its rays of heat.

I glanced back at Orion, finding him standing at the entrance to the cave, begging him to come closer with my eyes, but he didn't move, as if he didn't feel he should step further into this sacred place of my ancestors. But he belonged anywhere that I was, including right here.

Beyond the rising flames which licked the high ceiling were wooden bookcases, reaching up above me with ladders that climbed the stacks.

"These books belonged to the Phoenixes of old," Arnold explained. "They can only be touched by a Phoenix, so they have not been read in many centuries, my lady. The secrets found within them belong to you and your sister."

My lips opened and awe fell over me as I strode towards the books, my head tipping back as I took in the endless knowledge sitting there before me, a gift from my ancestors. And I wished that Tory was here to share it with me.

"The answer is here," I said to no one in particular. "It has to be." I turned my head, looking to Arnold. "I wish for Orion to read these books too. Can I let him touch them somehow?"

"M-My lady," he stammered in horror. "Allowing a Power Shamed Fae to do something such as that would be an abomination."

"But can I do it, Arnold?" I asked angrily and he bowed his head once more, nodding quickly.

"Yes, it can be done. You must simply take a book from the shelves and hand it to him, then the spell will release it."

"Thank you." I nodded to him in dismissal and he trotted away out into the tunnel muttering something about Power Shamed scum touching ancient and priceless books, making my hackles rise.

If these books were for me and my sister, I'd put them in the hands of whoever I damn well liked.

And there was no one I wanted to read them more than Orion.

"Are you sure, beautiful?" he asked as I walked straight towards the shelves.

"Of course I'm sure." I glanced back at him, arching an eyebrow. "Do you really think I'd keep them from you?"

"I am owed nothing from you and yet you have given me everything. I am always surprised at what you hand me so willingly."

"You are the most valuable man in the world to me, Lance, I wish that you'd see it the same way. Now come here, I'm going to hand you a book. Please don't get a hard on."

He smirked as he approached, moving out of the shadows as the flames danced over him, casting him in gold and red light.

They seemed to twist and move, almost bending towards him as he stepped around them and approached me.

"I think your ancestors are judging me," Orion said and I laughed lightly.

"Are you afraid they'll come back from the dead and teach you a lesson?" I jibed.

"I'm not afraid of anything when it comes to you."

I smiled, stepping onto a ladder at the base of the huge stacks and starting to climb, my eyes gliding over the old tomes all around me. I tried to read as many of the names on the spines as I could, not sure exactly what I was looking for but still climbing higher and higher as I searched, some strange stirring inside me guiding me onward.

There were all kinds of books on numerology, astrology, star signs, the constellations, and a whole range of magical spells and potions, and I was endlessly curious as to what secrets lay within them.

"What are you looking for?" Orion called up to me.

"I don't know," I admitted, feeling that strange pull in my chest again as it drew me toward something.

"Higher."

The ethereal whispered voice made me gasp and I cursed as I lost my grip on the ladder, slipping down several rungs and Orion cast air magic that pushed me back onto them.

"What the hell was that?" I hissed.

"A clumsy princess?" Orion offered.

"Asshole," I tossed at him. "And I didn't mean *that*, I heard a voice. Like the stars or…something. It told me to go higher."

"So go higher," Orion encouraged and I continue to climb until I made it right to the top.

There, alone on the shelf was just one book lying on its side. And I knew in the depths of my being I was meant to find this book. I reached for it, drawing it from the shelf, the binding made of some red woven silk that was so soft it almost slid from my grasp.

I could feel power humming within this book that resounded right down to my bones. And I trembled as I clutched it to my chest, feeling that same echo from my ancestors crying out through me.

"What is it?" Orion called up to me.

"A book," I called back.

"Very funny," Orion growled. "What's it called?"

"You're very grumpy today." I turned it on its side to read the name, finding nothing but a single flame there carved into the binding itself. I flipped open the front cover to read the first page and found the title glimmering in bronze ink that almost seemed to flicker with flames.

Fire in the Blood by Petonius Vega

My breathing hitched as I stared at those words, sensing I held a gift from the past in my hands that had meant to find me.

"Come down here, Blue," Orion urged.

"Alright," I answered, tucking the book under my arm and starting to descend the rungs, before remembering I had magic.

I let go of the ladder, plummeting several feet as Orion swore before I caught myself on a gust of air, floating down towards him and landing on my feet in front of him. I noticed his hands were raised a little and I tilted my head to one side.

"I can catch myself," I told him.

"You didn't before. I'm your backup parachute," he said seriously.

I reached out, pressing my thumb into the corner of his mouth and drawing it up.

"Don't forget to smile, it'll make me sad if you don't smile."

"It's hard to smile when I know the fate we face."

"Do you think I'm going to die?" I asked in a whisper, chewing on my lower lip.

"No. Because I won't rest until you're safe," he said fiercely.

"I am safe. I'm with you."

He smiled finally and I held out the book, offering it to him with my eyes alight. He hesitated, his hand lifting as if he were desperate to take hold of it, but he couldn't let himself do it.

"Take it," I insisted. "You're clearly dying to take it."

"Are you sure?" he asked. "I don't think you understand the magnitude of what you're offering me here."

"I do. And that's why I want you to take it."

Orion inhaled slowly then took the book from my hands, a hunger entering his eyes as they roamed over the ancient tome. "This is made from glendian silk," he said. "The silk worm which used to make this material died out hundreds of years ago."

"Is it expensive?" I asked curiously.

"You have no idea. The value of this book is immeasurable. And that's just based on the cover. I imagine what lays inside makes it far more valuable even than that."

"So let's find out," I said eagerly.

He chuckled and we moved across the room to an iron table, sitting at it side-by-side as Orion laid the book down delicately like it was made of fragile glass.

"I don't think you have to be so gentle with it," I said, reaching out to open it.

His fingers brushed mine and as we opened it at the same time, I swear a groan of pleasure left him from the combined contact of me and this book.

"Does it turn you on?" I murmured to him and he glanced at me with an intensity in his eyes that could have brought the entire world to its knees. But as I was the only one to witness it, it was just me who fell to ruin.

"Pay attention," he said sternly, his professor tone coming out to play and I liked that a lot.

In ways, being back at Zodiac sneaking around the school grounds to steal moments in his arms had actually been a simpler time. Now I had him to myself, and yet he still wouldn't declare me as his to the world because of his fall from grace, and that was something which pained me every day. At least back then, we'd had dreams of declaring our love to the world, now every time I tried to bring it up, Orion wouldn't indulge in those dreams with me. He said it was to protect me, and I knew he meant that, but having to keep hiding our relationship after all we'd been through was opening a wound in me that I didn't know how to heal.

His finger skimmed down the contents page like he was caressing the arch of my spine and I swear I could feel it, him touching me as he was touching that book. I pushed all thoughts of his Power Shaming from my mind, just enjoying his company as I remembered the agony of going so long without it.

"Should I be worried that you're going to leave me for a book?" I asked, a grin pulling at my lips.

Orion turned to me, still looking deadly serious. "I'll never leave you, Blue. Now stop misbehaving or I'll have to punish you."

"Is that a threat or a promise?" I whispered and his hand clapped down on my thigh under the table, the sting sending a flash of excitement through me.

"What's gotten into you?" he growled, not playing my game. "You find out you're cursed and you sit here smiling."

"I'm beside the love of my life in a magical library underground in a world I didn't even know existed a couple of years ago. I've always been an optimist, but now I have a real reason to believe in miracles."

"So you're certain we'll find an answer?" he asked like he wanted to feed on my positivity.

"No," I admitted. "I'm still terrified that we won't, but I'm equally hopeful that we will." He stared at me with the weight of the world in his eyes and I pushed my fingers into his hair, stroking gently as I hoped to dissolve some of his worries. "Why do you look so scared, Lance?" I whispered.

He raised a hand, his fingers locking around the Imperial Star at my throat and his knuckles turning white as his grip hardened on it. "Because the stars have taken everything from me. My dream, my free will, my status, my family," his voice thickened on that last word and pain sliced into my heart for him and all he'd lost. "And when there was almost nothing left to take, they gave me you."

I lowered my hand from his hair, wrapping my fingers around his fist that held the star like he was trying to hurt it.

"I thought perhaps the tide was turning in my favour, but now I fear that they've given me you only to have something more to strip away from me. I don't know what I did to offend them, but they have taken their pound of flesh from me regardless."

"I'm not going anywhere," I swore and he nodded, his expression settling into something demonic.

"I know," he said, his voice rough with grit. "Because I'm not going to let them take you from me, Blue, even if they come down from the heavens themselves to try and rip you from my arms. I am not named after the hunter constellation for no reason. I will make the stars my prey if they set you in their sights, and so help me, I will carve every one of them out of their seats in the sky and watch them fall."

He released the Imperial Star, his head snapping back around as he looked down at the book again and I was left breathless and staring at him, heat blazing up my spine and burning between my thighs.

He flicked firmly through the pages as he searched for something that could help us and I tried to get myself in check as I watched his jaw tick. But then a line from Gabriel's prophecy echoed in my mind and fear spilled into my soul.

"The hunter will pay the price," I whispered, fearing what that line of the prophecy could mean as I gazed at Orion. "What if it's you?"

His eyes flashed and he reached out to carve his thumb along my jaw. "That could mean so many things."

"But it could mean you," I pressed, fear making my breaths quicken.

"You'll drive yourself mad assuming the will of the stars," he said gently. "We can't say anything for sure."

"What's the point of prophecies if their meaning is unclear until they've happened?" I said in frustration.

"To drive us mad?" he offered playfully, but I couldn't summon a smile, too caught up in the idea that we were walking along a dark path toward a bitter fate we couldn't escape.

He took my hand, placing it against his chest so I could feel the powerful thrum of his heart. "I'm right here, Blue. Don't get lost in some imagined future that might never come to pass. Right now is all we have, so let that be all that concerns us."

He leaned forward, kissing me deep and slow with the taste of a better future on his lips. One where we were happy, where we loved each other from the core of our beings to the very edges of the universe. And it filled me with so much joy, that I remained there, holding onto it and making a silent vow to myself that I would fight for that future with everything I had.

I breathed a sigh of relief, resting my forehead to his for a moment before we broke apart and he turned back to the book. We sat quietly for a while, reading through the pages and though I was fascinated by the descriptions of the Phoenixes of old, we found nothing of use and I was just on the verge of suggesting we look at another book when Orion turned the page and a spell was laid out in front of us.

The power of the Phoenix tribe.
It is fabled that the flames of the Phoenix live in all of its Order, meaning the same fire burns in one Phoenix to the next. The result of this is a powerful energy which can be made stronger by the addition of one or more Phoenix flames.
This power sharing is also power enhancing, meaning the gifts of their kind can be amplified together. This technique could be used to fight off deadly Fae diseases or even break curses.

"Fuck yes," Orion whooped, smacking the table and a smile split across my face.

"Tory," I breathed.

"The two of you can fight it off together." Orion beamed so bright his dimple popped out on his right cheek. "Why didn't we think of this before?"

"Because we're idiots," I laughed and threw myself at Orion, hugging him as his solid arms folded so tight around me, I almost couldn't breathe.

When we'd read the page back to back and concluded Tory and I needed to try burning the curse away one day at a time until it eventually succumbed to our combined flames, Orion closed the book and got to his feet.

"Let's get back to The Burrows," he said. "You can start straight away."

I got to my feet too, heading over to the exit to ring the bell for Arnold with a much better idea in mind. "We're in the Library of the Lost, we can spare a little bit of time to explore."

Orion shot over to me, a glimmer of his old self back in his eyes as he took in those words. "Are you sure?"

"The curse could take weeks to burn through," I said. "It's not gonna make any difference if we spend a couple of hours here."

Orion's face lit up like a kid on Christmas morning and I grinned at him, bouncing on my toes as excitement poured through me too. "We deserve a bit of fun."

At the word fun, a beast's grin pulled at his mouth and his fangs glinted at me, making my stomach swirl with butterflies.

Arnold appeared with a loud moo, startling the hell out of me and I cursed him as he led us back into the tunnels and out of the labyrinth. We returned to the main library through the large doors and the two of us immediately darted off down a set of narrow bookcases where golden butterflies were dancing in the air and red flowers trailed above us on vines, blooming then closing again.

The magic in this place was surreal and I was soon lost in a maze of stacks, each turn making me gasp at the beauty of the place. There were water fountains that bubbled with tiny transparent dolphins leaping out of the water before swimming away into their depths, whole sections where grass grew up around our knees and we had to wade through it towards giant toadstools where we could climb up ladders and sit on their cushy surfaces. Another area had a treehouse with hidden doors in the trunk where books were nestled among nests of moss and twigs. Owls even hooted in the trees and an eagle came down to watch us as we lazed in a giant hammock hanging between two of the huge branches, both of us coiled together as we read a mortal book about a pair of twin girls, one of whom had been claimed by the royal Vampires who'd taken over New York City and the other had teamed up with the last slayer on earth who happened to be hot as hell.

A group of Sphinxes plucked books off of the shelves and lay down in the grass, looking enraptured while Orion murmured to me that their kind could step right into the pages of a story. They didn't just see it in their head, they lived every word, the whole thing playing out in their minds as if they were the main character, and that sounded pretty awesome. It must have been incredible to experience your favourite books first hand, to fall so deeply between the pages that it seemed as if those worlds really existed.

"Which book would you go into?" I asked Orion, brushing my fingers over the thick stubble on his jaw.

"There is no story I would choose to live in but ours," he answered simply, and damn this man to hell for his silver tongue. My heart all but packed up its bags and moved out of my chest to go and live in his instead. He already owned it that completely anyway.

Next, we headed upstairs to a place where clouds hovered everywhere and we could step right onto them, letting them carry us all around an area that had mirrored glass which reflected an azure sky back at us. The books were hidden between the mirrors, their covers transparent until they were within our grip, and I smiled at the incredible magic as we got lost in it, forgetting all about the problems that awaited us far above our heads.

When we came to a carved wooden door which was as large as a house, I glanced at Orion with a giddy look before taking hold of the bronze handle and turning it, finding the thing impossibly easy to move considering its size.

We stepped into a perfectly silent part of the library where books stretched out impossibly far in front of us on dark wooden bookshelves that rose up two floors above our heads. The floor was a rich red mahogany and we crept across it, glancing down the passages that led away into the cavernous room either side of us.

Orion tugged on my hand to get my attention and I glanced back at him, finding him pressing his finger to his lips with a smirk before lifting me up and shooting us away down one of the passages. He came to a halt, but his shoes slipped on the highly polished floor and we slammed into one of the bookshelves, sending the whole thing tipping sideways and spiling books all over the table and floor.

Orion caught hold of the shelf before the whole thing could go over, placing it back in its position with a resounding boom that echoed throughout the entire room.

"Woops," he laughed, putting me down and I lifted a hand to cast a silencing bubble. He knocked my hand aside, a roguish glint in his eyes. "Looks like no one's in here."

He pressed a hand to my chest and shoved, knocking me backwards onto the table, my ass hitting a book and my hand slipping on another one as I fought to push myself upright.

But Orion shot in front of me, kicking my legs apart and rearing over me, pressing me back down onto the books as he sank his tongue between my lips.

My heart beat matched the rampant beat of his own and excitement tangled with my veins at the thought of doing this here.

"I wanna hear what your screams sound like filling up this whole room and echoing back to me," Orion said against my mouth, nudging my knees apart as he stepped between them and slipped a hand up my skirt.

My back arched before he even touched me, his knuckles rubbing over the damp spot on my panties, my body always so ready for him. He growled carnally then pushed my panties aside and sank three fingers mercilessly inside me.

"Oh god," I gasped.

"Good girl," he growled, teasing me as he drew his fingers in and out of me so slowly I whimpered.

"More," I commanded, reaching for his belt, but he caught my wrist, placing my hand against the swell of his cock through his jeans and making me feel every inch of him through the rough material.

"If you want more, you're gonna ask for it nicely." He smirked, driving his fingers into me deeper and holding them there as I panted for him.

"Please," I said breathlessly and a heady look entered his eyes at me begging him.

He released my wrist and I kept my hand on his cock, squeezing and caressing him through his jeans while keeping one hand behind me to support myself, my body half upright as he stepped closer to spread my legs wider for him.

He pushed my skirt higher so he could watch his hand fuck me, a greedy look on his face as he wet his lips.

I held my lower lip between my teeth to stop myself from making too much noise, fearing the echo in this enormous part of the library, but Orion reached out, pressing his thumb down on my lip and yanking it free.

"Don't hold out on me, how will I know if you're enjoying yourself if I don't hear you scream?" he taunted, curling his fingers deep inside me as I swallowed another moan and bucked my hips.

"You know, asshole," I panted and he grinned, his face half cast in shadow as he leaned over me.

"Yeah, I know," he admitted, his thumb circling over my clit, making my whole body arch. "I know exactly what you like."

"Then give it to me," I demanded and he laughed loudly, letting his voice carry through the stacks and making a blush rise in my cheeks.

"Keep your commands for when you're ruling the kingdom, beautiful," he said, his eyes running over my body slowly, taking in everything before him before his gaze met mine again. "But when we're fucking, I'm in charge. And when you're a queen and everyone in Solaria worships you, I will be the only one allowed to worship you like this. Do you understand?"

He circled his thumb faster against my clit and I rode his hand, crying out and losing complete control of my body as my climax built so fast, I couldn't stop the noises leaving my throat, the sound echoing around the entire library. I could feel his eyes on me the whole time as I tumbled through a wave of pleasure, his fingers driving in and out of me until I was spent and collapsed on top of the books.

Orion pulled his hand free and took hold of my wrists, pinning them above my head and casting cuffs of ice around them, binding them in place with an ice chain and locking them against the table.

He squeezed my breasts through my top and took his time to drag his hands along the curves of my hips before spreading my thighs, tearing my panties clean off of me and stepping between them.

"I liked those ones," I complained as he pocketed the pale pink material with a light shrug.

"I prefer them in pieces." He freed his cock, watching me as he stroked the huge length of it and I shifted my hips in anticipation of him, my heart beating like crazy in my chest.

He lined himself up with my core, pushing the head of his thick cock inside me and making me gasp as he drove in so slow it made my head spin.

"Fuck," he groaned as he filled me up, his hands sliding beneath me to grip my ass and draw me flush to him.

A loud moan left me as he hit some deeply sensitive spot inside me and he thrust his hips to do it again, reading me so freaking well. It was like he was in tune with my body, knowing what I liked better than I knew it myself as he started to fuck me towards another high that was promising to throw me into oblivion.

I watched his powerful body move as he stood above me, his eyes burning into mine as I gave up on trying to hold my cries back, letting them fall from my lungs and getting off on how that made him groan. He was so hard inside me and my body was gripping him with every thrust, wanting more and more of his beautiful cock as he filled me up.

I tugged against the restraints he'd bound my hands in as he wet his fingers with water magic and started to massage my clit, light bursting before my eyes as I fell at his mercy. He was relentless, tormenting me with his body as he drew me close to the edge then pulled me back again, not letting me dive into bliss.

He smiled wickedly at me like he knew exactly what he was doing, which of course he fucking did. But when he finally pushed me off the cliff, I had to be grateful, because my orgasm hit me harder than a bus, pleasure pounding through me and humming within my veins.

He fucked me through every second of it as my moans echoed all around us, my legs locked tight around his waist as he drove into me again and again, his pace picking up as he chased his own release.

I burned through the cuffs on my wrists, rearing up and dragging him down on top of me, my hips moving in time with his as he lost control and the heat of his body weighed against mine. He was an animal, my wild creature born to rule my flesh and devour me like a god dipped in sin.

His shoulders tensed then he stilled within me, coming with a deep groan that lit me up from the inside out. His heat seeped between my thighs as he pumped in and out of me in two final drives of his cock that made me shiver all over.

His mouth found mine and I held him as the world seemed to fall entirely silent and all that existed in this cavernous room was us.

"I'd burn every one of these books for you," he said against my mouth and I pushed my fingers into his hair, sinking my tongue between his lips.

"When I'm queen, I'm going to buy you this library," I decided and he lifted his head, his eyes sparkling with surprise. "Then you can do whatever you like with these books, because they'll be all yours."

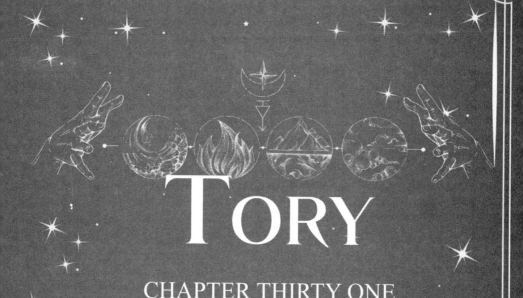

TORY

CHAPTER THIRTY ONE

I finished up my morning run with a sigh and dropped forward, bracing my hands on my knees as I caught my breath and Darius mirrored me at my side.

"You're determined to make me work as hard as I possibly can, aren't you?" he teased and I smiled at him.

"Well I can't go easy on you just because we're fucking," I replied.

"Oh, is that what we're doing?" he asked, his eyes flashing with that dangerous kind of heat that was probably meant as a warning but always seemed more like a red flag to the Tory bull within me.

"Did you or did you not spend the better part of last night buried between my thighs, Darius Acrux?" I taunted. "Because if you don't call that fucking then I don't know what it was."

Darius straightened and stalked towards me, his gaze dark and promising me I'd pay for that dismissive remark, but I was happy to stand my ground.

"No, Roxanya Vega, I don't call that fucking," he replied. "I call that worshipping my goddess. I call it making love to the most beautiful woman in all of Solaria, I call it penance for all the bad things I've done to you and the least I can offer in retribution for the harm I caused you. But most of all, I call it loving you with the intensity of the sun and the devotion of the moon because you are my end, baby. The only dream I never dared to have for myself. Yet here you are, within reach at all times. And you'd better believe I can't resist you now that I have you. I plan on marking every inch of your flesh so thoroughly with the memory of my touch that you'll never be able to forget it."

"Why would I ever forget it?" I asked him with a frown and his brow lowered as he continued to hold my gaze.

"We're at war, Roxy," he said slowly. "And I can't believe that the stars would be so kind as to let us all see the other side of it. One way or another, I will take on my father and destroy him to negate the threat he poses to all of us. But that pledge doesn't come without risk. You have to know that."

"Well I forbid it," I replied, moving forward so that I could taste his breath on the air between us and fisting my hand in the sleeveless hoody he'd worn to run in.

"I wish that you could. But either way I intend to live every day to the fullest of its potential and to do all that I can to ensure we win this war."

"Like training me and your brother until all hours and using magic to stop yourself from sleeping?" I asked, arching a brow at him because if he thought I hadn't noticed the fact that he'd basically gone on a sleep strike since we'd arrived at The Burrows then he was mistaken.

Darius hesitated then sighed, reaching out to wrap his large hand around my throat and tilting my chin up as he held me there. It was dominating and possessive, but it was somehow tender and loving too, the caress of his rough fingers against my pulse point making my heart skitter and my cocky front slip away as I fell into the intensity of his gaze.

"I just don't want to have any regrets," he murmured, drinking me in. "I need you to know how much I love you. I need you to understand that the only place I would ever want to be is right here with you, no matter what happens. And if I do die in this war, taking on my father, then I need you to understand how much I loved you-"

"Stop talking like that or I'm gonna have to smack you," I warned and he breathed a laugh.

"Of course you would resort to violence to prove how much you don't like the idea of me getting hurt," he joked.

"Yeah well, death can't have you because I already staked my claim."

"Bullshit," he replied, his fingers shifting so that he tilted my chin up and lined his mouth up with mine, letting me feel the brush of his words against my lips. "If you'd claimed me then we'd be married already."

A breath lodged in my throat and a surprised laugh spilled from me. "You're insane. I'm nineteen."

"Twenty next week," he pointed out and I shook my head, but not as forcefully as I should have.

"Why not just go the whole hog and you can knock me up too?" I challenged.

"If you're offering I wouldn't complain," he replied, his hand brushing against my flat and very much unoccupied stomach, his voice so fucking serious that I could only part my lips in shock and stare at him.

"Maybe just the wedding then," he conceded with a dry laugh as he leaned forward to claim a kiss from my startled lips and I half shook my head and half melted into a puddle for him.

"You're fucking crazy," I muttered as he drew back.

"No, Roxy. I just know what I want and it's you. In any way I can have you and every way you'll offer. So if I can get you to be my bride then I'll fucking take it. If you never want to get married, then I'll take that too. If you didn't want me this close and all I was left with was the option to watch you and hunger for you from afar the way I had to when we were Star Crossed, then I'd take that as well. It's you, Roxy. Only you. So here I am and I'm yours. The rest of it is up to you."

I drank in the honesty in his dark eyes like I was a sponge in such desperate need of it that all I could do was soak it up and let it fill all of those dark, unworthy corners of my heart which I'd believed were an unchangeable part of me for so long. I'd never even dared to hope for someone to love me the way he was professing to right now and looking at it in his gaze unlocked something in me which I'd feared I would never come to have.

"There is only him," I breathed, lingering in that look he was giving me and knowing that I was in trouble with this man. Because he was right. No matter how long I planned on dragging this out and trying to convince myself that we were taking our time and getting to know each other better, I already knew all there was to know of him. Hell, we'd been shacked up together for almost six months and there was never a day where this heat between us had dimmed or my hunger for him had faltered. We were all in. So marriage, kids, all that crazy shit that people did when they knew they'd found the one was on the cards for us if we wanted it. But I was still planning on winning this war first.

Darius broke a smile, tilting his head to the side as he looked me over and slowly removed his hand from my throat, releasing me from the spell of his touch.

"No weddings, got it," he said, smirking at me with that cocky look in his eyes which I knew meant he thought he'd won a point here, but I wasn't going to let him leave me on the back foot.

I leaned in close and kissed him again, the demand of our lips and the scratch of his stubble making my skin prickle before I stepped back and offered him a single word.

"Yet."

I turned on my heel and strode away while the shock settled into his features, and I laughed as he called out after me.

I made the ground shake at his feet as I took off running back towards The Burrows, another laugh tumbling from my lips at the game as he took chase, shooting water after me which splashed against the air shield I threw up at my back.

I made it into the farmhouse, racing through the door past the startled looking guards and swinging around a corner before yanking open the doorway hidden behind the grandfather clock and leaping through it.

I slammed the door behind me and ran a few more steps down the darkened tunnel then skidded to a halt as the sound of his footsteps thundering along behind me made my pulse skip.

I pressed my back to the stone wall, casting a concealment spell around myself and wielding my earth magic so that the rock wall grew around me, shifting to hide me from view a moment before Darius threw the door open.

He took off running down the corridor and I held my breath, working to hide my presence as he drew closer to my hiding place and I stifled a laugh. But just as I thought I'd gotten away with the game, he jerked to a halt, his arm flying out and hooking me around the waist as he yanked me against his chest.

"You can't hide from me, Roxy," he growled, kissing me hard before I could reply and pushing me back against the wall.

I moaned into his mouth as he gripped my thighs and lifted me up, crushing me against the stone and kissing me breathless as his hard cock ground against me and let me know exactly what he was thinking of doing instead of getting breakfast.

"You need to work on your concealment spells," he murmured against my lips.

"No doubt you could do better," I replied.

"I could conceal us so well that no one would even hear you screaming as you came all over my dick, let alone see you panting for me against this wall," he said cockily and fuck me, I was tempted to take him up on that offer.

He kissed me again as I locked my ankles behind his back, moaning at the feeling of him grinding against me as his powerful body pinned me to the wall, but before I could get too lost in that idea, a strangled scream and beastly howl echoed through the tunnel and made my heart freeze in my chest.

We broke apart breathlessly, both of us looking down into the darkness of the tunnel where the unearthly howl sounded again.

"That doesn't sound like a Werewolf," I said, gripping Darius's forearms as he continued to hold me against the wall.

"No, it doesn't," he replied with a frown.

The scream came again, pleas for help filling the air and making a shiver dart down my spine.

Darius released me in an instant, my feet hitting the floor as a growl spilled from his lips and his eyes shifted into his golden Dragon form, the beast in him rising to the surface of his skin.

"Stay close and stay behind me," he commanded.

"That'll be a fuck no, dude," I replied, shouldering him to one side as I took the lead and started running down the tunnel with him at my back.

Darius breathed down my neck as he was forced to follow me and we turned down a side chamber where the screams were getting louder and more desperate. They cut off with a gurgled cry which turned to choking and the roar of some enormous Order form rattled through the air, making my spine straighten and magic flare in my fingertips as we closed in on the source of the sound.

We made it to the end of the passageway which was used to store supplies and I reached for the handle of the slightly open door where the sound of a huge creature ripping into flesh greeted us.

Darius caught my shoulder and shoved me behind him as he stepped through the door first, fire flaring in his other fist and making me squint against the sudden brightness of the light in the dark tunnel as the back of a huge, hairy beast was revealed beyond the stacked crates of supplies in the darkest corner of the room.

"Hey!" Darius barked, the fire shining brighter, but as the beast whirled around it knocked into the crates, sending them flying towards us and making me throw my hands up to protect us with a blast of air as we narrowly avoided getting crushed.

The moment they'd stopped falling, I dropped my shield and Darius vaulted over the closest crate, cursing as he reached the far side of the room and I followed quickly, bile rising in my throat as I spotted the bloody remains of the woman who I had to assume was the one who had been calling for help.

"It went that way," Darius said, leaping over more crates and charging down another tunnel which led off of this one.

I knelt down, feeling the woman's wrist for a pulse but finding none as

I took hold of her arm, the blood from the huge claw marks which had been torn into her chest soaking into the knee of my leggings.

I stood again and turned to run after Darius, knowing there was nothing I could do for her now and taking chase after the sound of his footsteps which were heading away from me into the dark.

Darius swore up ahead and I ran after him as fast as I could go, rounding a corner and almost slamming straight into him as I found him standing at a section of intersecting passageways and scowling around at them.

"I dunno where the fuck it went," he said, casting an amplification spell but all that brought to us was the sound of people heading to the dining hall and making noises in their chambers, nothing of the beast we'd been chasing.

"What the hell was it?" I asked, looking around like I might spot some clue as to which passage it had taken but there was nothing to make any suggestion as to where it had gone.

"I dunno. I only caught a glimpse of it. Something big and hairy - a Monolrian Bear or a Cerberus maybe."

"A Nemean Lion could be that big," I breathed, looking around. "Should we keep hunting?"

Darius considered that for a moment then shook his head. "Let's go warn the others, if there are more of us looking for it then we will have a better chance of tracking the thing down."

I nodded my agreement and Darius took my hand, tugging me along behind him as we took off running back towards the main section of The Burrows.

We headed through the slowly gathering crowd in the dining hall then ran into the royal quarters and kept on straight towards Darcy and Orion's room.

Darius hammered on the door, yanking it open and breaking through the spell put there to lock it when they didn't reply quickly enough.

"I'll bite ya ass," Orion slurred sleepily as he shoved himself upright in the bed, blinking at us in confusion.

"Wake up. There's been another murder," Darius demanded, tugging me further into the room and slapping Seth on his hairy ass where he slept in his shifted form at the foot of the large bed.

"Where's Darcy?" I asked, looking around in alarm and Orion frowned as he glanced at the other side of the bed just as Darcy pushed the blankets off of her head and peeked out at us.

"Here," she muttered, scrubbing sleep from her eyes in a daze. "Did you say murder?"

"Yeah. And we saw the thing that did it, though we didn't get a great look, but it was a big Shifter with a massive hairy back so we can narrow it down a bit," Darius replied as Seth shifted and sat up to look at us, his dick on full display.

"It killed a woman in the supply caverns near the entrance to the tunnels," I added. "We heard her screaming for help but didn't get there in time."

"Alright. Let's get back on the hunt," Orion said firmly. "I'll go get Cal and we can make a plan."

"Since when did you start calling him Cal?" Seth asked, a whine in the back of his throat but Orion shot away without comment.

"It's probably just a blood brother thing," I said, dismissively. "Can you put your dick away now?"

"I call him Cal," Seth complained, getting to his feet and looking like he wanted to go chasing after Orion to join in with them.

"Everyone calls him Cal, dude," I pointed out, but Seth just tipped his head to the roof and howled.

"Let me get dressed and I'll be ready to go," Darcy said, hopping out of bed and moving to get some clothes while Darius grabbed a pair of sweatpants from the floor and tossed them into Seth's lap.

"Stop sitting there naked in front of my girl or I'll burn it off," he muttered distractedly, turning to look at the door just as it pushed open and Caleb and Orion shot inside laughing and nudging one another.

"What's the joke?" Seth asked, jumping up and pulling his pants on while looking between the Vampires with hope in his eyes.

"You kinda had to be there," Caleb laughed, shaking his head as he exchanged a look with his new bestie and I rolled my eyes at them.

"Is everyone ready to go?" I asked and the others agreed, though Seth was still pouting as we headed out of the room in hunt of the others. Max had taken to helping Geraldine with her bagels in the mornings and Hamish and Catalina were always overseeing the kitchens too, so we made our way back to the dining hall quickly.

Caleb and Orion raced ahead of us to let the others know what was going on and by the time we caught up, Hamish was amplifying his voice throughout the entire rebel sanctuary and demanding everyone return to their rooms once more.

"Who needs help from a little one?" Washer called, pushing his way through the crowd towards us in a lycra leopard print shirt with a zip down the centre of it in place of buttons. A zip which was open so low that his freaking nipples were on display. He was looking extra sun baked thanks to the nice weather we'd been having which had drawn him out to naked sunbathe at all hours of the damn day on the roof of the barn outside. He claimed he went up there for privacy, but it just meant that all of us flying orders were gifted a free show of his teeny weeny whenever we came in to land after exercising up there which was just freaking great.

"Ew, no," I said, shifting away from him but his gaze zeroed in on us all the same.

"Oh, poor, sweet girls, are you in need of some help processing the trauma of there being yet another murdered body amongst the people who followed you here in hope of refuge?" he asked, opening his arms for a hug and I bristled at that suggestion.

"It's not on us that there's some psycho running about this place," Darcy said angrily. "And no, we don't want any help processing anything from you."

Washer sighed and turned away to go offer his slippery hugs to some other Fae and I watched him sashay away with a shudder.

Darius and Orion started barking orders to everyone on how they wanted the search conducted and I offered to show Hamish where the body had been left.

Darius caught my wrist and tugged me close, kissing me hard and looking into my eyes. "Stay with Darcy and use your Phoenix fire on any asshole who so much as looks at you wrong."

"I'm a big girl, Darius, I got this," I assured him, and he narrowed his eyes at me before nodding sharply and turning away to start the hunt once more.

"You need the breakfast of queens before you head off on your gruesome quest, my ladies!" Geraldine cried, thrusting two plates of buttery bagels at us and I accepted mine with a word of thanks, my stomach rumbling after my run this morning.

The other Heirs and Geraldine headed after Darius and Orion, and Darcy moved to my side, giving my fingers a little squeeze as I headed back through the tunnels towards the body.

"Are you okay?" she asked as I took a bite out of my bagel.

"Yeah. Just a little freaked out that this thing is still roaming the tunnels and we haven't caught it yet," I replied as Hamish started muttering about all of the vengeful, fruit based punishments he planned on offering the scoundrel who had done this once he apprehended them.

I made it through my own bagel and Darcy offered me hers as she noticed me licking my fingers, claiming she was still full from her dinner, and I wasn't gonna complain about free food so I gladly accepted it.

When we reached the room where the woman had been killed, we hung back, letting Hamish head inside to investigate and waiting as he cried out in horror at the sight of the butchered body.

"How are you feeling today?" I asked Darcy as we lingered in the corridor, unsure how to help any further now and wondering if we should go join the others on the hunt.

We'd been working to try and burn the curse out of her every day, merging our Phoenix fire and encouraging it to rush through her body in a similar way to how I'd managed to burn the Dark Coercion from Darius and his family. We were hopeful that it was making a difference, though it left her feeling wiped out every time we finished.

"Better I think," she said. "Though I'm still exhausted."

"You sure that doesn't have more to do with the Vampire in your bed?"

"With Seth sitting there with front row seats? No thanks." She wrinkled her nose and I laughed at that visual.

"Yeah...I get that. But maybe some more rest will help?" I suggested and she sighed.

"I don't want to rest - I want to fight," she replied firmly and I nodded, agreeing with that.

"Well if it isn't my favourite sisters," Gabriel called and we both looked up as we found him striding down the corridor towards us, shirt off, wings out. "Destiny is calling your names."

"What's that supposed to mean?" I asked, kicking off of the wall I'd been leaning against to see him better.

"The stars haven't told me much, but they did say this: it's time for you to visit The Palace of Flames."

Darcy's eyes widened in surprise and her lips popped open. "Really?"

"I thought that place was just ruins now?" I asked, a shiver of anticipation running along my flesh.

"It is," Gabriel agreed. "But apparently the ghosts of your ancestors have some secrets to share with you."

"Right now?" Darcy asked and he nodded.

"I've left a note for the others. Come now, or fate may shift again and you'll lose this chance."

I exchanged a look with my sister but we were both already moving towards him, the heat of our Phoenixes burning brightly beneath our skin at the thought of heading to their homeland.

"Sounds like we need to get going then," I said excitedly and Darcy grinned widely as we hurried to join our brother.

Gabriel slung his arms around our shoulders, guiding us towards the exit and leading us back outside through the farmhouse until we made it to the other side of the barrier where he pulled a pouch of stardust from his pocket.

"Shouldn't we fly to save the stardust?" Darcy asked, twisting her fingers together.

Since Lionel's restrictions had been put on the stuff, we were finding it harder and harder to get enough to complete supply runs for the rebels, and we had all taken to travelling without it as often as we could manage.

"Not on this journey," Gabriel replied. "But I'm certain it will be worth it."

He tossed the handful of glimmering stardust over our heads and we were whipped away through the stars before finally landing in the sweltering heat of a jungle with animal sounds all around us and humidity making the air seem to press in on us from all sides.

"Where the hell are we?" I asked curiously as Gabriel set off through the trees, seeming to know exactly where he was going, either through the help of The Sight or something else.

"We're somewhere in the far south," he hedged. "Likely not even in Solaria anymore, though I don't actually know for certain. I only know how to get here thanks to my visions letting me *see* enough to travel here via stardust and I haven't visited often. Once, several years ago I was in desperate need of something to help me free my mind from the bonds of a monster and the stars told me to come here. That's where I got my Phoenix Kiss." He held his hand out to show me the tattooed ring of Phoenix wings which circled his finger much like the one I'd gifted to Darius in the form of a bangle.

"Was there a Phoenix here who gave it to you?" I asked, my eyebrows arching as hope filled me, but he quickly shook his head.

"No. I took the ring from the hand of a skeleton I found within the ruins below the actual palace. It would seem that the gift returns to its metallic form upon the death of the person who was offered it, meaning I could claim it for myself. I suspect the magic in it is hundreds if not a thousand years old and yet it still burns with all the heat of a shooting star."

"That's incredible," Darcy murmured, her arm brushing mine as we walked side by side.

"It is. But I would hazard a guess that it is only one of countless treasures hidden here within The Palace of Flames. But I don't believe that any of those secrets are intended for me."

"You think our ancestors wanted us to come here?" Darcy asked, her voice filled with awe though my natural cynicism had to lay doubts to that suspicion.

"This place has lain in ruins for hundreds of years, Darcy. I seriously doubt they've been waiting for our slow asses to show up here all that damn time. More likely they'd offer up this same chance to any Phoenixes who had Emerged in the time since their kind fell. But considering the fact that there haven't been any of our Order born in all that time, it's fallen to us instead."

Darcy and Gabriel exchanged a look which I knew was about my sceptical attitude and I flipped them off, causing them to snigger at my expense as we kept pushing through the overgrown jungle towards something Gabriel seemed certain was there - despite the fact that there was nothing to suggest we would find anything but more lush greenery ahead of us.

A shock of power suddenly rolled over us and I sucked in a breath as it hummed and buzzed through my flesh, feeling like the touch of a thousand kisses on my skin and making my hair damn near stand on end.

"Descendants of the royal line," a voice filled with unearthly power spoke within my mind and one look at Darcy confirmed that she could hear it too. *"Bringers of a new dawn. Seekers of the past."*

I gritted my jaw as the power thrummed with more energy, making my whole body tense up as it seemed to dig its way right down to my bones, hunting down the heart of me and measuring what it found.

"The time for you to rise is close."

The power released its hold on me and I stumbled forward a step, catching Gabriel's hand as he held it out to me like he'd already seen me falling and was waiting to catch me. Darcy fully collided with him and he held her on her feet too, chuckling a little as she swore.

"The magic that lingers here is ancient and impossibly powerful," he said, like that wasn't terrifying at all. "Come. The Palace of Flames is waiting."

"Because a palace waiting for us isn't at all creepy or concerning," I muttered, following as he walked on. "Inanimate objects just hang around and wait for us now."

Darcy breathed a laugh and I grinned at her as we strode forward along a path which was lined in bronze metal that peeked out from beneath the overgrown foliage. My entire body seemed to buzz with a vibrant kind of energy as if the stones themselves were sentient and they knew that we were here.

"A lot of the palace is beneath the ground now – there are tunnels which lead to any number of places, though the few times I have visited here before, the stars guided me exactly to where I needed to go," Gabriel explained as we reached a fork in the path, one trail leading right towards what looked like a dark cave which cut into the rocks while the other twisted left where I swear I could sense a huge building just lurking out of sight through the trees.

"We need to go that way," I said, pointing to the left where an enormous golden gate stood closed and tangled with vines and other jungle greenery. It was almost impossible to make out and yet the moment I looked at it, I just knew it was there, almost like I'd been here before but I sure as fuck hadn't.

Darcy nodded her agreement, clearly feeling the same pull on her power that I was, the sensation tugging like a cord tied behind my navel, urging me onwards.

As Gabriel pulled a final swathe of vines aside, I couldn't help but suck in a breath as my gaze fell fully upon the ancient entryway to The Palace of Flames.

"Wow," Darcy breathed while I cursed in a way that was a whole lot less civilised.

The jungle had done a good job of trying to conceal what had clearly once been a stunning palace built with yellow stone which sparkled with veins of quartz and looked golden in the light of the sun that blazed above us through the trees.

Gabriel stepped aside as Darcy and I strode forward, moving towards the gate while the thick foliage brushed at our legs, leaving them damp with moisture.

A monkey started hollering in the trees above us and I craned my neck to look up, spotting some colourful birds sweeping between the branches and making my eyes widen with wonder.

We made it to the gate and I reached out to grasp it at the same moment Darcy did, connecting to our earth magic and encouraging the vines to slither off of the metal, making the jungle retreat until the tall, golden gates stood clear before us.

The moment we withdrew our hands, the gate parted, swinging open with an echoing clang which made the animals in the jungle screech and race away through the trees.

A courtyard opened up beyond it, the walls of some huge structure just visible on the far side of the cobbles.

"This is where I leave you," Gabriel said, drawing my attention back to him where he stood behind us.

"Leave?" Darcy questioned sadly and he nodded.

"You will stay here until you have unlocked the secrets of your kind and learned to fight like your ancestors once did. In fire, blood and bone. The Phoenix will always rise."

Those last words rang with a toll of truth to them that had my hair standing on end as the creature within me awoke, raising her head to the challenge that had just been laid out for us.

"How long will that take?" I asked and Gabriel concentrated for a moment as he sought out the answer from the stars themselves.

"It's hard to tell. A month, a year...the power will take time to understand and accepting it is half the battle. There are lessons you must learn here and it is up to you how fast you do so. Find your inner Fae and listen to them. The guiding star will bring you to a place of peace and when the time is right, you will emerge ready to fight on."

"A year?" Darcy balked. "We're in the middle of a damn war, Gabriel. And I don't want to be away from everyone for that long." She was clearly thinking of Orion and I felt the exact same way about Darius. We'd only just gotten our shit together, I didn't want to be away from him for who knew how long.

"Yeah, that's insane," I said, taking a step away from the gates though that cord which seemed to be trying to draw me through them yanked harder at my resistance. "We can't just disappear for some ridiculous amount of time while Lionel is out there doing fuck knows what-"

"This is important," Gabriel said firmly. "If you turn from those gates now, they will close forever. The stars are offering you this one chance and if you turn from this path, I *see* only darkness in your futures. You need the knowledge hidden here. You need to finish growing into the Fae you must become if you ever hope to take the crown and rule with the true grace and power of queens deserving of it."

"But...there's nothing here. No one has lived here for a thousand years - what are we supposed to eat?" I asked because this place might have been beautiful and fascinating and all that jazz, but a luxury holiday destination it was not.

"The stars will provide," he replied mysteriously, and I narrowed my eyes on him because that was bullshit.

"The stars have only ever provided me with grief," I muttered as Darcy looked around at the gates again.

"I can feel the power of this place," she said in a low voice. "Do you think we can really learn all there is to know about our Phoenixes here?" I could see the hope glimmering in her eyes and I knew she was thinking of the curse, wondering if this was the place where we would figure out how to end it for good so that she could return to her full strength, ready to ride into battle and rip Lavinia's damn head off in payment for landing her with it.

"I can feel it too," I agreed, my irritation over the ridiculousness of us having to stay here for some extended period of time without coffee melting away as I began to wonder if this really could be where she needed to come to end the curse. We were working daily to burn through it, but she had read that a tribe of Phoenixes could do that. We weren't a tribe, we were only two. Maybe here, we could find some stronger power to help us. To help *her*.

"It's time for you to claim all of your strength," Gabriel said firmly, and I blew out a long breath as I looked through the golden gates to the cobbled courtyard beyond. There was an open doorway on the other side of it set between two pillars which held more of the golden bricks, casting the interior of the palace into shadow so that we were unable to see what lay within. But I knew we couldn't investigate any further than that. Stepping beyond the threshold of this gate would be us making a choice, and I got the feeling that we wouldn't be able to change our minds once it was made.

"Tell Lance not to worry about me," Darcy said, making up her mind. "We'll work hard to learn everything we can here and return quickly."

I nodded my agreement, swallowing thickly as I prepared myself to step over the threshold.

"Do you have a message for Darius?" Gabriel prompted me and my skin prickled at the idea of that.

"Just...tell him not to be a dick while I'm gone," I muttered.

"Seems unlikely, but I'll tell him," Gabriel replied. "Shall I pass on a message of your unending love too or just the dick thing?"

I cut him a narrow eyed look and he broke a laugh.

"Fine," I huffed. "Tell him I love him *and* he can't be a dick while I'm gone. Good enough for you, asshole?"

"It brings a tear to my eye," Gabriel said, placing his hand on his heart mockingly and I rolled my eyes at him.

Gabriel moved forward, wrapping the two of us in his arms and squeezing us tightly before placing kisses on our heads.

"You'll be the best queens Solaria has ever had," he said fiercely, keeping us in the cage of his arms a moment longer as I breathed a laugh.

"Have you *seen* that?" Darcy asked curiously and he grinned as he stepped back.

"No. But I feel it in my soul."

Darcy gave me a hesitant smile, reaching out to take my hand and I turned back to look at the gates once more.

"Well, here goes nothing," I said in a low voice and we stepped forward over the threshold.

Magic rang through the air, making my body burn hot with the heat of my Phoenix and forcing the shift on me so suddenly that it burned right through my clothes, coating my body in blue and red flames and making my wings burst from my spine.

Darcy gasped as she was forced to shift too, her hand tightening around mine as the gates clanged shut at our backs with a finality that left me in no doubt that they wouldn't be opening again until we had finished whatever our task here was.

"Welcome home, fire born," a commanding, female voice called, the air trembling at the sound which seemed to come from all around us and from nowhere at once. *"It's time for you to learn the path of the flames."*

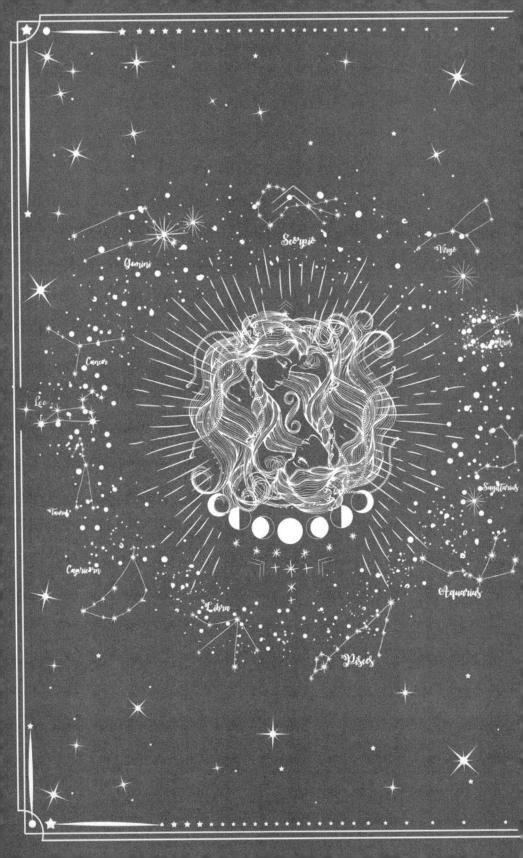

DARCY

CHAPTER THIRTY TWO

We walked through an overgrown courtyard, but with every footstep we took, the vines and weeds retreated, exposing an ancient mosaic on the ground of a Phoenix dancing with its own flames. A stone fountain stood at the heart of it, a Phoenix bird rising from the centre of it and as we approached, fresh water bursting from its beak.

"There seems to be a theme here," Tory muttered.

"Phoenixes?" I guessed through a laugh and she snorted.

We turned towards the dark doorway which was thick with shadow, creeping inside and the moment our feet touched the flagstones, fires burst to life in the sconces all along the walls.

We followed the fire deeper into the ancient palace, turning past another old courtyard in the centre of it where a tall tree stood, casting it in shade. On its branches were large green mangoes and I wondered if that was what we were going to be eating down here.

Despite the place seeming to come alive at our touch, I didn't understand what we were supposed to learn from simply being here.

Two stone doors opened ahead of us and we shared a look before tiptoeing through them and gazing around at the enormous throne room we were in. The throne was made of a ruby red glass, its back carved into the shape of two huge Phoenix wings. Upon it, lay a single feather, the bronze colour seeming to glint with a fire that burned within it. An arching window beyond the throne sat high up on the pale walls and sunlight filtered through the room in slanted rays.

I stayed close to Tory as we approached the throne and I reached out to touch the feather.

The moment my skin connected with it, the feather fluttered away from me, spinning up in the air right before our eyes as a shimmering red and blue light built around it.

We staggered backwards as the feather suddenly shifted and a goddess of a woman took its place, sitting on the throne with her bronze wings stretched out either side of her, her body clad in armour similar to the kind Geraldine had gifted us. Her hair was as dark as charcoal, her skin a rich brown hue and she had a mouth that seemed used to smiling. At first it seemed like she was solidly there until her wings folded behind her and I realised I could almost see through her.

"Descendants," she sighed, her beautiful features lifting with happiness, her eyes so bright they burned. "Finally, you have come."

"Um, hi," I said and Tory raised her hand in a two finger wave.

The apparition looked between us then threw her head back and laughed so loudly it filled up the room.

Tory and I shared a glance, backing up another step as the woman got to her feet, smiling eagerly at us.

"You don't know who I am, do you?" she asked and we both shook our heads, but then I frowned, realising she did seem kind of familiar, though I couldn't place her. "Perhaps this will help you." She raised a hand flicking her finger and a beautiful crown appeared there that was so stunning it stole my breath, the platinum set with deep red and blue stones which made the fire coating my skin flare hotter.

"You're a queen?" Tory guessed and I gasped as I suddenly remembered where I'd seen her before. In Lavinia's memories.

"She's the Vega queen I saw in Diego's hat. She's the one who banished Lavinia to the Shadow Realm," I said and the queen's eyes darkened at that name.

"Yes, I am Avalon Vega," she confirmed. "Or at least, I was. Now, I am nothing more than a spirit summoned back to this place to assist my descendants." She smiled warmly at us, reaching out to touch my cheek and I shivered at the tingling against my skin, though I didn't feel anything of her fingers. She touched her hand to Tory's shoulder next and my sister shivered as the queen assessed her.

"Lavinia has risen again, yes?" she asked, a bite to her tone.

"Yeah, she's risen alright," Tory said as her upper lip curled back. "And she's playing house with Lionel Acrux."

"Acrux," the queen growled. "Yes…I see it now. The stars are offering me the knowledge I need to help you. So many years," she sighed. "Empires have risen and fallen in the time I have been gone." She gasped at something, then her eyes snapped to the Imperial Star hanging from my throat. "You possess it."

I touched the star protectively, nodding as the queen stepped closer with a hunger in her eyes. I wasn't going to be letting some back-from-the-dead ghost woman steal it.

"You must never let it go," Avalon said firmly, looking between us. "It will be your greatest gift when you ascend." She reached out, brushing her fingers against it like she wished she could take hold of it.

I shifted back a little, clearing my throat. "We had to go through a lot to get this."

"Yes, there is always a price to possess greatness," she said, her hand falling to her side as she looked between us once more. "Goodness…you will pay such a price for one of you to rule. What a curse twins have when they vie for the same goal."

My hand shot out the same time Tory's did, our fingers clasping in unity.

"The only reason we're going for the throne is to destroy Lionel and Lavinia so we can restore peace to Solaria," Tory growled.

Queen Avalon smiled sadly. "For now, but when the time comes, you will both want the throne, and you will fight to claim it from each other."

"We'll never fight each other," I said fiercely.

"Power is the root of our kind," Queen Avalon said softly. "There is no shame in choosing it over our siblings. It is the way of Fae. I fought my brother for this very throne," she said.

"Well, we're not like you," Tory said and the queen's eyes flashed onto her, but not with anger, just curiosity.

"Perhaps…or perhaps not," she said. "Either way, I have much to teach, much you need to know if you are to defeat my old rival."

"What happened to us? To the Phoenixes?" I asked. "Why did they die out?"

She hesitated for a second before answering. "I died before our kind was lost."

"But you said the stars have filled you in on the years that passed after you died. So what happened?" Tory pressed.

"I…cannot say."

"Because you don't know, or because you won't tell us?" I asked in frustration.

"I do not know," she said then swept past us, her wings passing through our bodies as she practically glided across the floor. "Come now, I have much to teach you. You must be trained in the ways of our kind. You must learn of our gifts, you must be ready for any opponent."

"How did you know we'd come here?" Tory called as we jogged after her our skin still burning with the fire of our Order.

"It was a prophecy gifted to me by a great Seer," she said without looking back. "I knew one day my descendants would rise, and I knew you would come to me ignorant and in need at a time when Lavinia returned from where I banished her. I bound myself to this place when I died so that I could return to train you, to teach you to fight as I can fight, to rule as I have ruled."

"Keep the broken promise."

The whispered words echoed through my head and Tory stiffened as if she'd heard them too, looking to me in alarm. Those very words had been spoken to our father Hail Vega from the Imperial Star.

"Did it just…" I looked down at the star, taking it into my palm as we walked, the flames on my fingers licking it fondly while leaving it and the chain it hung from intact.

"Come now," Queen Avalon called like she hadn't heard a thing, drifting out of the room and leading us into the courtyard where the large fruit tree stood. "It is time for your first lesson."

The woman came to a halt beneath the tree, raising a palm and casting a ghost of Phoenix fire in her palm. The flames shifted, growing larger and larger before splitting away from her body into a fully fledged Phoenix bird, the creature flying all around us, spilling trails of blue and red fire everywhere it went. It opened its beak and released a beautiful cry that filled the air and sent a quake through the entire palace.

I shared an excited look with Tory and we waited eagerly to be taught how to do that.

Queen Avalon smiled at us. "This will take some time to learn, but the power of your Phoenix fire cannot be fully unlocked until you are able to set it free like this."

"We're ready," Tory said and I nodded, raising my hands in preparation.

The queen of old moved toward us and my heart hammered in anticipation of all we were about to learn. And I realised that within these walls, the grip of the curse barely seemed to have a hold on me at all. So perhaps when we were done here, I'd break free of it for good.

ORION

CHAPTER THIRTY THREE

"**I**'m gonna gut them," Darius growled in my ear as he clung to my back and I shot around The Burrows at high speed, hunting for the murderer as we had been for the past couple of hours.

The asshole had run from the scene of the crime, but they couldn't be far. They had to be somewhere close and the metallic scent in the air said they were still wet with the blood of their victim.

We'd been stalking these tunnels back and forth, checking every room but then the patter of footsteps up ahead had drawn me this way, and I was ready to finish the traitor who lived among us.

"You gut them after I rip their limbs off," I suggested and Darius chuckled darkly.

We rounded into a large cavern which had been set up as a kitchen, stone worktops everywhere and metal utensils hanging on the wall.

The sound of running water made my head snap around and I spotted Justin Masters by the sink, cursing as he scrubbed red stains from his sweatshirt.

I slowed to a halt and Darius dropped down from my back as I set Justin in my sights. Justin looked up at us, yelping in alarm and splashing water everywhere as he fought to turn the tap off, but instead turned it on full blast.

"You scared the crap out of me," he hissed, managing to shut the water off at last. "What are you doing down here?"

He grabbed a towel, drying his hands and folding his arms, covering up one of the larger red stains on his sweatshirt.

"Looking for a killer," Darius purred.

"Well good luck with that." Justin turned away from us, marching in the direction of the exit on the other side of the room.

I shot past him in a bolt of speed, stopping dead in front of him and tipping my head down as I exposed my fangs. He backed up a step in alarm and I glanced over his head as Darius closed in on him from behind.

"What do you want?" Justin demanded, trying not to look me in the eye. "I can't believe they even let you walk around The Burrows with free reign," he muttered. "It's uncomfortable for everyone to look at you."

I snarled and Darius released a growl that rumbled through the room, grabbing Justin's shoulder and yanking hard enough to spin him around to face him.

"What's with the stains?" he demanded and I leaned closer to sniff a dark blotch of red on Justin's shoulder.

"It's blood," I confirmed and Justin jerked away from me, realising how close I was, but finding himself bumping into Darius's chest instead. He was trapped between two predators and there was nowhere for him to run.

"I cut my hand, that's all," Justin insisted.

Darius grabbed his hands, examining them and Justin tried to yank them free.

"I've healed it now, obviously," Justin said quickly. "I think I cut an artery because it spurted everywhere."

"How convenient," I drawled and he flinched, glancing back at me.

"I don't know what you're talking about," he said, but sweat was breaking out on his brow and I knew we had him.

"What's your Order, Jacob?" Darius demanded.

"C-cerberus," he stuttered, starting to sense we were the danger in the room. "And my name is Justin. Why are you asking that?"

"Because a large beast is going around killing people in The Burrows," I said, fisting the back of his sweatshirt and tugging him towards me so I could speak in his ear. "Another victim has been found and now we've discovered you here covered in blood."

"If I'd killed them in my Cerberus form, my clothes wouldn't be bloody, would they?" he hissed.

"They might if you'd left them close by for your getaway," Darius said, grabbing hold of Justin's throat and squeezing.

I fisted my hand in his blonde hair, making him curse and Darius and I yanked him back and forth between us like lions with a bone as we both hankered for this kill.

"Stop!" he wailed in terror and a twisted satisfaction ran through me. "P-please, I didn't kill anyone. You can't prove it."

"A Cyclops could," I pointed out.

"But I think we have enough evidence to put you down anyway, Jeremy," Darius added and we shared a savage smile.

"N-no, please, just let me go," he begged.

"You like to kill your victims by ripping them apart, mauling them with tooth and claw," I growled, my hand ripping at his hair so hard, it was coming loose at the roots. "Maybe we'll do the same to you."

"It's only fair, Joseph," Darius agreed, his monster on full display.

"Holy raisins on a sandy flan!" Hamish burst into the room followed by Geraldine. "You cannot kill him, there must be a formal trial. We are not coots in a coop, we have to act within the laws of our kind, or what are we but cowboys riding wayward goats beneath the moon?"

"Papa is right," Geraldine insisted, hurrying forward and picking up a kipper laid out in a trough of ice by the sink. She whacked Justin around the head with it, unleashing a screech worthy of a barn owl. "But if you are responsible for this, you unholy woodlouse, I shall shove this kipper so far up your sailor's crocket, that it shall never see the light of day again!"

"I didn't do it!" Justin yelled, his hand going to the wet, red mark on his cheek as Geraldine whacked him with the kipper again and again, saying a word with every strike.

"I. Shall. Bury. You. Like. A. Questionable. Orange. Laid. Out. For. The. True. Queens. To. Sup. Upon - Hear. Me. This. Day. And. Hear. Me. Ever. More."

I stepped back to enjoy the show as Justin repeatedly took a kipper to the face then she started on his balls, slamming the whole fish against his junk and making him cough and fall to his knees.

"I'm innocent," he rasped as Geraldine propped the kipper up on her shoulder like a weapon.

"We shall soon see which way the whelks fall," Hamish said, puffing out his chest and grabbing hold of Justin's arm. "You're going to be locked up like a beetroot in a jam jar for the safety of the true queens and their people." He dragged him out of the room and Justin looked back at Geraldine imploringly, but she just turned her back on him and placed the kipper back in the trough.

"He always did give me the colliest of wobbles," she said with a shudder. "Perhaps my lady rivers were always telling me that a snake was lurking in my waters. A woman must never ignore the slithers in her rivers, I fear I have let the true queens down." She fell to her knees, burying her face against Darius' thighs and clinging to his pants so hard that they started to fall down.

"By the stars, Geraldine," Darius muttered, trying to pull his pants back up, but Geraldine clung on so tight they slipped down with his boxers, exposing his bare ass. "Geraldine!"

He managed to get them back up as she let go of him, lunging at me and trying to get hold of my pants instead, but I shot away with my Vampire speed, coming to a halt beside Darius, our shoulders resting together.

"Let's go tell the twins," I suggested and Geraldine wailed, throwing a hand against her forehead.

"Oh, but you don't know," she gasped, shuffling toward us on her knees. "The thoroughbred steeds of my gentle ladies have been left unawares."

"Unaware of what?" Darius gritted out.

"Our ladies Tory and Darcy have been swept away upon the wings of fate. Gabriel returned to tell us just moments ago after he delivered them to the doors of destiny."

"What are you talking about?" I demanded.

"They have travelled to The Palace of Flames where their ancestors resided so many centuries ago to learn the ways of their kind. Our fine and gallant Gabriel believes they will be there for some time. Perhaps even months."

"Months?" Darius choked out. "You're joking," he snapped. "Tell me you're joking."

A dangerous fire lit in his palms and Geraldine shuffled backwards on her knees with a wail. My gut sank and my arms went slack at my sides as sadness washed through me. Blue was gone? For *months*?

"Oh, but I am not. And yes, we shall miss them greatly, but we must also praise the stars for their kind and wondrous gift!"

"No," Darius barked. "Tell me where they are right now."

"I do not know. The location of The Palace of Flames has long since been lost to all memory and some say it is just a myth of a legend of a rumour," Geraldine said dramatically. "And Gabriel will not offer the location, not when they are on such an important quest. We must await them here and think of them often, sending out positive vibes into the ether towards them, so that they may-"

"No," Darius snapped, pointing at her. "Where's Gabriel?"

"I do not know. He disappeared like a wraith into the night after he told us the news, claiming he had another important quest from the heavens to attend."

"He's hiding from us," I gritted out. "But I'll find him. Get on my back, Darius."

Darius leapt up without a word, latching his arms and legs around me and I shot out of the kitchens at speed. At least if we could find out where they were maybe we could visit them. How could Blue have left without coming to see me first? It wasn't like I begrudged her learning about her kind, and frankly I was fascinated to hear about the secrets of that palace, but couldn't she have given me a heads up?

"GABRIEL!" Darius bellowed, amplifying his voice with magic so it echoed all around The Burrows and the bastard would know we were coming.

We came to a halt outside Gabriel's room and Darius blasted it with fire, a Dragon's roar leaving his lips, but it billowed across a firm air shield and sparked out of existence just as fast.

I let him down, frowning at him. I mean shit, I was pissed they'd gone without saying goodbye and I would miss Blue like hell, but he was acting like Geraldine had said Tory would never return.

"Chill, man, what's going on?" I asked him as he started pacing back and forth in front of the door.

"She's not going to be back for months," he spat. "I don't have months."

"What's that supposed to mean?" I asked in confusion and he shook his head, smoke spewing from his lips.

"I'll miss her, that's all," he muttered.

"Yeah and I'll miss, Blue, but...maybe this is a good thing. They'll learn more about their Order. Maybe they'll uncover new gifts that can help us with-"

"I don't care," he snapped, his eyes shifting to the golden eyes of a Dragon. "She needs to be here. With *me*." He strode up to the door, hammering his fist on it. "Gabriel! Come out and face me."

"He's busy," a male voice carried to us and we both snapped around, finding a golden haired Lion Shifter standing in the shadows, leaning against the wall with one leg kicked up.

"Leon," I said in realisation, striding towards him. "Where's Gabriel?"

"He could be in his room. He could be miles away. Who can say?" he said casually, pushing his fingers into his long mane.

"You can say," I insisted.

Darius slammed his fist against the barrier to Gabriel's room again and a feminine moan carried from beyond it.

"Gabe's busy," Leon said with a smirk.

"And what are you, his bodyguard?" Darius spat at Leon.

"I'm just a mysterious Lion, lurking in the shadows with many secrets to his name," he said in what I guessed he thought was a spooky voice. He folded his muscular arms, pouting at us when we didn't immediately respond to that. "Don't you want to know my secrets?"

"Is one of them where Gabriel is?" I asked.

"Yes…and no," he said, tossing a grin at Darius as he narrowed his eyes at him.

"If you know, then tell me right now," Darius commanded, his shoulders pressing back and a look of his father entering his eyes. A loud groan sounded that definitely belonged to Gabriel and I muttered a curse under my breath.

"Wow, I'm quaking in my little puss-n-boots," Leon chuckled. "Gabe's gone, dude. He's either in that room fucking his wife into another realm, or he went swimming with the dolphins in Sunshine Bay. Who can really say?"

"You," Darius snapped. "*You* can say. And I can hear them in there, so I know the answer anyway."

"Do you?" Leon asked, waving his hands and wiggling his fingers. "Or is it all just an illusion?"

I ran a palm down my face and sighed, knowing in my heart that we weren't going to get to Gabriel. He'd have *seen* every route we took to try and reach him, and my shoulders dropped as I accepted that.

"Come on, man. Let's go," I said to Darius, but Leon's hand swung out and slapped me.

"Hey," I barked.

"Do you feel that, Lance? That's the strike of fate." He gripped my shirt, yanking me close to his face as he smiled like the Cheshire Cat. "And I'm it's messenger. Ride me towards your destiny. Ride me!"

"For the love of the moon, Leon." I shoved him back. "Personal boundaries, remember? I don't know how many times I have to say it."

I turned and started walking away, drawing Darius after me as he gave up on trying to get to Gabriel with a huff.

"But what about my secrets?" Leon called after us in desperation, but we simply kept walking. "I have a secret quest set for us by Gabriel," he said excitedly, blurting it out as he accepted we gave no shits.

"Fuck Gabriel," Darius grumbled and I clapped a hand to his shoulder.

"They'll be back soon, brother," I said, hoping my words were true.

"Not soon enough," he said, hanging his head and I went to ask him what was really troubling him, but Leon collided with us, breaking us apart and slinging his arms over our shoulders.

"Gabe said I needed a couple of recruits for our quest, so I thought this would be a great opportunity for me to get to know some new friends."

"Yeah, sure. See ya," Darius growled then strode off down the corridor, smoke billowing out behind him before he disappeared into a fog of it.

"Wow, that was dramatic," Leon breathed, leaning close to my ear. "Guess it's just me and you then, shamesy."

"Shamesy?" I growled.

"Yeah, like Power Shamesy. I thought I'd make a cute nickname out of it, so it didn't seem so, you know…devastating."

I shrugged him off, folding my arms. "Is there really a quest?"

"Of course there's a quest," he said, rolling his golden eyes. "What do you take me for, shamesy?"

"I'd really prefer if you didn't call me that," I said flatly.

"Who else shall we bring with us?" he barrelled on as if I hadn't spoken.

"What even is this quest?" I asked in frustration.

"Oh my stars, I didn't even tell you about the quest yet." He leapt in front of me, pressing his hands to my shoulders. "Gabe says you're looking for some gemstones, right? Right?"

"Right," I agreed, frowning at the swerve this conversation was taking.

I still hadn't made any solid progress in my research with tracking down the Zodiac Guild stones, though I had quite a few leads to follow up after Eugene and his friends had sent across some information from the Library of the Lost on gems that could possibly be the ones we sought. But with the lack of stardust and the fact that I was chasing trails which had gone cold hundreds of years ago, it was pretty hard to get anywhere with our search.

"And they're extra special gemstones, right? Right?" Leon pushed.

"Right." Would he ever get to the point?

"Well." He stepped closer, glancing left and right before cupping a hand around his mouth. "I know where one of them is. And usually I wouldn't give up any of my family's stolen treasures – we are the best thieves in Solaria after all – but my dad had this one all locked up in a special place and I'm owed a little revenge against my dad."

"Because of your brother?" I asked sadly. Roary Night had turned out to be a decent ally in Darkmore Penitentiary, and I had to admit the reason that he was in there turned my goddamn stomach.

"Yeah, Dad won't even speak to him, because of the shame. I guess you know a lot about shame so you probably understand that, shamesy. I wanna get revenge on him for being such a dick…" Leon said, sadness crossing his features, but then a smile split across his face again just as fast. "So I wanna thieve from my thief father and give you his treasure for your rock collection."

"It's not a rock coll-"

"It'll be the most prized rock in your rock collection," he announced proudly, turning and strutting off down the tunnel ahead of me and I figured fuck it, and didn't bother to correct him.

Leon was wearing snug jeans which clung to his thick thighs, his muscular frame filling out his white t-shirt. His golden hair practically shone in the light of the sconces around him and I shook my head at the guy, a smile lifting my lips for a second. He had grown on me a little since he'd befriended Gabriel, especially since he'd stopped being such an uber fan of mine because of my Pitball status. Of course, now he was living the dreams I'd once had for myself so I guessed I should have been the one fangirling over him these days. And now I was Power Shamed too, I was hardly the celebrity he'd first met all those years ago when his academy had done an exchange programme with Zodiac Academy.

I shot after him, not wanting to pass up the opportunity to get hold of another gemstone and he tossed me a roguish smile.

"So who are we recruiting?" Leon asked.

"Let's bring Caleb," I decided.

"Yes – I love Caleb! And he's your sanguis frater now too, right?" he cooed, turning to me and reaching out to brush his thumb over the pinprick silver marks on my neck.

"Yeah." I batted his hand away. "Gabriel told you?"

"Yup. But he says I'm not to keep going on about how cool it is because Vampire covens are bad and if I make it sound too cool then other Vampires might get ideas about joining up which apparently isn't a good thing – but I have to wonder if he's right about that, because it seems kinda like a good thing to me and I want my favourite Vampire to have all the good things."

"It's against the Vampire Code for a reason," I said, knowing that was the truth even though I couldn't say I hated it so far. "There are issues with pack hunting and bloodlust and-"

"Those sound like good things to me, shamesy. Maybe Caleb will agree and we can get you a new recruit. Let's go find him!" he ran off down the passage and I shot forward, picking him up and throwing him over my shoulder as I raced towards the royal quarters while Leon whooped.

I placed him down outside Caleb's room and rapped my knuckles on the door. It opened and Caleb beamed as he spotted me.

"Sanguis frater!" he cried excitedly and we hugged. "Did you watch that documentary on that blood river in eastern Voldrakia I told you about?"

"Yeah," I said as we released each other. "It got me so thirsty, I had to wake Darcy up to feed from her."

"Yeah, that shit got me so thirsty too. I knew I was gonna feed on the next person I saw until I bumped into Washer," Caleb said, wrinkling his nose.

"Ergh, Nova made me feed from him once for a class demonstration," I said in disgust. "He ground himself all over me and my fangs wouldn't extend again for a week."

"Shit, he gave you fang fear?" Caleb gasped.

"Massively," I said and Caleb turned to Leon, hugging him too.

"Oh, I bet fang fear is the worst," Leon said sadly. "Lions get mane fear if someone touches our hair without permission. It happened to me once... I've never really gotten over it." He shuddered and Caleb pressed a hand to his arm.

"That must have been awful," he said as Leon nodded sadly then Seth suddenly popped his head out from under Caleb's arm through the door.

"I got pube fear once when someone got their pubes tangled with mine while we were going at it. It. Was. Awful," he said, smiling as he looked around at us all to join in.

"That's not the same at all," I said irritably and Seth whimpered, looking to Caleb.

"Yeah, you can't compare those things, man. It's actually kind of insulting," Caleb said with a frown.

"Actually you can," Leon jumped in. "I once got my pubes tangled in a lot of cutlery, and now I can't even have a spoon down there without getting pube fear."

"How the hell did you get cutlery tangled down there?" I asked I confusion.

"Were you playing chip-chop pube?" Seth asked knowingly.

"Exactly, dude!" Leon cried. "Do you know how many people act like they don't even know what chip-chop pube is? It's a classic game."

"A classic game involving pubes and cutlery?" I scoffed, folding my arms.

"What are the rules?" Caleb asked in amusement.

"You have to see how much cutlery you can hang from your pubes," Leon explained.

"It only counts if it stays hanging for more than ten seconds," Seth added.

"What, so…your dicks are just out while you play in front of other people?" I asked, unsure why I was curious about this game because I definitely didn't plan on giving it a whirl.

"Yup," they said at the same time and I looked between them as they grinned at each other, sensing the two of them together would be like mixing two very explosive potions in the same cauldron. They were both just so… peppy.

"So shall we go?" I asked and Leon looked to me.

"Yes! Let's go on an adventure," Leon said brightly.

"Ooh, what adventure?" Seth asked, padding closer to us eagerly.

Leon explained as we followed him down the passage towards the exit and we were soon outside, the summer sun shining down on the bright green grass, daisies and dandelions popping up everywhere.

The guards shot me glowers, turning to mutter with one another and I ignored them, so used to being treated like that now that it didn't even massively register to me anymore.

We made it beyond the boundary and the Lion Shifter took out a pouch of stardust as he turned to us.

"You've got a whole pouch?" Caleb asked him in shock.

"I kept it for a rainy day, and my Lion senses tell me it's gonna rain really hard today," Leon said and I glanced up at the clear blue sky, the songbirds dancing across it and the sun which burned so brightly a raincloud had zero hope of forming under its gaze.

"Yeah, looks like it," Seth agreed conspiratorially. "So where are we going?"

"To my hometown," Leon said. "Alestria." He tossed the stardust over us and we were dragged away, transported through the stars and deposited in a dark alley where the scent of piss hung thickly in the air.

"Ergh, are we in hell?" Caleb muttered, stepping closer to me like I might be able to ward off the stench. "Oh my stars, is that a shit? Like a Fae fucking turd, right there by that dumpster?" He pulled his shirt up over his nose and I couldn't really blame him.

"It's the magic of Alestria," Leon cooed. "Between the grime, the piss and the shits that hobos do in alleys, there's something really special about this place."

"I think I like it," Seth whispered and Caleb and I shared a look.

Leon walked over to a drain, dropping down to his knees and casting some spell, his hand weaving back and forth above the metal before it began to shimmer. He took hold of it, pulling it up to reveal a ladder leading away into the dark.

"You know, I think I'd rather go back to The Burrows and have a scalding shower that'll burn a layer of my skin off," Caleb said, backing up but I pressed a hand to his shoulder and pushed him forward.

"Come on, princess, you can handle a little dirt," I taunted and Seth looked back at us, nodding eagerly.

"We can tick it off our bucket list, Cal," he called.

"I don't have 'crawl into a shit pit' on my bucket list," Caleb said, shaking his head but he let me guide him over there all the same.

"It'll be one of those tales we tell for years to come," Seth encouraged. "Like that time I was on the moon and I stuck my dick in a crater."

"You did?" Leon asked, looking at him in awe as Seth nodded proudly. "Holy shit, tell me everything. What did it feel like? Did you get magical dick powers after?"

I groaned as Seth jumped on the opportunity to tell someone new his moon stories and I worked to zone him out as Leon led the way down into the sewer and Caleb reluctantly followed.

I cast a Faelight as I stepped off of the rungs at the bottom and looked around at the dank tunnel we were in, a river of water rushing along beside us. We followed Leon down the narrow path beside it, his and Seth's voices echoing around us as they laughed and shared stories, and I walked with Caleb as he worked hard not to touch anything and muttered promises to burn all the clothes he was wearing the moment we got back to The Burrows.

As Leon and Seth turned down a tunnel to the right up ahead, I lost sight of them and realised Caleb wasn't beside me anymore. I glanced back, finding his head and one arm tangled in a thick cobweb that hung down from the ceiling.

"Fucking, argh," he grunted, trying to burn it off of him, but only getting himself caught in more of it as he nearly burnt off his own eyebrows.

I jogged back to him as I went to help, casting an ice blade in my hand.

"Hold still, Cal," I encouraged and he did, grimacing as I carved through the sticky web and shuddering full bodily as he jerked away from it, peeling the last of it from his hair and flicking it off of his hand.

I examined the web for a second, not liking the size of it or the way it disappeared into a wide hole in the wall above us. It could have belonged to a harmless weaving spider, but my gut clenched at the other possibility. Gnarla spiders were rare as hell, but their webs were notoriously sticky and a place like this was perfect for something that size. I just prayed to the fucking stars I was wrong about that assessment though.

"Let's keep moving," I urged, the sound of Leon and Seth's voices lost to us now and I didn't think we should be apart, not when every cop in the kingdom was hunting for us.

We used a burst of Vampire speed to chase after the others, turning into the tunnel they'd taken but finding it empty.

I slowed to a halt and Caleb spat a curse as he stopped beside me and his foot sank into a murky puddle, shaking his leg out and using fire magic to dry it off.

"Fuck my life," he grumbled, looking utterly disgusted with this entire situation.

"Seth!" I called into the dark tunnel ahead, growling when he didn't answer. There were forks in the tunnel here, leading off in several directions. Where the fuck had they gone?

"Fuck this. If they've left us, they can meet us back at The Burrows later," Caleb said, but before he could turn around and go through with that plan, a roar sounded and the shadowy figure of a monster with ten arms came at us from the dark.

"Shit," I snarled, raising my hands and blasting it with air magic. It toppled immediately, laughter rising from it and I realised it was Seth and fucking Leon as I sent my Faelight flying over them.

Seth had cast vines in his hands and had apparently been sitting on Leon's shoulders because now he was stuck beneath him with his thighs clamped around Leon's ears. The two of them laughed like crazy and Seth's vines whipped out around him, one of them hitting the water and sending a splash up which slapped Caleb in the face.

"Argh!" he cried. "That got me in the fucking mouth, you motherfucker."

Seth howled a laugh, untangling himself from Leon and clutching his side as he got to his feet, but Caleb shot forward, slamming his hands into his chest and sending him flying backwards into the river of sewage with a huge splash. A bark of laughter left me as Seth's head came up and he bobbed away on the tide with a yell of horror.

"You asshole!" he shouted as Cal and I cracked up.

Leon got to his feet, racing after Seth and hauling him out of the water, drying him off with the heat of his fire Element, cracking up too.

"I'm gonna be diseased. I'll get Faeitis. Faeiphylis. Fucking pink eye," Seth cried in a panic.

"You're fine, dude," Leon said easily. "This water's clean. The river of shit is in the next tunnel over."

"Thank the stars for that," Caleb muttered as he dried his hair with fire magic.

Leon led us on into the tunnels and we finally made it to a huge door with a wheel in the middle of it. He turned to us dramatically, his golden eyes glinting. "Beyond this door lies years and years of family heirlooms, things my ancestors stole, many of our prized possessions."

"How can they be heirlooms if you stole them?" I asked and Leon shushed me.

"Touch nothing in here, for you will set off a curse that will make your eyes fall from your head and your nose cave into your face."

"Seriously?" Cal balked. "I'm not going in then."

"Nah, just kidding." Leon laughed. "But if you try to steal anything I'll know, and I'll fucking murder you and everyone you love." He smiled lightly then turned and pressed his hand to the door, magic sparking out from beneath his palm then the wheel began turning of its own accord at a rapid pace. The door clunked as it unlocked and he pulled it wide, revealing a trove lit by everflames.

We followed him inside and my jaw slackened at the endless wonders in this room. There were chests overflowing with jewels, a shining crown sitting on top of a stack of shelves which held all kinds of potions and rare artifacts, even a whole suit of armour which was blood red and held the Leo constellation on its chest.

"Lucky we didn't bring Darius, he would have tried to claim all of this from you," I said and Leon growled at the idea of that.

The Lion headed over to an old wooden cabinet, unlocking it with a small key he took from his pocket and pulling out a silver box from inside. He flipped it open, revealing all kinds of gemstones there and he rifled through them, taking out the most perfectly cut of all. It was an oval topaz stone which was golden brown in colour and glittered with the magic that lived within its depths.

I reached for it, the hidden Guild mark on my arm itching like it knew what this was, and the whispers of the stars seemed to hang in the air for a second, urging me to seize it. But Leon closed his fingers around it tightly before I could.

"You owe me something for this," Leon announced and I looked to him with a frown.

"What?" I demanded.

"The truth about what happened between you and Gabriel the night he visited you at Zodiac Academy five years ago and he developed a mysterious aversion to proballs. I know something happened, Lance Orion. So help me, I want that secret."

I jerked my hand away in horror. "No," I hissed. "I'm taking that to the grave. I swore it to him."

Seth and Caleb looked to me curiously, but I folded my arms and shook my head.

"No secret, no stone," Leon said airily, shrugging his shoulders and I growled.

"We need that stone. I'll just tell Gabriel to take it from you," I said and Leon gasped, holding his hand to his chest in offence.

"You wouldn't," he hissed.

"I would. It's either that or you hand it over." I held out my palm and Leon looked conflicted, still holding onto it tight.

"I want your Ryan Luxian Pitball League card," he changed tact.

"That's a collectible," I said in frustration, not to mention the guy had been my favourite player growing up.

"It's that or I'm gonna swallow it and you can dig it out of my poop." Leon held the stone to his open mouth in a threat and I cursed.

"Fine," I huffed. "You can have the card, just give me the stone."

"Sure." Leon slipped it into his pocket. "We can make the trade later."

I growled and he grinned at me.

"Can I have this hat?" Seth asked and we turned, finding him wearing a ridiculous red cowboy hat with leather tassels hanging from it. "I've always fancied myself as a hat person."

"You look ridiculous," Caleb said with a snort.

"Sure, man," Leon said easily.

"How come he doesn't have to dig it out of your poop because he's not giving you anything for it?" I tossed at him.

"Don't be such a sourpuss, shamesy," Leon said, slinging an arm around me. "You're still my favourite." He licked my face. "Oh wow, you can really taste the shame on you." He licked me again. "It's like cinnamon and failed dreams."

"Alright, back it up, Lion," I warned, bitter over the shamesy comment and not thrilled about the saliva either.

"Sorry, didn't mean to shame you, shamesy," he murmured like he really was sorry, though calling me shamesy wasn't exactly helping his case. "I think you could bottle it as a scent actually, it's kind of alluring. You could call it eau de toi-regret."

"Thanks," I said dryly. "I'll do that once I've finished setting up my own failed dreams clothing line."

"I think you're really onto something here, Lance," Leon said seriously. "You could sell it to all the other losers. There's not many as shameful as you, but you could expand into washouts, has-beens and even junkie deadbeats."

"I can't wait," I said hollowly.

We headed out of the trove and Leon locked up the door tight as Seth toyed with the tassels hanging from his new hat and Caleb shook his head at him with a smile dancing around his lips.

A scuttling sounded somewhere above us and I glanced up at the pipes winding overhead, glancing at Caleb to confirm he'd heard it too. I flexed my hand, bringing magic to my fingertips as we pressed on, the scuttling carrying off somewhere ahead of us.

We rounded the next corner and Seth howled in fright. "Holy mother of an eight legged cunt!"

My eyes fell on the enormous gnarla spider blocking our exit, its white eyes flashing our way and its huge hairy legs scuttling forward, its pincers snapping and a horrible grunting noise coming from it.

Caleb charged forward and punched it in the face with a flaming fist, sending it flying backwards with the force of his Order. The spider righted itself and I gasped as I noticed more climbing the walls and the click of spiny legs hitting the floor behind us made me twist around.

"Don't let them bite you," I called. "Their venom will make your lungs burst."

"Ahhh!" Seth charged into battle, blasting one spider into the water with his air magic and I took on the one in front of me, casting a spear of ice in my hand and launching it towards its head with precision. It slammed into its ugly face and it screeched as it died, but another took its place in an instant.

Leon hurried forward at my side, sending a blaze of fireballs flaring down the tunnel, the heat of his power warming my cheeks as the spiders scurried away from his flames while others were consumed in the blaze.

I knocked another one of the beasts down into the water with a gust of air while Caleb burned a path right through them.

"Go!" Cal roared and I grabbed Leon, throwing him over my shoulder as Caleb grabbed hold of Seth and we shot away as Seth shouted, "Yee-ha!"

We made it back to the ladder as the sound of the scuttling monsters chased us and I sped up the rungs, shoving the drain cover open at the top as I climbed out.

Caleb appeared right after me with Seth clinging to his back, his hat tassels fluttering around in the breeze as Leon jumped down from my back and slammed the drain closed, sealing it up again with a spell.

"Dere's spiders down dere in dat hole," a gravelly male voice made me whip around and I found a naked hairy dude standing there with a whole array of cutlery hanging from his pubes.

"Oh my stars, he's a chip-chop pube champion," Seth gasped, starting to applaud the man who was clearly high on something as he started spinning in circles and pointing at the sky.

Leon threw stardust over us and we were carried away back to The Burrows, my retinas forever burned with the image of the forks and knives wrapped in that man's pubes, but relief pouring over me too. Because we now had another gemstone, and despite the need to scrub myself clean and the fact that I had to give up my prized Pitball card to claim it, I had to call it a win.

I sat in bed, missing Darcy, thankful Seth had gone to spend some time with the Heirs this evening. I turned the beautiful topaz gemstone over in my palm, zoning out as I wondered what Blue was doing.

A soft knock came at the door and I called out for whoever it was to come in, finding Darius there as he stepped into the room with a forlorn expression on his face.

"Do you want company?" he asked and I nodded, shoving the covers back beside me in an offering.

Darius pushed the door shut, kicking his shoes off and getting into bed beside me. The familiarity of his company made me instantly relax and I leaned against him as he shifted closer to me.

He sighed heavily, sadness spilling from him and tainting the air.

"I know, brother," I said. "Hopefully they'll be back soon."

Silence fell between us, but it was the kind that was so familiar to me, it wasn't at all awkward. Darius and I had always been able to share the same space in quiet contentment, and I was so fucking glad that was still the case now the Guardian bond was broken.

"You know I love you, don't you, asshole?" Darius broke the silence after a while and I looked at him in surprise.

"Are you about to ask me to elope with you now Tory's out of the picture?" I teased and he thumped my arm.

"I'm serious," he growled and my brows raised as I sensed something was up.

"What's going on?" I asked and he shook his head marginally before huffing out a line of smoke.

"You just never know what's going to happen. And the second I get a chance to go after my father, I'm going to take it. I don't know if I'll survive that, Lance, so I'm saying what has to be said in case I don't."

My chest constricted at the thought of losing him, and though I knew he was right and that any of us could be in peril any time we stepped outside The Burrows, it was also easier to pretend that wasn't the case than to say goodbye every time someone I cared about walked out the door.

Of course, at that thought panic welled in me over Blue having left without me seeing her, but Gabriel had taken them somewhere far away and he'd have *seen* that they were safe there. At least, I fucking well hoped so.

I considered saying something stupid to lighten the mood, or taunting him more for saying he loved me, but as I met his pained gaze, I found I couldn't do that. And instead, I leaned my head against his and sighed, "I love you too, brother."

"In this life and the next," he swore, my chest tightening at the words because it sounded like he really thought he needed to say them. But the man I knew wouldn't just give up on hope like that. Where was the arrogance? The self assurance? The utter confidence that he could win this? I needed to remind him of who the fuck he was and how certain I was that he would win that fight just as soon as we could destroy Lavinia and allow him to have it.

"You're bigger than him," I said firmly because it was more than true now. He'd let me measure him in his shifted form last week and by my calculations he was over a ton heavier than his father in Dragon form and nearly six feet longer too.

"And still growing," he replied, a faint smile on his lips though it didn't touch his eyes like even that fact didn't make him feel any more confident.

"Stronger too," I added. "Plus now that the twins are off learning from another teacher, I'll have more time available to dedicate to you. And we have plenty of bones so we can get back to honing your skill with borrowing Elements from the dead."

His smile grew more genuine at that and he nodded. "I would enjoy seeing the look on his face when I wield dark magic against him," he admitted, his eyes brightening at the idea.

"That's my Dragon," I said, slapping his arm bracingly and he snorted in amusement.

We broke apart and I reached into the nightstand drawer.

"Are you getting the lube?" Darius asked and I barked a laugh.

"No, I'm getting the vibrating Mammoth Shifter tusk you enjoyed so much last time."

Darius chuckled as I grabbed hold of Diego's hat, turning back to face him and my eyes fell on a dark figure standing in the doorway, the door wide open as he stood staring at us.

"Fucking hell," I cursed. "What the fuck are you doing, dickwad?"

Seth stepped into the light with a whimper, eyeing the bed. "Can I join? I haven't had pack snuggles in ages. My skin's getting touch starved and Cal and Max went to bed."

"No," I said instantly but Darius flipped the cover down beside him.

"Come on then," Darius patted the space, and I clenched my jaw as Seth shoved the door shut then whipped off his shirt, sent his shoes flying in two different directions and dove onto the bed beside Darius. But instead of staying there where I could ignore him, he climbed over Darius and started nestling his way between the two of us.

"Oh my stars, this is so comfy. Isn't this the best?" He tugged the covers up around us and nuzzled into Darius's head before trying to do the same to me. Which I certainly did not allow.

He tucked his hands under the blankets and started wriggling, bringing up his hand again a second later with his sweatpants and boxers in his grip, tossing them across the room on a gust of air magic.

"By the stars, are you naked?" I seethed, trying to move away from him as he rubbed himself against me. I swear I could feel the side of his fucking ass cheek on my leg. "Stop it this instant." I shoved him hard against Darius and he tipped his head back with a mournful howl.

"I have to have full bodily contact," Seth complained. "It's a need of my Order. You guys can get naked too, I don't mind."

"Fuck no. Go find some Wolves to rub yourself on, for the love of the moon. Or I bet Washer would be up for a cuddle with you," I suggested.

"Or just shift if you have to be fucking naked," Darius commanded and the shift rippled down Seth's flesh, nearly shoving me out of the bed entirely as a massive white Wolf appeared in his place and the bed creaked from the weight of us all. His tongue lolled out of his mouth and he swiped a paw at Darius who rolled his eyes before tickling his chest.

Seth promptly fell asleep, but his tail kept wagging under the covers, making the bedsheets ruffle.

"I don't know what I'm more uncomfortable with, being in this bed with that animal or putting on a hat that hasn't been washed for months, maybe years," I said, eyeing the thing in my hand.

"Can't you use your water magic on it?" Darius wrinkled his nose.

"I'm afraid I'll wash the souls right out of it," I said, imagining hearing Diego's tiny screams as he raced away down the drain and deciding against that idea. "Anyway, let's see if Diego has anything more to offer us." I pulled on the hat and held out my hand to Darius.

Just before I was dragged into the shadowy depths of the enchanted knitwear, Darius gripped my hand tightly and he was pulled along with me.

I expected to hear Diego greeting us, but the voice that spoke took me by surprise.

"At last, I've been waiting for you to come here," the unfamiliar voice said and my heart leapt.

"Who are you?" I demanded, though it was more of a thought than me physically voicing it.

"Miguel Polaris," he said, sounding nervous. "I'm Diego's father."

I immediately pulled back, panic rushing through me. "Let's get out of here, Darius," I commanded, withdrawing from this dark place we were floating within.

"No – wait! Listen to me," Miguel begged. "You were there the night I was freed, Lance Orion. The night Darcy Vega killed my wife Drusilla with her Phoenix fire."

I paused, sensing Darius pulling on my psyche urgently, but then I recalled this man shouting at us to run that day, like he'd wanted us to escape that place.

"What do you want?" I asked hesitantly.

"I want to repay Darcy for what she did. She returned my mind to me. Drusilla had me bound to her control by the will of the Shadow Princess. Many years ago, I was captured and enslaved by her, for my power is strong and so long as it runs in my veins, my strength aids the Shadow Princess. Drusilla wanted to birth a son equally strong, combining my power with hers, but I was simply a pawn, fed so much of the shadows that I was drowned in them. The darkness infected my mind for so many years as Drusilla prayed to Lavinia to keep me drunk on their endless power, to keep me compliant and practically braindead. But now Drusilla is gone and I have awoken. I see my life clearly for what it has been. My poor son is dead. I hardly got to know him at all and now I have nothing left but an ache for vengeance in my heart."

"How can we trust you?" Darius hissed. "You could be working for them."

"I can do no harm to you here. All I can do is show you memories of the past. I was never weaved into the web of souls, but I managed to save a thread from Drusilla's glove when she died that has since allowed me to connect to this place, to my son."

"Please listen to him, Orion," Diego's voice came out of the dark, a plea so desperate in his tone that I knew I had to give Miguel my attention.

"Alright," I said. "What is it you want to show us?"

"You must understand that the Nymphs are not all loyal to the Shadow Princess," Miguel said hurriedly. "Many of us are enslaved as I was, but many more are in hiding."

"Wait, what if Alejandro is able to hear this discussion?" Darius hissed.

"He cannot see anything but the memories in the web," Miguel promised. "And he is no longer uploading memories here himself, believing it a pointless endeavour now that his sister is dead and there is no information to be shared."

"So what is it you want to tell us?" I asked.

"I know what you are doing," he said excitedly. "You closed one of the rifts and have weakened the Shadow Princess. She is most aggrieved, and it has been hard to hide my jubilation and pretend I am still a slave among her ranks."

"What do you know about the rifts?" I asked hopefully.

"I don't know their locations, but I do know how you can find them. You see, I was there the day Vard was gifted a shadow eye. I know of its power. And I believe it can be used to find the rifts."

"Are you saying we need his eye?" Darius asked in confusion.

"Yes," Miguel said eagerly. "It is no normal eye, it's infected with the shadows. If you could make a spyglass strong enough to hold it, I believe it could show you the locations of the rifts."

"How are we supposed to get close to that asshole?" Darius asked.

"Perhaps you can think of some way," Miguel said anxiously. "For if you can find those rifts and close them, you will be able to block Lavinia off from her power."

My heart drummed harder at that. If we could weaken her entirely, cut her off from the shadows, then not only could we end her, but it could also destroy the shadow curse she'd laid on Darcy once and for all.

"Mierda, I must go," Miguel said anxiously. "I will try to contact you again soon. Viva las verdaderas reinas."

His presence vanished and I pushed away from the connection to the soul web, my eyes blinking open as I fell back into my body and yanked the hat off my head.

I looked to Darius across Seth's sleeping form, a fierce purpose resounding between us.

"How the fuck are we going to get that shadow eye?" Darius murmured.

"We have to find a way into the palace," I said thoughtfully. "So we just need a plan and the balls to pull it off."

LIONEL

CHAPTER THIRTY FOUR

I sat in the smaller of the two offices I knew resided within the Palace of Souls, despising that I still couldn't gain access to Hail's quarters and his main study which likely held countless secrets within its depths. But I would crack my way in in time, and at least for now I could revel in dominating this space that he had once occupied too. Hopefully he was watching me from beyond the Veil, seeing the man I had become and seething with vitriol over the better Fae who had won his crown.

I dominated the oak desk that ran the length of the enormous window on the back wall, my fingers flexing across the grain of the wood. The light was crisp, casting shadows through the room including those of the Hydra heads that made up the iron chandelier above. I'd toyed with the idea of gutting the palace, stripping out the mark of the old king entirely, but there was something abundantly satisfying about sitting in the place of a man who'd once thought he was far greater than me.

But Hail had been a puppet of my design and this whole ascension would have gone much smoother had he not married that whore of a queen from a savage land. She had made things far trickier for me, her Sight a difficult obstacle to navigate. But eventually, I had found ways by allying with the Nymphs and using the shadows to hide my plans, a thing even a powerful Seer like her could not foresee.

Their deaths should have been the end of my troubles, but now their daughters had returned to lure away my Heir and his Guardian with their pussies. No matter though, I had things under control. I would soon produce another Heir to ensure the Acrux line was upheld, and those who opposed me would be crushed beneath my heel and ground into the earth like the worthless ants they were.

And better still, they were playing into my hands by closing that rift to the Shadow Realm.

Lavinia had complained of the weakness it had brought on in her and that was something I was most pleased about. Because she could not control me as easily now, and she had spent much of her time alone and plotting some hateful vengeance against them, which equalled her staying out of my way.

I still needed her, but I needed her on a leash, one I could yank tight whenever it suited me. But let them weaken her for all I cared, then when she was malleable again, she would be easier to control.

I'd have to keep an eye on the situation though. I couldn't have them taking the Shadow Princess from me entirely, but for now I would let them believe they had gained an advantage over me while in fact they had just made my weapon easier to wield.

A knock came at the door, the light knuckled rapping familiar enough to let me know it was my butler Jenkins.

"Yes?" I barked.

"My King, Stella Orion is here to see you," he replied and a weary sigh left me.

I considered turning her away as I had been doing for some time now, but then again…Lavinia wasn't as easy to force beneath me and fuck as she had been when Clara had inhabited her.

I growled low in my throat, wanting to exert my power. I'd have liked to have women brought to the palace in droves, the most beautiful in Solaria. I was the king, after all. I should be burying my cock in whoever I liked, but the first time I'd had some brought here, all five women had been found mutilated in the entrance hall.

Lavinia had stood among their corpses, smiling menacingly as she stood drenched in their blood, a lump of flesh gripped in her hand with a savage bite taken out of it.

I had not brought a single woman here since.

But Stella could come and go as she pleased and she was a beautiful woman, one I had long enjoyed the company of even if I had grown bored of her over time. And Lavinia was currently nowhere to be seen. My cock was already aching to be inside a warm body, because Lavinia's was cold and unwelcoming. I needed the hot flesh of a Fae to sate me, and it looked like it was time to get what I wanted.

"Let her in," I called and the door opened, revealing Stella as she stepped into my office in high black heels and a fitted white dress which hugged her perfectly fuckable body.

"My King." She bowed her head and I leaned back in my seat as I watched her walk towards me, admiring her tight figure.

Once upon a time, she and I had studied together at Zodiac Academy alongside Hail Vega, the other Celestial Councillors and Azriel Orion. Of course, back then I had merely been the spare, below their notice most of the time while my older brother Radcliff lorded it over me, believing he would always be the most powerful Fae in our line and that I would never pose any kind of threat to his position.

Of course, he'd died choking on that belief, staring up at me in horror as he awoke one night finding I had dropped a norian wasp into his bed while he slept, his hands locked to his sides with my air magic, preventing him from healing himself of the severe reaction he had to it's sting. With healing magic, the norian wasps's sting wasn't much of a threat to most Fae, but for anyone who didn't manage to heal away the effects of it, they suffered a slow and agonising death as their internal organs swelled and swelled until they burst. The process took almost an hour to kill a man as big as my brother had been, and it had been quite the shock to my parents when they found him the next morning. Everyone believed he must have been tapped out and stung in his sleep, his tongue too swollen to call for help by the time he woke from the agony of the sting.

But that hadn't been the way it had happened at all. Oh no. My big, powerful brother had been awake for the entire thing, woken by the sharp snap of his limbs being immobilised by my power and the angry red and black wasp trapped against his chest within a glass.

He had cursed and screamed while he died, all of it contained within the silencing bubble I had cast while I watched his agony play out within his eyes, and I was filled with the satisfaction of knowing he would never again refer to me as Lame Lionel. I'd mocked him over that as he choked on his own blood and begged me to heal him. *"Who's lame now, Radcliff?"*

His dying reply had left a bitter taste on my lips though. *"You are,"* he spat around his swollen tongue. *"You're unFae, unwanted, and will always be Lame Lionel no matter what you achieve."*

His girlfriend had sobbed so loudly at his funeral. I couldn't recall her name now but I remembered well how I'd comforted her, taking her to his room so that she could claim something to remember him by. I fucked her on his bed while I watched the tears spill down her cheeks as she tried to bury her grief in affection for me, and I buried my cock in his woman proving just how lame I wasn't.

Stella had always shared my vision for the world, she had been a perfect accomplice in many ways. Her obsession with me had always been useful to my needs and she'd been happy to play the part I created for her in my rise. She even married Azriel Orion so that she could grant me access to the research he was doing for the king, helping me find out more and more about the shadow realm and creating our plans to steal their power for ourselves.

The Orions had long held an alliance with my family in the past, teaching us the ways of dark magic, but Azriel had grown distant with me after Radcliff had died and I'd taken my brother's place as Heir, his little friendship with Hail always taking precedent over his commitments to the Acruxes. I'd found my way to trap Azriel in the end though, manipulating him into assisting me by encouraging his marriage to Stella. I recalled how easy convincing him had been with a smirk on my lips.

"You know, Azriel, I think you would benefit from a little time with your nose out of a book and some time spent in the company of a beautiful woman. I shall have to introduce you to my dear friend Stella Columba - she is a powerful Vampire and should be more than interesting enough to give you some reprieve from the monotony of all those books you love so dearly." I smiled encouragingly.

"I don't know that I'm entirely suited for marriage," Azriel said with a nervous laugh. *"Most women find they don't like having to compete for my attention with my love of knowledge."*

"Nonsense," I purred. *"She would be the perfect fit for you. I'll set it up."*

They'd been married within the year. And the fool had even believed Stella loved him. Right up until he'd walked in on her sucking my cock during their anniversary dinner, that is. I swear I saw his heart crack in two right as I spilled my seed all over her lying tongue. The fool had killed himself with a wayward spell not long after that, so he hadn't suffered the heartbreak for long. A pity really. He'd always been resistant to my kinship, but in the end I'd bound his son to mine in an act which had always felt like such sweet revenge for Azriel's insolence.

The fool had even believed Stella loved him. Right up until he'd walked in on her sucking my cock during their anniversary dinner, that is. I swear I saw his heart crack in two right as I spilled my seed all over her lying tongue. The fool had killed himself with a wayward spell not long after that, so he hadn't suffered the heartbreak for long. A pity really.

"It's a pleasure to see you," I purred, my gaze dripping over Stella's full tits and the tight nip of her waist. I wanted to fuck with the savagery of my kind today, I wanted my name falling from those full lips while she suffered through the might of the Dragon King.

"A pleasure you could have had many times before now," she said, a stern edge to her voice and my eyebrows arched at her icy tone.

"Bitterness doesn't suit you, Stella," I warned, straightening my tie as my fingers twitched to punish her.

"I've stood by you for years. Do I not deserve a moment of your time these days?" she asked, hurt crossing her features.

Women were always so tiresome with their emotions.

"What do you call this, if not a moment of my time?" I loosened my tie, pulling it free from my neck and undoing the top buttons of my shirt, the Dragon in me heating my body with the desire to have her.

"It has been hard won," she said, pausing before the desk and dropping her eyes to a silver cigar box on the desk. There was an engraving of a Hydra on it wrapped in the embrace of two wings. "Do you ever think about them? What we did?"

"You hardly did anything at all. It was I who dealt with them," I growled and her dark eyes raised to meet mine.

"I taught you all you know about dark magic," she hissed and I sat up straighter in my seat, her tone making the fire in me burn hotter.

"You were useful, now you are less so," I said with a shrug, rising from my seat so I was looking down at her, my shadow falling over her and swallowing her whole.

I'd always allowed Stella to speak more candidly with me than most, but something about the sharpness to her eyes today riled the beast in me.

"What have you come here for, Stella? To try and claim some of my glory?" I scoffed, moving slowly around the desk as I approached her, my gaze falling to the swell of her tits again.

"Of course not," she muttered, dropping her gaze from mine and twisting a bracelet on her wrist. "I've come to ask for mercy."

"Mercy?" I chuckled at the word. "I have no bone to pick with you, Stella."

"Not mercy for me," she said, her eyes raising to mine again. "For my son."

I growled, stepping closer to her as a dangerous energy rose in me. "Your son is a traitor to the king."

"I know," she breathed, her throat rising and falling as fear crept into her features. "I'm not asking for a pardon. All I ask is that if he is caught, he will not be killed. I have already suffered the loss of my daughter, to lose him too-"

I struck her, my hand smacking hard enough across her face to leave a blazing red print there.

"Foolish woman," I spat. "Cut out your attachment to him at the root. He has dirtied your name even more so than his father did. Your womb has failed you. You'd do better to burn the crops it has reaped."

Tears swam in her eyes as she looked back at me, touching the place I'd hit her as her lower lip trembled. I reached out to push a lock of raven hair behind her ear which had swept across her face, stepping closer to her and breathing in the luscious scent of her skin. I loved when they put up a little fight, it made it all the more satisfying when I was inside them. Stella had always been so boringly willing, but her resistance now was definitely more appetising. I knew what she really wanted anyway, because who wouldn't desire the attention of the Dragon King all to themselves?

"Now be a good girl and please your Lion, hm?" I rolled down my fly, dropping one hand to squeeze her tits while she stiffened and tried to back up. But I caught her waist, not letting her go as I took her hand and brought it to the mighty swell of my cock.

"That was an order from your king," I purred, leaning in to inhale the sweetness of her fear.

"Daaadddy," Lavinia's voice sailed through the air, seeming to carry on some ethereal wind and my spine straightened. "I've been a bad girl, Daddy. Come fiiiind me." A giggle followed that noise and I reluctantly took my hands off of Stella, frustration filling me as I pushed her back and tugged up my fly.

"We'll have to meet somewhere more private," I muttered. "I'll summon you when the time is right." I brushed past her, marching open the door as I went in search of my psychotic housemate, my cock still ragingly hard from its unfulfilled needs.

As I strode down the echoing halls, the sound of Lavinia singing to herself reached me, and my Atlas buzzed in my pocket.

I took it out, a sneer lifting my lips as I found my emails filling up over some article that had been published online about me. My PR team were looking to put a spin on it already and I hurriedly brought up the article to see what all the fuss was about.

Catalina Acrux lives!

A shocking discovery has been made that is set to rattle the nation. Catalina Acrux - wife to King Lionel Acrux – was previously thought dead after a tragic accident at The Palace of Souls. However, she has not only has been found alive, it's been declared that she has dissolved her marriage to the king and re-married a known Vega supporter and rebellion leader, Hamish Grus.

I froze, every fibre of my body turning to solid, unyielding ice as I stared at the photograph accompanying the article of my wife – my fucking *wife* – alive and well looking as stunning as she had the day I'd made her my bride in a wholly different wedding dress and on the arm of that disgusting rebel *Grus*.

A Dragon's bellow spilled from my chest as my eyes roamed back and forth across the article, taking in every detail as rage clawed up my spine.

The wedding was attended by none other than the two Solarian princesses, Tory and Darcy Vega, as well as Hamish's daughter Geraldine Grus, the four former Celestial Heirs, Caleb Altair, Seth Capella, Max Rigel, and the two sons of the false king himself Darius and Xavier Acrux.

The photos demonstrate a strong alliance between the Heirs and Vegas twins, and since their disappearance after the battle at The Palace of Souls, it is clear they have formed a bond which could rock the foundations of the kingdom.

Catalina was available for comment, and the secrets that she has unveiled about the false King Lionel Acrux paint him in a terrifying light which is set to lose him support in droves.

Catalina has stated that Lionel 'Dark Coerced her into doing anything he desired', and that she was subjected to 'unspeakable cruelty under his control'. Perhaps one of the most harrowing moments of her account was when she spoke about her ex-husband's business friends, and how he secured deals with high up officials like Gregory Gander, Percy Nostar, and Christopher Bloodstone, by forcing Catalina to offer her body to them, using his dark magic to 'keep her compliant'.

Catalina bravely detailed her years of abuse while her new husband Hamish Grus remained at her side, their hands clasped together in a union that spoke of a deep and caring relationship between them.

Darius and Xavier Acrux also gave their accounts of years of mistreatment, painting a frightening picture of a violent father who created a fearful home for his family with little stability and constant pressure to perform.

Xavier discusses how his father kept him locked up in Acrux Manor after he Emerged as a Pegasus, subjecting him to the wicked and previously outlawed practise of Order Reassignment. We're as yet unclear to the reason his father would take such measures, but it is possible he planned on casting an illusion over his second son to make him appear as a Dragon to avoid admitting his true Order. This of course begs the question as to why the so-called king would want to do such a thing and suggests that his Orderist laws are based on prejudices more than legitimate facts as he claims.

The Daily Solaria has reached out to King Acrux for comment, and we will wait to hear his response. What we know for sure, is that the false king who paints himself as a great ruler, appears to be nothing but an abuser with years of shameful secrets to his name. One can only wonder at what else he is hiding, and at a time of great unrest in the kingdom, we must ask ourselves who it is morally right to align ourselves with.

Click here to watch the full interview with Catalina Acrux and her sons Darius and Xavier Acrux.

(All statements have been verified by reputable Cyclops and former FIB agent Blane Moonbead.)

By Tyler Corbin

I threw my Atlas so hard that it smashed to pieces against the wall, scattering along the hall as I roared my utter fury into the palace, the whole place shuddering around me.

"Daddy, what's the matter?!" Lavinia cried and I strode toward her voice with my hands curling into fists, about to head through the door ahead of me when it slammed into my face so hard it broke my fucking nose.

"Argh!" I shouted, clutching my face and healing the wound before throwing my fist into the door.

The fucking palace was shutting me out of more and more rooms, and I pummelled the door with my knuckles as I fought to get through it.

"JENKINS?!" I yelled for my manservant, needing him to bring me my stardust.

I was going to head to the press and make sure every single piece of that article was undermined. I'd have every upstanding Fae in the kingdom speak on my behalf to besmirch every one of that filthy Pegasus's words.

I gave up on the door which had closed itself to me and turned down the next corridor, taking the long way round towards Lavinia's voice, wanting to throttle her to shut her up.

My eyes fell to a trail of blood along the floor as though someone had been dragged down it and a frown gripped my features as I quickened my pace and followed it.

"Jenkins!" I shouted. "Who left this fucking mess here?!"

My foot slipped in the blood and I spat a snarl as I nearly fell on my fucking ass before using air magic to keep me upright and hurrying along after the blood trail. "JENKINS!"

The blood swerved left into a room and I threw the door open, smoke seeping between my teeth as rage clouded every thought in my head. And there stood Lavinia in a mist of shadow with Jenkins held above her head, her hand buried in his chest as he jerked and thrashed, unable to scream around the shadows pouring into his mouth. His arms were missing and I spotted them on the floor, half eaten like raw meat.

No, he was my best man. My most loyal servant. "Wait!" I ordered, but Lavinia just smiled like a witch and ripped his heart clean from his chest, letting him fall to the floor, his legs snapping on impact.

She tossed his heart away and dropped over his body, taking a bloody bite out of his side as I stumbled a step back, my spine hitting the open door as she pinned those wild eyes on me.

"I'm going to eat him bite by bite," she said, laughing manically and I raised a hand, fire blazing at my fingertips as I prepared to defend myself.

"Why?" I gasped. "Why him?" Of all the people in this world, Jenkins was the one I would likely miss the most. He was relentless in his attention to detail, unwavering in his worship of me, as perfectly enraptured with my power and violence as a man could be, a devoted fan of the brutality of Pitball, the most flawless shoe shiner I'd ever known, and there was no Fae in the whole of Solaria who could rival his calligraphy skills. To put it simply, he was irreplaceable. And of all the worthless Fae in this fucking palace set to serve us, this bitch had chosen him to play out her vile games on. Why did the stars curse me so?

"I should kill you for this!" I bellowed, my rage exploding from me as I took a step towards her, intent on putting her back in her fucking place and punishing her for stealing my best man from me.

But then that traitorous shadow hand of mine slammed down hard between my thighs and I wheezed out a cough, falling to my knees and extinguishing the flames in my palm as I cupped my crotch.

Lavinia jerked her chin and the door was slammed shut behind me by a tendril of shadow, two more taking hold of me and dragging me across the floor towards her.

"Stop," I snapped, throwing out my hand again and blasting her with fire. She deflected it easily, her shadows swallowing up the flames as she stalked toward me, her face and body wet with blood.

"You forget who I am, My King," she sneered, blood running down her chin as she prowled closer, her eyes a roiling storm of shadows. "I am the Shadow Princess, ruler of my realm and soon to be your queen. I am done waiting for my crown and I won't suffer the pain of my shadows being ripped from me without being allowed to drown my grief in blood."

Panic welled as she latched whips of shadows all around my body, binding my arms to my sides as I fought to blast her with my magic. But she was an unstoppable force, a creature so powerful I was suddenly at her mercy and I wasn't sure what she was going to do.

"Enough! I am your king," I barked as she stood above me, bending me right back onto the floor.

"Yes, you are," she said, licking the blood from her lips. "And I owe you an heir, Daddy."

She released my right arm and took hold of the shadow hand she'd gifted me, forcing me to unbuckle my pants and free my bruised cock.

"No, stop," I rasped as she made me pump it forcefully up and down for her, watching me with glee in her eyes while she made me do it so roughly, I feared she'd rip it right off. "Please, Lavinia," I gasped in panic and she offered me some reprieve by having me stroke it more gently.

"Make me your queen," she hissed, the threat of refusing her clear in her eyes. "You have put it off long enough."

"We need a minister," I blurted, hunting for a reason to stall her.

"The word of the king will be enough to bind us beneath the eyes of the stars," she replied, a feral look in her eyes as she waited for my agreement, and I could tell that I'd pushed her for as long as I could with this. She wouldn't wait anymore and perhaps with the announcement of Catalina's union to that fucking rebel Grus, a royal wedding was just the publicity spin I needed to draw attention away from it.

"Alright," I conceded, trying to ignore the way my fucking shadow hand was still tugging at my manhood. "I'll set it up for the weekend. A huge celebration, the whole court in attendance and-"

"No," she snarled, bearing bloody teeth at me. "Tell the stars now, Daddy. I want my crown."

I swallowed thickly, staring up at her as she cocked her head and my hand squeezed my cock a little harder like she was warning me of what would happen if I refused, and I gave in.

"By the power of the crown," I called out, tipping my head back to look up towards the heavens and crying out in alarm as Lavinia smashed a hole in the roof with her shadows so that I could actually see the stars. "As King of Solaria, I choose to bind myself to this woman in marriage. Let us both enter this union with clarity and honesty and forever be linked by the stars."

Lavinia clapped excitedly, tipping her head to the sky too and repeating the words in reverse. "I choose to bind myself to my king in marriage. Let us both enter this union with clarity and honesty and forever be linked by the stars as he makes me his queen."

I felt the slap of that bond fall upon us like a crash of thunder rumbling ominously throughout my soul and as I looked up at my new bride, she smiled a wicked, bloody, triumphant smile at me, urging my hand to move faster up and down my still flaccid shaft.

"It is done," I breathed, watching as she dropped her head back and a crown forged of shadow grew to rest upon her brow, making her moan as she began to run her hands down her chest.

"I just want to please you, Daddy," Lavinia purred, the cloak of shadows on her body falling away to expose her naked flesh. She was bloody and beautiful and maybe having a queen this powerful wasn't such a bad thing, so long as she truly wanted to please me. She was mine to own, mine to ruin if I decided it, and as she released me from the shadows and allowed me to rise, I let myself indulge in looking at her lustful body.

She stroked a hand down my chest, her fingernails cutting through my shirt and tearing it off of me as she looked up at me with wide eyes, the crown on her head clearly tempering some of that rage in her and reminding her of her place. A queen's job was to serve her king after all.

I started to get hard at last as her nipples brushed against my chest and she moaned softly, dropping her bloody mouth to my throat. Her skin was near translucent, darkness writhing through her veins in place of blood, but there was something endlessly seductive about owning this powerful being.

"You killed my butler. I will never find anyone good enough to replace him," I hissed, reaching up to lock my fingers around her throat.

"Then you'd better show me how bad I've been, Daddy," she said, biting her lower lip and I couldn't deny I liked having this hold over her.

Besides, I was the Dragon King, if anyone could tame her it was me.

I spun her around, shoving her against the wall to my right and pinning her firmly there. She pressed her ass back eagerly and I lined my cock up with her entrance, a rush of power rolling through me at taking control of her, of reminding her that I was her king.

I was inside her within one hard thrust and I growled, taking my rage out on her over that article, over Jenkins, my fingers bruisingly tight on her arms as I crushed her to the wall and she cried out like the rougher I was, the more she desired me.

"I'll give you an Heir," she moaned. "I will please you, My King. Just give me your seed and I shall grow us a boy more powerful than any you have spawned before."

415

"You'd better produce one soon," I snarled, fucking her harder at the thought of that. A replacement to the treacherous creatures who had abandoned me for the Vega whores. A true Heir who I could trust to rule in my stead the way this kingdom needed to be ruled as he fulfilled my legacy.

"You have had plenty of time to offer me one. So where is it?" I shoved her face harder against the wall and she moaned louder.

"I told you I would give you an Heir once I was your queen. Not before," she gasped.

"Well you're my queen now. So give it to me," I grunted, my cock close to bursting as I drove into the tightness of her body.

"As you wish," she replied, her words a violent promise which I failed to react to fast enough as I prepared to finish inside her.

Just as I was about to find my release, Lavinia took hold of my shadow hand once again, punching me in the head and I stumbled backwards from the force she used, roaring in rage as my cock was tugged free of her body and my legs hit a table behind me.

Lavinia flipped around, running toward me with a shriek in her throat and though I cast an air shield to protect myself, she tore through it like paper with her shadows, diving on me and forcing me down on the table.

She slammed her pussy down on my cock, bending it sideways and I yelled in pain before she grabbed hold of it and shoved it inside her, riding me hard while locking both of her hands around my throat.

"Stop," I choked out, trying to push her back as she bounced furiously on my lap, the crown on her head growing larger as she moaned in ecstasy. She lashed my good arm to my side while wielding my shadow hand so it tweaked my own nipples hard enough to almost rip them off.

"Lavinia!" I begged.

"Daddy!" she cried back as if my prayer for her to stop had been an exclamation of pleasure, and I wailed as she made me shove the shadow hand beneath me and spread open my ass cheeks.

"Stop – stop it!" I roared, trying to buck her off of me but it only spurred her on.

The next words died in my throat as she forced me to shove two shadow fingers up my own ass, the burning pain of it making me scream like a new born whelp.

Lavinia howled like a banshee, her pussy tightening around my cock to the point of agony. And suddenly she was forcing an orgasm out of me, one that somehow hurt like fire was tearing free of my cock as I spilled myself inside her, and she continued to bounce until I'd given her everything I had and my cock felt as though it was broken beyond repair.

I groaned in discomfort as she leapt off of me, leaving me bound there on the table, unable to move as the shadow fingers remained deep in my ass and my other hand was still latched to my side.

Lavinia moved around the room as the shadows danced across her skin, and a horrified realisation fell over me as her stomach started to swell and swell as though she were pregnant, but that wasn't at all possible.

"What's happening?" I asked, my voice coming out weak as I continued to strain against her hold on me.

"It's your Heir, of course," she said with a manic smile, clutching her belly as she dropped down on the couch and spread her legs wide so I had a view straight to her cunt. "He wants to say hello to his daddy."

"Stop," I begged, shaking my head, unsure what game this was but I didn't like it at all. "Let me go, Lavinia. I am your king – obey me!"

She moaned gleefully, clutching her swollen stomach as she spread her legs wider. "He's coming."

"Who?" I breathed in fear, but my answer was given to me in the most horrifying way as small shadow hands clawed their way out of her vagina and a blackened head swiftly followed, two blood red eyes locking on me as the thing clawed its way out of her, making her scream.

"He's here!" Lavinia gasped and I shuddered, trying to get free, but I was bound in place and she wouldn't let me look away.

The shadow creature dragged itself fully out of her body, the thing the size of a baby but nothing like one too. Its limbs were too long, its head too bulbous, and the moment it slithered free of its mother, it stood up on two legs, its eyes glowing red and its body smooth and wet with some black substance that dripped to the floor at its webbed feet.

"Say hello, baby," Lavinia encouraged.

"Hello Daddy," it growled in a voice made of nightmares and I screamed. I screamed and fucking screamed like I had never screamed before.

MAX

CHAPTER THIRTY FIVE

I lay in the pool of water in the bathhouse, using my hold on the Element to help me float on the surface of it. I was shifted into my full Siren form, navy blue scales coating my skin and quivers of pleasure tracing through them at the contact with the water.

I drew in a deep breath, working to close my mind and shut myself off from the incessant press of everyone's emotions which were working to alter my own feelings. It was exhausting being down here, so close to countless Fae at all times.

In truth, I had to work fairly hard to keep my mind clear of others' emotions at the best of times, and at Zodiac Academy I'd often struggled with this issue, the call of so many emotions drawing me from sleep or making it hard for me to concentrate as they brushed against my senses.

But down here was worse. At the academy I'd had King's Hollow to escape to, and my room in Aqua House was surrounded by water which dulled the press of external emotions far better than earth or air. Here I felt like I was suffocating with the pain of stubbed toes, indignance over portion sizes, unsatisfied lust and general frustration.

It had been a long time for so many rebels to hide beneath the ground, and the victories we won against Lionel as we tore down his Nebular Inquisition Centres only provided a small respite from the monotony of life hidden away from the world. I had it far better than most in the royal quarters, our space bigger and freedom greater but there was such a pressure of boredom and frustration coming from the rest of the rebels that it was growing harder and harder for me to block it all out effectively.

"I just heard from my mom," Caleb's voice interrupted my little haven of tranquillity, and I banished the flash of irritation that passed through me in favour of opening my eyes and looking to him in hopes of hearing some news from my family.

"Anything to worry about?" I asked, rolling over and swimming through the water towards him as he sat down on the edge of the pool.

"No. She says Lionel is still making sure they're busy with menial tasks, keeping his plans for the rest of the kingdom to himself while sending the FIB out on wild goose chases to search for information stolen by Sphinxes and Minotaurs even though no solid evidence of that has actually been presented. Oh and there was some bullshit party they all had to attend to celebrate his wedding to the shadow bitch."

"He's up to something," I muttered, feeling it in my soul and hating that we couldn't figure out what that something was.

"Yeah. Mom is going to keep trying to find out more, but I worry about her being so close to him. She said Hadley and the rest of the Spares have been put in special classes at Zodiac with that fucking troll Highspell. No one is allowed to question what they're learning but I can only imagine there is a whole lot of Lionel loving bullshit involved in it."

"I'd guess Ellis doesn't much mind that," I muttered bitterly, knowing my bratty little sister would be loving every minute of being treated as the Heir to my seat on the Celestial Council. But if she seriously thought she was going to be able to claim it from me without a fight then she was kidding herself.

"Yeah." Caleb sighed, sitting back and leaning on his hands as he looked out across the pool of water.

"What's up?" I asked, automatically pushing out to feel for his emotions, but he had them locked down just like he always did recently, and I couldn't help but frown at that. "You've been keeping me out a lot."

Caleb's brow dipped and he looked at me, seeming unsure if he wanted to speak about whatever was on his mind before throwing a silencing bubble up around us and leaning closer to where I sat within the pool of water.

"You know how I've been hunting Seth a lot recently?" he asked, dropping his voice even though it was unnecessary with the silencing bubble in place.

"Sure." The excitement Seth gave off whenever he came rushing past me running for his life from Caleb's fangs put a smile on my face every damn time I felt it.

"Well, I'm thinking about it a lot. Like, any time I'm not actively doing something else, my mind will wander and I'll start thinking about the rush I get when I'm chasing him, the way it feels to fight for the chance to sink my fangs into his skin and how good it feels to pin him beneath me and just take what I fucking want from him as roughly as I like. And I...I'm beginning to wonder if there's something more to that..."

"Oh yeah?" I'd caught more than the odd whiff of lust coming from Seth when he and Cal played those games, and I guessed I could see how the thrill of it could be getting the two of them all worked up. Especially seeing as we had all been trapped down here night after night listening to Darius and Tory practically break the fucking walls down with their passion while having very little outlet for our own needs. I'd managed to spend a single night worshipping Gerry's body after her father's wedding, but since then I was back living on blue balls mountain while she made me work my ass off for every scrap of attention I gained from her.

"Yeah and I'm getting kinda worried that maybe my mom was right."

"Your mom?" I asked in confusion.

"Yeah. I mean, I almost killed Tory by playing this stupid game. And sometimes when I'm in the hunt it's seriously hard for me to keep my head. I go all in with my bloodlust and I feel like it urges me to act in ways I wouldn't. Or…maybe that's just a load of shit and all it's really doing is revealing what I want the most, making it easier for me to see exactly what my deepest desire is." He frowned, glancing away again and I scrubbed at my chin.

"And you think that desire is Seth's blood?"

Caleb's lips parted like he'd been going to agree then he leaned in a little more. "Not just his blood. I want to own him. Like make him mine in some primal way that can't be questioned by anyone or anything. I felt a little like this when Tory was my Source, but it's so much more intense with him. Like just the thought of anyone else biting him or laying some kind of claim on him makes my fucking blood boil. I have to fight against the urge to just grab him and lock him away where no one can find him. The other night he went and ran beneath the moon with Rosalie Oscura and her pack and I paced my fucking room for two hours before snapping and shooting out there to find him. He was in full Wolf mode so the fight we had was epic, but when I finally managed to force him beneath me and sank my teeth into his neck, I swear I hit nirvana. And I thought that was all I needed but when Rosalie called Seth back out to run with her again once I was sated, it was all I could do not to attack her. I just can't cope with the idea of anyone trying to have him in any way, it's driving me nuts." Caleb's fangs snapped out and a snarl escaped him as he considered that and I raised my hands in surrender.

"Calm down, man, I have no interest in biting your precious Source."

He breathed a laugh and I smiled back.

"It sounds like Vampire stuff. Maybe just talk to Orion about it? It could be to do with your Vampire coven thing?" I suggested.

"Yeah," he agreed, looking up like he was hoping his new little pal might appear at any moment and I shook my head at the total one eighty they'd taken in their relationship. They'd gone from bitter rivals to fucking besties with no more than a little love bite shared between them, and I couldn't even doubt their new bond because I could feel it humming between them as if they'd been best friends since they were kids. It was kinda weird, but they seemed happy enough and it wasn't like anything all that terrifying had happened to them - they'd just lost the urge to constantly compete with one another for blood sources and had found a way to bond over all things Vampy in doing so.

Caleb looked around, cocking his head as he listened to something I couldn't hear and he got to his feet.

"Gabriel just arrived at the dining hall and he has some plan to help us get the shadow eye," he said, beckoning for me to get out of the water.

I sighed, pulling myself out of the pool and shifting back into my Fae form before using my water magic to dry myself off and dressing quickly.

We hurried down the sweeping tunnels towards the dining hall and found Gabriel surrounded by a group of rebels who were all listening to him with rapt attention, their excitement spilling through the air and brushing against my skin.

Cal nudged me to point out our group and we slipped through the crowd towards them as Gabriel gave the rebels his instructions.

"I need each and every one of you to make a plot to assassinate the false king's Seer Vard over the coming month," he was saying. "You can choose any time to strike and come up with the darkest and most gruesome methods of attack that you can manage. It is imperative that you make this your priority. We need him dead, and we need it to happen as soon as possible."

Murmurs broke out between the crowd as their moods turned bloodthirsty, hungry and determined. I exchanged a surprised look with Caleb as we made it over to our group and Gabriel came to join us.

"Won't Vard *see* all of them coming?" I asked in confusion and Gabriel grinned demonically.

"Oh I'm counting on him *seeing* endless versions of his death in his very near future," he agreed.

"If he can *see* them coming then how do you expect them to succeed?" I pushed.

"I don't," he replied simply. "I only wish for him to be so distracted by all of the death threats he *sees* coming his way that he doesn't *see us* coming when we strike at him tonight."

"So we're going to kill him?" Darius asked, sounded all too ready for that idea.

"No," Gabriel barked. "And don't you for one second plan to either."

"Oh good golly, I think I get it!" Geraldine cried, bouncing in her seat and drawing my attention to her tits. "This is an old fashioned distract and dongle move, isn't it?"

"It is," Gabriel agreed.

"What the fuck is that when it's at home?" Orion asked flatly.

"It's when you tell someone to expect a slap to the face, but surprise them with a Long Sherman up their begonia instead!" she explained like she was talking to a child and Xavier neighed a laugh.

"Exactly that. But instead of getting anywhere near Vard's rotten begonia, we're going to sneak up on him and steal the shadow eye right out of his sub-standard Seer's face," Gabriel said proudly.

"So you want us to steal his eye without killing him?" Seth asked like he thought that was an impossible task.

"Oh Seth Capella, anyone would think you have never plucked an eye from a conniving little Roger before," Geraldine chastised. "Sometimes, I think you boys are as wet as a kipper in the morn."

"Are you saying you have experience of plucking people's eyes out?" I asked her, half grossed out and half turned on by the idea of that. Geraldine in badass warrior mode was pretty much my ultimate wet dream - and I had it really damn often.

"Lavinia and Lionel will need to be drawn away from the palace to give you the best chance of striking at him. Vard will no doubt lock himself away in his chambers the moment he starts getting visions about all of these death threats against him, so he should be simple enough to find."

"And I can get us into The Palace of Souls thanks to the ring Tory made me which gives access to the king's secret passages," Orion said, his eyes brightening at the idea of striking at them right at the heart of their power.

"Precisely. I think you, Darius and Geraldine should head after Vard and the rest of us will attack the new Nebular Inquisition Centre that Lionel just opened to the west of Tucana," Gabriel said.

"Have you *seen* a way for us to take it down then?" I asked because we'd been trying to figure out how to rip that place apart since it had been built.

Lionel had clearly grown tired of us destroying his detainment facilities and had built this latest place with so much magic that the rebels had yet to come up with a viable plan for destroying it and freeing the prisoners he was holding inside without triggering the defences which would kill all of them instead.

"Yeah, with the help of my family, I'm confident that we can get the prisoners out of there," Gabriel confirmed and my blood started to pump faster at the thought of heading into the fight once again.

"Oh I do love a good showdown," Geraldine squealed, clapping her hands.

"Geraldine will be in charge when you get to the palace," Gabriel ordered, making both Darius and Orion's bloodthirsty grins turn to scowls.

"Why?" Darius demanded.

"Because she is the most unpredictable. Besides, I know that she understands the plan - you can't change your minds and decide to kill him or he's going to *see* you coming. He has to be so overwhelmed by all the death threats that he can't *see* a simple injury so you can only plan to take his eye."

"We have to leave him alive?" Darius asked, looking pissed as all hell about that. "Do you know what that sick fuck did to Roxy?"

Xavier whinnied sadly, looking to his brother with an ache in his eyes.

"Believe me, I know," Gabriel growled, his brotherly love for her clear in his tone but he stayed firm in his decision. "His day will come, but it can't be today. We need his eye more than we need his death. I can't *see* the shadows and it's the only thing that will be able to lead us to the rifts, and I can *see* a future where we have used that eye to find them and have succeeded. I've had my family testing the holes in his capabilities with non-lethal attacks and I can confirm that he never *sees* them coming. He's not fucking fit to put his ass on the Royal Seer's chair and I'm looking forward to proving it when you pluck that fuck ugly eye from its socket."

"So that's why your little gang of hooligans have been slapping Lionel with shit pies to the face, making him trip and fall into questionable puddles and throwing Dragon dick dildos at his head during his public appearances?" Seth asked, his eyes filling with understanding. "You were figuring out the limits to Vard's abilities."

"Exactly," Gabriel replied proudly. "And when I sat watching the slow-motion replay of that big, glittering, plastic pegasex doll dick slapping him around the face at the official coronation for his shadow queen last night, I knew it was time."

"I provided the extra glitter for that," Xavier said proudly and I snorted a laugh as he puffed up his chest.

"Anyway, point is, we need his eye and we absolutely can't kill him. Got it?" Gabriel pushed, looking around the group to make sure we were onboard with his plan.

Darius didn't look happy about it, but he nodded once in agreement and Geraldine leapt to her feet.

"Oh joyous day! I'll go get my great grandmama's eye scoop and meet up with you dastardly fellows by the boundary in a jiffy." She took off without giving any of us the chance to question her on the eye scoop thing, but I had to assume that was just some weird turn of phrase.

"I guess we're going to destroy a psycho king's holding cells then," I said conversationally as we headed away to our rooms to grab our weapons.

"And oh, what a night it will be," Seth sang happily as he bounded ahead, and I couldn't help but grin at the challenge we were facing.

DARIUS

CHAPTER THIRTY SIX

We crept along the stone passages which crisscrossed beneath The Palace of Souls with Geraldine in the lead singing some strange as fuck song beneath her breath while I bit down on my tongue and tried to force myself to follow her without complaint.

But it was fucking hard.

She had literally changed direction down here for no reason at all three separate times and even though I knew that her choices were leading us further from Vard's rooms instead of closer to them, I couldn't say a damn word against it.

"Are you sure this is the way you want to go?" I asked through gritted teeth while Orion smirked at me, knowing full well that this was pissing me off to no end. But seriously? Was I really going to have to follow her commands throughout this entire trip even when I knew she was making insane moves that just dragged this whole thing out? "I feel like we should be trying to take a more direct route-"

"Of course you do," Geraldine sighed, sounding utterly exasperated with me even though I'd only opened my mouth a total of three times during the hundred instances I'd wanted to since we'd entered these tunnels. "Because yours is the linear and simple mind of a well-bred dairy cow. When you see the grass you want to go directly to it - no matter if a bog monster awaits you in the swamp ahead."

"In what way are we risking running into a bog monster?" I hissed and Orion chuckled.

"We aren't," she replied hastily. "Because we are swimming the fair and tranquil waters of lady fate and her whims alone shall guide us to success tonight."

I gave up on trying to reason with a mad woman and just kept my internal grumbling within my own head as she found a hidden staircase and led the way up it. Up and up and up, far beyond the second level of the palace where I knew Vard's rooms to be.

"Avast!" Geraldine announced suddenly, pulling a door open and tossing a tapestry aside as she stepped out into the palace. "Onwards dear brother and my faithful sharp tooth, there is a game afoot!"

We hurried out into the corridor behind my insane stepsister, and she took off towards the far end of the hall with purposeful strides.

My fingers flexed for the feel of my axe in my hand but I left it strapped across my back, knowing I was already going to be tempted enough to cut Vard's fucking head off when I saw him. I didn't need the added temptation of having a weapon to hand to make it easier to do. I had to keep repeating that in my head though.

Do not kill the motherfucker who helped torture the woman I love. Do not kill the motherfucker who helped torture the woman I love. Do not kill the motherfucker who helped torture the woman I love.

But I could sure as fuck butcher him a bit in payment for what he'd been a part of doing to her.

A scuttling sound made me whip around as some dark shadow caught the corner of my eye and I frowned, almost certain I'd heard something there as I felt the weight of eyes on my back.

"Did you hear that?" I muttered to the others, knowing our silencing bubble would keep my words private.

"Yeah," Orion replied, his sharp gaze scouring the far end of the hallway as that feeling of being watched increased.

"I sense a crafty cretin in the wings," Geraldine whispered, removing her flail from her back and swinging it menacingly as she stepped in front of us to get a look. "If we are ambushed, then you must run sweet brother, for my lady requires your services more than she is in need of mine, so I shall take the fall if it comes to such a fate."

"My services?" I asked, still frowning down the hall and finding no one there.

"Yes. You do warm her cockles in a most pleasing way. Even if you are a bothersome beast, you clearly know your way around her lawn."

"Err, thanks?" I glanced at Orion who seemed way too fucking amused by this whole thing and shot him a scowl.

"Please do not accost my ears with tales of your wally-whacker. I do not need the visual inspired by such recounts to press in on my mind, causing incestuous thoughts of your performance."

"We aren't actually related so they wouldn't be inces-"

"Yonder. We must forget the possibility of a wandering Norman following us and keep on with our task." Geraldine turned suddenly and shoved her way between me and Orion, shoulder checking both of us and knocking us aside as she stormed off in the opposite direction to the noise I'd been certain I'd heard.

"You heard the lady," Lance said. "Yonder."

I snorted and turned to follow her, my mind instantly falling on the thought of us taking Vard by surprise which was quickly followed by the desire to dismember him for the things he'd done to my girl.

"I brought my sun steel sword so you can cut him up good," Lance said conversationally as we walked. "I figured it was the least he deserved for what he did to Tory."

"Seriously?" I asked, feeling way too thrilled about the idea of being able to permanently scar that motherfucker than was probably healthy, but I wasn't gonna psychoanalyse myself over the fact.

"Yeah. I know you have to be aching to finish him. Hell, I'd gut him myself if I could. But maybe Tory will be able to claim the honour when she returns."

"Whenever the fuck that is," I growled, my mood instantly souring as I thought of the month I'd already lost with her. "I missed her fucking birthday."

"I know, brother, I missed Darcy's too. But Gabriel is certain they have to do this. They need to learn everything The Palace of Flames has to offer if they're going to be strong enough to take down Lionel and-"

"It's not the same for you," I snapped, realising I shouldn't have said it as his gaze darkened and he bared his fangs at me, but he didn't know the truth. I hadn't just missed her fucking birthday, I'd missed the only birthday of hers that I would ever get a chance to celebrate with her properly. I'd lost my shit entirely that day, shifting and flying away from The Burrows, determined to find my father and destroy him so that she could return to me and I could make full use of the small amount of time I had left with her without the dark cloud of his presence still hanging over us.

But of course that hadn't worked out. I'd flown halfway to The Palace of Souls before Gabriel had shown up like a bat out of fucking nowhere and told me that my future would end that night if I continued along the path I was on.

So I'd been forced to turn back, unable to bear the thought of never seeing her again even if I had been willing to take the chance with my own life to destroy the man who had dominated and destroyed so much of it. But I couldn't bear losing her without a goodbye. Just like I couldn't bear watching the weeks, days, hours and seconds tick by without her, knowing with such certainty that my time was running short.

I had just under five months left and it was never going to be enough, but now even the short amount of time I did have was being stolen from us, and Gabriel still had no answer as to how long I would have to wait for her to return. He'd even admitted that there was a chance it would be after Christmas which meant I may have already stolen my last kiss from her lips, her last smile, laugh, all of it over before it had even really begun and I was so furious at the stars, myself and everything in between that I couldn't even keep this secret to myself properly anymore.

"How isn't it the same?" Orion growled, grabbing my arm and wheeling me to face him while Geraldine headed on down a set of stairs as if she couldn't even hear us. "You think because she was your Elysian Mate that makes your bond to her stronger than mine is to Darcy?"

I opened my mouth, half willing to agree to that just so that I could feel the force of his rage and let it distract me from this endless agony I was in over the time I was losing with the only woman I would ever love. But then I hesitated, almost spilling the truth before realising that that would be selfish too. I'd kept this secret for a good reason because we all needed to be focusing on the war, not wasting time trying to fight the stars on my fucking hopeless fate. I'd made my choice and I was going to have to own it.

"It's not that," I gritted out, forcing myself to keep my head despite my desire to lose it. "I just know I'm going to have to go up against Lionel soon and I feel like I could be losing the only time I'm going to get with her. There are no guarantees I'll win that fight even with you teaching me the dark magic I'll need to give me an edge and you know it. So if it comes down to that before she returns then I might not get the chance to say goodbye."

I knew it was a dick move to offer him a half truth like that, but I had to hope that they would all be able to forgive me and understand my reasons for lying in the end.

Lance relaxed, his brow furrowing as he shook his head. "You will win that fight when the time comes for it," he said fiercely. "We just need to get Lavinia out of the way first then you'll have the shot at Lionel which you're owed, and you'll see him bleeding out at your feet for all the things he has caused you and the rest of us alike. Tory will be back before you know it and you'll be able to look forward to a future where you create mini Dragons and Phoenixes to chase around after each other in a kingdom which thrives in peace."

I locked my jaw, unable to say any more about Roxy or why I couldn't look forward to any of those things in a dream or otherwise and I nodded once.

Lance made a move to turn away from me but I caught hold of him, making him meet my eye again.

"You have always been a brother to me," I said roughly. "And the love I feel for you is mightier than any bond placed upon us ever could have forced us to feel. If I do die, I want you to know that-"

"Darius, don't-"

"Look after her," I growled, taking his hand in mine and forcing him to make this vow with me. "If I'm gone, promise me you'll do all you can to help her move past it and see her happy again. Love her like a brother and help her find…peace beyond me. Swear it. I need to know she won't be alone without me."

Lance looked like he wanted to protest but then the same fear and darkness that consumed me so often these days shifted in his gaze and he nodded.

"Only if you swear to do the same for Darcy if the worst happens to me," he replied.

I should have told him I wouldn't be around to do that, but I didn't, knowing that I would keep this vow in this life or the next anyway and needing him to make it for Roxy's sake.

"I swear," I agreed and as he did too, a flash of magic clapped between our palms that bound us to it.

I dragged him towards me by our clasped hands and wound my arm over his shoulders, hugging him tightly for a brief moment before releasing him, hoping he hadn't realised that I was trying to give him a goodbye in case I didn't get a chance to give him another before my time was truly up. Because I knew that if Christmas rolled around and my countdown came to an end, I wouldn't spend my final day surrounded by the people who loved me. I'd fly to the Palace of Souls and give all I had to make sure my father and his fucking minions were destroyed along with me.

We parted and took off after Geraldine, hurrying to catch up to her and spotting her just as she reached the third floor of the palace and headed out into the corridor there. It was still an entire floor above Vard's sleeping quarters, but I couldn't be bothered to try and ask her why she was taking yet another indirect route, instead trying to remind myself that Gabriel had *seen* this working so long as we stuck with her.

"Oh sweet onions on a basket of rye!" she exclaimed as the door swung shut between us and Lance and I broke into a sprint, drawing our weapons and gilding them in Phoenix fire as we burst through the door at her back, finding ourselves in a huge chamber with a floor length painting of the dead queen hanging from the wall before us.

Geraldine had thrown herself to her knees and was murmuring praises to the dead woman despite the fact that she was clearly no more than paint on canvas, and I muttered a curse at her ridiculous ways as I sheathed my axe once more, extinguishing the flames.

I had to assume that this was one of the rooms which had locked itself to my father as it seemed untouched. It was still full of things which related to the Savage King and his queen and I wondered briefly why we were being gifted access to it.

"Geraldine, I don't think we really have time to be praising random paintings," I said.

"Oh you cod bellied, Dragoon," she sighed. "You are so irksome sometimes it is hard to function at all around your overbearing, borish ways."

"We literally came here to get a shadow eye," I hissed. "Not to take a fucking tour of the palace. Who knows how long the others will be able to keep my father and Lavinia away from here?"

"Fine," she gasped with a tone that said she found me irritating as fuck and I sighed, biting my tongue in favour of just getting this shit over with.

We made a move to head on again, but Geraldine screamed suddenly, raising a hand and pointing a shaky finger at the wall. I turned towards it, reaching for my axe then hesitating as I realised what she was pointing at. A pair of glimmering silver wings had appeared on the wall below the painting, a hum of energy about them which made them hard to ignore.

"Darcy told me that Queen Merissa left visions for her marked by a symbol like that," Orion breathed, stepping towards the marking with a look of awe on his face.

I arched a brow in suspicion. "Why would the queen have left a vision for us to find?"

"You are right," Geraldine breathed. "You are most unworthy, a scaled salamander of suspicion, spawn of the false king, an unequal rapscallion of a man. And let us not get started on the Power Shamed scandal in the room."

"Alright, Grus, that's enough," Orion grumbled as he stepped forward with his hand outstretched and I followed.

The moment my fingers brushed the stones, I was drawn into a vision which stole my breath as I was gifted a peek at a life that could have been.

"This future was stolen from us all," Merissa Vega's voice echoed through my skull and my jaw fell slack as I watched a lifetime of memories on fast forward where the Vega twins had been raised with me and the other Heirs.

Lance and Clara had grown up with us too, all of us spending countless hours in each other's company, growing together and planning for a life where we were united as the force of power destined to rule Solaria.

I was gifted visions of Roxy and I, looking younger than we were now, drawn to each other time and again, sharing our first kiss in this very palace during her fifteenth birthday party and getting caught by her father who damn near bit me in half as he chased me the hell out of there.

Lance and Darcy fell for each other when he came home on his first break in the middle of a pro Pitball season and had a whirlwind romance which the press were all over like a rash. Roxy and I kept sneaking around, trying to fight what we were to one another because of our positions and what it would mean for the Celestial Council.

But in time we stopped fighting it and my lips parted as I watched image after image detailing the way I'd given up my seat for her, marrying her and handing my position to Xavier in my place.

The entire kingdom was at peace and in love with their princesses. When it came time for them to ascend, I was right there at Roxy's side while Lance stood by Darcy. And everything was so fucking good that I could almost taste it. This future which had never truly been on the cards for us thanks to my father.

Geraldine began to sob as the vision faded, murmuring her love for the true queens over and over again while I tried not to grieve a life I would never get the chance to live in any way. Because my death was coming on swift and certain wings. I wouldn't be in any version of Roxy's future now. But as the impression of that vision lingered within my mind, I began to wonder if a future with the two of them claiming the throne really would be as bad as I'd feared.

With the other Heirs there to guide them, perhaps they could learn what was needed for the rule of our kingdom. But I wouldn't be around to find out if that was the future they would face or not.

And though the ache of grief over everything I'd never had weighed heavily in my chest, I couldn't help but wonder what would happen if I truly did manage to destroy my father and tear him from this world before I was forced to follow him beyond the Veil. Because just maybe, once I was gone, the age of the Dragons would fall, and it would be time for the Phoenixes to rise once more.

SETH

CHAPTER THIRTY SEVEN

Dante swooped overhead, electrocuting a whole line of Nymphs as they ran to intercept the escaping rebels. He'd taken down half the fence with his lightning powers and we'd done the rest of the work, slicing through the magical boundaries beyond it just before Lionel and Lavinia had shown up to rain down death on as many people as they could.

The rebels' magic was locked down, their hands in glowing blue cuffs, but Caleb had shot between the guards, stealing their keys and freeing as many rebels as he could get to. The more of them that reclaimed their magic, the more the tide turned in our favour, but the Nymphs were arriving in droves following their queen and I didn't know how long we'd have the upper hand.

Washer and Max stood by the broken fence behind me, using their Siren allure to draw all the rebels towards them, feeding them a sense of freedom which I felt humming in my own chest. They cast shields and ice barriers around them to protect themselves from any enemy strikes too.

Xavier swooped low over the escaping Fae, kicking his hooves at the FIB agents who raised their weapons against the fleeing rebels, whinnying loudly in encouragement. There was a sharp metal spike encasing his horn that the twins had made for him and it was alight with Phoenix flames. He neighed in delight every time he shook his mane and the glitter from his hair made the flames burn with the colour of a rainbow. He'd looked pretty ridiculous when he'd strapped that thing to his head in his Fae form, but I could admit it looked kinda badass now. Especially as he worked to hold the FIB off as he'd been tasked. But me? I had the most important job of all.

"Awoo!" I howled in my Fae form, cupping my hands around my mouth as I stood on top of one of the muddy huts the imprisoned Fae had been forced to sleep in. And as Nymphs turned their attention towards me instead of the rebels trying to break past them, I created a powerful illusion of those very people, splitting away from the real path they were taking and leading the Nymphs in several directions, their huge probes swiping through the air and slashing through nothing but my illusions. Far beyond them on the other side of the compound Lavinia and Lionel were chasing more of my illusions in circles, carving through nothing but sweeping droves of magical casts instead of the Fae we were all working to rescue.

I laughed at the chaos, catching sight of Cal as he moved like the wind between the real rebels, freeing their magic so they could defend themselves. Clouds of smoke and flashing light exploded across the huge compound as the Fae took revenge for their treatment in this hellish place and I grinned at their efforts.

My gaze hooked on a couple of little kids running hand in hand towards Max and Washer, nearly falling time and again as the crowd stampeded past them, my smile falling away.

"This way! That's it, move your hineys!" Washer encouraged as he beckoned the rebels past him to where Leon and his family were working to disguise them with spells and hide them from view altogether.

I growled as a man's knee smashed into the back of one of the kid's heads and the two of them fell sprawling into mud.

I howled, but this time it was a real Wolf's howl as I pulled my clothes from my body and dove forward into the fray, my gigantic paws slamming into the mud as I ran against the tide of fleeing Fae to reach the kids. The Phoenix fire gauntlets on my hands had shifted to accommodate my paws, but I kept the flames unlit as I ran through the sea of our allies to ensure I didn't hurt anybody.

Screams rang out ahead of me and a huge shadow blotted out the moon as a massive Nymph stormed through the crowd, knocking Fae down and ramming its probes into their chests.

People fell against me, terror everywhere and magical casts going up into the air which only caused more danger as explosions of fire and ice blasted over the crowd.

I barked loudly to try and tell them to stop, ducking my head as an ice ball fell from the sky and took out a guy beside me. I leapt over two women in front of me, landing right over the huddled bodies of the two children as the Nymph reared above them and its branch like arm smashed into my head.

I stumbled sideways with a yelp, but I didn't fall, leaping up and slashing my claws down its chest with a savage snarl, the fire igniting across my gauntlets and burrowing into its body.

The Nymph shrieked in pain, stumbling back and I pressed my advantage, jumping up and biting its throat while tearing at its body with my claws. Something snapped beneath the pressure of my jaws and the Nymph exploded into ash, my paws hitting the ground as I turned back towards the kids amidst a cloud of dust and embers, nudging them with my nose to get them up.

The boy was a little older and tugged his younger sister up by the hand, their tiny fingers knotting in my fur as I helped them climb onto my back.

Then I stood up to my fullest height and charged along with the crowd towards the shattered fence, Max and Washer's powers falling over me and making my heart sing. Freedom was close, we were so near.

Max's eyes fell on me within the surging rebels and he ran forward to meet me, pulling the kids from my back and holding them to his chest.

"I'll get them out of here. Cal needs help," he said urgently, turning and running beyond the fence.

His final words left me with a sense of terror in my chest as I leapt up on top of one of the sheds to see across the compound to find him.

Caleb was fighting three Nymphs, moving fast and slashing at them with his twin blades, but he couldn't hold all of them off, even with his speed. And as one of them smashed a fist against his head which knocked him clean off his feet onto his back, I howled loudly, hoping he'd hear, that he'd know I was coming. Then I leapt off the roof of the shed, my paws thumping to the ground. I was already running, tearing towards my best friend and the guy I loved so deeply that the thought of losing him completely terrified me.

I howled again, promising I was close, then sprang into the battle to help, colliding with the Nymph closest to him and taking the monster to the ground. I slashed my claws so hard across its face that I saw bone. The beast died on my next strike, ash exploding out around my feet as I turned back, finding a Nymph with its probes pressed to Cal's chest who was lying still on his back, his eyes shut, his lips pale.

I howled my desperate fear as I ran towards him, seeing absolute murderous red as I collided with the Nymph before it could get its probes into Cal's chest, biting down on its whole head until a vile crunch sounded and my victim burst to ash.

The final Nymph turned tail and ran, but I didn't let it go, charging it down with its friends' blood on my lips and my teeth bared for the kill.

I sprang into the air, landing on its back and knocking it to the ground with a heavy crash. I shifted back into my Fae form, unleashing my gauntlets on the back of its head as I punched and punched with all the fury of a man's soul who'd been ripped from his body. And if Cal was dead, then it might as well have been.

The Nymph died with a pained wail and I fell into the mud, shoving myself up, covered in filth and blood and grime. I ran back to my friend, wiping the ash from my eyes as I dropped down beside him, ripping his shirt open and placing my hands to his chest as Xavier swooped overhead with a furious whinny, slamming his horn into the chest of another Nymph as it ran at us, killing it with a fatal blow and dropping glitter over us as he passed by.

Healing magic swept out of me as my magic connected to Caleb's and I released a groan of complete relief at knowing he was still with me.

"Cal, come back. Wake up," I croaked, offering him wave after wave of healing magic and feeling a head injury healing over as his eyes flickered and opened.

"I knew it'd be you," he said, his voice dry as a sideways smile hooked up his lips. "It's always you." Then his eyes widened in fear as they moved to look over my shoulder and he grabbed hold of me, rolling us over so he was on top of me and a gasp got stuck in my throat as I saw Lionel Acrux bearing down upon us in the sky, his jade green scales glinting as fire bloomed from his open jaws, aimed directly at us.

A dome of thick soil shot up around us, turning to stone just before the blast collided with it and Caleb gritted his teeth as he fought to hold it in place. I pressed a hand to his arm, offering him my magic and his barrier came down in an instant, a moan of pleasure leaving me as our power washed together and

I tasted the strength of him on my tongue.

The stone turned to an impenetrable metal, flashing silver with the power of our combined earth Elements as we kept Lionel's fire from touching us and a few of Caleb's golden curls fell forward to brush against my forehead, our breaths shared within the same small space as we fought to protect each other.

An angry roar carried from beyond our barrier and the two of us laughed headily.

"Let's tunnel out and let him waste his power trying to get in here," Caleb suggested and I grinned, nodding my agreement. But neither of us moved and suddenly the space felt so small and his body weighing me down was making it harder for me to breathe.

"Cal," I whispered. "I've been meaning to tell you- I mean, Darcy thinks I should. And Orion too actually, and Tory now I mention it. And anyway, well now might not be the best time, but-"

The dome was suddenly ripped off of us and Lionel appeared with his claws wrapped around it, a Dragon's grin on his scaly face as he found us exposed beneath it. Caleb threw one of his twin daggers with a yell of rage and it lodged in Lionel's cheek, making him roar in anger as he stumbled back, swiping at his face to dislodge it.

"We gotta get underground!" I grabbed hold of Caleb's shirt and made the earth drop away beneath us, burying us from sight and the soil heated around us as Lionel's flames tried to follow.

But we sank deeper and deeper until the two of us were carving out a tunnel, on our feet and running hard and fast to try and get some distance between us and that psycho lizard.

"We need to lead him away from the rebels," I said urgently and Caleb nodded, a look passing between us that said we definitely might die today, but both of us started tunnelling upwards at the same time, knowing neither of us were never going to just hide away underground.

"You're the best Fae I know, Cal," I told him earnestly. "And I fucking love you with all my heart."

"I'm gonna make you repeat that once we get out of this, Seth," he said, giving me one of his cocky grins, but it fell away as we closed in on the surface, and he gave me an intense look. "But just in case, I want you to know that I wouldn't pick anyone else in this world to die beside. You're my ride or die, you know that? I fucking love Darius and Max, but you and me? We've got something special that I can't even explain sometimes."

"You think so?" I asked, wondering if he was saying what I thought he was saying.

"I know so," he growled. "You're like my Nebula Ally on fucking speed, man."

My throat thickened as I accepted what he was implying. Ally equalled friend. And I didn't know why I'd expected him to say something different. I realised I didn't really care in that moment though. I was fucking privileged to be Caleb Altair's friend, and if that was all we were ever destined to be then that was enough for me. Because I'd spent most of my life loving the moon without ever resting a paw on its surface. So Caleb would be my new moon, my unreachable love hanging over me in the sky. And I would show up to watch it night after night with no resentment in my heart, just a lone Wolf on a mountain, trying to get close enough to bathe in its light.

ORION

CHAPTER THIRTY EIGHT

Seeing how our lives could have been without Lionel plaguing every move we made left me with a crushing weight in my chest over all he had taken from us. From the twins. They hadn't deserved to suffer the life they had. They hadn't deserved the shitty foster homes and no stability, they hadn't deserved the poverty, the nights going hungry, the lack of any kind of parental love to surround them.

It still angered me to this day to think of them in the conditions I'd found them in. That cold apartment with mold on the ceilings and my girl in those well worn bunny pyjamas with a look that said I'd just stamped on her last nerve.

Fuck, if I could go back and do it all different I would. I'd walk into their place, sit them down and fucking hug them for one. And for two, I'd bring the Heirs there with me, and I wouldn't let them leave until the lot of them had bonded. Everyone could have saved themselves a whole ocean of heartache if we'd figured all of our shit out sooner.

But I'd learned a long time ago that hindsight was the enemy of the future. We couldn't go back, what was done was done. What was lost was lost. Our feet were facing forward and the doors behind us were sealed shut. I may have had enough regrets to fill the sky, but they were as useful to me as carrying around a ton of rocks on my back. And mostly, I'd set them down and left them in my past. But seeing that vision had reminded me of all the ways Lionel had been responsible for so much of the torment in our lives.

It had been strange to see myself in a world where my life had never been ripped away from me though, coming home from a Pitball tournament only to meet Blue and find ourselves enthralled with each other. How much easier it would have been for us if that had been our fate…

Would she have preferred that version of me? He'd looked happy, stress-free, no hint of darkness in his eyes. This version of me was hard and cold at times, but she was the one who broke through all of that. She was my sunshine after an eternal winter, and I didn't know whether to grieve the life we'd missed out on or be thankful that we had still found our way to each other regardless.

In the pit of my gut, I felt a strange detachment to the man I'd seen in that vision too. He wasn't me. I'd parted ways with him the day Clara had died and Lionel had bonded me to Darius. And if he wasn't me then that meant Darcy wasn't herself in that vision either. She was a girl raised in Solaria, she'd had the gleam of privilege about her that the Heirs often carried, and I wasn't sure this version of me liked it. I wanted *my* Blue. The one who had come to this world ignorant and who I had watched blossom into a Fae queen. Our story wasn't pretty, and it certainly wasn't easy. There was struggle and divide, arguments and pain. But it was ours, down to every gritty detail, and I found I wouldn't have exchanged it for that pretty, simple life I'd just seen. I was possessive of my Blue, and maybe it was selfish of me to think that way after all she had been through, but there wasn't a single thing I'd have changed about her, and to become who she was today, she'd had to be broken, put under pressure so she could emerge like coal into a diamond.

"Oh how easy it all could have been, as simple as a sandworm riding a sea breeze," Geraldine sobbed.

"Those people aren't us," I voiced my thoughts and Darius looked to me with a frown.

"At least they had a future," he muttered.

"So do we," I hissed. "Stop talking as if your fate is sealed. You *can* defeat Lionel."

He shrugged and Geraldine wiped her eyes on her sleeve, sniffing deeply. "Perhaps you are right, Orion, perhaps this is the better way. The juiciest grapefruit is never hanging at the bottom of the tree after all."

"That actually makes some sort of sense," Darius said in surprise.

"Flabberjacks! Of course it makes sense you overgrown crouton!" she clapped him around the ear. "Now come, we have to move yonder."

"I'm really unsure of the meaning you're putting on the word yonder," Darius muttered.

"Yonder, as in 'let us delve into the cracks of the great yonder', you frallycake. I don't know how I can be any more clear," she scoffed, heading from the room and we shared a glance before taking off after her.

We hurried along the cavernous halls of the palace and a creeping feeling ran up my spine, my heightened hearing picking up a scuttling sound somewhere behind us once more.

I whipped around, drawing the Phoenix sword from my hip and Darius reacted in the same moment, lifting the axe from his back. I gazed into the shadows beyond a cracked open door, trying to see through the dark, but it was so thick I couldn't make out anything at all.

"Why do I feel like we're being watched?" I whispered and Darius nodded, taking a step towards that door, but I caught his arm and drew him back.

"We should stay on track," I said, tightening our silencing bubble around our group. "But keep your wits about you."

He nodded and we turned to follow Geraldine, finding her prancing off down a huge staircase that was covered in a deep blue carpet.

We treaded quietly after her and I kept glancing back over my shoulder, keeping my ears trained on anything behind us in case I heard that strange scuttling again.

Geraldine turned down a corridor at the bottom of the stairs and we kept close at her back as she picked up her pace.

"His quarters are down here," Darius encouraged.

"Yes, yes, you bothersome bandicoot. I will get us to our destination. Simply lay your fate in my hands and I shall not lead you astray." Geraldine turned right down a corridor as Darius hissed at her that she was going the wrong way, but after several random turns, we arrived back in the same corridor and she walked up to a door, pausing with her hand pressed to the door as she worked to disable the magical locks and alarms on it before pushing it open.

"Ah yes," she purred. "The greasy-haired codswallop rests his scar-shamed face upon a lagaluffin."

"What the hell's a lagaluffin?" I whispered, moving forward to peer over her head into the dark room.

"I think she means a pillow," Darius said as he knocked the door wider so he could see too.

Vard was asleep on a fourposter bed, facing towards us with his eyes shut and his brow furrowed like he was plagued with nightmares in his sleep.

The bloodlust rose in me as the urge to kill this scum filled me and I followed the others into his room, the three of us approaching him like wraiths come to steal away his soul to hell.

I drew the sun steel sword from my hip and passed it to Darius. "Make him pay," I growled and he nodded to me as he slinked closer to him.

But before he could make it there, Geraldine dove onto the bed, straddling Vard and slapping him forcefully around the face.

"Ah!" he cried, his hands raising to blast her off of him, but she tethered them to his chest with vines and cast a dick-shaped eggplant in her hand before shoving it deep into his mouth to silence his screams.

In the next second, she'd taken a silver item from her pocket which resembled an ice cream scoop and she rammed it into his eye socket with a precision which suggested she'd done this before.

Vard screamed against the eggplant, thrashing like mad as Geraldine pressed a lever on the scoop and a snap sounded as the thing closed around his shadow eye.

I stared on with my mouth agape as she ripped the whole thing from his face in a stream of blood and held it up victoriously while he screamed around the vegetable gag in his mouth.

"Bleed for the pleasure of the Grus line, devil man!" she wailed. "I declare this eye a possession of the true queens!"

Vard flailed and sobbed against the eggplant as Geraldine dismounted him, taking a plastic bag from her pocket and shoving the eye into it before ziplocking it tight. The grotesque red eye was surrounded by shadow, coils of it hanging from it like tiny feet as it wriggled angrily inside the bag.

"Ergh." I recoiled as she pocketed it then the sound of Vard screaming even louder came to me and I realised Darius was on the bed, shearing one of his fingers off.

"Holy fuck," I gasped, shooting forward as Darius tore open Vard's shirt and started carving a crisscross of deep cuts into his chest, making a savage grin fill my lips as his blood spilled and he roared in agony beneath him.

"That's a warm up for what I'll do to you in future." Darius spat on Vard's face then got down from the bed, tossing the finger into a glass of water on Vard's nightstand and wiping the blood from his hand down his pants.

He passed me the sun steel blade and I leaned down and added a few more slashes to Darius's artwork on Vard's chest as Darius watched with a dark laugh, knowing this was never going to heal. He'd bear those scars until the day one of us came to kill him.

I wiped the blade off on Vard's bedsheets before placing the sword back in its scabbard and turning my back on him.

But I frowned as I realised Geraldine wasn't there.

"Where the hell did she go?" Darius whispered and the two of us ran out of the room, checking the corridor but finding that empty too.

A scuttling noise drew my attention to the ceiling and I swore as I found Geraldine bound in a web of darkness, her body glued in place and tendrils of shadow gagging her as she tried to shout a warning to us.

A rush of movement behind me made me whip around and some dark creature collided with me.

I hit the ground with a growl, shoving it back, its jet black body slick with some gloopy substance. It was half man, half monster and I threw it off of me in horror as I realised its face was a weird combination of Darius and Xavier's, sending it tumbling down the stairs to my left as it shrieked and shadows swirled around it.

"What the fuck is that?" I shuddered as Darius tugged me to my feet.

The thing flipped over backwards on the stairs, its arms and legs lengthening as it scuttled up towards us, its head spinning on its neck and a huge black tongue lashing out of its mouth left and right.

"Ah!" Darius dove at it as it leapt from the stairwell, slashing his axe and severing its arm, making the creepy creature stagger away from him and lunge towards me instead.

I raised my Phoenix sword, tearing forwards in a burst of speed to meet it and ramming the blade straight up underneath its jaw, slicing through shadow and bone.

The creature shrieked as it leapt away from me, springing over my head as black blood sprayed across the tiles and it grabbed hold of the wall, scuttling up it like some kind of fucked up spider and hurtling towards Geraldine as she thrashed against the shadows which held her in place.

Darius threw a handful of flames between it and her and the creature screamed, lurching backwards and losing its grip on the ceiling.

It fell towards me with a howl and I shot aside before I could end up crushed beneath it, swinging my sword at it as more black gloop and blood sprayed up mine and Darius's legs.

Darius swung his axe at the thing but it rolled aside, the blade ringing out loudly against the tiles as it leapt to its feet.

It screamed as it came for me, the grotesquely familiar features of its face making me recoil as it reminded me of my best friend and I shot towards it once more, driving my blade home in its chest with a grunt of effort.

It fell to the ground at my feet, making a horrible rattling, grunting noise as it died.

"Phew." I stepped back, grimacing at the black goop which coated us and Darius swung his axe, beheading the thing to make sure it was definitely dead. The vile creature bled a puddle of black blood around our feet and we exchanged a look of shock.

"Ahhh, my ladies, I love you!" Geraldine cried as she fell from the ceiling as the shadows released her and I whipped out a finger, catching her easily on a gust of air and setting her down beside me.

"Oh, gracious, I have been saved by a dashing yet unfortunately shamed Fae," she gasped then her gaze fell to where the monstrous creature had died and she stomped her feet in the blood like a kid playing in a puddle. "I have to say, I thought that beastly vagabond would pose more of a challenge, but what luck, it appears to have been an easy kill after it caught me unawares."

"Yeah, I really thought that was gonna pose more of a challenge," Darius said thoughtfully. "But then bam, thwack, splatter, dead."

"Definitely seems like it should have been harder," I agreed, relieved that it hadn't been. "What the fuck was it though, and why did it look like you?" I grimaced and Darius shuddered.

"Don't know, don't care, frankly, brother. Let's get the fuck out of here," he said, leading the way down the stairs and we pulled tapestries aside until we found a way down into the tunnels.

"Into the night we go!" Geraldine cried as we ran along in the dark. "With a shadow eye in our pocket, and another slap delivered to the false king. Oh-ho!"

CALEB

CHAPTER THIRTY NINE

Seth howled as he ran, his hands cupped around his mouth and the sound making adrenaline spill through my core as I raced back and forth alongside him, casting more and more illusions of people running from the ruins of the Nebular Inquisition Centre as I prayed to the moon that Max, Xavier and the others had managed to get the real prisoners away.

"Long live the rebellion!" Seth yelled, a laugh tumbling from his throat as Lionel roared so loudly the earth rumbled beneath our feet.

The jade green Dragon released a powerful stream of Dragon fire in our direction and I shot towards Seth as it was directed his way, catching his hand and lending him my magic as he threw a powerful air shield up at our backs, shielding our false crowd of escapees as well to maintain the illusion.

The rush of his magic tumbling through my veins made me suck in a sharp breath as I felt the solid power of his earth magic along with the pure and wild freedom of his air.

Seth threw a grin my way as I kept hold of his hand and I pulled on the connected thread of our power and urged it my way instead. He followed my lead, pushing his power into me and the rush of it made me heady as I threw a hand out and blasted Lionel with the full force of my fire magic, hiding sharp arrowheads cast from stone within the flames as he rushed towards my attack without even trying to avoid it, believing his fireproof hide would be enough to protect him.

A furious roar burst from his lips as the arrowheads pierced the scales lining his face and I whooped in victory as my Phoenix blade was knocked free and I shot beneath his scaley belly, catching it before it could hit the ground.

I tugged Seth on, glancing back and finding blood dripping down the Dragon king's face as he turned and wheeled away from us, charging across the night sky with a bellow of rage as I caught sight of the Nymph army taking chase after us.

My victory crow was short lived as I caught sight of the shadow bitch tearing through the sky behind him on a cloud of darkness, her hair and shadowy clothes whipping out around her and revealing her naked body in flashes of pale skin piece by piece. There was a black crown upon her head which seemed to seep darkness deeper than the night itself into the air surrounding her.

Her face was set in a furious mask, and I gritted my teeth as I drew on all the magic in my possession, holding it ready for an attack as she swooped closer.

I called fire to my fist once more, using the added might of Seth's power to make it burn hotter and hotter and yanking him around to stand and face her as she flew closer.

"Let's see her burn, Cal," he growled, his tone all Wolf as he drove the power of his magic into me even harder and she swept straight for us.

Lavinia shrieked as she raised her hands too and I launched the fireball at her just as she threw her shadows at us.

The combination of the attacks collided with a tremendous boom, the shockwave slamming into us so hard that we were flung from our feet and tossed backwards into the air.

Seth kept hold of me as we were thrown away and he took hold of the air which surrounded us at the last moment, slowing our fall just enough for me to throw my hand out and command the ground to soften at our backs.

We hit it hard and bounced against the spongy texture of the soil, our hands wrenched apart by the impact as I was sent rolling away across the ground.

My concentration broke for a moment and the illusion of the escaping crowd flickered in and out of existence. It was only for a fraction of a second, but the roar of feral fury Lionel emitted was enough to let me know he'd seen it.

I cursed as I realised I'd fucked our entire plan, but before I could figure out how the hell we were going to keep the attention of our enemies now, Lavinia released a shriek of agony so loud that I swear the sky rattled from the force of it.

"Our Heir!" she screamed, shadows wrapping around her as she launched herself up and into the air, shooting towards Lionel and abandoning her fight with us like she'd forgotten it entirely.

I pushed to my feet and raced over to join Seth, offering him a hand and tugging him upright as Lionel turned his furious gaze our way once more. But as he beat his wings and bared his fangs at us, he suddenly jerked around, turning away again, his shadow claw held out before him like there was some invisible tether lashed to it which forced him to head after Lavinia instead of pursuing his fight with us.

"Oh my stars," Seth breathed. "We just scared them away."

Half a laugh tumbled from my lips as we watched our enemies retreating, Lionel roaring furiously as he flew away, but I didn't get the impression that that was what had happened.

As Lionel made it to Lavinia's side there was a flash of stardust and the two of them disappeared into the grip of the stars, the oppressive feeling of the shadows lifting as she disappeared and leaving me to draw in a ragged breath of relief.

"I'm guessing they just figured out that the palace is under attack," I muttered, concern for our friends eating at me as I watched the sky for a moment before the howl of a Wolf caught my attention and I looked back towards the ruins of the Nebular Inquisition Centre where the FIB were still on the hunt.

Nymphs raced towards us too and my heart lifted as I realised they were all still fooled by the illusion we'd created and that the others must have cloaked the real rebels and made it away from here as planned.

"Wanna lead the authorities on a merry little dance?" Seth asked, his eyes glimmering with mischief as he looked at me in the starlight and I smirked at him as I nodded, turning back towards the illusion of our escapees who were all still running and screaming in the opposite direction to the real Fae who were hopefully well on their way to The Burrows by now.

"Let's see how well I do as the prey instead of the hunter," I agreed, concentrating on my illusion and raising the volume of the sound they were making so that any Vampires who happened to be working for the Fae Investigation Bureau would be sure to hear them.

Seth cast an illusion around us, making it appear that we were nothing more than a patch of long grass to the side of the road, and my fangs tingled as I waited for them to come.

It took no more than a few seconds for the Vampires to arrive, six of them shooting across the open field towards the town where I'd sent my illusions running, their uniforms marking them out as first line agents.

But as they got close to passing us, I closed my fist, making the ground fall away from them in a massive crater, the screams of one of them filling the air while the others fought to save themselves instead of panicking.

Seth took full advantage of their distraction, flicking his fingers and stealing the air from their lungs as he raised them up to hang before us and we stepped out of our hiding place.

The agent closest to us widened her eyes as she thrashed and kicked against the magic which held her while the man to her right had the cheek to throw a spear of wood our way.

I dismissed the attack with a flick of my wrist and grinned at the six of them with my fangs on show, reminding them that they were in the presence of the most powerful Vampire of my generation as I tied them with vines of my creation.

The moment they were fully restrained by my earth magic, Seth let them breathe and dropped them on their asses on the far side of the huge crater I'd torn into the ground.

"Y-you're Caleb Altair," one of the men gasped, looking all kinds of fucking terrified which was actually a pretty nice ego boost.

"We're just doing our jobs," a woman pleaded, her wide eyes fixed on me.

"I'm also here," Seth growled, drawing their attention for a moment but they all quickly looked back to me.

"Don't take offence, buddy. It's a Vampire thing," I teased him and he growled like a Wolf, letting me know he was less than impressed about that. But I'd been with him around Werewolves plenty of times and had literally been shoved aside as they fought over the opportunity to suck his cock first, so this was nothing.

"Seems like everything's a Vampire thing these days," he muttered.

"What's that supposed to mean?" I asked with a frown.

"You know what I mean. Me and Lance were supposed to be building a BFF moon friends bond and you and me already had our special only for us bond, but then you two had to go getting cosy in that temple and now I'm the odd Wolf out while you giggle about blood and biting and...*fangs* all the damn time."

I arched a brow at him. "Are you jealous?" I asked and he huffed out a breath.

"No. What gave you that impression?"

"Umm...Mr Altair?" one of the FIB agents breathed and I turned back to look at them. "Are you going to kill us?"

A howl sounded from across the field and I looked past the agents we'd caught to see the second wave racing our way, Werewolves, Nemean Lions, Monolrian Bears and Manticores charging towards us in shifted form, taking up the hunt. Beyond them the Nymphs were charging our way too, but they were cumbersome and built for strength over speed so I wasn't too concerned about them reaching us.

"No, we aren't going to kill you," I said, looking down at the agents before us once more. "I'm passing on a message. The false king will fall and those who stood beside him will be remembered. If you want to keep your positions once we reclaim our kingdom then I suggest you give some serious thought to aligning yourselves with the rebellion."

"And you can tell that to your boss as well," Seth added.

They all stared up at us in wide eyed fear like they didn't believe we were really going to just leave them there, but I wasn't going to start killing FIB agents when I had a choice in the matter. Besides, they were just doing their jobs by following the rule of the king, so I figured they could have this one chance to realise that they needed to follow more than just the line of command if they wanted to end up on the right side of this war.

I flashed them a grin which was all fang and they blanched as they were forced to bow their heads to my position of power above them then I shot towards Seth, tossed him over my shoulder and sped away into the night before the second wave could arrive – or worse, the Nymphs.

I raced away into the streets of the town where we'd sent our illusions running, taking control of them again. I made them scatter so that they didn't all just disappear at once and the FIB would be kept busy trying to hunt them down for long enough to be certain that the others had time to escape and make it to The Burrows.

Once I was sure the false trails had been left well enough to keep them distracted, I took the small pinch of stardust we'd brought with us from my pocket and tossed it over our heads.

We arrived back at The Burrows in a flash of starlight and I let Seth down again, my attention caught by the sight of the Storm Dragon breaking through the clouds overhead and coming in to land.

I spotted my cousin riding on his back before noticing the countless tiny creatures who covered his scales too.

Dante landed on the hill beside the forcefield and I watched as what must have been a hundred Tiberian Rats in their shifted forms all scrambled to climb off of him, scurrying down his legs and making it to the ground in a wave of rodents so thick that I was afraid to move in case I stepped on any of them.

A flash of light drew my attention and I turned as Geraldine, Darius and Orion appeared, looking more than a little worse for wear with blood splattering them all and black ichor coating both Darius and Orion, but the victorious looks on their faces let me know this whole thing had been a success.

Gabriel swept overhead, his smug grin telling me all I needed to know about how well that had just gone, and as Washer started calling out for all the new arrivals to follow tight on his tail to get inside, I decided I didn't need to linger out here any longer than was necessary.

I jerked my chin to let the others know where I was headed, and Darius nodded his agreement as I caught Seth's arm and nudged him towards The Burrows.

"Are you good?" he asked me as we carefully stepped over Tiberian Rats and passed through the protective barrier, almost colliding with Hamish Grus as he came jogging out with boxes of clothes ready and waiting for the Shifters to use once they returned to their Fae forms.

"Yeah man, thanks to you," I said, knocking my arm against his and he smiled as he bumped against me in return, nuzzling his head against the side of my chin and bringing a smile to my face as we walked.

"I was pretty heroic, wasn't I?" he mused, pushing his fingers into his long hair which was tangled with at least as much dirt as I could feel clinging to mine.

"Shall we head to the bathhouse?" I suggested as we walked through the farmhouse and he opened the hidden door behind the grandfather clock, holding it wide for me to pass through before moving to walk right beside me again once we entered the tunnels.

It was weird how much I accepted his Wolfy ways really, enjoying the feeling of him brushing against me as we walked instead of distancing myself from him like I would have done with pretty much any other Fae. But with Seth it was different. I liked it. And as I thought about the risks we'd taken today and how many more we would likely face before the end of this war, I couldn't help but fear losing him.

We made it to the bathhouse and I yanked off the torn remains of my shirt, dropping my pants next and glancing over my shoulder at Seth as I didn't hear the sound of him undressing behind me.

My gaze locked with his and my skin prickled at the heat in his eyes as I caught him running his attention over my back, trailing it down to my ass before snapping his gaze up to meet my eyes.

"Are you checking me out?" I teased, my blood heating a little at that idea.

Seth's lips twitched then he raised his chin, jerking a nod at me and just owning his behaviour like it didn't mean anything.

"Don't pretend you don't know how hot you are, Cal," he said. "I doubt there's a man or woman in Solaria who hasn't fantasied about you."

"Including you?" I asked, the words coming unbidden to my lips and

451

making Seth's brows rise as I caught him off guard with the question.

But before I could get my answer, Darius, Orion, Xavier and Max strode into the room, all of them loudly discussing what they'd been through tonight as they began to strip down and Seth tore his attention from me, placing it on them instead.

I moved across the pool, sinking into the hot water and sighing as tension ran from my flesh as I let myself relax.

I dipped beneath the surface, grabbing a washalilie and scrubbing it through my curls as I worked to get the muck and dirt free of them.

By the time I came up for air, the others were all in the water too, scrubbing the evidence of battle from their skin and still swapping tales.

I listened to Max and Xavier describing the panicked dash across the wilderness to get the bigger Shifters back here while my gaze trailed to Seth who was struggling to scrub all of the dirt from his long hair. A frustrated whimper escaped him as he worked and the third time he swore at the tangles, I took pity on him, knowing he was used to his pack grooming him and shit like that and I knew he'd been missing them a hell of a lot since we'd arrived in this place.

"Come here," I said, catching his elbow to get his attention and tugging him towards me as I took the foaming flower from his hand and turned him away from me so that I could help him.

"Seriously?" he asked, giving me the puppy eyes over his shoulder and I nodded indulgently, casting a brush into my palm with my earth magic and coating that with the suds from the washalilie before starting work on combing the tangles from his long, dark hair.

"There was some fucked up shadow creature in the palace," Darius said as he scrubbed at the black ichor which seemed to be clinging to his skin like oil and Orion was struggling with the same problem.

"Really?" Seth asked curiously. "Like a big hairy shadow beast that likes to prey on the souls of the irritating? Killing Karens everywhere and bringing an end to their reign of boring fucker nonsense?"

"That might have been less creepy," Orion replied dryly. "This thing was the size of a man with a face that looked weirdly like Darius and Xavier. It was scuttling about like some kind of spider, clinging to the ceilings and shit."

"What the fuck?" I asked, yanking a little too hard on Seth's hair and quickly apologising as he whimpered.

"What was it?" Max asked, his brow furrowing.

"I don't even want to know. But we killed it good so whatever it was, it isn't anymore," Darius said, his lip curling back in distaste.

"Lavinia and Lionel left the fight in a hurry and she was screaming like a stuck pig on Christmas Day," I said thoughtfully. "You think that thing was connected to her? Like a manifestation of the shadows?"

"Well, if it was then that's only more evidence of her power growing. So thank fuck we got hold of that shadow eye. Hopefully now we can track down the rest of the rifts and close them, cutting her off from her power and leaving the two of them vulnerable at last," said Orion.

"Yeah. Then I can kill my father and Roxy can get her ass back in my arms where she belongs," Darius said with a growl.

"Shit man, you're taking this possessive stuff a bit far. I mean, I know you're missing her and I'm guessing going cold turkey on all the sex you guys had been having has to suck, but you need to hold it together," I said. "What's a few months in the grand scheme of things?"

Darius pushed his tongue into his cheek, smoke coiling from between his teeth before he blew out a harsh breath and banished it.

"I just spent a long fucking time thinking I'd never be able to have her," he said with a shrug, his hand going to his shoulder where the flames of the Phoenix tattooed on his back were just visible. "I don't like wasting the time we've got."

Seth howled and Max reached out to brush his hand against Darius's arm, sending a wave of relaxing emotions from his body which struck us even more potently through the water.

I sighed as I let his gifts take effect on me too, dropping my mental barriers and letting him push that feeling into me, wanting to loosen the knot of tension which seemed to have me tied up within it all the time recently. I had so much to worry about with most of my family still so close to Lionel, Hadley being groomed for a position on the Council which he was unlikely to ever take up and my mom in clear danger just because of how powerful she was. I wouldn't put it past Lionel to turn on all of our families eventually, wanting to wipe out the lines of every Fae who was strong enough to pose a threat to him.

And on top of that, I was worried about my friends here. We were rebels, on the run from a mad man who had already issued each and every one of us with a death sentence if we were caught, and tonight we had come pretty damn close to meeting that fate.

So I let the lure of Max's Siren gifts sink into my skin and bathed in that feeling of utter relaxation as I banished the brush in my hand and trailed my fingers through Seth's hair instead. His posture stiffened in surprise as he glanced over his shoulder at me again.

"You want me to stop?" I asked, wondering if I was letting the Siren lure push me too far. It wouldn't be the first time. When Max had first Emerged, he'd loved practicing on all of us and I'd gotten a little addicted to letting him use these kinds of gifts on me until my mom had realised and forced me to work harder at blocking him out. There was just something so fucking nice about letting a Siren sweep your worries and inhibitions aside though and now that I was confident in my abilities to push his influence back out again if I wanted to, I didn't see the harm in indulging from time to time.

"Don't stop," Seth murmured and I continued to toy with his hair, a smile pulling at the corners of my lips.

Max smirked at me as he read my mood and he shifted, his navy scales rippling along his body and making me groan as the power of his magic intensified and my whole body felt like freaking jello as I relaxed even more, my eyes hooding with the feeling as I leaned against the edge of the pool and continued to play with Seth's hair.

Seth glanced between me and Max, a grin finding his lips too before he lowered his shields as well and I watched as his pupils slowly dilated and he moved to lean against the edge of the pool beside me.

Max dipped beneath the water, disappearing for longer than he would have been able to in his Fae form as he revelled in the kiss of the liquid against his scales before surfacing on my other side and draping my arm around his shoulders.

"I'm pretty sure I should be pissed about this," I muttered, feeling high as a fucking kite as he drew even more of my worries from my body, seeming to carve them right out of my bones and leaving me feeling so chilled that I was close to falling asleep.

Max just chuckled as he stole my magic like a total asshole, but I couldn't summon the energy to care, concentrating on the feeling of Seth's soft hair as I twisted it between my fingers and Orion started talking.

"Fuck, it's been a long time since I let myself relax like this," he muttered.

"I don't think I've ever felt this relaxed in all my life," Darius sighed and that made me feel shitty for him for half a second before Max stole that away too.

"I love you guys," Seth said dreamily. "Even you, Lance. I know that your snappy snaps are only ever meant with love."

"They're not," Orion mumbled.

I breathed a laugh, my fingers stroking through Seth's hair before brushing against the back of his neck and I felt a tremor run through his body where his side was pressed to mine which made my sleepy smile widen.

"I was so cool today," Xavier said sleepily. "Did you see how cool I was, guys?"

We all murmured agreements, a few snorts of laughter passing between us as we lazed in the fog of Siren magic, drinking in the taste of victory in the air.

"Well," Geraldine's voice called to me from beyond my chilled out bubble and I fought to get my eyelids to peel open again. "If I'd known there would already be so many salacious sausages at this party, I wouldn't have brought more."

The sound of her heavy metal breastplate hitting the floor made my eyes finally open and my brows went up as she whipped her shirt off and flashed all of us her huge tits without so much as a warning.

"By the stars," Orion muttered but he was drowned out as a Max lunged away from me, cutting off his Siren gifts so suddenly that I felt like I'd just been punched in the dick as all of my own emotions and worries came slamming back into me with the force of a meteorite crashing into the earth.

"Fuck," I wheezed and Seth howled beside me as Darius growled angrily.

Max leapt from the water so fast I could have mistaken him for a damn Vampire as he whipped a towel from the pile beside the door and wound it around her so tightly that her arms were pinned to her sides.

"What in tarnation and the name of the solitary sun beam do you think you are doing, you irksome eel?" Geraldine cried. "I need to wash the evidence of battle from my nipoleans and I won't be ushered away by your flipper dippers!"

"Fine," Max snarled. "The rest of you are done, so fuck off and let Gerry have a bath in peace."

"Seriously?" I grumbled. "I'm not interested in her tits, no matter how nice they might be, dude. Does it really matter?"

"Don't talk about her fucking tits," Max hissed and I rolled my eyes, sensing defeat in the air as Darius gave in and got out of the water.

"Ooh, hotdogs!" Seth cried as he noticed the huge platter of food that Geraldine must have brought with her.

"Well, I thought we all deserved a victory feast after our delightful dalliances tonight," Geraldine purred, her eyes sparking. "I am all of a fluster recounting the way I popped that shadowy eyeball right out of that dastardly scullion's face and I want to rejoice in celebration."

"The second you got naked it became a celebration for two," Max said firmly. "So the rest of you assholes can take your food to go and fuck off."

"Fine by me," Orion said, shooting out of the water and wrapping himself in a towel while Max shielded Geraldine's eyes, and she cursed him for stealing her visage of the man meat on show. He grabbed himself a hotdog and left, and I kinda missed my sanguis frater already.

"Does that command include me?" Washer's voice came from the water and I cried out in shock as I spotted him emerging from the centre of the pool, his cyan blue scales on display and his hair plastered to his scalp as he looked at us.

"Ahh!" Seth yelled in alarm. "How long were you under the fucking water?"

"Only a teeny weeny while," Washer said, striding towards us with droplets rolling down his scales as Max quickly slapped a hand over Geraldine's eyes to shield her from the sight of his shrivelled dick. "I hurried down here to wet my willy right after the battle. Did you expect me to announce myself when you all arrived?"

"Yes," I barked instantly, wrapping a towel around my waist as the others hurried to do the same, and Xavier whinnied in alarm as he lost his grip on his.

"Oh I meant to say, Xavier, that is a mighty man package you have there," Washer said as he looked right at his dick while he struggled to yank his towel back up, accidentally stepping on it in his haste and neighing in frustration as he fought to cover himself. "I counted all thirty sparkling gems in order of the rainbow front to back while I was dilly dallying beneath the waves."

"Oh stars no," Xavier gasped, managing to grasp his towel at last and taking off running out of the room without another word.

"Wait a moment, dear boy!" Washer called as he jumped from the water too, grabbing a peach coloured cock sock which he rolled on to cover his junk before taking off after Xavier and leaving us all behind in horrified silence. "I wanted to speak with you about proper cleaning practices for those shiny baubles!"

Xavier neighed in fright and I laughed as the sound of him tearing away was swiftly followed by a door slamming and Washer muttering something about the ungratefulness of the youth these days.

"Right," Max said, looking to me, Darius and Seth as he continued to shield Geraldine's body from us. "You three can fuck off now too."

"Alright, alright," I agreed, heading for the door as Geraldine batted his hands away.

"I spoke to dear Gabriel about the shadow eye," she called after us.

"He warns everyone to stay away from it until we can encase it in a night iron spyglass so that we can make use of it. If not, it will crawl right into your face, devour your own eye and take its place just like a wallysnapper in the dew. Be warned."

"Fuck that," I muttered, shuddering at the thought and happily taking her warning to avoid that thing until it was contained and even then, I was happy to let someone else look through the spyglass because I wasn't risking it clawing its way into my fucking face for anything.

I followed Seth out of the room, grumbling about the way Max had just stolen my buzz as I took some hotdogs for myself.

I strode out of the bathhouse with Seth and Darius, the three of us quiet while we ate the food which was damn good, and we slowly made our way back to our rooms.

"Well, I'm gonna go and have a pity wank while cursing the stars for taking my girl away from me for fuck knows how long," Darius joked as we made it to his room and I laughed, clapping him on the shoulder as I finished the last bite of my food.

"She'll be back in no time, man. Then you can get back to making the rest of us feel like shit because you're getting laid so fucking much while we suffer on with the bluest balls in the history of testicles."

Seth barked a laugh and we walked on alone as Darius headed into his room, looking fucking miserable and making me wonder if there was something else bothering him. Though I guessed we all had plenty to be keeping us up at night, so I shouldn't have been surprised that he was clearly worrying about things.

We made it to my bedroom door and I opened it, stepping inside and catching Seth's hand as he tried to say goodnight.

A lump hitched in my throat as I looked down at his fingers caught between mine and I flicked my gaze up to his earthy brown eyes, hooking a smile onto my lips as I tilted my head in offering.

"I may or may not have a bottle of Orion's bourbon in here," I said, releasing my grip on his hand. "If you fancy celebrating the fact that we didn't die tonight?"

"So you're not just looking for an easy drink from my veins?" Seth teased, though he followed me inside all the same, closing the door behind him with a click that made my pulse spike.

"Not just that," I agreed, my gaze shifting over his neck as I felt the dull ache in my fangs. Between the fight this evening and Max draining me, I was running pretty damn low, but in that moment, I was more interested in his company than his blood.

I turned away, moving across my room and grabbing some clothes from the closet, pulling on a pair of black jeans and tossing Seth some grey sweatpants. I turned my back on him, dropped my towel and dressed in a flash of speed. I didn't bother with a shirt because it was always warm down here and as I spun back to face my best friend, my gaze caught on the V of his abs which dipped below his waistband.

I moved past him, grabbing the bottle of bourbon from my nightstand and taking a swig from the neck before holding it up to his lips. His throat bobbed as he swallowed a measure, taking the bottle from my grasp, his fingers brushing against mine. I released it slowly, my eyes still on him as he lowered the bottle, his lips wet with the liquor and drawing my focus.

"Did you see the look on Lionel's face when you stuck him with your Phoenix dagger?" Seth asked, smirking at me as he offered me the bottle again and I took it, placing it on my nightstand instead of drinking and nodding as I dropped down to sit on my bed.

"He looked like he was gonna shit a fucking brick," I laughed.

Silence fell between us and I frowned at the odd tension that grew in it. I'd noticed it more and more often recently, like a question that hung in the air between us, waiting for an answer I wasn't sure I had. But as I looked at him again, the dark stubble lining his jaw and the strong cut of his muscles, I was starting to think I knew. I just wasn't sure what the fuck I was supposed to do with that.

"I've been thinking of getting a tattoo," he said abruptly, dropping down to lay on the bed beside me and breaking the silence like it had been assaulting him and he'd just had to do it.

"Oh yeah?" I asked, resisting the urge to look over his body as I considered that. "Of what?"

"A moon," he said with a grin, and I snorted because I should have known that.

"Where?"

"That's the problem - I can't decide. Where do you think it would look best?"

I ran my tongue over my teeth and slowly dropped my gaze to his chest, feeling like he'd just given me permission to do something I'd been fighting the urge to do since he'd moved into that position.

I reached out and brushed my finger against his pec, frowning as that didn't seem right and trailing my hand to his bicep instead.

"Oh, I know," I said as it came to me and I grabbed him suddenly, making him gasp as I flipped him over onto his front beneath me, moving to straddle him and sitting on his ass as I pressed his shoulders down into the bed. "Here," I said, brushing his long hair aside and drawing the shape of a crescent moon on his skin with my fingertip right between his shoulder blades.

Seth's skin peppered with goosebumps and a growl escaped him. But not a growl that was warning me off, more like one which was urging me on. But what was it that he wanted me to do?

I hesitated there, buying myself a moment by painting the shape of a moon onto his skin again, my gaze catching on his neck as he buried his face in the pillows and released another low growl which made my cock twitch as he fisted his hands in my sheets.

He looked fucking good like that, pinned beneath me and at my mercy.

I leaned in, my lips brushing his neck as my fangs snapped out and I breathed in the scent of him.

Seth stiffened beneath me as I pushed my face into his hair, my mouth grazing his neck as the need to bite him damn near overwhelmed me.

But before I could follow through on that urge, Seth bucked his hips and knocked me off of him so that I fell back on the mattress at his side.

"Is that what you want?" he demanded, standing suddenly, a growl on his lips as his chest heaved up and down and he glared at me with a silver glint

457

in his eyes betraying the Wolf beneath his flesh. "My blood?"

"You know I want your blood," I said, tilting my head to one side as I took in the anger in him, and I tried to figure out what had sparked it.

"And what else?" he asked. "Because every time I convince myself that this is enough for me, you do shit like this and I just...I don't think I can keep on having my heart jerked about like a fucking yoyo not knowing if it means more, or..."

"Or what?" I asked, pushing myself up to stand before him as he raked a hand through his long hair, his eyes full of anguish.

"Tell me what you want, Cal," he begged, a whine in his throat which turned to snarl as I frowned, and he turned for the door angrily.

He gripped the handle and made a move to jerk it open, but I shot forward and tugged his hand away from it, stopping him.

"Don't go," I demanded, knowing I didn't want him to leave even if I wasn't sure about the rest of it.

Seth turned to me, his back pressing to the door as he looked into my eyes and I found myself caught in the intensity of his gaze.

"Bite me," he demanded. "Take what you need from me and then I'll go."

I moved suddenly, gripping his biceps and shoving him back against the door as the monster in me rose to the surface of my skin at that offer, hungering for his blood with an intensity which almost owned me.

But instead of lunging for his throat, I hesitated there, my gaze roaming over the thumping pulse in his neck before dropping down lower, drinking in the defined cut of his powerful body, skimming past that V which dipped down beneath his waistband and onto the pale grey material which clung to him in a way that made it impossible to miss the swell of his thick cock within it.

Suddenly something in me seemed to shift, something I'd been feeling but not thinking for so fucking long that it was like a light switching on inside my fucking dumb brain as I dragged my gaze back up to his once more, finding him watching me with this guarded look that made my throat tighten.

"I just haven't been with anyone in a really long time," he breathed, shifting like he was going to rearrange his dick in his pants, but I tightened my hold on his biceps to stop him. "And with my pack I got used to... Fuck, please don't let me ruin us."

I ignored his words, shifting a little closer to him, my body eating up the space between us one tiny bite at a time as I leaned in, my attention falling to his throat once more as my fangs fucking ached for a taste of him.

"Please, Cal," he said, the rough edge to his voice making every hair on my body stand on end as I leaned in a little more, coming closer and closer to crossing that divide between us which I hadn't even realised I'd been yearning to tear apart. "Just take what you want," he demanded again.

I shifted forward with a growl, dipping my head as I aimed for his throat, my fangs grazing his skin and making him tense in my hold in anticipation of the bite he thought was coming.

But he hadn't demanded I bite him. He'd told me to take what I wanted and right now there was something I wanted far more powerfully than his blood, no matter how thirsty I was.

My mouth met with his skin as I flattened him against the door, our bodies pressing together in a way that had my fucking heart jack hammering at the newness of it, the promise, the temptation, the fucking danger. Because this *was* dangerous. This was free falling with no parachute or air magic in sight and hoping to hell there was a soft landing at the bottom because I knew there was no turning back from this line once I stepped over it. But I also knew I wasn't going to be able to back off now.

I kissed Seth's neck as I pinned him to the door, my fangs scratching against his flesh without piercing it as I held him there, tasting him and groaning as the most intoxicating feeling ran through my body in response.

Seth fell still, his back ramrod straight as I kissed him again, running my tongue up the side of his neck and growling with desire as my dick hardened inside my jeans.

Seth sucked in a breath as I moved my mouth to his jaw, still unmoving as I kissed him again, the rough scratch of stubble against my lips at once alien and exhilarating as I explored this new desire in me and found myself wanting more and more of it.

As I made it to the corner of his mouth, he cursed, the taste of his lips teasing me as I got the briefest brush of them against my own. But it wasn't nearly enough.

"Fuck," he murmured. "Stars, please don't let this be a dream. Make it real. Make it-"

I silenced him as I turned my head and crossed that final barrier, ignoring the fact that he was my best friend and that I'd only ever hooked up with girls before, ignoring the fear that this might break something between us because I needed it too fucking much to let any pointless doubts like that take it from me.

Even so, the kiss I gave him was hesitant at first because I couldn't help the one doubt from creeping in that could actually ruin this moment. Because if I'd read him wrong and he didn't want this at all then there was a chance that he was about to push me away, tell me to stop, steal this fantasy before I'd even taken a moment to indulge in it. Maybe it really was a pack need that had been driving that lust in his eyes and it hadn't been about me specifically, but I really fucking hoped that wasn't it.

My lips met with his and I swear a fucking explosion went off in my body, every nerve ending firing off at once as a whole lifetime of loving him echoed through the foundations of who I was and twisted itself into this new beast, this perfect possibility which I was afraid to even put a name to.

But I didn't need a name for what I wanted in that moment, because as my mouth tasted his, I could fucking feel it and all I needed to know was that I wanted more.

I pressed myself into him more firmly, kissing him harder and parting my lips as I teased the seam of his with my tongue.

But Seth didn't react at all and as that one terrifying doubt pushed in on me, I drew back, looking at him with my heart racing and my skin burning and my fucking cock driving into his leg so obviously that there was no mistaking it.

I opened my mouth to apologise or ask him why he wasn't kissing me back or fuck knew what, but it didn't matter because as I made a move to step away, he caught hold of my belt and dragged me back against him again, kissing me so hard that it was bruising and my whole fucking world caught alight alongside my flesh.

Seth pushed his hand into my curls, fisting them tightly and parting his lips at last so that I could taste his tongue as it swept over mine, and I knew in that moment that I didn't care if this was terrifying because it was so fucking good that I never wanted it to stop.

He kissed with a hunger that made me think he'd been wanting this for just as long as I had. I'd just been the dumb fuck who had been too blind to notice what was right in front of me.

He turned us, slamming me back against the wall and going all Alpha on me as he growled in a possessive way that got my fangs tingling and my cock throbbing with the desire to put him in his damn place.

His hands were suddenly on my body, roaming down my chest and finding my belt which he unbuckled so fucking fast that I barely had time to consider what he was doing.

My whole body tingled with an urgent kind of need as he rolled my fly down and his hand pushed beneath the waistband of my boxers, fisting my cock and making me groan as he broke our kiss and looked at me.

"You really want this?" he asked, rolling his thumb over the head of my dick in a way that made it jerk in his grasp.

"I want you," I confirmed, my mind wheeling with what that meant because I hadn't really thought this through, and I was suddenly thinking about how many guys Seth had fucked and realising that I was out of my depth here because I wasn't even sure where to start.

"Fuck, I could come from hearing those words alone," Seth growled, knotting my hair in his free hand once more and kissing me so hard that I forgot about getting this wrong because it felt so fucking right.

His hand worked my cock like he instinctively knew exactly what I liked, and I couldn't help but drive my hips forward as the feeling of his big hand surrounding it turned me on so damn much that I began to fear how long I could even hold out for.

I pushed all of my hesitation aside as I reached for him too, sliding my hand into his sweatpants and finding him rock solid within them, the tip of his dick beaded with precum which I smeared all around the head of his shaft before slicking my hand down it.

Seth growled into my mouth, pumping me harder and making my head spin at his expert touch as I kissed him with a demand that I was desperate to satisfy.

He broke away suddenly, his mouth moving to my neck before he dropped it to my collar bone then my chest, working his way down and tugging my pants lower as he went, still pumping my dick even as I lost my grip on his.

He dropped to his knees and looked up at me with a wicked grin, licking his lips and making my cock jerk again. My dick was sliding between his lips in the next heartbeat, a growl of desire escaping him which made my hips thrust forward instinctively, a shiver of pleasure racing through me as I felt the bite of his stubble grazing along the length of my shaft.

Seth gripped my ass in his hands and pulled my hips further forward still, taking me right to the back of his throat and I groaned, his name tumbling from my lips like a fucking prayer.

He started moving then, sucking and licking me like he couldn't get enough and I was left leaning against the wall, watching him suck me off with my heart thrashing so hard I feared it would give out because I was pretty certain the sight of him taking my dick was the hottest thing I'd ever witnessed.

I let him lead for as long as I could force myself to, but as he shifted a hand to caress my balls, I snapped. My hand took hold of the back of his head, fingers tightening in his long hair as I thrust my hips forward and began to fuck his mouth.

He didn't even balk at my demand, his eyes on mine as I watched him, wishing I could record this moment to play it over and over again for myself because I knew that this was never going to be enough.

I thrust in harder, deeper, loving how he took me and cursing as I fought to hold myself back, make it last. But Seth wasn't going to be so easily dominated, and as I drove my cock to the back of his throat again, he shifted the hand which still gripped my ass and drove two fingers straight inside me.

I came instantly like he'd found some fucking switch to my oblivion, and a low groan of ecstasy escaped me as I was overwhelmed by the pleasure he wrung from me, jerking forward with a growl of satisfaction as my orgasm took me by surprise. He swallowed greedily, claiming my pleasure for his own as I slumped back against the door, panting in the aftermath of what he'd done to me as he flexed his fingers inside my ass and somehow made the bliss linger in my flesh as I fought to catch my breath from that explosion of pent up need.

Seth withdrew slowly, making my whole body shudder with bliss as he did so and I watched him as he stood before me once more.

He kissed me again and I tasted myself on his lips, the thrill of that so intoxicating that all I could do was bathe in the feeling of it as I dragged my tongue over his, slower this time like we were both saving the pure perfection of that moment.

Seth pressed himself against me and I felt the keen swell of his erection driving into my hip and I knew we weren't done. I wanted to do that to him. I wanted to make him feel the way he'd just made me feel.

But as I pulled back and broke our kiss, concern built in my chest and I was left feeling like some fucking virgin as I looked into his eyes with a frown pulling at my brow as I tried to figure out how to tell him that I had no fucking idea how to suck his dick like that. I didn't want to fuck it up and Seth had a whole lot of reference to compare me to if I was fucking awful at it.

"Seth," I said, my voice rough as I scrambled for the words. "I...I don't know-"

"What?" he breathed, pulling back as if I'd smacked him and my chest tightened further as he stared at me like that.

"What you just did to me," I began, not knowing how to finish that without making myself sound like a fucking idiot. Because now that I'd let that concern creep in, it was all I could think about. I was remembering all the times he'd told us about how hard he'd come when Frank sucked his cock, or how much he'd loved fucking Maurice in the ass when he'd been trying to act like an Alpha all day, telling us how well he took it and how good he was at it, and I felt completely and utterly out of my depth. "I just don't think-"

"Fuck, I'm so stupid," he breathed, backing up suddenly and I frowned as I missed the feeling of his body against mine. "I shouldn't have done that. It's my fault. I'm just missing my pack and I haven't gotten laid in a long time, and I shouldn't have...*fuck*. Just forget it happened. You were horny and it's in my nature to satisfy the members of my pack. That's all."

"That's all?" I questioned as my heart crushed to dust in my chest, because that hadn't felt like it was fucking all. It had felt like waking up after sleeping way too long and finally realising what I'd been aching for.

"Yeah. I literally suck all of my friends' dicks aside from you guys and that's just because you're into girls. It was just a BFF BJ. No biggie. In fact, I'm gonna go and offer Darius one." Seth yanked the door open and held his hand up with his two fingers extended in farewell.

"Is that the peace sign?" I asked in confusion because he'd just made me come so hard, I'd seen fucking stars and now he was acting like a nineties baby at a Spice Girls concert.

"Yeah. I peace sign all of my BFF BJ buddies. Now you know."

The door slammed behind him before I could question that, and I was left leaning against the wall with my whole body still trembling in the aftershocks of what he'd done to me and my heart thrashing with the bitter sting of rejection.

"Oh," I breathed to no one at all because Seth had gotten what he wanted, flipped my entire world upside down and left me with a peace sign and my cock out all alone in my room. "Fuck."

SETH

CHAPTER FORTY

I wandered through the dark tunnels, dragging my heels as my heart sank like a stone into a cold, cold pool in my stomach. Caleb's words spun around and around in my head like a washing machine set on a spin cycle of hell. *"I just don't think-"*

I knew the end of that sentence, I knew it in my gut, my heart, my dick, my fucking soul. *'I just don't think we should have done that.'* That was where he'd been going with that sentence. I'd seen it in his eyes. I'd seen the change, the exact moment he'd realised he'd made one, giant irreversible mistake. And I was that mistake embodied.

Instead of telling him the truth like maybe I should have, I'd tried to cover my ass. I'd tried to lie as well as I could possibly lie, and told him I give the peace sign to all my BFF BJs. I'd said I might go offer one to Darius. Like that was an entirely fucking normal thing for me to do and wasn't completely fucked up.

The peace sign? The fucking peace sign?? Now I was gonna have to commit and try to bring the peace sign back, offering it out to random guys whenever Caleb was around to keep up my lie, bind it in sun steel and never let it break. I had to go Rambo on this lie, gut every crumb of honesty and leave a trail of bloody truth in my wake until only the lie remained.

I had to commit so hard, because if Caleb ever questioned me, if he ever figured out the truth, I'd die. And not just in a dramatic metaphorical way, I would literally die. I'd walk straight out under the moon and ask her to end me, because I was not living in a world where I lost Caleb Altair.

Even if I was in agony for the rest of my life and had to bottle this secret up in my chest forever until it devoured my heart and left nothing but bitterness behind it. I'd have to stomach seeing Caleb marry some girl, attend his wedding with a smile on my face, watch him have children with her, all the while remembering how I once sucked his cock and offered him the peace sign, pretending it meant absolutely jack shit to me.

I'd grow mean-tempered, lonely and I'd never marry, too full of spite to do anything but just fester in my own feelings. And on the last day of my life, when I was old and grey, and living alone in a palace full of beautiful things I'd collected to try and fill the void in me, I'd take a knife, cut out my heart and leave it on Caleb's doorstep. Then, and only then, would I let him know that I had loved him so deeply, so unrequitedly that it had destroyed me every day of my life since our moment together in his room.

Or maybe he'll be done with me now and never want to speak to me again.

Oh stars, I've fucked up everything. I've lost Cal forever.

A mournful whimper left my lips and I shivered in the freezing air as I delved deeper into the dark, my body aching for the contact of a pack surrounding me. It was my nature to seek the comfort of Wolves but I didn't have a pack down here, not ones I could turn to right now anyway. The Oscuras welcomed me in whenever I really needed the comfort of other Wolves, but they had their Alphas already and I just didn't feel any desire to challenge for control of them. Besides, if I headed down to see them, I'd just be looking at Rosalie remembering the way Caleb had looked while we fucked her together. My soul burned to cinders as I thought of him and his love of vaginas and I realised I'd probably end up trying to rip her throat out if I went to her now.

I couldn't talk to Max or Darius about this, and now Darcy was gone there was no one else to talk to. Orion was the only one in this whole place that even knew about my feelings for Caleb, but he didn't want me. He'd turned away my affection time and again and I couldn't handle any more rejection right now. So I found my way to the darkest, loneliest corner of the entire Burrows and dropped down to sit there and whimper, the mournful sound pouring out of me as I fisted my hands in my hair and buried my face in my knees.

I'd lost him. This was it. I'd gone from nought to blowjob in sixty seconds. I'd taken a train to Dicklick Kingdom without even having a full stopover in Kiss County. I should have spent more time in his mouth, making sure he wanted this. I could have done so many things with my tongue between his lips and figured out if he even wanted me to go on a quest south. What had I been thinking? I'd just gotten so excited. But that was always my problem, wasn't it? I was a stupid mutt who only needed a tiny bone offered to him to send him into overdrive. And Caleb had had a massive bone. It was my nature to want to bury it somewhere, but my mouth clearly hadn't been the best option.

I'd overstepped the line and now he was going to retreat from me. I must have read the room completely wrong, and now I felt like I'd fucking sexually harassed my friend. It must have all been about my blood. He must have gotten confused for a moment and, like an asshole, I'd let myself believe it was me he wanted, and now what? How were we ever gonna move past this?

The sickening truth fell over me, because I knew we were *never* going to move past this. I'd single-handedly whacked our friendship over the head with a cock shaped hammer, dragged it out kicking and screaming into the woods, finished it off with another bloody strike to the head, then buried it six feet underground. It was friendicide. Fucking murder in the friend degree.

I slowly started pulling down my sweatpants, figuring I might feel better if I just shifted and went topside to run under the moon. At least the moon would listen to my woes, she was always so faithful in her companionship.

"Do I even wanna know why you're crying and stripping in the dark?" Lance Orion's deep voice dripped over me, and my head snapped up as a whine got trapped in my throat.

"I'm not crying," I said thickly, pulling my pants back up. "I'm whimpering."

"Same difference, mutt." He took a bite out of a burrito in his hand and I frowned at him.

"Why are you eating down here all alone?" I deflected from my issues.

"Because I was still hungry after the hotdog and eating alone in the dining hall is a special kind of hell for me when everyone treats me like a fucking pariah," he muttered, taking another bite of his burrito and swallowing it down. "So I made myself a snack in the kitchen – well, technically, I scared a little Mouse Shifter into making one for me." He chuckled. "So I suppose I'll leave you to cry."

"Whimper," I growled.

"Uhuh," he said lightly, turning away from me.

"Wait," I called. "Did you...hear me whimpering and come to check if I was okay?"

"Absolutely not," he said dismissively, but surely his Vampire ears had picked up my whines? He must have known it was me, he must have wanted to help. And if he wanted to help, then maybe he'd give me what I needed.

I pushed to my feet in desperation, jogging after him as he started walking away, and the fact that he didn't shoot off with his Vampire speed gave me an absolutely certain answer that he wanted to comfort me.

"You must want company. You're missing Darcy," I said and he ripped into his burrito more aggressively, not replying. "Maybe sometimes I could sleep in with you at night? I could put an illusion on my hair so it looks blue and if I put on a high pitched voice too then maybe-"

"I'm gonna stop you right there, Seth," he cut over me after he'd swallowed the food in his mouth. "There are no circumstances - and I repeat – *no* circumstances, in which I would allow you to pretend to be Darcy so you could cuddle me in our fucking bed."

"Okay," I sighed, hanging my head.

"Why don't you go and bond with some of the Oscura Wolves if you need that kind of attention?" he suggested.

"Because I need more than snuggles, and cuddles, and nuzzles," I said sadly. "I need to talk about what happened while I'm doing all those things."

"What do you mean?" he asked and I looked to him with my eyes large and my lower lip quivering.

"I did something terrible," I whispered.

"What?" he demanded, but I shook my head.

"I can't, Lance. I can't say it. Not without snuggles. I need to feel safe while I say it."

"Then go say it to one of the Heirs," he said firmly, but I whimpered, shaking my head again.

"I can't," I croaked. "It's about Caleb. And now Darcy's gone and – and-" I tipped my head back and howled, my pain spilling out of me and filling every corner of this freezing, dark section of The Burrows.

Orion slapped a hand over my mouth to silence me, finishing his burrito as his eyes narrowed on me. He sighed long and wearily, slowly removing his hand from my mouth.

"I am only going to offer this once, and only because Darcy would ask me to if she could."

"What?" I breathed.

"You may come to my room and have one small, short-lasting hug," he offered and I gasped, throwing myself at him in excitement as I bounced up and down, knowing my tail would be wagging a mile a minute if I was in my shifted form.

He shoved me off of him with a growl.

"What did I just say?" he snapped.

"One hug. Got it." I backed up, practically bursting with the need to be held as he released another long sigh and started walking away into the dark.

I followed him all the way back to our room and Orion locked the door firmly behind me like he was afraid someone might walk in on this moment. I reached for my waistband, about to drop my pants when he pointed at me and barked, "No. Clothes on, Capella. Let's not make this weirder than it already is."

"Okay," I agreed. "Where do you want me? Big spoon position or little spoon? Or we could do topsy-downsies? Or upsy-topsies? Ooh, what about the double-inward spoon with a little leg hitch action?" I got onto the bed, patting the sheets beside me in encouragement and Orion remained by the door, looking like he was questioning his life choices.

"I will lie there." He pointed to the empty space beside me. "And you may put *one* arm around me."

"Can I hitch a leg?" I asked pleadingly.

"No."

"Not even one tiny little thirty second leg hitch?" I begged and he ran a hand down his face, but I could see him resigning himself to this.

"Fine," he gave in, moving to the bed and I hurried to switch off the light before diving back onto the mattress and putting the lamp on instead.

"Why did you do that?" he growled.

"Mood lighting," I said. "Every hug has its own mood, Lance. By the stars, does Darcy get moodless hugs from you? I really need to give you my hug manifesto. It'll change your life."

He laid down on the bed, his head propped up on the pillow and I crawled towards him as he eyed me like a piranha on its way to bite his dick off.

"Relax," I growled, pressing his shoulders down into the pillow and massaging them. "I can't hug you like this. Stop tensing."

He ground his jaw then his body went more slack and I smiled, taking hold of his right arm and drawing it out to the side before I started crawling around in circles in the space his arm marked out.

"What the fuck are you doing now?" he asked irritably as I scratched at the sheets, moving around and around in a ring.

"Checking for snakes, Lance. By the stars, this is snuggle safety one-oh-one." Finally satisfied, I laid down in the space beside him, resting my head on his shoulder, laying one arm over his body and hitching my leg up over his thigh.

"Now close your right arm around me," I whispered and his lips twitched in resistance before he did as I said, holding me against him and I finally relaxed, shutting my eyes as my thrashing heart finally started to slow.

I lay there, drinking in the feeling of being cuddled while my Order instincts settled down and were finally sated.

"So are you going to tell me why you were crying?" he muttered.

"Whimpering," I corrected, keeping my eyes shut as my chest pinched with pain again, remembering Caleb's bitter rejection and feeling that hurt wash through me in wave after wave. "Oh Lance, I've done something so fucking stupid."

"What?" he grunted and I took a shaky breath.

"I gave Cal a Tiberian tip swirler," I admitted.

"A what?"

"A Likranian lip dipping dong dancer," I explained better.

"In a language I can fucking understand?" he demanded and I huffed heavily.

"A blowjob, Lance. A fucking blowjob."

"Right, okay. And why has that left you devastated beyond all reason?" he asked in confusion and I howled long and low right in his ear, making him wince away, but I held on tight.

"Because he didn't want my blowjob," I admitted on a whimper. "The look he gave me, Lance, it was like -like – the apocalypse had befallen his cock. Oh my stars, I'm the acockalypse," I said in horrified realisation.

I hugged him tighter, hitching my leg higher and nuzzling his shoulder as I stole the comfort I needed and Orion's chest heaved up and down, his jaw ticking away like a tiny little clock in his face. "I can normally read people so well. I swear I thought he gave me the green light. He kissed me. He kissed *me*, Lance! With tongue and everything. Then he gave me the BJ eyes – I'm always so good at spotting the BJ eyes."

"I'm really not the best one to talk to about shit like this," he said. "I think you should tell Max and Darius. They'll know what to say."

"No," I growled. "I won't. I've already ruined one friendship, I'm not dragging everyone else into this and ruining things with them too. But how can I fix things with Cal? What can I do-awoooo." I broke into a sad howl.

"Stars give me strength," Orion said under his breath, but he didn't let go of me as I curled myself tighter around him and panted heavily against his ear. "Look, I'm sorry Seth, but it's happened now, so the best thing you can do is to have it out with him. Tell him how you feel, apologise for shit getting weird and try to figure out how you can both move on from there. You've been friends long enough that your bond should be salvageable regardless. He's probably feeling shitty about this too."

I nodded, whining softly. "Or how about I bury my feelings, act like it never happened and hope all our problems magically go away?" I suggested.

"I don't think that's-"

"Yeah, that's what I'll do, thanks Lance. That's great advice," I said decisively, snuggling in as I prepared to have a snooze.

"That wasn't my advice," he hissed, but I was already falling asleep, finding some peace in the arms of my new friend and thankful that he'd come up with a plan that could really help me.

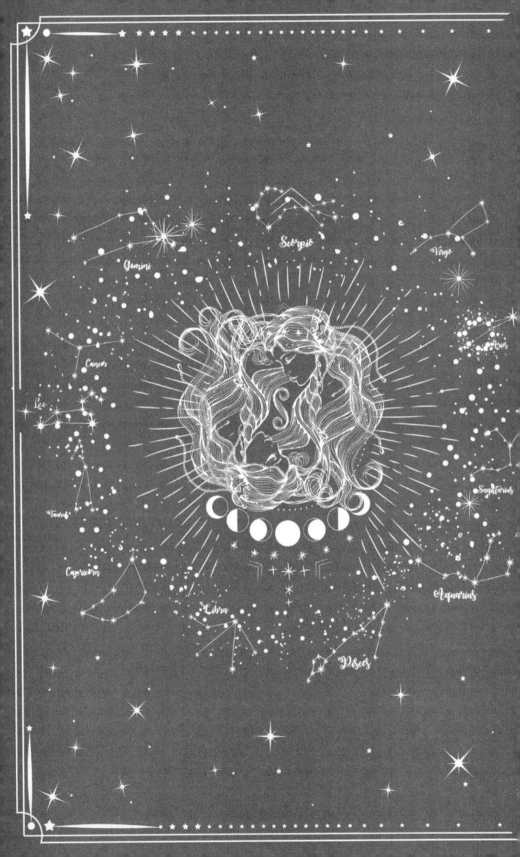

TORY

CHAPTER FORTY ONE

Four months was a hell of a long time to live on a heathy diet of things we could grow. Particularly mangoes. Fucking mangoes. If I never saw a mango again after this, then I would be one happy Fae.

Of course, the limited menu was somewhat tempered by the fact that we'd been working our asses off to learn the ways of our ancestors and we were now beyond proficient in swordplay, archery, brawling and could even wield a bunch of weird weapons with reasonable skill like a flail, mace or spear.

It was pretty badass and I had no complaints about learning these things, but I was growing restless stuck in this palace. Sure, it was beautiful and we had spent the first weeks exploring it during any free moments we got from our training, and I'd even grown used to wearing the tunics and long dresses which we'd found stored in a chest that had been spelled to keep them fresh and clean so long ago that time had forgotten them. But it didn't feel like home. The jungle courtyards and oppressive heat were just too alien to me and though I enjoyed them to a point, I was aching for some change in the weather, some variation in the temperature and most of all, I was desperate to see Darius and the rest of our friends.

Days of worrying about how they were doing and what was happening in the war had turned to weeks and months with no answers for us and no way to leave this place and find out. The golden gates were firmly sealed and Queen Avalon had made it clear that the moment we left, the spell holding her ghost or spirit or whatever the fuck she was in this place would shatter and she would be gone. That meant this was our one and only opportunity to learn from her and so far she wasn't convinced we'd learned enough.

On top of the training we'd been doing, we'd spent hours working together to try and drive our Phoenix flames through Darcy's body and burn the curse from her and we were certain it was working.

She didn't tire or weaken nearly as often as she had before we'd come here, and her magic was holding up well to the vigorous routine that Queen Avalon had us abiding by.

Every morning when we woke, we met her in a grand hallway where the walls were lined with carvings representing the zodiac and long windows looked out into the jungle where we practiced casting our Phoenix magic in ways I'd never even imagined we could before.

We had learned to create weapons the way Darcy had already figured out, honing that skill and imbuing them with our fire magic in more subtle ways too so that we knew how to provide our army with the means to stand against the Nymphs and win. Rather than focusing on one mighty weapon the way Darcy had for the Heirs, Orion and Geraldine, we had learned how to gift a smaller amount of our flames to a larger amount of weapons at once, enough to arm the rebels when the time came for them to use them against the Nymphs. It was the kind of advantage we desperately needed to be able to face Lionel's army on a battlefield and it was so reassuring to know that we were learning things that really would change the way this fight went.

Queen Avalon had also taught us more about the magic of the Phoenix Kiss, though she warned us not to offer it out unless we had no other choice as it stole an ember of our own flames which could never be returned to us. We'd figured that out too, but the way she spoke about it was like she was afraid of that, hating the idea of giving some of her fire to another Fae and could see no reason why we ever would.

She taught us to create Chalices too, some of which could burn away the effects of most poisons if someone ever tried to slip something into our drink, though neither of us wanted to carry around some fancy ass chalice all the time to drink from even though Avalon encouraged it. As well as that, she guided us in the ways of casting flames we could track, placing them in jars and hiding them away from us all across the palace until we'd felt out our connection to every one of them.

Queen Avalon had clearly been a cold leader who ruled with an iron fist and a heart as unmovable as I'd been warned my father's was, and as time had passed, the two of us had begun to question some of her lessons. She had been unforgiving and swift to execute anyone who stood in her way or who didn't fall in with her laws, and she urged us to do the same.

There was also an ongoing undercurrent of competition from her too, and the way she assessed our skills made my skin prickle as she continued to insinuate that one day the two of us would end up fighting to claim the throne alone.

But that day would never come, no matter if all the stars in the sky predicted it. I would sooner end my own life than turn on my sister and the fact that she couldn't understand that bond between us only made me think of her as weak. In the way that a lot of Fae were weak because they were selfish. Their thirst for power gave them the excuse to do terrible things and I for one felt that needed to change.

Kindness wasn't weakness which my sister had shown me more often than I could count. And neither was knowing when to concede that you were wrong. Arrogance was one of the founding problems of the Fae society and the two of us made a vow late one night that if we took the throne, we would never just blindly follow our own desires when making decisions for the people of our kingdom.

Once we had exhausted our Phoenix fire, we were gifted a short break to eat - which was all too often including mangoes - before we started our physical fighting training. Queen Avalon insisted that that order of things was correct because in battle, we would only resort to the use of a weapon once our Order gifts were exhausted beyond use and we needed to build up our physical strength and learn to endure the exhaustion brought on by wearing out our Phoenixes.

It had seemed near impossible at first, my limbs feeling weighted with lead once my Phoenix ran out of power, but the more I pushed through the feeling, the more I'd been able to achieve, the longer I'd been able to keep fighting. Queen Avalon fought us herself, her skills profound and seeming impossible to match and her weapons somehow colliding with our own while sailing through our flesh without harming us if they made contact with our skin.

I was in a state of constant exhaustion, but I also felt more connected to my Phoenix than ever before and I was revelling in the feeling of getting to know just how powerful I was.

The clash of metal rang through the air as the ache in my arms intensified and I bellowed my defiance as Queen Avalon started to force me back, making me retreat several steps as she swung her sword at my head.

I ducked low, swinging my blade high to meet the blow she swung next and twisting away from her before running at her with a roar of determination.

Queen Avalon met the strike of my sword but as I got in under her defence, I grabbed the dagger at my hip and drove it home in her chest with a furious snarl.

I felt the strike connecting with her body for the briefest of moments before she shimmered and lost her corporal form, making me stumble forward a couple of steps as I panted and grinned my victory across the room at Darcy who had leapt up to applaud me.

"Good," Queen Avalon said as she reappeared, the small praise always a hard earned thing and my smile widened as I pushed some loose strands of dark hair out of my eyes and sheathed my weapons once more. "You have both impressed me with your dedication and the way you handle yourselves. Poise, strength, and unwavering will are what is needed to claim the crown and you both have it in spades. So let us see if you are ready to head back to your war and claim it."

She turned and swept from the room, her fighting leathers shimmering and shifting until she was wearing a golden gown instead which clung to her lithe figure and trailed out behind her with beautifully embroidered detailing.

The straps of the dress had been designed to allow her wings to remain out at all times and she encouraged us to do the same, leaving our wings in place as often as possible to help us get to know them better. And she'd been right, having them out so much meant I had gotten used to the weight of them, gotten better at moving them, strengthening them through the hours we'd spent flying and perfecting all kinds of acrobatic skills. I'd even fallen asleep with them still out more than once, enjoying the silken feeling of my bronze feathers as they caressed my skin.

We'd spent hours flying with her through a huge obstacle course which had been created for our kind too, breaking through barriers with our fire, getting to know the span of our wings as we dove through gaps and learning how best to glide, freefall and manoeuvre to make ourselves almost impossible to target during a battle.

And once we were utterly exhausted and couldn't so much as lift an arm to fight, we sat and studied Phoenix lore. There were all kinds of legends about our Order, some of which had even slipped through into stories in the mortal realm, but it soon became very clear to us that a lot of them were nothing but a fantasy. We weren't immortal - which I for one was damn pleased about. Why would I want to live forever and watch everyone surrounding us die anyway? That sounded like its own kind of hell to me. I wanted life not stagnation, and I was more than a little relieved to find out that there was absolutely no truth to the story. We couldn't revive the dead either which was a little more disappointing especially while we were caught up in this war with a monster who wanted us all dead. But it was absolutely undisputable, we weren't necromancers, we were fire born.

Our tears were in fact useful in other ways though, able to be used in the creation of elixirs which cured several deadly Fae diseases. That was where the healing rumours had stemmed from, but in fact it was the magic of our fire that aided in the destruction of those diseases as it burned through the affliction in much the same way as we had been working to burn through Darcy's curse.

One of the things we'd known nothing about before coming here was the power of our song. When used correctly, our fire could create a bird which released a song capable of rallying armies and destroying despair, it could help block out the sensation of pain and instil courage in the hearts of Fae. There were even tales of particularly gifted Fae of our Order who had been able to create a Phoenix song so pure that it could create power of its own.

I glanced at Darcy as she walked at my side, thinking about the way she'd won her bout with Queen Avalon too by managing to get behind her and drive her sword straight through her back. We'd been a force to be reckoned with before coming here, but now? Now I felt like we could take on the entire world and win if we set our minds to it.

Queen Avalon led us to her throne room, and I felt the power of this place wrapping around me like a warm hug, the sconces blazing with fire and working to recharge our magic the way they did in every part of the palace. I could hardly even remember what it felt like for my magic to run low.

"There is one final test which you need to pass in order to prove that you have full command of your Phoenixes," she said as she dropped down to sit on her throne, her gaze assessing as it roamed over the two of us. "One of you must claim the crown."

She waved a hand and there was a grinding of stone as one of the flagstones by her feet dropped down several inches before shifting aside to allow a podium wrapped in flames to rise up from within the hidden space, a glimmering platinum crown adorned with blood red and deep blue stones resting on top of it, a mirror to the one she appeared to be wearing.

"Solaria's crown is still locked away inside The Palace of Souls," I said, looking to the beautiful crown for a moment before raising my eyes to meet hers once more. "This won't make either of us a queen."

"No," Queen Avalon agreed on a sigh. "The seat of power once rested here, but with the end of our race, my descendants emerged in other Orders and they abandoned the home of our kind, fearing this place held a curse which had been the cause of the demise of the Phoenix race. They built a new palace to the north where your parents resided and continued to rule from there, forging a new crown, a new throne and a new world in the wake of ours. But that which is forgotten is only ever lost until it is discovered once more. But for one of you to ascend, you need to rise above all others. Including one another."

Silence fell as neither I nor Darcy made any move to fight or to claim the prize she was offering.

"Keep the broken promise," the whispered hiss of the Imperial Star insisted urgently, its voice making my skin prickle as it sounded within my own head, the queen still seeming utterly oblivious to the fact. It had been urging us to do that ever since we'd first arrived here, but we had no idea what that meant, only that there was yet another piece of this puzzle which we had yet to uncover.

"And if we won't take it?" Darcy asked, ignoring the star in favour of the challenge the queen was setting us.

"Then you will remain here," Queen Avalon replied. "And I will continue to train you day after day, year after year until one of you finds the resolve of a true Fae and steps forward to fight for what is rightfully yours. Only one may ascend."

Her words were like lashes against my spine and I straightened angrily as I took in that crown and the fact that it was our only way out of this place. We had done what was asked of us here, learned what we needed to and now it was time for us to return to the war. We'd wasted enough time. And we weren't going to linger here any longer.

"Fine," I said, fixing the queen in my dark gaze. "We'll fight for what is rightfully ours."

Darcy straightened beside me, surprise flickering over her features for a moment as I turned to look at her with a challenge in my eyes and as she met my gaze, understanding registered in her, causing her lips to tilt up in a savage smile.

"Alright," she agreed. "You asked for it."

The queen smiled triumphantly as she waited to see which of us would emerge from this victorious, but I wasn't going to wet my blade with the blood of my other half. She said only one could claim the crown? Fine. Because we had always been two halves of one whole and if she thought that her challenge would be all it took to divide us then she had judged us poorly.

I turned my gaze onto the queen, sidestepping towards my sister and holding out my hand for her to grasp.

Our power merged instantly and the queen sat up taller on her throne, her lips parting on a complaint that we didn't allow her to utter as the power of our Phoenixes blended and a roaring inferno built between us.

Higher and higher the flames burned within my soul until I couldn't hold them back anymore and they tore from my body with a force that almost knocked me from my feet, red and blue flames erupting from the very core of my being and colliding with the same power as it exploded from my twin too.

As the flames met, they merged, wings erupting from them far broader than any I'd ever conjured alone before and then the rest of the fire kept building until an entire Phoenix bird was born of the flames.

It looked almost like an eagle, though its face was still humanoid and resembled the two of us, and as it raced towards the queen she screamed in fright as though it could truly harm her.

It flew forward, wings beating so powerfully that my hair was blown back by the force of it as it soared towards the high roof of the throne room. My whole body buzzed with the strength of the power we were summoning, and my grip on Darcy's hand tightened to the point of pain as we clung to each other and urged our flames on.

The Phoenix released a musical cry of victory as it dove from the sky like a hawk closing in on its prey, and the queen raised her sword as it dove on her.

An explosion rocked the foundation of the palace as they collided, the queen, the throne and the crown all consumed by the blast as Darcy and I were flung from our feet and sent crashing to the ground with the last of our power ebbing.

My gaze darkened as I hit the floor, consciousness dancing in and out so that the only thing I was certain of was the feel of my sister's hand still locked in mine.

I wasn't sure if I actually passed out or not, but as I peeled my eyes open and found Darcy's uncertain gaze meeting mine where we lay on the cold stone floor, a smile lifted my lips. Because no matter what that outburst from us had caused, I knew that we still had each other and nothing could tear us apart, especially not some fucking crown.

Darcy returned my smile and I pushed myself up beside her, looking over to the now empty and blackened throne just as a metallic clang rang out from somewhere in the distance, the creak of hinges following it and making my skin prickle with awareness.

Darcy stood first, heaving me up with her and we strode forward, the silence in the wake of so much power pressing in on us as our footsteps echoed across the flagstones.

The queen was gone. I could feel it in my heart, I had no doubt that it was true and as we made it to the throne, I spotted the crown sitting in her place, the circle cut exactly in two and the stones set within it seeming to burn with the flames which had tried to destroy it.

I reached out tentatively, picking up the left side of the crown as Darcy took the right, the metal oddly cold despite the heat it had just survived.

"Many will fall for one to ascend."

The words of the prophecy echoed through the air surrounding us and I laughed in the face of the stars.

"I already defied you once," I called out to them, tightening my hold on my half of the crown. "So fuck your idea of fate."

"We'll make our own destiny," Darcy agreed and we exchanged a dark smile before turning and heading out of the throne room, striding through the palace towards the golden gates which I knew in my heart would be standing open to let us leave.

But as we stepped out into the wide hall which led to that courtyard,

I paused in surprise, finding it transformed, a cascading waterfall of golden liquid rushing through the centre of it forming a hole in the roof and pooling across the stone floor.

The sound of whispering carried through the air as if the room was filled with a thousand voices, despite the fact that it was clearly empty, but I got the feeling that it was the stars who were watching us now, waiting to see our next move, trying to decide our fates once more.

A stone tablet lay before the tumbling golden liquid and we moved towards it, finding words scratched into it with what looked like charcoal.

A true Fae takes fear captive and refuses its call.

Well, I had to say I liked the sound of that. I glanced at Darcy and she shrugged, striding into the golden water and making me jog to catch her just in time for us to step beneath the waterfall together.

A moan escaped my lips as it rushed over my body, washing far more from my skin than dirt and sweat, stripping away doubts and fears and leaving me feeling rejuvenated as I stepped back out on the other side of it.

Everything we'd been wearing had somehow been washed away too and we emerged beyond the falls naked with only the pieces of the crown left intact as the loose tunics we'd been wearing for our training and the weapons we'd been carrying disappeared as if they'd never been there at all.

I raised a hand to my throat, relieved to find the ruby necklace Darius had gifted me still hanging there just as the Imperial Star remained around Darcy's neck and we exchanged a bemused look as we used air magic to dry our skin.

Hanging by the arching doorway which led outside were two stunning floor length gowns, one an icy silver inlaid with deep blue crystals and the other a pale gold decorated with blood red rubies, each in the style of Queen Avalon with thin straps and a long train which left space for our wings to remain on show at our backs.

We moved forward and I claimed the red and gold dress as Darcy claimed the silver and blue. We dressed ourselves in them, calling our wings back into existence as we finished and turning to look at each other as we did so.

"Wow, we actually look like princesses at last," I said on a laugh and Darcy grinned, holding up her half of the crown.

"We'd look the part even more if we had tiaras," she said, conjuring a tiny vine covered in little white flowers to hold the half of the crown on her head and I followed suit, making my flowers red instead to match my dress.

"Let's go," I said, holding my hand out to her and we walked out into the sun of the courtyard and straight through the golden gates without looking back.

The time had come for us to return to the war and now that we had full control of our Order forms, I was more than ready to end it for good.

It took us the rest of the day and all of the night to fly back to The Burrows, using the location spell to keep us on course and warming our skin with fire magic as we powered on hour after hour.

By the time we crested the final ridge and the mountainous landscape which hid The Burrows from view was revealed, I let out a whoop of celebration.

Darcy laughed at my side and we dropped from the sky, passing right through the magical barrier and landing before the farmhouse where a group of rebel guards damn near crapped their pants as we took them by surprise.

"The true queens!" one of them gasped and in the blink of an eye all five of them had prostrated themselves on the ground at our feet, murmuring thanks to the stars for our safe return and begging us to bless them with our divine touch.

Darcy gave in and brushed her hands over them, but I wasn't really up for touching random strangers in the false belief that I might somehow bless them so I just complimented them on the great guarding job they were doing and moved on.

I stepped past them and opened the door, denying their requests to make an official announcement of our arrival and heading through to the grandfather clock with Darcy close behind me.

I pulled it open and stepped into the enormous, stone tunnel, wondering if the others would be having breakfast or if they'd still be in bed and hoping for the former.

"I can't wait to eat something overly processed and covered in sugar," I groaned hungrily and Darcy nodded eagerly.

"Doughnuts, or pancakes, or just a big fat bar of chocolate," she agreed dreamily.

"Yes. All of it. I wanna eat until I pop and then I'm gonna find Darius and lock myself in a room with him for a week."

"Seth is not staying in my room this week either," Darcy agreed decisively. "If him and Caleb haven't sorted their shit out yet then he can just go sleep on the floor in Max and Xavier's room. I need Lance all to myself."

Somehow, we didn't end up passing a single Fae on our journey through the tunnels and we stepped into the dining hall where a few people were already eating and I spotted Geraldine across the room, carrying a tray of buttery bagels.

I called out to greet her and her head snapped around so fast I was surprised she didn't give herself whiplash. She released a full pterodactyl screech which made several other Fae slap their hands over their ears in alarm.

I started laughing but then she clapped the back of her hand to her forehead and honest to shit fainted, a cascade of buttery bagels tumbling over her where she fell and burying her alive.

"Geraldine!" Darcy cried out, taking off towards her, but before she could get more than a few steps, a blur of motion appeared and Orion swept her off of her feet, kissing her so hard that it must have hurt.

"You're back," he gushed as he drew away again to study her, his eyes roaming over her dress, the half crown and the defiance in her eyes before flicking to me and taking in those changes in me too.

"Hey," I said with a wave, trying to ignore the butterflies in my stomach as I looked beyond him for any sign of my big, bad, tattooed asshole of a boyfriend and feeling like some dumb lovestruck girl as my heart began to thunder like a galloping stallion at the thought of reuniting with him.

Seth howled loudly as he ran into the room followed by Max, Caleb, Xavier, Sofia, Tyler and a whole bunch of other Fae who all clamoured to get close to us.

We were hugged, screamed at, hugged again and basically handed around like a pass the parcel as everyone lost their shit over our return, and I was relieved when Geraldine appeared to crush me in her hold and sob all over my dress about how the world had been a dull and vacant place without us in it.

But despite how thrilled I was to be reunited with everyone, there was really only one person I wanted to see, and he still hadn't appeared.

Gabriel grabbed me next, his entire family dog piling me and telling my how much they'd missed me while Leon whispered into my ear that he was proud to be best friends with the true queens.

"Where's Darius?" I begged of my brother, unable to hold my tongue on the damn question anymore as I squeezed my nephew tightly in my arms and placed kisses on his cheeks while he giggled.

"We caught the murderer not long after you all left, and I suggested that he take a shift on guard duty last night."

"Why?" I asked as Darcy made it close enough to us to listen while Orion held onto her possessively, "Who was it?"

"Justin Masters," Gabriel said with a frown and Geraldine burst into tears beside us which were punctuated with words that I could just about make out.

"I have brought such shame on you, my ladies," she wailed. "My own betrothed was a snake in your lawn, a tiger in your pie, a worm in your oatmeal!"

"Seriously?" I asked in surprise. "Justin? But he's such a wet blanket."

"We caught him covered in blood and there hasn't been a death since he was apprehended. The plan is to execute him once the Cyclopses get some proof out of his head, but there was a debate over who had the authority to order that seeing as the true queens weren't here which means he's become a low priority," Orion explained and I wrinkled my nose at the thought of having to order an execution.

"But why did you tell Darius to guard him last night? Didn't you *see* us returning?" I asked Gabriel as he plucked his son from my arms and tickled him.

"Because I wanted everyone else to get the chance to say hi to you before he steals you away," he said with a knowing grin.

"You knew they were coming back?" Orion demanded angrily and Gabriel just shrugged.

"Maybe."

"Then why didn't you-"

Orion was cut off by the sound of a Dragon's roar which echoed throughout the entire dining hall and made dust tumble down from the vaulted stone roof.

"Move," Darius barked, his voice so thick with Coercion that almost all of the rebels fell under the sway of it and got the hell out of his way despite their mental shields. Although maybe they were just terrified of standing before him come to think of it.

My flesh heated as I caught sight of him carving his way through the crowd, a whole head taller than almost everyone and twice as broad too. The muttered goodbyes from my friends barely even registered as my whole world seemed to narrow down to just him and me.

"Leave," Darius commanded, the Coercion slamming into everyone in the entire room as he threw a hand out and hit them all with a repulsion spell to keep them away too.

Orion laughed as he swept Darcy into his arms and shot out of the room and everyone else took off without another word as Darius strode towards with me with such dark intention in his gaze that I couldn't even draw breath.

He didn't pause a single beat as he came for me and he collided with me in a fit of passion that had his hand fisting in my hair and yanking my head back for his kiss before I'd even fully registered the feeling of his arm banding around me.

I moaned into his mouth as the fire in my flesh burned out to meet his, and he drove me backwards, crushing my wings against the wall as he hoisted me up and sank his tongue between my lips with a feral and possessive growl that had my core soaked and my pulse rioting with a need for him that went beyond all comprehension.

He lifted me up, kissing me harder as he ripped his belt open and dropped his fly, his solid cock driving against my panties with a demand that I was desperate to meet. Darius ripped the material aside and slammed into me with a growl that rocked the foundations of my fucking soul and I cried out, my pussy clamping tight around him and my whole body trembling with the power of this beast of mine.

Darius remained there, his cock deep inside me as he used his hold on my hair to break our kiss and force me to meet the raging vortex in his eyes which had shifted to reptilian slits, the taste of smoke coating my tongue as I wetted my bruised lips.

"You don't run off on me like that again," he growled, the demand making my spine arch as I balked against the idea of him trying to own me like that.

"I-"

He silenced my protest with a hard thrust of his hips and I gasped as he fucked me into the wall, forcing me to look at him with that hold on my hair while my fingernails bit into his chest hard enough to draw blood through the white shirt he wore.

"Swear it," he snarled, thrusting his hips so hard that it was punishing and my mind spun with the delicious almost pain of it as he stole my fucking breath with every deep drive of his huge dick inside me.

I wanted to argue, to tell him he didn't control me and to call him some kind of asshole based insult, but as that rage in his eyes gave way to a desperate kind of fear which he'd been masking with fury, I gave in.

"I swear," I gasped, fisting my hands in his shirt and tugging him closer. "I'm yours. I'm here. I won't leave you behind again."

Darius growled, his eyes flashing in triumph as he stamped his lips to mine and released my hair so that he could grasp my other hip in his hand too.

He fucked me so hard that it was all I could do to cling onto him, to taste his lips and bathe in this pleasure as it built and built in my body with alarming speed.

I came with a cry which he swallowed with his kisses and he drove himself into me one final time as my pussy clamped tight around him, releasing a roar as he came too, filling me with his seed and making me feel like the only woman in the entire world as he clung to me like I might disappear again at any moment.

We stayed like that, panting heavily and inhaling each other's air as he pressed his forehead to mine and kept me in his strong arms.

"Then again, if all of our reunions are like that…" I teased, but he just growled.

"No. I'm not losing a single second more with you, Roxanya. You just earned yourself a Dragon sized stalker and I won't be going anywhere until death rips me from your arms. Even then I'll try to stay, I'll be the air on your cheeks and the light on your skin, never leaving you no matter where you go."

"Don't talk like that," I protested, winding my arms around his neck and drawing him into my arms as I breathed in that cedar and smoke scent of his skin and something in my heart just slotted right back into place.

"We should go," he muttered, though he didn't seem inclined to release me, but seeing as we'd just commandeered the entire dining hall to fuck in, it seemed like a good idea for us to leave before anyone got hungry and tried to come back.

"Where are we going?" I asked and he pulled back to look at me again, his eyes deepest brown once more.

"Out," he said decisively. "I'm taking you on a date."

"Really?" I asked, my brows rising. "Isn't there war stuff which I should be getting involved in and-"

"No," he snapped, raising his hand to straighten my tiara before lowering me to the ground and buckling his pants again. We were still fully fucking dressed and I couldn't help but blush as I glanced around at the empty room, knowing every fucker who had been in here when I arrived would know exactly what we'd been doing. "You've been gone for months so they can cope without you for another day," he said firmly. "And it's long past time you got to ride that fucking bike I bought you."

My eyes widened with excitement at that idea and I honest to shit squealed like Geraldine at a bagel buffet.

"Really?" I asked, feeling kinda like a naughty kid about to skip class.

"Really," he said firmly, taking my hand and leading me towards our room. "You're gonna have to take that crown off though, princess, because where we're going, you'll require a helmet."

"And where's that?" I asked, grinning at the thought of it even though I knew the others might be kinda pissed at us for sneaking off. But it had been so long since I'd spent any time with my Dragon and we were overdue this date, so I wasn't going to argue against the idea.

"The mortal realm," he said firmly. "I'm gonna take you out for fast food and a day of racing that beautiful beast of yours to your heart's content.

Then I'm going to pay for us to spend the night in the fanciest fucking hotel in New York City and spend the entire night bending your body to my will and making up for all the time we've missed out on during the last four months."

"Okay," I agreed, licking my lips because that sounded like fucking heaven. "Can we start off by getting pancakes?"

"Baby, if you want pancakes then I'll happily buy you a whole damn pancake house. I'm spending the day in the company of that smile on your face and the night bathing in the sound of your screams. Your every desire is my command and I'm making sure they're all fulfilled today." Darius tugged on my hand to make me move faster and I bit my lip at the mere thought of that.

"Well in that case, I'm all yours."

GABRIEL

CHAPTER FORTY TWO

"**D**on't you wanna stay and hang out with your new friend?" I asked Orion as he walked beside me out of the dining hall, pointing at Seth with my coffee mug who was chatting with Rosalie Oscura.

He glanced back at him then gave me a dry look. "He's not my friend, Noxy."

"Right," I said knowingly, seeing a whole different kind of future for them in my mind. "And I'm not your Nebula Ally."

He groaned. "Please tell me the mutt isn't destined to win me over?"

I laughed. "Not necessarily, but there's definitely a chance."

"I'll work harder to crush that chance," he said with a smirk. "Apparently I don't do friends unless they're forced on me like you and Darius, and now Caleb too."

"I wasn't forced on you," I said.

"I could argue the stars forced you on me," he tossed back.

"I could argue they forced you on me." I gave him a look as I remembered the night he'd been slipped a lust potion back when I'd met him at Zodiac Academy, and he'd fallen for me hard until I could get him an antidote.

He barked a laugh. "Yeah, well we're taking that night to the grave, aren't we?"

"So long as we take the proballs incident to the grave too," I muttered and he nodded seriously at me. I never wanted to think about that again. It still gave me nightmares. My dick had PTSD.

"For someone who has no friends, you seem to have an awful lot of them," I taunted and he shoved his shoulder against mine.

"No I don't."

"I think you've gone well over your quota of wanting 'no more friends than you have fingers', if I remember correctly."

"Whatever. Seth Capella isn't joining the ranks," he said firmly.

"Then why did I have a vision of you cuddling him all night long while

Darcy was away?"

"Oh fuck off," he muttered. "I said he could have one hug and we both fell asleep, that's all. Anyway, what are you, the friend police now?"

"I'm actually quite enjoying watching you fall in love with all the Heirs," I teased and he growled in warning.

"Watch it, Noxy. Cal and Darius are the only ones I have time for."

"You laughed for five whole minutes after Max told you about the Vampire who went to the mortal realm and made everyone believe he was the real Edward Cullen by covering himself in Pegasus glitter."

"That shit was funny," he said defensively. "It's not him I like, I liked the story."

"Then why do you always laugh at his jokes?"

"Jokes are funny, Gabriel," he growled. "That's why they're called jokes."

"Orio, I was just like you once, unable to let people in and working so hard to pretend I didn't care about anyone who tried to get under my defences," I said seriously and he looked to me with a frown. "I just don't want you to lose out on the best friendships of your life because you're a stubborn asshole, or worse, something awful happens and you lose the chance to form them forever."

"I've got Darcy, her sister, you and your family, Darius, Xavier, Cal, isn't that enough?" he asked, proving his stubbornness.

"Yeah, it's enough," I admitted. "But there can always be more." He shrugged and I clapped a hand to his back. "Anyway, tell me about you and my sister. Are you treating her well, because you know I'll destroy your life if you're not," I said through a dark smile.

When Darcy had gotten back, I'd checked her over for signs of the curse with Orion, and found no definitive trace of Lavinia's grip on her. She claimed her power felt restored and though my Sight wouldn't offer me much in the way of an answer to confirm she was truly free of the curse, I was hopeful that my sisters' Phoenix fire could fight it off.

"Of course I am," he said firmly. "And you can hardly destroy my life, Noxy, what are you gonna do? Take away my status and make everyone repulsed by me? Oh wait, too late."

I dug my fingers into his back, my wicked smile growing. "I'll burn every book you love for starters."

He inhaled sharply, looking to me in horror. "You wouldn't."

"I would. I'd rip those pages right out and make those hardbacks scream."

"You're a monster," he cursed.

"So, she's happy with you?" I pushed and a crease formed on his brow.

"Well, yeah. Mostly, I guess."

"What do you mean?" I frowned.

"I mean…" He looked to me. "And don't go after my fucking books for this, but I know she's not exactly happy with my stance on our current situation."

"Meaning?" I pressed and he sighed, looking pained as his dark eyes bored into mine.

"She doesn't care about my Power Shaming because she hasn't grown up in this world. She doesn't understand how deeply this will affect us. Always. I'm never going to be accepted in society again. When this war is over, and pray to the fucking stars, the Vegas ascend to the throne, what then? I can't stand at her side, she'll lose the support of her people. She'll be ridiculed. What if she resents me for that? She deserves an easy life, a partner she can openly be with without the judgement of the whole fucking world."

I tried to *see* more of that future he spoke of, but the fate was too weak, barely plausible at all while Lionel sat on the throne.

"So what are you planning? Because I swear to the moon, Orio, if you leave her-"

"I won't leave her," he promised. "But I'm happy to remain in the background, let the world believe we're not together."

"Like you're attempting to do here in The Burrows?" I scoffed and he nodded. "You should be proud to claim her as yours."

"I am," he snarled. "But you can't deny this situation is putting me in a difficult position. What would you do?"

I thought on that, thinking of my wife and imagining what it would be like for us to face this kind of trial. And dammit, Orion was right. I wouldn't allow her to be dragged down by the weight of my shaming, but still...there had to be some better answer than this.

I looked to the stars for guidance once more and *saw* such a mixture of fates that I winced away from them. There was so much death in my visions these days. I'd *seen* my family and friends die countless times in countless ways and sometimes I wished I could just switch off my mind and live in the now. It must have been such fucking peace during this war to at least have the hope that everything would be alright. But for so many people in this place, it seemed it might not be.

"I guess I would do what you're doing and my wife would give me hell for it," I admitted and Orion snorted a laugh.

"Yeah, well welcome to my world," he said and I guided my Sight towards this situation specifically, trying not to *see* too far so that I didn't get caught up in the chaotic visions of war.

A small pocket of possibility opened up before me as I watched Orion claiming Darcy as his publicly before the rebels and the outrage that caused in response, but my sister was smiling like it was the happiest moment of her life and my heart tugged, knowing their whole relationship had been lived between secrets. She deserved better. She deserved the whole damn world. Just like Tory did, but holy fuck had Darius gone and made a shit show out of their fate. I could only put out so many fires, and his was a raging inferno I couldn't control.

As the vision continued, I watched the rebels withdrawing from Darcy, only following Tory's command as more and more of them turned their back on her twin. I saw Orion begin to hate himself for what he'd done, his self-blame driving him to drink away the guilt of ruining her claim to the throne.

I came back out of that possible future and smiled sadly at my friend. "Just love her with all your heart, Orio," I sighed, knowing I couldn't interfere with their fate. They had to make their own decisions, overcome their own obstacles. But it left me with fear clutching my heart for them.

Were both of my sisters going to end up broken because of the men they'd chosen to love? It didn't bear thinking about, but the stars probably wouldn't let me avoid it.

"Always," he promised.

We made it to the long passages where the classrooms were located and I headed into the one assigned to me while Orion followed.

"What's the word on Justin Masters?" he asked.

"Still nothing yet," I said gravely. "The Cyclopses won't stop trying to get some hard evidence or a confession though."

"If Hamish would just let me inside his cell, I'd get it out of him in minutes," he said with a glimmer of malice in his eyes.

"Yeah, and you'd add another crime to your collection. Are you sure you wanna be a murderer?" I asked.

"What's one more little crime? I'm on the run anyway," Orion said with a shrug and I laughed.

"Do you wanna stick around for today's lesson?" I asked him. "I could use a hand teaching them ceromancy."

"Sure," he agreed and I headed over to my desk, a flash of a vision tearing through my head a beat before my chair burst into flames.

"What the fuck?" I cursed, placing my coffee mug down on the desk and rushing around to put the fire out. But the moment I got that one under control, my whole chalkboard went up in flames.

"Orio!" I barked for help as small fires burst to life all around the room and a flash of who was responsible filled my head. "Xavier – what the hell?!" We finally got the flames under control, and I turned, finding Xavier standing by my desk with his cheeks flushed and an awkward smile on his face.

"Just a little joke," he said innocently and I noticed Tyler and Sofia stepping into the classroom. They weren't really supposed to have joined this class, but Xavier had asked for Sofia to join and after my agreement, Tyler had shown up too and refused to leave. The Sight told me it wasn't a fight worth having, so I hadn't bothered to send him away since.

"Hilarious," Orion deadpanned, moving to perch on one of the desks and fold his arms.

"Well I'd give you detention, but I'd rather gouge my eyes out than spend an hour of my evening watching you do some menial task," I muttered, picking up my coffee and swallowing down the last of it. A strange taste lingered on my tongue for a second and I smacked my lips together before my eyes shot up to Xavier, his cheeks, ears and neck now bright red. "Go and sit down." I wafted him away and he trotted to his seat beside Sofia near the front of the class.

Tory, Darcy and the Heirs arrived followed closely by Geraldine as she sung a loud ditty about the moon coming down to a royal ball and I waited for them all to drop into their seats before picking up a bunch of candles from my desk.

Orion snagged them from me, handing them out to everyone a little aggressively as he tossed them down on everyone's desks. But as he approached Darcy and she held out a hand to take one, he moved it out of reach and tapped his lips, smirking at her. She stood from her seat, kissing him as she reached around his back to snatch the candle from his hand.

"You might be free to kiss in class now, but that doesn't mean you should," Max called to them and Orion stood upright, locking him in his sights like prey.

"I'll do whatever the fuck I please, and if you want me to continue teaching you so that you don't miss out on your final year of studies, then I suggest you keep your opinions to yourself," he said through a deadly smile and Max rolled his eyes, but didn't say another word.

"I think it's romantic!" Geraldine gushed, cupping her chin in her hands. "A shamed, repulsive Fae professor claiming a princess when the whole world would rather he didn't."

"Geraldine," Darcy hissed.

"Forgive me, my lady. Have I spoken out of turn?" she gasped.

"Don't call him repulsive," Darcy insisted.

"Oh my holy biscuit box!" Geraldine gasped. "Forgive me, dear Darcy. I shall pick a more fitting word in future. Ghastly perhaps? Or abominable? Maybe the word pugnacious would be more to your tastes?"

"He isn't those things," Darcy growled.

"Oh – I -um- apologies - blast my baking goods," Geraldine seemed to glitch out, caught between the cultural norm to turn on Power Shamed Fae and the desire to please her queen. His shame was something I could handle easily enough. He was my Nebula Ally and I was far too powerful to let something like that get under my skin, which was the same reason the Heirs weren't bothered by him. Many Fae believed the company of a Power Shamed Fae brought down their own status, but I didn't give a fuck about any of that. I'd stand by Orion through anything, he'd always done the same for me.

"Let's begin, shall we?" I suggested, letting Orion off the hook as he stared coolly at Geraldine, but as everyone turned their attention to me, Tyler gasped and pointed at my crotch.

"Oh my stars, sir, are you keeping the beast from the east in there?" He took out his Atlas, snapping a photo and I looked down, finding dark hairs sprouting out from the top of my waistband, my crotch bulging a little.

"What the-"

The button on my jeans suddenly popped off, flying across the room and hitting Seth right in the eye.

"Why?!" he cried as he clutched his face and my zipper flew open.

"Orio," I gasped, complete panic filling me at the thought of what was happening.

"Dude, have you got a Pomeranian in your pants?" Tory balked.

Orion gaped at me and I forced myself to look down again, a noise of grief leaving me as my jeans burst fully open at the front and hair sprouted thick and fast out the top of my boxers which were barely containing the rapid growth.

The Heirs started roaring with laughter, but this was no fucking joke. My pubes were growing at the speed of light and as I tried to stuff them back down into my boxers, the material split apart, freeing the hair which was sprouting like a wiry black bush.

Tyler fucking Corbin was recording every second with a manic gleam in his eyes and I cursed, turning my back on the class, casting a pair of silver scissors in my hand and starting to slice through the hair so it floated down around my feet.

"Are you okay, Gabriel?" Darcy called in concern.

"Someone slipped me a potion!" I barked and Orion shot to my side in concern.

"What can I do, Noxy?" he asked in earnest.

"Get them all out of here," I begged and he nodded, turning back to the class.

"OUT!" he bellowed in his best professor tone.

"No way, I wanna see this play out," Darius said with a smirk in his voice and if that Dragon wasn't already doomed, I would have killed him right then and there.

"Is he shearing his pubes off?" Sofia whispered to a round of raucous laughter.

I gave up trying to cut them with the scissors, the pubes getting out of hand, growing faster than I could keep them back. They were climbing towards my chin and I shoved them down with a noise of anguish, whipping around as rage burned through my limbs.

"Who did this?!" I bellowed, trying to *see* the answer, but all that came to me was a vision of my pubes getting out of control and I gasped, turning to Orion again. "Get something to stop them growing," I begged and Orion nodded, shooting out of the classroom and leaving me exposed to the whole room of laughing assholes. Even Darcy and Tory were cracking up and I growled at my sisters before striding towards Tyler with the intention to snatch that Atlas and break it. But before I made it there, my pubes went through another huge growth spurt and I cried out as they expanded around me and I spluttered as they grew up to my face and got stuck in my mouth.

I fought them back as I tried to see beyond them, the only sound reaching me the endless laughter in the room and suddenly my pants were splitting down the middle and falling to my ankles as the pubes curled around my back and started extending in every direction throughout the room.

My only saving grace was that the pubes were so thick, my cock was no doubt hidden within them, but as I felt the hairs pressing against my desk and it screeched along the floor from the pressure of them, I knew it was barely a saving grace at all.

"Help me!" I demanded, managing to carve a space in front of my eyes so I could peer out and I saw my sisters coming to my aid while the rest of the class fell apart in their seats.

Tory and Darcy cast shears in their hands, chopping away at the pubes before giving that up, sharing a look and raising their hands.

"Trust us, okay?" Darcy asked and I *saw* what was about to happen a second too late to stop them.

"No – wait," I gasped as they used fire to consume the pubes, the hairs swallowed up by the flames in a flash, burning all of my clothes off in the process and stopping just short of my cock.

I stood naked in front of everyone with smoke coiling up around me, the scent of burning pubes hanging in the air while my sisters exchanged a smile of satisfaction, and I exhaled out in relief, sure that had stopped it. Even as Tyler bounced in his seat and angled his Atlas down at my dick, I knew there were worse fates than this.

Xavier was laughing his ass off beside him and as my gaze locked on him, I *saw* the truth. I *saw* him placing a potion in my coffee, so I knew it was him. I knew what he'd done. And as his eyes fell on me, his laughter fell away, because he knew I'd realised it too.

"XAVIER"! I roared in anger, taking one step toward him, but then the pubes exploded back into action, seemingly spurred on by the fire that had stolen them away as they grew so fast, I was lost within them in moments, the weight of them pressing me down as I fell on my ass and I heard desks screeching everywhere as the pubes forced them back.

"Ah – run! The pubes are coming for us!" Caleb cried and the sound of footsteps racing for the door carried to me.

"Sorry, Gabriel!" Tory cried as they abandoned me.

"I'm coming!" Orio's voice reached me and the sound of something swinging and slashing reached me before Orion appeared, cutting his way through the forest of pubes which must have filled the whole room now. His face was strained as he fought to get to me with the sun steel blade in his hand, the pubes driving him back time and again as he gritted his teeth and battled his way towards me. "Hang on, Noxy. I'm almost there."

I reached for him in desperation, the pubes pushing me down time and again so I kept losing sight of him, but my warrior of a friend kept fighting his way towards me, braving the sea of my pubes which tickled his face and got in his mouth.

He spluttered and powered on, cutting his way towards me until his hand reached for mine and I latched hold of it tightly.

"Don't let go," I begged, like Rose trying to cling to Jack at the end of Titanic. But we all knew how that had turned out.

"I won't. I've got you," he promised, as he tried to pull me from the pubes which were trying to carry him away on a tide, his hand squeezing as he dragged me towards him.

But the tide was too strong and he was being forced backwards as he held out a potion with his other hand, offering it to me. I reached out with my free hand to grab it, but the pubes formed a wall I couldn't get through.

"Orio!" I cried.

"Noxy!" he called in return as his hand started slipping out of mine.

He fought his way forward once more, the potion now bobbing along on a gust of air he cast, bringing it to my lips.

"Open your mouth," he commanded and I tipped my head back, doing as he asked. But as Orion flipped it upside down with his air magic, the cursed pubes intervened, knocking it to one side and the potion spilled into my eye instead, the liquid stinging like a motherfucker.

"Ahh!" I wailed, the burning intensifying.

I could feel Orion's hand slipping further from my grip and I held onto his fingers with all I had.

"Don't let go," I growled again, squinting out into the pubes as my eyes burned and I hunted for him.

His face appeared through the pubes once more, his eyes full of apology as he shook his head.

"I'm so sorry, Noxy." His fingers slipped from my grasp and my friend was swallowed away into the black forest of pubes like a monster had drawn him into its depths.

I shouted after him in desperation as the pubes thickened so much that I was plunged into darkness. And only one thought remained with me there.

Xavier Acrux is going to pay.

XAVIER

CHAPTER FORTY THREE

I cantered down the corridors in my Fae form with a neigh of victory as Sofia ran at my side, pink glitter cascading from her blonde hair as she smiled.

"You really did that?" she laughed.

"Yeah, and he's gonna freaking kill me when he gets out of there," I said with a snort of laughter.

"You're so funny, Xavier," she said with a wide grin.

"Oh yeah?" My chest puffed up as we turned another corner and slowed to a halt. We were both breathless as we hid in the dark and adrenaline was coursing through my veins.

"How did you do it?"

"It was all about distraction," I said with a shrug. "I got someone else to make the potion, then I left the opportunity to chance."

"That's genius." She smiled, her eyes dipping to my mouth and suddenly I was moving toward her, aching for her as I slid my hand into her hair and pressed her back against the wall.

A small gasp escaped her and I gave her a moment to push me away, but she didn't.

My throat bobbed as I stared down at this perfect creature who'd captivated my dreams. She was the most beautiful mare I'd ever seen, and I couldn't believe the way she was looking at me right now.

I threw caution to the wind, leaning down and pressing my mouth to hers, stealing a kiss that didn't belong to me, but I took it all the same. She resisted for half a second then melted against me, drawing me closer as passion and need drove us toward each other.

"Tyler," she said against my mouth.

"Forget Tyler," I insisted.

"Hard to forget him when he's standing right here," Tyler growled then he grabbed the back of my shirt, ripping me away from Sofia.

I turned to him, stamping my foot in rage and our foreheads slammed together as we whinnied furiously at one another.

"The rest of us are also here," Darius said, scaring me out of my damn mind as I whipped around and found him, the twins and the other Heirs all waiting to get by. In my lust, I had totally forgotten that we'd left the classroom together and like a fucking awkward duck, here I stood, making a damn scene, blocking the tunnel so they were all just forced to watch me.

"Oh, er, sorry," I said. "I'll let you guys go."

I took a step to my left but so did Darius. I jerked to a halt and moved right but he did that too, the awkwardness intensifying as Tory sniggered beside him. The third time it happened, Darius huffed a cloud of smoke into my face, grabbed my arms and lifted me up, planting me against the wall so that the entire group could file past us.

I glared at Tyler through the line of them as they went and the moment they'd all headed off down the tunnel, we lunged at each other again, our foreheads butting, whinnies filling the air.

"You think you can touch my girlfriend and get away with it?" Tyler snarled.

"She wants the strongest Pegasus, Tyler, and that's *me*," I insisted.

"Stop it," Sofia snapped. "I like both of you, okay?" She tried to pull us apart, but we ignored her, our heads knocking together once more as we fought for dominance, trying to force the other one to submit.

I was so sick of Tyler acting like I was less than him. My instincts demanded I crush him beneath me and claim my rightful position as Dom of our herd. I'd fallen for Sofia a long time ago, and yeah maybe I knew it wasn't my right to move in on another guy's girl, but this was more than that. It was a need of my Order. I had to claim her as I had to claim the Dom position. And it wasn't some primal claiming either, I loved Sofia. And I wanted her as mine in every way. To fly at my side as my mare and ride through clouds and rainbows together.

"That's it," Sofia huffed as Tyler and I started shoving each other. "Until you can figure this out between you two, I'm done."

"What do you mean done?" Tyler rounded towards her in alarm.

"Done, Tyler," she said firmly. "I can't handle all this aggravation anymore. I'm barely even glittering lately, I need a relaxed environment. This isn't healthy for any of us." She sighed, looking between the two of us with want in her eyes then she turned and walked away from us with a sad whinny, disappearing after the others who had headed towards the dining hall.

"Now look what you've done." Tyler shoved me in the chest and I stumbled back into a wall. "Everything was fine until you showed up with your stupid quaffed hair and your hot as fuck abs, and now your fucking dijazzle to top all other dijazzles. It's bullshit. And you know what?" He grabbed hold of his shirt and pulled it off, tossing it away. "I'm done with this game. You wanna try and take my position, then come at me Xavier!" He slapped his hand against his bronzed chest. "We fight and whoever wins claims the Dom title once and for all and the other one has to suck it up and never challenge the other again."

"Fine by me," I said, pulling my own shirt off and stamping my foot in preparation of the fight.

"Oh, hey there boys," Washer purred as he appeared at the end of the corridor in his speedos, a towel draped over his arm. But he wasn't heading to or from a bathhouse in this tunnel so why the fuck was he dressed like that? "Do you need someone to referee your little spat? I'd be more than happy to offer my assistance."

I wrinkled my nose and Tyler folded his arms like he was trying to cover up some of his muscular chest.

"Come now, let's see you limber up first," Washer encouraged before starting to do lunges. "Follow my lead. Like this. Get deep into the glutes."

I glanced at Tyler as he grimaced.

"Wanna go to my room for the fight?" Tyler muttered and I nodded quickly, the two of us turning and cantering away from Washer as fast as we could.

"Don't be like that!" Washer called after us. "At least remember to oil up your bodies before you get started, it'll help keep your movements nice and fluid."

"Ew," I ground out.

Tyler shuddered and I was relieved when we made it to his room and he pushed inside. I followed him, rolling my shoulders as he kicked the door shut, ready to go full wild mustang on his ass.

Tyler picked up a bottle of oil from his nightstand squirting it over his chest and rubbing it into his skin.

"What are you doing?" I asked in surprise, my gaze falling to the firmness of his muscles as the oil highlighted them all.

"Washer's a perve, but he's also right about the oil thing," Tyler said.

"Why do you have that lying around?" I asked in confusion and he gave me a filthy look.

"You are such a little virgin, Xavier," he said with a grin and I realised the oil had glitter in it that sparkled against his skin.

"Fuck off," I snarled. "I'm not a virgin."

He whinnied a laugh. "It's sad how much you deny it." He tossed me the bottle of oil and I poured a load of it in my hand, glossing it all over my chest and arms.

When I looked up, I found Tyler adjusting his sweatpants and kicking his shoes off.

"No magic," he said. "Let's just beat the fuck out of each other and see who's the top stallion."

I swallowed thickly at that, but raised my chin at the challenge and nodded. I could take him on, I'd been keeping up with training here, doing morning workouts and pushing myself hard daily to stay strong. Darius had been more than happy to help me out with building a regime and if I could keep up with his relentless drills then I could do this. But from the look of Tyler's muscular frame, he was probably working out just as much.

I tossed the oil onto the bed and we eyed each other for a moment, the tension in the room prickling against my skin.

"Come on then," he goaded me, opening his arms wide. "Or is the little spare, Xavier Acrux the virgin too afraid to fight me?"

I whinnied in anger, charging towards him and throwing a punch that crashed into his gut. He doubled over, but smashed a fist into my kidney in response, making pain radiate through my side. I shoved him away from me and he landed on the bed, bringing his legs up and slamming his bare feet to my chest, making me stagger backwards.

He lunged at me with a neigh of fury, his fist ramming into my jaw and I responded with an equally hard blow to his ribs. He grabbed my shoulders and I grabbed his in return, trying to fight him back as our hands slipped and slid over our oiled up skin.

I dug my nails in as he reared forward and bit my shoulder, a neigh of rage leaving me as I shoved him back and swung a punch at him. But I missed and he leapt at me again, his weight knocking me into a table and sending a bunch of shit falling off of it with a crash that echoed off the walls. A tarot deck went flying, cards spilling all over the floor and The Tower looked up at me like it was fucking mocking us with its predictions of destruction and chaos. But that was fine by me, because this fight had been a long time coming.

I threw my shoulder into his chest, knocking him back as I dug my heels in, thinking of Sofia as my instincts burned and flared. I had to force him beneath me. I had to make him submit.

The backs of his knees hit the side of the bed and he fell down beneath my weight as I clambered on top of him, driving him down into the mattress and throwing a punch into his face.

"I'm the Dom!" I snapped and his lips parted as he stared up at me then he bucked his hips, knocking me off of him as he turned and rolled onto his knees, making a move to escape me.

I pounced on him again, forcing his head down into the sheets. "Say it. Say I'm the Dom, Tyler. Say it."

I let go of his head so he could look back at me and say it. But instead he turned his head and his gaze fell to my crotch and I followed his line of sight, realising I was rock hard, the outline of my cock pressing against my sweatpants.

Heat burned lines across my cheeks as Tyler's eyes lifted to mine, but he wasn't looking at me with a mocking smirk like I expected, I found a pool of lust in his eyes.

"You're not the Dom unless you prove it," he croaked and I knew what he was saying, what he was asking of me. A moment of silence hung between us where the fight shifted to something else, and the energy in the room burned in a whole different way.

"Prove it," he demanded again and suddenly I was shoving him back down against the sheets and grabbing the bottle of oil from the bed, driven on by instinct alone. I freed my jewelled cock, pouring the sparkling oil all over it before yanking his sweatpants down.

"Do it," Tyler groaned, his words a plea and a demand at once.

I didn't let myself consider a single doubt before I was lining my cock up with his ass and driving it inside him, forcing him down beneath me and thrusting my hips as a neigh of pleasure fell from my lips. And oh my fucking stars that felt so good, my dick wrapped tight inside his body like it had been made perfectly to fit right there, and the way he groaned my name said he felt the damn same. Why had I never done this before? Why the hell had I held off on this feeling of ecstasy?

"I'm not a virgin anymore now, am I Tyler?" I laughed lustily, my blood thrumming with the perfect feeling of my cock inside him as I began to move.

"Fuck you." He groaned, pressing his ass back against me and meeting every drive of my hips as I held him beneath me and I gasped at how good this felt, lost to a haze of desire and rage and instincts that made my head foggy.

"Who's the Dom?" I demanded again through breathless pants as I pinned him down and rocked my hips faster.

"You are," he replied through a moan and I replied with a neigh of pleasure as I felt myself teetering on the edge of oblivion. There was so much pent up rage and anger between us and it was making me lose my mind now it was culminating in this perfect act which felt so star damned inevitable, I had no idea how I hadn't seen it before.

"You're the Dom. Oh my stars, you're the Dom," Tyler said breathlessly.

Those words made me finish with a loud whinny, stilling inside him as I reared over him, pressing him firmly down beneath me and panting as I came down from the high that was making my veins buzz better than any rainbow I'd ever flown through.

But as my thoughts realigned, I looked down at Tyler and realised what I'd done.

"Oh fuck," I breathed. "Sofia."

"Xavier," Sofia's voice reached me in reply and my head whipped around as I found her standing in the doorway, her eyes dragging over us in shock.

"I'm sorry," I blurted as Tyler lifted his head and looked to her too.

"Shit, Sofia, baby. It wasn't planned, it just happened. I don't even know how it happened," he garbled.

She stepped into the room, kicking the door shut behind her and pulling her dress off in the next move. Her tits were bare and the tiny sparkly pink g-string she wore clung tightly to her pale skin as she walked towards us.

I eased my hips back, releasing Tyler and pulling my sweatpants up as he rolled over and I slid off of him as I knelt on the bed.

"What are you doing?" I asked around a lump in my throat and she walked past us with a mischievous gleam in her eyes, heading through an archway in the room and the sound of a shower carried to us.

Tyler shoved off of the bed, tugging his pants up as he ran after her and I raced after him too, unsure what to fucking do. Anxiety warred in my chest, but my veins were buzzing too, solidifying my position as Dom of the herd. As much as I wanted to feel bad about this, every part of my Order was telling me it was right. And it was confusing as hell.

There was a shower there carved into the rock, water falling from a pipe which must have been made with earth magic, tumbling down over Sofia in a spray as she washed herself, caressing her breasts with her eyes shut and her head tipped back.

Tyler looked to me as we stood shoulder to shoulder before her and she finally opened her eyes, biting her lip and beckoning us closer.

"Both of us?" I asked and she nodded, all hesitation abandoning me as we moved as one into the shower and she sank her tongue between Tyler's lips.

"He Dommed me down, it was instinct," he said and she leaned back, capturing hold of my hair and dragging me closer.

"I know, I saw," she panted as my hands fell to the soft curves of her waist as the water washed over me heavily. "And I'm happy. Because this is the answer we've been looking for."

I met Tyler's gaze again and his throat bobbed as his eyes dipped to my mouth and Sofia pushed our heads close together. His mouth pressed to mine and I accepted his tongue between my lips, kissing him and finding my heart rate picking up again.

I'd thought about guys before, even jerked off over these kinds of fantasies plenty of times, but since I'd fallen for Sofia I'd been more caught up in the idea of her than exploring those desires in me. But as I kissed him harder and thought of how fucking good it had felt being inside him, I knew that this was what I'd been hungering for in all of those tension filled moments we'd shared. My feelings for Sofia had clouded that desire to me, but now that I'd given in to it, I knew I wanted more. And as my cock got solid again and Sofia pressed her ass back against me, I knew I was all in with this arrangement. It felt so damn right, I couldn't believe I hadn't noticed how much Tyler had appealed to me before. I'd been so caught up in trying to dominate him that I hadn't even realised what else I'd been hungering for from him.

I broke our kiss, leaning down to kiss Sofia instead and she moaned against my mouth as Tyler gripped my sweatpants and yanked them down. I kicked them off and groaned as he washed my body with soap, his hand slipping over the ridges of the gemstones on my cock and making me ache for more. He slid the tiny g-string off of Sofia, tossing it at our feet and baring her gem encrusted pussy to us both, making me so hard I ached.

Tyler moved behind me, his mouth on my neck as he pushed Sofia forward so she had to brace herself against the wall, then he gripped my cock again and guided it to the hot wetness of her pussy.

"Like this," Tyler growled, driving his hips against mine and forcing me inside her with that single hard thrust, making Sofia cry out and a neigh of pleasure tumble from my lips.

Tyler gripped her hips, pulling her back to meet every one of my thrusts as he continued to drive against me from behind, showing me how to please her as she moaned both of our names.

"Stars, that's so good," Sofia sighed and my chest swelled as Tyler took hold of my hand, guiding it around her waist and over the gemstones adorning her pussy then onto her clit.

He moved my fingers in circles and she shivered with pleasure for us before he let go of my hand and left me to keep up the rhythm, building her towards ecstasy as her pussy gripped tightly around my shaft, every one of the gemstones in my Jacob's ladder grinding inside her in a way that had her falling apart for me.

I reached behind me, my instinct to please my Subs driving me on as I forced Tyler's sweatpants down, and gripped his cock in my fist. He groaned deeply, moving to my side to watch me and Sofia as he let me take the reins, and his eyes became hooded as he watched my dick driving in and out of her while my fist glided up and down his length.

Sofia came with a shudder, her moans filling up the space as her pussy suddenly clamped down on my cock and I gasped as she forced me to come with her, driving my hips forward a couple more times as I rode out the wave of pleasure, unable to believe how good this felt.

I pulled out of Sofia and she turned to us with desire in her eyes as she reached for Tyler's cock too and we worked together to please him, our fists slipping up and down his length until he was coming against Sofia's thigh and the three of us collided in a desperate, messy kiss as the hot water raced over our flesh.

My heart was pounding to the most thrilling tune it had ever known and I knew this was right where I belonged, the three of us finding the most perfect harmony between each other. And though I may have become the Dom, I'd never expected things to go this way, we were falling into a natural order that pleased our inner Fae and had found a way to balance the urges of our kind. And holy fucking shit, it felt like heaven.

I galloped through the halls, hunting for everyone as my dick tingled with the amount of sex I'd had today. I was a sex stallion, I mean a stallion of sex, or a sex horse, gah fuck it, I wasn't a virgin anyway and that was all that mattered. I was *sooo* not a virgin.

I whinnied my joy as I heard the sound of people talking up ahead, recognising Orion's voice as he said, "This changes things."

I rounded into the passage, glad he was there most of all because he was the one who'd called me out in front of everyone for being a virgin, and now he was going to eat his words.

I leapt out into the passage, placing my hands on my hips. "Ha-ha! You can't use my blood anymore for your elixir, Orion. I had loads of sex. Loads and loads of sex. With a guy *and* a girl. I double dicked and double dipped and all the doubles and had my dick in all the holes, Orion. *All* of them."

Orion looked to me in shock as did the rest of our group who were standing around him, but none of them smiled and Darius carved a hand down his face, shaking his head.

"Someone just *died*, Xavier," Max hissed and Orion stepped aside, revealing a bloody body behind him on the floor, also unveiling my mother and Hamish standing beyond the corpse.

Mom was pale as she looked to me. "That's wonderful news, sweetie, well done you. It sounds like you did a great job too, but we'll have to discuss it later, okay?"

No...no. Not again.

I didn't want to discuss my sex life with my mom. I'd just told her point blank I'd fucked a guy and a girl in all the holes. *Oh my stars I just said 'all the holes' in front of my mother.*

"I'm sorry, I didn't mean- by the stars, I thought the murderer was caught," I rambled, backing up as I stared at the bloodbath between them all.

"Looks like Justin Masters wasn't the killer," Tory said and Geraldine shrieked, holding a hand to her forehead.

"That wigworm has been abused so terribly for his crime. And now he must be an exonerated insect, set free to fly like a beetle to the sky," Geraldine said, falling against Max and sobbing against his shoulder.

"What the hell are we gonna do?" Darcy questioned anxiously. "Why can't the Cyclopses find who's doing this?"

"Bless my hyacinth, we must intensify the interrogations," Hamish said. "We will begin at once." He took my mom's hand, heading off down the corridor and a few rebels hurried forward, covering the mutilated body with a blanket while everyone else started walking my way.

I turned, finding myself face to face with Gabriel, his upper lip curling back in a snarl as he took hold of my arm. "Hello, you little shit."

Oh fuck.

"Do you know how long it took for Orion to get me out of that pube forest?" he hissed.

"Um…a while?" I rasped.

"Long enough for me to nearly choke on my own pubic hair, Xavier. Long enough for that," he growled, taking out his Atlas, bringing something up on it and showing it to me. "Get your little asshole of a friend to take this down."

"He's actually my Sub now," I said with a hint of pride in my voice as I looked at the video Tyler had just posted to FaeBook.

"I don't care if he's the son of the moon itself and has come down to earth to gift us all with moon magic, Xavier. You will tell him to take this down."

I nodded quickly as I read the FaeBook post Tyler had put up online, the video of Gabriel playing beneath it, his pubes knocking Geraldine to the ground as she ran for her life, wailing about dying the way she'd always feared she would. She crawled towards the door in desperation, her hand outstretched as she began to disappear into the dark hair before Max dragged her free, promising she wouldn't die this way and they made it out of the room.

Tyler Corbin:

Things got #hairy in class today when there was a #pubetastrophy after @ Gabriel Nox tried to teach us the importance of keeping a tidy bush. His pubes quickly got out of control and his #wangwig went from a #furryfriend to a #bristlybeast in less than a minute. Quick to act, Lance Orion dove in to help only to find himself amBUSHed as the #cockcarpet smothered him and he found himself with his friend's #willywhiskers in his mouth and nowhere to go. Despite how hard Orion battled the #peenpelt, he was lost within the #deeppubesea and we have yet to lay eyes on him since.
#youhairedithererefirst #thelostfurld #bashedbyyourownbush #deathbyphallusfuzz #willthepubenatorbeback

Carson Alvion:
Justice. *bush emoji*

Mikaela Colgan:
Orion can come battling into my bush any time he likes! #bravethebush #bushbandit

Leon Night:

HAHAHAHAHA Orion is buried in Gabe's #cocklocks

Erica Collins:
*I miss you, Leon. Why won't you answer my calls???? #Mindyforlife
#thislionessislonely #cryinformylion*

Savannah Desiree:
*Holy moonstones! I'd dive into that #pubacioussea to rescue the #hotharpy
any day of the week*

Jasmine Andrea Ray:
Snip for Gabriel! We'll all pitch in! #I'llbringmyclippers #finderskeepers

Marta Segura:
*That's what you call a hairy situation #savethehotprofessors
#itsnotlearningunlessmyloinsarea-burning*

Telisha Mortensen:
*Don't wanna make it weird, but I'd EAT my way to Gabriel and Orion in that
pubalicious room #dontknockittilyoutryit #furryfeast*

Zian Williams:
I hope there's no minocrabs in there! #thecrabsareaftertheabs

"Sorry?" I tried as I swallowed a laugh, wondering if I should explain the deal I'd made for my dick gems, but Gabriel didn't seem in the mood to see them all right now, so I decided not to get them out.

"You're not sorry," he growled. "But you will be." He shoved me towards the bloody mess left by whatever had attacked the dead Fae as their body was carried away by the rebels. "Clean that up without a single drop of water magic."

"But-" I gasped, and he pushed me to my knees in front of the carnage.

"I can do a whole lot worse," Gabriel warned and I sighed in resignation, starting to clean up the mess. But as he walked off with the rest of our group and I was left trying to deal with the blood and gore strewn across the ground, I still couldn't help but feel that this was one of the best days of my life. And I muttered to myself, "Worth it."

GERALDINE

CHAPTER FORTY FOUR

I paced my room, pondering the meaning of all things as I tapped the shadow spyglass in my palm, enjoying the satisfying thwack the eyeball made within it every time I shook it hard enough.

The thing was a tricksome beast which had already tried to crawl into my face thrice when I worked to contain it within this night iron – a metal specifically designed to hurt nymphs, targeting the shadows and nullifying them - but now that I had it properly contained, I had nothing to fear.

And yet that hadn't brought us any closer to our goal and I had taken this one challenge upon myself because I knew in the bottom of my beetroots that we would never win this war without succeeding in this endeavour.

We needed to get our sticky fingers on a map of espial to be able to use this dastardly eye to track down the rifts. But the darn things were rarer than a Dragon's uterus these days and there were only five known to be in existence, all of which were owned and heavily guarded by the FIB.

Just thinking of those dastardly Daniels got my crockpot boiling at the knowledge that they were still following that false filibuster of a king and doing his bidding no matter how nefarious his intentions were. They really made my gobble wobble and I was determined to snaffu one of those maps of espial right out of their hands at the soonest opportunity.

The problem was, dear, sweet, flappy Gabriel had only managed to *see* one of the maps which was held by the highest division of the FIB and every plan we had come up with to claim it had ended with him foreseeing our failure. And death. Much death. Honestly the little nutmuffin had looked quite aghast at that vision and I'd firmly suggested he go for a lie down to get over it much to his refusal. But he really looked like a wet Sally and I'd needed him gone so I'd wafted him on his way all the same.

It really was one big hairy Dragon nut to crack, and I was just tooting my horn over the time we were still wasting while we tried to come up with a plan that wouldn't fail.

A knock at the door sounded and I sighed, moving to open it and tossing the spyglass down on my comforter, the eyeball bouncing around in it like a moist ping-pong ball in a tumble dryer.

"Hey there, sugartoot," Papa said kindly, knocking his knuckles against my chin. "Are you ready?"

"Oh, heavens have mercy," I gasped but I followed him out into the hallway all the same. Because I may not have been able to get my deft hands upon a map of espial to help my queens locate the shadow rifts and bring down that conniving crumb, Lavinia, but I could make amends with my intended. Though I could admit to myself that I was loath to do so.

Papa gave me a look from the corner of his eye as we walked, his assessing gaze making me all cumbersome and I tripped over my own feet, only saving myself a fall onto my petunia as he caught hold of my elbow and righted me.

"You know, if this betrothal no longer suits you-" he began, but I cut him off with a gasp.

"Sweet sourcrout whatever gave you that idea?" I gasped.

"Well, I'm not blind, honeybutton, I see the looks you share with the Rigel chap and I know he has a dastardly opinion about the throne, but perhaps that's not such a bother. It is clear our ladies will rise regardless and once he has been cowed down by the sweet and stern hand of fate, he may become a suitable match for you."

"But what of Justin?" I cried. "Poor, sweet, foolish Justin who was so wrongfully accused? What kind of lady am I if I do not return to him now after all he has suffered?"

"Popkins…"

"No. I cannot waver on this," I replied firmly, though my bottom lip did quiver some and as we turned into the tunnel where Justin's cell was housed, he let the subject drop like a leaf into a well.

It wasn't just my own lady whims which held me to this engagement, it was my dear momsy too. Upon her deathbed, when the cruel and long-lasting Faeitis had eaten into her bones and stolen her away from us upon the wings of the star-guided nightjar, she had asked me to always stick to my word. For there was nothing worse in my sweet Mama's eyes than a tongue which spoke in reverie of one snowbell, only to pick another. She was the epitome of a loyal, faithful woman, my guiding star in all the years since she had passed beyond the Veil into the arms of our shining fate-weavers. And if I were to go back on my word to Justin, what would she think of me?

Papa hurried forward, unlocking his cell door and releasing Justin, apologising to him and explaining the fact that another body had been discovered while I lingered in the wings like a fart no one had noticed yet. But as his gaze rose to meet mine, I knew the stench of betrayal had found him.

"Oh sweet salamanders," I said. "Can you ever forgive me for believing you capable of such heinous and brutal acts?"

Justin's brows arched in surprise, his simple face a picture of confusion as he found himself free, Papa removing the magic restricting cuffs that had been used to contain him with a key from his pocket.

"Did you catch the real culprit?" he asked, not answering my question and I sucked in a shameful breath as I shook my head.

"Whatever will it take to earn your forgiveness?" I begged of him and he blushed a little as his gaze dropped to the bounty of my bosoms, letting me know he desired a reward of the flesh.

"Bagels!" I cried, so loud that Papa darn near fell over and Justin flinched. "This man needs a bagel if ever I saw a man in need of one."

I turned sharply and hurried away, hearing Justin's footsteps hounding me as my ears burned with the terrifying prospect of allowing him to water my lawn.

I ran like a peacock on a tennis court, leading him to the dining hall where I bellowed at everyone in attendance to applaud him and apologise for ever doubting his stalwart heart before escaping through the crowd to the kitchens.

A sob caught in my throat as I began to prepare the dough, beating it like a lizard on a tumbleweed as I worked to create my signature bagels. But today's batch were sure to be a failure. Because my tears were going to add more salt than a barracuda with a bum rash and there wouldn't be a Fae who ate them who didn't know the truth soon.

"Gerry?"

My heart stilled at the sound of that voice and I sucked in a sharp breath, freezing where I was and wondering if I hadn't just conjured the idea of him into my mind.

"Gerry, talk to me."

I felt him at my back even before he touched me, his hands finding my forearms and sliding down my skin until his fingers met with mine and he began to guide me in the dance of kneading the dough.

"I can feel your heart breaking," he murmured in my ear and I heaved another sob as I closed my eyes and leaned back against him, focusing on the feeling of the dough between our fingers and his chest pressed to my back

"Who am I if I am not a lady of my word?" I asked, feeling the heat of his breath on my neck like a dawn crested feather spinning through the air.

"You're Geraldine Grus," he replied. "And you're fucking everything to me."

My fluttering heart free fell to my nether regions at those words and I broke for him, opening up like an egg cracking apart and offering him a view of my yolky insides.

"But you are a cad and I am a lady," I breathed. "We are as unlikely as a fish and a dandelion finding truest love."

"Well this fish would grow legs and crawl from the water to sit with you, dandelion."

My throat bobbed and my fingers stilled in the dough.

"And what if the wind blows and my seeds take flight?" I murmured.

"Then I would grow wings and follow you to the moon," he replied. "Because nothing in this world means more to me than you do, Gerry. And there are no differences we can't overcome to be together."

I turned my head, my eyes cracking open and swimming with tears that revealed a watery view of his handsome face.

"Then meet me on the moon," I breathed, agreeing to something I knew I shouldn't and parting my lips for the caress of his mouth. Would Mama hate me for this, would she curse my name once, twice, three times beyond the Veil and call me a tongue twizzler of a tuppence?

He kissed me like I was a hogmoth dancing in the nether breeze and I kissed him like he was a mongoose who just needed love.

It was sweet and honest and utterly ours and as our hands returned to kneading the dough, I fell into the rhythm of baking with him and together we made the butteriest bagels that I ever had made which we devoured together away from the crowd. And not a single crumb was offered to Justin's thin lips.

LIONEL

CHAPTER FORTY FIVE

Istood with my hands clasped at the based of my spine, staring out into the
sheeting rain that beat down on the glass of the royal conservatory. The
doors before me held the near transparent images of a Hydra and a Harpy
within the glass, and I watched as rain droplets drizzled over them, the king
and queen appearing to weep before me. But not even that could bring me any
satisfaction this morning.

"The wind is blowing in from the east, my king," Vard offered from
somewhere behind me and I sneered, whipping my head towards him as rage
coursed through me. I'd had him tortured for his failings, allowing my son and
his companions to get into my palace and cut the eye from his worthless face.

"If you cannot offer me a useful prophesy before the week is up, I will
have you sent back to the dungeon and you will remain there until my torturer
pulls something useful out of your head."

"A-apologies, sire," he simpered in fear. "I am still adjusting to The
Sight without my shadow eye."

I turned to face him, letting my arms fall to my sides as I approached
this weasel of a man before me. The shadow eye had been of much concern to
me. I had no idea why it was worth risking breaking into the palace for. What
did my son think he was going to use it for? Vard had assured me they could
not use it to predict the future unless someone placed it into their own head.
Perhaps that was their plan. My son was heartless enough to force that fate
upon someone, and that idea unsettled me. For if my enemies could *see* the
shadows, my movements could be predicted.

"Do you know why you are not dead, Vard?" I asked icily and he started
trembling and shaking his head at me. "You are not dead for one reason and
one reason only. A more skilled Seer has not yet presented themself to me. But
I assure you I am looking, so you'd either better find a way to procure yourself
another shadow eye, or become a better Seer without one, because your fate is
otherwise decided. And I promise you, you will scream for weeks until I allow

you passage beyond the Veil for the problem you have caused me." I back handed him with heat blazing along my skin and he wailed as the flesh of his right cheek was scalded badly.

I glowered as I stalked out of the conservatory, my new manservant Horace hurrying forward with a glass of whiskey on a golden tray. I accepted it, sweeping past him. He was adequate, but Jenkins had been of a particular calibre that couldn't be replicated. He had been in ownership of a sadistic soul which had pleased me some, and he had been so in tune with my needs that I had barely noticed them being fulfilled. I had already had Horace punished twice for his errors, but he appeared to be willing to correct himself. Which was a trait I appreciated in my subordinates.

"My King," Lavinia's voice carried from the winding stairway to my right which was covered in deep black carpet.

I looked up, finding her draped in shadow and making my skin prickle with the unease of her proximity. One good thing had come out of the Vegas' attempt to thwart me. They may have taken the shadow eye from the face of my Seer, but when we had returned here to find the monstrous Heir she had provided me with butchered, I had to admit I was relieved. When she had offered me a child, I had assumed it would be Fae, but my blood curdled in disgust at whatever that shadow creature had been. It was no pure blooded Dragon, that was for certain. So good riddance to it.

I had a new plan for an Heir now, one I would not breathe a word of as I conducted what needed to be done. I would have that repugnant girl Mildred Canopus inseminated with my own seed. All I was in need of was a pure blooded Dragon womb to carry my Heir, I did not care for the woman who housed it. And I certainly wouldn't need to plunge my cock into that vile looking girl to achieve it. I just needed to figure out how to convince my new queen to accept the idea so that I could be certain she wouldn't kill the owner of the womb I required. There were no alternatives to the Canopus girl after all.

"Come lie with me," Lavinia commanded, letting her shadow dress fall away to reveal her naked flesh.

I kept my poise, though inside I shuddered. She was of no appeal to me since I had seen that repellent creature crawl from her body into this world. Not to mention the way she had used my flesh for her own pleasure and the agony it had caused me. No. I did not want to risk my cock by driving it into her again, no matter how attractive she might seem at times.

"I have business in the city," I said firmly, turning my back on her and striding away, leaving her shrieking in anger, but at least she didn't try to wield my shadow hand against me.

An entourage of FIB agents were waiting for me outside and I drew my air shield tighter around me as I let my gaze dip down to the ass of the beautiful Agent Francesca Sky as she opened the back door of the car for me.

"Good evening, your highness," she said dutifully as she turned to me, her eyes on the ground and her head bowed. Her dark hair was woven into a braid and I indulged in the image of wrapping it around my fingers as she sucked my cock, wondering if I could steal her away after the interview tonight.

"Join me for a drink after the show," I insisted and her eyes snapped up to meet mine, a flash of something in them which could have been fear. And I quite liked that look on her.

"Just me, My King?" she breathed in confusion.

"Just you," I purred.

"I have to work," she said quickly, and for a millisecond there was a flicker of defiance in her gaze. But it was nothing I couldn't easily stamp out.

"I am the king, and I command that you are unengaged." I stroked a finger along her cheek before ducking into the car and she snapped the door shut after me.

I was driven to Tucana and I ran my palm down my crisp white shirt, adjusting my dark red jacket as the car door was opened. I stepped out into the chaotic light of camera flashes, the rush of anti-magic spells falling over me.

I indulged the crowd, offering photographs and perfectly designed quotes written by my PR team which would fill the papers tomorrow. I was the most popular man in the kingdom, everyone wanted a bite of me and I let them have it as I fed them my most winning smiles and basked in the glory of my reign.

They asked about my queen, and I told them she was overtired, but would soon be on her feet again. This was my night after all, and I'd had no intention of bringing her here to claim any of my triumph for herself.

When it was time to head inside, I walked up the red carpeted stone steps into the grand theatre set up for the event with my entourage in tow. The FIB remained close, but not so close that they blocked the photographers as I turned and offered a final wave to the crowd who cheered raucously. Then I was escorted inside and led down a glitzy corridor full of golden sculptures which called to the inner Dragon in me.

I was led backstage for a while, but it wasn't long before it was time for my moment in the sun. The theatre was fit to bursting with my supporters, and as I waited by the stage to be announced by my good friend from The Celestial Times, Portia Silverstone, I bathed in the excitement in the air.

I was at the height of my career, this moment years in the making and tonight my life would be celebrated in an interview that would go down in history. It would be broadcasted live to the entire kingdom, all other shows cancelled in favour of it, and an order in place to ensure every Fae in Solaria had their eyes glued to it. To me. Their ruler, the greatest king to ever have lived.

"So without further ado, I welcome to the stage our most magnanimous, our glorious, our eminent and powerful, King Lionel Acrux!" Portia cried and I slapped on my best smile as I strode out onto the stage, the entire audience rising to their feet to clap and cheer me.

The seats rose up high to wide balconies above, and in the gold rimmed boxes were Pitball stars and celebrities, all watching me, their attendance non-negotiable after I'd sent the personal invites to their doors. In the front row of the closest balcony was the Councillors alongside the new Heirs to their seats, Ellis Rigel, Hadley Altair, and Athena Capella.

Portia was wearing a dark blue dress which clung to her curvaceous body as she bowed to me in greeting and sat down on a green velvet chair. I unbuttoned my suit jacket before dropping into the much larger, wingback chair opposite her.

A table sat between us with a glass of what was no doubt my favourite whiskey already waiting for me next to Portia's glass of wine and I picked it up, sipping the fine nectar. The woody undertones rolled along my tongue as the crowd simmered down and took their seats once more and I placed the glass back on the table.

Behind us was a huge screen which filled the entire back wall of the stage; a black and white photograph was on it, the picture of me standing regally on the eastern balcony of The Palace of Souls, gazing off into the distance while I rested one elbow on the railing and my chin upon my fist. It was finery at its best. And beside it were the words, *An evening with King Lionel Acrux. The man behind the crown.*

Ah, the struggles of my life had finally paid off at last. I'd fought for this moment with everything I had. As a boy, I had acted out this interview in my room countless times, and now it was coming to fruition, all my efforts paying off. I was being celebrated as I ought to have been celebrated for so many years. They saw me now, they saw my power and they cowered beneath it. And I was sure this would be a night I'd never forget.

Portia started out with a few simple questions, warming the crowd up as I offered light-hearted stories from my youth, from the time I went hunting a near extinct species of desert hawk and mounted the last of their kind on my wall, to the time I'd had a hotel built in my name in northern Baruda that overlooked the most beautiful lake in Solaria. Of course, I'd had to grease a few palms to stop the townsfolk from trying to intervene with that project, their complaints of my tower blocking their own view to the water almost throwing a spanner in the works. But I was more than used to getting my way.

"So tell us more about your years at Zodiac Academy," Portia asked, the questions deepening now as we got to the root of my success. "Is it true you were bullied by the Savage King and his friends?"

"Bullied?" I scoffed. "I have never been bullied a day in my life, Portia. No, I think what you are referring to are the rumours that Hail Vega was jealous of me, and acted in response to those feelings during our time together at the academy."

"And are those rumours true?" Portia asked curiously.

I let a sad mask fall over my face and nodded. "Unfortunately, Hail saw the greatness in me. It was a great shame as I only ever wished to be allies, but alas, it seemed he couldn't handle gazing upon my power. It is why he targeted me so at school, altering my perfect grades so that I would appear less of a threat to him. He wanted to hold onto his status, but it seemed the stars had other plans in the end."

"Goodness what a scandal," Portia gasped and I felt the crowd hanging on every word.

"Perhaps, but I suppose it isn't too surprising to discover the Savage King was savage in his youth too," I said, quietly loving that I was tarnishing Hail's name even more than I had managed while he lived. "He was the Captain of the Pitball team too and refused to let me play despite my proficiencies in the game."

"You were proficient in Pitball?" Portia asked curiously and suddenly the crowd started laughing and I jerked around to look at them in surprise, noticing their gaze was on something over my head. I turned, finding a video of me at Zodiac Academy the day I had tried out for the Pitball team.

Hail was throwing pitballs my way lazily while I failed to catch every single one of them, falling in the mud more than once as rage built on my face. I was sucked into that memory, anger spewing through my blood now as the laughter grew more raucous in my head. The sound started playing on the video as Hail ran out of pitballs and I bristled at his voice.

"I thought you said you were good at this," Hail laughed and my right eye twitched with the memory of those very words.

"I am good. I'm the best," the young version of me insisted in a growl.

"Maybe you're better at defence then. Try and stop me tackling you," he commanded, immediately charging me down. I cast air magic left and right, but he avoided every shot and collided with me like a battering ram, my back slamming to the ground beneath his weight and a scream left me that sounded entirely feminine, causing the laughter in the theatre to amplify.

The video ended and a line of smoke left my nostrils as I snapped around to glare at Portia. Who the fuck had gotten hold of that video? And how dare she think it appropriate to play it during this interview!

I contained myself, keeping my head and not letting anyone see my inner distress.

"Are you sure you were proficient, My King?" Portia asked, a teasing lilt to her voice and I allowed a light laugh to fall from my lips as my hands tightened on the arms of my chair.

"I had come down with the Fae flu that very day," I worked to play it off as the crowd settled down. "I assure you I destroyed him on that pitch not a week later when I had recovered, but Hail swept my second try-out under the rug, not wanting to be put to shame by my talent."

"I see," Portia said lightly. "Well, let's move on to another important relationship in your life. Your brother Radcliff Acrux tragically died when he was just twenty, but he must have held a big influence on you before then?" she asked and the screen thankfully changed, but my gut clenched like a hard ball as it filled with a photograph of Hail, Azriel, Tiberius, Antonia, Melinda and Radcliff all arm in arm as they smiled widely in their muddy Zodiac Pitball uniforms together.

"Indeed," I said, nodding sadly as I turned my head away from that image of my brother smiling with his friends, taking satisfaction in the fact that he and two of the other Fae in that image were now dead in the ground. "Radcliff was a good brother, but he hid his weaknesses well. This is the first time I am speaking about this but...when I was just about to be Awakened, Radcliff confided in me saying that he felt he had to bluff his way into being an Heir, that he had convinced Father he was the strongest in the family, when really it was I he saw the power in. Upon my Awakening, he came to me once more and asked me if I would play down my power for a few years so that he might enjoy being Heir a while longer - for it was all he ever wished to be, though he knew in his heart I could take it from him at a moment's notice, and that in time, I would. I, loving my brother dearly, promised to keep the truth of my immense power secret until it was time for me to ascend and beat him in a fight to take his place. But of course, the most unfortunate of events later occurred, stealing him away before his time, and leaving me with no choice but to take up the baton without ever fighting him for his position." I looked directly into the camera, pretending to wipe a tear from under my eye. "I know tonight you will be watching me from beyond the Veil, Radcliff, and I want you to know, I will rule well, and I will bring endless glory to the Acrux name for us both."

Applause rang through the room and Portia smiled sadly.

"Yes, indeed, it was a most terrible tragedy, but one that has not gone by without scrutiny," Portia said, sending a prickle up my spine.

"Scrutiny? What scrutiny?" I played dumb. I'd seen the bullshit printed in The Daily Solaria, the conspiracies that pointed at a covered up murder. But no evidence had ever been found, and I certainly didn't want to discuss such things live on fucking television.

Portia pointed to the screen again and I was suddenly faced with the swollen features of my brother Radcliff after his death, the gruesome image causing the crowd to gasp and mutter.

"The sting marks were solely located in this one spot," Portia said, a ring appearing around the blistered red sting marks on Radcliff's chest. "And some biologists claim the norian wasp stings erratically, that it wouldn't sting in a localised place repeatedly unless it was held in place by magic, or perhaps a jar-"

"Preposterous," I blurted, waving a hand at her as heat flared within my limbs. What the fuck was this? Was she accusing me of something? This was meant to be my night of celebration, how dare she bring my brother's death into it?

She moved swiftly on, detailing my strengths at school and the awards I won in the art of illusion and Coercion, and I relaxed as I drank in the praise, enjoying sifting through the memories of my ascension to greatness, letting go of the anger I'd felt over the Radcliff questions. I supposed Portia had a duty to get a reaction on such a critical moment in my life; I was likely being sensitive due to the secret nature of his death.

"Upon your graduation, you had officially taken the place of your brother as an Heir to the Celestial Council and Hail Vega was set to ascend to the throne and take over from his father. It seemed your bond with Tiberius Rigel, Antonia Capella and Melinda Altair had solidified, and your public appearances alongside Prince Hail were widely publicised." A stream of newspaper articles ran across the screen with shots of us all standing as one, showing our unity to the little crowned prince who was set to seize the throne. But even back then I had had plans of grandeur far greater than the boundaries set for me. Why should Hail take all the glory? Why settle for second best when I could have first place?

"A bond we share to this day." I lifted my drink in toast to the Councillors up on their balcony and they smiled tightly, raising their drinks in return to me as the audience clapped and cooed.

"And yet," Portia interjected, making my eyes snap back to her. "When we delve deeper, it appears that bond wasn't always in place."

"How do you mean?" I laughed lightly, taking a long swig of my drink as I set this woman in my deadly gaze.

"Well, let us take a look at this exclusive undercover footage from the graduates party at Zodiac Academy," Portia announced and a new video started playing that made my blood freeze within my veins. Because that night still left a shudder in my soul, it still drove its way into my nightmares, it was one of the things I'd held firmly in my mind when I'd watched Hail and his wife die.

I sat in a cordoned off booth in The Orb while some lout must have recorded me in secret on their Atlas. I had a girl on my lap who I planned on taking back to my room, and I wish I had sooner as I spotted Tiberius jogging up to me excitedly.

"Hey, they want you to get measured outside in your Dragon form in front of everyone. The cheerleading squad wanna know if you're bigger than Radcliff now," he said keenly and I pushed the girl from my lap, jumping up in excitement.

"Well of course they do," I said, pressing down my shirt and following Tiberius through the crowd as the sly Fae who was recording followed. They turned the camera back on themselves as they went and Hail gave a thumbs up to the camera, making the crowd chuckle.

I shifted in my seat, shaking my head at Portia and covering my microphone as I leaned towards her. "This is unsuitable. Have it turned off immediately," I commanded.

"It will endear them to you," Portia said, not bothering to cover her mic and I swallowed a curse, heat blazing along my veins as the Dragon within me begged me to deal with this.

"Stop this instant," I hissed, but the video was getting to the worst part already.

I was outside, up on a platform of earth magic Melinda had cast as most of the academy gathered around to watch. I stripped out of my clothes, my body on full display along with the giant cock that hung between my thighs, enhanced just a little with an illusion – there was no harm in that, every hot blooded male was guilty of it.

"Portia," I snarled, smoke spilling from my nostrils as the crowd cooed at my giant appendage, and I would be more than glad for the video to end there, but it did not.

The younger me was about to shift when vines shot out of the crowd from Hail's hands, pinning me down and magic washed over me as he stripped the illusion from my penis, showing its true size while casting a magnifying spell before my cock so it could be seen by everyone in the crowd and Tiberius lit it up with Faelights. Hail burst out laughing along with the crowd and the young version of me screamed as I thrashed against the vines and managed to burn them away to dust, grabbing my boxers and pulling them on.

"Definitely not as big as Radcliff," Hail called, those words echoing on in my mind eternally.

I felt the shame of that day washing over me, the sheer embarrassment as Hail roared a laugh and ran forward to clap me on the shoulder like it was all some game.

"Oh don't be lame, Lionel," he sighed as he took in my rage and those words sent a ripple of blazing heat up my back.

"Lame Lionel!" Tiberius laughed as he leapt up beside the young version of me. "Isn't that what Rad used to call you?"

The students all took up the chant, calling it out over and over and I snapped, throwing my palms into Hail's chest and making him stagger back as I left burning marks in his shirt.

"It was just a joke between friends," Hail said, healing the burns like they didn't bother him at all. "You burned off all my hair last week. This is payback."

The young version of me seethed, staring at this motherfucker who dared toy with me, and I recalled deciding in that moment that if he thought we were friends, then I would be the best friend he had ever had. I would get closer and closer to him until I could drive a knife into his back and watch him scream for me.

Laughter echoed through the theatre and I snapped out of the horrified reverie I was in, dragged into reality where my nightmare was coming to life again before my eyes. The crowd were laughing, crying out Lame Lionel over and over again and Portia clapped along like it was a fun little fucking ditty.

"ENOUGH!" I roared a Dragon's roar, my voice resounding through the entire theatre until everyone in the room fell deathly quiet and stared at me in shock.

I realised I was on my feet and I rounded on Portia as she stared at me with a little fear in her eyes. But no, this wasn't right. I was live on TV. I was not a monster in the public eye. I was a composed, highly regarded Dragon who commanded the respect of everyone in the kingdom.

I laughed a little tightly, the sound forced as I tried to keep myself together. "Perhaps we can move on?" I suggested, sinking back down into my seat, trying to work out my best angle here. "Those times are somewhat sensitive. Forgive my outburst. I grieve Hail daily so I can get a little emotional recounting our friendship."

"Of course," Portia said, bowing her head. "Apologies, your highness. We only wanted to show things weren't always rosy between you and the other Councillors, and perhaps this shows a hint of the Savage King's savagery too."

I felt she was trying to cool my temper, feeding me what I wanted to hear, but it worked regardless, helping me find my composure as I played it off, pushing a hand into my hair and smiling roguishly.

"Ah, yes. He could be savage indeed. This was nothing, I saw many cruelties dealt by his hand. And of course, to place a shrinking potion on my penis in front of everyone was in fact one of his more light-hearted jests." That ought to squash any rumours of my cock's size. It wasn't small anyway, I was just a very large man so it seemed that way at first glance.

Portia encouraged me to start recounting more stories and I made up lie after lie on the spot of Hail bullying students at Zodiac Academy, sometimes offering my own truths and attaching his name to it instead, and soon I was feeling much better again as more videos were played of me taking charge of the Dragon Guild, of attending parties with famous Fae and of my marriage to the most beautiful woman in the land, Catalina Nightbell. Of course, the wedding footage held a bitter taste to it now as I thought of her fucking that rebel, Grus. But I would soon return her to our marital bed and remind her of exactly who she belonged to. It was only a matter of time.

"As thanks for all you have done for the Dragons of the Guild, they have put together a very special surprise for you tonight," Portia announced excitedly and I perked up at that.

"Oh?" I inquired. I wondered if they would gift me some grand treasures, a golden statue of me perhaps?

"If you'll turn your attention to the screen, you'll find a message from one of your Guild members," Portia instructed and I sat back in my seat, smiling as I waited to see what one of my Dragons had to say about me. Perhaps he would speak of the gleam of my scales, or the strength of my roar. Or maybe it was the power of my Dragon fire he would focus on.

Dante Oscura's face appeared on the screen and I stiffened in my seat, my hands tightening to fists as I stared at the rebel who had deserted me.

"Portia," I spat, but Dante's voice echoed through the room, drowning me out and making sure his words were heard by all.

"Buona serata Solaria, I want to send my regards to the false king. A long time ago he bound me to his Guild and made me his little cagna. I've always made sure to have dirt on my enemies, and now that I've turned my back on him and he no longer holds sway over me, it's time to air Lionel Asscrux's dirty laundry. Long live the true queens." A video started playing of me fucking a woman, bending her over as I grunted and pushed her down on a bed, and fear snaked up my spine and left me helpless as I stared in horrified realisation of what this video was. It was a fucking set up. Years ago, that motherfucking Dragon had tried to fight back against me, and this was what he'd come up with to try and buy back his freedom. For so long, I had had enough sway with him to keep this under wraps, but he no longer had reason not to release this video he had recorded of me. And now I could do nothing to stop it.

I rose from my seat, waving my arms as I stood in front of the screen to try and end this madness.

"Enough! Draw the curtains – the interview is over!" I yelled, but no one listened, even my FIB agents were slow to act as they moved down the aisles, glancing between one another.

"End this show – stop this immediately." I swung towards Portia, pointing a finger at her, wishing I could use my magic to incinerate her here on this spot, but the anti-magic spells in place prevented me from doing so. "ARREST HER!" I shouted and the agents started moving a little faster, but not nearly fast enough for my liking. They were the only ones in here capable of moving against her right now, with their weapons strapped to their hips, they could take her down in an instant.

A horsey neigh filled the air and the crowd gasped in reaction to the video and I turned, not wanting to look but for some reason I did as I found that moment replaying before my eyes once more. The girl shifted just as I came inside her and slapped her ass, turning into a star damned fucking glittery Pegasus. The entire world was watching this, seeing me fuck her in her horse's ass and groan my release throatily before I realised what had happened, as if I had wanted to fuck her in her Order form like it was some fetish I held.

I started screaming and thrashing in the video, trying to get away from her before the whole thing started playing again. It had been a complete set up, and now I was set up again by that asshole of a Dragon who I should have had put in the ground the first day I'd met him.

I rounded on Portia as she got up, my hand locking around her shoulders as she backed away, a look of flight in her eyes.

"You'll pay for this," I hissed as the crowd laughed louder and suddenly a chant sounded from the balcony above me led by Hadley Altair, Athena Capella and her brother Greyson beside her. "Lame Lionel, Lame Lionel, Lame Lionel!"

The crowd picked it up and I lost my grip on Portia as she darted away.

"STOP!" I commanded in a roar, rage pounding through my chest as those words echoed everywhere around me. "I am your king! You will respect your king!"

Portia was almost off the stage and I pointed at Francesca Sky who was nearest to her.

"Get hold of her!" I ordered, but Francesca was slow to react, focusing her attention on holding the crowd back instead, making me spit a curse as Portia made it to the edge of the stage.

A swarm of FIB agents appeared beyond her, corralling her back towards me and I clenched my teeth and bared them at her, excited by the coming pain I was going to inflict on this turncoat woman when I got her in a holding cell somewhere out of sight. Somewhere she would never, ever return from.

A roaring, crashing noise filled the air as a dagger of lightning exploded through the wall to my right, followed by the almighty bellow of thunder and the Storm Dragon himself appeared, forcing his giant, navy body through the hole in the side of the building.

The FIB aimed guns at him on my command and a blast of electricity tore from their tasers, slamming into his chest, only making him roar a laugh as his storm powers absorbed every bit of it without damage.

I pulled at my own clothes as he swooped down, preparing to shift and rip this piece of shit apart myself as the crowd ran for cover. But before I could, I was knocked back by several agents as they shoved me towards the edge of the stage.

"You need to get out of here, sire!" one of them cried as I struggled against their grip.

"The rebels are here," another said anxiously.

Dante leapt down, dropping his wing and Portia dove onto it, clinging on tight as she scrambled up onto his back like he was some common pack mule and I spat a snarl as the agents continued to wrestle me out the way of danger. But I would face it head on. I would destroy that blasted Dragon and kill every member of his family in a bloody massacre he would never forget just as soon as I found them.

Dante turned and leapt back out of the hole, disappearing into the raging storm beyond just like that and I was left roaring my anguish to the stars, vowing on every last one of them that I would have my revenge for this. And it would be a merciless, gory thing.

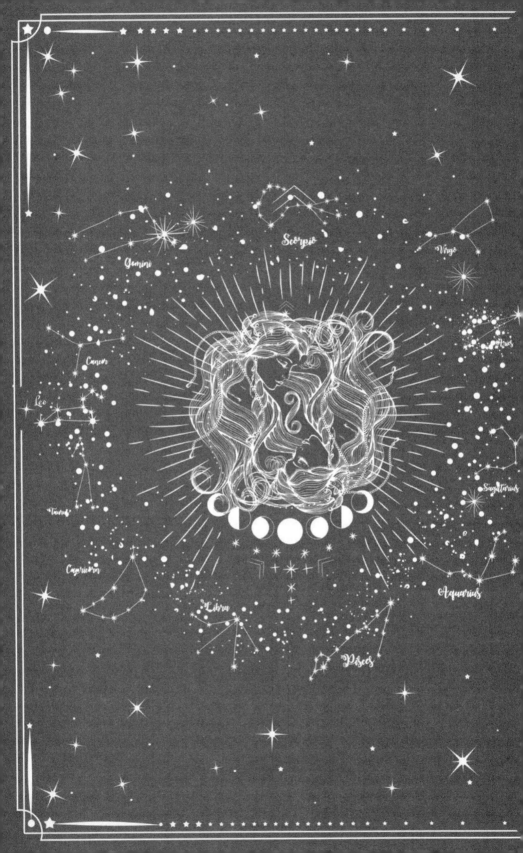

DARCY

CHAPTER FORTY SIX

I headed to dinner, unsure where Orion had gotten to and taking my Atlas out to shoot him a message. No response came and I pouted, but my mood brightened as I checked FaeBook and scrolled through post after post about Lionel's humiliation at his interview, #lamelionel trending like crazy.

Gabriel hadn't told us a single word about it, but he'd been heavily involved in the plans to sabotage the whole thing and had encouraged us to watch the interview before disappearing off with Dante last night. We'd laughed our asses off the entire time, and when they'd all shown up back here with Portia Silverstone in tow, the whole of The Burrows had erupted in cheers. I was never going to forget the way Lionel had squirmed on that stage, and it had made me proud as hell to see my dad tearing him down to size at school – like, *literally* down to size.

I pushed my Atlas back into my pocket and turned down a passage that was a secret shortcut to the dining hall which me and Tory had created to make it simpler to get there and back from the royal quarters. The darkness was thick down here and I cast a Faelight above my head, the amber orb bobbing along above my head, pressing the shadows away in a ring around me, but beyond them I could see nothing at all.

Something moved up ahead and I squinted towards it, wondering if some of my friends were here, but when I called out, no one replied.

I guided magic to my fingertips, thinking of the brutal murders that had been happening down in these tunnels, my pulse rising as I prepared to blast an attacker into the afterlife. I wasn't afraid to keep walking. I'd been trained by a queen of old. I knew the depths of my power now, and I could take on some cowardly Fae who slunk through the dark and cut down my allies.

"Come out," I commanded in a growl.

A whoosh of air made my hair swirl around me and I sucked in a breath, turning sharply, certain something had passed me. And it had felt awfully like-

"You shouldn't be wandering around in the dark alone, Blue. What if there was a monster lurking down here?" Orion growled and a relieved laugh left me as he came up behind me, closing his arm around my waist in a snare, his fangs grazing down my neck.

"Then I'd kill it," I said, a shiver darting along my flesh as I let my head fall to the side in an offering.

"And what if the monster is me?" he asked, his breath on my neck making me heady as he toyed with biting me.

"You're not a monster, Lance," I teased and a rumble of a growl in his chest made goosebumps rise across my skin.

"No? But you're a princess, so maybe I'm the cruel beast who wants to keep you locked up in a tower."

"You wouldn't be able to keep me locked up," I countered.

"True..." he conceded.

"So what's your next move?"

"I suppose I'll be your vicious attack dog and destroy anyone who touches you," he said, a grin in his voice.

"You could get arrested for that," I said lightly, fighting another shiver as he dragged his fangs up to the sensitive skin behind my ear.

"That would be quite awful."

"Yeah, I can imagine," I said dryly and he laughed deep in his throat.

As he went to bite me, I twisted fast in a move Queen Avalon had taught me, wrenching myself out of his hold and turning to face him, my Faelight following me as I backed up with a challenging smile on my face.

"Come bite me in the dining hall," I offered and the playful look in his eyes melted away.

"You know I can't do that."

"Well maybe it's the only place I'll let you do it in future then," I said, anger igniting in me. I was so sick of him acting like we weren't a couple in front of the rebels, always shifting away from me whenever I tried to take his hand or lean in to kiss him.

"Blue," he growled.

"Lance," I growled back and he sighed, stepping closer to me as I stepped away.

"You know why it has to be this way."

"Fuck what everyone thinks," I huffed, my thoughts spilling out in a torrent. I was tired of abiding to the rules he set, letting him dictate how this relationship was going to be. "I'm giving you everything I am, but you only give me part of you in the name of protecting me. Are you really planning to walk away from me if I one day gain the throne?"

He paused, his silence speaking volumes and making rage spew like lava through my veins. "I will always be here for you."

"It sounds awfully like there's a 'but' hiding in there."

"Darcy, it's what's best."

"For who?" I snarled. "Because the best thing for me would be to stop living under a veil of secrets. I want to claim you as mine in front of everyone in Solaria, but you won't let me."

"Because it would destroy you," he snapped.

"Let me be destroyed then," I growled. "I would rather be judged for living a life of my choosing than have to lie about you, to have to watch you pull away from me every time some random Fae looks at us. I don't care what they think."

He shook his head. "I won't be responsible for your downfall."

"You're not responsible for shit, Lance. You just won't let me make the choice I want to make. It's my downfall, so let me have it if I want it."

"You don't know what you're saying," he hissed, stalking towards me as I continued to back up. "Solaria needs you more than I need to claim you in public."

"Or maybe you just don't want me in public," I spat, knowing it was just coming out of anger, but I said it anyway.

"Oh don't be a child," he said dismissively.

"No, maybe there's something to it, Lance. I've always been your dirty little secret. Maybe you like the thrill of sneaking around. Maybe that's the appeal for you."

He shot toward me in a blur, shoving me up against the wall and baring his fangs in my face. "Don't belittle what I feel for you. I would tear down mountains for you. The stars look my way in contempt, resenting me for getting to love you while they're way up there never feeling anything real, never touching anything as beautiful as you. I am the object of their envy because they can't have you while you're down on Earth in the cage of my arms, but if they're waiting to claim you in death, they will find me right beside you, guarding you even then. Because no one will take you from me, and no one will love you as fiercely as I love you. Where you go, I will follow. There is no force powerful enough in this life or the next to tear you away from me. So don't you dare question my love for you."

Tears were pooling in my eyes and I shoved at his shoulders, needing air to breathe, but he wouldn't let me go.

"Then why can't you love me in front of the world?" I whispered, my voice cracking on those words. "You say you love me more than anything, but you keep our love hidden like it's something shameful. Do you know how much it hurts me that you expect me to accept that the man I love won't touch me in front of anyone but our inner circle? It kills me."

His face twisted in pain at my words, his eyes a sea of agony and confliction as he stared at me.

"Let me choose my fate. If I'm to be ruined, then so be it, but let me be happy in my fucking destruction," I demanded.

He leaned in close, his mouth against mine in the softest of kisses which tasted an awful lot like heartbreak.

"I'll see you later, Blue." He stepped back and before I could answer, he'd shot away into the darkness in the direction I'd come from, leaving me with tears falling down my cheeks and my heart cleaving apart.

I wiped away my tears, standing up straight, not really feeling hungry at all anymore, but still heading in the direction of the dining hall all the same, wanting to see Tory, my friends. I made sure I had myself together as I arrived in the large cavern and spotted everyone sat in front of a large buffet laid out on our table by Geraldine as usual.

I headed over to them, slapping on a fake smile as I took a seat beside Tory, but the moment she looked at me, she gave me a twin look that said she knew something was up. I shook my head marginally and she squeezed my hand under the table, a promise in her eyes to talk to me later if I wanted to. She knew me so well, but honestly I didn't see the point in talking about this. Orion had made up his mind. He was never going to stand at my side and say he was mine to the world, because he believed doing so would be the end of my bid for the throne. But what right did he have to decide that for me?

I picked my way through my veggie burger, trying to laugh and smile along with my friends as they shared jokes about Lionel's interview and discussed our next move against him, but my heart was heavy and I wasn't really engaged at all.

Seth came to sit at my side, whimpering softly while Max looked over at me with an expression that said I wasn't doing well at keeping my emotions hidden. I didn't know why I'd even bothered to try and hide it at all. They all knew me too well.

Caleb was sat at the far end of the table from me and Seth, and I looked to my Wolf friend beside me with a sad smile, knowing he was hurting inside. He'd told me everything that had happened between them and I wished I could help, but honestly it sounded like they needed to talk it out and Seth wasn't willing to do that. So instead, the two of them barely spoke, or when they did they acted overly civil, pretending nothing was wrong at all, but quickly heading in different directions the moment they could escape each other's company. It was painful to witness.

Geraldine took out the spyglass with the shadow eye in it, slamming it down on Darius's plate.

"Oh for the love of fuck, Geraldine. Why?" Darius complained, the burger on his plate completely ruined as the eye swivelled back and forth inside the spyglass on top of it like a grotesque slimy animal.

"Because I am making a statement, you buffoon of a Dragoon." She rolled her eyes like Darius was the one being unreasonable and Tory cracked up, earning her a narrowed eyed look from her boyfriend.

"We must push on to find a map of espial," Geraldine said.

"And do we need the fucking shadow eye on my plate to discuss that?" Darius growled.

"Of course we do, you lout of a lizard," she said firmly. "Has our Power Shamed ally heard from his contact at the FIB yet? Can she procure us a map?"

"No," Darius said. "Francesca hasn't responded to his message."

"Fucking Fran," I muttered and Tory glanced at me with a nod of solidarity.

"Fuck her up the butt with a coconut," Tory added.

"And a pineapple," Seth added. "And a bushel of prickly pears."

"And a rotten carrot," Tyler called across the table and I looked over at him, his hand on Xavier's on the table while Sofia sat on Xavier's other side, nuzzling him with a look of contentment on her face.

I was super freaking happy for them but also like, fuck my life. Because it was just another perfect relationship on display for everyone to see. Xavier was showing off his Subs at every chance he got, and they were doing the same to him in return. My fingers tightened around my fork as I gritted my teeth so hard it hurt, and Max raised his eyebrows at me.

"You okay there, little Vega?" he asked. "You're giving off murderous death vibes, it's kinda ruining my appetite."

"Sorry," I murmured, trying to focus enough to put up a barrier and keep my emotions from leaking out towards him. My Phoenix could stop him invading my feelings, but I still had to have magical barriers in place if I didn't want him to get a taste of my emotions.

I sighed, stabbing my burger moodily, giving up any pretence that I was enjoying myself and Seth nuzzled into my head.

"You okay, babe?" he asked and I shrugged.

"Oh my stars," Seth whispered, tugging on my sleeve but I ignored him, attacking my burger more viciously.

"Oh shit," Tory gasped.

"Is he drunk?" Cal laughed.

"He's walking straight, I think he's sober," Darius chuckled and Seth continued to tug on my sleeve, but I jerked my arm to stop him.

"My lady!" Geraldine gasped, half mounting the table as she waved her hand to get my attention. "Your one true love and shameful Vampire is here making quite the hullabaloo!"

My head snapped up as I frowned, spotting Orion striding through the cavern shirtless with 'I love Darcy Vega' written on his bare chest in what looked like lipstick. He jumped up onto a table and the rebels all gasped, trying to ignore him as he kicked their dinner plates and sent their cutlery and food flying everywhere.

"Burnt strudels on the eve of my Great Aunt Tulip's grave!" Hamish wailed from across the room, jumping to his feet and Catalina tried to pull him back down into his seat.

"I can't sing, or dance, or write poetry so I'm just gonna shout this really, really fucking loud," Orion announced, looking right at me with a smirk on his lips. He raised a hand to his throat, casting an amplifying spell before tipping his head back and hollering so loud that the roof of the cavern rattled. "I am in love with Darcy Vega, heir to the throne of Solaria, daughter of the Savage King – who by the way was tricked by Lionel Acrux into being an evil sonuvabitch. And I know you all think I'm a complete waste of oxygen." He kicked a bread roll into Justin Masters' face and it bounced off his forehead as he tried not to react. "That my shame is infectious and you don't want it anywhere near you, let alone your precious princess." He leapt from one table to another, making his way towards us and I got up, a smile nearly splitting my cheeks open. "But it turns out she wants me anyway. And I'm done making decisions for a girl who has always made better ones than I do. So if this is what she wants, then she can have it. Because she owns me right down to my black heart." He leapt forward again, a round of cursing and outrage sounding as he landed on my table, looking down at me and holding out his hand with a piece of paper folded inside it.

I took it with a curious frown, unfolding it and realising what it was as my heart hammered out a wild and desperate tune. On the surface was my final I.O.U. from the ones I'd gifted Orion for his birthday last year.

I.O.U.
One kiss anywhere you like.

527

"This cannot be!" someone cried in anguish.

"Crabcakes through my mail slot, please stop this madness," Hamish begged as he lumbered his way towards our table.

"Papa!" Geraldine flew out of her seat to halt him. "They are in love. And Mama always said love is like a peppercorn buried in a salt pot."

"But sweet Gerrykins," he rasped, bringing his handkerchief to his mouth. "I cannot stand to look at it."

"Then don't look," I growled, taking Orion's hand and letting him pull me up to stand in front of him.

He gripped my waist and yanked me flush to his body, his warmth surrounding me and the scent of cinnamon hanging in the air.

"You owe me a kiss," he purred, a devilish gleam in his gaze.

"Where do you want it?" I asked, high on this moment as raindrops pattered in my gut.

He tapped his lips, his smirk still hitched in place and I swear I was never going to get enough of this man.

"Are you sure about this?" I whispered as the crowd muttered and cursed him.

"No," he admitted seriously. "I'm so terrified of what this will mean for you, Blue, but I'm so much more terrified of hurting you. So if you want this, then it's yours. Besides, now the decision is made, I get to do what I've wanted to do since I first laid eyes on you."

"And what's that?" I asked, my hands sliding over his broad shoulders and looping around his neck as I zoned out the cries of disgust around me, focusing on him and nothing else. He was all that mattered anyway.

"Kiss you in front of the world, and show them that you're *mine*." He leaned down and I offered him my mouth and everything else I was made of right down to the dust that made up my bones. Our lips collided and I swear I could feel the stars watching, their whispers hanging just on the borders of my hearing like they were conspiring, and I prayed they were done working against us, because we'd suffered enough, and it was our time to be happy.

His tongue met mine in firm strokes and my sister whooped loudly, pounding her fist on the table, the Heirs taking up the cry and all my friends were suddenly working together to drown out the rebels.

I swear I had never felt so much joy in all my life as I did then, and I hoped it was never going to end.

"Crustaceans on a cracker," Geraldine gasped. "And then where did the second Long Sherman go?"

Sofia giggled, releasing a horsey snort as she pointed at her ass and we all fell about laughing.

We were having a girls night in Geraldine's room, using Angelica's surprisingly extensive collection of nail varnishes and beauty products to pamper ourselves. Geraldine had just finished freshly dyeing my hair blue and it glittered around my shoulders as I dried it with air magic, the loose waves falling gently down my back.

"Perhaps I shall dye my hair a more flamboyant colour," Geraldine said thoughtfully as she sat opposite me and Tory on the bed.

"You'd suit scarlet," Angelica suggested.

"Nonsense! And have my hair look like a boiled lobster to attract more hungry hammerfish to my shores? You're being nonsensical, Angelica," Geraldine said, shaking her head fiercely.

"How are things with you and Max?" Tory asked.

"Oh my lady," Geraldine sighed. "I am of a dither! Maxy boy has declared himself ready and willing to service my lady garden at my beck and call. And oh, how I wish to grant him the keys to its wild meadows and wandering daffodils forevermore, but alas…I fear I must marry Justin Masters instead."

"Ew," Tory breathed. "He's so *nice* though. He literally held a door for me while I was a hundred yards away from it. I had to walk so. Fucking. Far. To get there. And he still waited." She shuddered.

"That's not exactly a bad thing, Tor," I snorted. "And Darius holds doors for you all the time."

"Well yeah, but he does it obnoxiously. So it's not the same at all," she said, tossing her hair and I laughed.

"I see what you mean, Justin has no edge. He's…" I tried to find the word.

"Dull?" Geraldine offered. "Boring beyond what should be possible within the realms of our kind?"

"Err, yeah," I admitted and Geraldine wailed like a half strangled goat.

"Can't you just break the wedding off?" Sofia suggested. "I'm sure your dad won't care."

"Papa has given me his blessing to end the engagement. But I am a lady of my word, and what am I without my word, Sofia?" Geraldine gasped, clutching a hand to her chest in horror.

"What if we break it off for you?" I suggested. "Like a princess declaration thingy?"

"You would do that for me?" Geraldine breathed in awe. "You would stand between me and a loveless marriage to a hapless worm and decree it as disbanded? You would banish the worm to a faraway land so that I may never have to fret over the loss living in his beady snail eyes?"

"Err, the banishing part seems a bit overkill, but we can do the decree thing," I said with a shrug.

"Holy shit, have we had the power to decree stuff this whole time?" Tory gasped. "I wanna decree that no fucking decaf coffee is allowed to be served next to the caffeinated goodness."

"And so it is decreed." Geraldine slapped her knee even though I was pretty certain that Darius got all of Tory's coffees these days anyway.

"Can I decree that everyone stops pointing in horror at me and Orion whenever we touch?" I grumbled.

Geraldine reached out, patting my knee with sympathy in her eyes. "No, my sweet and gentle Darcy. You can only decree things that are possible within the realms of reasonability."

I growled, messing up the pink paint I was coating onto my nails and using water magic to correct it. "Dammit."

"Can I ask you guys a question?" Angelica squeaked and we all looked to her, smoke pluming from her nostrils for a second as she turned bright red. "As you know, I'm having relations with a dashing Minotaur, and everything's been great sexually, but last night he asked to do something that I'd never heard of before and I said I'd think about it, but I'm not sure…and maybe one of you have tried it."

"Is it the flipping dipstickle?" Geraldine asked and Angelica shook her head. "The backwards fornicator? The sprouting duck tail?"

"Um, no," Angelica said. "He said he wants me to shift into my Order form, so he can climb up my tail and ride me like a cowboy."

My jaw went slack as everyone stared at her in shocked silence.

"So…one of you guys must have had Order form sex, right?" she asked hopefully, looking from Sofia to Geraldine.

"Hang on, he wants to fuck you while you're a massive Dragon?" Tory blurted.

"Like, in his Minotaur form or Fae form?" I asked in horror, unsure why it mattered or which answer would be worse.

"Um, the second one," she whispered, her cheeks getting pink. "So none of you have ever…"

"Let someone service my petunia while I am a giant three headed dog?" Geraldine cried. "Certainly not, Angelica."

"Well, I've had my wings out during, but I don't have a dog vagina… so it's not really the same," I added.

"Oh," Angelica breathed.

"I let Tyler stick a few sugar lumps up my butt once, but I wasn't in my Pegasus form," Sofia offered and we all fell apart laughing.

We continued pampering ourselves through the evening and I headed to bed at midnight, smelling like vanilla and looking forward to waking Orion. I'd put on a silk blue teddy which was nearly transparent, and I closed my white dressing gown around it as I jogged down the cool corridor to my room. I'd bribed one of the rebels to get me some more fancy underwear on their last supply run too to replace the ones Orion had destroyed, but he'd already massacred a few of them. It would have been kind of annoying if it wasn't so hot.

I stripped out of the gown as I made it to our door, tossing it onto the floor and taking a moment to draw my hair forward over my shoulders and fluff it up a little before stepping into the room. The bedside light was on but I frowned as I found the space empty.

I grabbed my Atlas from the nightstand, typing out a message to Orion but I got distracted as a drumming started up inside my head and I was bathed in the absolute feeling of needing to go somewhere. I just wasn't sure where that somewhere was…

I threw my Atlas on the bed and turned towards the door, hurrying out of it as the urgency intensified and I walked down the icy tunnels on bare feet, too distracted to will fire into my veins to warm me.

I blinked and I was outside, my feet sinking into the mud left behind after last night's storm and guards shouting to me beyond the rising drums in my head. I'd somehow lost track of the time it had taken for me to walk out here and though I knew deep down that something about this could be dangerous, I still couldn't tear myself from the path of fate which was guiding me forward.

"Princess!" one of the guards cried, trying to run forward and grab me as I headed to the barrier, but I flicked a finger, knocking her back with a gust of air.

I headed through the boundary and let my wings burst from my back as I stared up at the impossibly clear sky, the stars seeming to shine brighter than I'd ever seen as I took off towards them. They were whispering, plotting, speaking my name and beckoning me onward as I flew far and fast, pushing myself hard as I sailed over the dark and sleeping land below.

I lost track of time once more as I found myself flying above a city, the lights twinkling and glittering in the windows.

I circled down, the pull in my chest intensifying until I spotted a grassy hill rising up behind a tall building at the edge of the city with trees dotted across it. I wasn't afraid as I landed, my feet pressing down on the golden leaves and crunching under my weight. The wind picked up and carried the fallen leaves around me in a circle, marking out a ring that seemed to hum with expectant energy.

My wings flexed against my back as my gaze rose to the stars and I felt their unimaginable power weighing down on me, making my heart beat to a beautiful, hungry pace.

Destiny was calling to me and I knew I stood right where it wanted me to be. I could feel fate wrapping around me, binding me to this moment. And for once, I was sure this wasn't some curse or cruel twist of fortune. This was a gift from the stars, and they were about to ask something of me which I had to answer. And as I watched the sky, it started to shift, the heavens rearranging until the Gemini constellation sat right next to the Libra constellation, glittering so brightly it was hard to keep staring.

My breathing became shallow as it pooled out before me in a fog, because I suddenly knew what was happening. I'd been taught about it in class, Tory had described it to me, I'd even dared to wonder if Orion and I might be Elysian Mates too on occasion, but to actually find myself offered this bond with the man who owned my heart still left me speechless.

"Hello, Blue."

I dropped my head, finding Orion there before me, his breaths coming heavily as if he'd run all the way here and I supposed he had. He stepped into the circle of peace carved out for us and suddenly the world beyond the ring of leaves blurred and we were captured in a dome of starlight, standing before one another with no one but the stars to watch. The air was perfectly still within the bubble of calm, and everything was so quiet it was like the world had been wrapped in cotton wool.

I stepped forward, our hands clasping and his eyes igniting as his gaze fell down me. "You must be freezing."

"I can't feel anything but this moment," I whispered, staring up at my soulmate. The Fae chosen for me, perfectly designed to match me in every way. And as I looked up at the stars, I had to wonder if they were truly spiteful, or if they just had a twisted way of leading us to our destinies. "They made us for each other."

He nodded, a smile spreading across his face as he drew me closer and I could hardly breathe with how much I needed him in that moment. The stars were whispering our names, driving us together, offering us a life united, bound and promised to one another in every way. And though I didn't need the stars' acknowledgement of our love to be happy, now we were here I couldn't deny the rush I felt at the idea of having him marked as mine. Of laying a permanent claim to this man who had brought so much good into my life that it made me feel like rays of sunshine lived within my flesh.

"Tell me this is real," he murmured, tucking a lock of blue hair behind my ear. "Because I fear the stars are playing wicked games with me again."

"It's real," I said through a grin.

"Well then, Blue." He stepped closer to me, swallowing up the space dividing us until my blood was heating and every part of my body hummed with the need to be closer still. "Will you kiss me and be mine in every way imaginable? Will you accept a grumpy asshole of a Vampire as your one true mate?"

I smiled up at him, my toes scrunching in the dead leaves beneath my feet as my wings fluttered a little. "I will. But only if you'll accept a clumsy nerd of a princess as yours."

He leaned down, our lips a hairsbreadth apart, the stars' whispers filling my head and urging us on, begging us to be together. But they didn't have to beg, I'd chosen this man long before this moment, this was just the icing on the cake.

"I'll love you 'til the world is dust," Orion breathed and those words sent a delicious tremor down to the centre of my being.

"I'll love you even beyond then," I answered and our lips collided as we accepted this bond and a ripple of power blazed through my body as the stars threaded our souls together.

Our tongues moved in perfect synchrony, and I moaned as the most powerful urge drove me toward him. Our kiss deepened and I felt it everywhere, sending quivers skipping through my skin. The bond roared and I fell into a frenzy as he groaned, pressing his hand against the base of my spine and pulling me firm against him. But I needed more, so much goddamn more.

My fingers ripped at his clothes as he growled into my mouth and tugged my lower lip between his teeth. His hand clasped my breast and his thumb scored over my hardened nipple through the thin material, drawing another moan from my lips. But as I considered pulling his clothes off and fucking him right here on this hill, the sound of sirens rushed in on me and our lips broke apart.

Flashing red and blue lights made me freeze and my head whipped around as I took in row after row of FIB agents standing around us on the hill with magical guns in hand.

"Lance Orion and Darcy Vega, stay where you are!" a large man cried, his voice amplified by magic. "You are under arrest by decree of the king."

Orion tugged me closer to him and I cursed the fact that we had no stardust as a line of FIB started closing in on us.

"Shit," I growled, letting my wings stretch out as I held onto him and prepared to take flight. But then a dart pierced my neck and Orion snarled furiously, ripping it out of my skin and tossing it aside just as one was shot into his own neck.

I met his gaze in horror as I felt my Phoenix being locked down deep inside my chest as the Order Suppressant kicked in, my wings falling away.

"What do we do?" I gasped as I raised my hands in preparation of a fight, but he pushed them down, shaking his head with a frantic look on his face.

"They'll kill us if we fight," he warned and suddenly the agents were upon us, pulling us apart and snapping magic blocking cuffs onto our wrists.

I was spun around, finding myself in the hands of Orion's ex Francesca Sky, her jaw falling slack as she looked at my eyes.

"You're his Elysian Mate," she rasped in disbelief, then towed me along and I looked back for Orion in fear, relieved to find him being marched along right behind me. For a moment I was captivated by the silver rings circling his dark eyes, glinting at me like starlight.

My skin was still burning and itching with the need to be closer to my Elysian Mate, the bond between us flaring so sharply I almost cared more about getting back into his arms than I did about the fact that we were being arrested and likely walked to our doom.

Francesca guided me into the back of a cop car on a track halfway down the hill and Orion was shoved in after me, the door snapping shut and locking tight.

I immediately lunged at Orion, swinging my leg over his lap and he dragged me against him with a growl of need, his cock hard between my thighs as our mouths fell together and we kissed like the only source of oxygen in the world lay between us.

"Hey!" a man barked as he dropped into the driver's seat, banging the bars between us and the front of the car with a baton. "Enough of that."

Francesca got into the other seat, staring at us as I turned my head but Orion grabbed my face, forcing me back around to look at him and sinking his tongue between my lips again.

"Lance!" Francesca snapped. "This is serious. Do you understand what's happening right now?"

"Perfectly. I'm being arrested while I'm trying to fuck my mate," he growled against my lips, his hands sliding up the back of my little nightgown, grasping my ass and making me moan loudly.

"Stop it!" the guy shouted again, whacking the baton against the bars once more. "You'll be split up if you can't control yourselves."

We ignored him, our animal needs blocking out all else as we fought to get closer to each other, kissing and biting and grinding on each other as the car drove off down the track.

"Did you know you were right outside an FIB precinct?" Francesca called.

"Fucking stars," I cursed as Orion slid his fingers between my thighs and found me bare and soaked for him.

"Mine," he growled, driving two fingers into me and I gasped, riding his hand and panting as I bit down on his lower lip hard enough to draw blood. He tasted his own blood with a groan and pumped his hand harder, the two of us completely lost to each other, unable to even think about the fact that we were in a cop car with two agents right there in the front of it.

"Fuck, I need to be inside you," Orion exhaled and I reached down to his waistband, unbuckling his jeans, planning to grant him that wish but then the car came to a halt, the door was flung open and I was yanked out of it.

I growled and kicked like a wild thing, slashing my nails down the arms of whoever had hold of me but then a taser slammed into my side and I screamed, my knees slamming into concrete and splitting open as the electricity burst through my limbs. My mind was in a daze as I blinked away the darkness, looking up and finding Orion punching the guy who'd tasered me, beating the shit out of him as he went completely feral and I smiled at my savage mate as someone pulled me upright again.

I found Francesca looking me over in concern. "The stars have cursed us all by bringing you here," she whispered.

"Then let us go," I snarled and she almost looked like she wished she could.

It took three agents to get Orion back under control and I looked up at the huge building in front of us with FIB stamped above the doorway.

We were marched inside, Orion's shirt torn half off of him and his shoulders heaving as he looked back at me, and somehow all I felt was a rush of desire at the sight of those silver rings glinting at me and the carnal look of need in his expression.

We were marched past a desk and through several security doors before the two of us were shoved into a barred cell together. Eight agents stared in at us while one of them locked the door tight and I stood in a patch of moonlight that filtered through a barred window behind me.

"We'll have to contact the king," one of the men said anxiously.

"He's at a press conference," another said in concern. "We're not supposed to bother him."

My heart juddered with fear for a second, but then I looked at Orion and the mate bond flared once more, driving me towards him.

I forgot about the onlooking agents and ran to him, leaping up and wrapping my legs around his waist, our mouths coming together in a furious kiss that lit me up from the inside out.

"Are you sure we should leave them together?" one of the agents said uncertainly.

"This is the only spare cell we have after the Sphinx raid we did this afternoon," another answered as Orion slammed me up against the bars and a dong reverberated throughout the whole cell. I pulled off the remnants of his torn shirt, moaning at the heat of his muscular body meeting with mine.

"We, um, will need you to help us fill out some paperwork," one girl tried addressing us and Orion broke our kiss, my lips bruised and swollen, but somehow I just wanted more. More of his passion and strength, more of everything he had to offer me.

"GET OUT!" he roared. "Anyone who stays is going to see me fuck my mate. And if you stay, I will mark you as dead for laying your eyes on her skin. I will hunt you to the ends of the earth to ensure I get my cut of meat from you."

"Lance," Francesca hissed. "You need to calm down, you need to focus."

"OUT!" I yelled at her and she backed up like I'd slapped her.

The agents all shared a look then shrugged and scarpered from the room. Francesca was the last to go, looking to Orion with some hint of loss in her eyes and I bared my teeth at her, my hand sliding possessively around the back of his neck and she bowed her head and ducked out of the room, leaving us alone at last.

Orion was already dropping his fly and he laid me on a hard wooden bench at the back of the cell, gripping my hips and guiding the tip of his cock to my entrance.

"Let me see those eyes, beautiful," he commanded and my gaze flicked up to meet his as I panted and bucked my hips, needing him to stop taunting me.

He took in my Elysian rings with a groan of desire, cupping my chin in his hand as he turned my head left and right to examine them, and then he made me cry out like a girl possessed as he drove himself into me with an earth-shattering thrust, every inch of him sheathed deep within me. He gripped my hips, spreading me even wider for him as he pulled himself out of me agonisingly slowly, watching me like a hawk hunting in the sky.

"Fucking perfect," he sighed, then slammed into me again, making my back arch against the bench and my cries filled the whole precinct as he unleashed the full force of his inner animal on me.

My hips worked to meet every thrust of his and suddenly he slowed right down, his hands pressed above my head and our bodies working in the most delicious fucking way together, his hips rolling and grinding until I was seeing stars, my head falling back as pleasure spilled through me and my body trembled in the wake of his power over me. I was still coming when he pulled out of me even though he wasn't done, tugging my nightgown down to free my breasts, sucking one of my nipples while toying with the other.

I could feel him everywhere, my skin electrified from him as if his magic was skittering under my skin, but I knew that couldn't be possible with the magic cuffs blocking off our power.

He dropped further down my body until his tongue was assaulting my clit and he feasted on me like my pussy was the source of life, my thighs wrapping around him as he licked and nipped and teased me. He swirled his fingers in my wetness, sucking them into his mouth with a hum of satisfaction before driving his tongue into me, lifting my ass with his hands so he could spread me out for him like a fucking buffet.

I came twice more before he sat up, wiping his glistening mouth with the back of his hand and smirking at me like a prime asshole. God, those silver rings looked good on him. They were like diamonds encrusting his pupils, so bright it was as if they held moonlight within them.

He bore down on me once more, but I moved fast, jumping up and pressing my hands to his shoulders to make him sit on the bench, his back to the wall. Then I knelt over him, gripping his hard cock as I looked directly into his eyes and guided him inside me once more.

The most sexy fucking sound left his lips as I took him all the way in and started rocking my hips, our mouths almost touching as we just stared at each other, our hands roaming, caressing and fire trailing up my spine as pleasure rolled through my body.

I couldn't think about anything but him as he sucked his thumb then placed it against my clit, letting me grind on his hand as I climbed towards another impossible high, and suddenly I was coming again, my body tightening around his solid length and he grabbed hold of my ass, guiding me up and down as I rode out the wave, forcing me to go to the pace he wanted as he fucked me from below and took total control of my movements. He drove into me with an intensity that told me he was on the verge of coming apart too, my pussy squeezing every inch of him as he watched me like I was a divine being born to rule him.

His head fell back against the wall as he finished with a final firm thrust of his hips, and I felt the deep heat of him spilling inside me and slicking between us, his breaths coming heavily as he groaned like he was in nirvana.

As my forehead fell against his, I knew we weren't even close to done, because this need inside me was still blazing. So the world would have to wait for us to be done with each other, because I wasn't going to part from his body until I physically had to stop.

He scored his thumb up between my shoulder blades as my hips started grinding, a villain's smile on his lips as he made me shiver. "Wasn't that enough for you, mate?"

"Not even close," I panted, feeling him getting hard again for me already and I leaned forward so all I could see were those shining, star-gifted rings in his eyes.

"When I'm done with you, Blue, you'll never get the feel of me off of your skin."

DARIUS

CHAPTER FORTY SEVEN

I flew through the sky with my wings beating hard and a storm brewing all around us which sparked off of my scales and made my skin tingle.

We were less than a mile from the FIB holding cell now and Gabriel's warning rang in my ears. *"Fly hard and fast and don't waste time being subtle."*

Easily done.

Roxy soared ahead of me, her bronze wings reflecting the first flash of lightning like light glinting off of metal as she raced ahead of me, only half shifted so that her flames wouldn't give her away.

The Storm Dragon flew above us, so high that I couldn't see him when I glanced up into the ever darkening sky, providing the cover we needed to pull this off. I cursed the fact that we didn't have any stardust left at our disposal thanks to the new laws, but we didn't have far to go. It had been just over fifty miles away from The Burrows which with the speed we were travelling had gone past in under twenty minutes.

Barely a mile lay between us and them now, and there was no chance in hell that I would fail in this task.

Thunder boomed overhead and the rain burst free of the clouds like the sound had been heralding its arrival. I resisted the urge to roar as I flew as fast as I could, chasing after the girl the stars had chosen for me and who I had stolen back from them after they cursed us.

"I see it!" Roxy called above the sound of the storm, pointing towards the ground and tucking her wings in tight to her sides as she plummeted out of the sky at a ferocious pace.

I followed her lead, snapping my wings shut and diving down after her, allowing myself that roar at last as I spotted the FIB compound below, the building squat and constructed from grey brick.

"Which way is west?" Roxy called, making me snort a laugh and I pointed it out with one clawed foot, indicating the wall closest to us which Gabriel had said held the cells where they were being detained.

She grinned in that Savage Princess way of hers which got my blood pumping like nothing else on this earth, and threw her hands out with a furious cry, a bird of red and blue flames bursting from her palms as she directed her power at the wards surrounding the building.

I didn't slow as I passed her, chasing after her Phoenix fire and scrunching my eyes up as it crashed into the barriers with an echoing boom which short circuited them and blasted them clean out of existence.

I roared loudly, hoping Lance and Darcy would understand the warning as I turned at the last second and slammed straight into the side of the building, taking out the wall and sending bricks flying in every direction.

Roxy flew at my back, her hands raised as she used her earth magic to grab the falling wall, directing every last brick to the outside of the building and making sure we didn't accidentally crush the people we'd come here to rescue.

"Holy shit," Lance gasped and I spotted him and Darcy scrambling to get up from the floor inside. Darcy pulled down a nearly transparent blue nightgown while Lance yanked up his pants, his chest bare and his shirt discarded somewhere beyond them.

Were they fucking kidding me right now? Had they been going at it while my father was on his way here to execute them?

"Hurry!" Roxy called to them as I wheeled away from the wreckage and I spotted Lance clambering out over the heaped bricks, his hand locked in Darcy's as he tugged her up beside him, the rain sheeting down on them.

Their magic was blocked off with cuffs as we'd known it would be and Roxy dropped to her feet as I was forced to fly back up into the air again, circling around to grab them on my second fly by as FIB agents rushed out of the building with shouts of alarm and guns in hand.

"Don't fight us and you won't be harmed," Roxy called loudly as she threw a solid air shield up between us and the agents.

"Lance!" one of the agents yelled and my gaze caught on Francesca as she came running up behind her colleagues.

As I looked at her, her eyes began to merge and she shifted into her Cyclops form, a shockwave of psychic power blasting from her so suddenly that I barely had a chance to flinch before it struck.

But in place of the attack I had expected, I watched as the rest of the FIB agents all fell like dominos, crashing to the ground in a heap and twitching there beneath the force of her attack.

I landed heavily on the ground, a snarl tearing from my lips as Roxy continued to shield all of us and Lance and Darcy made it out of the wreckage to my side.

"I have the map of espial you asked for!" Francesca called as she came to a halt beyond Roxy's shield and my girl looked back over her shoulder towards Lance in a question as she continued to keep her back.

"Let her through," he commanded and Roxy dropped the shield, backing up to stand at my side as Francesca ran forward, pulling a long metal tube from her back pocket and holding it out.

"You really think you can end the war with this?" she asked, her eyes

540

shifting apart once more as she looked at her Nebula Ally with hope in her gaze that made my heart twist with emotion.

"Yes," Lance said firmly. "This will let us destroy Lavinia and once she's cut off from the shadows, we will be on an even playing field once more. The false king will die and the true queens will rise."

I growled at the conviction in his voice, but I wasn't even certain I disagreed with that assessment anymore, my gaze on the woman I loved as she stood before me like the royalty I knew she was. But it didn't really matter what I thought anymore anyway. I had a few months left on this earth at best, so I wouldn't be here to see the world which would rise after my father's downfall. My only desire now was to watch him die before I succumbed to the deal I'd struck with the stars.

"Then take it," Francesca said in a growl. "And make it hurt when you end him."

Lance accepted the container which held the map of espial, throwing his arms around her and squeezing her tight as Darcy stepped closer to them too.

"Here," Francesca said as she stepped back, taking two syringes from her pocket. "It's the Order Suppressant antidote." Lance stabbed one into his own arm like a savage and depressed the plunger before doing it more gently for Darcy.

"Come with us," Lance begged but Francesca shook her head.

"They won't remember that I was the one to attack them, I'll forge new memories in their heads to cover for what I did," she said. "And I can do more good here. I've already thwarted countless wrongful arrests. I need to stay."

"Thank you," Darcy breathed, wrapping her arms around Francesca too and making the Cyclops gasp in surprise. "This will be the thing that turns the tide of this war."

"We need to go," Roxy said firmly, her eyes on the stormy sky and I knew she was thinking of Gabriel's warning, knowing my father would be here at any second with his shadow whore likely right beside him.

"Stay safe," Lance commanded, and Francesca quickly unlocked the cuffs on his wrists before offering Darcy the same, the two of them leaping up onto my back as thunder crashed overhead once more.

"You too," she called and I took off into the sky with Roxy at my side, turning back for The Burrows and speeding away into the storm while Dante kept it raging overhead and flew back with us.

The rain crashed down with furious intent but as we left the FIB precinct far behind, my heart soared with joy because not only had we saved Lance and Darcy from a fate worse than death, we'd just secured the very thing we needed to bring about the end of this war and the downfall of the man who had worked his hardest to ruin my life.

ORION

CHAPTER FORTY EIGHT

Darius swooped through the boundary surrounding the Burrows with Tory flying by his head and Dante circling down after us, his storm powers still rattling through the air and rain drenching us through.

Darcy and I hadn't even bothered to shield from the drumming rain, her body wrapped around mine as we kissed, the bond still crashing through my body like the thunder in the sky. I couldn't get enough of this girl, my fucking Elysian Mate.

A shockwave rolled through us as Darius landed and it took everything I had to part from her and climb down from his back. I tossed the tube containing the map to Tory, barking a command at her to keep it safe as she caught it and I held my arms up for Blue as she hopped down and let me catch her.

"Jesus, Dante, calm it on the rain!" Tory cried as Dante landed heavily beside Darius, electricity darting down his navy scales as he released a growling Dragon's laugh. The two of them shifted into their Fae forms, running inside after Tory and I grabbed Blue's hand keeping her close as we chased after them, sharing a grin at what was coming.

I pulled her inside out of the storm, finding the others drying themselves off while Darius and Dante got dressed and started talking excitedly about their flight together.

I looked down at Darcy, her nightgown now fully transparent, slick to her skin from the rain, her dark blue hair drenched and dripping. She looked hot as fuck, reminding me of the time she'd come to me in a storm back at Zodiac Academy, the night we'd crossed the most forbidden of boundaries between each other. It was so clear to me why we had never been able to stay apart from each other. We were inevitable, a fate waiting to happen. But as tempting as she looked right now, my thoughts were also starting to clear since our mating, and I realised she was not to be seen like this by anyone else.

I grabbed hold of her, threw her over my shoulder then shot away, speeding past our friends and down into The Burrows, shouting to them that we'd come see them in a bit, before running all the way back to our room where I threw her on the bed.

I cast a lock on the door and silenced that area so we wouldn't be disturbed by anyone knocking then prowled toward her.

She looked so star damned fuckable that I buried myself in her for another twenty minutes before I allowed her to escape me. I washed us both with water magic and dried us with air, the scent of the storm leaving us at last. Then I spent the next five minutes healing every mark and bruise I'd left on her body, replacing each one with a kiss. Finally, I fetched some lacy black underwear and a long sleeved silver dress from the wardrobe and handed it to her with a grin.

"Put this on."

"And why am I dressing up?" she laughed as she did as I said anyway, and I watched her hungrily as I grabbed some clothes for myself.

"Because I want to present you to everyone in The Burrows as my mate," I said, raising my chin with pride and she smiled up at me, a pink blush building in her cheeks.

"But it's the middle of the night," she countered and I shrugged, determined of this and she bit her lip, giving in to my demands.

When she was finished dressing, I circled her, humming my approval as I buttoned up my jeans then pulled on a nice black shirt.

Darcy immediately stepped forward to do up the buttons for me and I watched her with my heart thrashing like a caged animal. When she was done, I shot to the wardrobe and grabbed a bottle of bourbon hidden in there, twisting the cap off.

"I want to drink and be fucking merry, beautiful," I said, taking a long swig as I grinned at her. I didn't even give a damn that we'd most likely scraped by death tonight, because it seemed the stars were on our side at last and I was wide awake and ready to fucking party.

"Then screw it, let's be merry." She beamed.

I snagged a pair of black heels out of the wardrobe, and gestured for Darcy to get on the bed. She watched me with amusement in her eyes, sitting down on the edge, but I pushed her to lay all the way back, sliding her heels onto her feet then leaning over her and tipping a measure of whiskey into the hollow of her neck. I licked and sucked it out then sank my tongue between her lips, giving her a taste too as a sultry moan left her.

I kissed my way to her neck, my fangs lengthening and my heart rate elevating at the thought of what I wanted.

"Bite me," she ordered breathlessly and I did, my fangs sinking in deep, drawing a gasp from her lips as her sweet blood hit my tongue and I groaned in rapture. She wasn't just my blood Source, she was the source of all things pure and good in my life, and I would never get enough of her taste.

Before I could get my hundredth boner of the night, I drew back and pulled her to her feet, making her twirl under my arm as I assessed her, loving the way her ass filled out that dress and the heels made her legs look extra long. I healed the mark on her neck and sucked the last of her blood off my thumb as I drew my hand away, my magic reserves swelling.

"You're a fucking delight to behold." I pulled her towards the door. "Are you ready to tell everyone what happened?"

"Yeah, but I think they might be pissed we disappeared," she said, opening the door and I found myself looking at an angry Tory with her arms folded, the Heirs at her back and Geraldine pulling at her hair with anxiety.

"What the hell?" Tory demanded and Darcy rushed forward and grasped her hand.

"I'm sorry, Tor," she said quickly.

"Why are you dressed up like that?" Tory demanded then she gasped, yanking her sister forward and gripping her whole head as she looked into her eyes. "Wait – what? Seriously!?"

"Yep," Darcy laughed. "It happened before the FIB caught us. The fucking stars gave us our moment right outside a freaking precinct."

"What moment is this you speak of?" Geraldine barrelled through the Heirs as they tried to get a look at Darcy and Darius muscled his way forward too, grabbing my arm and yanking me close to look into my eyes.

"Holy fuck," he gasped then he punched me in the shoulder, making me curse before he dragged me in to a tight hug.

"Flog my seaweed sprouts!" Geraldine bellowed as she made it in front of Darcy, shaking her and starting to sob as she drooped all the way down to the floor. "By the gleam upon the moon's rump, it cannot be! My lady Darcy has had her moment of the divine. She has been called under the stars to be bound to her Orry man!" she wailed, clawing her way up Tory's legs as she sobbed and buried her face in Tory's wings which were folded at her back.

Seth howled his excitement, leaping forward and snaring Darcy in a hug before coming for me like a bounding puppy, nearly falling over his own feet as he collided with me, forcing Darius aside.

I was so fucking happy that I didn't even push him off, I just clapped him on the back and suddenly Cal slammed into me, hugging me too before him and Seth exchanged an awkward look and released me at the same time. Max stepped forward next, congratulating me before hugging Darcy tight and I realised Geraldine had fainted, her arms strewn above her head and her mouth agape where she lay on the floor.

Max snagged the bourbon from my hand, a grin on his lips. "So we're fucking partying, right?"

"Right," I agreed.

"Awooo!" Seth howled and I fucking howled too because why the hell not?

The Heirs joined in and Darcy and Tory did too until our voices were echoing all around the royal quarters and beyond, the sound turning to laughter. I crouched down, casting a splash of cold water against Geraldine's face and she woke with a wail, lunging at me and wrapping her whole body around me, nearly choking me out as she sobbed.

"Oh, your curse is lifted, I no longer feel the need to look over your shoulder and imagine you are anyone else but the Power Shamed Fae you are – were!"

"What do you mean?" Darcy gasped, dropping down beside her too as she helped prise her off of me.

Geraldine wiped the tears from her eyes, clutching Darcy's face as she stared at her Elysian rings in wonder. "My sweet, dear, queen, he has proven his worth. He has risen up the food chain like a whelk to a whale."

"What are you saying, Geraldine?" Orion demanded.

"Don't you see, my beautiful fanged forager?" she rasped, clasping my face with her other hand as everyone else leaned closer. "This will exonerate you. For how can you be shamed for foul-playing fornication when you have been chosen by the stars as my lady Darcy's one true mate? No one in Solaria will question their decision. You are a fine and true steed, and you will serve my lady well, you will set the ultimate of fires in her loins, you will birth heirs born of valour and loyalty. Your story shall be made into a ditty that will be sung from every hill in Solaria." Tears rolled down her cheeks and I looked to Darcy in shock, unsure if this was true and if I could bear getting my hopes up in case it wasn't.

"What's all this ruckus?" Hamish's booming voice carried to us and everyone stepped back as I drew Geraldine to her feet and wound an arm around Darcy's waist.

Well, I guessed this would be the test that proved it.

I looked to Hamish as he bustled along the corridor towards us in a stripey night cap and matching open-toe slippers, his chest hair peeking from beneath his gown.

"Gerrykins, move away from that Power Shamed cret-" he was about to retch when he paused in front of us, his gaze settling on my eyes then moving to Darcy's, then back to mine.

His mouth opened and closed, gaping like a fish out of water, all words abandoning him.

"Papa, the stars have chosen our lady Darcy an Elysian Mate," Geraldine cooed.

"Well bless my salty crackers on a bed of kale. Twist my dough balls and call me Uncle Dunberry. Tickle my turnip and bury me in a pile of battered beetroots." Hamish reached towards my eyes like he was close to the sun and couldn't resist a feel of it, but before he could touch me, his eyes rolled into the back of his head and he collapsed to the floor in a heap.

I snorted a laugh, serving me a glare from Geraldine as she ushered Max forward to help her pull her father to his feet.

When he woke again, he lunged at me, picking me up in his huge arms and spinning me around and around.

"Oh-ho! My boy! You're saved! Rejoice we shall! Let us sound the bells, let us ring the cherryhocker and bang the drumble to celebrate this finest of days! Oh-ho! Oh-ho!"

He placed me down and I smiled awkwardly before he lunged at Darcy, swinging her around too and Geraldine grabbed hands with Seth and Tory, forcing them to make a ring-around-the-roses circle and join hands with the others. Even Darius let himself be dragged around so it was just me, Hamish and Darcy in the middle as Hamish threw his head back and amplified his voice so it carried out through the entire Burrows.

"Rejoice - rejoice! You must awaken! It is time to celebrate this most momentous of occasions, for our Princess Darcy Vega has found her Elysian Mate!"

There was a moment of quiet then a stampede of footsteps sounded out all around the tunnels, the excited chatter of people carrying from every direction. I laughed as our friends swept us along in the direction of the dining quarters, keeping a tight hold of Darcy as our fingers threaded together. I watched her as she laughed, unable to believe the stars had really offered me her like this. I'd always known we were meant for each other, even wondered if we could be Elysian Mates, but until they'd proven me right, I had never felt worthy of her.

Now, I wore the rings which told me I was enough, that said I could give her everything she deserved, and I would honour this bond with my entire life. I would spend every day worshipping my queen, my mate, and I would know with all my soul that there was no other Fae in this world who could do a better job of that than me.

We made it into the dining quarters where Fae had already arrived, looking to us through sleepy eyes as curiosity filled their expressions.

"Joyous day!" Hamish cried. "We shall have a feast, and we shall drink until we cannot drink anymore. Come, gather, fetch whatever you can as an offering to our queen and her mate."

The rebels ran forward to obey, looking over everyone's heads and craning their necks to try and get a look at us both. I felt more observed than I had been the entire time I'd been here and I found I wasn't entirely comfortable with the attention, but anything was better than being fucking Power Shamed, because with each passing glance came smiles and waves and kisses blown our way.

They were looking me in the eye and they saw someone worthy again. They saw a Fae whose status had not only been returned to him, but had just gone up the power rank several levels by being mated to a Vega princess.

Someone placed a glass in my hand and I realised the Oscura Wolves were here, led by Dante and Rosalie with bottles of Arucso wine in their grasp.

"Drink, amici. Che le stelle benedicano ogni giorno che condividi insieme," Dante said in his native tongue, filling my glass and Darcy's before filling a golden chalice in his hand. I didn't know what he'd said, but I liked the sound of it, so I was happy to drink to it.

We clinked our cups to his and I gulped down the sweet wine, finding the Wolves breaking into dance as someone got music playing and the lights were turned down low.

Gabriel appeared next, clasping the back of my neck and resting his forehead to mine for a moment with a big ass smile on his face before leaning down to kiss Darcy's cheek.

"The stars hid this from me," he laughed. "I thought your relationship was doomed."

"Thanks for telling us." Darcy punched his arm and Gabriel chuckled.

"I always hoped a new path would arise for you both. I am so damn pleased."

Leon barrelled past him, licking my whole face before descending on Darcy and I wiped the saliva off my face, not even giving a fuck about it as an Oscura Wolf filled my glass again and I took another long swig.

"I got you gifts!" Leon announced, placing a wreath of gaudy flowers around my neck with a little picture of Darcy glued to it. He placed one over Darcy's head with a photo of me that was definitely the one posted on the Zodiac Academy website. I looked like a grumpy asshole in a suit. "I had a couple of Mindys put them together super fast, they came out great though, didn't they?"

"Wonderful." I plucked at the hideous thing, but didn't bother to take it off.

"Mindys?" Seth asked in confusion as he stepped up beside me nibbling on a doughnut with his red tassled cowboy hat in place on his head. "What are they?"

"Just Fae who wanna serve me," Leon explained simply, his eyes slipping up to the hat. "The hex hasn't set in then yet?" He asked in a mumble.

"What?" Seth asked, clearly not hearing him.

"Nothing – ooh conga line!" Leon bounded away to join the Oscura Wolves as they lined up, grabbing Rosalie's hips and kicking out his legs as they all started congaing around the room.

"Oh Lance," Catalina sighed as she approached us next and I was distracted from what Leon had said. Darius's mother took hold of mine and Darcy's hands as she gazed between us with watery eyes. "I'm so happy for you."

"Thank you," I said as Darcy moved to hug her tight and my heart squeezed with affection for Catalina. She'd become very precious to me in the time we'd spent together down here, and I couldn't help but think of her like a parent. She drew me into her arms next, placing a kiss in my hair and I held her against me, breathing in her scent as the comfort of her aura surrounded me.

She headed off to dance with Hamish as he reappeared dressed in a brown suit with a bright pink bowtie at his throat. Most of the rebels were half dressed or in their pyjamas, joining in with the celebrations as the party quickly grew wild.

Some of the Oscura Wolves got hold of us, throwing us above their heads with air magic and bouncing us all across the heads of the crowd, Darcy's laughter making the bond burn even brighter at how happy she was.

When we were back on our feet, we danced and danced, our friends joining us until we were surrounded by the best people I knew and had fresh drinks in our hands.

As the night wore on, and I became progressively less sober, it seemed every rebel in The Burrows wanted to come and talk to me, praising the stars for releasing me from my shame.

It was sort of a backhanded compliment, but I took it because fuck, I'd never imagined this reality existed for me. Since I'd been convicted, I'd assumed I'd cursed myself for good one way or the other. I'd sacrificed a lot that day in the name of my queen, and I had to wonder if the stars had always been planning to hand it back to me. Because as I mapped out our relationship together, I could see the tests we'd faced. From fighting to stay together even when it was against the law, to facing Seth's wrath when he discovered us, to the day Kylie had exposed us and I'd made my choice to protect Darcy instead of dragging her down with me.

Blue had always stood against anyone who went against us, she'd even demanded I claim her in front of the world knowing my status would destroy her. And I had to think that me finally submitting to her wants and letting go of the control I'd tried to hold onto might have been the final test. I'd stood with her in this hall, declaring her as mine while she declared me as hers in return despite the fact that we knew it wouldn't be easy, that we knew the world might turn on us. But instead of the life I'd expected to be handed because of that, the struggle of watching Darcy be ridiculed by the press, and the possibility of her losing support from her subjects, the stars had decided on a different fate for us. And hell, I hated those twinkly assholes sometimes, but their gifts certainly did go some way toward making up for their bullshit.

Darcy was pulled away from me across the room, accosted by her own swarm of rebels and I kept meeting her gaze, not even really hearing what the guy in front of me was saying.

I had trinkets, pins and badges all over me, offerings from the rebels like I was some sort of god they wanted to worship, and Darcy was gathering a large pile of gifts that seemed to be a mix of anything the rebels could come up with either with their magic or from their own possessions.

At some point Geraldine appeared with a buffet made up entirely of ring-shaped food, all of it sprayed silver, from doughnuts to bagels, party rings, to onion rings.

One of the Kipling brothers who'd worked on my court case stood near it all, looking at it in horror like it offended him somehow, but I had no idea why, though he looked more interested when a tray of large cakes were brought out which had silver rings marked on the icing.

I lost all interest as Tory appeared in front of me. She'd changed into a fitted red dress and had painted silver eyeliner onto her eyes.

"We're playing dares," she announced, pointing over at the Heirs and a group of the Oscuras, including Dante and Rosalie.

"Is that an invitation?" I asked, swaying a little as I stepped toward her. Oh shit, drunk feet.

She reached out, pinching both of my nipples and twisting hard enough to make me snarl. Then she turned and ran away with a wild laugh, darting back to the others and I realised I was the subject of her dare.

"Well, I'll fucking dare you...I mean, play dares, and then you'll see, because I'll be the dare king-" I slurred a little then my eyes met Darcy's again as I found her surrounded by a circle of adoring fans. She bit down on her lip and beckoned me over to her.

I shot forward, but didn't see the table in front of me so I went flying over it, crashing to the floor and taking down three chairs with me. But I didn't let that slow me down for long, knocking aside the hands of the people who tried to help me up as I scrambled to my feet, finding Seth sitting on a chair in front of me with a plate of food on his knees, wearing bright red cowboy boots that matched his hat.

"Where'd you get those?" I balked.

"Where'd I get what?" he frowned then barrelled on. "Oh by the way, I came up with another nickname for you: Professor Not Shamed," he announced excitedly. "Isn't it great?"

"No," I grumbled. "I wanna be something good. Why do you have to bring my shame into everything, Seth. Why?"

"Because of your shame."

I growled. "And now it's gone. And I'm not even a professor anymore, so call me something that I am."

Seth assessed me with narrowed eyes like he was thinking really hard on it. "Vamp-ring-eyed-drunk-asshole?"

I gave him a flat look. "I hate you."

"Nah, you don't. Okay, okay, I can do better. I'm gonna name you The BFV – The Big Friendly Vampire. It encompasses your bigness, your friendliness, and your Vampiness."

"Since when am I friendly?" I scoffed, though I guessed this nickname wasn't so bad.

"Since you cuddled me when I needed someone more than you can even imagine," he said quietly and I stared at him in surprise as he cleared his throat. "You're the rootinest tootinest guy I know."

I swear for a second he had a twang of an accent about him on those final words and I frowned. Odd.

But I was too distracted by Blue again to question it as she gave me the flutter eyes and I sped away from Seth across the room to join my mate.

"Hey beautiful." I swung her around, knocking the rebels aside as I stole her from them, tearing across the room to join our friends as I tucked her under my arm. I placed her down on a chair beside Tory as Seth came bounding over too with his plate of food in his grip. *Wait, was he wearing that huge horseshoe belt a minute ago?*

We all started chatting about anything and everything as we dared each other things whenever we remembered to play the game, but mostly I just soaked up the company of everyone I loved around me, feeling like nothing in the world could ruin my mood ever again.

"-but I mean *hypothetically*," Max was saying across from me in the circle. "If you could have any other Order what would it be?"

"It's an insult to the Fae realm!" Geraldine barked. "No such thing is possible and it offends my ears to even deliberate it, you scullion of a scoundrel."

"It's a game, Gerry," Max said in exasperation. "It's not real, I'm just saying if you *had* to."

"Then I would be a Cerberus." She lifted her chin with pride.

"But you are a Cerberus," Max sighed, running a hand down his face.

"And a Cerberus I will stay," she announced.

"Fine," Max gave up, looking to the rest of us. "What would you all choose?"

"Pegasus," Darius said easily. "Just to double piss off my father."

Xavier snorted a laugh. "You'd be a shit Pegasus."

"You'd be a shit Dragon," Darius tossed back and they shoved each other lightly.

"I'd be a Lion Shifter," Caleb said. "I could use their Charisma powers to form an army of servants and I've already got the best hair, so I'd easily fit in."

Seth looked over at him with a small smile, but when Caleb looked back, he glanced away again and awkwardness filled the air. I was pretty sure only Darcy and I noticed it as Seth looked our way, and I had to admit I felt a bit shit for the guy.

"I'd be one of them too," Tory agreed. "They sleep in the sun all day to recharge their power, right? That's right up my street."

"Lionesses tend to serve Lions though, baby," Darius pointed out and

Tory wrinkled her nose.

"Ew, I take it back," she said quickly and Darius sniggered.

"What would you be?" I nudged Darcy and she sucked her lower lip, drawing my attention to it and making my cock twitch in response. "A fluffy little Bunny Shifter that I can put in my pocket?" I teased and she laughed, shooting me a glare as she pushed me back.

"No chance," she growled and I could see she was a predator through and through these days. I fucking loved that about her. The sweetness on the outside hiding the wild creature within. And I enjoyed luring it out to come and play with me.

"I want to know what it's like to be one of the animal shifters," she decided. "Maybe something furry and vicious - like a Bear Shifter!"

"Or a Wolf," Seth jumped in. "We could go running beneath the moon together – awooo!"

"Awoo!" Darcy answered with a laugh and I grinned at her.

"Oh what fun." Geraldine clapped. "But by my mulberry bush, there is no true Order better suited for the queens than their rightful, honourable Order, the gallant Phoenix."

"It's just a game, Gerry," Max insisted.

"And I am just a krill riding a lump of driftwood into the great beyond, Maxy boy, but a sealess plankton I can never be," she said.

"What the hell does that mean?" Max balked and I frowned too. I had no idea what Geraldine was going on about at the best of times, let alone when I was wasted on Oscura wine.

"Tell you what I wouldn't wanna be," Darius said, wrinkling his nose. "A Cyclops."

"Now, now, don't go Order Shaming, you big Dragoon. There is merit to all Orders," Geraldine insisted.

"I'm not against their Order, I just don't want a bug eye," he said.

"Oh my stars, Lance, did Francesca Sky get her bug eye out when you rammed in her backdoor?" Seth blurted and before I could cut him down to size myself, Darcy raised a hand and blasted him with water, sending him flying across the room as he howled in fright and fell down among Gabriel and his family.

I turned to Darcy, finding her expression feral and leaning forward to steal a kiss from her wild, snarly little mouth.

"There is no Fae in this world I want but you," I said against her lips, soothing her and her shoulders relaxed.

Seth came running back over, drying himself out with air magic, his hair flying out about his shoulders as he straightened his cowboy hat and I noticed he was wearing a red leather vest, his shirt now missing and his muscles on display. Where the fuck did he get that?

"What the hell are you wearing, man?" Max asked him as he approached and Seth looked down, seeming to notice his attire for the first time.

"Woooah," he cooed, and his jeans suddenly shifted into red leather chaps. He turned around with a gasp, shaking his butt to reveal that they were in fact assless chaps.

Caleb's lips popped open as Seth wiggled his ass back and forth in them, admiring himself as spurs appeared on the back of his boots.

"What in tarnation is happening?" Seth said, his accent changing once more to something more country and he touched a hand to his mouth in shock. "Did you hear that?"

Leon hurried over through the crowd as he spotted Seth, laughing his ass off and smacking him on the back. "It got you!"

"What got me?" Seth asked in confusion.

"The hat. The guy who owned it was a Bull Shifter named Bo Vine. He had one dying wish and it got trapped in this hat when he went out of this world, trampled by his own Cow harem when they were startled by a roaming Lion Shifter." He shook his head sadly. "Tragic."

"Was the Shifter you?" I deadpanned and Leon looked to me, aghast.

"What are you implying? That I crept onto Bo's land to steal his special leather hat and accidentally killed him?" Leon gasped.

"Yes, that's precisely what I'm implying," I said and he held a hand to his heart like I'd wounded it.

"Lance Orion, you have no proof and nothing to go on. I don't know anything about Bo's death, but I do know he was a mean asshole who liked to shoot pigeons from his window and once got arrested for molesting a drainpipe. So are we sorry he's dead? Are we? Or is that unknown, nameless Lion a hero?"

I gave him a flat look as the Heirs sniggered.

"I think I suit this look." Seth continued to wiggle his ass. "Can I keep all of it?" He looked to Leon with big eyes, but Leon shook his head seriously.

"Bo breathed his final wish on his dying breath – not that I was there to hear it - but *apparently*, he said he always wanted to ride a Pegasus in his finest red leather attire, and sing Cotton Eye Joe by Rednex as loud as he could." Leon frowned at Seth. "And if you don't live out his wish the leather will bind to your skin, turn to acid and melt away your bones."

"Ah!" Seth yelped and Caleb shot to his side, reaching for the hat.

"Take it off," Caleb growled, but Leon shoved him back with a cry before he could get hold of it.

"No! The wish must be fulfilled!" Leon yelled. "If you take any of the clothes off, you'll set off the curse and the leather will bind to your-"

"My skin. Got it," Seth ground out. "So what do I do?"

"Fulfil Bo's wish," Leon breathed mysteriously, pointing dramatically at Xavier who sighed, getting to his feet.

"Come on then." Xavier started stripping and Seth hurried forward, hitching a leg up over his hip before he'd even shifted, his ass cheek popping fully out the side of the chaps.

"Dude." Xavier batted him away. "Gimme a sec."

Seth whimpered as he stepped back, waiting as Xavier leapt forward and shifted into his Pegasus form, and Seth hurried forward to climb onto his back.

Tory ran over to the Oscuras who were playing the music, speaking with them and a second later Cotton Eye Joe by Rednex started playing and Xavier took off, flying over us as a lasso popped into existence in Seth's hand and he started swinging it as he belted out the lyrics like his life depended on it – which I guessed it did come to think of it.

I glanced at Darcy as she cracked up beside me, snorting a laugh myself at the ridiculousness of this situation. Tory came jogging back to our group, laughing at Seth as he circled above and dropping back into her seat.

"Will that shit really burn his skin off?" I asked Leon as he stepped closer to us, grinning from ear to ear.

"Yep," he said. "I wear the hat on my birthday every year. I swear I can hear Bo singing along too from the grave. You could say I gave him the greatest gift a person can give someone."

"What, death?" I asked.

"Oh Lance," Leon laughed, heading back off into the crowd as Xavier came down to land and Seth slid off his back, his clothes returning to normal as he pulled the hat off.

"I think I wanna do it again," Seth said, slowly lifting the hat up to his head like he was going to put it back on.

Caleb shot to his side and ripped the hat out of his grip, burning it to dust in his hand and walking back to his seat without a word, leaving Seth staring after him in confusion.

"Let's do some more dares," Xavier suggested as he shifted back into his Fae form, and pulled his clothes on.

Tyler and Sofia hurried over from the buffet, handing him a plate of food and offering him kisses that he accepted with a smug grin on his face. It was cute to see him so content within his herd at last, a natural order found between them.

Gabriel swooped over on his wings, landing behind Xavier and leaning down to speak in his ear. "You still owe me, kid, so I will make the dare, and you will pull it off."

Xavier jumped in alarm, looking up at him with a whinny of apology in his throat.

"Alright, alright," he agreed and Gabriel smiled satisfactorily and leaned down to whisper something in his ear.

Xavier neighed a laugh then nodded his agreement, jumping up and heading off to do whatever Gabriel had asked. My Nebular Ally moved to sit on my other side, smiling at me in a way that said he was as drunk as I was.

"Hey, Professor, check this out." Tyler tossed me his Atlas and I caught it out of the air before it hit me in the face, arching a brow at him.

"I'm not your professor," I corrected.

"But you still teach us shit." Tyler frowned like he couldn't get his head around that.

"That's different," I said dismissively.

"How?" he demanded, ever the fucking earwig in my ear.

"Because it is, Corbin," I barked, on the verge of stealing house points when I got hold of my tongue to stop myself and Tyler laughed at me.

"Such a professor," he muttered and I sighed, looking down at the Atlas he'd passed me as Darcy leaned closer to read the article on the screen.

Lance Orion is exonerated by the stars!

A miraculous night has turned into a miraculous dawn for a former professor at Zodiac Academy and once popular rising Pitball star, Lance

Orion, after he was called beneath the stars with none other than Darcy Vega in a Divine Moment set to rock the nation. When the question of fate was asked of them, they leapt eagerly into each other's arms, only to find themselves surrounded by the FIB, stunned and apprehended.

The two lovers with silver rings in their eyes were dragged mercilessly into a cell under the false king's orders. But all was not lost as a gallant breakout occurred and they made their escape from certain death before the Dragon King could arrive to no doubt execute them both.

The revelation comes alongside a story that will shock Solaria and leave them swooning over the star-bound couple who have fought through thick and thin to be together. After battling their feelings for one another at Zodiac Academy, they eventually gave in to their star-driven urge to be together. However, the law which kept Lance Orion from claiming a student as his partner eventually caught up on them and Orion was taken to court for his crime after Kylie Major reported them to the FIB.

But as the truth is unveiled now, we discover the story he spoke upon the stand was none other than a lie to protect the woman he loved, and save her from disgrace by claiming that he Dark Coerced her into having relations with him. A lie which shackled him to a twenty five year sentence in Darkmore Penitentiary and left him Power Shamed and ruined beyond all shadow of a doubt. And yet, today we learn of the great and unimaginable sacrifice he made for the Vega princess to keep her name clear by placing a burden upon himself that some would shudder to even consider.

Since his escape from house arrest at The Palace of Souls, he has been subjected to the full weight of that shaming, his name dragged through the mud time and again while the Fae around him shunned and ridiculed him. But now in a wild twist of fate, the stars have placed a bond upon him and his one true love, lifting the shame from his soul and shining a light on him for all he sacrificed for his Elysian Mate.

Darcy Vega was available for comment, stating that 'Lance is the most devoted, noble and selfless man I have ever met, and I am privileged to be his Elysian Mate'. She also said 'he holds a value to me that's worth more than the sun itself, and I will spend my entire life loving him as he deserves to be loved'.

I looked up at that, finding Darcy beaming at me, her eyes bright and full of emotion as a lump rose in my throat.

"You said that?" I asked and she nodded, leaning in to kiss my cheek softly.

"I meant every word," she swore and I stared at her, speechless before looking to Tyler.

"I was hoping to get a comment from you," Tyler asked. "So I can get it published by the morning."

"I don't know what to say," I said, slumping back in my seat and running a hand over my hair, at a loss, my mind still processing that this was really happening.

I was free of my shame, I had the most unbelievably astounding girl as my Elysian Mate and now the whole world was going to know I wasn't some monster who'd abused her.

"Yes you do." Gabriel murmured to me, a knowing look in his eyes and I breathed a laugh as the words came to me.

Tyler tapped on his Atlas as I spoke, jotting them down as I said the only thing I could really say, "I'm the luckiest man in the whole fucking world."

CALEB

CHAPTER FORTY NINE

The celebrations were pretty intense and I couldn't help but grin, in part because I was pretty fucking wasted but also because things were just going well for once.

My sanguis frater had found his redemption in the Elysian Mate bond and I was bathing in the joy and love being thrown their way by all of the rebels as they seemed to have instantly forgotten that he'd ever been a Power Shamed loser at all.

Hamish had been sobbing so damn much that Catalina had ended up taking him to bed early, and she hadn't even pointed out the hairy balls Xavier had cast on his chin as a dare set by Gabriel. The massive balls had wobbled with every shuddering sob he took, and I had to think it was justice for how he'd treated my blood brother over his Power Shaming. I got the feeling Gabriel had *seen* it that way too as he'd kept running around the hall with Orion earlier, pointing them out to everyone, the two of them cracking up time and again like little kids.

I was enjoying a beer from my seat to the side of the room while I watched the others dancing and I soaked in the sound of fun and laughter all around me. Xavier was caught in the middle of a Tyler/Sofia sandwich, the two of them kissing his neck and releasing happy little whinnies which kept resulting in puffs of glitter flying out over the entire crowd and pretty much everyone in the dining hall was sparkling at this point.

It was almost as though there wasn't a war raging on beyond these tunnels at all. Almost.

My smile fell away though as I caught sight of another pair of dancers across the room, Seth's arms looped around Rosalie Oscura as she moved to the music like she was born for it, her body swaying to the beat and hard not to notice. Except she wasn't the one I was staring at. No. My eyes were on Seth's hands as they skimmed her ass and she tipped her head back to howl loudly, causing Wolves all around the room to follow suit.

They looked good together. Perfectly fucking matched. Two gorgeous, powerful Werewolf Alphas who would no doubt produce the strong kind of offspring his mom and dad would freaking love to fawn all over.

I bit my tongue against the frustration I felt at watching them together, my jaw ticking as another Werewolf girl with long, dark hair moved in to join them followed by a guy with blonde curls who Seth gave a fucking peace sign to in greeting.

Fucking perfect.

My dick throbbed in my jeans as my smile slipped away and I couldn't force out the memory of having him on his knees before me. How fucking good his mouth had felt wrapped around my cock and how spectacularly fucking dumb I'd been to start thinking it had meant something more than that to him.

Sex was like eating to Werewolves. If there was a member of a pack who was hungry, they fed them, and if there was a member with a hard cock, they sucked it for them. End of. I doubted he even remembered it now, my dick lost in a sea of cocks and pussies which he'd had before and since.

I was such a fucking dumbass.

"Why the frown?" Tory asked, a hiccup escaping her as she dropped down into a chair beside me and placed a cake on the table in front of her. It was a gooey chocolate cake which looked fucking delicious, but weirdly had a hole in the middle of it and it looked like it might have been sat on too.

Tory shoved it to the far side of the table with the tips of her fingers, shuddering a little as she left it there and turned those big green eyes on me, waiting for my answer. She looked good. Happy. And there was something about her that lightened the ache in my chest a little because her and Darius really deserved that.

"Nothing. Just trying to decide if I wanna hook up with anyone tonight," I lied, my gaze moving across the room again to where Rosalie was still dancing with the other Wolves, but Seth was gone and I had no idea where he was anymore. Not that I cared. But that blonde dude had disappeared too and there was a lump rising in my throat which made me feel kinda sick.

"Rosalie is looking stupidly hot tonight," Tory said, her gaze following mine as she got the wrong end of the stick, but I didn't bother to correct her. "I think I have a girl crush on her."

"Yeah," I agreed, not saying anything more than that because despite her being right, Rosalie just wasn't who I wanted. "What's with the cake?"

Tory's smile turned wicked and she leaned in close to whisper in my ear. "It's a trap," she said excitedly.

"For who?" I asked.

She glanced around before answering, keeping her voice low once more. "Seth. He keeps stealing all of my goddamn snacks. And I've just been introduced to Orion's lawyers – Darius has already got them working on the paperwork to declare their Elysian Mate status and have the Power Shame thingy wiped from his records."

"You're losing me," I admitted, glancing at the squashed cake once more.

"Well, one of them has a cake fetish. As in, he doesn't get hard for anything without a fondant topping. He was finished with that one." She inclined her head towards the cake and I wrinkled my nose as the hole in the middle of it suddenly made a whole lot of gross sense.

"No way."

"Yes way. And I still haven't gotten revenge on Seth for pissing on me that time. So he has this coming."

"By the stars," I muttered, wondering if I should warn him, but Tory's eyes narrowed dangerously as she realised I might.

"This is Fae on Fae, Caleb. Don't go selling me out."

"Fine," I agreed, though as I eyed the cake, I had to wonder if I could keep my word on that one.

Before I could make that decision, Seth appeared from the crowd, a grin on his face as he spied the cake and I had to fight not to show the relief I felt at realising he hadn't gone off with that blonde dude after all.

"That is *my* cake," Tory warned, pointing her finger at Seth as she hiccupped again. "You can't have any."

"Oh yeah?" he asked, the challenge in his eyes saying he was gonna dive right into that thing headfirst at any moment.

"Seth," I warned, unable to let this happen. "Don't-"

"So now you're on her side?" he demanded in outrage. "After I shared that mega bar of chocolate I found in her room with you?"

Tory gasped, pressing a hand to her chest as she glared at me in accusation. I mouthed an apology to her and Seth took the opportunity to lunge for the cake.

"No!" I yelled and Tory cried out too.

"I changed my mind, it's too gross!"

But Seth already had the cake half way to his mouth, it was too late, or at least I thought it was.

Tory shot him in the face with so much water that he tumbled backwards off of his chair and hit the floor with a crash that rattled the tiles beneath our feet and the cake was sent flying away into the mass of dancing bodies.

"It was a sex cake," Tory explained, a laugh falling from her lips as she got to her feet. "I couldn't go through with it."

"Why?" Seth demanded.

"You peed on me," she replied, the two of them glaring at each other before he barked a laugh and leapt upright once more.

"Well maybe I'll do it again!"

Tory shrieked and took off into the crowd, Seth chasing after her as she stumbled more than a little in her high heels and he howled like he was on the hunt.

My fangs prickled at the sight of her running, but as I pushed myself to my feet, I remembered my promise to Darius about hunting her and curled my hands into fists as I fought to get hold of my instincts.

I crossed the room to get myself another drink, spotting Rosalie Oscura once more as she danced with the blonde dude, and I wondered if I should try to hook up with her again myself. The best way to get over someone was to get under someone else after all. So why did I have about as much interest in doing that as I did in eating that cake?

I spotted my cousin across the room and shot over to join her, downing my beer on the way and falling into the seat at her side as she gave me a little salute in greeting and continued listening to the story Leon was telling her.

"Hey, lost girl," I said in greeting, my nickname for her bringing a smile to her lips.

"Hey, little cousin," she replied and Leon gave me a nod, not pausing for a moment in his story telling.

"-then a man leapt out of the bush with a badger on his ass and beer balanced on top of his head," he said dramatically, gaining more of my attention as he balanced his own drink on his head and Dante called bullshit on his story, causing the two of them to fall into a spat which I watched with amusement.

I sat there with them as Leon moved from one tale to the next, each of them getting more ridiculous until I had no real idea if he was even telling the truth anymore. But no matter how many times he made me laugh, my attention kept straying back to the dance floor where Seth was once again dancing with Rosalie and her Wolf pack.

They kept brushing their hands over his arms and chest, drawing him into their pack and howling in excitement the longer he stayed there. It was fucking annoying.

I tore my gaze away from them one last time and repositioned my chair so that I wasn't able to see them at all, my skin prickling with the desire to turn around and look while I fought with everything I had not to do it.

A girl suddenly dropped into my lap, a giggle falling from her lips as she fluttered her eyelashes at me and reached out to stroke my jaw.

"Hey, I'm Lucy and I'm extremely flexible," she purred. "Wanna find out how much?"

The desire to shove her off of me rose up forcefully but I stopped myself short of doing it as I tried to consider her offer. Seth clearly wasn't interested, so was I just gonna sit over here, listening to Leon's ridiculous stories all night before going off and sleeping alone? I mean, the girl was hot, I couldn't deny that and the way she bit her lip made me think she'd be a fucking firecracker in the sack, but...

"Not tonight, sweetheart," I said, getting to my feet and offering her an apologetic smile as I placed her down on hers.

I needed to Fae up and own my shit though. Because if I wasn't going to bury my problems with a night in this girl's bed then I was going to have to just face them head on. Which meant I needed to talk to my best friend.

But as I turned back to the dance floor, ready to go over there and demand he come talk to me, my heart sank like a stone.

Seth was gone. And so was Rosalie Oscura.

A cold and empty feeling began to grow in my chest as my pulse pounded in my ears and I scoured the room for any sign of them, finding nothing at all. They weren't here. And I hated the thought of where they could be so much that my fangs snapped out at the mere idea of it.

I strained my ears, focusing my attention on the rooms closest to this one and trying to listen out for him, but I heard her instead, Rosalie's voice raised in a pitchy moan.

"Yes, like that," she panted. "Show me how much you want to please me."

A snarl escaped me and I shot towards the sound of her moans before

I could overthink it because I couldn't let this happen. Not without at least asking him if there was any chance he felt the same way I did and wanted something…more.

Fuck.

I shot down a dark tunnel and skidded to a halt outside a door which was cracked open enough to let me hear Rosalie's moans loud and clear.

I threw the door open with a growl, my heart shattering as I took in the sight of Rosalie in the dark room, sitting on the edge of a table, her skirt shoved up and her hand fisted in Seth's long hair as he feasted on her pussy and made her moan loudly again.

"Dalle stelle…yes, like that," she urged in that husky voice, her hips grinding against his face as he licked and sucked at her and she panted loudly for him.

But as I felt like my entire fucking chest was about to cave in, a feminine moan reached my ears which sounded nothing like Rosalie and my breath caught as the girl spoke.

"You taste so good, Alpha," she moaned. "Come for me, say my name as you come on my face."

"I don't know your fucking name," Rosalie cursed. "But maybe if you use your tongue for something more useful than speaking, I'll remember it afterwards."

"Okay." The girl dove between Rosalie's thighs once more, moaning as she got back to eating her out and I reached out to flick the lights on because I had to be certain, but the hope in my chest and what I could see of the dark room already had my heart lightening.

"Ah, stronzo, what the fuck are you doing?" Rosalie snapped as she looked over at me, pushing the girl's head back down between her thighs as she made a move to look around too. "Don't stop," she added and the Wolf on her knees got right back to fucking her with her mouth.

"I was looking for Seth," I said, figuring I might as well own it at this point as I took in the empty room around them and finally accepted that he really wasn't here.

Rosalie's lips curved into a sly grin and she nodded. "Of course you are, siete destinati l'uno all'altro."

"I don't know what that means," I admitted, glancing down at the girl on her knees for a moment as Rosalie bucked her hips and moaned once more.

"You will. I can always tell," Rosalie replied cryptically.

"So…you and him haven't…"

She barked a laugh, holding my eye and not seeming to give a fuck that we were having this conversation while she had her thighs clamped around some girl's head. "No, Vampiro. As much as I might yearn for the taste of an Alpha, I don't want to try and claim one who isn't meant for me. I haven't fucked him since we were all together at your academy last year and I have no intention to be with either of you again now."

"O…kay. Well, I'll leave you to it," I said, fighting a smile at her candid reply and reaching out to flick off the lights.

Rosalie didn't respond, instead tipping back onto the table and commanding the girl to use her fingers too before moaning even louder than before as she clearly followed her instructions.

I pulled the door closed on the sound of the two of them getting more into it and set my jaw as I made a decision. I was going to find Seth tonight and I was going to end this awkwardness between us one way or another. Because I was done being without him and that meant we needed to figure this out.

SETH

CHAPTER FIFTY

I slipped back into the room I shared with Darcy and Orion – well, the one I *had* shared with them until they'd kicked me out when she came back from the Palace of Flames. But I was tired of sleeping on the floor in Max and Xavier's room even if I had made myself a nice cushy, moss nest in there. I couldn't talk to Max about my issues. No, I needed to be around two people who knew the truth and would wanna chat away the rest of the night with me about it until I felt a bit better.

But as the door opened a beat later and Orion and Darcy came crashing into the room, half ripping each other's clothes off as they kissed, I wasn't sure they'd seen me.

I waited for them to notice me, my arms hanging at my sides as Orion pushed Darcy down onto the bed and hitched her dress up, the two of them acting like they were addicted to each other. But they'd done plenty of fucking, and I had to get this off my chest.

I opened my mouth, but wasn't sure what to say so I closed it again as Darcy encouraged Orion to roll onto his back then tore his shirt open and started kissing her way down his body, his eyes on her as lust sparked in his eyes.

I considered fetching some of the snacks I'd stashed under my bed and waiting this out, not wanting to be rude considering this was their mating night and everything, but as Darcy undid his fly and I took a step backwards towards my snack stash, the movement caught Orion's attention and his gaze shot onto me like a bullet.

"Seth!" he roared and Darcy's head snapped up but she squeaked as her hair got snagged in Orion's fly.

"Ow, ow, ow," she hissed as she fought to get it free and Orion sat upright, trying to help her.

"Oh, that's a tricky one, I've dealt with it a bunch of times though, I can get free for you." I hurried forward, reaching out to help but Orion smacked my hand away and I whined.

"Why'd you do that?" I demanded and he growled at me.

"Because I don't want your hand near my cock," he spat.

"Well then I guess I'm gonna go snippy snip on Darcy's hair like old times," I joked but the two of them didn't like that joke.

"You are not snipping my hair, Seth Capella," Darcy warned. "Or I'll snip your balls off."

"Then let me jiggle it free. I have the magic touch," I promised and Darcy sighed, nodding to Orion to make him back off, but wincing as she made her hair pull against the zip.

I leaned in close, my face right in front of Orion's cock which was still rock hard and bulging against his jeans.

"For the love of the moon," Orion sighed as I took hold of Darcy's hair and gently did a twist and pull move which had saved many a Fae's hair. There was nothing worse than a hair snag when you were trying to get down and dirty.

"That's it," I said as it loosened.

"Maybe pull it that way," Darcy suggested, my head knocking against hers.

"Just get it over with," Orion encouraged.

"I need to slide it this way then use my teeth a little," I said.

"Yeah, like that," Darcy said excitedly as the hair started to come free.

"Almost there," Orion said as he watched us and my head bobbed up and down as I tugged it softly between my teeth while wiggling the end of it which was snagged.

"What in the love of fuck is going on in here?" Caleb's voice rang through the room.

"What does it look like?" I said through a mouthful of hair.

"It looks like you're sucking off our old professor with his fucking mate," Caleb barked and strong hands latched around me just as I got the hair free.

Darcy squeaked with joy as she sat upright and I was dragged across the room by Caleb and thrown against the wall. He pinned me there by the throat, his eyes full of hostility.

"Cal," I choked out, trying to get his hand off of my neck as he stared at me with something burning deep in his navy blue eyes. And it looked a lot like hurt.

"My hair got caught in Lance's zipper," Darcy explained, grabbing Caleb's arm and trying to pull it away from my throat.

Caleb's grip slackened as he glanced over at Orion whose cock was still very much in his pants as he shifted up the bed.

"Do you really think I'd let the mutt near my dick?" he scoffed.

Caleb dropped his arm, releasing a long breath and I realised his shoulders were shaking.

"Cal, what's going on?" I asked, my voice thick as awkwardness descended on us fast.

I had no idea how to talk to him anymore, like the moment I'd put his cock in my mouth had changed everything. And I wished I could fucking take it back. Because my worst fears had come to life and I knew I was losing him more with every day that passed. But now he'd shown up here. and I couldn't figure out what the hell he was thinking.

"You're my Source," he barked suddenly, wheeling around and looing to Orion. "I'm taking my Source," he announced and Orion's eyebrows arched.

"Sure, sanguis frater," Orion said easily. "Enjoy."

His eyes moved hungrily to Darcy and Caleb suddenly picked me up like a fucking baby, one arm under my legs and his other around my back.

"What are you doing?" I whispered in confusion.

"I'm hungry," he muttered then stepped out of the room.

"C'mere you," Orion growled, shooting towards Darcy who laughed giddily as he threw the door shut behind us, the sound of a lock clicking following us.

Caleb put on a burst of speed and the next thing I knew, I was being tossed down on his bed and he was pacing before me like a wild animal.

"Are you looking to fight me?" I asked, my shoulders squaring as my Alpha instincts raised their head, responding to the fury in his eyes.

"No," he seethed. "Just shut up and listen to me for a second."

"Okay, but-"

"Seth," he snarled, rounding towards me as I moved to sit on the edge of the bed. "You're my best friend and I don't want to lose you. We grew up together. We've been there through the good and bad for each other, so one meaningless blowjob doesn't get to ruin that."

I nodded slowly, my throat so tight it hurt, the word meaningless circling in my head like a vulture come to feast on my broken heart.

"So how do we move past this? How do we get back what we had?" Cal demanded, leaning down so he was nose to nose with me and I suddenly couldn't draw any breath at all. Because I knew there was no way for me to go back, I was done for, a damned Wolf who'd already pledged his heart to his best friend and there was no taking it back. But I had always been so very fucking good at pretending.

"It doesn't have to change things," I said. "I fuck all my friends," I insisted, feeding him that line of bullshit again. But it was the only one I had which saved my pride. Because if I admitted that I was hopelessly, relentlessly in love with him, then everything would change permanently between us. He'd dance around my feelings, try to say it was alright while withdrawing from me and feeling awkward about getting too close to me again. So if I could convince him it had meant absolutely nothing, then maybe we could find something salvageable in that. Even if the idea of him regretting what had happened destroyed me inside. "I just thought maybe you felt awkward about it, so I was giving you some space, but I mean it. It's easier for me to count the friends I haven't fucked than the ones I have. Like I think I'm down to seven now…"

"Right," Caleb hissed, returning to pacing. "So it was just a one time thing. Just a stupid decision while I wasn't thinking straight because I was hungry, and you were offering out pity BJs like you do with your Wolf pack whenever one of them hasn't gotten laid in a long time."

I hesitated, every piece of my nature wanting to say no. No, it hadn't been like that for me. I'd wanted to make him feel good because I fucking loved him, and I'd thought for a second that was what he wanted too. But I'd gotten carried away and now I felt kind of sick as I feared what he might think of me for doing that. Maybe he thought I'd taken advantage of him, mistaking his blood boner for something more. And maybe that *was* what had happened. Maybe I'd wanted him so bad and had dreamed about that moment for so damn long, that all rational thought had abandoned me because of how much I'd wanted to believe he liked me back.

"Yeah," I rasped, the truth too bitter a thing to air. "That's all it was."

I hated those words leaving my mouth. They tasted like ash and soot and fucking death. The death of any chance of anything ever happening between us again. And it hurt, by the stars did it fucking hurt. I could feel that door closing, locking tight never to be opened again. I didn't know if this was more painful than living with a small ray of hope that he might like me too, or if knowing he didn't was akin to the absolute shattering of my soul. Either way, I was vacationing in Spain without the S.

"Right," he said again.

"Right," I echoed once more and he came to a halt before me, his fingers curling and uncurling, and he was just so achingly fucking gorgeous that it broke my heart all over again as I stared up at him.

"I'm hungry," he said. "Will you still be my Source, still take part in the hunt with me?"

I almost said no for my own sake, knowing it was going to be ten times worse to feel his mouth on me now knowing how certain it was that he didn't desire anything from me but my blood. But I was also a selfish, selfish loser and still wanted to steal those moments with him even if they only ended up crushing my heart a little more.

"Sure," I said lightly like it meant nothing.

He wet his lips, his gaze falling to my neck. "I have a lot of feelings I need to work through tonight," he said. "Vampire feelings. I've been away from you for too long, and as my Source I need to…do some stuff. Okay?"

"Okay," I agreed so fucking easily that it was sad really. Because if Caleb needed to tie me to the ceiling by my ankles and wrists and drain my blood like a sacrifice to a god, then slap my ass and call me Mr Willing.

His eyes glinted then he lunged at me, his body pressing me down into the sheets as he grabbed my wrists and pinned them above my head. My breaths came unevenly as I bucked my hips, not wanting to play victim, my instincts too fierce to let him just have my blood like that.

I rolled us over, wrenching my wrists free of his grip and pinning his wrists to the bed instead.

He bared his fangs at me and I smirked over my victory before he bucked me off of him, yanking his hands free and punching me in the kidney.

"Motherfucker," I wheezed as he threw me off and I hit the floor face down, rising up onto my knees before a heavy weight slammed down on top of me.

Caleb gripped my hair in his fist, his knees pressing hard against the insides of mine to keep me down and I gave up trying to fight as he wrenched my head sideways and dug his fangs into my throat.

A traitorous moan left my mouth and his hips ground forward at the sound, his cock hard against my ass as I panted and tried not to get confused again.

It's about my blood. Just my blood.

He drank deeply, holding me at his mercy while I fought not to give too much attention to how much I loved the feeling of his mouth on my skin and he didn't pull back until I was a little woozy. He stood up, taking my arm and pulling me upright too before tugging his shirt off and dropping his pants.

"Um…" My gaze fell down his sculpted body, my cock throbbing and my head a fog of confusion.

"We're going to bed," he said.

"Right," I muttered, pulling my own clothes off until I was just in my boxers and his gaze skimmed down the outline of my cock which was saluting him, and I cursed it for trying to give the game away. We needed to have a serious dickscussion, because I couldn't go around visiting boner town while Cal was looking.

Caleb said nothing, leading me to the bed, whipping the covers back and pointing.

"Get in," he commanded and I arched a brow at him, but did as he said.

He followed me, pushing me so I rolled away from him before wrapping his arms around me and drawing me flush against him, my back to his chest. His fingers traced over the bite mark on my neck and I shivered as he healed the wound, trying to ignore the rush of blood to my dick and the feel of his hard muscles moulding against mine.

"You're my Source," he said in my ear. "And you're my best friend. So you're gonna stay here with me from now on."

"Yes, master," I whispered.

"What?" he snapped and I chuckled.

"Joking," I said and he broke a laugh, his body relaxing as he kept me firm against him.

It wasn't like we hadn't snuggled before, but something about this felt more intentional, and I had to keep reminding myself that this was a Vampire Source thing that I would probably never understand. But I wasn't going to complain about it, because for the first night in more nights than I could count, I finally felt peaceful, able to drift off almost instantly as I was held by the man I loved, even though I knew he could never truly be mine.

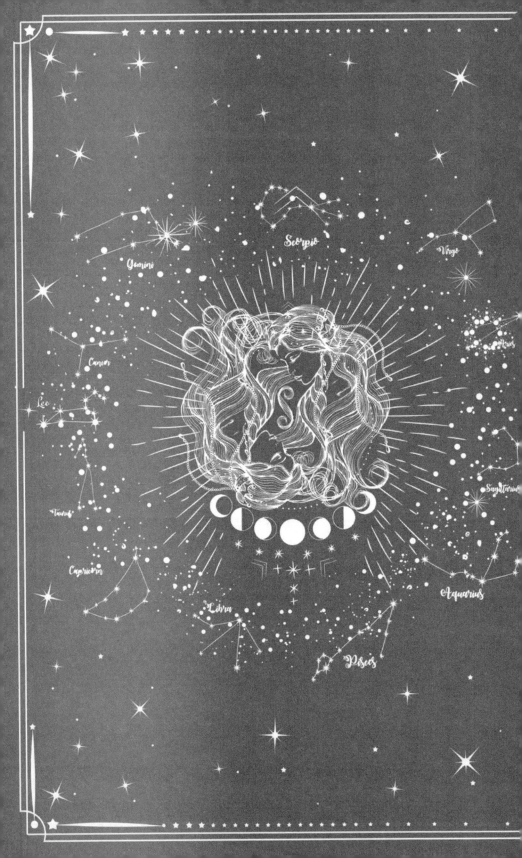

TORY

CHAPTER FIFTY ONE

I groaned as I woke, the chuckle of a smug Dragon asshole rumbling through my brain and making it rattle as my parched tongue clung to the roof of my mouth like cottonwool and I reached around blindly for a glass of water.

"Here." Something hard and cold met my lips and I parted them to suck on the icicle like a dying woman, the cool water melting into my mouth and alleviating some of the self-inflicted issues I was currently suffering from.

"If this icicle looks like a dick, I'm going to be pissed," I muttered around it before sucking on it again.

"I could make you one of those if you like?" Darius offered in a teasing tone. Then I could use it to-"

"Dude. Do I look like a woman wanting some double penetration with a side of frost bite to the vag in this moment?" I asked, snatching the icicle from his hand and cracking my eyes open as I continued to suck on it.

Darius tilted his head to one side as if he couldn't decide on that and I slapped his arm, forcing myself to sit up with a groan.

"Okay, so perhaps not right now," he conceded. "But maybe after you've drowned your hangover in greasy food…"

I smacked him again but my smirk turned somewhat flirtatious as I gave the idea a little more of my attention before shaking my head and banishing it. I'd learned that lesson the hard way - literally. Indulging any of his fantasies for more than eight seconds resulted in him playing them out on my body. And I wasn't really complaining about that, but right now I needed to pee, eat and mentally process the level of shame I had exposed myself to last night.

There were memories of me and Lance crawling around under tables while trying to hide from Seth that kept playing through my head on repeat and I shuddered as I thought of the prank I'd almost played on him too. I mean, he totally deserved it for that time he peed on me, so I guessed I would have to call us even now, but he was likely still pretty pissed about it.

"You wanna skip our run this morning?" Darius asked as I got out of bed and started hunting for some clothes. I was wearing one of Darius's shirts but my panties were long gone and I had some rather vivid memories of him bending me over the bed and making me scream for him after we stumbled back here last night, not to mention the ache between my thighs which he'd left behind as evidence. I was pretty sure he'd put my half crown from The Palace of Flames on his head for some of it too, laughing through my curses and making me come so hard I forgot to complain about it.

Honestly, if we'd met in the mortal realm, I probably would have had a rest schedule planned out for my vagina between rounds with him. But as I could heal that shit, I was good to go on demand instead and as my gaze fell on his bare chest and the icicle I'd abandoned on the bed, I started to give his suggestion some consideration.

No, Tory. Don't let him tempt you back in before breakfast.

"Food first. Then the creepy map thing," I said decisively. "We have shadow rifts to close up today."

Geraldine had taken charge of the map of espial last night, telling me she would take the greatest care of it and saving me from having to be responsible for the thing, so I wasn't complaining.

Darius drew his bottom lip between his teeth as he continued to watch me from the bed and I narrowed my eyes as I looked at him, sensing there was something he wasn't saying.

"Spit it out, big man," I demanded and his gaze snapped up from my legs to my eyes as he sighed.

"When we close those rifts, Lavinia and my father will be vulnerable at last," he said. "Which means it will be time to strike at them."

"Yeah, that's the plan," I teased.

"Roxy…I want you to agree to let me be the one who goes after Lionel."

I frowned, the desire to see that lizard asshole's head ripped off and laying at my feet rising in me fiercely for all I'd suffered at his hands, but as I opened my mouth to demand I get a shot at him, I hesitated. Yes, I'd spent months in the company of that twisted motherfucker and I'd suffered massively in that time, but Darius had endured a lifetime of that. Even my treatment at his father's hands circled back to him really, Lionel had struck out at the people surrounding him to hurt him too. Me, Orion, Xavier, Catalina. He'd been suffering since the day he was born under the rule of that tyrant so was it really my place to try and take his death from him?

"And what would that make you if you were the one to kill the king?" I asked in a low voice because there was more to this than just figuring out which of us deserved the killing blow more.

Darius exhaled slowly, his gaze staying fixed on mine. "A man worthy of you," he replied. "Or at least I hope it would. If I could claim vengeance for the suffering he's forced upon you and everyone else. If I could turn the wrath he's always offered me back on him and end him and his power for good, then I would like to think I might have done enough to make up for everything else."

I moved towards him, reaching out to cup his cheek in my palm and feeling the intensity of our souls reaching out towards one another as the love between us crackled in the air.

"Killing him isn't what makes you worthy of me," I said, my thumb tracing over his cheekbone as I drank him in. "This love between us is what proves that. You've given me something I never dared hope for and I know you're still not perfect, but I don't want perfect. I want your flaws, your temper, your power, and your passion. I want *you*, Darius Acrux. Not a white knight who slayed a Dragon for me."

A smile lifted his lips and he pushed to his feet so that he could kiss me with an intensity that made my pulse race and crash like thunder in my chest. Or at least it did until my stomach growled loudly and he broke away from me with a chuckle.

"Let's go get you fed, baby," he said seriously and I nodded as I finished up my clothes hunt, putting on a teal sweatpants and crop top set before tying my dark hair in a messy bun and pulling on some snuggly socks.

Darius dressed in a grey tank and black sweats too, dropping a huge arm around my shoulders as we headed for the door and leading me outside into the corridor.

"This way, my lady!" Geraldine cried and I turned, looking along the tunnel to her room where she stood in the doorway, waving me over. "Oh and you too, you dastardly Dragoon, I hadn't noticed you there!" she added, though that made no sense because Darius had been standing between me and her and he was fucking huge, but I just smirked at him as I turned us her way and the scent of food filled the air.

An honest to shit moan escaped me as we reached her doorway and the scent grew stronger, my gaze falling on the table she'd cast in the middle of the room in place of her bed and the one beyond it which was laden with food. All the best, most unhealthy, greasy food and not a fucking mango in sight.

"Fuck me, Geraldine, you created heaven in here," I groaned eagerly as I ditched Darius and headed straight for the food.

"No, my lady. I created a war council," she replied triumphantly. "And we have been slaving away since the crack of dawn to prepare this feast for it."

"We?" I asked in confusion before almost jumping out of my damn skin as Max stood from behind the table, a plate of pancakes in his hand which he placed down amongst the feast.

"It was three in the morning, not dawn," he grumbled, wiping his cheek with the back of his hand to remove a smear of flour while only making it worse. "And you made me leave the party to do it. If I'd realised what you'd meant when you invited me back to your room to mix your muffins, I wouldn't have come. I assumed you weren't actually talking about muffins."

"Whatever else would I have meant?" she asked him.

"Sex, Gerry. Sex."

"Oh, you are so vulgar at times. Now don't be a wet willy at the dining table, you will make the food all sombre," Geraldine cried, flapping a washcloth at him like she was trying to waft the complaint away on the breeze.

"Well whatever it is, I'm here for it," I said enthusiastically, piling my plate up with so much food that I knew I'd seriously struggle to eat all of it, but that was a challenge I was willing to take up.

I moved around the room to take a seat at Geraldine's war table and she directed me into a chair with a high back and intricate carvings all over it of things like Phoenixes and crowns and a group of guys who looked suspiciously like the Heirs all bowing low to two queens.

Geraldine shrieked as Darius made a move to take the matching chair beside me and chased him away from it, directing him onto a three-legged stool on my other side which matched all the rest of the seats around the table in their plainness.

As I started to eat, Geraldine moved to take the metal tube which contained the map of espial from her nightstand and pulled the map out of it with a dramatic flourish, flicking her wrists so that it unfurled before her as she laid it in the centre of the table.

I paused with my fork halfway to my mouth as Geraldine reached out to place her finger on the map of Solaria, a beat of magic pulsing from her which seemed to activate the thing. My lips parted as mountains and forests grew from the page, rivers started to move, waves crested in the sea and clouds formed to hang in an imitation of the sky above it, some of them white and fluffy, others dark and spilling rain or flickering with lightning.

"Wow," I breathed and Darius's hand slipped over my thigh beneath the table as he gave me a light squeeze.

"I forget how damn mortal you are sometimes," he teased but as I looked up at him, I found nothing but fondness in his dark gaze as he watched my fascination like it was more interesting than the map itself.

"That thing is cool," I protested just as the door opened and Darcy walked in with an, "Ooooh."

Orion chuckled as she hurried over to get a closer look and he moved away to get her food together for her as Caleb and Seth strolled in too.

"Gather round, gather round!" Geraldine called loudly. "Fill your bellies and let us prepare to peer through the eye of our enemies."

"Is Xavier coming?" Darius asked, looking around for any sign of his brother but Caleb shook his head.

"There was so much fucking whinnying and moaning going on in his room, man. He's way too busy to be joining us any time soon."

"Then he shall have to go without," Geraldine announced with a wave of her hand. "If his jolly dipper is taking precedence over this task then so be it."

"Can we not with the jolly dipper talk while I'm eating?" Darius muttered and Geraldine sighed like she thought he was being dramatic.

Everyone grabbed plates of food and I focused on eating as she whipped the spyglass from a drawer in her nightstand next, not wanting to look at the gross eye which was suspended in the end of it as I ate.

"Who would like to peruse the downfall of the false king?" Geraldine offered, holding out the spyglass as she dropped to one knee and I wrinkled my nose in distaste.

"Fuck no," Caleb said through a mouthful of toast. "You told me that thing will crawl into my face and devour my eye if it gets the chance. My eyes are too pretty to be devoured."

"Yes, *if* you give it the chance," Geraldine sighed like she was addressing a simpleton. "But I have utter faith in the spyglass which contains it. I am at least forty percent certain that it cannot escape and crawl into anyone's faces. Never fear."

"Forty percent is not good odds," Seth balked. "I don't want it near my face either."

"Give it here," Darius said with a huff, holding his hand out for it but Geraldine's gaze slid from him to me and Darcy as a little whimper escaped her.

"It should really be an honour for the true queens," she said and I glanced at Darcy who physically recoiled.

"Fine," I said, trying to ignore the way the thing was looking at me as she pointed it at me. I reached out to grab the metal tube which contained it so that I didn't have to suffer through her sobbing about the shame of someone else doing it before us.

"I don't think that's a good idea, Tor," Darcy said, shaking her head in refusal.

"Neither do I," Darius agreed, snapping his hand out to try and snatch it from me but I yanked it aside, my stubborn streak flaring at his demanding tone.

"Well tough shit, asshole," I said, leaning away from him so that he couldn't steal it from me.

I raised the spyglass cautiously, not quite touching it to my face as I peered through the glass at the other end of it to the shadow eye and I sucked in a sharp breath as I found myself looking through the creepy thing.

The world seemed darker through it, hazier somehow. And as I turned it to face the map, I saw things I hadn't before. A dark coil of power hovered over The Palace of Souls which I could only assume was due to Lavinia herself. But as I turned my focus from that, I noticed more slithers of shadows dotted around the map, the rifts revealing themselves one by one until I counted out seven of them.

"There," I pointed and Geraldine squealed as she grabbed a standard paper map and marked the location on it with an X. "And there," I pointed out another which looked like it was hidden within the depths of a canyon that had been formed in reddish rock to the east of the kingdom.

I continued pointing them out until she had them all marked down and handed the spyglass to Darius as he held his hand out for it to take a look himself, muttering about me being a brat while I shrugged innocently.

I wiped my palm on my pants once I released it, glad to be rid of the thing and shuddering at the memories brought on by the sight of that damn red and black eye.

Max stood and moved towards me, placing a hand on my shoulder as the memories pressed in on me and the sounds of my own screams rang in my ears. He didn't steal the emotions from me like he once had done for me though, he just helped me as I used the memories to fuel my rage towards Vard, Lionel, Lavinia and their whole regime, vowing to see them fall no matter what it took from me to do so.

"So what's the plan?" I asked, looking over at Orion and he frowned in concentration as he scrutinised the map Geraldine had drawn out.

"Without stardust it will take us weeks to travel to some of these locations. Unless we could get hold of an aircraft maybe, but it will be damn hard to board one without the FIB noticing," he said in frustration. "And if we want to hit them all at once like we planned to then that means us splitting up for that amount of time too."

"This whole stardust situation is a bitch," Caleb grumbled and I knew the fact that they hadn't managed to get their hands on more of the priceless substance had been causing a lot of issues while Darcy and I had been gone.

"We only need one bagful," Darius growled. "We have to be able to get our hands on that much to-"

There was a knock at the door and we all looked around as Gabriel opened it and stepped inside.

"Noxy," Orion greeted warmly. "Where have you been? We started without you."

"Sorry," Gabriel replied. "I had to make a deal with a seriously irritating Lion Shifter who had been keeping this 'for a rainy day.'" He tossed a bag of stardust onto the table between all of us and I grinned widely as my eyes fell on it.

"That's enough, isn't it?" I asked, looking to Darius for confirmation as he took the bag in his hand and weighed it.

"Yeah, I think it will be. Only just though and I doubt more than two people can head to any one of the locations with this amount."

I glanced around our group but Gabriel interrupted before I could make any kinds of plans about the way we would need to divide ourselves to get that done.

"Seth and Orio should go to this one in the desert," he said. "You'll need speed and a strong shield, though I can't tell much more. Then Geraldine and Darcy to that one. Darius and Max over in that cavern. I can get some members of my family to help take out the two in the north and the one in the snowfields by the Polar Capital, and Tory and Caleb can handle the one in that canyon."

"I'm going with Roxy," Darius demanded.

"No. The cavern will require brute strength and the canyon needs speed. If we split up the way I suggest I see a possible future where we all return here later on tonight. Any other combination and the fates shift, making it less and less likely that we will succeed."

Darius looked ready to argue but I punched him in the bicep. "Don't you think I can handle this?" I demanded, making his brow furrow.

"I just want to be there to protect you."

"Well you heard Gabriel, if you change up the dynamics you're putting her in danger," Darcy said firmly and I couldn't help but grin as my twin got my back.

"Fine," Darius said after scouring the table for an ally and not finding one. "Let's get this over with then."

"Does anyone need to go over the way to use the binding needle again?" Orion asked, his posture tight with tension as he placed a box on the table and opened it to reveal the additional binding needles he'd been creating in anticipation of this. There were ten of them in total, though luckily we wouldn't need that many and the others had all been taught enough dark magic to successfully sew the rifts closed when we reached them. He'd been planning to teach me and Darcy too but we hadn't gotten enough practice in yet, so I was going to be handing that task over to Caleb.

"I'm good," Darius confirmed and the others all nodded their agreement as we stood.

"Alright then, let's go." Gabriel turned and headed back out of the room, grabbing a couple of bagels as he went and Seth sidled around the table to join Orion, looking like his damn tail would be wagging if he had been in his Wolf form.

"I can't believe we're mission buddies," Seth whispered loudly, nudging Orion who didn't return his smile. In fact, the look he was giving him was kinda like an anti-smile if that was even a thing. "It must be fate."

"Well, I guess I've used up all my good luck gaining my mate so I was due some bad to balance it out." Orion strode from the room and I giggled with Darcy as we headed off to grab our weapons.

"This could be it," she breathed, taking my hand and squeezing my fingers tightly. "If this works, we could be taking Lionel and Lavinia down and claiming our throne back before the year is out."

My brows rose at the idea of that. I hadn't really let myself give too much thought to the possibility of what our world might look like if we really did win this war. I was too caught up in the endless struggle to get to that point to really spend any time thinking about what would happen when we did, but she was right. Everything might just be about to change, and I suddenly found myself unsure of what that would mean.

We'd come to a level of peace with the Heirs which I'd grown so used to that I'd forgotten that they were against us too when it came down to it. What was that going to mean for the six of us once Lionel was out of the equation? What would it mean for me and Darius?

I followed Darcy with that gut churning thought on my mind and tried my hardest to push it aside. Because no matter what might come after this war, we still needed to win it. And today we would be striking a brutal blow.

The stardust dropped us from its grasp at the foot of the huge ravine where I knew the rift was hidden and I gasped as I craned my neck back to look up at the sliver of blue sky so far above my head that it made my head spin.

"The Ravine of Cragoon is over three miles deep at its lowest point," Caleb said as he followed my gaze and moved a little closer to me.

"So what are the chances that there isn't anyone down here then?" I asked, looking down and taking in our surroundings.

The rocky walls gave way to a vibrant woodland which seemed to be thriving in this little paradise, hidden away from the world. There were birds chirping in the trees and small mammals darting around between the undergrowth and I could hear the distant sound of running water too.

"There is an old legend that an ancient and forgotten tribe of Fae lives down here somewhere," he replied thoughtfully. "Though no one has ever managed to gain evidence of there being any truth to that. But the entire ravine is protected by Solarian law to keep visitors from coming down here and destroying this precious habitat. You have to get special permission from the royal line to even set foot down here and since the Savage King died, there hasn't been anyone to grant access to explorers who may have wanted to find out more."

"How would anyone know they'd come here?" I asked curiously as I looked up and down the ravine, wondering where to start our search. "Is there a magical alarm?"

"Yeah. But it alerts my mom rather than Lionel since your family was killed so she will have recognised my magical signature and shouldn't raise the alarm."

"Let's hope not," I agreed with a feeling of foreboding rattling through my limbs.

"Hop on then, we can search much faster at my speed than yours." Caleb turned his back on me, patting his shoulder and I moved closer so that I could jump on, wondering if our history made this weird or not.

"We're cool, aren't we?" I asked him to make sure and he glanced back at me with a confused look before catching on to what I was really asking.

"Yeah, don't you worry, sweetheart. I have someone else fucking with my feelings these days."

"Is that what you think I did to you?" I asked uncomfortably and he snorted.

"A little. But not in any way I didn't want. And honestly? I think no matter what the stars had intended for you and Darius there never could have been a long term for us. So let's just keep it as fond memories that we never mention to your boyfriend because I don't want him to BBQ me, and stay comfortably in the friend zone."

"Sounds good to me. So are you going to tell me who's messing with your emotions now?" I asked.

"How about I tell you once we close this rift?" he suggested, his smile slipping. "Because I don't even know where to start with it and this is probably more important."

"Okay," I agreed and he shot away without another word.

A laugh was ripped from me as I clung to him, my eyes squinting against the onslaught of air as we raced between trees, leapt over a river and sped through the entire canyon so fast that my brain was left spinning as he skidded to a halt on the gravel which lined the edge of the river and let me down.

Water crashed past us in a rush, the drop to it making my pulse thump harder as I looked into the churning rapids and felt the cold spray on my face.

"Well, that's a bitch," Caleb said, pointing to a spot about six feet above the tumultuous water and making me curse as I spotted the flicking darkness which marked the rift's position in the world.

"You're going to have to trust me, dude," I said as I took in the challenge and wrapped Caleb in my air magic before plucking him off of his feet as he pulled the binding needle from his pocket.

"And you're going to have to hold me incredibly still," he replied as I lifted him to hang above the water before the rift.

"You sound like you don't trust me," I said.

"It's not about trust. It's about me getting sucked into the fucking Shadow Realm if you screw up. So don't screw up, Tory. I have too fucking much to live for."

I snorted as I concentrated on holding him still and Caleb reached out to start stitching the cut between realms back together.

"This is going surprisingly well," I called out to him as I looked around at the trees, wondering if I should be bracing for an attack. But the birds continued to sing and the sun continued to shine down into the ravine from far, far above and there was nothing to suggest that was going to change.

I flinched at the sound of a breaking branch, looking around in alarm as I fought to hold Caleb perfectly still, my heart racing as I hunted for any sign of something approaching us through the trees.

It was hard to listen for movement over the roar of the rapids so close to me and my eyes darted left and right as I scanned my surroundings, bracing for an attack and calling my Phoenix to the surface of my skin as I waited for whatever it was to burst from the forest.

Had Caleb been wrong? Had that warning been sent to Lionel after all? Or were there Nymphs hiding here between the trees, waiting to pounce?

I was so on edge that when Caleb called out to me, I flinched so fucking hard I almost fell over my own feet while standing freaking still.

"That's it," he announced.

"Seriously?" I asked in surprise, rounding to face him and drawing him back to land with my air magic.

"Yep. Orion made such a fuss about how hard that was, but I think he must have just been looking for an ego stroke because that was a piece of cake. Of course, there was all those dark artifacts at the last one and yada yada, but whatever. I totally aced that."

I blinked at him for several seconds, unable to believe that something had just gone to plan for us so easily.

"Looks like the stars are finally favouring us," I said with a breath of laughter.

"Let's hope they're favouring the others too," he agreed, moving close to me and taking the tiny pinch of stardust from its bag.

I took hold of his arm to make the journey even easier, hoping we had enough stardust to make it the entire way and Caleb tossed it over us.

My gut lurched as I was tugged into the embrace of the stars, spinning in circles which made me dizzy before finally tumbling from their clutches where the two of us fell on our asses in the lush grass outside The Burrows.

"Fuck. Now I remember why I hate travelling with stardust when you don't have enough of it," Caleb groaned as I let myself fall back and laughed, watching the clouds rotate above me and remembering lying in the grass like this with Darcy when we were kids.

We'd spin around and around until we fell over then watch the heavens twist and turn for us like we were on a ride at a fair. Of course that had been about as close as we'd ever gotten to a fair so maybe it wouldn't have felt like that at all, but it was what we imagined at the time.

Caleb cursed and I looked around just as Darcy appeared out of thin air, falling right on top of him with Geraldine at her side, tumbling down too.

"Oh holy man abs, I have died and gone to buns heaven!" Geraldine cried as she face planted Caleb's stomach and Darcy apologised as she scrambled away from his crotch while I just laughed at them.

"Did you do it?" I asked.

"Yep," Darcy agreed. "I guess the Nymphs didn't know about that one or something because it was just sitting there waiting for us."

"Ours too," I told her, pushing to my feet as the air rippled again and

Gabriel appeared with Leon beside him, the two of them quickly explaining how badly guarded their rift had been before Dante and Rosalie reappeared too, confirming they'd closed theirs as well.

My heart lifted with excitement as I turned to look for a sign of the others returning, hope burning through me at the thought of us managing this so fucking easily.

But those hopes were dashed as Orion and Seth appeared, Seth howling loudly while Orion apologised to him, the scent of burning hair and blood clinging to them strongly enough to catch in my throat.

"-told you it was an accident! It's not like I meant to do it," Orion barked.

"I know what this was, Lance Orion. It was hairmocide pure and simple!" Seth snarled and as he turned to look at us, a gasp escaped me as I took in the right side of his head where almost all of his long, brown hair had been burnt clean off of his head. His face was stained with soot and he was drenched from head to toe in water.

"What happened?" Darcy asked as she hurried forward, giving Orion the once over while searching him for injuries.

"Your clumsy boyfriend sheared half my fucking hair off with his Phoenix fire sword," Seth growled though the sound turned into a whimper as he pawed at his ruined hair.

"No. You were the dumb fucker who did a hair flick in the middle of a fucking battle," Orion snapped. "How was I supposed to know that I'd end up beheading your hair as well as the Nymph?"

"Your rift was guarded?" I asked anxiously as I looked around for any sign of Darius.

"Yeah," Orion confirmed. "But we managed to close it before too many of them could come for us."

"We were working together like a dream team," Seth said wistfully. Darcy let out a little squeak of excitement as she looked between the two of them hopefully and Orion gave her a look that said 'no chance'. "Right up until he decided to play Sweeney Todd with my luscious locks anyway."

A snigger drew my attention over my shoulder and I found Gabriel standing there with his fist pressed to his lips as he and Leon both worked really damn hard not to fall apart entirely while looking at the state of Seth's hair.

"You knew!" Seth accused suddenly, raising a shaking finger to point at Gabriel as he spotted him laughing and I fell apart too as I realised he was right. Gabriel must have *seen* this coming and hadn't done a damn thing to stop it.

"Serves you right for cutting my sister's hair off, mutt," he taunted and Dante boomed a laugh behind him just as Seth lunged.

Gabriel was already sidestepping him before he even got close and I watched them with amusement for a few minutes while Seth tried his hardest to punch Solaria's greatest Seer in the face without success.

But despite my amusement over seeing him get another taste of his own medicine, I couldn't fully focus on their to and fro while my mind was consumed with fear for Darius.

I caught Geraldine's eye across the group, seeing her own fear for Max in her features and I moved to her side, nudging her with my elbow.

"They'll be fine," I said, as much to myself as it was to her.

"Oh, I'm certain of it, my lady," she agreed enthusiastically. "I'm more concerned about mortal wounds or maiming than I am of death. Lost limbs or jagged gashes, half eaten appendages or-"

"Yeah, I get it," I said, my voice a little harsh as I willed her to stop.

"Oh sweet heavens, I am so sorry. Of course your Dragoon is most unlikely to have been half eaten or to have had a foot cut off or a finger shoved up the bombardier of a badger, or-"

A flash of light ended her terrifying ramblings and I squealed like a love struck idiot as Darius and Max finally appeared, darting forward to throw myself into my Dragon's arms before skidding to a halt before him as I took in the sticky green substance which covered him from head to toe.

"You could have mentioned the fucking eperious slug which lived in that cesspit of a cavern, Gabriel," Darius growled angrily, his chest rising and falling heavily as he dripped slime all over the floor.

Max was covered in the sludge too and he wiped it from his face aggressively, flicking it from his fingertips so that it splattered the grass beside him and I took a measured step back. The hug could wait.

"Oh right, yeah...sorry about that," Gabriel said with that knowing asshole glint in his eyes again and I snorted my amusement before I could stop myself.

"You *saw* that too?" Darcy asked him, biting her lip to hold back her smile.

"What's an eperious slug?" I asked curiously, taking another step away from Darius as he tried to wipe some more slime from his body, but it seemed to be sticking.

"Oh it is a most gruesome of beasts," Geraldine supplied. "A huge and carnivorous slug which is big enough to eat an entire minivan in one bite when at full size. It likes to dwell in dark, dank caverns and wait for creatures to wander inside unawares. Then it pounces, traps them in its slime and devours them whole where they will be slowly dissolved within its stomach acid over a period of around a week. It is said to be a most horrendous way to die."

"Yeah, it would have been," Darius growled. "But we managed to blast our way out of the fucking thing eventually - it took almost every drop of magic I own to do it though."

"The slime burns," Max groaned and Gabriel laughed louder. My brother could be such a dick sometimes. I kinda loved that about him though. "I need to get inside and wash it off."

"Not on your Nelly!" Geraldine cried, raising her hands and blasting the two of them with so much water that they were knocked clean off of their feet by it and sent tumbling away down the hill as they yelled at her to stop.

She didn't stop though, not until every bit of slime was blasted from them and they were left panting and cursing in a puddle of mud at the foot of the hill.

"I can't have The Burrows full of that foul slime," Geraldine explained as if her actions had been perfectly reasonable and I shook my head at her as I jogged down the hill to help Darius to his feet.

He looked all kinds of pissed as he stalked back up the hill, scowling at both Gabriel then Geraldine before turning his attention to Orion who was the only one who was managing to rein in his laughter.

"We closed the rift despite the fucking slug," he said firmly. "So is that it? Have we done all we need to do to weaken Lavinia?"

"I think so," Orion confirmed. "I can check the soul hat and see if Miguel can confirm it, but if it's worked then we can get the rebels ready to march at last. We can bring the war to Lionel's door and finally rip the crown from his unworthy head."

"I have a better plan," Darius said. "As soon as my magic is replenished, I'll go to him myself. We don't need to risk the army in a war against him if I can just take his head. I'm bigger than him, just as strong and I have far more desire to win than he could ever muster. I can end this entire thing tonight and we can be done with this fucking war for good."

"No," I snapped as the others all voiced protests too. "Just because Lavinia will have been weakened by this doesn't guarantee she isn't a threat at all anymore. And what about Vard? Or Lionel's Dragon guild? You can't just expect us to agree to you flying off to face all of them alone."

"Well if it fails then you can go ahead with your plan to bring an army to his gates," Darius replied firmly. "But it has to be worth taking the chance. This way the only life we're risking is mine and-"

"I'm not willing to risk your life, Darius, what is so hard to understand about that?" I demanded and his eyes flashed with his Dragon as irritation rose in him because I wouldn't just let him take charge of this. But he wasn't in charge here and there was no way in hell that I would be letting him do something so dumb as to fly off into a fight he couldn't possibly be certain that he would win.

"Better my life than any of yours," he barked back and Gabriel sucked in a breath, his eyes clouding with a vision and distracting me for a moment as Orion looked to him too.

"How can you suggest that your life is worth less than any of ours?" Seth asked and I looked back at Darius furiously as I waited for that answer.

"It's not worth less," he growled. "But Christmas is right around the corner anyway, so it makes sense for me to just-"

"What the fuck does Christmas have to do with anything?" Max asked, his expression pinching like he'd read some emotion he didn't like the taste of.

"I just have to face my father before then," Darius said angrily, smoke coiling between his teeth as he glared at us like he was challenging us to question that.

"Why?" I asked. "Who the fuck cares about Christmas while all of this is going on?"

"I do," he replied, his gaze meeting mine and pain sparking there for a moment before his anger devoured it just as fast.

"Well I don't care what bullshit timescales you've put on Lionel's lifespan," I replied. "Because this isn't up to you and you're not fucking flying off into the night on some suicide mission. We need to make a plan to bring this fight to him the way we have been preparing to for the last year and-"

"I don't have that long Roxy," Darius said, moving forward and grabbing my arms as he forced me to look at him again.

Ice formed around my heart at the look in his eyes and a breath fell from my lungs as I stared up at him, feeling this moment hanging on a knife's edge as I hesitated on the question which I knew I had to ask next because I didn't need The Sight to tell me that I wouldn't like this answer. I could already feel the pain of it humming in the air, waiting to devour me.

"Why?" I breathed and something in his gaze shattered as he opened his mouth to give me my answer.

"Because I'm dying, Roxy."

Silence weighed heavily all around us, the kind that stung and rang on and was filled with an eternity of nothing because breaking it was only going to make his words into a reality.

"No you're not," I denied, taking hold of his forearms and squeezing so tightly that my fingernails marked his skin. "You're right here before me, solid and unbreakable. You're not dying, Darius. There's nothing wrong with you."

"I made a deal with the stars," he breathed. "Last Christmas when the fight broke out at The Palace of Souls, Gabriel took me to the Caves of the Forgotten and he led me to a room where I made a deal with a star to save your life."

"No," I said, shaking my head as those words crept into my skull and took root. "No." I refused the truth of what he was saying to me because it made far too much sense.

"The bonds," Darcy breathed as her hand landed on my shoulder and she moved up behind me, lending me support while the injustice of it all built in my veins, the reality, the fucking truth.

Darius was nodding even though I was shaking my head. "They showed me your death. Both of you. And they offered me a chance to save you, to twist fate and give us a shot at defeating my father. Every bond placed on us broken and a single year to prove I could have been a man worthy of your love, Roxy."

"No," Orion snarled.

"A year?" I gasped, my heart hammering as I realised how fucking close we were to that time coming to an end already.

"That's why you were so angry when they went to The Palace of Flames," Orion said in realisation, his voice cracking. "Because your time with her was being stolen?"

Darius nodded, but he didn't look away from me, taking my face between his hands and willing me to understand this fucked up choice he'd made for me without even doing me the curtesy of letting me know about it.

"No time with you would ever have been enough, Roxy. You have to know that. A year, a lifetime, a fucking eternity would never be enough. But I couldn't let you die. I had to make the choice. I had to-"

My fist snapped out and I punched him so hard that I was pretty sure something broke in my hand as a scream erupted from me that defied all logic or reason or understanding, and was instead filled with the pain and terror of knowing that I was so close to losing him already.

The only man I would ever love. The only one I ever wanted. The one I fucking needed with every fibre of my soul. And he'd lied to me about this. Let me waste months that I could have spent searching for a solution and leaving me with weeks to find one instead.

It was too much. Too fucking much.

"You didn't have the right to make that choice for me," I hissed, blood from his busted lip staining my knuckles as I backed up a step and he just stared at me with heartbreak in his eyes which I didn't want to face because he was the one who had done this to us and it wasn't fair for him to look at me like that.

"Roxy," he began but I shook my head fiercely.

"No," I snarled, all of my hurt and fury and pain over this fucking lie lashing at him within that single word with enough force to make him flinch.

I shook my head as I took another step back, looking at this man I thought I knew so well who lied so fucking easily to me like he was a stranger, because that was what this felt like. The actions of someone I didn't even know. Or worse than that, the actions of the monster who had always been destined to destroy me in the end.

And with my heart breaking and soul shredding, so much anger burning through me that I couldn't even bear to look at him, my wings snapped out and I took off into the sky, flying the fuck away from him and all of it, the fucking war, his fucking father and my goddamn heart which was ripping into a thousand pieces as tears spilled down my cheeks and were stolen by the freezing cold bite of the wind.

ORION

CHAPTER FIFTY TWO

I stared at Darius, shocked into silence as fear made my lungs cease to work. Darcy headed after her sister, her wings bursting from her back as she chased her into the sky and I took a step towards Darius, but the Heirs got there first, surrounding him like a pack of Wolves and demanding answers. I couldn't hear them though. I couldn't hear anything but the ringing in my ears as I tried to process the fact that one of my best friends in the whole world had traded his life and was going to fucking die.

And the worst thing was, I should have known. I should have realised the bonds wouldn't be broken for nothing. And deep down, maybe I had. Maybe I hadn't pushed him on the subject because I knew there was a price and I couldn't bear to know the truth of it. Or maybe I was just a shitty fucking friend who hadn't realised this whole star damned time that there was a secret lurking in his eyes. Because it was so fucking obvious now. He'd been evasive, he'd made comments I'd shrugged off, he'd even said goodbye to me though I'd put that down to him talking about worst case scenarios, but now it made a whole lot of sense that left my head spinning.

"Noxy," I turned to Gabriel and he reached out with pain in his eyes, gripping my arm as Leon gathered up Rosalie and Dante, the three of them heading away inside. "You knew?"

"I'm so sorry, Orio," he breathed. "Really. I am. It wasn't my place to say."

I nodded, my head hanging as Seth's mournful howl filled the sky and I felt the pain of that noise cleaving my chest right open down the centre.

"There's no way to stop this?" I asked Gabriel even though he'd said it already, but I had to hear it again, because surely there had to be a chance. Even one percent of a chance. Some fate that could spin on a coin and change for him. But he just shook his head sadly, closing that tiny window of hope in my heart and bolting it shut.

The Heirs took it in turns to embrace Darius and Caleb went to sit on a boulder, his head sinking into his hands as Seth hurried to sit at his side and nuzzled into him. Max spoke in a low tone with Darius, his hand on his arm like he was syphoning away some of the emotions raging within him and I picked up the odd words about him offering to make this easier for everyone if that was what Darius wanted. But I didn't want that. If this was really going to happen, then I was going to face every soul wrenching slice of it. I wasn't going to shy away from the pain, even when it was the most tempting thing in the world to cling to denial and use it as a pacifier. But Darius's eyes said it all and as he met my gaze and inclined his head in an offer for me to come closer, I gave in to the need in him, striding forward and wrapping my arms around him tight.

"Fuck you," I snarled in his ear and he clapped my back as emotion burned all the way down my throat into the pit of my stomach.

"I'm so fucking sorry, Lance."

"You don't get to be sorry, you asshole," I ground out. "Because I know why you did it."

"You'd have done the same thing," he said and I wanted to punch him in the head, but instead I held him more firmly, refusing to let go, terrified of the moment hanging over us in the future where I'd never get to hold him like this again.

"What can I do?" I asked helplessly, wanting to solve this like I always wanted to solve everything. I wanted to dive into my books and search for an answer, I wanted to shake Noxy until he came up with one too, because doing nothing wasn't an option.

"Don't change," he begged. "Don't treat me like a dying man. Just be you, the Lance Orion I fucking love, who tells me when I'm being an asshole and tries to convince me to share the throne with the Vegas."

I laughed weakly, still not letting go of him.

A horrified whinny broke through the air and I turned, finding Xavier there running along with Catalina at his heels. Caleb stepped out after them, a grim look on his face that said he'd fetched them and told them the news.

"Darius, tell me it's not true," Xavier demanded and I released his brother, letting Xavier step up and grab Darius by his shirt, fisting it hard as he bared his teeth at him.

"I'm sorry, Xavier," Darius said heavily as Catalina collided with him, sobbing so loudly it seemed to fill up the whole world. And when Darius explained once more, Xavier sagged against him, clinging to him as he cried into his brother's chest and somehow that was worse than feeling it myself. Seeing everyone fall apart around him. It was like standing at his wake, only he was alive and staring back at us. But his fate was just as sealed, just as impossible to change.

Gabriel slid a hand onto my shoulder and guided me away. I knew I had to give Darius time with his family and the Heirs drifted after us too. And as we headed inside, I glanced back at my friend, knowing I would never be ready to say goodbye to him.

DARIUS

CHAPTER FIFTY THREE

I sat in my bed draped in gold and feeling like the world's biggest asshole as I just bathed in the silence that had followed me facing the truth of my situation at last. I'd tried to stay with my friends and family but after a few hours, my mom's tears and their devastated expressions just got too much and I begged for some time alone.

But now that I *was* alone, I was starting to think that it was worse. I wanted them around me, to bathe in their presence and soak it all up while I could. But that was exactly why I hadn't told them about this before now. Because they wouldn't act that way anymore. I was the doomed man now, biding my time until death came for me.

The fear, pain and pity wouldn't be banished from them, and I would never again get to spend time with them without its company.

I was grieving that loss as I sat there. The simple joy of spending time with the people I loved without them knowing our time was running short.

But I was missing Roxy most of all.

I hadn't healed the split lip she'd given me. The small sting of pain an all too little reminder of what this would do to her. And I hated myself for that more forcefully than I hated myself for every other awful thing I'd done in my life combined.

If I tried to consider our roles in reverse, knowing that I only had weeks left before her death and that I'd be facing a future without her beyond that, I couldn't breathe. The mere thought of living without her was a horror unlike any other I could imagine, and I knew it wasn't a future that I would have been able to bear. It terrified me that I might be destined to leave her in even an inch of the pain that I knew I would suffer when being torn from her embrace when my time came and the stars collected on this debt I owed them. It had seemed like a long time when I'd agreed to it, but now? Now it was a drop in the ocean of the endless amount of love I wished to share with that girl. She deserved so much better than this fate. So much fucking better than me.

There was a knock at the door and my pulse quickened as I called out that it was open, hoping like a fool that it would be her, that she would have returned and would be in my arms again where I needed her.

But of course it wasn't her. That wasn't her style. She was hurt which meant she was angry, and fuck knew how long she would maintain that rage for or how long she would keep away. And I got it. I wanted her to have that time to rage at me if she needed it, to fucking hate me all over again for doing this to her, but I was also running so low on time with her now that the thought of days or weeks going by without her forgiveness terrified me far more than the fate that awaited me on Christmas Day.

I didn't fear death. But I did fear a destiny which meant I never got to kiss her goodbye.

Darcy stepped into the room, her eyes red and puffy but her expression firm.

"Hey," I said lamely, unsure what I was supposed to say to her, knowing she must hate me too for what I was doing to her twin. Hurting her all over again after I'd sworn I never would.

"Darius..." she said softly, her gaze moving over me as she hesitated a moment before darting forward and throwing her arms around my neck as she lunged at me.

It took me a couple of seconds to return her embrace, the shock of it catching me off guard as I'd expected anger from her too.

"Thank you," she breathed against my ear, a tear falling on my neck as she squeezed me tightly. "I can't imagine how much you must have been hurting, keeping this secret for so long and I hate that you made this deal, I hate it so goddamn much. But I get it. You did it for her. Because you love her. And I can't be angry at you for making this sacrifice to save my sister's life no matter how bitter the price may be."

I sighed, relaxing into her embrace as I let that pain in my chest lessen just a little, holding onto that one fact which I'd clung to throughout all of these months every time I'd been tempted to fall into the trap of fear over my fate. Because I didn't regret my choice. I would have made it again a thousand times over for her. For them.

"I did it for you too," I told her. "The stars showed me your death on the cards too, little shrew. And I couldn't have that."

She sobbed as she clutched me harder, more tears falling against my skin as she held me like she really cared about me. And I realised just how much I cared about her too. She was like a little sister to me now. My silly little shrew of a sister who ran me around in circles as easily as breathing.

"You're a good man, Darius. So much better than the monster who tried to forge you in his image. The world will be a far emptier place without you in it."

I wasn't sure what to say to that, though the words meant more to me than I could describe, especially coming from her. She saved me from trying to answer them by pulling back, cupping my cheek in her hand and smiling sadly.

"She loves you so much that she doesn't know what to do with it all," she breathed. "Don't hate her for being angry."

"I could never hate her," I murmured and she nodded, getting up and backing away.

"She could never hate you either. Even before, even when she wanted to with all her heart. She didn't, Darius."

The door closed behind her and I was left with those words and the endless regrets I had over the way I'd treated Roxy when we'd first met. Everything between us could have been so different if only I'd found a way to defy my father sooner. Though I knew now that regrets weren't worth the memories they lingered in.

I sighed, getting up and hauling my chest of gold into my arms before pouring the lot of it across the bed so that I could replenish my magic faster. Not that I intended to head out after my father now. I couldn't risk death without trying to fix this with Roxy. Without saying goodbye to her properly before I went.

I tugged my shirt off and sat on the bed again, placing more rings, necklaces and bangles on before picking up a golden crown and looking at it thoughtfully. Somehow, I didn't want to feel the press of it on my head tonight.

I hadn't ever been born to wear a crown. All I really wanted was for Solaria to be ruled by people who knew what was best for its subjects. And I had to accept that whatever way this war went now, that was never going to be my fate. I wouldn't share the throne with the other Heirs, I wouldn't take my place on the Celestial Council. I wouldn't even see in the new year ever again.

This was it for me. My final days on countdown and all I could hope was that I would at least see my father fall before I left this world behind and passed beyond the Veil.

I closed my eyes and I didn't even bother to fight sleep as it pushed at me, the exhaustion I felt from using too many wakefulness spells and anti-sleep draughts weighing down on me after so many months of avoiding it. I hadn't wanted to miss a moment of the time I had left to me, but now I found myself wanting the escape of sleep at last.

I wanted to leave this empty room behind and dream of the girl I loved, have her in that way if I couldn't hold her close in reality.

I drifted off quickly, but my sleep was far from restful, plagued by nightmares or visions of Roxy grieving me when I was gone.

But as I fell deeper into the despair which was summoned by knowing how much I was going to cost her, I was called back from the brink by the sound of a door clicking closed.

I jerked awake, a small cascade of gold coins falling to the floor as my eyes found hers across the room and I fought to hold myself still, staring at her as intently as she was staring at me.

"I'm so fucking angry with you, Darius," Roxy breathed, her voice laced with pain which I wished I could banish.

"I'm sorry, baby," I said, knowing it didn't fucking matter how sorry I was.

"I'm really, really angry," she reiterated, her wings flaring at her spine as fire danced in her eyes. "But...I'm not going to waste the time we do have on that feeling."

"You're not?" I asked, my throat bobbing with hope at that idea, and she shook her head as I moved to sit up.

"We have a war to win," she said firmly, taking a step towards me.

"Hamish and the others are already working on the details. We will bring the fight to The Palace of Souls before the week is out. Darcy and I will have hundreds of weapons to bless with our flames to help arm the rebels against the Nymphs so that they can stand against them. And you will swear to me that you won't attempt to go after Lionel before then."

I stared at her as she took another step closer, the distance between us dissolving as she made her demands of me, and I found all of my desire to fight her just fading away. I'd made this deal for her. She owned me anyway. So why keep fighting against the commands of my queen?

"Okay," I agreed.

Roxy stepped forward and pushed her hand into my hair, tilting my head back as she looked at my eyes and I fell into the trap of hers. Those endless green eyes which held my entire soul captive and owned every piece of me entirely.

"Are you wondering what they would have looked like ringed in silver for you?" I asked her and her lips lifted a little as she shook her head, her wings flexing at her back.

"No. I don't want the stars to choose you for me, Darius. I chose you for myself and that's exactly how I like it. Fate doesn't get a say in it. You're my mate because *I* picked you, not them. You're my match because *you* proved that you were the only one for me, not destiny. Our love burns hot with unmatchable passion and eternal devotion as endless as the entire universe because we fucking fought for it in a way no other Fae have ever done before and none ever will. You're not some gift from the stars to me, Darius. You're the spoils of a war no one else ever could have won but us. So I'll take your eyes as endlessly dark as the day you first set them on me. And if the stars come offering us rings in them again, I'll give them the same answer as I did before. Because no, I don't want them to choose you for me or me for you. I don't want them to do a damn thing for us. We don't need them. I made you mine without them and I'm yours without them too."

"So goddamn stubborn," I commented and she gave me the ghost of a smile.

"I just know what I want."

Her hand dropped to skim along my jaw, her eyes moving over my face like she was committing it to memory and as much as I loved the feel of her attention being focused on me, I hated the reason behind it. I hated that she needed to be able to remember me and that this moment and any other I stole with her between now and my end was limited.

Her hand trailed down my neck, fingertips gliding over my shoulder and caressing the ink there, her chin dipping as her gaze roamed lower, drinking me in inch by inch until her hand made it all the way down my arm and she was clasping her fingers with mine.

"Swear it," she said, her tone unwavering and her gaze hard. That was my girl. Any softness was always tempered with steel and she might have been back here, might have wanted to hold me close and kiss away the hurt of this, but she was still angry as all hell with me and I knew I deserved it.

"You don't trust me?" I asked.

"After finding our you've been lying to me throughout our entire relationship? Strangely, no, I don't." Her eyes flashed with Phoenix fire which made my pulse spike and her wings shuffled a little, the sound of rustling feathers drawing my gaze to them.

"Our relationship started long before I got hold of you in my arms," I protested.

"Well if you would like me to count all of the days I spent expecting you to hurt me in any and every way you could imagine then that won't help your case much. Besides, this is arguably the worst thing you've done to me," she replied.

"Roxy," I breathed, my voice breaking on that name, a plea there for something though I wasn't certain what I could possibly ask of her now.

"Swear it," she repeated, tone unwavering and I gave in because when it came down to it, I would always do anything for her.

"I swear I won't go after my father before the battle," I replied, magic crashing between our palms and binding me to that oath.

"Now swear you won't allow this fate to pass," she said, her tone darkening and something sweeping through her eyes which reminded me of the shadows. There had always been dark in her though, exactly like there was dark in me. No doubt it was part of the attraction.

I wetted my lips, my heart tearing open at that demand in her eyes and the fact that she wanted me to make a vow like that at all.

"You know me swearing that won't change it," I said softly.

"I know you're giving up," she replied in a deadly calm tone, though I could see the pain in her green eyes. "And I know that the man who fought so damn hard to claim me from the stars wouldn't just give up on me that easily."

"That's what you think?" I asked, my blood heating at her suggestion as she just arched a brow at me and didn't take those words back.

"I think you got too used to taking a kicking when you lived with your father, Darius. So now, instead of fighting this with all you have you're just rolling over and taking it."

"You're a bitch sometimes," I growled.

"That doesn't make me wrong," she replied, shrugging one shoulder.

"What do you expect me to do, Roxy?" I demanded, my temper rising despite myself.

"Well you defied the stars for me once already. So what's once more?" she asked.

"This fate was the price of that defiance," I said, my soul aching at the words I was having to speak, but I'd thought about this. I'd thought of nothing *but* this for months on end and I couldn't see any way to change it. "I was gifted a year to love you and that's what I've done."

"If you love me so much then why are you so set on leaving me? Destroying me?" she asked icily.

"I'm not," I protested.

"So swear it, Darius."

"Gabriel already looked into my future. He knows there's no way around this. No way out of it. My fate is already decided. Even if I'd told all of you months ago, he knew as well as I did that all it would do was distract you from the war because you'd all have been looking for a way to change this fate and there isn't one. Don't you think I would have done everything in my power to change it if I could?"

"Apparently not." Her fingers tightened around mine and I growled at her, letting her see the Dragon in me but she just flexed the bronze wings at her back in reply, letting me see her monster too.

Roxy took a Lapis Lazuli crystal from her pocket, turning my hand over and painting the constellation of my star sign on it before painting her own hand with hers. She arched a brow at me as she took my hand again, the demand clear that she wanted me to make a star promise with her.

I looked at this woman, this princess, this ultimate fantasy of mine and she stared me down as she waited me out, knowing that when it came down to it, I could never deny her anything she desired of me. So if she wanted me to swear I'd pluck my fucking soul from the grip of the heavens after I died and return it to her keeping where it belonged then I'd swear it. No matter if I was just one man going up against all the stars in the heavens for her, because there was no fight I wouldn't face in her name. No matter how impossibly the odds were stacked.

"I won't allow this fate to pass," I said.

"Neither will I," she replied darkly and I gasped, trying to snatch my hand from hers but the magic clapped between us before I could pull away and she was left standing over me, smiling triumphantly and waiting for me to lose my shit over what she'd just done.

"Did you seriously just curse us both?" I demanded as I snatched my hand away from hers and she tossed the crystal aside.

"No," she replied. "I intend to keep that vow."

"And what if you can't? I can hardly release you from it beyond the grave."

"You won't need to if you stick to your word."

"What you're talking about is impossible," I insisted.

"*We* were impossible once, Darius Acrux. So don't try to put limitations on what we can or can't do."

My throat bobbed as I looked at her, wanting to break that vow out of fear, but wanting to uphold it even more out of love. Because of course I didn't want to die. I didn't want to lose her. I wanted to agree to every want she had of me and promise her the entire world at her side.

"I love you, Roxanya Vega," I said, my voice raw with the truth of that. "No matter what happens with this fate, the war, my father, the throne, all of it pales beside my love for you. And I know I'm not good enough for you but that just makes it all the easier for me to worship you the way you deserve because I won't ever stop trying to live up to being the man you deserve to have. Not until my dying breath and beyond that too if it's what you want."

"*You're* what I want," she replied firmly.

Her palm moved to my chest and she pushed me back so that I shifted to sit against the headboard, my gaze latched to hers as she slowly stripped out of the clothes she was wearing, dropping them to puddle at her feet and stepping free of them in her matching black bra and panties.

My gaze roamed over her deep bronze skin, taking in the swell of her tits and the rise and fall of her heavy breaths before dropping to the hourglass curve of her toned waist and round ass, descending to that tattoo which bound her to me and made my fucking heart sing every single time I laid my eyes on it.

She was right. The stars couldn't have this. They couldn't take us away. It was too powerful, too beautiful, too fucking right. And I wouldn't let them have it because it was mine. She was my most prized treasure and I would hoard her away from the sight of the stars themselves if that was what it took to keep her.

Roxy moved onto the bed, climbing into my lap and dropping her forehead to rest against mine as she closed her eyes and breathed me in just like I was inhaling her. She was intoxicating, this creature of mine, soul destroying, heart breaking, endlessly everything.

I ran my hands up her spine beneath her wings until I found the place where they joined with her shoulder blades and I started to run my fingers back and forth along that ridge of skin and feathers.

"Mine," I murmured, repeating what I'd said to this girl more times than I could count now, but it had never felt so brutally honest.

"Even beyond the Veil," she breathed and I nodded, turning my face and kissing her neck beneath her ear, making her shiver for me as I continued to massage that sensitive spot where her wings emerged from her back.

Roxy shifted her hips over mine and I groaned as she rode over the solid ridge of my dick within my pants, a breath drawn in between those most kissable of lips as she felt how much I wanted her in every atom of my body.

I moved my mouth to the corner of her jaw, kissing her again and she rocked her hips once more, this slow, sensual movement which made a growl build in the back of my throat as coins cascaded from the bed beneath us.

I found the corner of her lips and kissed her once more, my stubble biting against soft flesh and the taste of saltwater coating my tongue as a tear tracked down her cheek.

"I love you," I swore to her, knowing I couldn't take that hurt away with those words but hoping she felt the truth of them all the same.

"I love you too," she replied, turning her head to meet my kiss and the taste of her tears passed between us as I kissed her so sweetly that it made me ache. I could feel every heart breaking thump of her heart where my hand still caressed her spine, her whole body seeming to thrum with that pulse which held so much fear and sorrow.

She parted her lips for my tongue and I deepened our kiss, wishing our first could have been like this, that she could have felt how much she meant to me in it instead of only ever seeing the worst of me.

But that wasn't true anymore. I stood before her ripped open and without barriers and still she was here in my arms, her hands clasped behind my neck as she held me close and kissed me like I was the sole reason for her existence. I was the empire she was looking to conquer. I was the destiny she had picked for herself. So if she needed me to keep fighting for us beyond this life then I would. I'd fight to stay and I'd refuse to leave even when the heavens came to drag me from this unworthy body, even if it cost me my place in the afterlife.

Because an eternity with the stars meant nothing to me in comparison to a life in her arms.

Roxy rolled her hips once more and I groaned with the need to have her. It didn't matter how many times we came together, I always hungered for her like this and now more than ever I needed to feel our bodies connected as one.

I ran my fingers down her spine as I continued to kiss her tears away and I slowly unclasped her bra, dragging it down her arms and tossing it aside as my hands found their way to her nipples.

She moaned softly as I moved my fingers over her pebbled flesh, her nipples two hard and aching points which I tugged and teased before breaking our kiss and dropping my mouth to suck one of them between my lips.

Roxy arched back, her long hair tumbling down her spine as she continued to rock her hips against mine to that slow and heady rhythm which had my cock straining for more against the fabric containing it.

The noises which filled the air from her sultry lips made my flesh come alive and as I moved my mouth to her other nipple, I dropped my hands to grip the sides of her panties and began to roll them down.

Roxy drew back, standing once more and dropping her underwear, watching me as I took my pants off too and her gaze fell to my dick as it was revealed, her tongue wetting her lips as she climbed back onto me.

I kissed her again as she moved to straddle me, the slickness of her pussy grinding up the length of my shaft and making us both shudder with the need to claim one another.

My cock found her entrance without either of us needing to guide it, her spine arching in the most seductive way as she leaned forward and the tip of my dick moved inside of her.

"There is only you, Roxy," I said, finding her evergreen eyes and holding them. "The stars can have it all, everything else of me but you."

"There's only you too, Darius," she replied, her hands moving to my shoulders as she sank the rest of the way down onto my cock, a moan escaping that perfect mouth of hers which made my entire body tremble with want for her.

She held my gaze as she started up a slow rhythm on top of me, tears still slipping free to roll down her cheeks every few moments, but as I was consumed by my need for her, they began to sizzle away to nothing when they fell against my chest, the heat of my Dragon burning through my skin as I came undone for her.

Roxy's eyes blazed as the heat between us continued to rise and I dropped my fingers to her clit, devouring her moans of pleasure with my kisses as I began to rub slow circles around the sensitised spot in time with the rhythm of her hips against mine.

Her palms pressed to my chest and the weight of her magic against mine had me cursing as I dropped my barriers and let her in, the combined heat of our magic tumbling through my core like liquid flames.

The heat between us continued to rise as I moved my hips to her rhythm, guiding her with my hands on her as I started to drive myself in deeper, making her breath catch with every deep thrust of my cock inside her.

I could feel the pressure in her body building and building like a coil just begging to snap and continued to massage her clit as she fought against that pleasure, growling her name in demand as I drove up into her and kissing her hard until she finally fell apart for me.

But as her pussy pulsed and squeezed my shaft, the heat between us grew even further, the flame she'd gifted me with that Phoenix Kiss rising up in my chest to meet with her own flames once more and suddenly, we were burning.

I cursed as I broke our kiss, my eyes widening as I looked at the blue and red flames which had consumed not only her flesh, but mine as well, this fire between us catching light and claiming everything around us just like we were claiming each other.

Roxy rolled her hips again and a Dragon's roar escaped me as the burn between us ran through my veins making every single point of contact between us buzz with a pleasure unlike anything I'd ever known.

Her wings spread wide at her back, the fire gilding them so beautifully that I could only stare at this stunning creature and marvel at my luck for making her mine.

Roxy moaned as she rode up and down the length of my cock and I thrust up into her, staring at her as she cried out for every drive of my cock inside her and I felt the gold coins melting beneath us with the power of our flames.

The red and blue fire was interspersed with the gold of my Dragon and there was something so captivating in the way it coated her flesh that it was all I could do to stare at her and try to make this moment between us last and last eternally.

But of course, my body could no sooner hold off her destruction than I could stop the days from passing us by and as I continued to fuck her deep and slow, I knew I was closing in on my end.

I pushed up to kiss her again, the tears burned away by the fire now so that all I could taste on her lips was the desire and love I felt just as keenly for her.

I gripped her ass and rolled us over, pinning her wings beneath her as I hooked her leg over my arm and drove my cock in just right to make her gasp my name for me as I found that perfect spot inside her body and delivered her all the pleasure that I could manage.

Roxy's lips found mine once more as I drove my hips down on her, keeping up that slow torment as I kissed her deeply, my tongue dancing with hers as I thrust into her one more time and she came for me so beautifully that I had no choice but to join her in her climax.

I kissed her hard as I came inside her, filling her with my seed and marking her as mine as her pussy pulsed around me and the flames between us finally died out.

We fell panting onto the bed which still dripped molten gold to the floor, and I couldn't even find it in me to care about my destroyed treasure as I wound my arms around her and held her so tightly that I could almost convince myself I would never have to let go.

"Marry me, Roxy," I said, knowing it was unfair of me to ask but doing it all the same. Because there were a lot of things I wasn't going to get to do with my life now but I didn't want to miss out on that.

"Stay with me, Darius," she replied, asking me to do the one thing I was almost certain I couldn't. But if there was any way in which I could, then I'd do it for her.

"If I can then I will," I replied honestly, hating that I couldn't swear it any more definitely than that.

"Then I'll marry you," she replied. "No bullshit. Just us."

"Really?" I asked, my chest swelling with the idea of that, of her being mine in such an unmovable way.

"Really."

I woke in the arms of the woman I loved with melted treasure coating the bed and sticking us to the damn mattress.

Roxy groaned as she woke too, one of her legs also stuck in the now solidified gold though the rest of her body had been draped over mine, so she'd escaped the worst of it.

I wasn't really sure where to start with trying to fix it, but she just rolled her eyes at me when I made a comment about it as she lifted her hand, using her earth magic to take control of the metal and force it all back into the form it had taken before we'd managed to turn it into a molten gloop. She tossed the coins and jewellery back into the treasure chest beside the bed with a flick of her wrist then got out of bed before I could stop her.

"We need to plan our attack on your father today," she said, moving across the room and opening the wardrobe, flicking through her clothes aggressively.

"We do," I agreed, trailing her movements with my eyes and trying not to focus on how many more mornings we had left before the stars came to collect their debt. Because I knew they would. I could make as many vows as I liked and fight as hard as I was capable of, but in the end I saw no real way out of this fate for us, despite how much I wished there could be.

"So we need to hurry." She took the long, golden dress she'd worn back from The Palace of Flames out of the wardrobe and dressed in it while I continued to watch her. "I'm pretty sure you shouldn't be looking at me, dude."

"I'm not your dude," I growled irritably. "And why shouldn't I be looking at you?"

"Have you changed your mind already?" she asked curiously. "Because you're the one all set on marriage. I'm perfectly content living a life of sin."

"Truly?" I asked, suddenly feeling a whole lot more awake as I pushed myself upright.

"I told you, no bullshit. You want to do this, or you don't. I'm not doing the whole massive crowd and virgin white thing either. You can take me as I am or not at all."

"You know how I like to take you," I said roughly and she offered me a smirk in return.

"Let's go then. I already texted Geraldine and the others so no doubt she's freaking the fuck out and making some insane preparations with zero timescale. I don't want to give her long enough to make it fancy."

"Heaven forbid," I teased.

"War council starts in half an hour," she tossed back and I arched a brow.

"You're serious," I stated.

"Are you going to become a Vega or what?" she asked irritably and I could tell this whole thing was pushing her out of her comfort zone, but there she was, looking good enough to eat and waiting for me to marry her.

"You'll be an Acrux," I corrected and she gave me a wicked smile.

"Oh no. I know how it works here. The couple takes the name of the most powerful Fae in the relationship. And that would be me in this scenario."

My lips parted in surprise as she said that and I realised she was right. My whole life there had never been a prospect of there being a mate for me who could be the more powerful party, so I had always assumed any wife of mine would take my name. But her claim was true. Then again, she still hadn't taken me on and won, so I was unlikely to bow to her power any time soon.

"You'll have to put me on my ass before I'll admit that's true, baby," I replied.

Roxy glanced at the golden clock which sat on the nightstand and sighed. "No time. We can figure out the name thing after we kill your father then. His severed head can sit and watch me kick your ass so he gets a front row seat to the moment when his precious Heir is forced to bow at long last and the final shred of hope for his empire dies. It'll be romantic."

"Fuck I love it when you talk like a psychopath," I said.

"I do it a whole lot more since I met you," she replied.

A frantic pounding at the door drew our attention and she sighed.

"That'll be the bullshit. Hurry the fuck up before this whole thing gets too weddingy."

"Stars forbid," I agreed sarcastically and she flipped me off before heading to the door where Geraldine's shrieks of excitement pierced the air so loudly that I feared for my eardrums.

I caught sight of Darcy and Sofia there too and raised my hand in greeting half a second before Roxy was tugged outside and the door was slammed in my face while Geraldine commanded me to scrub my eyes of the sight of her queen.

That girl was honestly fucking insane but I could admit that she was growing on me a little.

Xavier, the Heirs and Orion arrived within another few minutes as I was buttoning my shirt and I couldn't help the shit eating grin that pulled at my lips as they all leapt on me, howling congratulations and slapping me on the back. Seth had shorn his hair down on the side that Orion had burned, with braids winding across it and through the other side of his hair too. Darcy said he looked like a Viking warrior, whatever the fuck that meant, and despite us mocking him for it, I was pretty sure we all quietly thought it looked damn good on him.

I headed up out of The Burrows, finding my mom and Hamish in the farmhouse which hid it from view with Gabriel and his family and she rushed at me as she saw me, wrapping me in her arms and telling me this was the proudest day of her life.

I crushed her in my embrace, trying not to feel the resentment I harboured over the years that had been stolen from us by my father in favour of just holding tight to the time we'd been gifted now.

"I'm so proud of you," Mom breathed, clutching the front of my shirt and looking up at me with tears in her eyes. "Your father worked so hard to make you into a mirror image of the man he was but despite all of the odds set against you, you fought off the weight of his influence and grew into your own man. A man who could win back your heart from the clutches of the stars themselves. A man who is worthy of the love of that girl out there."

I pulled her into my arms as those words touched a chord deep inside me and plucked on it with a resounding note that echoed right down to my bones. Because those words embodied everything about what I had been trying to prove I could become over this last year and hearing them from the lips of the woman whose love I had been denied for so long meant the world to me. We should have been gifted more time to enjoy together, but if I could believe those words then at least I could pass out of this world knowing that I'd done enough to prove what kind of man I could have been to everyone around me and they could remember me as a man who was worth remembering.

Roxy was waiting for me at the furthest edge of the boundary which surrounded The Burrows where the hills dropped away to reveal the stunning view beyond where eagles swooped across the landscape and every shade of autumn bloomed across the trees, their leaves racing through the sky on the cold wind that promised an end to their glory.

My eyes fixed on my girl as I closed the distance between us with the others clustered behind me, striding through a field of stunning wildflowers which had definitely not been there the last time I'd been out here.

Roxy looked to me with a smile tugging at the corner of her lips, now wearing a stunning blood red dress made from hand stitched lace which left her back bare and had a train which swept out around her feet. Her long, dark hair had been pinned up with loose curls escaping to caress her neck and her face was painted with makeup, her eyes lined in black and lips ruby red like the pendant she wore around her neck for me.

Fuck knew how Geraldine had transformed her in the ten minutes since I'd last seen her or where the hell she'd found that dress but my pulse hammered hungrily as my eyes feasted on the sight of her waiting there for me.

Geraldine started sobbing loudly and Darcy beamed with tears in her silver eyes which I knew were for our situation, but I couldn't focus on that in that moment. All I could see was *her*. The girl who had owned my heart before I'd even met her.

"Aren't you supposed to walk the aisle to meet me?" I asked as I closed in on her, my brothers and family clustered close.

"I told you, no bullshit," she replied with a shrug and I noticed the bouquet of roses that had been tossed by her feet, a breath of amusement leaving me as I looked at this woman who I wanted to offer eternity to, trying not to let my heart break at the knowledge that our happily ever after would end in a few short weeks.

"Are we going for traditional vows?" Geraldine choked out but Roxy shook her head instantly.

"No. I'm just going to stand right here and tell the world he's mine. If anyone refuses to take my word on that then they can bring it up with me themselves."

"Always so aggressive," I teased as I moved to stand over her, noticing the flawless makeup and perfectly styled curls in her ebony hair which shifted in the cool breeze that danced all around us. Geraldine really did work fast under pressure.

"Says the Dragon who tried to drown me."

I shook my head, unable to believe she would bring that up right now while simultaneously wondering why I hadn't known she would. This fucking girl would be the end of me. But I was alright with that.

"Do you have rings?" Darcy asked me as Lance moved to drape an arm around her shoulders, looking at me with an expression that told me he was both happy and devastated. Which was pretty much the sentiment of all our guests unfortunately.

"He's a treasure obsessed Dragon, you know he's got rings," Caleb joked and I breathed a laugh, pulling them from my pocket and offering Roxy the one meant for me to wear.

She eyed the simple platinum band for a moment, looking up at me in surprise and I shrugged. "You said no bullshit."

A smile broke across her face like sunshine through the clouds and she took it, stepping in to me and taking my hand, pushing the ring onto my finger without so much as a proclamation.

"I claim this man to be my husband," she said, a ring of power to her voice which defied the heavens themselves to deny her.

"I claim this woman for my wife," I replied, taking her lead and slipping the ruby inlaid ring onto her finger in return and giving her a hungry smile.

Geraldine started gushing about our union and the stars and some shit which I guessed was her way of making this whole thing official, but I wasn't able to concentrate on a single word of it as I swept my girl into my arms.

Roxy's eyes burned with love for me and I dipped my mouth to claim hers, unable to believe that I would be this damn lucky as I found the woman of my dreams in my arms and my ring firmly placed upon her finger. She lifted her chin to meet me, her fingers curling into the front of my shirt and I closed the last remnant of distance between us, kissing her breathless beneath the grey clouds without a single fucking star in sight.

She'd been right about that. We didn't need fate or rings in our eyes to know that we belonged to one another. And right here, without any of that, I felt the power of our connection far deeper than any bond could have granted us as I laid my claim on the woman who I had hungered for for so damn long.

And I knew that even death could never tear our souls apart again now.

CALEB

CHAPTER FIFTY FOUR

The war council had taken all goddamn morning, partly because we had to wait for over an hour for Darius and Tory following their wedding after he dragged her into their room on our way back to it to consummate their damn union.

We'd spent that time trying not to notice the way the walls were rattling while also working hard not to fall into the trap of agonising over Darius's fate.

I'd been awake all night with the others discussing it and we had all finally agreed to focus on this battle before we turned our attention to changing his fate.

Gabriel had been working hard to *see* the best way to success for us with that and eventually we'd all landed on the fight happening in a week.

Without stardust to transport our army, we were going to have a whole lot of work to do to bring the fight to Lionel though, so we planned on getting the rebels underway over the next few days and we'd spent the afternoon taking part in a huge rally to get all of them hyped up for the battle.

But after hours of listening to them chanting their support for the true queens and feeling like extras to this entire war campaign, I was starting to feel the results of missing a night's sleep.

"Just think, we could be back home again within a week," Max said as he moved to stand at my side, pressing a hand to my shoulder and helping me to feel refreshed and wakeful once more.

"It's hard to imagine that," I admitted, the sounds of the rebels celebrating filling the tunnels and echoing all around my skull. There were more than a few drinks being consumed and it was clear that this entire thing was going to have descended into a rave by nightfall, but I found it hard to muster the strength to join in with the celebrations.

"We'll figure it out," Max swore, feeling my fear for Darius through his touch and I looked at him hopelessly, willing that to be true, but I just didn't see how it could be. "He still has weeks left for us to find a solution. We're the most powerful Fae in Solaria - there has to be a way to change it."

"I really hope you're-" I cut myself off as a buzzing sensation raced across my skin, warning me that the leather journal my mom had given me had a new message waiting for my attention. "My mom just sent us a message," I said and Max's eyes widened in fear the way they did every time she made contact. There had never been a problem with our families before, but we were all expecting Lionel to turn on them at any given point so that fear for their safety never diminished.

"Where is everyone?" I asked, looking out over the crowd of yelling, bloodthirsty Fae and spotting Seth and Darius on the far side of the room but I couldn't see any of the others.

I grabbed Max's arm, hoisting him over my shoulder and shooting through the crowd - possibly knocking a couple of people over among the tightly packed bodies - before coming to a halt before the other Heirs.

"Hey, what's up?" Seth asked, looking between me and Max and clearly noticing the unease in our expressions.

"I have a message waiting for us from my mom," I explained.

"Then let's go read it," Darius replied. "The twins have been swallowed by the crowd anyway and Lance is making sure they don't get swamped. I think this thing will be going on for the entire night at this rate."

"Come on then," I agreed and I turned, leading the way to the royal quarters and heading to the room I shared with Seth.

It was pretty difficult for me not to think about how good his mouth had felt against mine in this very room, not to mention the other parts of my body too, but since I'd gotten him to come back here, we'd been careful not to get close to crossing that line again. We still needed to talk more about it really, but I was stalling on that, trying to get to a point where I didn't think about him every time I jerked off, so that I could discuss it without the fear that I would end up making a fucking idiot of myself over it.

I shot across the room as the others stayed by the door and I carefully pulled the leather journal my mom had given me to reflect the words of her scribing stone out from its hiding spot, removing the magical locks and concealments I had in place to protect it.

The message was waiting for me on it and my heart froze to ice in my chest as I read it.

Lionel has summoned us to his manor, but something is wrong. He has Hadley and the others and won't let us see them unless we go to him. I fear what he is planning.

"Fuck," Max cursed as Seth howled.

"What do we do?" I asked, my pulse racing.

"We go to them," Darius replied firmly, looking between us. "I won't let my father take your families from you."

I swallowed thickly, wondering if we were insane to be considering this, but we were the strongest Fae of our generation and we had been working to hone our fighting skills for almost a year in anticipation of this exact kind of situation.

"Should we try to find the others?" Seth asked, looking towards the door.

"Fuck knows where the Vegas and Geraldine are," Max said. "Last I heard, Gerry was getting them to individually bless every fucking Fae down here with their touch. Tory looked less than pleased about it, but Hamish insisted too and they headed off into the tunnels with them."

"I could probably find them," I suggested, knowing I could shoot back and forth throughout these tunnel networks without too much difficulty though they were pretty damn extensive now.

"We could cause a panic if the rebels realise we're leaving," Max pointed out. "I say we just go. We all know we're going to do it regardless, so why risk causing the army to freak out when they need to be preparing for war?"

"Yeah. I'm with Max," I agreed, my fear for my family driving me to act now.

"We don't have any stardust," Darius pointed out. "But I can fly us there. It will take an hour or more from here."

"Then let's go," Seth said firmly. "We'll be back here with our families, safe and sound before the rally is even over and then they'll be ready to fight with us too. It can't fail."

We looked between each other, knowing there were definitely a lot of ways that this could go to hell, but we also knew that we had no choice. This was family. They needed us.

I nodded my agreement and we all broke apart to gather our weapons and change into clothes which were fit for a fight. I snatched my twin blades from my nightstand and called out to let the others know I would meet them outside when they were ready.

It took a few circuits of the tunnels before I found Gabriel and I damn near crashed into him as he stepped into my path, a knowing look on his face.

"You're leaving?" he asked, his tone filled with concern.

"My mom and the other Councillors are in trouble. Lionel has them headed to Acrux Manor for something bad. Can you *see* anything that can help us?" I asked.

Gabriel frowned as he leaned into his gifts, hunting for the answers I needed before shaking his head in defeat and offering me an apologetic look.

"That place is hidden within the shadows," he said. "But I can *see* many paths for your future beyond tonight so I don't think you will die in this endeavour. Unless something changes of course."

"Super reassuring," I muttered.

"I try," he replied dryly.

"Can you tell the others where we've gone?"

"The twins won't be happy," he warned.

"No, but this is family, they'll understand."

He nodded and I clapped him on the arm before shooting away from him, speeding through the tunnels, out of The Burrows and through the enormous forcefield which protected this place where I found Darius already shifted into his huge golden Dragon form with Seth and Max on his back with Darius's clothes bundled in their arms.

"Gabriel couldn't *see* anything to help us," I explained as I leapt up onto him too.

"He never can when it matters," Seth muttered and I sighed in agreement, taking hold of one of the huge spines on Darius's back as I settled myself behind Seth, unable to help looking at the shorn side of his hair and the braids weaving across it.

Darius took off into the sky with a defiant roar and a burst of Dragon fire which promised a swift and brutal end to anyone who stood in our way and I just hoped we could make it there in time to see that promise fulfilled.

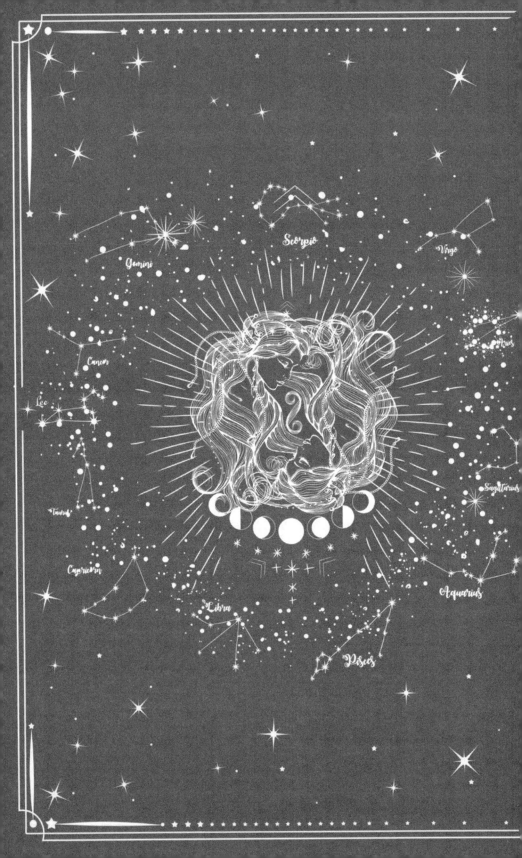

DARCY

CHAPTER FIFTY FIVE

"This way!" Geraldine cried, leading Tory and I through the tunnels where we ran our hands over the heads of the rebels as they bowed to us to 'bless them.'

I knew I didn't have any kind of real power to offer a blessing, but I also knew the power of belief. And if they thought this would help, then I guessed it did.

Tory begrudgingly joined in too and I kept casting concerned glances her way, thinking of Darius, my chest crushing every time I caught sight of the pain in her eyes. It was hidden beneath a hard wall, but I could read my sister like a book. And honestly, I wanted to be done here so I could just take her flying with Gabriel and go somewhere quiet where I could hold her in my arms. Or maybe she'd want to return to Darius as soon as we could leave the rally. All I knew was that she'd just married the man she loved right after finding out that their time together was running short, and now she was having to put her heart aside in favour of the war. I hoped Lionel burned for all the destruction he'd caused when this was done.

I was relieved when Geraldine called out to demand a break for us and led us back to the dining hall, through to the room at the back of it which had been reserved just for us. There were comfortable chairs and a silencing bubble in place to give us some semblance of peace and Tory groaned in relief as she moved towards a chair sat by a raging fire which looked like a real slice of heaven.

Geraldine patted me on the head fondly then turned and trotted back out of the room gasping something about a royal snack being required urgently.

Orion was having a tense looking discussion with Gabriel and as Tory slumped into her chair, I moved to join them. Orion's arm slid smoothly around me and I stole a moment of relief in his hold, resting my head against his shoulder and closing my eyes, not even hearing what he was talking about with my brother as my pulse seemed to drum too slowly in my ears.

The longer my eyes stayed closed, the more exhausted I felt, and as I tugged on my magic, intending to cast a wakeful spell to give me a boost, what came in its place was a wave of burning hot rage. I was angry at this war, at fucking Lionel and the threat that hung over us all, which put every single person I loved in danger.

"The Heirs are gone, they left a couple of hours ago," Gabriel's voice cut through the fog of my thoughts.

"Gone?" Tory gasped, sitting upright with her eyes widening. "What do you mean gone?"

"Their families are in danger," Gabriel explained. "Darius went with them to help."

"In danger how? When will they be back? Why didn't they come get us?" Tory demanded in a panic.

"I am fairly sure they will return," Gabriel said.

"*Fairly* sure? That's not good enough," Tory snapped. "Is that like the way you were *fairly sure* taking Darius to bargain with the stars was a good idea last Christmas?"

My eyes shot open and I lunged at Gabriel with a snarl, shoving his chest with flames in my hands and he cursed as he stumbled back.

I gasped as I realised what I'd done and Orion pulled me away from him.

"Sorry, I didn't mean to do that," I said in horror as Gabriel healed the burns on his chest, his shirt smoking where I'd singed right through it.

Gabriel frowned at me and I realised Tory was looking at me in surprise too, making shame burn along my neck as her anger with Gabriel fell away in favour of concern for me.

"I'm sorry," I repeated.

"What's wrong, Blue?" Orion turned me to him, looking at me with worry instead of the anger I should have seen there.

Gabriel stepped closer to me, cupping my cheek as he looked into my eyes and I felt like he was looking directly into my soul as he hunted for something within my gaze.

"What is it?" Tory demanded of him, but Gabriel shook his head, a frown crossing his features.

"I can't *see...* " he murmured though the frown on his face meant that wasn't at all reassuring.

A boom sounded that resounded through the entire Burrows, the tremor rocking the ground at my feet and a chill washing over me that froze me to my bones.

"What was that?" Tory gasped, but the answer came in the form of shouts going up all around the tunnels.

"The wards are down!"

"The boundary has fallen!"

"Prepare yourselves!"

Then screams, pitchy, blood-curdling screams.

The sound was coming from somewhere above us in the tunnels and panic washed through me like jet fuel catching fire.

"Go!" I cried, racing for the door and my family fell in around me as we ran out into the dining hall.

"It's the Nymphs – they're in the tunnels," someone burst into the hall and started working to seal the exit with his earth magic.

"Stop – you'll seal us all in." An older woman near to him pulled at his arm.

I could see that chaos was about to unfold and as more screams carried through the tunnels – closer this time – I knew we couldn't stop the tide of monsters that was coming. But we could get the vulnerable away from the fight and intercept our enemies head on ourselves.

"Dante!" I shouted as I saw him, running to his side as the Oscura Wolf pack drew tight around him.

"Get the children and elderly out of here. We need to make a new tunnel," I said quickly.

"I can do that," Rosalie said as she took to his side.

"I'll stay with them and protect the kids," Leon said fiercely, fire igniting in his palms.

"Tunnel out the back wall." Tory pointed and they ran off to get started, a bunch of earth Elementals hurrying over to help.

I turned to Orion, trying to keep calm as more screams sounded out in the tunnels. "Get our armour and weapons," I directed. "We'll head for the exit to stop them and block their way in. Meet us there."

He nodded before shooting away out of sight into the passage and I turned to Gabriel, his eyes moving back and forth as he hunted the stars for answers. But when he came back to us, his features were grave.

"I couldn't *see* them coming," he cursed. "And now I *see* so much death, I cannot bear it."

"Is Lionel here?" Tory demanded, a growl to her voice.

Her answer came in a bellowing roar from the surface and every Fae in the room looked up, before a swarm of them came running towards us.

"My Queens, what do we do?" one of them called, while others cried out for more direction.

I shared a look with Tory, unsure if I was truly ready to lead an army into battle, but it didn't look like we were going to get a choice in the matter. And if Lionel was here, then a fight was coming, and we had to do our best to lead it.

"Hamish!" I cried and he burst out of the crowd. "Arm the rebels. Get the blades we imbued with our fire and make sure everyone has one."

"Yes, my lady." He ran back off into the crowd, drawing a group of people around him to help, including Washer and some of the Oscuras.

"We have to stop the Nymphs from getting in here," Tory called.

"Follow Tory and I to destroy our enemies!" I yelled and a cheer of ascension went up that rattled the roof.

"I'll follow you shortly." Gabriel ran over to his family, speaking with them urgently and my heart squeezed with dread as my gaze fell on my little nephew. A snarl spilled from my throat. I would not let any harm come to him today.

Tory and I let our wings burst free of our backs, the dresses we wore allowing for them to spread wide either side of us. We took off above the rebels, swooping through the door and calling out for our people to follow.

Mothers pushed through the rebels with their children, trying to get them out of the way as Dante, Leon and Rosalie Oscura worked together with the earth Elementals to deepen the new tunnel in the back wall and usher all of the families through it.

A surge of bloodthirsty eyes looked up at us as the Fae who wanted to fight spilled out into the passage beyond the dining hall and we led them away from the vulnerable, hurrying towards our enemies to stop them.

As we flew through the winding tunnels, rage burned along my veins and fire spun within me like an inferno. This place had become a home to us, somewhere full of light and laughter and love. And I was not going to see it fall.

We flew over Hamish and Washer as they handed out swords to the front line, arming our people as we raced on and anyone who had a blade in their grip followed.

I pressed two fingers to my throat, casting an amplifying spell so my voice rang back to the rebels, glad Orion had taught me how to do it properly. "Lionel may have found us, but what he doesn't know is that he's standing on a nest of wild creatures! We are a family forged in the dirt, ready to fight with everything we have for the people we love! So let him hear us coming, let us roar like the beasts we are when we're together! And let him fear the trembling at his feet, for he has awoken us, and we are ready to fight with tooth and claw!"

The rebels roared in response, the sound filling up the corridors just as we rounded another passage and a line of Nymphs descended on us.

Tory grabbed my hand and our Phoenixes collided, a burst of blooming fire tearing out of us and slamming into the first wave of Nymphs. We took two down with the blast and the rebels pressed forward, swinging their blades as Phoenix fire ignited along the metal and slashed through the Nymphs.

The horrifying sound of Nymphs rattles carried through the air, locking down my magic and the magic of anyone close to them, making me growl a curse.

Tory and I blasted Nymphs with our power as we continued to fly, pressing on toward the farmhouse, desperately needing to seal the entrance to The Burrows as fast as we could.

Our Order powers rushed together once more and the Phoenix bird burst from us, my heart thundering up into my throat as I watched it sail away, colliding with one Nymph then the next, taking them down as they were turned to ash that scattered over the crowd who swarmed chaotically below us.

"We have to destroy Lionel," Tory snarled.

"Let's get to the surface," I said in agreement and we flapped our wings, moving faster through the passages. The cry of battle went up all around us, the glint of fury in the eyes of our people below us, their courage bolstering my own as the two of us swooped along above the masses.

More Nymphs barred the way forward and raging fights broke out everywhere in the passages as we flew, casting our Phoenix fire at any Nymphs we came close to and banishing them into death.

Their rattles echoed through the atmosphere, locking down our people's magic and weakening our forces just like that. More and more of our allies were shifting and we cried out to anyone who had yet to do so, urging them to take on their Order forms or keep fighting on with their Phoenix flame swords.

As we made it to the passage that led outside, we found carnage awaiting us.

Geraldine was already there with her armour in place and her flail in hand as she fought to keep the Nymphs back. They were fighting their way through the archway where the grandfather clock had been, the whole wall of earth now ripped apart to leave a gaping hole into the farmhouse. We flew forward as Geraldine worked to seal up the hole alongside another group of earth Elementals and Tory and I dropped down before her.

"We'll make a wall of Phoenix fire, stand back," Tory commanded and they hurried to obey as we raised our hands together as another tide of Nymphs dove forward to try and make it through the hole.

A billowing plume of fire tore away from us and the Nymphs shrieked, some dying in the blast as the fire curled around the entrance in an impenetrable wall and the tide of Nymphs was finally halted. The rattles fell away as they retreated from our flames and my magic returned to me, power crackling at my fingertips.

"Kill any of them who remain in the tunnels – the breach is sealed!" I cried, amplifying my voice once more so all the rebels could hear.

"Geraldine, get everyone enforcing the roof here, don't let anyone tunnel in," Tory commanded.

"Yes, my lady," she said, her eyes fierce as she started directing people to tighten up the defences.

"Blue!" Orion shouted, shooting up behind us with weapons and our armour in his grip.

"Thank god." I stripped out of my dress immediately.

Tory snatched a blade, cutting the red lace of her wedding dress open instead of wasting time with the ties and we pulled our armour on, sheathing the new blades we'd made for ourselves while Orion held his sword at the ready, a darkness in his eyes that I felt in my own soul.

Xavier and Sofia appeared riding on the back of Tyler in his silver Pegasus form, galloping towards us. Xavier had his metal Phoenix fire helmet strapped to his head, ready for when he shifted, and he looked to us as Tyler slowed to a halt.

"We have to get to the surface," Xavier said urgently. "We have to get to my father."

I nodded as Orion tossed Xavier and Sofia a couple of blades.

"Geraldine!" I called, an idea coming to me and she ran to us in an instant.

"How can I be of service?" she asked.

"We need to make a tunnel up to the surface so the rebels can get out and fight," I said.

"Absolutely, let me assist you. And once it is done, I shall follow at your backs like a nighthawk and cry to the moon the toll of death!"

I nodded to her as a line of rebels built behind us, all armed and looking ready to bleed for victory.

"Follow us!" Tory cried. "We're going to the surface! Fight for the world Lionel has stolen from you. Fight for our right to peace, and happiness, and a safe place for our families to live. Fight for every ounce of love in your heart, and fight for the love in the hearts of those who stand at your side. But most of all, fight for the good that has been ripped from our grasp, and fight for our goddamn freedom!"

"For freedom!" they yelled in reply and Tory and I blasted a hole in the wall to our right, cleaving it apart with earth magic, creating a path big enough for the rebels to follow as Geraldine widened it all around us.

Orion stood at my back with his sword raised and we shared a look that said we'd fight with all the fury of our love out there today. I'd fight for them all, for him, my sister, for my brother, for the family I'd found in Solaria and who were so precious to me, it was easy to stand here, ready to die for them.

"Stay close," I breathed and a promise flared in his eyes.

"I'm always in your shadow, you only have to look to find me there," he said, raising his chin with a flare of determination in his gaze.

"Love you, Tor," I whispered to my sister and she looked to me with that same love blazing in her eyes.

"Love you, Darcy."

We sprinted up the dirt path as everyone ran at our back, the ground opening up above us as we blasted through it. And suddenly we were outside, the cool autumn air whipping around us, the long grass stained red with blood and complete havoc descending in an instant.

I let my wings spread behind me as the Nymphs shrieked and Orion charged forward with a burst of Vampire speed, swinging his flaming Phoenix sword and slamming it into the chest of the closest monster.

I took off into the sky, wheeling up behind a Nymph on the breeze and blasting its head with Phoenix fire, a shout of rage leaving my lips. As it turned to dust and Tory ran to meet another Nymph, my eyes flickered over the field of our enemies, my gaze falling on Lionel in his jade green Dragon form as he snapped a man up between his jaws and swallowed him whole. A line of rebels must have gotten out here when they'd shown up, but it had clearly been a bloodbath, because bodies lay everywhere and the last of them were being hunted down and slaughtered.

I stared at the forces Lionel had brought here in hopes of destroying us, my heart pounding as I took in the sight of thousands of Nymphs and the legion of Dragons who stood at their backs, waiting with bared fangs and claws to strike at us the moment their king commanded it. He was letting the Nymphs run riot, but this was just child's play compared to what he had in store for us.

A roaring, bellowing cry came from the rebels at our backs, our army spilling from the ground as they followed Tory and I into the fray. A charge of Centaurs galloped past us with swords raised and they were followed by a group of Minotaurs who pounded their chests and mooed furiously as they ran.

Gabriel came sprinting out of the tunnel, taking off into the sky with his dark wings flexing, and I saw the terror in his eyes which spoke of how pained he was that he hadn't been able to *see* this coming. But my brother couldn't predict the shadows, and it was clear Lionel had hidden behind them tonight when he'd planned this assault.

We pressed forward, needing to create space for our army so that they could emerge from the tunnels to face our enemies and I snatched a smaller blade from my hip, throwing it with a yell of exertion and it wheeled end over end before driving straight into the eye of a Nymph making a charge for my mate.

Orion carved down the Nymph beneath me as it wailed and my heart wrenched as Tory flew ahead of us, diving down into a fight of her own as a swarm of rebels followed her.

A group of Nymphs surrounded Xavier and Sofia on Tyler's back below, and I flew towards them, drawing the sword from my hip and swinging it with a precision taught to me by Queen Avalon. The sharp, fiery blade sliced through skin and bone, carving the head from one of the Nymphs and ash burst into the air as it died.

Tyler galloped forward, his head bowed and his horn driving into another Nymph's chest, knocking it down and trampling it before the three of them cantered off deeper into the battle.

A Nymph reached for me in the sky, its probed hand swiping for my leg and I slashed my blade at it with a cry, severing its probes before driving the blade into its head. Embers exploded around me and my gaze locked on Orion as he killed with the wild and vicious savagery of his kind, cutting down his enemies and mercilessly ending them with powerful strikes.

Fear daggered through my heart for everyone I loved and my eyes fell on Lavinia as she stood on a tower of shadow, picking off the rebels one by one with blasts of her dark power, a malicious grin on her lips.

"Lead the way, Blue!" Orion shouted from the ground, my loyal mate ready to fight at my command. "I'll follow you."

I nodded, locking another Nymph in my sights as it took down two of our people, my teeth bared with hate.

My Phoenix fire blasted the Nymph apart as I spotted Tory locked in a fight a hundred yards away, her wings flashing with fire as she burned through Nymphs and tried to drive them back to make way for our forces.

Orion cut more of them down beneath me while I finished them with fireballs and the edge of my blade as we pressed forward.

Hamish and Catalina appeared beneath me, their hands locking as a tremendous challenge bellowed from the rebel leader's lips and the next thing I knew, the whole hillside behind them broke apart and rocks and dirt were ripped from the ground, revealing the whole host of our army beyond them, making my heart lift with the strength burning in their eyes. We could do this, we could really win this.

Catalina yelled out in challenge as she swept her free hand forward, sending all of the dislodged rock and soil crashing towards the enemy army, forcing Lionel to roar in rage as he raced skywards to avoid it and the ranks of Nymphs below him took the hit, screaming as they died.

The earth Elementals within the army cast huge stone slopes out of the remains of the tunnels and the rebels bellowed their challenge to the false king and his foul army as they ran up out of the ground to meet them on the battlefield.

My gaze fell on Lionel and Lavinia as rage coiled through my veins like a snake and an animal raised its head within my chest as I promised them their deaths tonight. Because I would not see anyone I loved die, I'd fight with every ounce of fire in my blood until I saw our enemies bleeding and destroyed at my feet.

They were about to find out what it meant to go against the descendants of the last Phoenix queen.

DARIUS

CHAPTER FIFTY SIX

It hadn't taken me long to break through the wards my father had left in place to protect his old home and the four of us crept across the sweeping grounds of Acrux Manor with our breaths held in anticipation and the need for vengeance pumping through our veins.

"I'll be glad to finally have our parents away from that asshole," Seth muttered as we moved through the dense woodland to the rear of the property, circling the lake and closing in on the manor house as quickly as we could while still remaining cautious.

"I'm just worried about what he's done to our siblings," Caleb said and I growled at the thought of him hurting Hadley or the others.

Max remained quiet and I knew what was on his mind without him needing to voice it. His father would still be resolutely backing him, but his stepmother and Ellis were likely more than happy with this current arrangement which put his younger sister in his place. We'd discussed it more than once over the past months. And as much as there had been no love lost between Max and his father's wife, Ellis was a different story. Yes, she was irritating and obnoxious and they butted heads all the time, but she was still his blood. Still his father's daughter. And I knew he was worried about the idea of her choosing to side with Lionel and what that might mean long term in this war.

"This way," I urged, leading them around the lake, using the full force of my power to shroud us in shadows and divert the attention of any unwanted eyes on us.

There was an old rabbit trail which cut through the undergrowth along here which Xavier and I had often used to slip between the formal path which ringed the lake and the wildness of the woodland where we preferred to play and pretend that we were free.

It had been a long time since we'd made use of it, but I found it all the same and Seth used his earth magic to widen it enough for us to pass through.

There was a heaviness in the air which seemed to grow thicker the closer we got to the manor, and I fought a wave of nausea which pressed into me the closer I got to those walls which had been my prison for so long.

I hated this fucking place. I hated the monster who had made it hell for my mother and brother too. And even now, when I was just here to sneak inside and take something from that monster instead of being forced to return like a dog on a leash, I couldn't shake off that feeling of foreboding which had long since accompanied my approach to those dark walls.

A high-pitched scream bit into the air and we jerked to a halt as we listened, the sound echoing out around us before dying away in an agonising wail.

Seth's face paled and Cal reached out to grasp his shoulder as we all recognised his mother's voice in that scream and the fiery pit of rage in my gut burned hotter at the mere thought of what was going on in that fucking house.

"We have to keep our heads," Max said firmly, pushing a sense of calm and courage over our small group as Seth bit his tongue on a mournful howl.

"We'll get them out of here," I vowed, turning my attention to the manor again and eyeing the tall tower where I'd once resided.

"If we can get up to the roof of my old room then I can get us inside," I said.

"I can get us up there," Max replied confidently and Seth nodded his agreement.

"Then it's on you and me to keep us shielded from view, Cal," I said, turning to look at him as he pushed his blonde curls out of his eyes and assessed the distance between us and the house. It was a long run across open ground, but there was little we could do about that.

"I'll shoot everyone across the lawn," Caleb said decisively. "It'll be a lot easier to hide us for a shorter burst like that."

We nodded our agreement and he shot forward, hoisting Max from his feet and speeding away across the lawn in a blur that I lost sight of within moments as the combination of his speed and their magic made it impossible to track them.

"I'm gonna enjoy looking at your dad's corpse when this is all done, Darius," Seth said in a dark tone. "Sorry if that's a weird thing to say, but I really hope he gets cut up into tiny little Dragon sush-ahh!"

I snorted as Caleb grabbed Seth next, speeding away with him so fast that I barely even caught the movement and I braced myself as I waited for him to return for me last.

Caleb's shoulder slammed into my gut and he hoisted me off of my feet, shooting across the lawn so fast that I could see nothing at all but a blur of movement surrounding me until we were suddenly whipped off of the ground and were sent soaring into the air.

The air magic guiding us upwards, catapulted us past all ten floors of the tower and before my brain could even figure out what way was up, I found myself crashing down onto the stone platform at the top of the turret and the wind being driven from my lungs as Seth landed on top of me.

"Well, I seriously doubt anyone saw that," I grumbled as I fought my way out of the pile of bodies and we got to our feet once more. "Now we just need to make it inside without triggering any magical alarms."

"We need to hurry," Seth urged, moving to my side as I reached out with my magic to hunt for the taste of my father's power. "I have a bad feeling about this."

"Well that makes all four of us," Max muttered darkly.

XAVIER

CHAPTER FIFTY SEVEN

"**G**et to my father!" I demanded of Tyler as he galloped through the battle.

I held on tight to Sofia's waist as Tyler let out a whinny of determination, weaving left and right through our allies and enemies, leaping over bodies and using his horn to swipe aside anyone who tried to attack us.

My gaze was set on my father as he blasted a line of rebels with his Dragon fire, soaring overhead, his huge wings stirring the air around us and I urged fire into my veins to fight away the cool wind.

"Be careful," Sofia begged as she turned to look at me, kissing me hard and I squeezed her tight, knowing it might be the last time I got to do so before I broke apart from her and rose to my feet on Tyler's back, adjusting the horn helmet on my head which had been made for me by Tory and Darcy with their Phoenix fire.

Tyler neighed in encouragement, but I could hear the fear lacing that sound as I leapt upwards, pulling my clothes off as I shifted into my lilac Pegasus form and racing into the sky after Lionel, my wings bursting from my back and a furious neigh escaping my lips.

My heart thumped violently in my chest like it was fighting against the decision I'd made, like it knew these might be its final beats. But I didn't care. I wasn't going to stand by and watch my father kill these people. I was tired of his tyranny, tired of hiding in the dirt and tired of waiting for the world to end. In a way it was a relief to find him here now, a relief to face him at long last.

I swept up behind him, staying in his blind spot and ducking his tail as it whipped out furiously behind him. He lowered his head, hunting for more prey below and I swung under his belly, angling my horn just right as I beat my wings hard to make it beneath his chest. I shook my head to ignite the Phoenix fire on my horn and a swirl of red and blue flames flared along it in an instant.

He still hadn't noticed me and hope sang a tune in my veins as I dipped my head, lining my flaming horn up with his black heart, ready to drive it through scales and bone to finish him.

Then I kicked my legs and beat my wings, coaxing all the power I could into the blow.

Father turned at the last second and my horn slammed into him off centre. But it still drove in deep and he roared in agony as I yanked my horn free and beat my wings hard, preparing to slam it into him once more, hitting the target I was so desperately aiming for.

I lunged at him to strike again, but one of his talons hooked around my leg and he threw me through the air, making my stomach lurch in fright.

I spun in a barrel roll, my wings flexing as I worked to get control of my descent and I narrowly missed the snapping of his jaws as I managed to fly upwards, my hooves smashing down on his skull as I used him as a springboard to get higher.

He bellowed another roar and the heat on my back warned me of the fire chasing my tail as I raced for the sky, a whinny of fear leaving my throat as I smelled singed hair, glancing back to find my tail on fire.

I whipped it hard until it went out and made it into the cloud cover with a breath of relief leaving me, thankful a water Elemental had cast a small storm here so I could use it to hide.

The cries and screams of the battle were muffled up here and though I was covered, I also couldn't see my father, his deep growl rumbling through the air around me.

I turned left and right, unsure what move to make next and suddenly two jade green eyes peered through the thick mist at me.

Fire blasted my way, lighting up the clouds in orange as I tucked my wings and dove from the heavens, plummeting towards earth as fast as I could.

The way the air dragged and shifted around me made me sure he was right on my tail, and I shot side to side as fire bloomed past me, so close to consuming me it was all I could do to keep moving.

I stretched my wings out at the last second, pulling up from the dive, and twisting back to face my father. I slammed into his side, his huge body taking much longer to manoeuvre the way I could, and my fiery horn sank into his flesh once more, cracking the scales along his ribs and the sweet scent of his blood made me whinny in victory.

I flew higher, running up his side, my hooves bashing against his body in bruising strikes as I charged towards his head, my breaths falling heavily from my nostrils in a fog of white as I focused on my target, galloping up his spine with victory humming my name.

I'd drive my horn into his skull and finish him.

I wasn't his victim anymore. I was a survivor of his reign, and he would rue the day he ever dared to try and dismiss my kind as weak.

But just as I prepared to strike him, a tendril of shadow came out of nowhere, locking my front legs together and making a neigh of fright leave me as I tripped, tumbling over my father's head and whinnying in horror as one of my wings got lashed to my side too.

I heard Lavinia laughing as I fell and I kicked my back legs feebly, my other wing stretching out in the hope of slowing my fall before I crashed to the ground.

I slammed into the dirt and the front talons of Lionel's shadow foot raked across my side as he held me down, agony spilling through the wound as his weight pressed onto me and my ribs snapped beneath his tremendous bulk.

I whinnied in pain, my eyes falling on Sofia and Tyler as they galloped towards me through the press of fighting bodies. She blasted fire magic from her position on his back as they fought to reach me, but they were going to be too late. And my gaze begged them to run, because I knew they couldn't face my father and win.

A line of Nymphs charged into their way, blocking their path to me and forcing them into a fight I prayed they'd win. Sofia raised a flaming sword and Tyler neighed furiously as he reared up, but another group of Nymphs arrived and I lost sight of my Subs beyond them. Panic bloomed within me, and I hoped to the stars that wouldn't be the last time I'd see them in this life.

Lionel reared over me, a rumble of rage sounding through his huge body before his jaws clamped down around my wing and his head whipped sideways.

Agony seared along my side as he ripped my wing free, tearing it away from my body so that it fell into the trampled long grass beside him and shock juddered through my entire being as I could only stare at it in horror, the lilac feathers stained red as they fluttered in the wind pathetically like a broken bird.

Blood poured and panic blossomed inside me as I stared up into the merciless eyes of my father, knowing he would make this hurt as much as he possibly could before he sent me beyond the Veil.

Lavinia released me from the shadow binds as her attention was snared by a line of rebels, but there was no way I could get up with the weight of a Dragon pressing down on me. And as my death closed in on me on all sides, I knew this was my end.

A furious neigh cut through the air and my eyes locked on Tyler as he came sailing down from the sky with Sofia on his back, his hooves slamming into Lionel's head. My father snapped his jaws at them and I whinnied to them in desperation for them to flee. But it was clear they weren't going to abandon me.

The weight lifted from my side as Lionel turned, taking off into the sky to try and catch them, but I couldn't get up to help as I watched him follow the two Fae who held my whole heart towards the stars.

DARIUS

CHAPTER FIFTY EIGHT

Cold air billowed around us where we stood on the turret above my room, and the others kept a lookout for signs of anyone noticing us here while I worked to get us inside. There was a door up here which led down into my old room, but I'd long since figured out that my father had placed detection spells and magical alarms on it to keep him informed of my movements.

I moved to the side of it instead, ignoring the door and activating the magic I'd left there which made the bricks rumble and part for me, bypassing my father's magic and allowing me entry into my old rooms.

The others followed me into the dark and I hurried down the twisting stairway, a feeling of deja vu stirring my senses as the familiarity of this, coupled with the length of time it had been since I'd returned here mixed into something that sent the hairs along the back of my neck standing on end.

I moved into the dark space, passing the familiar layout of my furniture and quickly moving to a safe which I had concealed beneath a flagstone by the foot of my bed as the others followed.

I unlocked it, grabbing the fat pouch of stardust from inside and smirking triumphantly as I wondered if I could try and break into Father's vault and steal a whole lot more of it while I was here too. This bag wouldn't be nearly enough to transport our army, but if I could get my hands on his stores, then I could use his own beloved form of transportation to relocate an entire legion of so called 'unworthy' Fae with it. There would be some sweetness to that act which was hard to ignore.

I snatched the few pieces of treasure I had hidden in the safe too, jamming them into my pockets greedily as the Dragon in me practically purred with happiness over being reunited with it.

"Holy shit," Galeb breathed and I looked up, my flesh prickling at the fear in his tone as I spotted him by the window on the far side of my room which looked down onto the internal courtyard far below us.

I shoved to my feet and jogged over to him, tugging the curtains wider so that I could see down there too.

My lips fell open at the sight that awaited me there, and I could only stare on in horror as I took in the altar of coal black stone which now dominated the courtyard, a swirling vortex of shadows hanging in the air above it which pulsed and hummed with that dark power which I'd been able to sense since we got here.

But that wasn't the worst part. My breath stalled as I looked down at the row of Fae who were lined up on their knees before the altar, their hands outstretched in what looked like an offering, their wrists cut and shadows latched to the wounds as they shuddered under the power of the dark magic.

I recognised the other Heirs' parents and their siblings too, each of the spares latched to that vile thing by shadows which seemed to be drawing on the raw essence of their power before feeding it back out into the sky.

"Lavinia found a way to connect herself to the shadows again," I breathed in horror as realisation dawned and the magnitude of this fucked up situation fell on me. "She must be drawing on the shadows via this, using their power to fuel the opening and allow the darkness to slip through to our realm once more."

"Why isn't it killing them?" Max ground out and I could tell he was on the verge of snapping and tearing straight down there to rip his father from the hold of the dark magic which contained him and freeing him from Lavinia's power. But we all knew it wouldn't be that simple. And who knew where the rest of their families were? There was no sign of Seth or Caleb's fathers, and where were their other siblings? Were they even here in the manor?

"I think it is," Seth whispered, pointing to a cloaked figure as he strode forward, his arms raised into the air while he called out praise to the Shadow Princess before descending on Caleb's brother Hadley and angling his chin up.

Hadley's face was written in agony and my heart hurt for him as I watched Vard forcing a vial of something into his mouth before a flash of green healing magic blazed in his palm and he pressed his hand to Hadley's side.

"What the fuck is he doing to him?" Caleb growled, his grip tightening so hard on the window frame that a chunk of the wood shattered in his fingers beneath the force of his gifted strength.

"I think it must have been a blood replenishing potion," Max said, frowning as he used his Siren gifts to feel for the answer. "He's regaining strength rapidly."

"They want to keep them alive to suffer on with this," I growled. "They clearly need their power to channel the shadows to Lavinia and don't want them dying."

"What about their magic?" Seth demanded. "It isn't endless. Once they're burned out, then what?"

But the answer to that became clear as a Nymph strode out of a dark corner, a man clutched in his grasp who kicked and thrashed and started begging for mercy. Vard moved forward with a knife raised, cutting into the man's arm and he screamed bloody murder as he was forced towards Hadley, the wounded arm shoved against his mouth.

Hadley tried to fight against his instincts, shaking his head and cursing in a raspy voice as he fought against the beast within him, but he was clearly in need of the magic and with the shadows latched onto his own power, he was growing frantic with the need for blood.

Vard shoved the man's arm to his mouth again and Hadley snarled as he ripped into his flesh, drinking deeply as he recharged his magic, and the foul hold of the shadows tightened their grip on him to feed their queen.

"The Sirens are being fed with pain," Max rumbled, pointing out movement on the other side of the courtyard where two Nymphs were torturing several Fae, their mouths parted in screams which must have been shielded by a silencing bubble because I couldn't hear them at all.

"And they're making my family run," Seth said, the horror in his voice turning to rage as the ground beneath Antonia's feet began to move under the power of an earth Elemental's magic, creating a rolling wheel which forced her legs to move against her will, replenishing her magic as she ran beneath the moon.

"Come on," I growled, turning from the view of that horror show and gritting my teeth in determination as I moved towards the door, fully intending to head down there and rip every single Nymph and follower of my father apart in a bid to rescue my friends' families.

But I only made it a few steps when the sound of an Atlas ringing cut through the air and I looked around in surprise, frowning at my nightstand where one of my old spares had been left, still plugged in and clearly forgotten.

Max went to stride past me, but I caught his arm, my skin prickling with the feeling that that call was important, and for a moment I swear I could hear the stars whispering amongst themselves all around us.

"It's Gabriel," Caleb said as he shot across the room to check the caller ID and he answered it before we could register our surprise at that.

"Darius?" Gabriel barked as Cal put the call on speaker and we all moved closer as I answered.

"We're all here. What is it?"

"The Burrows are under attack and your father is here," he said urgently and any last remaining shred of hope that I'd been holding onto withered and died with those words. "Lavinia must have planned this. I didn't *see* it coming until they were already here," I could hear the anguish in his voice, but that didn't make the news any easier to bear.

"What's happening?" I demanded, the beast beneath my skin writhing with the need for blood.

"His entire Nymph army and his Dragon guard are attacking," Gabriel said quickly. "We're meeting them in the open field and the twins are leading the charge. I think Lavinia lured you away from here to turn the odds in their favour."

"Or to trap us," Seth growled and my hand tightened into a fist as I considered that. The Councillors had clearly been here for a while which meant that message Cal had received had never come from his mom. "They want to add us to that shit fest down there."

"Fuck," Max breathed in agreement and a growl rumbled through my chest.

"I'm still not leaving without my family," Caleb said firmly, and my heart felt like it was being ripped in to two directions because as much as I understood that, I needed to get back to that fight, I had to be there to stand beside my girl, and I needed to be the one to take on my father.

"Fate is twisting too fast for me to keep track of it," Gabriel said. "But Darius, you need to return now or Xavier will die. His fate is set unless you can change it. He's gone up against your father, but I've seen his fate, he can't win. I'll leave you to decide on the rest, but Darius - you only have six minutes."

The call cut out as the sound of screams filled the background of it and I looked up at my brothers in horror as the magnitude of how spectacularly wrong this had all gone pressed down on my shoulders like an endless weight.

"Go," Max commanded. "We can stay here and save our families. Your brother needs you."

The others nodded their agreement and I lunged at them, wrapping them all in my arms and crushing them against me as we embraced for what I feared could be the final time.

"I have loved you all like family from the day that I was born," I said firmly. "No matter how this plays out, know that."

"We love you too, brother," Caleb replied and Seth howled mournfully as I pulled away, taking the stardust from my pocket and grabbing a fistful of it for myself before tossing the bag to Max.

"We'll throw you to the border," Max said, shoving me back towards the twisting staircase which led to the roof, and we raced up them at a fierce pace.

"Good luck," I said, taking off in a sprint and launching myself from the edge of the parapet just as Seth and Max threw a blast of air magic out to catch me and hurl me away from the manor at a ferocious speed.

I crashed through the barriers which prevented travel via stardust at the edge of the property, and threw the glittering substance over my head in the next breath, the stars whipping me away from Acrux Manor and sending me straight into the heart of the battle.

I emerged above the fight, the clash of magic and swords clanging below me as the rebels fought against my father's army with the ruthless need to survive which all Fae held deep within their hearts, their weapons flashing with Phoenix fire.

I shifted as I fell, my enormous golden Dragon form tearing from my body as I locked eyes on my father, the asshole snapping his jaws at Tyler who was flying with Sofia on his back. Tyler put on a burst of speed, and my father gave up on him, turning and diving towards the ground. He landed with a tremendous thud and my heart lurched with terror as I spotted him closing in on Xavier in his Pegasus form sprawled in the mud. My brother tried to get up, but Father slammed a clawed forefoot onto Xavier's side, his beautiful Lilac body pinned beneath the bulk of the jade green Dragon who I despised above all other things in this world.

A roar of challenge escaped me and father whipped his head sideways, a scream of pain escaping Xavier as the Dragon who had sired him tore his beautiful lilac wing from his back with the movement, blood and feathers flying through the small space which divided us, the wing landing with the other one which he had already severed.

I dove hard and collided with him.

My bones rattled as I sent him crashing away from my brother who lay bleeding and broken in the dirt, and the pain in my heart bled into a fury unlike anything I'd ever felt before as I swore one thing to myself which I was determined to follow through on, no matter the cost.

Lionel Acrux would die tonight, and I would be the one painting the world crimson with his blood.

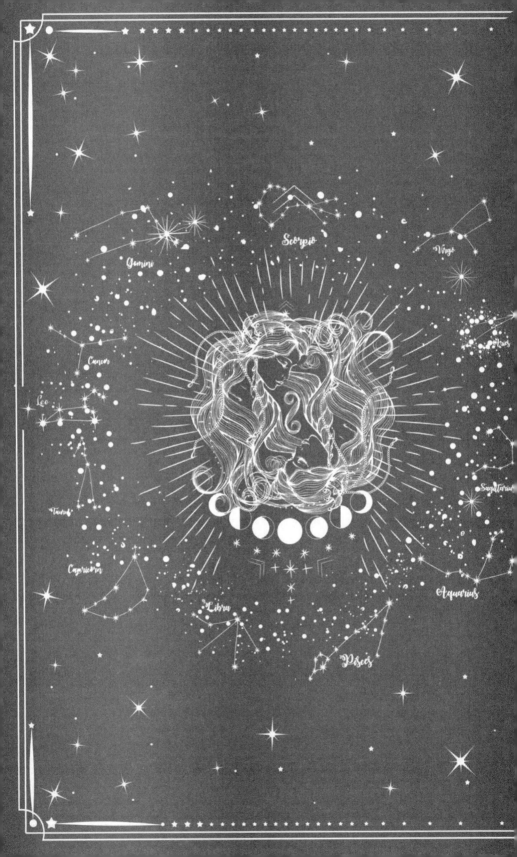

DARCY

CHAPTER FIFTY NINE

Ash and blood speckled my cheeks as I fought on the ground beside Orion, back to back as we were accosted by a ring of Nymphs. Fire scored out from my hands in a blaze of death, taking down three of them at once and darkness curtained my vision for a moment as I stumbled forward.

A Nymph's probed hand slammed into me, knocking me onto the ground but suddenly my mate was there driving his sword deep into its chest with a roar of anger that shook the foundations of my being.

I regained my feet fast, drawing on the power within me as fire weaved along my blood and begged for the death of my enemies. I blasted a Nymph to my right as Orion finished off another and he shot to my side, his breaths coming heavily.

We found ourselves among the rebels in a moment of reprieve as we healed ourselves of aching limbs and any wounds we'd gained in our last fights. I'd dropped my sword at some point and I ran over to pick it up where it was lodged in the ground, caked in mud and the blackish blood of Nymphs.

Orion spun his own sword in his hand, a knife in his other as he prepared to charge back into the battle and we shared a look that sent a shiver to the edges of my flesh. I flexed my fingers, magic tingling in them once more as the rattle of Nymphs died away around us, the delightful sound of their deaths filling my ears.

"Ready, beautiful?" he asked.

"Let's make them scream," I said just as a grey Dragon swooped overhead. Its jaws widened as it unleashed a line of hellfire down on us and the surrounding crowd, making my heart stall.

I acted fast, raising a hand and guttering the flames with air magic, a scream of defiance leaving me as I stole the air from the beast's lungs too, cutting off its ferocious roar.

Then I sheathed my sword and raised my other hand, wielding the air around the Dragon, taking control of its enormous body and pulling it from the sky with my muscles tense and burning, sending it slamming down into a pond beyond the fight and letting go of it.

The Dragon skidded through the water, droplets spraying up everywhere as it thrashed, but I held onto the air in its lungs, stealing it all away as fury burned a path up my spine as it panicked and kicked.

My power suddenly locked down inside me and I gasped, my knees buckling and a ringing sounded in my ears.

I was half aware I was on the ground, my hands sinking into the mud while the din of the battle droned on around me.

"Darcy," Orion gasped, grabbing onto me and drawing me back to my feet.

A quake ran through my body and I clung to him as I fought back the cloying darkness seeming to rise within me. But as I latched onto the shining silver rings in his eyes, my strength returned to me in a rush and I gripped his arms tighter, grounding myself in this moment.

"What happened?" he demanded, and I realised he'd cast a solid air shield around us, buying us a moment from the battle.

"Nothing," I said, needing to get back to the fight.

"Don't lie to me, mate of mine," he snarled, seeing right through me as he gripped my face in his palm.

"Alright, I'm not sure," I admitted. "It felt kind of like..." I looked to Lavinia who stood on a tower of darkness beyond the endless line of Nymphs, my upper lip curling back. "It felt like her," I spat. "I want to get to her, Lance. I want her to burn in my fire."

He looked over his shoulder towards her, hatred twisting through his eyes as he bared his fangs. "I'd like to see that myself, Blue," he said darkly.

"Then let's move." I let go of him and he dropped the air shield, forging my way through the rebels as Orion moved at my back, his sword raised as we set Lavinia in our sights.

Darius was in a furious fight with Lionel, the huge forms of the two of them colliding in the air and my breath caught as I pointed him out to Orion.

"Darius is here," I called over the clamour of the battle, praying he could win the fight with his father.

Orion yanked me back against his chest a heartbeat before three Nymphs came barrelling through the crowd, knocking several Fae down beneath them and driving their probes into their chests.

A snarl escaped me and I raised my hands, releasing an inferno on the closest one while Orion moved to intercept another. The rebels all looked to me for orders, and I was more than willing to give them as I called out for them to cut down our enemies.

"Close ranks, don't let them get to The Burrows!" I shouted.

"Yes, My Queen!" the rebels yelled, diving into battle with no fear in their eyes and my heart swelled as I witnessed the ferocity of my people.

Washer was riding on a wave of water, his body covered in the light blue scales of his Order and his clothes discarded. He cast whips of water which carried his Phoenix sword, sending it blasting into the chests of Nymphs before recalling it to him.

"Take a teenie weenie bit of that – and that!" he cried as he stabbed them, his skill and accuracy something to be admired.

The rebels took down the third Nymph with cries of my name on their lips, and when we'd laid out our enemies, Orion and I forged on.

Fae raced past us in countless Order forms, and it was hard to know who was with us and who was against us as a clash of fur and horns and magic collided everywhere.

Orion cast an air shield around us as we left the rattle of the Nymphs behind and I offered my own power to the shield to keep us safe as we picked up our pace and ran towards Lavinia, taking down any enemies we could along the way as I shouted out encouragements to the rebels.

I hunted for Tory as we went and saw her flying up over the head of a huge Nymph, battling to take it down and relief filled me to see her fighting like the warrior Queen Avalon had taught her to be.

I swore as a tide of rebels pushed back against us, slowing our movements as a row of Nymphs blocked their way forward and I looked to Orion, an idea forming in my mind.

"We can tunnel to Lavinia," I said. "If we can get beyond her, I can come at her from behind."

"I'll move us fast," Orion agreed, but before we went anywhere, I raised my hands and cast a tornado with my air magic, the monstrous vortex descending from the sky and slamming into the Nymphs who were attacking the rebels before us.

They were sucked into my power, the spinning grey storm making my hair fly around me as I poured my strength into it. The Nymphs shrieked as they were thrown to the ground, leaving them vulnerable as our allies fell on them, using the weapons we'd blessed with our fire to destroy them, my name carrying to the sky again as they shouted it in praise.

I disbanded the huge tornado with a breath of exertion leaving me and Orion gazed at me like I was a goddess of hell brought here to eradicate our opponents. And that was just what I planned to do.

I turned my hands towards the ground, carving a tunnel beneath our feet and racing down into it while Orion followed, and I closed it up behind us. I cast a Faelight as the muffled sound of the battle echoed around us through the dirt, and I took in the blood speckles on my mate's cheeks as he waited for my next command.

"Let's hurry," I urged and Orion picked me up as I scored a path beneath the earth and he carried me along it at a furious pace.

The rumble of a thousand footfalls and the clash of the battle made the earth tremble around us, and my heart dipped with fear for my friends. But they were strong, I'd seen them fighting and had watched as they felled their enemies time and again. They could handle this battle, we'd been training for it for months and though it had been sprung on us, it didn't mean we weren't ready. *We can do this.*

When I was sure we had to be beyond Lavinia, Orion came to a halt and I turned my hands towards the dirt roof above us as he placed me down on my feet.

"Wait," Orion growled, yanking me into a kiss that stole away every inch of fear in my body. It was barely a couple of seconds, but offered me endless courage as we broke apart, my lips burning from the contact of his.

"Give her hell, Blue."

"For Clara," I swore and his eyes blazed with emotion at his sister's name as he nodded.

I gave him a fierce look that swore I could do this, not letting myself dwell in dread about what might await us above ground as I turned my hands to the dirt and blasted it apart.

Orion lifted us out on a gust of air and I spread my wings as I raised my hands higher, finding us behind the towering darkness that Lavinia stood upon.

I didn't hesitate for a single moment. I flew upwards with fire swirling along my limbs, burning in my very soul as I built a blaze of Phoenix fire in my hands which could level a fucking town.

I came to a halt, hovering right behind her, and a twisted smile pulled at my lips.

Goodbye, shadow bitch.

I released the fire, the short range blast sending me flying backwards through the air as the fireball collided with Lavinia, and I raised a hand to shield my eyes against the flames. I beat my wings to counter the blast, my gaze adjusting to the brightness as I flew forward with a ruthless determination to end her.

Her body was consumed within it and Lavinia shrieked and wailed, the dark tower beneath her crumbling away within my flames. I followed her towards the ground as she fell with a scream and triumph scored through my blood. Fire exploded from me once more as I circled down after her like a bird of prey and she hit the ground with a thwack, her body jerking and writhing within my Phoenix fire.

I came to a halt above her as I beat my wings, unleashing all I had on this monstrous bitch for all she'd done to me, to my friends, to Clara.

"Fuck you!" I cried, frying the monster who'd dared tried to curse me, who'd thought she could win with her brutality and darkness.

But she was nothing compared to our light.

My power stuttered out and my wings fluttered away as I went to land beside her, hitting the ground awkwardly, but managing to stay on my feet. Panic rushed through me as I reached for my Order, but my Phoenix didn't answer the call.

Orion was at my side in an instant, watching as Lavinia burned and the rebels cheered nearby, the tide of the battle finally turning in our favour as I struggled to catch my breath.

I'm tired. That's all it is.

Just breathe.

Orion cast a shield of air around us, holding the Nymphs back who tried to dive in to save their princess, but she was still burning within my fire and I wasn't going to let anyone take her death from me now.

Lavinia's screams died away and my flames simmered all the way down, leaving a husk of charred bones in their wake, and though exhaustion was falling over me and I couldn't reach my Phoenix at all, I laughed my relief, my complete fucking joy. Because she was dead. Fucking dead and gone and without her, Lionel was nothing.

"You did it," Orion laughed like he'd known I could and I turned and threw myself at him, hugging him tight as a choked sob of happiness left me. He kissed my cheeks, my head, anywhere he could get to as I buried my face in his chest and breathed in the scent of cinnamon and fucking victory.

"It's over. She's gone. That fucking nightmare is dead," I sighed.

"Wait." Orion stiffened and pushed me back, forcing me to turn and look at the bones once more. And the smile slid from my face as I found them standing there, a skeletal hand pointed at me as shadows wrapped around the horrid creature and clad Lavinia's bones in skin once more.

From the bottom up, she was remade, her body reforming as the shadows twisted and writhed around her like a living beast and Orion and I backed up in horror as her face was reforged. Dark hair grew out the top of her skull, dancing in the ethereal wind her shadows created and as the darkness cloaked her in a black dress, she looked to me with a vicious sneer on her lips.

She was still pointing at me in a way that made my heart turn to a lump of solid ice in my chest.

I raised my hands as Orion raised his sword, but no Phoenix fire came out, no whisper of magic, nothing at all.

Lavinia twisted her fingers and something twisted in my stomach in response, making a gasp of agony leave me as I doubled over.

"Stay back!" Orion shot forward with a yell of defiance, his sword raised and flaming with the gifts of my Order and a scream of fear left me as Lavinia's eyes snapped onto him. But as he swung his blade, she just knocked him aside with a blast of shadows that made him hit the ground hard.

A tendril of shadow ripped the sword from his hand, turning it back on him and holding the tip of it to his throat. She carved his air shield to pieces around us with her dark power in the next moment and we were exposed, at her mercy.

"For the true queens!" one of the rebels bellowed, racing forward to attack Lavinia but she sent shadows his way which cut him in two right down the middle, blood spilling and making me wince in terror as I continued to try and will power to my hands in desperation.

Lavinia walked towards me, unleashing her shadows on the crowd to my left and screams of terror carried through the air as they ripped my people to pieces.

"Stop!" I cried, looking to Orion in anguish as he struggled on the ground, panic making me shake as I saw his end so clearly that the fear nearly drowned me.

"Vega filth," Lavinia spat, glaring at me with a sea of venom in her eyes. "You think your Phoenix is stronger than my shadows?"

I flexed my fingers, begging my Phoenix to rise or my magic to return, but it was as if neither of those things existed in me. I was a mortal willing power to come to me which didn't live in my bones, and it looked like Lavinia knew it.

"Did you think you had beat my curse?" she asked with an evil smile pulling at her mouth. She twisted her hand through the air again and I was yanked forward by some dark pit inside me, pain making me scream as I clutched my stomach. "Your Phoenix has put up a good fight, I'll admit. It wasn't meant to take this long. But now you're here and my power is far greater than ever, you cannot stop it."

"What have you done to me?" I gasped.

"Come out, come out, wherever you are," Lavinia sang as she ignored my question and I could feel claws ripping up my insides, making me scream once more as some dark thing seemed to crawl its way through my chest.

"Stop," I groaned, staggering as the pain became nearly unbearable.

"Let her go!" Orion bellowed, but I was fully in Lavinia's grasp now and as she came to stand before me, I saw a chasm of hatred in her eyes.

"Ambres tenus avilias mortalium avar," Lavinia growled and my head fell back so I was looking at the sky, rage opening up in my chest and darkness racing into the place where my magic should have lived.

"Stop," I begged again, my voice nothing but a puff of air leaving my lungs, my whole body taken charge of by her.

"You've been a bad, bad Vega. If you want to save all these people, then why have you been hurting them?" Lavinia purred.

Memories unfolded before my eyes and I watched in horror as I saw myself turning to smoke in mine and Orion's room, slipping away under the door in the night with bloodlust rising in me. I was soon outside beyond the farmhouse behind the first set of guards who'd been found murdered. I followed one of them all the way to the barn and suddenly the smoky form my body was in shifted into a huge beast. I was coated in thick black fur, my paws equipped with razor sharp claws. And I was full of nothing but anger and hunger and hate.

No, that's not me.

But it was. I was that beast and it had been responsible for the murders. *I* had been responsible. For all that death and pain and fear.

I watched the memory as I dragged the first man into the barn, killing him with claws and teeth, his screams echoing around me and drawing the other guards. But the moment they arrived, they fell prey to me, their power nothing compared to mine as I ripped into their bodies, devouring pieces of them while leaving the rest strewn across the hay in the carnage.

Memories tore through my mind of each of the murders, of me slipping in and out of our room in that smoky form at night then slicing into the victims I found. And all that I felt was rage. It was consuming and blinding and it ate away my power, my Order. Every time I killed, it grew a little stronger, and my magic was tugged from my grip more firmly. My Order had fought back, I could feel the beast's rage at that, but now I stood before the queen of shadow and she owned this monster in me. This creature which had stolen away everything I was, and it wanted more, so much more.

"The Shadow Beast has taken root in you," Lavinia purred as I snapped out of the memories and looked at her in terror, shaking my head in refusal of what I already knew was true. "It feeds on your power piece by piece by piece. You fought it well, but not well enough. And now it is sated and you are nothing but a mortal bound to a beast. And that beast is *mine*." Lavinia twisted her hand again. "Come out and play, beastie."

"No," I gasped in terror, raising my hands again, trying to will my Phoenix to the surface, but it was gone. Like it had taken flight from my body and abandoned me, and I had never known anything so terrifying as this reality.

"Get away from her!" Orion cried and Lavinia glanced over at him where he was bound in her shadows at the mercy of his own sword, then she looked back to me.

"I think the beast is hungry. Novus estris envum magicae. Avilias avar!" She flexed her fingers and suddenly my rage was all consuming and my flesh was tearing apart, my armour bending and buckling as an enormous monster fought its way out of my body. The armour was forced off of me, falling to pieces around me with a series of clangs as they hit the ground, the sound like a toll of death to come. The necklace at my throat snapped and the Imperial Star tumbled away, lost to the mud.

My huge paws slammed into the earth as I towered above Lavinia and every part of me was forced to let go as the animal took over on the inside too.

Lavinia let Orion get up, offering him his sword too and my mate immediately pointed it at her.

"Release her from this curse!" he ordered, slashing the sword at her, but Lavinia knocked him backwards with a wave of her hand like he was nothing but a mild irritation.

"You'd better stop her before she hurts your little friends," Lavinia taunted.

"I'll never hurt her," he snarled and she considered him, pointing me towards the rebels as my gaze turned that way and I salivated with the amount of prey I could see before me.

I prowled towards them with nothing but hunger and death within me, my mind a haze of darkness.

"No – Blue! Look at me!" a voice reached me, but I could no longer place who it belonged to.

I started to run towards the crowd as anger billowed up inside me and set my veins alight. I was hungry, so endlessly hungry I ached. And as I collided with the Fae and the first blood was spilled by my claws, I howled to the moon and felt the darkness within me deepen.

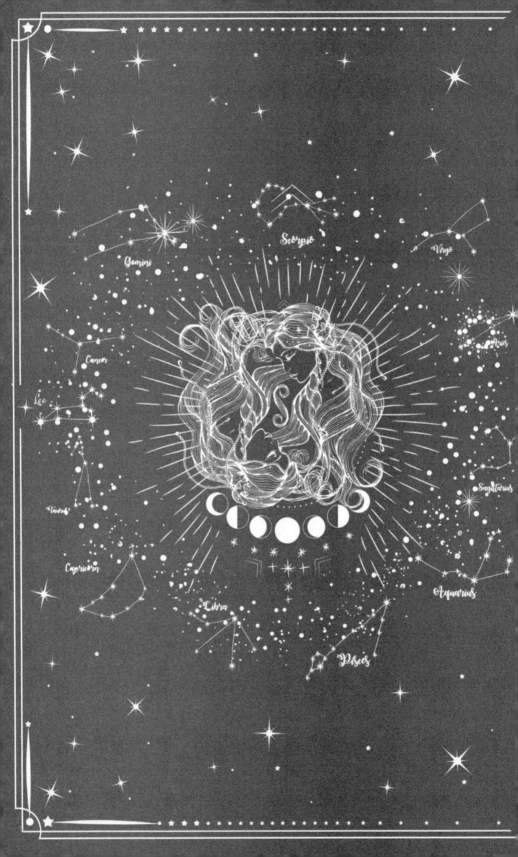

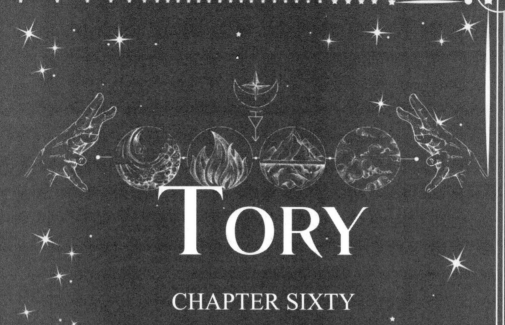

TORY

CHAPTER SIXTY

I fought with the rage of a queen protecting her kingdom and the power of a monster born to bathe in the blood of its enemies. And I had so many fucking enemies. Lionel and Lavinia were only at the top of a very long list, and I wasn't even going to get started on the fucking stars.

They watched us now, twinkling in the perfectly clear sky, enjoying the show as the Fae whose fates they twisted so carelessly with their desires fought for their lives down here in the mud. They didn't care who was the victor here. They only came to watch the carnage they had orchestrated.

I fought with fire and fury, using the power of the blaze to keep my magic fully charged at all times while blasting great holes in the ranks of our enemies, yet still they came at us from every angle.

We had been caught entirely unaware and with our army still mostly trapped underground, bottlenecked in the tunnels and only slowly making their way up here to join our ranks, we were at a serious disadvantage.

My gaze caught on Catalina and Hamish as they ripped the hillside apart with their earth magic, freeing more rebels from the tunnels beneath while shielding against the Dragon Guild who swooped overhead in their shifted forms, aiming to burn our army with their Dragon fire before they could even fully join the fight.

The heavy power of Nymph rattles sounded over and over again, making the magic inside me flicker to an insistent beat whenever I got too close to one of them, but my flaming sword was already wet with the blood of their kind and any who made the mistake of thinking I could only fight with my magic found out they were wrong the hard way.

The huge Nymph who seemed to lead their ranks was still in my sights, but he had moved further away, charging towards the far side of the battlefield where the Tiberian Rats were making a stand led by Eugene Dipper.

My heart swelled at the courage of our army as I found them fighting all around me, but still the sheer numbers of Lionel's followers was terrifying.

A roar unlike anything I'd ever heard before shook the ground at my feet and I turned to my right as the rebels there screamed, trying to run from whatever had caused that sound.

My eyes widened as I spotted the source of their fear, a huge beast tearing through their ranks with claws of shadow and the soulless eyes of a nightmare. It was as big as a Monolrian Bear Shifter and resembled their kind a little too, its black fur wet with the blood of the Fae it had killed.

I raised my hand with a bellow of challenge escaping my lips as I called on my Phoenix and red and blue flames ignited in my fist, building and building until I released it with a blast of energy which almost knocked me from my feet.

A bird born of fire erupted from my hold, crying out in its eerily beautiful voice for all the rebels to hear, bolstering their morale as it swept over their heads and flew straight towards the creature of shadow who had come to destroy them.

The beast looked up as the Phoenix fire bore down on it, its eyes moving to me, a glint of silver in them which almost made me pause as a shiver tracked down my spine.

My attack slammed into the creature and it roared as it was hurled from its feet, crashing backwards into the ranks of Nymphs and crushing them beneath it, shattering bony limbs and making them scream in pain.

I started running towards it as it scrambled to get up, a frown burrowing into my brow at the fact that it had survived that strike. I held my sword ready and yelled out a challenge.

The rebels tried to move aside as I ran at them, but I ignored them, leaping up and using my air magic to propel myself over their heads, gripping my sword in both hands and swinging it above me as I prepared to make the killing blow.

Something slammed into me with the force of a car crash, and I was knocked off course with a curse of pain, tumbling to the ground beneath a powerful body and losing my grip on my sword as we skidded across the dirt.

I snatched a blade from my hip, jamming my knee into the ground to stop our roll and swinging the dagger at the neck of my opponent, my eyes widening in alarm as I recognised Orion.

I managed to halt my attack at the last second, the tip of my blade grazing the corner of his jaw and drawing blood as I snatched it away and I sucked in a sharp breath.

"Holy fuck, I almost killed you."

"The beast is Darcy," he barked, not even seeming to give a fuck about the blood I'd just drawn from him. "It's the curse. Lavinia has forced it to manifest within her and I don't think it's the first time."

I jerked my head around, looking through the crush of fighting bodies towards the beast as it got to its feet once more, my lips parting in horror as I took in what he was saying.

"She's the one who was killing those Fae in The Burrows?" I breathed and Orion nodded as I looked back down at him.

"I think so. But I don't think she knew it was happening. She seems utterly lost to the curse now that she's in its hold. I'm going to get her away from here. You have to win this battle, Tory. You have to lead them to victory."

I swallowed thickly as I took that in, throwing a shield of air magic up around us as I got to my feet and offered him a hand up too.

"No pressure then," I ground out, glancing at the carnage which surrounded us.

"You can do it," Orion said, gripping my arm and making me look at his silver ringed eyes where I found a whole lot more faith in me than I had in myself, and I swallowed thickly.

"Please save her, Lance," I breathed unsure if he would even be able to hear me over the raging battle, but he nodded firmly.

"I'll do whatever it takes."

"Do you need more power?" I asked as the beast roared and I looked towards it once more, wondering how the fuck he planned on getting her out of here.

His answer came in the sharp sting of his fangs sinking into my neck and I gritted my teeth as I tightened my grip on my sword, my gaze falling on that huge Nymph once more just as he shifted back into his Fae like form and a snarl pulled at my lips as I recognised Alejandro.

"Don't die," Orion commanded as he released me, and I met his gaze one last time.

"You either." I dropped the shield protecting us and he shot away towards Darcy as I forced myself to let him help her without me.

I hurried over to reclaim my dropped sword, raising it and fixing Alejandro in my sights as he began to throw handfuls of wild fire magic at the rebels who fought against the Nymphs on his flank.

Fire magic he'd stolen from my father when he killed him. Magic I'd make him pay for taking in blood and bone.

"Tonight, you die, asshole."

GERALDINE

CHAPTER SIXTY ONE

I had seen it all. My lady Darcy turning into a beast of the backwoods, and her Orry man chasing after her into the fray. I had to run to her, to tame her like a wild mustang in my pastures.

I ran forth as the giant beastly creature that my dear Darcy had turned into feasted on our people. She resembled a large black bear with shadows that danced along the edges of her fur like a creature from the deep chasms of Bagamagooth.

"I am coming, hold on my lady!" I cried.

I spun through the air with the name Vega on my lips as I swung my flail, the spiked ball whacking into the goonish face of a Nymph and turning the brute to soot. It was a small victory among a field of desolation and as Darcy rampaged among our people, I could see our doom rising like the moon over a stormy sea, marking us for passage beyond the Veil.

Orion cast air shields over the rebels to keep Darcy away from as many of them as he could, but she tore through them time and again.

I took down another Nymph with a shriek and a swing of my loyal weapon, the Flail of Unending Celestial Karma delivering death to our enemies like it was born to protect us.

"Take that you rapscallion of the underlings!" I cried, wiping my brow as I pressed on, my sweet Darcy now coated in blood as pieces of the rebels went flying overhead and the wailing intensified.

I had an inkling of what had brought upon this change in her. Lavinia was clearly to blame. I had seen their interaction, though I hadn't heard even a whisper of a word over the tumult of the battle.

Orion was fighting to push her back, his arm already bleeding from a swipe of Darcy's claws, and I screamed like a Grebe of the Garbles as I fought to reach them. I would not see her Elysian Mate fall beneath her claws or watch her tear his head from his fine body, but alas! I could not seem to move any faster, pushed back by the rebels who turned and ran from their queen as she slashed them to pieces.

But I would not cower like a gnat before the jaws of a dragonfly, nay! I would come to my lady's aid. I would yodel her name to the sky and beg the stars to free her from this terrifying form which had gripped her body.

Orion managed to cover another line of the rebels with air magic, giving them a chance to escape, then he cast ice to try and bind Darcy's legs, holding her down.

I yelled in encouragement, but Darcy broke through the ice and slammed into a row of rebels, taking them down beneath her paws.

"Oh golly guacamole on a gecko."

I made it closer and blood splattered my face as Darcy shook a man between her jaws. My dear lady's eyes swirled with the darkness of the heinous shadow witch who had done this to her and I vowed to save her.

Orion leapt onto Darcy's back, his hands knotting in her fur as he wrenched her head sideways, forcing her jaws away from the rebels and allowing them a chance to run. But run I did not.

I dug my heels in, my shoulders ramming against the rebels as I fought the tide of bodies which pushed past me, not allowing them to sweep me away with them like a lost coconut to sea.

Darcy shook her head so hard that Orion was thrown off of her, hitting the ground on his back with a crack that told me some vital bone had broken. And as he growled through the pain of it, I saw he was unable to move, his sword lost to the dirt of the battlefield as his Elysian Mate stepped forward to deliver the killing blow.

A gasp lodged in my throat and I jammed my elbows into the rebels around me, forcing them aside, breaking through their ranks like a pea bursting from its pod and at once I was running again, my flail held aloft as I waved it and screamed loud enough for the sun to hear me where it slept beyond the horizon.

Darcy lifted her head, turning her eyes on me instead of Orion and I kept running towards them, my flail still waving but with no intention of hurting my lady. I was caught within confliction as she bared her fangs at me, and I saw my death shining at me like two pebbled diamonds in her eyes.

"You shall not harm your Orry man!" I wailed, diving forward, my feet leaving the ground as I spun in a somersault, head over heel before landing on Orion and healing him with all I had to give.

He grunted as the snapped discs of his spine fused back together and our eyes met a moment before sharp claws pierced my armour like a hot knife cutting through butter, digging deep into my shoulder and throwing me off of him.

I sailed through the air, losing my grip on my flail, time seeming to slow as the hot gush of blood rolled down my back and the sky and the earth merged together as one.

I scented a river of death upon my flesh and wondered if my time was near as I hit the ground, rolling down a muddy bank, a sea of blood and mud flying up around me as the wind was forced from my lungs.

Perhaps Mama was close, waiting to offer me her hand and guide me into the stars. But I would not go quietly, I would fight until there was no more fight in my bones. I would battle on like the brave warriors of old and stand as unwaveringly as a mountain before the moon this very night.

I lifted my head, trying to get up and the most tremendous boom sounded as Angelica hit the ground before me in her giant red Dragon form. She roared as Mildred's huge brown Dragon landed atop her, the ugly beast ripping into her throat with sharpened tooth and bloody claw, and my dear Angelica's roars extinguished in her throat, her final breath rolling over my cheeks as she died and that foul Mildred tore her head from her shoulders, bellowing her victory before taking off into the sky.

Anguish, grief and utter devastation tangled inside me as I forced myself to my feet, and healed myself, spotting Orion taking chase after Darcy on the battlefield, his shirt half torn off and soaked in blood.

Tears ran down my cheeks as I stared at my dear friend Angelica with a sob in my throat like a frog on a lily pad.

"Sweet, darling Angelica!" I wailed, my tears coming hot and fast as I looked to the sky, my gaze narrowing on Mildred as I branded her with a curse of my own making. "You shall die by my hand, and you shall suffer before I send you into the nether world screaming and burning from the inside out! Hear me this day! I shall avenge my ally who was stout of heart and held more worth in her toenail than you shall ever possess!"

SETH

CHAPTER SIXTY TWO

"What do we do now?" I growled, desperate to charge out there and grab my family, and my friends' families too. And where the hell were the rest of our families? Were they in this house? Because I sure as shit didn't know where to start looking for them if they were, and the idea that maybe they'd been disposable, that maybe Lionel had gotten rid of them kept swelling in my mind and making me want to charge into battle without thought. But I had to keep my head. I had to force down my emotions into that dark pit inside me and do what I did best. Pretend I was a fucking cold hearted, blood thirsty asshole who could take anything in his stride without flinching. So that was what I was gonna do.

We'd made it downstairs to a lounge where we could see out into the courtyard. I was kneeling behind a couch with Cal pressed up on my right and Max on my left, a whine in my throat as a silencing bubble surrounded us along with a thick concealment spell that blended us right in with the furniture. We'd watched Vard leave, leading a large group of Nymphs with him as they headed towards the front of the manor, muttering about the new arrivals being here soon and we'd quickly figured out that we must have been those new arrivals. Which meant they were off preparing their trap for us far too late. Sucked for them that we'd already made it into the house then. I guessed stealing Vard's shadow eye had made him the shittest Seer this side of Solaria. But it was a small victory in the face of all this.

"There's so many of them out there," Max said in frustration. "We need to draw them away."

"And we need a binding needle to close that rift," I replied. "Do you think one of us should stardust back to get one?"

"We don't have enough stardust for multiple trips," Max said with a frown.

"Wait, Stella's house is right next door," Cal said in realisation.

"And?" I asked.

"And Orion told me all about how there's a secret basement in there full of all his dad's old dark magic equipment," Caleb explained. "It's hidden behind a secret panel in the hall under the stairs."

"Of course your bestie told you that," I muttered, though okay, yeah it was handy.

"What if there's no needle?" Max said worriedly.

"They're one of the most commonly used objects in dark magic – Orion has been telling me loads about it. So it's worth a shot," Cal pushed.

"But we still need to draw those Nymphs away from the altar before we can even get to that rift," I said.

"How about I set a fire?" Cal suggested and I considered that.

"They won't all leave for that, maybe a few but…" I shook my head.

"I could try and manipulate their emotions, get them subdued," Max said thoughtfully. "Maybe I could even send them all asleep if I had enough time."

"You'll send our families asleep too and that could put them in more danger with that fucking altar thing," Cal hissed.

"I've got it," I announced, sitting back on my heels as the two of them looked to me. "I've got voice mimicking perfected. I can cast an illusion, pretend I'm Lionel long enough to call them away from outside to give you guys a chance to go get a binding needle and free everyone."

"That's not a totally terrible idea," Caleb conceded. "But if they figure it out and use their rattles on you, you're fucked."

"You think I can't handle a bunch of Nymphs?" I scoffed, though my heart thudded out of rhythm for a second at the intense look he gave me.

"Just be careful," he growled, reaching out to squeeze my hand and the point of contact sent an arrow of heat through my chest.

"Always am." I winked then worked to cast the illusion. It wasn't perfect considering I couldn't mimic Lionel exactly. He had spells working to stop me from doing so, but as I cast a large cloak around me and pulled up the hood, I reckoned I'd pass. It was dark out in that courtyard anyway, and my voice mimic would be perfect.

"Ergh, you look freakishly like him," Cal said with a wrinkled nose.

"I am a tiny-cocked iguana," I spoke in Lionel's booming voice. "How's that?"

"Perfect. Now fucking go." Max shoved me and I leapt upright, walking with my shoulders pressed back as I headed to the door and threw it open in a dramatic move worthy of the asshole himself.

"What the fuck do you think you're doing?!" I roared, making the Nymphs stiffen in alarm at seeing me.

"Doing what Lavinia asked of us," one of them answered in a grunting voice.

"And is Lavinia your king?" I barked and a few of them exchanged glances at that. "Well?!"

"No, your majesty." The nearest one bowed his head and I patted him vaguely on the shoulder, before realising that was probably not a Lionel move, so I wiped my hand off on my cloak with a grimace. "Get inside this instant. We need to talk. All of you!"

I pointed and the Nymphs hurried to obey, bowing their heads obediently as they darted past me, though a couple stayed behind to watch the shitshow which was taking place around the altar, and I guessed I'd have to trust the others to deal with them.

I started to follow the Nymphs inside, glancing over at where Max and Cal were hidden, praying to the stars that they could get our families away from that hellish altar quickly.

I followed the Nymphs into the corridor, continuing to point them along as I swept past them, getting turned around in the endless halls despite how many times I'd been here as a kid. I shoved through a door that I was pretty sure was a dining room, but instead turned out to be a large bathroom.

Balls.

They all filed inside after me and I tugged my hood closer around my face. The bright lights in this room would be a dead giveaway if these assholes looked too closely at my face.

Right. I'm in a bathroom full of monsters. Now what?

I cleared my throat, swiping my finger along a gold tap and tutting as I inspected it, trying to buy myself a moment to think.

The Nymphs exchanged a glance and I knew I was running out of time here. I had to come up with some plausible reason that I'd just led them all into this bathroom.

One of the Nymphs started looking at me a little too closely and I ducked my head, clearing my throat again as I leaned down and pretended to inspect the tap, eye to spout.

"This is no good," I tutted. "No good at all."

"Um, forgive me, my king, but what is no good?" one of them asked, and hell he had a good question which I didn't have an answer to.

"The taps of course," I growled. "They do not gleam as they should gleam."

"Perhaps you could take that up with your servants, your highness?" a Nymph suggested.

"INSOLENCE!" I bellowed, grabbing a towel and whipping him with it, but the movement knocked my hood back and my concealment spell was unveiled in all its not-quite-rightness.

"Wait, who the fuck are you?" one of the Nymphs snapped. "You're not our king!"

"Oh my stars, it's a Vega!" I roared, pointing behind them and like the idiots they were, they all turned and I fucking ducked and ran, blasting them aside with air magic and shooting myself out the door on a furious breeze.

I slammed the door behind me, welding it shut with earth magic, sealing it tighter and tighter with metal until the whole door glinted with it before releasing the concealment covering my body.

A weight slammed into it followed by another and another, but my door didn't shift.

"Ha!" I cried in excitement, but then a bang sounded as one of the Nymphs broke through the wall, stepping out into the hall with his buddies spilling after him and I yelped in surprise, turning and running back down the halls. But I didn't turn towards my friends, I delved deeper into the house, throwing magic back over my shoulder as a sea of Nymphs chased my tail.

I blasted doors apart and threw furniture into their way, tossing vases and priceless heirlooms everywhere as I smashed the place to bits in an attempt to slow down my pursuers and keep ahead of their deathly rattles which would lock away my magic.

"Seize him!" someone shouted from a set of open doors to my right and I spotted Vard striding into the house, pointing right at me with a furious expression on his one-eyed face.

I lifted a vase from a table with a gust of air magic, slamming it into his head and making him curse as he shot a blast of fire after me. I ducked it and kept running, howling loudly in encouragement for them to follow. Because so long as they were chasing me, they were nowhere near my family and friends. And I hoped to the fucking moon that they were in the process of getting the fuck out of here.

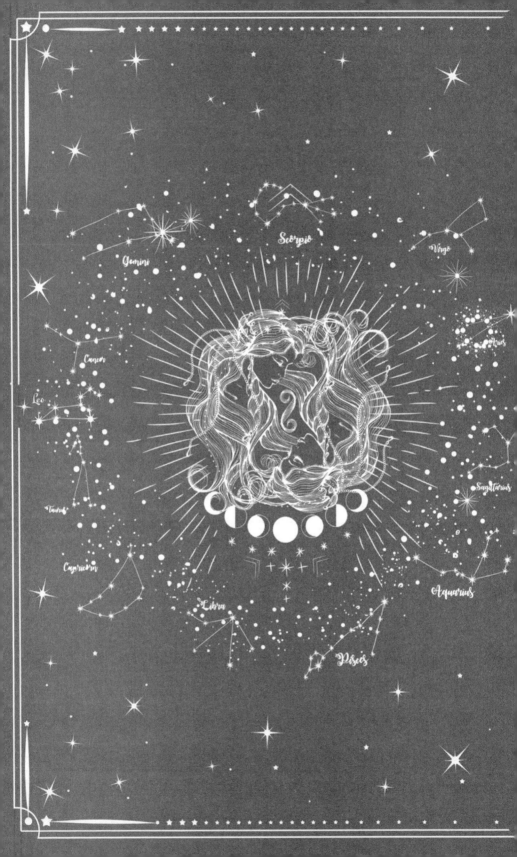

DARCY

CHAPTER SIXTY THREE

Rage spewed through my mind like acid and a wave of it drove me forward as I stared between the Fae on the ground, tearing through their ranks, the taste of so much blood sending me into a frenzy.

I wanted more. I needed to fill this dark and ceaseless need in me to destroy, ravage, and scourge the land.

The fangs in my mouth tasted of venom, the sharp and bitter tang rolling over my tongue and causing endless pain and suffering to whoever was lucky enough to live on after my bite. But they wouldn't live for long. Not when the black and tainted poison slid through their veins and claimed them as another victim of mine. Of hers.

Lavinia's whispers carried in my ears, her voice urging me on and my soul was so deeply tethered to hers even when some part of me reared up and fought against listening to her commands. But it was impossible to refuse them, her words making a fire burn in me that could never be put out, but it wasn't the fire I knew, it was a wicked thing that devoured every good piece of me whole.

A man appeared before me, his arms outstretched and a plea in his silver ringed eyes. I swiped at him, my claws slashing against a fierce air shield which I fought to tear through, driving him back as I snapped and snarled, trying to break through his defences as he battled to keep them in place.

"Blue!" he shouted, the word pulling on something deep inside my chest, but then Lavinia's whispers grew louder and my hatred thickened.

"Kill him. Kill them all," she urged inside my head. My mistress. The guider of my being, the one who had me chained and bound to her in ways that felt so deep I could never get them out.

I tore through his air shield and he shot away with a burst of speed so my paw crashed against the ground instead of striking him. I growled, turning my gaze on a silver Pegasus as he cantered along the ground, rounding up the rebels and pausing to let several of them climb onto his back. Beyond him was a pink Pegasus doing the same, already taking flight and I swiped at her as she flew towards the clouds, catching hold of her hoof and dragging her back out of the sky.

I threw her to the ground and dove forward to finish the kill but the silver Pegasus charged at me, driving a horn into my arm and making me roar as I backed up. The pink Pegasus scrambled upright, turning tail and running while the silver one galloped after her.

I chased after them, gaining on them as they stretched their wings and took off towards the sky, but I was faster, leaping forward to drag them back into my paws and finish them for good. But something grabbed hold of my fur from behind, yanking me down and throwing me to the ground.

The silver-eyed man appeared again as I shoved myself to my feet, snarling at him as he lashed ropes of air around me, trying to chain me to his will.

A girl with a flail appeared, casting vines of earth magic, binding me and bringing me to the ground as I fought their magic, anger rippling up my spine as the girl built a muzzle to close my jaws tight and yanked my head down to the ground.

The man rushed forward, kneeling in front of me and placing a hand to my head as I battled to get myself free. I needed to feed, to draw as much blood as I possibly could and sate the shadow queen who owned me.

I growled as the man spoke to me, not caring to hear, but it was impossible to ignore.

"Come back to me, Blue," he commanded. "Look at me. You know me."

He leaned close so all I could see was his eyes and for a moment I was sure I knew him. The anger inside me started to recede and the growl in my throat died as I tried to place him, unsure why it felt like this man owned me as deeply as Lavinia did.

But then my mistress spoke once more, her voice filling my head and drowning him out.

"He is your enemy. Bite, rip, kill. Spill the blood of the rebels and you will be rewarded."

I reared up as energy burst through my veins, shadow and darkness spreading inside me like oil pouring through my blood. I broke out of my binds, snapping them all at once and lunging towards the man before me.

My claws ripped into his sides as I trapped him in my paws, making him roar in pain for me as I dragged him close and opened my jaws, tearing the muzzle apart as I went to rip his head from his shoulders.

Something sharp slammed into my upper leg, again and again and I howled in anger, dropping my prey and rounding on the girl with the flail.

"Forgive me, lady Darcy," she half sobbed as she turned and ran. "I cannot let you hurt the man chosen for you by the stars!"

I leapt after her, a snarl on my lips as she cast walls of ice behind her to slow me down, but I rammed through them all, shards flying everywhere and cutting into my legs as I kept charging after her, only to find myself tumbling into a huge chasm in the ground.

I howled in anger, slamming to the bottom of it and looking up at the girl as she stood at the top of the hole, working to cast a magical net over the chasm to keep me held. But I was a creature of the shadows, a monster of the night. And I would not be held.

I sprang up, climbing the dirt walls and clawing my way higher as she hurried to trap me. But I got there before she could, slicing through her cage with my sharp claws and catching hold of her leg as I scrambled my way out of the hole. I knocked her down beneath me as the flail slipped from her grip and I saw the whites of her eyes as realisation filled them.

"I do not die in vain! Into the evermore I go - I love you, my lady!" she cried as I closed my teeth around her body, ripping and tearing until her screams were cut off, tossing her away from me like a ragdoll as she left a trail of blood through the dirt then fell into the hole she'd cast to trap me, tumbling away into the dark.

I lifted my head and howled to the night over my kill. And when I finally looked down again, I found the silver-eyed man holding a flaming sword above his head to gain my attention, waving it left and right.

I took off through the battlefield, leaving the other rebels behind as the voice in my mind urged me to finish this one off and feast on his blood.

And I was a slave to that command.

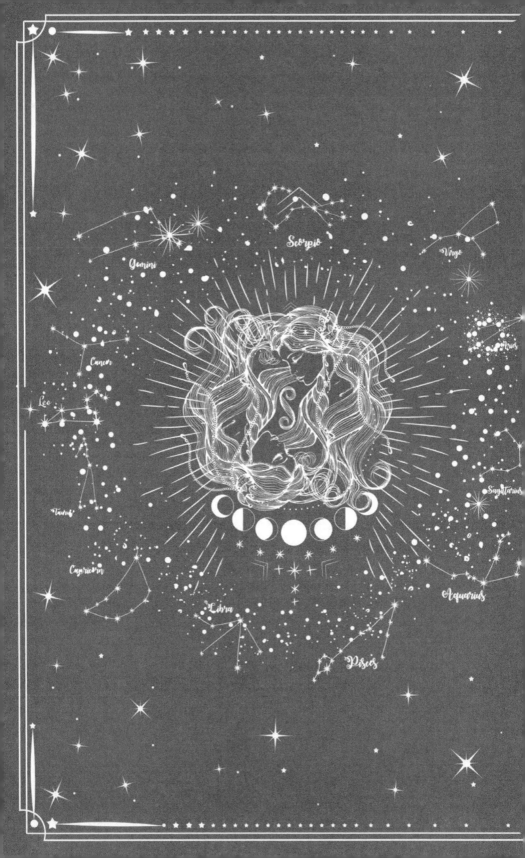

TORY

CHAPTER SIXTY FOUR

Fire magic slammed into my air shield with such force that I was knocked from my feet, my armour ringing with a metallic dong as I crashed down on my back and I snarled as I rolled in the mud and blood which coated the ground, shoving to my feet once more before summoning my wings from my spine and taking off into the air.

The fight was still raging all around me and I cursed as Dragon fire was blasted my way by one of Lionel's fucking fan club members, ducking the attack with my speed rather than wasting the energy on shielding and throwing shards of ice and wood back at the red beast, aiming at its wings and eyes.

The Dragon roared in agony as the magic skewered the thin membrane of its wings and I followed my attack with a blast of air that sent the beast soaring out over the ranks of Nymphs so that it crashed down into them as it fell instead of hitting the rebels.

I'd lost sight of Alejandro in the melee again as he kept shifting in and out of his Nymph form to attack in different ways, the Nymphs at his command allowing him through their line while I was forced to face it time and again.

A loyal band of rebels had formed at my back, adapting to my fighting style and battling alongside me to help me gain ground with every minute that passed, and I offered Justin a grim smile as he set a Nymph alight with his fire magic and sent it screaming back into the fold of its brethren.

An earth shattering roar filled the air and I looked across the battlefield to the hill where Lionel and Darius had taken their fight, the flash of gold and green scales in the moonlight slick with what had to be blood.

My heart squeezed with fear for my mate, but I forced myself to have faith in him just as he would have to have faith in me to see this fight through. Though as I looked down at my people and took in the seemingly endless swarm of Lionel's army advancing on them, I had to admit that I was starting to fear the outcome of this battle.

I sheathed my sword and called on my water magic as I held myself suspended above the fight, drawing my power to the tips of my fingers and holding it there until I swear I could hear the rush of water pulsing against my eardrums, the strength of it threatening to overwhelm me.

I released a tidal wave on the Nymphs before us, my hair whipping back with the force of energy I exerted and a feral snarl burning from my lips as it crashed into them, washing them away and driving them into the mud of the battlefield. I took hold of that mud next, dragging as many flailing bodies as I could down into it, my fists clenching and limbs trembling with the force of my magic as I drowned them in the mud and bought my unit some small reprieve from the fight.

I dropped from the sky to land before my people, finding Catalina among them as she threw wooden spears one after another at the retreating backs of the Nymphs who had managed to run from my attack, taking them down while Hamish kept his hand on her shoulder, lending her his power.

"That's it, Kitty! Poke them full of more holes than a fig bush!"

My eyes darted back and forth over the battlefield as my little unit of Fae all looked to me for my next orders and Justin moved closer, raising a metal shield and holding it protectively like he was hoping to shield me from an attack if one came, the glint of a Phoenix fire blade in his other hand, held ready.

I spotted Alejandro to my left as the sound of screams grew unbearable from his direction, Eugene's battalion all shifting into their Tiberian Rat forms and scampering away in horror as the Nymphs ran at them with their rattles choking the magic from the air.

I opened my mouth to direct my group that way, but before the command could escape me, Gabriel dropped from the sky like a bullet, landing before me in his fully shifted Harpy form with his black wings flaring at his spine and his body coated with the silver armoured scales of his kind. His chest was heaving, blood splattered his cheek and the look he gave me was laced with all the terror of whatever he'd *seen*.

"Call a retreat," he demanded. "The day is lost, and the army will be wiped out if we linger. I can't *see* what the Nymphs are going to do but if we don't concede defeat now, there is no future left open to us where the army will be left standing."

"We're surrounded, Gabriel," I breathed in fear, keeping my spine straight in case anyone was watching me, but it was the truth. Lionel's army had encircled us before they attacked, and the only way out was for us to punch through.

"My family have taken a large group of earth Elementals back down into the tunnels," he replied with a shake of his head. "They're digging an escape route for us as we speak. I've *seen* the children and vulnerable escaping that way and there's a good chance the remainder of our army can make it out through them too. I just haven't *seen* what needs to happen to ensure that fate yet. But it's now or never, Tory, call the retreat or the war will be lost this night."

My eyes widened in horror at that suggestion but I didn't question him further, trusting in his gifts, pressing my fingers to my throat and amplifying the sound of my voice as I yelled out loud enough for our entire army to hear.

"Retreat! Return to the tunnels! Retreat!"

All around us, the rebels heard my call and suddenly they were racing back towards The Burrows instead of fighting to escape them, not one of them defying my command as they hurried to do as I'd ordered with the Nymphs hounding after them, hungry for their demise.

"Get a shield in place between our army and theirs to allow the retreat time to take place," I commanded no one in particular, but Hamish raised his chin in understanding.

"It will be done, my queen. Kitty and I will hold the line while our people make their escape."

"What are you going to do?" Catalina gasped, catching my hand as I looked away and she seemed to realise I wasn't going with them.

"I'll follow once this fight is done," I snarled, hunting the sky for Lionel or Lavinia but finding neither of them close to me. "If Lionel dies tonight then we can salvage this."

"But, my queen," Hamish gasped and I shook my head at him.

"That's an order. I need all of you to get our people out of here. Can I trust you to do that?" I fixed him in my glare, and he bowed his head as he gave in to my command.

"It has been an honour fighting for the true queens this day," he said and my heart swelled with emotion as I thought of Darcy, wondering if Orion had managed to return her to herself and hoping with all my soul that she was going to be okay.

"It's been an honour fighting with you too," I said firmly, gripping his hand in farewell and gasping as Catalina threw her arms around me.

"Make that motherfucker scream when he dies," she snarled and I breathed a laugh as I swore to try, releasing her quickly and turning back to face the fight.

"I beg permission to stay and fight at your side, my queen," Justin said, drawing my attention to him as he moved to stand protectively by me once more and I gave a nod, seeing the determination in his gaze.

"Let's see if we can end this thing."

I took off running with Justin a step behind me, my gaze falling on Alejandro once more as he appeared in the crowd of Nymphs who were chasing after the retreating rebels, the rattle of his kind echoing through my bones and making my magic shrivel away from me as I raised my sword with a bellow of challenge and ran forward to meet him.

MAX

CHAPTER SIXTY FIVE

Caleb shot us through the manor as I kept the concealment spells tight around the two of us and we raced to find what we needed. I hoped to fuck that Seth knew what he was doing in leading the Nymphs away because his crazy ideas were dangerous as hell sometimes.

"No time to be subtle about it," Cal called.

I felt the heat of his fire magic burning through his skin where I was perched on his back a moment before he blasted it into the wards surrounding the house where Stella Orion lived.

The heat of the flames kissed my skin as we shot through the barriers and detection spells, and I clung on tight as Caleb kept going, moving so fast that I just locked my gaze on the back of his head instead of trying to see anything around us to save myself the feeling of motion sickness.

We crashed through the front door and Caleb shot through the house, sending doors slamming against walls before finally skidded to a halt before a panel in the wall which I was guessing was the secret entrance to the basement. My eyes widened as we found Stella Orion standing there, her fangs bared and earth magic coiling in her hands.

"Step aside," I warned as Caleb bared his fangs right back at her.

"Why are you here?" she demanded.

"Move," Caleb growled.

"And what if I don't?" she breathed, and I sensed something beneath those words, my gift latching on to fear, hope, loss. What was she thinking?

"You'll die," Caleb spat, but still she didn't move, her gaze darting between us.

"Is that what you want?" I asked, tugging harder on my gifts and her eyes widened as she felt the pull of them.

"I want so many things," she hissed, and I felt an ache in her that burned right through me. "I want to go back to a time where the world wasn't full of death."

"Well you should have thought about that before you helped your Dragon pal to take over the motherfucking world," I snapped as I tasted the regret on her, the depth of it fuelling my power reserves.

She tried to snap her mental shields up against me, but I wasn't going to let that happen, holding on tight.

Scales rippled across my skin and I drew in a deep breath, inhaling the feeling of pain and grief which clung to her, and she released a choked sob as the vines in her hands fell away.

"We'll hurt you if you don't move," Caleb warned.

"Do what you want. I don't care anymore," she said, shaking her head. "My daughter is gone. My son hates me and the man I dedicated my life to has only ever been using me."

"Lionel Acrux uses everyone," I pointed out and a flare of defiance and heartache shuddered through her as she shook her head, but she couldn't hold her tongue now that I had my grip tight around her emotions and I coaxed more from her.

"He loved me," she said. "We were something special. At least we were until…"

Hatred and jealousy poured through her in a black and aching torrent, and I was gifted flashes of her memories, of Lionel with his new queen, the shadow bitch Lavinia, kissing her, praising her, marrying her.

"We need a binding needle to stop her," I said, suddenly certain that she would give it to us. "If we can cut her off from the shadows then we can kill her. Don't you want to see her dead?"

Excitement tumbled through Stella at that suggestion, followed by fear and a sense of loyalty to the man who had brought the shadow bitch here, but I fought against that feeling and focused on encouraging the vengeful emotions within her, the jealousy and hatred, gifting her visions of Lavinia dead and gone, her influence lifted from Lionel's shoulders.

Stella broke a sob as she stepped aside suddenly, leaving the way clear for Caleb as he shot past her down into the basement, returning only a moment later with a binding needle in his fist. A blast of earth magic burst from him and he bound Stella in vines as she cried out in alarm, unable to raise a hand to fight back while I held her in the lure of my gifts.

I pressed my power into her harder, forcing her to fall asleep and making sure she wouldn't wake for hours to come as she fell to the floor with a crash.

"Do you think we should kill her?" I asked, raising my gaze to Caleb who considered it for a moment before shaking his head.

"Let's leave that choice up to Orion. It's his bitch mom after all."

I nodded my agreement and he hoisted me off of my feet, shooting us back out of her house and tearing across the sweeping grounds towards the Acrux Manor.

I lifted us back up into the air as we approached the tower above Darius's room, and Caleb sped us back through the house until we were right outside the courtyard where our parents were still bleeding for the benefit of the Shadow Princess.

"You wanna stitch it or watch my back?" Caleb asked, the two of us glancing around fearfully as we heard Seth howling somewhere in the house, but it didn't sound like he was in trouble, more like he was on the hunt.

"I've got you," I said, turning my attention to the courtyard again as I set my gaze on my dad and gritted my jaw. There were still a few Nymphs out there, but they would be nothing to us.

I twisted my fingers and let water trickle from my fingertips, trails of it snaking out into the courtyard and heading for the Nymphs where they stood watch in their Fae-like forms. The water raced towards them until it found their boots then moved up and over them, the temperature warmed so that they wouldn't even notice as the drops of it brushed against their skin.

The moment I had contact with all of them, I tugged on my power, snapping my fist closed and taking hold of the blood in their veins, freezing it solid in a single heartbeat and all four of them fell crashing to the stone floor of the courtyard dead before they'd even realised that they were under attack. It took a good chunk of my power and I released a long breath from the exertion.

Caleb shot out ahead of me, leaping up onto the stone altar with the needle in his hand and started work on closing the rift.

I ran behind him, hurrying to my dad's side and grasping his arm as he raised his head to look at me in shock.

"Max?" he gasped, his skin seeming taut across his bones like the power of the shadows was sucking the essence of him right out of his skin.

I nodded firmly as I took in the blood and power which rose from the wound on his wrist, tugging him towards that foul entity. There were heavy chains bolting him to the ground so that he couldn't be sucked right into it and my gut twisted with hatred for the fucking assholes who had done this to him.

"We're gonna get you the fuck out of here. Then we can all go celebrate Darius killing Lionel together."

My dad's eyes widened at that suggestion and his gaze flicked to the doorway beyond me.

"Hurry," he hissed. "There are countless numbers of their kind here."

"Seth drew them off," I reassured him and Antonia whimpered in fear for her son.

"There are far more than those," Dad insisted, but before I could reply, a pained howl made fear drive through my heart and I shoved away from him, taking several steps towards the door before glancing back at Caleb in uncertainty.

"Go," he hissed, his gaze never wavering from the rift as he fought to push the needle through the barrier between our realms. "Seth needs you more than I do."

I hesitated but as I heard Seth howl again, my decision was formed and I took off running back into the manor.

A crash of magic made the floorboards rattle and I charged towards it, ice coating my fists as I prepared my own attack, but as I ran past the sweeping staircase in the centre of the building, a slice of pain cut into my shoulder.

I looked down at the tiny point of pain, watching as a single drop of blood spilled from the wound and sucking in a sharp breath of alarm as I whirled around to see a spear of shadows shooting straight for me from the courtyard.

Dark energy slammed into me so violently that it knocked me from my feet and I cried out as my magic was locked in its grasp, the unnatural tug on it dragging it from that tiny cut on my arm as the shadows locked onto it with an iron hold and I was suddenly wrenched backwards across the floor.

I fought and yelled as I tried to grab hold of something to anchor me as the shadows ripped me back through the manor and out into the courtyard, my fingernails splitting as I tried to grip onto the doorframe before I was yanked free of that too.

I bellowed a warning to Caleb as I was dragged across the stones towards the altar and he whipped around, dropping the binding needle as he leapt from the altar and taking hold of me by the shoulders as he fought to pull me away from the rift.

"I've got you!" he bellowed as I kicked and fought to stay away from it too.

"Cal, someone cut me," I gasped. "You have to-"

Caleb's cry of pain struck me like a blow to the heart and his grip on me suddenly faltered as the shadows slammed into a cut on his arm and began dragging him towards the rift too.

I yelled as I was pulled towards it once more, the cries of our families' anguish echoing in my ears as that dark expanse called me forth and offered me endless pleasure which I knew would only end in my destruction.

I thought of Gerry, of all the people I loved and I tried to cling to that love as I saw my end rushing towards me, but before I could be wrenched into oblivion, a manacle snapped closed around my ankle and I jerked to a halt, panting wildly on the floor.

Caleb met my eye as he found himself caught there too and the sound of heavy footfalls made me look around just as Vard strode out of the house with a look of merciless victory on his scarred face as a group of Nymphs dragged a beaten, bloody Seth out behind him.

Seth fought as they locked his ankles to a set of manacles too and I groaned as the tug of the shadows intensified and they latched onto my magic, using my power to feed their foul mistress.

"Looks like I saw you coming after all," Vard hissed and as he stepped forward to slice a blade along the curve of my wrist, a cry of agony escaped my lips which was torn away from me into the endless sky as my power was taken hostage and I was locked at the mercy of the hateful stars.

DARIUS

CHAPTER SIXTY SIX

I chased my father through the sky with the taste of his blood on my tongue and a hunger for his death in my gut which I was determined to see sated.

He roared in pain and anger as he was forced to flee, the long wound I'd gouged into his side dripping blood all over the hillside below us as I tore after him, determined to end this.

He was damn fast, but I was faster, and I bore down on him with my superior strength and size, roaring my victory as I collided with him and we fell tumbling from the heavens in a clash of claws and teeth.

I pinned him beneath me, lunging for his throat, my jaws snapping closed just short of it as he kicked me away again and I was knocked backwards, hitting the ground hard and rolling down the hill towards the fleeing rebels.

Father chased after me, his jaw wide as the screams of our army reached my ears and I shifted just in time to throw an enormous ice shield over the heads of them as he blasted his Dragon fire at their ranks.

I hurled spears of ice after him, snarling through the effort it took to maintain my shield while attacking him and cursing his cowardly fucking tactics as he wheeled away from me and flew overhead.

"Darius!" a girl's voice caught my ear as I prepared to follow him.

I turned, spotting Sofia there, her eyes wide and fearful as she tried to drag Xavier away from the retreating rebels as they raced past where he lay bleeding on the floor in his Fae form.

"Give him to me," I said in fright, running to her and grabbing his arm, pressing healing magic into his skin, though the bleeding wounds on his back only scabbed over a little, the deep blackened, slashes in his side seeming to suck the magic away from the wounds and stop any of it from healing.

"I think it was Lionel's shadow claw," Sofia sobbed, gripping Xavier's cheeks and pressing a kiss to his mouth. She had his Phoenix fire helmet hanging from her wrist and there was a mark on his head where it had been so tightly strapped in place.

Xavier groaned, blinking his eyes open and cursing at the pain he felt as his eyes moved from her to me.

"He ripped my wings off," he choked out, tears glimmering in his eyes which cut me to my fucking core.

"I'm going to end him," I swore, raising my head as a furious whinny drew my attention and a huge silver Pegasus galloped through the crowd towards us.

"Tyler!" Sofia cried and I stood, hauling my brother into my arms as the Pegasus came to a halt before us, kicking up mud which splattered across his pale legs alongside more than a little blood. He had a bag hanging from his neck, the strap half severed and a pair of jeans dropped out of it as he fell still, pressing his nose to Xavier's cheek as a whinny of alarm escaped him.

My chest tightened as I took in the sight of Geraldine sprawled across his back, her chest and side punctured with a tremendous bite mark and similar blackish claw marks were carved into her flesh as Xavier's.

She looked dead and I hesitated for a moment before reaching out to touch her, a sigh of relief tumbling through me as I found a weak pulse.

I tried healing her too, finding a similar barrier to my magic as there was in Xavier's flesh.

"Fuck the shadows," I bit out, fear tumbling through me for the other Heirs as I wondered what was taking them so damn long. Lavinia was still visible on the far side of the battlefield, flying above the Nymphs on a cloud of shadows which seemed specifically designed to taunt me with her power. I didn't know what the hell was happening with that altar, but it couldn't be good if she was still that powerful, and I hated the fucking stars for forcing so many roadblocks against us time and again.

"What do we do?" Sofia asked, looking to me for an answer I didn't have.

"You heard your queen," I said firmly, stepping forward to place Xavier on Tyler's back as well. "She called a retreat. So get back inside those tunnels and make sure the four of you get the hell away from here."

"What are you going to do?" she gasped, reaching out to place a hand on my arm as I grabbed the jeans Tyler had dropped and tugged them on.

"I'm too fucking stubborn to bow to the orders of a Vega, even if I do happen to love her more than the earth we stand on," I growled, hunting the sky for my cowardly father and spotting him standing on a hill beyond the ranks of Nymphs who still pressed forward after the rebels. He'd shifted back into his Fae form too, no doubt needing to heal the wound I'd given him, and he was now shrouded in a red cloak which marked him as the leader of the Dragon Guild.

"You're going after Lionel?" she breathed fearfully and I turned to her again, picking her up easily and sitting her on Tyler's back with the others so that she could make sure they didn't fall.

"I'm facing my fate," I confirmed before slapping the Pegasus on the ass like he was a common mule and barking a command at them to go.

Tyler took off with a startled whinny, beating his powerful wings and galloping away from me towards the tunnels which were their only slim hope of survival, and I wished I could do more than watch them go.

I turned from them and broke into a run, casting as I went and building a bridge of ice right over the heads of the Nymph army and blasting them with Dragon fire as they looked up see me pass.

The sounds of their screams coloured the air beautifully and a dark smile lit my features as I spotted my axe embedded in the ground ahead of me. I must have dropped it after I stardusted back here and the shift took hold of me, but there it was, blazing with Phoenix fire which stopped the Nymphs from getting close to it and waiting for me as if it too was hungering to feel the weight of it slicing through my father's neck.

I leapt from my bridge of ice, grabbing the axe and swinging it at the closest Nymph, taking its legs out and leaving it screaming as I ran on, charging up the hill where my father was waiting for me with flames dancing in his palms and a look of vile victory in his eyes.

He threw the flames at me but I didn't slow, calling on my Dragon just enough to gild my skin in golden scales for a few moments so that they could deflect the heat and save me from the burn of his attack.

I grinned at the look of utter shock on his face, thanking my perseverance to learn that trick and glad of the hours I'd endured in Gabriel's company to perfect it.

I burst from the embers of his attack with a challenging roar, swinging my axe for his head and he yelled out as he was forced to leap aside, ducking beneath the next swing of my axe and knocking it from my hands with air magic on the third attempt.

I pounced on him then, driving him down into the ground beneath me and slamming my fist into his face so hard I heard his teeth crack.

Lionel roared and thrashed beneath me, fighting back with all he had while I maintained my position on top of him through pure grit and determination, raining down blows on him over and over again until he finally managed to knock me onto my back with a blast of air.

An agonised roar rattled through the sky above us and I glanced up in time to see a grey Dragon hurtling through the air towards us, blood pouring from a savage wound on its throat.

I leapt aside and Father rolled away from me, the Dragon crashing to the ground between us with a resounding boom that made the hillside rattle before it shifted back into its Fae form and one of my father's obnoxious cousins was revealed.

Ignatius screamed as he bled out in the dirt and I cast a spear of ice into my fist, slamming it down in his chest to finish him while holding tight to the memory of him walking in on my father beating the shit out of me when I was ten years old. He'd met my eye, arched a single brow and had apologised for the interruption before backing out of there and leaving me to the kicking I was taking. And as he met my gaze with his final breath escaping him, I hoped he was remembering that moment too and seeing the monster who was created in that house because of the things he'd witnessed and ignored.

Father regained his feet in the moment I was distracted by killing his cousin and he snarled a challenge as he moved to strike me again. I wrenched the spear of ice from Ignatius's chest and hurled it at him with a furious cry, forcing him to lunge away and send an inferno of fire and air at me.

I dropped to my knees, shielding myself in ice and gritting my teeth as the dome of magic I held splintered and cracked beneath the onslaught of his power, my gaze fixed on the murky outline of his body which I could just see through the ice.

"Hiding from me, boy?" he taunted, just the way he used to taunt Xavier for trying to avoid him whenever he came home. But I'd never hidden. I'd always walked straight up to him with my chin high even when I knew I'd receive a beating, or when he had some cruel and unusual method of making me fight my fears in mind. I faced it like a Fae just the way I was facing him now.

"Just savouring the moment," I called back, sinking my fingers into the dirt and taking hold of the moisture I found there before sending it spearing up and out of the ground beneath him in a series of razor sharp spikes.

Father howled in pain as they cut him, his attack faltering and allowing me time to banish my shield.

A dark and dangerous smile lit my lips as I found Ignatius's charred skeleton before me, his body burned up in my father's fire magic. His bones were laid out like an offering and the words of the dark magic Lance had been teaching me in preparation for this day sprang to my lips as I snatched a thigh bone into my palm and ran my fingers over it in well practiced movements.

"Chiedo al buio di disturbare questo corpo dalla pace e di mettere la sua magia nel mio sangue," I breathed, the power of those words making a tremble run through my entire body and I sucked in a sharp breath as the magic stored within the bone was unleashed.

The bone began to glow with the power that was locked inside it as I wielded the dark magic to claim it for my own. My muscles bunched with the power of those words as thorny vines sprang from it, twisting around my fingers and slicing into my skin as the alien feeling of his earth magic drove its way inside of my body.

It fucking hurt as I absorbed the alien feeling of the earth element, like those thorns were clawing their way through every vein in my body and tearing them open, desperate to find a way back out again.

Father roared as he ran at me, his fists coated with fire as I dropped the bone and managed to cover my skin with my golden scales once more before his blow could land.

The crunch of his fist meeting with my jaw was swiftly followed by a roar of effort pouring from my lips as those thorn covered vines ripped their way back out of my body, gilded in the fire of my Dragon and ripping him off of me with such force that he was hurled away down the hill.

I took chase, letting him see exactly what he'd made me into as he fought to burn the vines free of his flesh and the stolen magic continued to rattle through my body.

We collided once more, a furious crash of fists and magic and hatred which set bones cracking and blood flying, and made the entire hillside tremble beneath the might of our power.

Father cried out in alarm as I managed to hook the vines around his throat, the flames burning him as once again he failed to pass the fireproof hide of my Dragon while golden scales armoured my flesh.

I dove on top of him, darkness swirling through my skin as I threw my fist into his face and tightened the hold of the thorns on his throat, his lips turning blue and eyes widening in terror as he finally saw his death in me, and it felt so fucking good that I wanted to roar my victory to the heavens already.

But just as I was certain I had him, the dark magic I'd cast burned out, my hold on the stolen earth Element falling away and the vines which were choking him turned brittle before shattering entirely. I lurched forward, tightening my hands around his neck instead, baring my teeth and driving him down beneath me as I fought to end this with a desperation which matched the frantic pace of my heart. But just as I was certain of my victory, Father drew a sun steel blade from a fold of his cloak, slashing it across my side and forcing me to throw myself off of him as blood spilled and the perilous metal cut me open.

I rolled away from him with a curse, snatching my axe back into my hold as I leapt to my feet and he regained his too. I threw a hand up to deflect the air strike he shot at me with more water, causing him to drench the hillside as our power collided and was sent off at an angle, drawing my gaze to the raging battle once more.

The Nymphs kept chasing after the rebels as the retreat continued, more and more of them making it below ground and away from their enemies, though I had no idea where they planned to go from there.

Father tried to strike at me with his air magic once more, whips snaking around to slash at my spine while I blocked him with a barrier of ice that cracked and splintered behind me under his assault, the sound reminding me of Roxy trapped beneath that pool.

A snarl escaped me at the thought of the man I'd almost become because of this demon, and I bellowed a challenge as I ran at him once more, swinging my axe with a brutal strike aimed to cleave his head from his body.

The axe slammed against an air shield which he held close to his skin and his eyes widened in alarm as I heaved it back and struck him a second time.

Again and again, my axe slammed against his shield while his muscles bulged with the tension of trying to maintain it, his face reddening and veins looking ready to burst.

He looked into the eyes of the beast he'd created and I knew he saw his death in them, the Dragon in me peering out with a hunger for his end more potent than I'd ever felt before.

He was here. Right fucking here and I could feel his shield breaking beneath the assault of my weapon as the Phoenix fire coating it made the air between us ripple with heat.

"All of this because of some whore?" he shrieked as he fought to hold me off, his composure slipping and the cowardly man I knew him to be at his core revealed to me. Because this wasn't a Fae who had stood up and fought to claim his power, this was a cheat and a trickster who was as unFae as they came. But here and now I wasn't giving him a choice. He was going to have to face me man to man, and I could tell by the terrified look in his soulless eyes that he already knew who would win.

"Roxanya Vega is no whore," I spat, my axe cracking against his shield with such force that I felt the vibrations of it rolling down my sweat slicked spine.

"I should have killed the Vega twins the moment they returned," he hissed, that hateful look in his eyes never wavering. But I knew what it really was now. Jealousy. He hated them for the very same reason that he had hated their father, his own brother and even me. Because he could see that we were more powerful than him and he would always just be a small man when he stood beside us.

The wedding band on my finger seemed to burn just as hot as those flames as I thought of all the things this man had done to the girl who owned my entire soul, my mate, my wife.

"I married her," I taunted as I swung the axe once more. "And when I return to her with your head hanging from my fist, I'll bow to her too."

My father's eyes flashed with unyielding fury at that suggestion and with a roar of his Dragon, he let the air shield between us shatter, lunging towards me to get beneath the strike of my axe and sinking his shadow hand into my side, his claws piercing the skin and stealing my breath from me.

I swung my fist into his jaw with all my strength, my axe cutting into the back of his thigh as we struggled to get the upper hand and he crumpled, screaming as he fell back, but his shadows thrashed and pulsed inside me as he forced them to take hold.

I arched my back with a bellow of pain as they battled to take control of me, the strength of them unyielding.

The fire from the Phoenix Kiss that Roxy had gifted me raced to meet them, burning them back with the fury of our love for one another, but in the moment where they held me at their mercy, my father swung his hand back and plunged his sun steel blade straight into my chest.

Everything seemed to still within me as I stared at him, the pulse I should have felt thrumming through my veins falling impossibly still as shock and an adamant kind of refusal stole through me.

For several achingly long moments, all I could do was stare at him in horror as I felt the blood spilling from that blow to my heart, staining my skin and stealing my fate once more.

This wasn't how it was supposed to end.

I'd always known that it would come down to me and him, but it should have culminated with this scene playing out in reverse.

"No son of mine will ever bow to a fucking Vega," Father snarled, his upper lip curling back as he looked my death in the eyes and claimed it for his own. "I offered you the world and you refused it, so now I'm taking back the privilege I offered you upon your conception. Return to the stars, Darius. Perhaps they'll be kinder to you in death than they were in life."

He shoved me away from him and I fell, my limbs not responding to my commands and doing nothing at all to stop me as I crashed back into the dirt and found myself staring up at the stars who had scorned me so fucking much in my too short life.

Lionel spat at me before he left and the only thing I could feel was the deep pool of blood spreading out all around me from the blade which remained lodged within my heart.

My lips parted on words I couldn't speak, and the crushing feeling of disappointment filled me as I realised I'd let her down again.

I'd offered Roxanya Vega the stars and delivered her nothing but dirt. I'd always known I wasn't good enough for her, and now my death had come to me in a rush as short and pointless as my life had been, and I hadn't even been able to gift her the head of the man who had hurt her so much.

I held on to the love I felt for her as I began to slip out of this world, stealing it away with me as I let myself sink into the sensation of being held tight within her arms and knowing it was the only place in this life or the next where I would ever want to reside.

I had never deserved her. But she'd been mine all the same. If only for the briefest span of time. So no matter how foul my luck had always been, I knew I had been blessed in that one, most vital way. I had tasted the heat of her kiss and drowned in the weight of her love, been consumed by it and owned by it and made whole by it too.

I wasn't a good man. And I certainly wasn't a perfect one. But I had been hers.

The stars began to blink out in the cruel sky above me one by one, like they were turning their attention from me now, seeing my failure and losing all interest in me.

But then a single point of light appeared which burned so much brighter than them that it cast them into the realms of irrelevance, and I saw her soaring across the sky burning hotter than the sun itself. She was so endlessly beautiful, so powerful, so strong.

My heart.

My love.

My queen.

And that was the way I wanted to leave this life, because when it came down to it, I knew that she was it for me. The only thing I'd ever truly needed and for the briefest span of time she had belonged to me. And that was enough.

There is only her.

ORION

CHAPTER SIXTY SEVEN

Darcy chased me out into the long grass far beyond the clash of the battle and I sheathed my sword when I was far enough away to protect the fleeing rebels, turning to face her, my heart clutched in the grip of the stars who watched from above, my fate about to be decided as I let her come to me.

I'd had to get her away from Geraldine, and I prayed she would be alright, but at least she stood a chance now that Darcy had followed me here.

I took a breath, planting my feet and knowing I may well be granted my own death in this action. But better that than see the woman I love fall into the darkness of that Shadow Beast for good.

As she set me in her sights, her black eyes barely glinting with the rings of our bond, she snarled and ran faster towards me. I was running out of time. And I knew my next action was a gamble that held my life within the roll of the dice I was about to throw.

"I'm not going anywhere, Blue," I said beneath my breath.

I cast an illusion at my back, painting out a thousand memories of us together, the reflection of our love rippling through the air. Our first kiss beneath the Acrux pool, the night she'd come to me with blue hair, the day the FIB had taken me away, the good, the bad and everything in between, right up to our mating, when we'd claimed each other under the watchful eyes of the stars. I bled for her here and now, offering every piece of beauty between us and every painful moment that was stitched into the fabric of my heart. We were made of these memories. It was our story, our beginning, but this was not our end.

I shifted the illusion, showing her a life not yet lived. The hopes I had for us, the things I had fought this battle for. She was the dream I had never seen coming, the purpose I'd been searching for. I didn't want the dreams of the boy I'd lost the day Lionel had bonded me to Darius anymore, I wanted these new dreams that were born from her. I had been dipped in darkness, painted in sin and hardened into something cold and unlovable. And yet she had found some way to love me and I was liberated because of it, rising from that inky blackness I had known for so long, and laid in the sun. But now she, my light, was draped in darkness and I would not abandon her for anything in this world.

So I showed her the life I wanted for us, I showed her the children I prayed we'd have and the laughs and smiles I swore I'd offer her. I showed her peace and love and countless days where no suffering lived and all that existed was joy. And I pledged that future to her this very moment. My life was an offering she could eradicate tonight, or else she could find a way back to me, and accept all I had to give while I still had breath in my lungs and beats left in my heart.

"I am yours. And this life can be ours," I called out to her. "You are mine and Lavinia will not take you from me!"

Darcy slowed before me, her eyes falling on those memories behind me as I stood in front of her with no shield, nothing but my hands raised before me in a gesture of surrender.

"Please see me," I rasped, terror lacing the words as she stalked toward me, wet with blood and towering above me so I was cast in her shadow.

I knew I would die here if she was lost. Because there was no place for me in this world without her.

"Blue, come back to me," I begged.

She lowered her face to mine and I was sure I was dead as I gazed up at her, my magic nearly entirely tapped out. And I would not wield my blade against her.

She shifted so fast, I inhaled sharply, finding her standing before me in the snow, naked and shivering, her hair no longer blue but deepest black, moving about her shoulders in the way Lavinia's moved. She was bloody and bruised, her legs and arms covered in deep wounds, and my chest ached at seeing her like that.

She raised her hands to inspect them, turning them over as if she didn't know herself and the fear I felt over that nearly destroyed me. But when she looked up, my girl was there.

"Lance?" she breathed, her hands beginning to tremble and I rushed forward in relief, crushing her against me and offering her the last of my magic to heal her, the well of power in my chest hollowing out.

She shoved me away suddenly, shaking her head and running a hand over her face as she looked back at the battle. "What have I done? Oh my god, Geraldine…"

"It wasn't you," I swore, stepping toward her once more, needing to make sure she was alright.

"It was," she said in horror, tears spilling out of her eyes.

I stepped closer to see the silver rings in them, and watched as they flickered, there one moment and gone the next. They blinked out like dying stars and my heart forgot to beat.

Fear pressed down on me, but I wouldn't break. I would be here for her through anything. Rings or no rings, it didn't matter to me. She was my mate regardless.

She gasped as though she felt it, her hand going to her chest. "I'm mortal," she croaked.

"No," I refused, capturing her hand and pulling her close as terror wound its way around my throat like a noose. "Look at me," I begged, but she wouldn't, her eyes on the blood staining her trembling fingers until I gripped her chin, forcing her to look up at me. "I'll fix this," I promised with all the grit I could muster.

"It's too late," she said in fear then pushed me again to get some space between us. "You have to get away. I can feel it coming back."

"I'm not leaving you," I snarled. "This curse doesn't get to break us."

"I can't stay here," she half sobbed. "I have to get away from you all."

"Blue, please. You can fight this. Just look at me. You can stop it from taking over again, I know you can."

But she shook her head, more tears flowing down her cheeks, carving tracks through the blood and ash staining her face and a growl of pain left me as I stepped forward and she stepped back.

"Please," she whispered, holding up her hand to ward me off. "Please stay away, I don't want to hurt you. Oh god…oh god, what have I done? All those people…" She fisted her hands in her hair, a noise of anguish leaving her and I shot forward, not caring what she asked of me, I wasn't going to leave her alone. She needed me more than she ever had in her life.

I held her against me as she came apart, sobbing against my chest and clinging onto me as I wrapped her in my arms and tried to figure out what to do.

"We'll run. We'll go somewhere far away together, okay?" I offered, but she drew back, taking in a shuddering breath as she stopped herself from crying.

"No," she said, the ring of a queen in her voice. "I have to go alone. If I hurt you, I'll never forgive myself."

"Blue," I growled, as her green eyes filled with so much darkness, they almost seemed black. "Please." I grabbed her hand, trying to hold onto her as she continued to back up and the shadows seemed to thicken around her.

"I have to go," she said.

"I'm not saying goodbye to you and you're not going anywhere," I demanded. "You'll have to summon the stars themselves to keep me away from you."

As if in answer to my words, a meteor tore across the sky, a fallen star leaving a trail of glittering fire in its wake as it streaked over our heads towards the mountains and collided with the side of one, sending a tremor rocking out through the earth.

I inhaled in shock. "What now? The sky is falling too?" I looked down at Darcy, finding her backing further and further away from me, an apology in her eyes.

"The monster is waking up," she said, her voice breaking and I looked down to find she'd bound my legs in shadows with the beast's power, tethered to the earth itself as I lurched forward and was yanked back by their strength.

"Wait," I gasped in terror as she turned, shifting into the huge black Shadow Beast and howling mournfully to the night.

"Darcy!" I bellowed, my throat ripping raw. I knew I was going to lose her in the next moment and I couldn't stand it. "Meet me tomorrow at dawn where the meteor struck!" I cried after her in desperation as she took off in the direction of the mountains, and I wasn't sure she'd even heard me.

I released a roar of anger, yanking against the shadows again and again, fighting to get free, my heart cleaving in two at the idea of us being torn apart.

I wouldn't let her go. I would follow her to the edges of the Earth, I'd follow her to the moon if I had to.

I used every ounce of Vampire strength I had left in me to rip the shadows off of my legs then looked to the mountains, my mate already long lost.

"Blue!" I yelled, panic potent within me.

I was about to shoot after her when my gaze moved to Lavinia among the last remnants of the battle.

I shivered as the stars seemed to lean closer, whispering among each other as they watched their playthings put on a show for them. I was so tired of being worn down, so tired of losing everything whenever I believed it was finally mine for good. I'd had to look into my Elysian Mate's eyes and watch her silver rings fade right in front of me, I'd seen her heart shatter the moment she realised what that beast had made her do and if this broke her, I'd break too.

I felt so exhausted fighting for a life the stars seemed determined to steal from us. Were they ever planning to just let us be? Or would life be one loss after the other?

"Are you happy now?!" I yelled at the stars. "Are we tortured enough for you yet?!"

It took all the strength I had to stay standing, my gaze falling from our shining makers and my thoughts shifting onto Lavinia again, a decision solidifying in my mind. She was the one who'd done this to Darcy. She was the creator of the curse so I would rip the answer to breaking it from her worthless lips.

I took a shuddering breath then shot forward with a surge of speed, tearing back to where the last of the rebels were retreating into The Burrows, knowing what I had to do even if the stars defied me time and again. Because yes, I was tired, but I was not defeated. I would not submit to this fate even when it broke every bone in my body and tried to force my back to bend. I would fight for another destiny, I would build one from the fabric of the sky if I had to.

Before I made it to the shadow bitch who I hated more viscerally than any other creature on this earth, my gaze fell on a body laying at the top of a hill beyond the raging battle, something instinctual within me drawing me towards it and making everything inside me seize up.

No.

The very foundations of my being were rocked as I staggered my way towards him, panic binding my limbs as I fell down at his side and grief choked all air away from me as I touched his face.

"Darius," I rasped, his skin icily cold and the sun steel knife in his chest so fucking deep there was probably nothing left of his heart at all. His eyes were shut, his features still, but even in death he didn't look restful.

Pain splintered through my body like a dagger cutting into my flesh again and again.

"I'm so sorry," I groaned, falling over him and hugging him to my chest, feeling I'd failed him.

I should have been here, I should have stopped this from happening.

I held him while screams still cried out around me as Lavinia worked to hunt down the last of the rebels and I knew death could sweep over me at any moment, but I had to steal this time with my brother, some part of me still praying he could come back. But I knew deep down that his soul was gone. Stolen away beyond the Veil. I could feel the emptiness of his body and it shattered a piece of my heart that belonged solely to him.

"Please wake up," I begged, unable to bear the weight of this loss. He was more than my best friend, he was one of the only good things I'd had in my life for so many years. We'd fought a hundred fights together and it seemed impossible to lose him now after all we'd been through.

I released a groan of despair as I forced myself to let go of him, laying him back down in the mud.

"I'll come back," I promised through a razor sharp lump in my throat. "I'll give you a proper burial, I swear it."

I lifted my head, barely able to make myself stand as I set my gaze on Lavinia across the snow upon her tower of shadows, chasing down a group of rebels with her twisted power. My hands shook and the freezing air cut deep into my bones as I drew my sword, casting a final look back at Darius and finding my heart so full of vengeance that I could think of nothing else. For him, for Blue.

My grief turned to the most bitter kind of rage I had ever tasted and suddenly I was moving, running with the speed of my Order towards the witch who had caused us so much pain. Who had bound my mate to her with a curse that could have destroyed her tonight, who had trapped my sister's soul within her and made her suffer for so many years.

With an almighty swing of my sword, I sliced through the shadows which held Lavinia aloft and she tumbled toward me with a screech of fright.

But of course, she caught herself before she hit the ground, hovering just a foot above it on a platform of shadow. I charged forward, the weight of grief and anger in my heart so heavy that it nearly drowned me as I aimed to kill her. She gasped as she lurched backwards to avoid the swipe of my blade and I swung it again with a yell of hate, using the speed of my Order to slash and cut, but she moved like the wind to avoid me.

My blade slammed into the flesh of her neck at last and she screamed as her head was nearly severed clean off. But as she rose up on another swirl of shadows to avoid my next strike, her dark power wound around her throat to heal the wound which didn't ooze even a drop of blood.

This monster was empty, no heart lived within her, no organs there to make her even close to living. She was made of rot and death, and so long as the shadows poured unendingly into her body, maybe she could not be killed. But I'd damn well fucking try.

"You feisty little hellion," she growled, lowering down before me once more and my fangs snapped out as I dove forward again, determined to make her scream if nothing else.

I tried to drive my sword into her chest with a shout of despair and anger erupting from my lungs, but she flicked her fingers and wrapped me in her dark power, wrenching the sword from my grip as if I was made of nothing but paper. And I guessed that was what I was, just a paper man, ripped and cut apart by the stars. I was forged by them, and they would crumple me in their fist the moment they were done with me. Perhaps Lavinia would be the one to do it for them.

"Well, well, well," she purred, rising up above me while her shadows coiled around me like a python, binding my arms to my sides. "I wondered when I'd be seeing you again tonight." She smiled wickedly and I bared my fangs at her, struggling uselessly against her hold.

"Tell me how to break the curse," I commanded and she smiled, floating closer to me and sliding a finger under my chin to make me look up at her sharply.

"I knew you'd come to me," she whispered, her skin writhing with blackish veins as she stared deep into my eyes. "Look at those rings," she hissed. "Pretty, pretty little silver treasures. But mortals cannot be mated to Fae, and when I am tired of playing beast with her, perhaps I shall recall my pet from her body and leave her to waste away as a weak human girl," she mocked. "Your princess's rings will be gone forever. Poof. Bye bye."

"Fuck you," I spat. "She's my mate regardless."

"Is she now?" she laughed. "And have you come to pay the price for your sweet princess, Lance Orion? I bound your blood to the curse after all."

My throat thickened at those words as I remembered the blood she'd spilled from me that day. So this was it? The answer lay with me? Well all the better.

"I will pay any price for her. Name it, and swear she'll be free," I demanded and she considered that, a look in her pitch black eyes that said this was what she'd hoped for all along. And it made my stomach twist that I was playing so easily into her hands, but Darcy had to be free. I would do whatever had to be done to ensure that.

"Why are you doing this to us? Why not just kill us and be done with it?" I snapped.

She shifted closer, all darkness and death clinging to her flesh.

"Because a Vega punished me once a long, long time ago. And it is my turn to repay the favour," she growled, vengeance sparking in her gaze. "I'll make them hurt, and squeal and writhe in agony in every way I can think up. And it is so very easy, little hunter. I've already turned one of them into a killer, a monster too, now all that's left is to take away her king like mine was taken from me."

"So it's my death you want?" I bit out, and though I felt numb to the idea of death right now, I was not numb to the thought of being parted from Blue because of it.

"Perhaps," she said through a smirk, sliding her hand down to my heart and I felt her shadows reaching into my body and making it beat painfully hard for her. I was sure I was about to die, the stars pulling on my soul like they were preparing to tear it from my being at any second. "Your blood is the price. Flesh, bone, heart, whichever way you want to offer it. You can cut your heart from your chest and give it to me raw and bloody if you wish."

My heart thundered as Lavinia released me from the binds of her shadows, offering me back my sword, but using her shadows to guide my hand so I turned the blade's tip against my own chest. I glared into her eyes, snatching the blade from her grip and pushing it hard against my flesh myself, not wanting the choice to be hers.

Pain flared keenly and I gritted my teeth against it, staring my fate in the eye and not cowering from its cruelty.

Blood spilled from the wound as I gave this offering without a shadow of doubt passing through me. It was easy when I thought of Blue, holding her in my mind's eye and not letting go as adrenaline burned through my limbs, begging me not to do this, but for her I'd do anything.

I'm sorry, beautiful. I'll wait for you in the stars.

She was my winged princess, the girl who had saved me from myself and had offered so much sweetness into my life, it was staggering to think I was the same person at all. She had made me into a man I had never thought I could become, and there was nothing I could offer that would repay her for that. But I could do this, because what was my life worth here in this world anyway if Blue was lost?

"Goodness," Lavinia purred, latching the shadows around my hand to stop me from cutting any deeper. "What a loyal little king. More loyal than my own."

"Do you want my heart or not?" I snarled and she shifted closer, tracing her thumb along the line of blood that had spilled down my chest, bringing it to her mouth and licking it away.

"Mm," she sighed. "So sweet, so tempting. But you didn't listen to me very well. I'll say it again. You may offer me the price in flesh, blood or bone. Personally...I think I'd like to take it from your flesh." She leaned down, capturing me in her shadows once more as she sank her teeth into the meat of my shoulder, and I growled in fury as she bit deep enough to draw more blood. Then she lapped at it like a heathen, making me shudder at the caress of her cold tongue.

"I don't know what you're asking of me," I hissed in disgust as she pulled away, licking her lips as a raw, depraved kind of lust filled her eyes.

"You will become willingly mine," she announced. "Your body will be my playhouse to do whatever I wish with. I may cut it, whip it, burn it, and fuck it if the notion takes me. And you will allow me to do so willingly, no complaints, no fighting back."

Bile rose in my throat as I glared at her, the weight of that price nearly too much to bear.

"It's that or death?" I asked, my voice a hollow, empty thing.

"Yes," she confirmed. "Or I can take the bones from your body one by one, crack, crack, crack, but that'll probably end in death too." She laughed lightly like we were having some perfectly normal fucking conversation.

"And if I offer you my body, how long do you want it for?" I growled, knowing death would be preferable to an eternity in this bitch's company. "When will Darcy be free of the curse?"

"Let's say...three moon cycles," she offered. "I can't say fairer than that. Then when I send you back to your Vega mate, her heart will shatter piece by piece when she learns of what you have given me."

"You underestimate us," I said, my tone rising with the strength of our star bond. "We can survive anything."

She grinned, but it was more evil than anything I'd ever witnessed. "We'll see about that, Lance Orion. So do we have a deal?" She offered me her hand.

"You have to make a death bond on this," I insisted, my heart beginning to beat erratically as it slowly accepted what I was agreeing to. "I need your word to be binding beyond a shadow of a doubt."

She rolled her eyes then ran her palm across my sword, slitting it open and grabbing my hand to do the same. Then she slapped her hand against mine, the icy, wet touch of her blood vile against my skin as our blood rushed together – though I wasn't sure hers was really blood at all.

"I swear upon the stars to honour the terms of our agreement," she purred. "Your body will be willingly mine for three moon cycles, and when that time is up, I shall release Darcy Vega from her curse."

"And you will release me from your captivity," I snarled and she smiled coyly like she hadn't been going to mention that.

"And I shall release you, Lance Orion, from my captivity. And if I do not uphold my side of the deal, I shall die."

"Can you even die?" I snapped.

"All beings can die," she said bitterly.

Magic hummed between us, confirming her mimicry of blood was enough to make this deal at least. But I knew there was one more part to this, a lump building in my throat as I accepted what I had to do.

"Do you agree?" she asked, victory burning in her eyes.

I hesitated, fear spilling through me at what I was about to be subjected too, but I had to. It was that or let Darcy be consumed by a curse which would tear away her magic for good. It would leave her mortal, not to mention that vile beast which was housed in her flesh and drove her against the people she loved. She was too good, too sweet to deserve that fate. And Solaria needed her more than she needed me right now.

Three moon cycles would pass. And no matter who I was when I came out of it, I would still love her. I would still be hers.

I knew my decision was already solidified, and that I wasn't going to pull away even though terror was snaking through my body. But I could survive three moon cycles in hell for Darcy Vega. It would be agony in its purest form, but my body was nothing. Blue owned the part of me that mattered. And Lavinia would never be able to touch it. At least this way ensured I could return to my girl, ready to love her with every thump of my beating heart. I just prayed that when I was one day reunited with her, she wouldn't blame me for this choice, and could find a way to forgive me.

"I agree," I said firmly and the bond snapped painfully between us, the stars whispering as the magic wound beneath my skin and hers, light flaring around our palms and our blood drying to dust.

She released my hand and I found a red star burned onto the inside of my palm, glowing there for a moment before sinking beneath my skin and disappearing. Lavinia watched as that same mark settled within her own flesh and a smile curled up her lips.

It was done. I was bound, chained and owned by this foul monster.

"Three moon cycles," she confirmed, reaching out to touch my throat and I felt a collar of shadow winding around it, cinching tight.

"There we are. All mine." She floated towards me, tugging on a tendril of shadow that connected to the collar like a leash and she jerked me toward her by it, taking out a pouch of stardust from the cloak of shadow around her body. "Let's go home, pet, I cannot wait to start breaking you in every way a man can be broken."

CATALINA

CHAPTER SIXTY EIGHT

Hamish's hand was locked tight around mine as the combination of our dwindling magic surged between us and we fought to hold back the Nymphs who chased our people in their retreat.

Hundreds had passed us as they ran deeper beneath the ground, following the tunnels which the Storm Dragon and his pack had carved to take them to safety away from this hell we fought in.

The rush had turned to a trickle now as the injured were either carried back or managed to drag themselves to safety. Some brave souls had lingered, healing as many as they could before their power waned, but now it was down to the two of us and our magic was fading fast too.

"We can't hold them off much longer, Kitty," Hamish ground out, his teeth clenched as he fought to use every drop of his power to keep the Nymphs from reaching us. The vines we'd cast wrapped tightly around more and more of them, hurling them away from the entrance to the tunnels and the last few rebels who raced towards us in need of an escape from the carnage Lionel had wreaked here tonight.

"I know," I gasped, a tear burning a trail down my cheek as I hunted for any sign of my boys among the survivors who still fought to get back here. "But I can't run. Not while they're still out there, Hammy."

"Me either," he agreed, his eyes shining with love for his daughter and my boys combined.

We'd created something pure, him and I. This little bubble of happiness built on nothing more than the foundation of love.

He had found me as a broken soul, my years of abuse at Lionel's hands leaving me a husk of the woman I'd once been. And yet he'd coaxed me back out of myself. He'd helped me find out who I really was without a command or bind to hold on me and he'd loved me as that woman. He'd shown me what true love really was and how endlessly beautiful it could be while I healed him of the hurt he'd been left with after losing his wife.

A fearful whinny drew my attention and my heart stilled as I spotted a silver Pegasus galloping towards us, a girl on its back blasting fire at the Nymphs who closed in on them as she cried out in alarm. The Nymphs released their rattle and the fire in the girl's hands died out just as I recognised her.

"Sofia!" I cried, throwing a hand out towards them and ripping a chasm through the ground with earth magic which sent the Nymphs to the right of them tumbling down into it with screams of fury while Hamish cast a battering ram into existence which crashed into the Nymphs on their left.

"He's coming!" Sofia yelled, but I didn't pay her words much attention as I spotted the two figures who were laying before her on Tyler's back, and I sucked in a sharp breath of recognition as I spotted Xavier's blood-soaked flesh.

"Hammy, they have Xavier and Geraldine," I gasped, my grip tightening on his hand as I urged the Pegasus to run faster while continuing to destroy the ground behind him to hold the Nymphs at bay.

Tyler whinnied in alarm as he galloped faster, kicking up mud and clods of grass all around him as he charged towards us with terror in his eyes and as I looked beyond him, I saw why.

Lionel rose up behind them, using his air magic to hold himself above the ranks of Nymphs who still fought to get to us and raising his hands as his gaze locked on the charging stallion and the Fae he carried.

"Cling tight, Kitty, we can hold off that rapscallion," Hamish said firmly, and though my heart trembled with fear at the sight of the man who had once owned me so cruelly, I raised my chin and tightened my hold on my husband's hand, lending him all of my power as he threw an air shield up behind our children to keep Lionel from hurting them.

Lionel cast fire at the shield with a force so powerful that it almost fell, but through pure determination and love for our children, we made it hold.

I sucked in a sharp breath as my magic reserves diminished, knowing I was running out and willing the stars to lend me the strength I needed to hold on just a little longer.

Tyler neighed loudly as he raced to meet us, the open tunnel standing wide at our backs, welcoming him in.

"Get on!" Sofia cried as they skidded to halt beside us and a sob burst from me as I took in the wounds on Xavier's spine, knowing exactly what must have caused them and who the culprit was.

Geraldine was deathly pale, the taint of poison hanging about her which made my heart knot with fear, and I reached out to brush my fingers through her hair before taking Xavier's hand and squeezing.

"We have to hold him off," I gasped as Hamish growled loudly, the tug on my magic intensifying to the point of pain as he fought to keep Lionel back.

"Mom?" Xavier groaned and I leaned in to press a kiss to his cheek.

"I have loved you unconditionally from the moment I first found out I was having you. You are my starlit boy, my light in the dark and I am so endlessly proud of the man you have become, my love," I said, feeling the cold taste of goodbye on my tongue and knowing it was the only way.

"Why are you saying that?" Xavier growled as he pushed himself to sit up, but I knew he knew.

"We can't all escape him," I said, my words falling to a cry as my magic shuddered and I knew we only had moments before it would gutter out entirely.

"Live brave and true, my sweetest girl," Hamish said gruffly, taking Geraldine's limp hand in his and squeezing tightly as a pained moan passed from her lips. "I know that you will overcome this evil in the end."

"Tell Darius that I love him," I whispered to Xavier, my heart shattering at the knowledge that I would never see my boys again while the force of Lionel's magic crashed against our shield with an unrelenting strength. "The two of you made my life complete even when I could never show you how much you meant to me. My love for you never faltered."

"Mom, please," Xavier's voice broke on that word and pain ripped through me because I knew I couldn't give in to what he wanted of me.

"Go," I said, my gaze snapping to Sofia's before I met with Tyler's wild expression. "And make sure you love him the way he deserves to be loved."

They still resisted, Xavier begging us to come with them and I gritted my jaw, steeling myself with all of the power I owned and lacing my voice with Coercion as thickly as I could manage, shattering Tyler's mental shield as I directed that power at him.

"Run!"

The command hit him hard and he took off in a gallop, tearing away into the tunnel at our backs while Xavier's cries of anguish carried back to me in an endless world of pain.

I turned from the tunnel as Hamish pulled the shield in tighter around us, our magic pulsing and cracking while Lionel continued to try and burn his way through it.

It was only a matter of time. We both knew what this was. A final stand but not one we could survive.

I pulled a small blade from a sheath at my hip and met Hamish's dark gaze as he looked to it.

"I won't risk him capturing me alive," I breathed, the pain of that commitment flickering in his eyes as he acknowledged it and drew his own blade too.

"I won't allow that either, my dear," he swore, knowing full well what I would be subjected to if that happened. I had suffered far too long at Lionel's mercy, and I would never be his plaything again.

"Together?" I asked, pain assaulting me as I looked at this man who had offered me the world and made my life complete long after I'd given up on any hope of happiness for myself.

"Always, Kitty. We are bound as one, you and I."

I pushed up onto my tiptoes to kiss him, tasting the sweetness of our love in his kiss as our magic stuttered and cracked for the final time, the shield falling apart under Lionel's assault and his flames burning out as he stepped through the smoke with a victorious smile.

"I never thought I'd see the day that my bride would betray me for the likes of this rebel piece of shit," Lionel sneered as we broke our kiss and turned to face him, still hand in hand and filled with defiance towards this false king. "I hope the taste of his cock was worth the suffering you will endure for it, Catalina. Because I plan on making you pay for every traitorous moment you spent away from me."

"You will never have anything from me again, Lionel," I sneered, letting him see the disgust and contempt I felt for him as my grip tightened on the blade.

"And you will never be a true king," Hamish spat.

Lionel laughed cruelly as he stalked closer to us, fire building in his palm as he set his murderous eyes on Hamish, and I knew he wanted to make me watch as he killed him. But I was done allowing Lionel Acrux to take from me. So he wouldn't be having a single thing more. Not even our deaths.

I looked away from the monster who had stolen my life from me and looked into the eyes of the man I loved for the final time.

"Into the evermore we go, my love," he breathed.

"Don't let go of my hand," I replied and the last thing I felt before I swiped my blade across my own throat was the tightness of his grip on mine. And as he plunged his own blade into his heart and we both fell to the ground together, we held tight to that promise and slipped into the embrace of the stars as one.

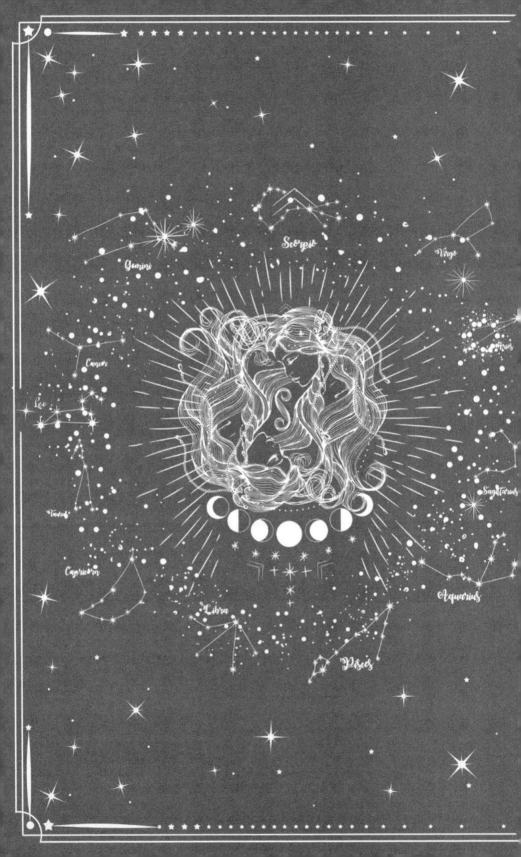

TORY

CHAPTER SIXTY NINE

The rebels had all run from me as I'd commanded, retreating to the tunnels and hopefully making it to safety. Only Justin and I remained on the battlefield, tearing through the Nymphs who came at us with the desperation of starving souls spotting the last scraps of food on earth.

I'd lost sight of everyone else and could only hope that they'd escaped as I focused on the one thing I was determined to achieve in this fucking hellish fight.

The Nymph who had killed my father would die before I left this place, and I didn't care what I had to do to make that so.

Alejandro released a rattle so powerful that it almost brought me to my knees as I ran at him. I encouraged the fire of my Order to coat my skin to combat his foul power as I raised my sword higher, wanting to feel the strike that killed him reverberating through my body when I landed it.

A flash of movement caught my eye and I whirled around, finding Justin there, his own sword swinging towards me and a look of fearless devotion in his eyes which made my heart skip a beat as I fought to get my guard up in time to block.

The Nymph's probes clashed against my armour and a chill hit me as I realised that would have been my damn heart if Justin hadn't been there to save me, his sword impaling the creature and spilling black blood to the dirt between us as our gazes met.

A howl of pain escaped him as the Nymph swung its probes at him instead and I drove my blade into the monster's heart, sending it spinning away into ash and embers as it died.

"Thank you, my queen," Justin gasped as he pressed a hand to his side to heal himself and I shook my head in refusal.

"I should be thanking you." I honestly didn't know why I'd ever believed he could be the bad guy because he was just too fucking nice to pull that shit off.

I turned my gaze back to Alejandro again, pointing at him with my sword in challenge and causing him to bellow right back at me as more and more Nymphs came at us. I was forced to shield us with my air magic, creating a dome of safety around us as we ran on.

But the further we went, the more the Nymphs released their rattles, the cloying power of them biting into me and trying to steal my magic away so that they could strike at us one last time.

Justin howled behind me and I turned to find him immobilised on his knees as the power of the Nymphs' rattles stole his strength and left him at their mercy.

I cursed as I threw my magic at him, hoisting him into the air and casting vines to wrap around his chest and creating a parachute out of leaves.

"What are you doing?" he gasped.

"Thanks for having my back, dude, but this is where you make your escape," I said, double checking that he was strapped in firmly as he shook his head in denial.

"I wish to fight at your side until the bitter end, my lady. I will be your steadfast and galant-"

"White knights just don't do it for me, Justin. But thanks and all that jazz. If I die, tell them I went out like a badass."

"Wait," he gasped but I needed to concentrate on the fight, and I couldn't do that while worrying about him, so I used every bit of my strength to hurl him up into the sky with my air magic and his screams shot up and away from me until I couldn't even hear them anymore. I left him with a strong wind blowing him in the direction I was guessing the rebels had run off to and the honest hope that he would be okay. He was just too damn nice to die.

The screams of the Nymphs soon drew my attention back to the fight and I turned to face Alejandro with a sneer pulling back my upper lip as I slammed my foot down and caused a huge fissure to open up between me and him.

The ground tore apart all around him, isolating him from the other Nymphs and I pushed my air shield out to encompass him too as I ran to meet him with my sword held ready and Phoenix fire burning through my veins like magma.

Alejandro screeched threateningly, lurching forward in his enormous form, the ground vibrating with each step he took and my heart thrashing to the heady tune of battle.

He swung at me with his probed fist and I ducked beneath it, my sword arcing overhead and carving his arm clean off so that it hit the ground with a thump behind me.

He whirled around with a roar of anguish, his other hand crashing into me and sending me tumbling to the ground, but I just kept rolling until I was between his legs and slashing my sword across the backs of them, making him scream even louder as he tumbled to his knees.

I leapt to my feet as he lurched my way and I kicked him with a defiant scream, my boot landing between his shoulder blades and sending him crashing into the mud before me.

I severed his other arm as he thrashed and flailed in the dirt, dancing away from him as his screams of agony made the air vibrate, and he suddenly released a rattle so potent that it choked the air from my lungs and locked my magic down deep inside me where I had no chance of reclaiming it.

He scrambled to his knees as my air shield fell and the other Nymphs all bellowed in victory as they surged towards me, but I wasn't even close to done yet.

"I am the daughter of the Savage King!" I roared, hefting my sword back and looking into his blood red eyes. "And I have come for my pound of flesh!"

I swung my sword with a furious scream, the blade cutting through his neck in a savage blow and victory singing through me as I ended his vile life in a spray of blood and vengeance. This beast had stolen my father's magic and I was setting it free now, tearing it from his unworthy body, and praying it might find him in the afterlife.

The other Nymphs were almost upon me, but as his head thumped to the ground, I leapt into the sky, my blazing wings burning bright and their screams echoing all around me as I rose above the battlefield of our failure with that single piece of glory clinging to my skin.

GABRIEL

CHAPTER SEVENTY

I caved in tunnel after tunnel, bottlenecking the rebels and sending them after my family who were far deeper into the network, carving an escape route away beneath the mountains. The relief at knowing they were safe wasn't nearly enough though, because the rest of the people I loved were still here, and it was all I could do to stay in the present moment and fight instead of falling into visions of the peril that surrounded every one of them.

I closed another empty tunnel, sealing it up tight with earth magic, trying to use it as sparingly as possible now to make sure I didn't run out.

"This way!" I called to a group of rebels as they came charging down the tunnel to my right and as they ran past me, I spotted Tyler in his Pegasus form, cantering towards me with three people on his back.

Geraldine was draped over his neck while Sofia clutched onto Xavier in front of her, his head drooping as healing magic flashed from her into him. Both of them were naked and I hurried forward to greet them, anxiety blazing in my chest at the paleness of Xavier's face and the stillness of Geraldine's body. I hurriedly cast a blanket of moss around them and Sofia shivered as she gripped it with a word of thanks.

Tyler snorted, rubbing his nose against me for a moment as I laid a hand to Geraldine's cool forehead and tried to cast healing magic into her flesh, concern rippling through me when it did little to help.

Xavier looked distraught and pain crushed my heart because I knew why, I had *seen* Catalina and Hamish stay behind, I knew what they had done for us. And I could not let their sacrifice be for nothing.

"What's wrong with Geraldine?" I asked in fear.

"She was attacked by a Shadow Beast," Sofia said with a whimper. "We pulled her from a chasm in the ground."

"Her wounds...they're not natural," I breathed.

"I have the same thing wrong with me, I think," Xavier said, his voice dry as he lifted the blanket to show me blackish claw marks on his side.

I tried to *see* how these wounds could heal, if either of them would survive them, but they were made of shadow and it was hard to *see* anything about tomorrow when so much death hung around us.

"Keep going," I urged, pointing them down the tunnel behind me. "Leon will meet you at the far end, go as fast as you can." I gave them an intent look and Xavier frowned at me, catching my arm before I could hurry away.

"Tell me how this ends," he demanded and I swallowed thickly. "Tell me everyone I love survives." He said it like he already knew they wouldn't, and I couldn't bear to reveal the truth to him.

"Xavier," I sighed, squeezing his arm as I gently pulled his hand off of me. "War is too chaotic to predict. I've *seen* everyone die this night, and many survive it. I can't *see* which of us will make it, but I swear I'll do everything within my power to save as many of us as I can."

Xavier groaned, his eyes fluttering closed then opening again, weakness clouding over him as Sofia offered him more healing magic and kissed his cheek.

"Stay together, and go as fast as you can," I urged and Tyler took off, cantering down the tunnel as I kept moving back in the direction of the battle, closing up the tunnels around me so only this one path remained.

I let myself fall into The Sight, fearing what I would *see* but knowing I had to look, to *see* who of my loved ones were still up there in that battle.

My mind moved towards Darcy first, because ever since the battle had started, I'd lost sight of her fate, darkness clouding it and making me terrified of what that meant. But even now, I couldn't reach her and I tried to still the panic in my heart as I turned my vision to Orion next, but his fate was equally dark, only glimpses of him offered to me, so much blood and pain surrounding his destiny that it made it hard to breathe. But he did live. I just couldn't *see* where he was.

Next, I looked for Tory and my heart juddered as I watched her fate play out. I *saw* Darius on the ground with a dagger in his chest and Tory's sobs filling the air. Pain slashed through my chest, because I knew Darius's death had already come to pass and it took all I had to keep pushing on with the vision, allowing it to unfold. I watched Lionel finding Tory buckled over in her grief, then I *saw* him bind her hands in air magic and drive a knife into her back.

I jerked out of the vision, panic flaring in my flesh as I took off running.

The air was thick with smoke as I climbed higher through the tunnels and I realised a section of The Burrows was burning. I blocked the tunnels where the flames licked the walls, keeping them from spreading into this final section that offered a chance at freedom. But as I used my vision to *see* how many more survivors were left, I knew this was it. No one else was going to make it down here and suddenly I couldn't breathe at all because I hadn't seen either of my sisters, I hadn't seen Orion.

I could not lose them.

I turned, my hands shaking as I followed the guidance of the stars, knowing my actions would save Tory but unable to *see* why.

I shattered the entrance to the tunnel, bringing it all down and sealing it with an ice and earth wall so thick it stole away the last of my magic. But it was done. The tunnels were closed and all who'd made it through were safe.

At least for now.

A deep and surprised laugh filled the air and cold water seemed to spill down my spine as I turned, finding Lionel Acrux there clad in a red cloak.

"The dead queen's bastard son," he said through a smirk. "And it looks like he's all out of magic."

My stomach clenched and the stars offered me a vision of my fate, a fate which would save Tory from death. And I shook my head at them and their devious ways, because I was the sacrificial lamb.

"I'm in need of a new Seer," he announced as he strode towards me, taking a pouch of stardust from his pocket.

I swung a punch at his face and he cursed as he stumbled back, blood spilling from his mouth. He raised a hand, stealing away the oxygen in my lungs and pressing a weight down on me with air magic that had me buckling to my knees before him.

He spat a wad of blood in my face, sneering at me as he bound me to him by ropes of air. "You will regret that, oh mighty fucking Seer."

He threw the stardust over me and I was torn away into its embrace with Lionel, my heart hammering as I called upon the whispering stars around me for a glimpse of the future. But they had nothing to offer but a vision of a future so desolate it crushed me.

So I turned my attention to those I loved who were left to fight this war, drawing on the power of the stars around me and forcing them to offer me a prophecy, an answer to this terrible destiny, a way for them to win. And as they answered my call, I sent the prophecy into the ether, gifting it to the one girl who I knew still stood back at that battle and who may find a way to unravel the stars' guidance. Then I prayed on everything I held dear, that she and her sister would one day find a way to cast a light through the dark and guide their people to victory.

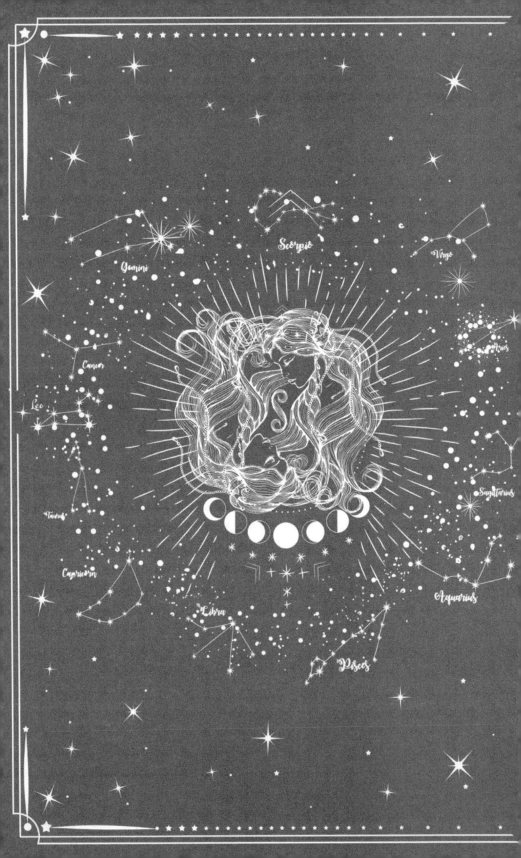

TORY

CHAPTER SEVENTY ONE

I soared above the battlefield with my flesh on fire and fury coursing through my veins as I took in the death that surrounded me, the last of the rebel survivors long gone and the Nymphs all fighting to break through into the tunnels.

I looked around for any sign of Lavinia or Lionel and frowned as I failed to spot them. In fact, the Dragons and Fae who had been fighting alongside them had gone too, not a single soul in sight surrounding me aside from the Nymphs who shrieked and howled for my blood. They reached up towards me from the ground with their probes as if their desire for my magic alone might be enough to pull me from the sky and into their embrace where my death would await me.

Fear speared through my flesh as I hunted for any sign of the people I loved, wondering if it was a fool's hope to believe that they might have made it back into the tunnels while failing to spot them anywhere out here.

The end of the battle had been chaos. I'd barely been able to keep track of the people right beside me, let alone anyone further out, and now I was left in the grip of terror as I hunted for any sign of my family and friends.

What had happened with Darcy and Orion? Had he gotten her away from the fight? Had he managed to return her to herself again?

My chest ached with concern for my other half and my pulse raced as I scoured the battlefield from above, my gaze moving over the dead and the bloodstained, trampled ground in search of any clue to her whereabouts, but there was nothing.

Where were Gabriel, Geraldine, Sofia, Tyler and Xavier? This frantic pounding in my chest was getting harder and harder to bear as my heart thundered in anticipation of an attack I couldn't see coming, like it already knew something I didn't and I was just struggling to catch up to it.

I hunted the land and sky for the sight of two warring Dragons, for a flash of golden scales or a powerful roar. A frenzied kind of panic was building within me as I beat my wings hard and swept across the battlefield, searching for Darius as my heart began to tremble in my chest, the lines of a fissure I refused to let burst open forming all around it.

A sudden sense of foreboding struck me deep in my soul at the emptiness I found in the sky and fear chased through me so potently that my hands shook with it.

"Darius?" I cried, adrenaline blazing through me hotter than my Phoenix fire as I hunted the battlefield for any sign of him, flying fast and searching with a desperation that made my skin prickle as I sensed the stars turning their eyes on me to watch. They knew. They fucking knew what fate awaited me once I found him, and they were creeping closer to feast on my destruction once it came for me.

My heart stalled in my chest as I spotted him, a breath sticking in my throat as ice tumbled through my veins and immobilised me. There he was, the man who had taken possession of my heart and ownership of my being, lying endlessly still on a hilltop far below me.

I dropped from the sky like a stone, the fire of my Order form extinguishing across my body as I free fell towards him with my heart in my throat and pain gripping me like a vice.

I hit the ground hard and dropped to my knees, a sob catching in my chest as I took in the sight of the sun steel blade which was lodged in his heart, and I shook my head in refusal of what I could see with my own two eyes.

"No," I breathed, the denial a curse on my tongue that tasted like agony as I reached for his cheek, the rough bite of his stubble grazing my palm and the cold touch of his skin sinking into my limbs and drowning me with a certainty which I refused to allow.

Pain shuddered through me so viscerally that I felt it like a tremor tumbling through my core, sending shockwaves out into the sky and throughout the entire world in its wake as it ruined me.

Tears pricked the backs of my eyes as I shook my head, refusing to accept this, leaning down to press a kiss to his unresponsive lips, the coldness in him sinking into my skin too and whispering goodbye on the wings of fate.

I pressed my lips to his harder, tasting blood on them and pain and an endless expanse of nothing, because I couldn't taste *him*. The reckless, brutal, beautiful man of mine who had taken all the worst in me and found a way to see it as his deepest desire. The creature who lit me up all the way to my core, who saw every piece of me and made it burn brighter for him while offering all of himself in return. My dark nightmare, my beautiful daydream, my stolen fate.

"Please," I begged, knowing the stars could hear me and falling back on their mercy as I kissed him again, willing him to return the pressure of his lips against mine, for his eyes of open and for him to be looking back at me when I broke this kiss. "Please, not him."

The weight of the stars' eyes on my back felt like it was trying to crush me into the dirt as they continued to watch my ruin with rapt attention and cold discard. They made no offer to me though. No words sounded in response to my plea, and the man I loved so desperately didn't stir beneath me.

My fingers brushed against his arm and a sob caught in my throat as I felt the cool metal of the Phoenix Kiss I'd gifted him there, returned to its bangle form following his passage from this world, another nail in the coffin of this unjust destiny.

The sound of the Nymphs screaming in excitement punctuated my grief as they came for me, seeing me vulnerable on the ground at last and racing each other to claim the prize of my power as my heart shattered into more pieces than could possibly be reunited.

They fell like grains of sand from my chest and scattered on the cold wind, hurtling out to find him beyond the Veil and beg him to return to me.

Rage rose within me with every passing second that I held his unmoving hand in mine, that I drowned in the agony of his death and refused to consider a future where I was forced to stand and leave him lying dead beneath me. The furious energy rose and rose until it was burning the tears from my cheeks and scouring the pain from my heart, leaving me consumed with anger unlike anything I had ever experienced before.

"This isn't our fate," I growled against his lips, my hand moving to grasp the sun steel blade which was lodged in his chest, the cold bite of the metal searing my palm with the sharp bite of reality as it mocked my requests of the stars and reminded me of what it had stolen.

I ripped the blade free with a growl of rage, breaking my kiss with the empty vessel which should have housed the man I loved as I turned my furious gaze upon the stars who continued to watch my destruction play out like it was nothing to them. Nothing at all in their eternal existence.

But they were wrong about that.

I wasn't nothing. I was fury and agony and untold power combined into a soul which they had tried to cleave apart too many fucking times already.

My sister was lost to me somewhere in the dark, my friends were all missing and facing their own fates with the odds stacked against them as always and this man of mine, this keeper of my heart and possessor of my entire being lay dead in my arms like a sacrifice to their cruel designs.

I shifted my hold on the weapon that had ripped from my arms and felt the cold kiss of the sun steel blade cutting into my palm as I gripped it tightly. I looked down at it as I felt my blood mixing with his along its sharp edge, my broken heart thrashing with the thought of a life lived without him.

Blood dripped between my fingers, his, mine, *ours*. There was magic in that. Ancient magic which I could feel thrumming through the air all around me and power built inside me unlike anything I'd ever felt before as I leaned into it. This wasn't my Elements or my Phoenix or any kind of magic I knew. It was raw, savage, the essence of all we were and all we'd ever be.

I looked up at the heartless sky with a curse on my lips and slit the blade deeper into my flesh, knowing that it would scar and welcoming the pain as I dropped the weapon and held my fist up to the stars for them to see the mixture of my mate's blood and my own running down my arm.

"I will tear the heavens apart for this," I snarled, flicking my free hand and using my air and water magic to send the droplets of our blood flying up into the sky for them to feast on. "I will shred your world to pieces and rip your hold on destiny from your fucking fists with blood and fire and vengeance for this," I screamed at them, power whipping all around me and making my hair billow in the force of it as more and more blood raced up towards the heavens. "On my life, I curse you. On *his* life, I curse you. And for our fate, I'll end you!"

The darkness rose within me as I fell into the despair of this end for us, Darius's body so cold and limp beneath me, his blood staining my flesh and his strong and powerful presence gone where I couldn't follow.

The Nymphs cried out in victory as they crested the hill, countless numbers of them descending on me with a hunger that went beyond all reason and a thirst for my death which I met with the rage of my grief.

The first of them reached us and as its probes brushed against the chest of the man who had owned my entire being, I lost the thin hold I'd been keeping on my restraint and an agonised roar of pain ripped from my throat. I tipped my head back and all of that unbridled power I'd felt building all around us exploded from my chest and echoed out across the entire battlefield and beyond.

A shockwave of red and blue fire exploded from me as I screamed my grief to the stars and the shrieks of the Nymphs rose in answer to me as they died beneath the full force of my power.

The blast tore from me like a supernova, leaving nothing but death and ash in its wake and I arched my spine as it spilled through me and into the world, carrying an endless echo of my pain with it to touch every corner of this star cursed earth and make sure that everyone residing on it felt it too.

I fell forward as the last of it burned its way free of me, sobs cutting from my body in harsh waves which wouldn't be denied as I fell over the body of the man I'd stolen back from the stars and pressed my ear against the heart which would never beat for me again, begging fate to change its mind while my tears were the only answer I was gifted.

But as I broke over the loss of the only man I'd ever loved, a deep, golden glow appeared before me, forcing me to raise my head and look at the prophecy which was painted for me across the sky.

When all hope is lost, and the darkest night descends, remember the promises that bind.
When the dove bleeds for love, the shadow will meet the warrior.
A hound will bay for vengeance where the rift drinks deep.
One chance awaits. The king may fall on the day the Hydra bellows in a spiteful palace.

AUTHOR'S NOTE

Hey there care bear…how's it going? You cool? Feeling a lil bit ragey? You wanna slap us with a kipper and call us a slippery salmon? Or is it worse than that? Oh shit…it's worse, isn't it?

Well let's look at the positives! Lionel got some fancy new wings to mount on his wall - yay! Lavinia got a cute little pet to take home, Darcy always wanted to find out what it was like to be a fluffy shifter and Darius got, well, he got some sparkly new friends to hang out with, wooo!

Okay, okay. In all seriousness, I know we bound you, gagged you and shoved you off a cliff into a pile of sharp rocks with this one. But on the bright side, there's one more book left in the series. And yes, maybe book 8 looks a bit like a psycho killer approaching you across those sharp rocks at the moment, with a knife in hand and a smile on his face. But let's not forget all the happies this book gave you too!

Xavier got laid – woohoo! And his spangly wangle will go down in history, PLUS he managed to prank the best Seer in Solaria. Gabriel is totally gonna be laughing about that while he's being brutally used against his friends and family by Lionel, right? And let's not forget that Caleb got his D sucked, even if that didn't quite go to plan, he's probably gonna be super happy reminiscing about that while he's in mortal peril, fearing his soul being sucked right out of his body, right? Right??

So here we are, you made it. I'd love to give you a medal or something because this book was the longest book we've ever written, and seriously, we've loved writing it so much. These characters own us body and soul, and we look forward to torturing them more – ah, I mean giving them happies – when the series concludes.

If you haven't pre-ordered the next book yet, then you can do so here. And if you'd love to hang out with us some more as well as a load of incredible readers who love books as much as you do, you can come and join us in our reading tribe on Facebook here.

That's a wrap for 2021 for us! But watch this space, because big things are coming next year and we cannot WAIT to share them with you.

Thank you for your continuing support. We're just a couple of sisters who sit in a room together chatting shit and drinking tea, and we so appreciate all the backing you give us as indie authors!

Lots of love from,

Caroline and Susanne xxxx

P.S. If you love Gabriel, Leon and Dante, find them in their own COMPLETE series (Ruthless Boys of the Zodiac) set five years before the Zodiac Academy series. And you might just find out that secret story Orion has on Gabriel…

ALSO BY
CAROLINE PECKHAM
&
SUSANNE VALENTI

Brutal Boys of Everlake Prep

(Complete Reverse Harem Bully Romance Contemporary Series)

Kings of Quarantine

Kings of Lockdown

Kings of Anarchy

Queen of Quarantine

**

Dead Men Walking

(Reverse Harem Dark Romance Contemporary Series)

The Death Club

Society of Psychos

**

The Harlequin Crew

(Reverse Harem Mafia Romance Contemporary Series)

Sinners Playground

Dead Man's Isle

Carnival Hill

Paradise Lagoon

Harlequinn Crew Novellas

Devil's Pass

**

Dark Empire

(Dark Mafia Contemporary Standalones)

Beautiful Carnage

Beautiful Savage

**

The Ruthless Boys of the Zodiac

(Reverse Harem Paranormal Romance Series - Set in the world of Solaria)

Dark Fae

Savage Fae

Vicious Fae

Broken Fae

Warrior Fae

Zodiac Academy

(M/F Bully Romance Series- Set in the world of Solaria, five years after Dark Fae)

The Awakening

Ruthless Fae

The Reckoning

Shadow Princess

Cursed Fates

Fated Thrones

Heartless Sky

The Awakening - As told by the Boys

Zodiac Academy Novellas

Origins of an Academy Bully

The Big A.S.S. Party

Darkmore Penitentiary

(Reverse Harem Paranormal Romance Series - Set in the world of Solaria, ten years after Dark Fae)

Caged Wolf

Alpha Wolf

Feral Wolf

**

The Age of Vampires

(Complete M/F Paranormal Romance/Dystopian Series)

Eternal Reign

Eternal Shade

Eternal Curse

Eternal Vow

Eternal Night

Eternal Love

**

Cage of Lies

(M/F Dystopian Series)

Rebel Rising

**

Tainted Earth

(M/F Dystopian Series)

Afflicted

Altered

Adapted

Advanced

**

The Vampire Games

(Complete M/F Paranormal Romance Trilogy)

V Games

V Games: Fresh From The Grave

V Games: Dead Before Dawn

*

The Vampire Games: Season Two

(Complete M/F Paranormal Romance Trilogy)

Wolf Games

Wolf Games: Island of Shade

Wolf Games: Severed Fates

*

The Vampire Games: Season Three

Hunter Trials

*

The Vampire Games Novellas

A Game of Vampires

**

The Rise of Issac

(Complete YA Fantasy Series)

Creeping Shadow

Bleeding Snow

Turning Tide

Weeping Sky

Failing Light